Bantam Books by Tom Deitz

BLOODWINTER

SPRINGWAR

Praise for

BLOODWINTER

"Deitz's skill at crafting a complex tale of men and women driven by warring emotions and rival ambitions anchors his fantasy visions in the reality of human experience."—*Library Journal*

"Both villainy and heroism go beyond stereotype [in] a well-crafted work that explores the nature of art."—*Locus*

"Tom Deitz is a fine storyteller in the tradition of the Southern mountains . . . with all its legends and magic transported from afar. Like his forebears, he can make magic with words."—Sharyn McCrumb, *New York Times* bestselling author of *The Ballad of Frankie Silver*

"Once again, Tom Deitz has proven himself a master of the fantasy genre. He has created a detailed, realistic world, characters who are both engaging and believable, and a compelling, fast-moving story that draws the reader in from the first page. I hope that the author will continue to explore this fascinating new world and its inhabitants in future books."
—John Maddox Roberts

"Deitz has always been a superb fantasist, but he's outdone himself in this richly developed, character-driven story!" —Josepha Sherman

SPRINGWAR

A TALE OF ERON

TOM DEITZ

BANTAM BOOKS
NEW YORK TORONTO LONDON SYDNEY AUCKLAND

SPRINGWAR

A Bantam Spectra Book / July 2000

SPECTRA and the portrayal of a boxed "s" are trademarks of Bantam Books,
a division of Random House, Inc.

Library of Congress Cataloging-in-Publication Data
Deitz, Tom.
Springwar: a tale of Eron / Tom Deitz.
p. cm.—(A Bantam spectra book)
ISBN 0-553-37864-3
I. Title.
PS3554.E425 S57 2000
813'.54—dc21   99-047800

Published simultaneously in the United States and Canada

Bantam Books are published by Bantam Books, a division of Random House, Inc. Its
trademark, consisting of the words "Bantam Books" and the portrayal of a rooster, is
Registered in U.S. Patent and Trademark Office and in other countries. Marca Registrada.
Bantam Books, 1540 Broadway, New York, New York 10036.

PRINTED IN THE UNITED STATES OF AMERICA

FFG   10   9   8   7   6   5   4   3   2   1

for
the folks on the forum:
many gone; none forgotten
and
in memory of Edge and Jen

ACKNOWLEDGMENTS

Soren Andersen
Stephen Andersen
Juliet Combes
Tom Dupree
Anne Lesley Groell
Brenda Hull
Linda Jean Jeffery
Tom Jeffery
Buck Marchinton
Deena McKinney
Howard Morhaim
Lindsay Sagnette

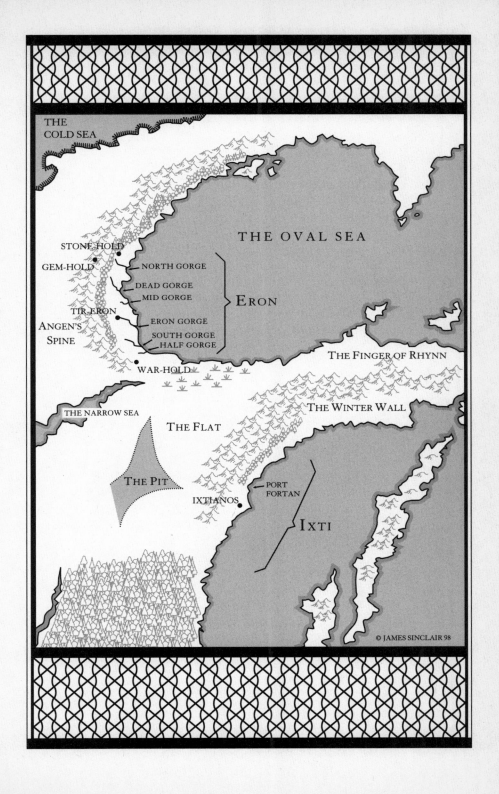

THE
COLD SEA

THE OVAL SEA

STONE-HOLD

GEM-HOLD

NORTH GORGE

DEAD GORGE
MID GORGE

ERON

TIR-ERON

ANGEN'S
SPINE

ERON GORGE

SOUTH GORGE
HALF GORGE

THE FINGER OF RHYNN

WAR-HOLD

THE NARROW SEA

THE WINTER WALL

THE FLAT

THE PIT

PORT
FORTAN

IXTIANOS

IXTI

© JAMES SINCLAIR 98

BLOODWINTER

~~~~~~~~~

The plague came and the plague went, and a third of the adult men in the cold, snowswept kingdom of Eron went with it, and one in nine of the women, with the bulk of all casualties in their prime. No clan or craft was spared in that land of scholar-artisans, but some were dealt harsher blows than others, with many crafts being virtually obliterated, while others—those that remained sequestered in the remoter winter holds—managed to survive relatively intact.

The upshot was an alarming decline in the population of that realm, which would not have been so troubling had Eron not possessed an adversary across the sands to the south: Ixti, which sometimes cast covetous eyes not only on the resources of its northern neighbor, but also on the works of its fabled craftsmen. And while Ixti, too, had felt the plague's lash, it was not so severe in that hot, arid realm, and so Ixti's population recovered more quickly.

It was in part to meet that threat (real or imagined—for an ominous desert called the Flat divided the two kingdoms, making casual contact difficult), that the High Sovereign of Eron, acting in concert with the Council of Chiefs, ordained that all Eronese women of childbearing age must produce at least three offspring. So it was that, eighteen years after the plague, young Eddyn syn Argen-yr, great-grandson of the Craft-Chief of his clan, and one of the three most acclaimed smiths of his generation, raped Strynn san Ferr of Warcraft, hoping thereby to get her with child and force her into marriage—for no Eronese children were allowed to be born without an acknowledged father, whether or not that man was the actual sire.

Strynn, however, had other plans, and promptly wed her childhood friend, Avall syn Argen-a, who was at once Eddyn's cousin, her own bondsister's twin brother, and (along with Strynn herself), one of the other two most accomplished smiths. Complicating matters was the fact that Avall and Eddyn each had a powerful patron within their mutual clan—patrons who had been rivals for three generations and had no qualms about using their talented two-sons to continue their decades-long game of one-upmanship. Eddyn's patron even commanded sufficient influence to save him from the exile normally granted rapists, but the whole affair threatened to cause sufficient trouble that the three—Eddyn, Strynn, and Avall—were dispatched to remote Gem-Hold-Winter to sit out the cold season, during which Strynn's child would be born. Nor would that time be spent idly. All three were assigned to complete one item apiece for the royal regalia: a sword, a helm, and a shield, each to be decorated with a gem of the craftsman's own finding.

And so, at the end of the autumn festival called Sundeath, Avall, Strynn, and Eddyn set out for Gem-Hold-Winter, in the company of more than a hundred of their countrymen. Among this number was a young man from Priest-Clan named Rrath syn Garnill, whose quick mind and interest in natural history had brought him to the attention of a secret cabal within that clan dedicated to preserving its ascendancy in an ever-more-secular age. A longtime admirer of Avall's, Rrath continued to shadow the young goldsmith—*until,* during an attack by a birkit—a wild carnivore something between a cougar and a bear—Avall seemed willing to let Rrath die rather than face the beast himself. Rrath promptly attached himself to Eddyn, who welcomed even that minor victory over his rival.

And there matters rested in Eron.

Meanwhile, in Ixti, Prince Kraxxi and his younger brother, Azzli, had begun to chafe at the restrictions of royal birth, as well as at King Barrax's obvious favoritism of Azzli, who was the child of love rather than politics. Eventually, neither brother could stand the tensions at court any longer, and so they conceived a plan to sneak into Ixti's wilder regions in order to hunt geens—man-sized reptiles that walked on their hind legs, and that were rumored to possess more than bestial intelligence. Such a foray would soon have been necessary in any event, all highborn young Ixtian men being required to kill a geen before they could be considered adults—and Kraxxi having just reached his majority.

Unfortunately for Kraxxi, the hunters became the hunted, and their camp was attacked by geens. Even worse, during the ensuing confusion,

Kraxxi accidentally slew his beloved younger brother. Since kinslaying was a capital offense in Ixti, Kraxxi found himself with few options, and chose what he considered to be slow suicide: daring the desert wastes of the Flat in hopes of reaching Eron, which he had long desired to visit. Though he began his journey alone, he soon found himself joined by his three best friends: Elvix, Olrix, and Tozri, a set of half-Eronese triplets who constituted his personal guard.

Against remarkable odds, all four reached Eron's southernmost citadel: War-Hold, where Avall's martially inclined twin sister, Merryn, had been stationed for the winter. And where Kraxxi, in his assumed identity of Krax, a merchant's son, managed to fall in love with Merryn, even as his royal father laid a price on his head.

And back at Gem-Hold-Winter, Avall had been reunited with his bond-brother, Rann, for whom he cared more than anyone in the world, and had met Kylin, a talented blind harper only a little older than he, Rann, and Strynn. In spite of their proximity to each other, Avall and Eddyn maintained an uneasy peace—until Avall, working in Clan Argen's private vein in the mines that mazed the hold's foundations, found a curious gem the like of which he had never seen. His initial intent was simply to mount it in the helm he was crafting for the High King, but in the process of fitting it, he let it touch an open cut on his hand—whereupon he found his senses altered, so that he could suddenly do much finer work than heretofore. Intrigued, he soon discovered that the gem had other powers as well, notably that it could confer the ability to share minds upon any group of people who primed the stone with blood. He and Rann were the first to join that way—by accident. But Strynn, from whom he had become somewhat estranged, was not far behind, and the two of them promptly began to grow closer.

Then came the great discovery. One night as Avall lay awake clutching the gem, he found himself in mental contact with his sister, Merryn, far away in the south. Thoroughly shaken, Avall quickly realized that control of instantaneous communication across great distances would cement Argen-a's position as most powerful of the three septs of Clan Argen, as well as ensuring its continued close access to the King.

Trouble was, Eddyn had spied on Avall and had discovered, to his dismay, that his rival was doing even better work than before—and doing it too quickly to be natural. Determined to locate the source of Avall's advantage, Eddyn learned of the gem—and drew the same conclusions as Avall regarding the role such a discovery would play in clan politics, namely that it would make *his* sept ascendant, as well as possibly redeeming his damaged reputation.

Meanwhile, Avall and Rann had decided to dare the unthinkable: a cross-country trek through the dead of winter to Eron's capital, Tir-Eron, in order to inform Avall's patron of their find. Little did they know, however, that two days after their departure Eddyn and Rrath would also leave Gem-Hold, seeking to waylay Avall's party and capture the gem for themselves. But even Eddyn was unaware that Rrath had a second agenda: to secure the gem for his own faction within Priest-Clan. For the gem, it seemed, provided strong evidence that the soul was not confined to the body and could perhaps access Eron's eightfold god directly, eliminating the need for Priest-Clan's intercession. Rrath therefore drugged Eddyn and the two of them detoured by a secret Priest-Clan holding, where they were interviewed and given a means of locating the gem, as well as a patrol of experienced warrior-priests to accompany them.

Nor were Avall, Eddyn, and their accomplices alone in having their lives disrupted by the gem. Kraxxi had been witness to Merryn's first contact with her brother, and had quickly determined how that had been accomplished. Realizing that instant communication would give Eron an advantage in any war, and knowing that his father desired war with Eron, Kraxxi decided to take news of Eron's new potential weapon back to his father's court, hoping thereby to gain a pardon for himself. And so he, too, set out in the dead of Eronese winter, heading south into the Flat, having tricked Merryn into facilitating his escape. Furious—and hurt, for she truly did love Kraxxi, and he her—Merryn pursued him, but was captured by outriders of the Ixtian army, who promptly took her to their main camp, where she was briefly reunited with Kraxxi. For his part, Kraxxi would say nothing save that he would speak only to King Barrax—who was not in camp. *Bloodwinter* ended with both Merryn and Kraxxi under threat of torture.

Back in Eron, Avall and Rann had encountered a hardy woodswoman named Div. But scarcely had that association begun when the party was attacked by birkits. During the ensuing struggle, Avall's blood primed the gem, and he found he could speak to the beasts mind to mind—and that they were, as Rrath suspected, semi-intelligent. Recognizing fellow hunters, the birkits called off their attack and offered Avall, Rann, and Div shelter from a blizzard in their den. During that enforced incarceration, Div and Rann became lovers, while Avall discovered that under certain circumstances it was possible to use the gem to draw energy from what he assumed was the Overworld—the realm of The Eight—thus confirming its use as a potential weapon.

Desperate to reach Tir-Eron at any cost, Avall, Rann, and Div continued on when the blizzard lifted, and soon reached the ruins of an abandoned way station. While preparing to camp there, they were attacked by mysterious, white-cloaked figures bent on acquiring Avall's gem. Div was shot with an arrow, and Rann clubbed to near unconsciousness, but not before he saw Avall also take an arrow in the back and fall from an escarpment into the icy waters of the river below.

Filled with despair at the loss of his best friend—and the gem, which Avall wore on a chain inside his clothes—Rann barely cared when their attackers were suddenly set upon by birkits, presumably those they had befriended earlier. All their enemies fled or were killed, but Rann scarcely had strength to drag Div to shelter in the ruins' basement and tend their wounds before yet another massive blizzard closed in.

Not all the attackers were dead, however. Though the ambush had been mounted by members of Priest-Clan's secret cabal, Rrath and Eddyn had also been present. Fleeing the carnage—and allies whose agendas seemed increasingly alarming—Rrath and Eddyn took shelter in a small boathouse near the ruined station, where the same blizzard that had driven Rann and Div to ground forced them to hold up for several days.

Eventually the storm passed, with Rann and Div being the first to emerge. Faced with a difficult decision, they finally agreed to return to Gem-Hold to inform Strynn that Avall was almost certainly dead—any hope otherwise being due to the fact that the gem conferred remarkable healing properties upon those who wielded it. Nor did Strynn accept Avall's death as given. Linking with Rann through another gem she had uncovered, Strynn was able to determine that Avall was alive but very, very cold.

As for Avall himself, he was indeed very cold—and very wet—and then, when both seemed certain to claim his life, he found himself suddenly warm again.

PROLOGUE I:

ORPHANS OF THE STORM

(western Eron, near Woodstock Station— Deep Winter, Day XXXIII—night)

~~~~~~~~~~~~~~~~

The lowest log in the wide stone fireplace collapsed to blocky coals, bringing down the sturdier wood atop it in a rush of sparks. A stretch of unseared bark reached well-banked embers and flamed up. Red glare danced around waist-high stone walls four spans long, above which more stone alternated with rotting shutters as tall as a man. Rough-hewn corner posts leered with the eyes and mouths of demons. More stared down from the rafters of the steep-pitched roof.

The sudden light roused the nearer of two young men huddled in furs beside the hearth. He blinked long-lashed lids, grunted, almost slept again—then recalled the plan he'd been formulating when the day's fatigue had claimed him.

He tensed, caught himself, and relaxed—slowly, lest his companion sense that aberration and awaken. A breath, and he opened his eyes, as alert as he'd been lethargic.

This was his chance. Maybe. If he were careful. If he didn't lose his nerve. If he didn't change his mind and choose escape over stealth or confrontation.

Escape . . .

He listened warily. One would be mad to dare what lay beyond these walls; what he could hear even above the crackling fire. The winds waged war out there, this latest sally winging in from the east, bearing new, seaborn snow to heap atop the days-old drifts that shrouded this wretched, abandoned place that had *not* been built as long-term shelter.

Not that he begrudged it. Still, their stony sanctum had been intended as *temporary* refuge in which riverside revelers could change clothes, eat light meals, and store boats.

In High Summer.

This was Deep Winter—and the direst part of that season howled without: a blizzard that had caught him and his companion unprepared. And for all that, they were luckier than some, whose corpses cluttered a sprawl of ruins a quarter shot upriver, victims of a birkit attack that might not be coincidental.

If the beasts were intelligent, as his floor-mate, more than once, had vowed . . .

No! He dared not think about that now, though those beasts—and those dead—were in large part why he was here. Him, Eddyn syn Argen-yr, protégé of the most powerful woman in Eron. The second-best goldsmith of his generation, by the ranking of his craft. And a proclaimed rapist, who'd only escaped unclanning and exile through that same kinswoman's machinations—and the fact that throughout his whole cold-blasted homeland there was a shortage of healthy young men, courtesy of a plague eighteen years gone by.

Eddyn syn Argen-yr.

The fool.

Holding his breath, he rolled onto his left side, giving that movement the casual crude grace of sleep. That faced him full toward the fire, perfectly poised to observe what he'd noted as he and Rrath settled in for a long, cold, and far too indefinite term of waiting.

Rrath's travel pack.

Not remarkable of itself, but inside the well-oiled leather were secreted certain herbs and potions with which Rrath and his dubious accomplices had kept Eddyn sedated into mindless pliancy, content to plod numbly through the silent empty woods between Gem-Hold-Winter and Tir-Eron.

Those accomplices were all dead now—the so-called ghost priests. And Eddyn had managed to shake off the soporific. He would *not* succumb again.

Slowly he eased his arm beyond his bedroll, grateful for proximity to the fire that kept the worst of the cold at bay. A wave of black hair slid into his eyes. He brushed it back, the better to assess his goal. A little farther, and . . .

Not quite.

Gritting his teeth, he rolled onto his belly, gaining a handspan's reach. Fingers stretched, and . . .

Success! Not the pack itself, but the flap above the side-bag in which the drugs were cached. The clasp was snug and took forever to free one-handed, yet he managed.

A pause to flex his fingers, and he eased them inside, feeling for a certain velvet pouch that wrapped a number of small glass phials. *Found it . . .*

But there was also a second pouch—which he hadn't expected. He snared both, wincing when glass clicked against glass as he withdrew them. Rich blue nap showed. Good: He'd found the right one. But this other—the red sylk—he'd never seen it before.

The fire popped. A coal spun toward him. He flinched—and lost his grip on the more slippery cloth, barely retaining the velvet. Glass shattered on the flagstones; liquid stained stones and sylk alike. "Eight," he swore silently. But maybe he could still cover—

"What?" a groggy voice mumbled at his back, issuing from a thatch of tousled mouse-colored hair shorter than his but thicker.

"*What?*" Again. More sharply.

"Fire," Eddyn grunted, as though he'd just awakened.

A squirm of movement became a panicked flurry. A hand clamped down on his forearm as Rrath flung his whole torso atop him in a desperate scramble to snare the scarlet bag. *"No!"* the Priest blurted, in something between a wail, a shout, and a yawn. Then: "Oh, Eight, not *that* one!"

But Eddyn was a third again Rrath's size and commensurately stronger, and in one smooth, practiced twist, he bucked his assailant aside then rolled atop him. Additionally blessed by a head start on alertness, it was a simple matter for Eddyn to pin the smaller youth beneath him: straddling his hips and forcing both arms against the floor. The surviving pouch was a hardness between his palm and Rrath's left wrist. By the resigned grimace contorting the Priest's bland features, Eddyn knew he'd won. "And why *not* that one?" he snapped. "Have I found *another* secret, Rrath?"

Rrath's eyes blazed with anger. "I can't tell you."

"Eight, you can't, you sneaky little turd. What was that stuff?"

"I *can't* tell you," Rrath repeated. "Remember what I said about conditioning? There are some things I literally can't reveal. But I can say that what you just destroyed will hurt you as much as it does me. It's . . . No, I can't say—I *can't*!"

"Try," Eddyn growled. "*Try* to tell me. Maybe then I'll believe you."

Rrath grimaced wretchedly. "That phi—"

He broke off, gasping for breath. The cords in his neck stood out like ropes. His jaw went hard. Panic washed his eyes.

"What—?" Eddyn demanded.

"What you saw," Rrath spat. "Paralysis of the throat and tongue. And pain in my head, like my *brain* was going to explode. I can't—"

"Not good enough," Eddyn retorted, oblivious to Rrath's discomfort. "What *was* that stuff? It has to be important, for you to act like this."

Rrath's breath was coming harsh and fast. He swallowed hard. "Compass," he gasped—then gasped again, louder, panting like a bellows. Eddyn could feel his pulse racing beneath his hand.

"What's that supposed to mean?" Eddyn persisted ruthlessly, increasing the pressure on Rrath's wrists. "How can a phial of . . . whatever it was be a compass?"

Rrath swallowed again. "Like calls to . . . like," he muttered, eyes going wide as he realized he'd managed the whole phrase. Then, almost recklessly: "I'm . . . a . . . weather-witch."

Eddyn's eyes narrowed in confusion, then widened in turn as realization dawned. He relaxed his grip minutely. "So you're saying . . . ?"

"I *can't* say," Rrath cried. "Not directly. Maybe this way, apparently. Obliquely. If it doesn't kill me with pain—which it could."

Eddyn gnawed his lip, fighting for patience. "So something in that phial was . . . like something else?"

Rrath's head rose once, as though to nod. But then he was gasping again. "I can't. Even that—"

"Like what, then? Like Avall? Or like the gem?"

Silence. Rrath was crying, almost sobbing. But then he took a deep breath. "Earth calls to earth," he dared, wincing in anticipation of what could not be feigned agony. His whole body shuddered again. Sweat shimmered on his brow.

Eddyn sat back, using that interval to thrust the remaining pouch down the neck of his tunic. He'd store it more properly later. Or destroy it. "Get up," he growled.

Rrath mumbled something unintelligible and wriggled out from under him, divesting himself of his bedroll in the process. Like Eddyn, he'd stripped to woolen hose and undertunic. Fortunately, Eddyn's had been belted; he could feel the pouch against his skin.

"Might want to stoke up the fire," Eddyn continued, his voice ominously soft. "Oathbreaking goes better in the light."

"And with something in one's belly," Rrath suggested hopefully.

"There's brandy."

"Not much *but* brandy, actually."

"Fetch it."

Rrath scooted off to retrieve the jug while Eddyn adjusted the fire, adding a piece of oak bench that would burn a good while. He had no idea how long this blizzard would last, and such resources had best be husbanded.

Red light became gold as Rrath returned. Side-lit, his smooth features looked very young. He was, too—within an eighth of Eddyn's age, since they'd both been part of the same Fateing. Eddyn doubted he looked much older himself, though he felt as if he were a thousand.

"Ask," Rrath prompted sullenly, uncorking the jug. "*Maybe* we can find a way around this, if you ask exactly the right questions. I don't think I can volunteer much at all."

Eddyn's brow wrinkled in thought. "So . . . something in the phial—some liquid—was like something Avall had, or else like something connected to the gem. And then you said earth calls to earth, and the gem came *out* of the earth, so that's probably what you meant. Right?"

Rrath didn't reply. Or couldn't. His mouth worked, but no words ensued.

"The phial had *liquid* in it," Eddyn stressed. "Which doesn't make sense—unless that liquid was connected to some liquid where the gem was found, except that I worked that vein myself and it was as dry as any of them are down there. On the other hand, something could be dissolved *in* that liquid. So . . ." He broke off, staring at Rrath again. "Weather-witches drink water from Weather's Well when they want to predict the weather—*find* the weather, so folks say. Everyone knows that. So if you drank from a Well that had . . . earth from the gem's vein dissolved in it, and then did the witching rite, you might—" He said no more, for he knew from the shock that crossed Rrath's face that he'd hit close to the mark. "That's it, isn't it?"

"I still can't tell you. Not that directly."

Eddyn eyed him carefully, his back to the fire. "It'll do," he conceded. "For now. For *now*," he repeated—and took a draught of brandy, straight from the jug. A deep breath, then: "When this ends—the storm, I mean—what do we do?"

Rrath looked startled. "Try to survive."

"And where do we do this surviving? Do we go forward, or do we go back?"

"That was . . . clearer before."

Eddyn glared at him.

Rrath snared the jug, drank deep, and leaned back, wrapping a fur around his shoulders. He rubbed his neck where finger marks showed red even in the firelight. But wouldn't meet Eddyn's gaze.

"The way I see it," Eddyn went on, "Avall had the gem with him when he fell. But it's always possible he could've given it to Rann or the woman. We haven't had a chance to search their bodies."

"If there *are* bodies," Rrath countered. "We saw them wounded, but we've no proof they're dead, and the cursed birkits wouldn't let us close enough to check before this Eight-damned blizzard hit."

"But they seemed to be protecting the station," Eddyn noted. "Which would imply that Avall's friends were alive—if your notion of birkits having intelligence is valid."

Rrath shrugged. "In any event, I doubt they'll come calling tonight. If we're lucky, the storm will finish them—unless they've gone to ground in the ruins."

"Which raises another question. When this thing lets up, what's to stop them finding us? They'd be as anxious to seek Avall as we are. They know he went into the river; that would lead them here."

"Supposing they're alive."

Eddyn shrugged in turn. "They're wounded, in any case. That gives us the advantage—assuming their four-footed allies were an aberration, which I'm beginning to doubt, since we know the gem lets people contact other minds. But even if we could best them, we'd still have to decide where to go. Thing is, some of your dead . . . *friends* would've been expected to report back to their hold. When they don't, more will be sent. That's how it works. If we go back, there's a good chance we'll run into them. I doubt that would benefit either of us."

Rrath nodded sagely. "But if we pushed on to Tir-Eron with Rann and the woman, we'd have to watch them every moment, never mind how we'd explain their presence and our conduct if we actually made it there."

"Besides which, we need to see if we can find Avall's body. He's still—he's still my kin, and I owe it to the clan to try to secure his remains."

An eyebrow lifted. "And if the gem happens to be among them?"

"Then this whole stupid mess won't have been in vain."

Rrath yawned hugely. "Suppose we ponder that tomorrow? I'm sorry, Eddyn, but I'm tired. I can't think. There'll be time to puzzle all this out, I promise you; time to consider every iteration until we're sick of them. But it's got to be close to midnight. We've been going steadily all day. I just lost a fight. I've to all intents broken a vow and barely evaded a compulsion, and have the mother of all great headaches to show for it. And of course there's no chance of me drugging you now. Or—" He paused, staring at Eddyn savagely. "Or of my murdering you in your sleep, just so you'll know. I swear on The Eight."

Eddyn huffed contemptuously. "And I'm supposed to believe that? After everything else you've done?"

Anger flashed in Rrath's eyes. "I didn't *like* doing it, if that helps. I'm not saying I had *no* choice, but in my case, you'd have done the same."

Eddyn didn't move. *"Would I?"* For a moment he thought to end it all here. It wouldn't take much to wrestle Rrath down again. He would resist, but Eddyn was stronger. Eventually he'd get his hands around Rrath's throat . . .

And be guilty of murder.

On top of rape.

And he'd be alone in the Wild in the heart of Deep Winter. There was only so much luck in the world. And so much forgiveness.

He tossed back a final hit of brandy in disgusted silence. Rrath spared him a last challenging glare and burrowed into the furs. Before long, he was snoring. Eddyn sat immobile, gazing at the fire.

Fire changed things. Melted metals or blended them into forms more biddable. It made meat fit to eat. But it rendered wood useless save as fuel.

So what did cold do?

It was like fire, actually. Cold killed and cold preserved.

Both changed things. Eddyn wondered how being here in the maw of Deep Winter was changing him.

PROLOGUE II:

CONFERENCES

(ERON: GEM-HOLD-WINTER—
DEEP WINTER: DAY XXXIV—MORNING)

~~~~~~~~~~

I don't like secrets," Crim san Myrk announced without preamble, letting the words fall like pearls into the musty air of Gem-Hold-Winter's least-used council chamber—the one expressly designed for what the previous Hold-Warden had called "invisible information." Nothing surrounded it on three sides but thick stone walls and double-paned windows looking on frosty morning air. Nothing rose above it, either, save a pyramidal wooden roof, painted on the inside with spirals and fabulous beasts. Even the stairs that climbed from the empty chamber below to the vestibule behind the single door were hinged to rise and fall by the Hold-Warden's key alone.

"I don't like secrets," Crim repeated, staring down her elegant nose at the other six people seated in an arc of leather-padded benches one step lower than her rail-rimmed dais. She was too old for this. Not in years—she was a fit and healthy forty-six—but in tolerance for exceptions to routine. Twenty years ago she'd have enjoyed the mystery confronting them. But twenty years ago was not now.

She sighed and adjusted her hood—worn up, to show that she acted in her official capacity as Hold-Warden. Her cloak of rank flowed around her, its gold and silver panels scarce less gaudy than the High King's Cloak of Colors.

The others stirred. Not from guilt—this was no summoning of errant parties to accounting—but from innate awareness that she knew, or suspected enough it was the same as knowing, that everyone present was party to secrets they'd be loath to share in the presence of others. Especially when those others were also rivals. Subchiefs acting without explicit authority from their seniors could be very closemouthed indeed.

She waited. Fixed her gaze on her next-in-command: the Sub–Craft-Chief of Gemcraft. Mystel held that rank, not for any administrative skill she possessed, but because she was the most accomplished gemsmith on the premises. As such, she was the weakest link, the one most likely to be swayed into betrayal, especially as she was also one in clan and craft with Crim, and thereby distant kin. And—almost—young enough to be Crim's daughter. She had the same black hair, too, but nine in ten of her countrymen had that—and dark blue eyes, slender builds, and angular faces.

But Mystel also knew Strynn san Ferr-a-Argen well enough that Crim suspected the two of confiding in each other. If she were lucky, Strynn might even have referenced certain . . . activities to which she alone was privy—and which no one this side of Tir-Eron was authorized to demand of her by threat or force.

So Crim had hoped, at any rate—until Mystel had failed to discover anything Crim didn't know already.

In any case, Mystel didn't reply. That fell to old Sipt, Sub–Clan-Chief of Ferr, which meant he was the oldest mentally competent member of that clan in the hold. And since Ferr was Strynn's birth-clan . . .

"Secrets," Sipt snorted with clear contempt. He was over seventy. Gray hair showed beneath his bloodred hood, but his body was lean and hard—as befitted one born to the clan that ruled Warcraft. "Rather we should discuss life and death! Whatever secrets you would have us divulge, if any there may be, the fact is that whether Avall, Eddyn, Rann, and Rrath are alive or dead, Strynn *is* alive, with another life inside her. We should take care that these . . . secrets do not also endanger her."

He paused to eye the two men sitting to his right, robed in identical Argen maroon, but with sleeves cut differently to denote their separate septs: Pannin syn Argen-a and Brayl syn Argen-yr: sub-sept-chiefs of Smithcraft's ruling clan. Pannin was older than Sipt, though still craggily handsome; Brayl, at fifty-five, was perilously close to pretty.

The remaining woman in the room, Lady Nyss of Priest-Clan, rang the silver attention bell attached to her chair, proof that she, at least, respected protocol. "So you're saying that whatever drove those others away—or led to their disappearance, since I'm not convinced we won't find their bodies in a storeroom—might also have reason to target Strynn?"

"Exactly," Sipt replied. "I—"

"You're already digressing," Crim snapped, rising and starting to pace. A window wall rose behind her, and the angle of the sunlight cast her into darkness cut out against light—which was intentional. "We need to lay out the facts in order, and who knows what. *Then* make some decisions."

"Fact one, then," Pannin began sourly. "As best we can tell, ten days ago Avall and Rann failed to appear for duty in the mines. Since both are reliable, Ayll asked after them, and was told they were ill of a flux and that Strynn was nursing them—yet no such authorization had been given her by Healing. A few days later, Eddyn and Rrath likewise went missing without excuse. Further investigation showed Avall and Rann *not* sick, but absent as well. Yet Strynn hadn't reported them gone, which was odd—since Avall would've had to leave the helmet he was making for the King unfinished—which I know he'd never do."

Crim's eyes narrowed. "And *how* do you know?"

"Because Avall cares about five things in the world: making, his bond-brother, his sister, his two-father, and his wife—in that order."

Crim lifted a brow at Sipt. "Would you concur with this, syn Ferr? More to the point, would any of your clan take exception to it? As an insult to Strynn, perhaps?"

"No one in Ferr is, or has been, insulted by Avall's treatment of Strynn," Sipt replied flatly.

"This may or may not be relevant," sullen old Ayll, who was Sub–Clan-Chief of Myrk, inserted roughly, "but the Night-Warden in the mines reported to me—belatedly, damn his hide—that when Avall was working there one night, he agreed to tithe everything he had in one very full bag in exchange for the lone item in the other. Since it was from the clan vein, the Warden agreed without inspection. But after that, he began to wonder if Avall might not have found something . . . special." He gave the word a particular emphasis, to let its import sink in.

Crim scowled. She, too, had heard rumors.

"Law would've let him keep it," Pannin observed.

"Custom required he report it to me," Crim retorted.

"Unless he intended it for the crown, which was also his option," Pannin gave back. "And he *was* working on a commission for the King."

"Which we ought then to examine," Crim told him, with a cryptic smile.

"Which you know we can't," Pannin countered. "No one is allowed to see a masterwork in process without the maker's permission. Even Strynn couldn't let you see it."

"But she could tell us if it included anything . . . special," Brayl allowed.

"So Avall may have found something out of the ordinary," Crim summarized. "He then disappeared, along with his bond-brother."

"And if he's gone, it's for something incredibly important," Pannin finished. "Nobody hies around in Deep Winter save for the direst of reasons."

"Which in Avall's case would be . . . ?" Brayl challenged.

"Something to do with his craft, I'd say. Half the people he cares about are here."

"Something that wouldn't wait until spring?"

"Maybe not—if someone else knew."

"Such as, perhaps . . . Eddyn?"

"Or that young Priest. What was his name again? Rrath?"

Crim saw Nyss stiffen. She was a territorial old lady. And now her clan was being implicated.

"So Rann and Avall *perhaps* discovered something in the mines that *perhaps* made them feel compelled to dare the Deep without telling anyone in authority, even in their own clans?" Ayll mused. "That sounds very foolish, very important, or both."

"Then Eddyn and Rrath got wind of it and decided to follow?" Mystel continued. "But why would they do that? There's no love lost between Eddyn and Avall; everyone knows that."

"To help them—or stop them," Sipt sighed. "That much is obvious. And given that they're from rival septs . . ."

"It implies that Eddyn and Rrath intended to stop them."

Ayll stroked his bell with a finger. "But why would Rrath go? He's got no vested interest in Argen's affairs beyond his friendship with Eddyn—unless they've become bond-mates."

Pannin laughed out loud. "Eddyn has no friends! Not that would dare the Deep with him. Whatever sent Rrath with him—if they are together— was a product of Rrath's own agenda."

"Or," Crim broke in pointedly, "Priest-Clan's."

Nyss's glare could've melted the rime on the windows. "If you can explain to me what interest Priest-Clan would have in Eddyn or Avall, I'd be glad to hear it."

No one answered.

Crim cleared her throat ominously. "Speaking of secrets, I, too, have a secret—one that was brought to my attention around midnight last night, and which I now lay before you." And with that, she reached behind her chair and retrieved something she'd concealed there, beneath a pall of black velvet. A pause to sweep them all with a searching glance, and she placed it on the rail before her. Eyebrows rose curiously, followed by six very audible gasps, as she removed the drape to reveal what had once been perhaps the most beautiful war helm ever seen in Eron.

Once.

Now it was a ruin: the panels dented and twisted, strapwork popped loose, and a series of intricate cast-bronze inlays smashed and flattened beyond repair. One of the earpieces had been ripped free as well, and the nose guard was pushed in. Brayl and Pannin were on their feet at once, dashing forward, emotions at war in their faces.

"Blasphemy!" Brayl choked.

"What are *you* doing with this," Pannin demanded in turn.

Crim regarded them calmly, as the others gathered behind them. "By blasphemy, I assume you mean the destruction of what was clearly a master-work such as few of any generation have seen."

Pannin glared at her. "That, and the fact that if it's what I think it is, it should *not* have been revealed even to this council without its maker's permission."

"Not even Strynn's," Sipt agreed. "Surely she didn't—"

"No," Crim assured him, turning her gaze to Brayl. "This was found in one of the ground-level storerooms by a cleaning crew on a routine sweep. It was inside an empty barrel, which, by our good luck, they had cause to move. I had it brought straight here. Strynn doesn't know about it . . . yet."

Sipt's face was grim as death. "But surely she knows it's missing. Or do you think— You're not saying you think *she* did it."

Crim shook her head. "Perhaps I should, but I don't. Nor do I think Avall or Rann did this wretched thing."

Pannin nodded slowly. "It would've been Avall's right, as craftsman, to do what he wanted with it. But there's no reason he'd hide it; he'd simply melt it down."

"But Eddyn—" Ayll began.

Brayl glared at him, then likewise nodded—sadly. "It would make sense, of a sort: Eddyn gains access to this helm, destroys it in a fit of jealous rage, then realizes what he's done and flees the hold."

"One more incentive," Sipt added.

"That little fool!" Brayl growled, as much to himself as anyone. "He's al-ready a rapist. Now he's—apparently—destroyed a masterwork. There's no way anyone can forgive this, if it's proven. He'll be lucky to get off with exile."

Nyss stroked her chin. "But why didn't Strynn report it stolen?"

Crim regarded her levelly. "That, my friend, is a very good question, to which the only answer I can supply is that she didn't want anyone to know, because she also didn't want anyone to know Avall was missing."

Mystel's eyes grew huge. "But that implies Avall and Rann left because of something even more important than the destruction of a masterwork. But what could *be* bigger than that? I—"

Brayl's face went suddenly hard. He rounded on Crim furiously. "You led us on!" he spat. "You had the helm all along—something you *still* have no right to see, even as it is—and yet you pretended you knew nothing about it. And you accuse us of harboring secrets!"

"I suspect everyone," Crim replied simply. "I thought one of you might let something slip. No one did," she added.

A gong sounded somewhere in the hold: token that the sun was now a hand above the horizon.

"And now we're out of time," Crim grumbled, "but perhaps we should consider this the first of *many* meetings." She gave the word as much implicit threat as she could muster. "Meanwhile, I'd suggest all of you find out whatever you can. Brayl, you and Pannin keep Strynn under close observation and report *anything* that doesn't violate clan security to me. The rest of you . . . Well, I said it before. I don't like secrets."

"And you?" Ayll inquired archly.

Crim managed a sly smile. "I will hear what you all have to say three days hence. After that . . . let's just say that it's well past time that I offered my condolences to the . . . widow." And with that, she rose and gestured them all into the antechamber.

"It's too bad," Pannin murmured to Ayll as they moved toward the door, "that torture is illegal."

Crim caught that comment and had to bite her lip to keep from laughing. She agreed. But she'd start her interrogation at a more rarefied level entirely.

In spite of the fact that he was her courtesy escort, Nyss found it hard to match paces with Sipt as they made their way down one stone corridor after another, first through Gem-Hold's attics, then through the living quarters. They didn't speak, though Sipt's jaw twitched once or twice, which made Nyss wonder what he might be provoked into revealing under certain circumstances, with particular stimuli.

In any event, she was grateful when they made one last turn, which put them in the common room outside Priest-Clan's suite. Its sigil glittered in the floor, worked in colored marble. Wood-paneled passages teed off to either side, and a light well brought indirect illumination from the rapidly rising sun.

She bowed her thanks and stole away, approaching her suite alone. The lock required two keys, for more reasons than personal security. Nor did she linger in her chambers longer than required to divest herself of cloak and hood, and to retrieve three black tiles, each a hand square, from a secret compartment in one of her bedposts. Thus equipped, she made her way into the bath, knelt, and pressed three other black tiles in one corner simultaneously. Each promptly lowered a finger's width. A deep breath, and she dropped the remaining tiles into the resultant recesses and pressed them down in turn.

Something clicked, and she rose to watch a section of the wall slide back, then aside, revealing a passage barely wider than her shoulders, lit by a lone glow-globe. She entered boldly, pausing only to confirm that the panel had closed behind her, then moved on—straight at first, then up a tightly coiled stair that made her wish she'd chosen house-hose and a short tunic instead of her robes of office.

Soon enough she found herself on the landing of another, better-lit corridor, paved with alternating bands of colored marble. She stepped on certain colors in sequence as she marched along, which would send word of her approach ahead. And was not surprised when the blank wall at the end of the corridor drew back to reveal an antechamber no more than a span square, but as luxuriously decorated as any she'd ever seen, where richness of materials was concerned. The door beyond opened into a room two spans to a side, lit only by a glass-brick wall fronting a light well that bathed the chamber in soft radiance.

A figure sat before it, enthroned in a limestone chair, hooded, cloaked, and with a mouth-mask raised, so that only eyes showed. Thus arrayed, it was impossible to determine the person's age or sex. Twin mugs of cauf steamed on a low table to the figure's right, one of which the host took in a gloved hand and raised in salute.

Nyss did the same. This was ritual. A pause for one sip—the sip of trust—and Nyss spoke without prompting. "They know."

"Ah, but *what* do they know?" the figure replied in a buzzy voice, courtesy of a metal screen affixed to the mask.

"They are questioning why Rrath would dare the Deep with Eddyn. They do not believe his friendship with Eddyn sufficient. And that implies some agenda of his own—which as much as implicates Priest-Clan."

"Can we stand the scrutiny?"

Nyss gnawed her lip for a moment before replying. "The surface can stand it," she said at last, "because the surface doesn't know the heart, and can therefore only speculate, not lie."

"And the heart?"

"The heart must continue," Nyss intoned the ritual words, almost as a sigh. "But it would be best if questions and eyes were directed . . . away from the heart."

The figure remained silent. "Is there other word?"

Nyss shook her head. "No, and we should've heard from Those Outside by now."

"There's been time," the figure acknowledged.

Nyss nodded solemnly. "There should have at least been messages, and none have come, either from the hold itself or those sent onward."

"Which would imply a . . . failure."

Another nod. "The question, then, is whose?"

The figure sighed in turn and took another sip. "The *question,* Nyss, is who, at this moment, commands the gem?"

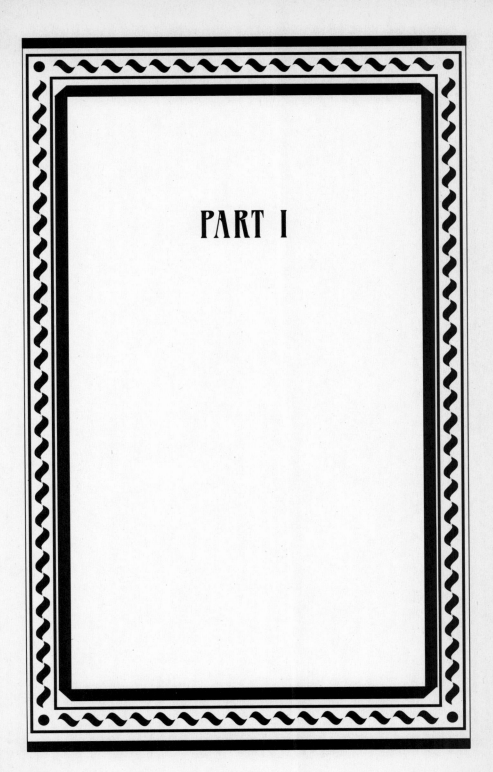

PART I

CHAPTER 1:

EMERGING

(western Eron: near Woodstock Station— Deep Winter: Day XXXV—morning)

~~~~~~~~~~~~~~~~~

Dawn had turned the snow pink. As pink as the tongue of the raccoon that licked rime from its fur, where flakes had sifted into its tree-trunk den during the daylong blizzard. It yawned sleepily, yet something suggested that the air had shifted toward warmth and light, if only briefly, and that this was a good time for foraging. Heaving its compact body out of the rough bark shell, it dropped into snow already frozen hard in only half a night.

A step. Another. A pause.

Something else was awake out here. Something that took no care for the noise it made. Something big, by the sound of it, and coming from that snowbank at the foot of the slope, the one with the peculiarly steep pitch and the overhang that made a cave beneath. The one from which . . . *smoke* was issuing. The raccoon danced back, alarmed. A shift of wind brought that stench more strongly, and with it came others: burned fish and something worse.

The noises increased: scrabblings, the rasp of tearing wood, and angry, guttural cries. A vertical line appeared in the cave's back wall. A hand thrust through, then an arm, as a much larger beast struggled through that slit. It was covered with fur in no pattern that made sense, and had a pale, thin, and very flat face, with big eyes and too little nose to matter.

It stank, too. Of sweat and dirt and death.

The raccoon returned to its den. This was no time for hunting.

Eddyn thought briefly of barring the door behind him and abandoning Rrath in the boathouse where the two of them had sheltered since that blizzard had come ripping out of the east two twilights ago, piling snow atop snow, up past the windows to the eaves—which was what happened when one built in hollows. Fortunately, the structure was sound, and the snow itself provided insulation, which was also fortunate, because there was little left to burn beyond the boats drawn up outside, and Eddyn didn't want to touch them.

Leaving Rrath, however . . .

That was a hard call. Companionship could mean survival when one was outdoors in Deep Winter. On the other hand, he wouldn't *be* here if not for the Priest. Too, Rrath's motives and actions were ambiguous at best, and while his fondness for Eddyn was real—and his hatred of Avall—he'd also shown no compunction about betraying Eddyn to the ghost priests, and drugging him to achieve that goal. In short, he was either very naive or very complex, but easy to underestimate regardless—which made him dangerous.

But Eddyn was stronger. And now that he controlled Rrath's cache of sedatives, he had that advantage as well. A day's worth of arguing coupled with a fair dose of intimidation as recently as breakfast had made that amply clear.

He hoped.

In any event, Rrath seemed cowed right now, judging from the way he was lurking back there in the gloom beside the single unburned table. "Is it . . . safe?" the Priest called tentatively.

Eddyn slogged farther onto the porch. The snow only reached to midcalf. "You tell me; you're the weather-witch."

Rrath joined him. "I have to be outside to do that," he murmured. His breath ghosted into the air as he tugged his hood closer around his face and reached back to snare their skis. He yanked at the door, but it was stuck.

Masking a surge of impatience, Eddyn jerked it closed. Eronese conditioning, if not Eronese Law, said that one should always leave a shelter as one found it. Someone else might need this place. Some *fool*.

"I could've managed," Rrath muttered.

Eddyn nearly hit him. Forced confinement with someone he had little cause to like had worn his always-volatile temper dangerously thin. "I'm sure you could," he growled as he stomped into the waist-high snow drifted around the porch. A pair of strides put him into knee-deep powder atop a hard-packed base. The river glittered a dozen spans beyond, totally iced over save for one narrow channel, courtesy of the steam venting upstream. Pines lined the gorge to every side: dark against the white.

"I was afraid you were going to—"

"I nearly did," Eddyn snapped. "Don't make me regret it."

Rrath glared at him, but his guileless features and youth made him easy to dismiss. "I think we're even," he dared at last.

Eddyn grunted. "Until we reach Tir-Eron."

"Assuming we do."

Eddyn dipped his head to the right, where an impressive escarpment glowered, easily six spans high. Snow softened scorched walls at its summit: the ruins of Woodstock Station, now abandoned. "Might as well get to it."

"But the birkits—"

"Even birkits go to ground in blizzards," Eddyn retorted. "The fact remains: Either the gem is up there, or it's in the Ri-Eron. And while I doubt that Rann or that woman who was with them had the thing, we'd be crazy not to check."

Rrath's eyes flashed challenge for one wild reckless moment, before their fire faded. "Apparently," he spat, "my choice is whether I'm killed by birkits, you, or my own clan."

Eddyn's face was like frozen stone. "That's a fair assessment." And with that, he started up the timbered slope.

Eddyn knew what they would find long before they peered over what had been the way station's outer palisade, but he motioned Rrath to caution anyway.

The tracks told it all: two fresh sets of ski trails from the station to the riverside, ending just out of sight of the boathouse, then footprints going back up, but angling away from the station. Birkit spoor in indeterminate number accompanied both sets, all several hands old.

So Rann and the woman had survived. They'd evidently risen early, skied down to the river to search for Avall's body, and, not finding it, had struck out overland, back into the Wild and heading west. Which made sense, given that both were wounded, and the woman would surely have a permanent shelter fairly close by. More to the point, they *hadn't* pressed on to Tir-Eron. By the look of the sky, he and Rrath shouldn't, either.

"Best I can tell," Rrath murmured, "Rann and the woman left at first light."

Eddyn peered over the blackened wood of the outer palisade. A courtyard lay beyond, clogged with drifted snow from which more blackened timbers rose—the remains of the station proper. And a wellhead. A messy maze of prints, human and birkit, already melting in the fickle morning light. The air was sharp and crisp, but without the deadly bite of the last few days. Eddyn didn't trust it.

Scowling, he began to skirt the wall, targeting what had once been a gate a dozen strides to the right. "We could follow," he observed, "but we've already argued that to death."

"Indeed," Rrath dared. "Of course, two days ago I could've told which way the gem had gone."

Eddyn didn't hear him, having slipped through the gate and entered the compound proper.

Eddyn flung a snow-caked white cloak over the frozen body he'd found sprawled atop a millstone, revealing a tan-green tangle of entrails where its abdomen had been. Fighting back an urge to vomit, he stalked off to the shelter of an arched alcove, facing into the sun. It was almost warm there; snowmelt ran in trickles across the blackened pavement, carrying soot with it, for the fire was barely four days old. They'd been poking and prodding through the ruins for almost half a hand.

It was strange, though, that neither that body—nor the three they'd found stripped to their small clothes in the cellar—had been savaged. They showed claw marks, true, and deep gouges from the fangs that had killed every one of their companions. But the big predators hadn't lingered to avail themselves of fresh, hot-blooded prey.

Which made no sense.

Not that anything else did, either.

When, Eddyn wondered idly, had reality come unraveled?

Rrath joined him, handing him a mug of something that steamed. Eddyn took the drink in a gloved hand and sniffed it suspiciously, then glanced uphill, toward where the ghost priests' camp had been. That, too, barely seemed real.

"So," Rrath ventured primly. "What do you make of the situation, since you seem to have claimed leadership?"

Eddyn stared across the snowy court, noting how blue the shadows looked against the white; how green the needles seemed on the trees. Recalling how red the ghost priests' blood had been when it splashed across the snow.

Shaking his head to clear it, he rose, squinting at the sun, which was approaching noon. "There should still be a fair bit of food around, fire or not. Best we stock up on rations, then head downriver, in case Avall's body has washed up. Not that I expect it to," he added.

Rrath gnawed his lip. "Or . . . we could just stay here in the Wild. We could find another station and weather the winter there, and . . ."

"We could not!" Eddyn huffed. "There's living and there's being alive.

You're letting fear rule you, and that'll get you killed. Except that it might get me killed, too, and that I won't risk. No, we'll press on to Tir-Eron and hope to catch up with Avall on the way—if he's still alive. In either case, I can tell Tyrill what I know and let her handle the rest." *And maybe buy forgiveness,* he added to himself.

"The river will take us there," Eddyn announced, after consuming the rest of the morning consulting the maps he'd salvaged from the ghost priests' camp. He thrust a sheet of parchment beneath Rrath's nose. They were back in the boathouse and the light was bad, for they were letting the fire coast down to embers. Even so, it was sufficient to show the wavy blue line that continued more or less southeast from Woodstock Station, through at least two more days' travel to the plains. Other abandoned stations were marked along the way, lavish reminders of the plague's depredations. A few fish camps were likewise indicated, but they'd be closed for the winter. Right at the point where the Wild met the plain, a tower was sketched: a winter hold.

"There'd be people there, if we need them," Rrath observed.

"Then we don't stop," Eddyn replied flatly. "We'd have no choice but to report to our sub–clan-chiefs, who'd ask all the wrong questions. Never mind that anyone in your clan could be a ghost priest agent."

"Eddyn—"

Eddyn rounded on him. "What're you going to say? That it's over? That you'll conveniently forget that you joined up with a bunch of people no one knows exist, who may be playing major power games here? Do you think they'll let you back out now? Eight, Rrath, who *can* you trust? The only protection you're going to get from here on out is from my clan–or the King. And neither of *those* is guaranteed."

Rrath didn't reply, though Eddyn gave him plenty of time. "The river's the straightest way," he said at length, "and the most level. I'd say we ski on it as much as possible, keeping watch for weak spots. Otherwise, we hug the shore. When we find empty stations, we avail ourselves of whatever supplies remain. Same for fish camps. When we near the hold, we travel down the opposite bank under cover of darkness. There're outbuildings on both shores. If we're lucky, we can shelter in one without getting caught. In any event, we have to get going. There's a fish camp that looks to be no more than a half day's hard trek away. We can target that, and if we make good time, we can think about pressing on to the next one. The map shows the river's fairly smooth that far: no rapids, so the ice should be plenty thick. And there're buoyancy vests in one of the boats we can wear, in case one of us falls through—though we should still travel with rope to hand."

Rrath eyed him neutrally, and the sky with more trepidation. "At this point, I'd simply say we should travel."

. . .

The sun was driving their shadows before them when Rrath and Eddyn finally swung around a particularly imposing granite spire—one of many that ornamented this section of the Wild—and at last caught sight of the snow-capped cluster of low stone domes that comprised the first fish camp. Their shadows obligingly swung left as they turned right, which took them off snow and across bare ice that showed green, and which snapped ominously as Eddyn's weight skimmed across it.

In spite of the weather, it had been an uneventful afternoon, if perhaps the most tiring of Eddyn's life. The frozen river had been monotonously smooth, and there'd been little to appreciate in the endless leagues of trees beneath whose shadows they passed. Trouble was, whichever of them was in the lead (they alternated once every half hand, and tried to keep four spans between them) had also to keep an eye out for patches of open water and thin or rough ice. Never mind checking every pile of flood wrack for signs of Avall. All of which tired the mind out of all proportion to the physical effort involved.

Not that they'd found any trace of his kinsman, or really expected to. His body, in all likelihood, was lodged beneath the ice. If it surfaced at all, it would be around Sunbirth, at the equinox.

There *were* hot springs, however, which often generated sufficient heat to permit stretches of open water. And there were animals that either dug down to water or broke through to it with their weight—sometimes to their detriment, as evidenced by the unfortunate elk they'd found drowned two hands back, supported above the ice only by its magnificent rack.

There were fish, too—a few: enormous, ancient catfish that rose now and then for a gulp of air to augment that which sustained them in the cold, dark depths where they drowsed away the winter unmolested.

But they were closing in on the fish camp now, and that promised sleep of a warmer kind, not to mention a reliable source of food in the form of salt fish stored away to season for the winter.

Eddyn and Rrath ate well that night and slept decently—in an actual bed.

The wind turned bitter the next day, and blew snow in their faces, forcing them to raise mouth-masks, wrap gauze around their eyes, and fret about their ears. Still, they persevered, not altering their pattern until the following evening, when another fish camp did double duty as a way station. And then the storm fell upon them in earnest, forcing them to remain where they were.

Nothing moved outside that second night, in all of eastern Eron.

CHAPTER II:

WISHFUL THINKING

(WESTERN ERON—DEEP WINTER: DAY XXXVIII—EARLY MORNING)

~~~~~~~~~~~~

The hold had been built as a hunting retreat in more prosperous times, and had been deserted eighteen years—since the household to which it was attached had succumbed, every one, to the plague. Four stone slabs, each rougher than the last, marked the ashes of a father, two sons, and a mother. There'd been no one to bury the daughter, but Div and her husband had found her bones in bed when they'd found the hold, four years ago. They'd also found the phial of poison.

It was *Div's* hold now, and typical of such places in the Wild. Which is to say it had thick, rough-log walls; many shuttered windows; steep-pitched roofs of split-board shingles; and a massive fireplace that heated a large common hall and ducted to smaller bedrooms and the bath. Div had lived there with a man from Tannercraft at first, and, later, alone. Now it was filled with her scourings from the Wild: tubers, nuts, and berries she scavenged in season; herbs to flavor the dried or salted fish and flesh that were her staples. And, stretched from countless frames and racked against the walls, the pelts of the beasts she hunted for the trade scrip that bought other food. Like barrels of flour and cauf, jugs of butter, and wheels of cheese.

The rest—notably beer and wine—she'd learned to make on her own from resources at hand. From the forest that enclosed her, ominous and silent, for shots unending.

Her untitled realm.

She was a middle-sized woman of twenty-five, lean and fit, with muscular arms and legs. She was also Eronese, albeit of Common Clan, which meant she had her fair share of beauty—dark blue eyes, black hair worn long for warmth, and fine bones masked by skin scoured rough by weather.

She'd had love and lost it, and had hope and lost it as well—and now, she thought, she might be regaining both. If nothing else, she'd renewed her sense of wonder, her feeling that mysteries beyond her ken still dwelt in the world unsuspected, and that she might yet achieve something worthwhile before she died.

An eighth ago . . . She'd been empty then: hunting competently, trapping often enough to ensure next year's trade; usually full, usually warm—yet listless and numb, with no ties to anyone alive. Her husband was dead of a wound acquired during a blizzard, when *no one* moved in the Wild. Her womb was bare, courtesy of a late-term miscarriage that had rendered her unable to conceive again.

But she now knew things and people she hadn't known before, and, for the first time in ages, felt some stirrings of passion.

So she sat on her front porch that morning, feet on the carved wood rail, gazing out at a grove of pines poking through snow that would've reached her thighs. The sky was blue as thick ice, and the mountains of Angen's Spine rose like a purple wall to her right. The air was crisp but bearable, and she'd pushed back her hood and unlaced her overtunic. A mug of mulled cider steamed beside her.

Her back itched, down by the crest of her hip, where an arrow had found her five days ago. She clawed at it through layers of leather, grateful for the fact that it had healed far faster than it ought, yet perplexed that it seemed to heal that way no longer, as though whatever had driven that healing had been exhausted.

She assumed it was a function of Avall's curious gem. The Eight knew it had healed him more than once, and seemed to work its . . . magic on her and Rann as well. But whatever virtues it possessed were locked within it, and in its absence—whether from time or distance—those powers were dissipating.

More proof lay before her.

A female birkit had ambled from the woods soon after she'd sat down, falling lazily at her feet in a wash of thick silver-white fur that a year ago she'd have been tanning this very moment. It was safe now, it knew, and had suffered her to run her hands through that marvelous pelt, feeling the strong heavy muscles that powered it. She'd even dared scratch between its calm green eyes. But when she'd tried to touch its mind, as the gem had previously allowed, she'd found only a blur of startled recognition.

So *that* was fading, too.

Rann would know for certain, but Rann was gone. She'd *urged* him to go—on to Gem-Hold while she stayed here to recover. He'd left the previous morning.

Rann . . .

Rann changed everything. He was young, beautiful, talented, and loyal. If not rich, he was at least attached by adoption to a powerful clan. He liked her enough to treat her as an equal, which was not a given with High Clan men. He'd also made love to her—at first from raw need and afterward as though he cared—though she had sense enough to know he'd likewise sought solace for the loss of his bond-brother, whose death he still denied.

Which was stupid. She'd *seen* Avall fall: on the brink of the escarpment one moment, then grasping his chest and tumbling over the next. Arrows had flown, and whether or not they'd caught him as they'd caught her, Avall *had* fallen into icy water.

No one survived such things.

But wounds like hers didn't heal in five days, either.

And women didn't converse with birkits.

So Div sat and pondered, and looked to the west, where lay hope in the form of Rann, on his way to Gem-Hold-Winter.

And then looked east, to where more hope, and yet *more* danger, lay: in Tir-Eron.

Which way she would go when the time came for going, she had no idea. But she knew she'd spent her last winter in the Wild.

(GEM-HOLD-WINTER—DEEP WINTER: DAY XXXVIII—MIDMORNING)

Strynn san Ferr was wondering if she should send a hall page in search of the breakfast that ought, by rights, to have arrived by now—one of the perks of being pregnant—when a knock sounded on the door to her suite.

Stifling a yawn, she rose slowly and made her way to the vestibule, wishing she felt less lethargic. Then again, she'd been lucky; most women in her condition were throwing up half their meals by now. "Who is it?" she called, having learned that caution when she'd pretended to nursemaid an Avall who was supposedly ill with flux. *That* little bit of subterfuge hadn't lasted as long as it might, she reflected. Not that she'd expected it to.

"Breakfast—lady," came a muffled reply—female, but no one she recognized.

She shot the bolt without thinking, and stood back to admit a page in gemcraft livery, bearing the delinquent breakfast tray. Too late she realized that the page was not alone, and who was looming behind her, though not in her official cloak and hood.

Crim, the Hold-Warden.

Strynn's heart skipped a beat. She should've expected something like this. After all, hadn't Pannin, Sipt, and Brayl all paid what they claimed to be courtesy calls during the last few days? Not to mention, Ikkin, Subcraft-Chief of Smith, and Nyss of Priest-Clan—who'd offered condolences for her loss and stressed the availability of her clan, should Strynn feel her soul in any way . . . encumbered.

Of course the subchiefs of Ferr, and Argen-yr and -a, respectively, had also managed to quiz her *quite* thoroughly on her whereabouts during a recent period. Which didn't surprise her, either, since she'd heard from her own sources that they were trying to account for every moment of her time since Brayl had last seen Eddyn. And there'd also been questions about Avall's progress on the helm, though no one had been tactless enough to request a viewing. Which was fortunate; she'd found the evidence of its destruction and hasty removal. It was the hardest thing she'd ever done *not* to report that to the relevant authorities.

The most ranking of whom was now waiting just beyond her threshold.

She wasn't up for verbal fencing this early, yet had no choice but to admit the Warden. But not until the breakfast had been deposited on a nearby table, and the page had bowed her way out, did Crim clear her throat, the meaning of which was clear.

"Lady Warden," Strynn murmured, "be welcome in these rooms, where I dwell by your largesse." It was the full formal greeting, which thereby indicated that she intended to play the following interview by ritual rules. There would be no confidences exchanged here today—not from her.

"I am honored," Crim replied tersely, stepping across the threshold. Only then did Strynn notice that she was carrying something at waist level. Something draped in a black-velvet pall, barely visible against a robe of the same fabric and color.

Her heart skipped again. Something about that shape . . .

"You look . . . pale," Crim continued, nodding to the page to close the door behind her. "Then again, you have been under a certain amount of strain."

Strynn looked Crim straight in the eye. "I assume this is not a courtesy visit."

Crim stifled a chuckle. "Oh, but it is, if you consider it courtesy to return lost property to those who have let it stray." She looked past Strynn, toward Avall's workroom. "I don't suppose your husband . . ."

"He's not here," Strynn replied. "I don't know when he'll return." Both of which statements were absolutely true.

"And you'll say no more until it may be said before King and Council, if I know you," Crim shot back. "Very well, I had hoped to win your cooperation, but I see it is not forthcoming." Without further comment, she set the draped object on the table beside the food. "May I sit?" she continued. "I haven't the patience for games, Strynn, and by the look of you, neither do you—at heart."

Strynn gestured to a chair, then, after a pause, claimed another. She didn't speak, however. This was Crim's gambit; let her play it.

Crim took a deep breath. A variety of emotions played across her features before they settled on weary honesty—which might be an act and might not. "I have one thing to say, Strynn," she began. "I don't give a bucket of frozen piss about clan politics. Whatever is between Avall and Eddyn and whoever else they've managed to involve in this little escapade of theirs is none of my concern. What *does* concern me is that four people under my guardianship in this hold have gone missing, and for that I will be held accountable. Granted, my clan and yours have anciently been allies, and Rann is even distantly connected to it, but I honestly don't care about that. I do care about my honor and my reputation. And, though I know it sounds hollow in light of what I've just said, I care about the lives of those who have . . . vanished. Don't you understand that, Strynn? One can spend every moment imagining plots, discoveries, deceptions, rivalries—dares. You name it. The fact remains that four young men I have no cause to hate and some cause to admire, if not love, based on the little I've seen of them, may very well be dead. I have to do what I can to locate them. I have no choice. It's my charge as Hold-Warden, my responsibility as clan-kin to one of them, and my duty as a human being. 'There are no enemies in the Deep.' You've heard that. I believe it's true. So if there's anything I can do to save those men's lives— *anything* at all, Strynn—please tell me. I'll muster this whole hold to search, if need be. It would be unprecedented, but I'll do it. My honor means that much to me."

Strynn didn't look at her. Her mind was racing. Crim seemed sincere. Report named her among the most evenhanded of Hold-Wardens. If she could trust anyone—and The Eight knew she was tired of bearing this alone, save for Kylin—perhaps . . .

But would Avall then forgive her? It would remove his awful secret from the control of her husband's clan. And if she hadn't told her own Sub–Clan-Chief, why should she now confide in Crim?

"I'm sorry," she heard herself saying. "I don't think there's hope of anyone finding them now. But I promise *you,* Crim, Ferr and Argen alike will be grateful for your . . . cooperation. You can only profit from my silence, and your clan can only profit from yours."

Crim's eyes narrowed, but finally she nodded stiffly and rose. "Consider what I have brought you," she said. "I didn't have to do that. And remember, Strynn, that by bringing you that, I have in effect brought you Eddyn's head. That's a nice symmetry, don't you think?"

Strynn—almost—smiled. "Spring approaches," she replied. "And I do thank you, Lady, for your concern."

"Spring approaches," Crim echoed, from the door. "Let us hope the melting snow brings no harsh surprises for either of us." And then she was gone.

Strynn locked the door and managed to eat her breakfast. But another hand elapsed before she dared remove the black-velvet pall from Crim's . . . gift. She spent the next half hand weeping.

CHAPTER III:

RING OF TRUTH

(THE FLAT—DEEP WINTER: DAY XXXVIII—MIDDAY)

~~~~~~~~~~

T wo rings.

Identical golden bands. Identical bloodred stones.

The black velvet on which they lay, a hand apart, set off their work-manship to perfection. *Eronese* workmanship: the best there was. Stolen or imported, it didn't matter. The candlelight that was their sole illumina-tion made them spark and glitter like things alive. And maybe, just possibly, they were.

Certainly everyone observing them had seen them move toward each other, so that the smooth-shaved faces bearing the cross-in-circle design had clicked together, as iron bars sometimes did.

Three people stared at those rings.

One was twice the age of the others, and ten years more. He was tall, fit, and dark-skinned—and not only from the ravages of sun and heat. His hair was barely a finger's width long, and the skin of his skull showed through. His brows were black, his eyes the same—in this light. He had little in the way of lips, but a frame of close-clipped beard compensated somewhat for that deficiency.

He wore rich clothes—sylks and velvets—but sand and sweat had stained his tawny undertunic. An indentation that would coincide with the rim of a helmet circled his brow, while another, in the shape of a buckle, showed beneath his chin. His name was Lynnz. He was War Commander of the Kingdom of Ixti—and also its chief torturer.

It was in that capacity that he was staring by turns at the two rings, and at the other two people sitting at either end of the low camp table. One was well dressed; the other desert-clad. One male and one female. And both—to judge by the expressions they were trying to hide behind stoic facades—very, very frightened.

"The rings know each other," Lynnz said amiably, in Eronese. "From there, it was not a large assumption—even before your actions confirmed as much—that you two know each other. Especially as there are only four rings like that in the world, and I know for a fact that their owners would never part with them, save in extreme duress."

The young man to his left, who was also his half nephew, didn't reply, though he desperately wanted to. Well fed and well clothed because he was also a royal prince, he was nevertheless exhausted—because he'd also been in self-imposed exile in the Flat—the vast wasteland between Ixti, which was his homeland, and Eron, where he'd sought sanctuary.

His name was Kraxxi, and a season ago his prime concerns had been boredom and worrying about why King Barrax, his father, favored his half brother, Azzli, over him. It was in response to the former that he'd joined the latter on an illicit hunting trip during which Azzli had been killed—by an accidental swipe of Kraxxi's sword.

Which was still kinslaying, which was a capital offense in Ixti, even for princes. And since there was reason to suspect the affair had not been entirely accidental, he had two reasons to exile himself. As someone once had said, suicide didn't have to be rapid. So he and three loyal friends had gone into the Flat and, against all hope, made their way to Eron.

Where he'd met the woman sitting opposite him, whose name was Merryn, and lost his heart to her soon after, even as he'd also found a possible way to regain honor in his homeland. At her expense.

Kraxxi wondered what she'd seen in him. Not much—if he'd looked then like he did now: wiry, almost gaunt; hairy-armed and -legged, where the men of her homeland were waxed sleekly smooth; chin and jaw dark with stubble they'd not let him shave for fear of what he might choose to cut instead.

He wasn't sure if he wanted to know what she thought of him now, and she, like he, was guarding her expression. He *had* loved her; that much was clear. But he'd had no choice but to . . . betray her, he supposed, caught between love of land and love of woman.

"Pay attention, boy!" Lynnz thundered.

Kraxxi blinked and, in spite of courtesy, yawned. He couldn't help it. They'd fed him well when he'd come stumbling out of the Flat three days ago. They'd let him bathe, and had given him fine clothes and a warm place to stay.

And denied him sleep since his arrival.

Even after Merryn had set fire to Lynnz's tent.

Then again, Lynnz *was* a torturer.

He wondered how they'd try to get at Merryn.

"I will speak only to my father," Kraxxi heard himself saying. Repeating the litany he'd been uttering anytime his acts or intentions were put to question.

It was the truth, too. What he knew—what he'd learned from Merryn without her knowledge—could make the difference between war and peace—though Kraxxi feared it was too late already. The force arrayed here—officially an intelligence mission—implied the former, but he didn't want to think about that. He looked at the rings instead, one of which had belonged to him, given to him as a bonding present by a friend who was blessedly far away. And then, surreptitiously, he looked at Merryn.

Even scoured by the wind and cold of the Flat, and covered with mud beneath a film of desert dust, she was impressive. She was tall for an Ixtian woman, though not for an Eronese—nearly as tall as Kraxxi, in fact. She weighed as much as him, too. And, like most Eronese, she had black hair and dark blue eyes, a slender build, and finely wrought features—fortunate, given how much the folk of that land treasured beautiful things and their making.

But there was more to her than beauty. She possessed a wildness, a rebelliousness—an unwillingness to be restrained by anyone or thing unless *she* willed it—that had called to that same latent impulse in him and wakened it to roaring life. For a while they'd been exotic curiosities to each other. And then they'd become lovers, without her knowing who he was, because he wanted her to love him for himself.

She probably *did* love him, too, else she'd not have come south seeking him. Not after what had happened. Or maybe she'd pursued him for revenge. That would be like her as well. But either way, whatever they did to him, he would not betray her again—ever.

"I'm talking to you, boy!" Lynnz all but yelled, reaching over to cuff Kraxxi, which made him realize he'd fallen into the dreamy lethargy of his thoughts twice in ten breaths. "I know about these rings. I know where you got yours. It would be good to know how the other came into this woman's keeping."

Kraxxi didn't reply.

"Shall I tell you?" Lynnz continued with wicked amiability. "A healer woman from Eron married a soldier from Ixti, who was attached to the royal court. She brought with her an odd red stone she'd found in that land, the parts of which, when broken, pointed to the other parts no matter where they were. In due time she had three children at one birth, who became friends with the king's son of Ixti. They ran wild, as children will, and she made the stone into four rings so that she could keep up with her brood. One of that brood, in turn, gave his ring to the son of the king as a sign of affection. That ring is yours, Prince Kraxxi."

He paused for a sip of pungent, resin-scented wine, which he didn't share.

"I will speak only to my father," Kraxxi mumbled wearily. Nor did he know, save that *he* hadn't given it to her. Merryn did not reply, either—or in any other way acknowledge their presence.

Lynnz sighed. "Well, the civilized option having now been exhausted, I suppose I must resort to alternatives."

Kraxxi felt his blood run cold, but tried not to show it. "I will speak only to my father," he said again. "I will speak—" He didn't finish, because, with a force that cut his lips, Lord Lynnz, Warlord of Ixti, slapped him.

Kraxxi slept, then. Or fell unconscious. It didn't matter.

(THE FLAT—DEEP WINTER: DAY XXXIX—MIDDAY)

The manacles were padded, and they hadn't left her naked after they'd stripped and searched her—which were about the only good parts of her current situation, Merryn had decided during her last lucid interval in the near-stifling darkness of the tent.

She hadn't revealed who she was, as far as she knew—not verbally, though Kraxxi had blurted out that she was "cousin to the King of Eron." But her captors had wasted no time in summoning someone well versed in Eronese clan tattoos to inspect the one on her left shoulder—which showed the characteristic insignia of Clan Argen, augmented by the knotwork border of her own sept, Argen-a, which presided over workers in precious metal. They'd know that, too, of course, since every clan controlled a specific craft. But what the tattoos did not reveal was that—though she'd been trained as a smith, she'd displayed an early aptitude for more physical arts, and when she'd come to her official Raising during the eighth after her twentieth birthday, she'd requested a tour at War-Hold. Which was where she'd met Kraxxi—and damn him for it, too.

Not that she wanted any of that known just now, though some of it was implicit by association, since War-Hold-Winter was the closest craft hold to the Flat.

As for the torture . . . It was odd. It was also subtle. Her captors clearly knew enough of Eronese training to know that she would've been conditioned to a high pain threshold indeed. And while there were certainly things they could do to surpass it, those things generally came with a cost— like a broken mind.

Of course they could always have threatened her beauty—since her countrymen (and herself, she conceded) prized aesthetics above all else. But that would also have been a last resort. Actually, she agreed with their methods: Use the subtle approach at first, the one least likely to do permanent harm— and, quite possibly, the one least likely to be remembered.

She'd resisted so far, but another round was surely about to begin.

They were using imphor wood, which was nothing if not versatile.

Back home in Eron, it was often used, illegally, before sports competitions, since it enhanced reflexes and deadened the pain response. A stick of it in the mouth during minor surgery served as anesthetic. But the fumes could *also* deaden the mind in such a way that a person felt compelled to tell the truth.

Fortunately, the more one took, the more resistance one built up, which was part of the training at War-Hold. But one must be careful for all that. Too much too fast made one reckless and wild—which got one killed. More—especially burned as incense—could make one hallucinate.

Whoever had been entrusted with her knew that very well indeed.

It had been deceptively simple at first. The search, and then the shift they'd given her to put on, and then the manacles, which gave her room to move somewhat, but which effectively pegged her spread-eagled on the carpeted floor of a thick-walled tent.

And then a brazier was introduced, full of smoking sprigs of very fresh imphor indeed—twig and leaf. It had smoked like crazy, and she'd tried not to inhale but ultimately had no choice. And eventually she'd found herself intrigued past endurance by the texture of the pile on which she lay, and how certain colors felt slightly different against her skin, and in trying to read the pattern through the flesh of her calves and thighs.

At some point, someone had removed the brazier, then returned to sit calmly at her feet, face shrouded by a veil of wet sylk. "Who are you?" that one had demanded. "Whence do you come? What is your connection to Prince Kraxxi? What is this secret he would convey?"

That was it. Over and over. She'd started to answer, too, but had become interested in the difference between dark blue and purple, and had begun explaining that instead, which had then prompted an ongoing analysis of how words felt on one's tongue, and the fact that they likewise had colors.

Eventually, her inquisitor had departed, and the air had slowly cleared. Too much imphor would do lasting damage—and most inquisitors only stayed until they began to feel themselves affected.

Her next dose would be stronger, though, and she dreaded it. The next level, so she'd read, usually involved the inquisitors trying to frighten the truth from one by playing on fears through verbal suggestions.

As if sensing that anxiety, the brazier returned, along with another one. Imphor and something else she didn't recognize. She closed her eyes, tried to sleep. Or pass out. Or go into trance. Anything that would wall away her mind. Along with that, she tried to take shallow breaths, and them as rarely as possible.

But the fumes, especially the new ones, were pervasive and not unpleasant, and before she knew it, she was inhaling ever more deeply, even as her mind recoiled.

And with those breaths came muttered words in soft female voices.

"Think of who you love, and then think of what you fear."

Repeated.

Endlessly.

She resisted, but she'd been raised to worship the arts, and one art was that of the storyteller, and so she began to construct images . . .

. . . a woman beautiful beyond description, for neither she nor anyone else could explain how Strynn—for so it was: her bond-sister—could have a face like most other High Clan women and yet surpass them all, to be accounted the most beautiful woman of her time.

They'd become bond-sisters at their first bleeding, and confirmed that bond every year after. Strynn had been gawky then, and Merryn often mistaken for a boy, so physical attraction clearly hadn't mattered. And though they'd pleasured themselves with each other, as bond-mates usually did, that had never been the basis of their affection.

But to lose Strynn—that was what she feared most. And yet she couldn't help thinking of that loss, and all the ways it could be accomplished. And so she saw . . .

Strynn working bare-armed before a forge, hammering out swords and daggers and axes. No, a particular *sword—and she was leaning far over the forge, and the fire was leaping up and raking that perfectly smooth face, and finding a hold in her hair, so that it, too, blazed up, and Strynn was screaming, and then her robe had also taken fire and she was all aflame, and nobody was helping, though many stood around to point and cheer. And then she glimpsed Strynn's face with the brow and lashes burned away, and the lips and nose starting to melt—and Strynn said one thing: "This is all your fault."*

And then Merryn screamed and closed her eyes, but what she found inside them was also Strynn . . .

. . . *lying in an odd sort of bed, her belly as big as the biggest summer melon. She wore a shift, but it was open around that swelling, and movement occurred there, like ripples in still water. Strynn's legs were spread, and she half lay, half squatted, so that the draw of the earth would help the baby out. But the baby wouldn't come, though Strynn screamed at it to be born, and cursed the midwives* gathered round, and then cursed Merryn's brother, Avall, who had put this baby in her . . .

Except that wasn't right. This was Eddyn's child, the fruit of his seed. Avall was only the acknowledged father, chosen to circumvent Eddyn's attempts to woo her.

And it didn't matter, because the child was coming out all wrong, and blood was coming, too: first a trickle then a gush that made odd harmony with the sound of Strynn's screaming, and then the baby's shoulders were free—but it was pushing out, and grinning a grin that looked exactly like Eddyn's, and then it tore at Strynn's womanhood and ripped her all asunder: a terrible gash from between her legs to halfway up her belly.

Strynn screamed. The baby laughed. And then Strynn died . . .

But the screaming never ended, and it took Merryn a while to realize that it was her own.

"Avall!" she shouted. "Save me!"

Merryn! he gave back, the merest whisper.

"Avall—!"

It was him, too: Avall speaking to her mind, through that strange bond born of a gem she had never seen. But though she felt him there, he was no longer responding. Still, wherever he was could only be better than here, and so she went to him—that which was most truly her did. And though it was cold beyond bearing where he was, Merryn found refuge there and rested.

"Is she dead?" she heard someone whisper, and that true voice sounded loud as thunder.

"No," another roared back. "But we dare not increase the dose until tomorrow."

"If you lie very still, it is less likely they will sting you," Lynnz advised, from where he leaned casually against the polished metal railing that surrounded the sand on which Kraxxi lay. Unlike Merryn, he lay in broad daylight, spread-eagled on sand, not carpet. And while tent walls rose around him, there was no roof, and the midday sun beat down on his flesh, every bit of which was ruthlessly exposed. That sun beat down on metal, too: an inward-sloping circle of oiled brass, designed to keep certain things confined.

Very large, very black, very deadly somethings.

"The scorpions don't generally start on anything important," Lynnz offered helpfully. "In fact, they'll ignore you entirely until you start to sweat. After that . . . they'll sample that sweat. And then they'll find they like the places where most of that sweat occurs, and notice how the skin tends to be softer there, and they'll start to . . . nibble."

He helped himself to a swallow of wine from a goblet on a camp table beside him. "They'll have trouble with your forehead because it's smooth, so they'll probably go for where the sweat pools by your ears—which are also just of a size for them to get their mouths around. Eyes . . . Probably not, there's something about them that repels them. Noses don't sweat much, but as the day gets hotter, they'll be looking for caves, and though these are much too big, they might want to probe inside your nostrils. Be sure not to sneeze. A sting in the face is very bad. Not treated, stings tend to fester, and then the flesh around the wound drops off. And that's with the small ones."

Another swallow, and for the first time, Kraxxi felt something brush against his bare thigh. Or had it?

It was as if Lynnz read his mind. "Was that real?" he wondered. "Or was that your imagination? Doesn't really matter, does it? Not when I'm giving you advice.

"Now, as I was saying, they like salt and soft places, and in the day, they like tunnels. So I'd be thinking about my armpits, which embody all three of those things—and you'll notice that we've made sure your legs are wide apart. There are all kinds of interesting dark and sweaty places down there."

Kraxxi tensed in spite of himself, then, as slowly as he could, relaxed.

"Did I mention," Lynnz purred, "that one of these is a female—with young? I've heard *they* like to burrow."

Kraxxi knew what Lynnz was doing: trying to instill fear in his mind, knowing that a person's anxieties could overrule actual facts, letting the person being tortured do all of the torturer's work.

He wasn't even that afraid of scorpions, beyond the usual healthy respect any intelligent person granted them.

Which didn't mean he liked them, or that he wouldn't be able to feel them doing what Lynnz had said. He was ticklish, too—extremely—and while he doubted they'd actually let him die, he also doubted they'd spare him pain. Nor was this Eron, where kings must be physically perfect in order to reign. Here it wouldn't matter if he had a nibbled earlobe, or eyelid, or . . . scrotum.

No! He was doing exactly what Lynnz wanted: thinking about what *might* happen, when none of it was a surety.

What *was* a surety was that they wouldn't let him die until he'd come face-to-face with his father. And if they thought he didn't know that word had gone out by the fastest messenger to inform Barrax of Ixti that his wayward heir had been found, they were more than fools.

So he had to endure—a while. Two days—four. An eighth at most—and somewhere during that time they'd surely expedite the interrogation by moving him closer to his father. Closer to Ixti.

And Merryn . . . He dared not think about her. She was strong, and they'd do nothing to her that would provoke a war. For though Ixti wanted war, they wanted it on their terms—and on Eronese soil. Eron come south was not an option Barrax would risk.

Besides, there was one thing Lynnz hadn't reckoned on before he'd begun this torture session, which was that Kraxxi had been deprived of sleep for days before it had begun. At some point his body would take over. And sleeping men chained to the ground could not be bothered overmuch by anything as minor as tickling.

Which was good, because he could hear something raking across the sand, not far from his left ear.

(THE FLAT—DEEP WINTER: DAY XL—EARLY EVENING)

Zrill's mount was not one he would have chosen for a wild midnight ride across the desert. As Lynnz's Master of Horse, he naturally knew more than a little about the suitability of mounts for situations, and would've picked something more surefooted, even were it slower, for any less clandestine activity. But since he *was* Master of Horse, no one dared question his choice of steeds. And since he was known to be a loner, no one questioned him disappearing into the desert, either. The official excuse was that every spare horse, even pack animals, had to be given rigorous regular exercise, and that Zrill himself would take beasts at random for long gallops, so as to assess their care and condition. But since Lynnz's infernal meetings and intelligence reports seemed to consume most of the day, the only time that could actually be accomplished was after the evening meal, which was traditionally served at sunset.

Taking an unimportant horse on an important mission was therefore a good way to disguise his trail. And thank the Gods for the steady desert wind that would either disperse his tracks entirely or fill them with what little drifting snow still remained on the Flat.

And it *was* an important mission, of that there was no doubt—though not one that would please Lynnz if he knew. Zrill reined in Obyll, the sturdy black mare, at the top of the long ridge southwest of Lynnz's camp, such that any observing his progress would see what they expected: him putting her through her paces.

Actually, however, it gave him a chance to note if anyone was marking his departure. The camp had a perimeter guard, though a sketchy one, since the Flat was no-man's-land, and the main threat that might be brought against it was not from man at all, but from nature. And sure enough, he could see the west guard marching his slow patrol in his gold-sylk winter cloak and high-domed, gold-washed helm. Not that Zrill could see those details, only the cloak as a splotch of light against darker tents, and the occasional gleam of firelight on the helm. A flickering behind the guard was his shadow, splashed by the largest visible moon across the landscape of tents.

It was too big a camp, Zrill thought: too big for mere reconnoiter. But of course everyone else knew that as well.

On the other hand, it was too small for an all-out attack. So what was it? He wasn't sure, save that it was certainly a monument to Lynnz's pride.

But he'd tarried long enough. The desert beckoned; the vast, blue-black arch of sky lured him on. Heels to Obyll's sides, he moved, down the stonier western slope of the ridge and into snow at the bottom. Not much snow—a hand's depth here and there in the most shadowed places—but enough to remind him that Eron wasn't impossibly far away, and that snow was a way of life there, though even Eron's folk had the sense to hide from it in their vast winter holds during what that land called Deep Winter.

The wind was from the south, though—from Ixti—and it carried with it the scents of coming spring. As if sensing that, Obyll snorted with what sounded suspiciously like delight, and of her own will strove to move faster. Zrill let her—cautiously, for stones could lurk beneath that snow. And worse. He'd heard rumors—things babbled by the Eronese woman in one of her torture sessions—that the Prince had lost a mount to a scorpion burrow.

And there were more scorpions here than farther north.

Still, he was young—twenty-five—and strong enough to survive even if he lost a steed. He was also well fed, and had more food in his saddlebags, and weapons, because no one left Lynnz's camp without them. Finally, he wore more clothing than might be apparent, because he was never certain when he might be marooned out here.

But for the moment, all was well, and so he and Obyll kept going.

He was still riding when midnight rose overhead. Desert still surrounded him, but it was flatter now, and comprised of sand interspersed with stone. One moon had set and two risen to replace it, washing the place with a strange admixture of shadows. But what drew Zrill's attention was a dark crescent in the landscape straight ahead, as though some vast *thing* had taken a bite from the earth—a crescent that a finger's farther riding revealed to be a declivity in the land. It was in fact the rim of the Pit, as the escarpment-edged depression that occupied most of the Flat's western half was called. And except for a few odd streams below that rim, it made the desolation of the Flat resemble a garden.

It was also Zrill's goal. He reined Obyll to a walk and nudged her north. He'd missed a minor landmark—the spires of wind-worked sandstone hereabouts looked too much alike in the dark—and had arrived south of his goal. Not that it was a problem. It was simply that he prided himself on not making such fundamental errors.

Mistakes got you killed; they got you found out and distrusted. Trust was very important to Zrill—and not only Lord Lynnz's.

He'd reached the rim now, and dared to peer over the cliff. It was fairly low here—only a dozen spans—and was marked and fissured with any number of depressions that looked like the start of a way down. Only one was, however, and he found it with little trouble a hand later, though he had to dismount to guide a frightened Obyll part of the way. The trail was narrow, and the moonlight too faint to show a clear way to the bottom. He therefore felt a certain comfort when, halfway down, a black-clad figure melted from the rocks to his right to block his path, face veiled by a black-sylk mouth-mask, but with a sword clearly visible.

"Zrill min Bizz," Zrill announced. "The scorpion stings its own kind."

"The sting is the child of the sword," came the reply.

The figure—he'd never known its sex—merged back into the shadows. Zrill exhaled a breath he didn't know he'd been holding and edged past.

A second figure intercepted him where the trail issued into a flat sand field at the foot of the cliff. The Pit swept away to the west, a featureless, dark-sanded abomination as anonymous as a waveless ocean.

"The sting is the child of the sword," he intoned.

"A child with a sword should be stung," came the reply.

And once again Zrill moved on.

The cliff to the right was pocked with caves at various levels, all of which he ignored until he rounded a certain head-high outcrop and turned sharp right, which put him face-to-face with one from which issued a furtive light. So little light, in fact, and so precisely located, that only one seeking it would notice.

He followed it into the cliff. Turned left, and relaxed as that light washed out to meet him, becoming brighter and clearer as he progressed. The cave walls changed, too, becoming smoother, squarer, and straighter, and he could hear voices now, and smell food. The scent of stables reached him as well, and then suddenly a tunnel opened to one side, down which he heard louder talk. A few paces farther on he passed an actual door, and then he was facing a much larger door indeed: gilded bronze twice as high as his head. Tunnels broke off to right and left. A sexless figure appeared from the right-hand one, to relieve him of Obyll, as another made to undo his mouth-mask.

He intercepted the black-gloved hand and drew it down. "Zrill," he repeated, and stopped where he was, arms folded, staring at the doors.

"A moment," the left one replied, and strode away.

More quickly than he'd expected, both doors parted down the middle, and as soon as the gap was wide enough to admit him, Zrill stepped boldly through.

Had he not known he was inside a cave, and many shots from civilization,

Zrill would've sworn he was in some princeling's pleasure dome. Marble surrounded him. The trickle of water reached his ears from rills hidden beneath bronze screens, exactly as in Barrax's palace. The ceiling was a sweep of white sylk that continued down the walls to define chambers, all kept carefully away from the myriad beeswax candles and the odd glow-globe imported from Eron.

A few people lolled about, but only a few. In spite of the luxury, the place had an austere feel, like a well-run military camp.

Which it was.

Zrill would've been impressed had he not been here before. And at that, there were a few things he'd forgotten, which always impressed him anew.

One of which was the way that Barrax, though he was king of Ixti, could often be found lounging casually about as though he were some particularly well-clad and well-groomed off-duty soldier.

The king saw him before Zrill was aware of his presence, and called the Horse Master by name, motioning him to the cushion opposite, in an alcove defined mostly by walls of sylk. A tray of cold meat sat there, surrounded by a crescent of sauces arranged from sweet to sharp.

Zrill met the king's eyes briefly, then withdrew his ceremonial geen-claw dagger and, with a formal nod and bow, laid it on the carpet before him.

"Step into my home," Barrax said, already reaching for a brass wine ewer from which he filled a twin goblet to his own.

"Majesty—"

"You rode shots to meet me and, king or no, it is I who am in your debt."

Zrill nodded and sat down, cross-legged. Barrax's face was intense. And though well combed, his black hair was in need of trimming.

A pause for the ritual sip of peace, and for another to slake his thirst, and Zrill set down the goblet. "This news shouldn't wait," he began. "In short, Prince Kraxxi has returned."

Barrax tensed, and his eyes flashed, but he showed no other reaction—which surprised Zrill. "Returned," he mused. "Was that the word you would choose?"

Zrill nodded. "He came out of the Flat five sunsets back. To my eternal regret, there was no way I could get away until now. Lynnz made me watch."

"Watch?"

"The . . . preparation. He treated him well—fed him, bathed him, kept him warm, and gave him fine clothes—but denied him sleep."

"For no reason?"

"Maybe for a reason. Kraxxi was there by choice, that much was clear. He was seeking you. The only thing he would say, when put to any question, was, 'I will speak only to my father.'"

Barrax snorted with laughter. "And of course Lynnz sent messengers immediately to the court at Ixtianos, where he presumes I am."

Zrill dared a chuckle of his own, having had some version of this conversation before. "Where he indeed presumes you are. Where a well-paid actor lives in luxury before he—"

"Not dies," Barrax finished for him. "Is put to sea and told to sail south and not return."

"Have any?"

"None of which one might speak." Barrax laughed again, but something about his expression told Zrill he was treading on dangerous ground. There were limits, he supposed, even to one of the few outside Barrax's circle to know that the royal court officially functioning in Ixti was a sham, and that Barrax had ordered his most trusted guard and staff, and all his southern levies, to meet him here, in this secret place in the Pit, while he took stock of the lord of his northern levies, Lord Lynnz. And waited.

"Is there more you would tell?" Barrax asked, filling another goblet for Zrill.

Zrill took it gratefully. "Aye, lord king, there is."

And with that he told all he had seen and witnessed about Prince Kraxxi and the woman whose name neither the prince nor the woman herself would reveal.

When he was finished, Barrax rose. "You have stayed as long as you dare," he said. "Would that I could reward you with rest as well as gold, but alas, that may not be—though you may certainly take that goblet as token of this meeting. For the rest . . . I go to ponder what this news might be that my son thinks will buy his life."

CHAPTER IV:

WITCHING

(WESTERN ERON–DEEP WINTER: DAY XL–MIDMORNING)

~~~~~~~~~~

Rrath awakened to cold feet, the scent of salt-dried fish stewing to palatability, and Eddyn sitting in the wide-open doorway studying the map. In spite of his bedroll, a layer of furs, and a pile of ratty blankets they'd found at this latest fish camp, he shivered. And would have feigned sleep longer, had Eddyn's sharp gaze not caught him with his eyes open.

"You have to get up sometime," Eddyn said mildly—disarmingly. Almost like a friend. "I let you sleep because you needed to. You've been pushing hard, for someone your size."

"I'm fine," Rrath snapped, finding no energy for politeness this early, even if both things were true. Eddyn *was* bigger—and stronger—yet they'd covered the same distance; it stood to reason he'd had to work harder to achieve the same results. At least they hadn't lacked for food the last few days, all of which they'd concluded at fish camps, which were generally well provisioned—if one didn't mind fish soup, fish stew, and fish chowder.

At least Eddyn was a competent cook.

Rrath wished, however, that he'd witnessed the preparation.

Sighing, he dragged himself out of the covers, found his next layer of clothing—leather leggings, knee boots, and snug undertunic—and began tugging them on. Eddyn put down the map and ambled over to the fireplace to scoop up a cupful of stew and pour it into a bowl for him.

"You having one, too?" Rrath inquired, as he found his top tunic and flipped up the hood, the better to shield his ears from the infernal wind that was also blowing smoke into his face.

Eddyn grinned, white teeth gleaming like the snow beyond the door. "Still don't trust me? If it'll make you happy, I'll have that and you can have another."

Rrath shrugged, but Eddyn helped himself to the first bowl and let Rrath fill a second. That was the trouble with all this: not trusting Eddyn. Of course Eddyn didn't trust him, either—with cause. But it really was unfortunate to be at heart a good person, as Rrath certainly considered himself, and yet be driven to do things that violated every ethic he'd ever learned in exchange for access to a dubious, unseen power that seemed increasingly unlikely to be forthcoming.

That *wouldn't* be forthcoming if word of how his first assignment had been botched reached the relevant authorities. As it surely had by now.

Of course, he knew certain things, too, but most of those he literally couldn't talk about. And even if he could, it was as much as his life was worth to reveal them.

All because he'd liked observing animals. Which had attracted the notice of a certain Life Priest named Nyllol, who'd put him in touch with *them*.

Who liked observing *everything*.

As much, apparently, as Eddyn liked observing the map, which he'd picked up again.

"I doubt anything has moved since the last time you looked at that," Rrath drawled, punctuating his remark with a swallow of peppery stew.

"I'm considering an alternate route."

"*Are* there any?"

Eddyn laid the map between them. "If we're lucky, we should reach Grinding-Hold tonight, which is right at the edge of the Wild, where the river drops down in cataracts that power the grinding wheels. Beyond are the plains. We could stay on the river and have easy going, terrain-wise, after we pass the hold—just continue skiing the river. But there's not much food or shelter through there, and we *are* in a hurry. So look: The river curves around right here; if we go overland, we could cut off a day or more."

Rrath studied him carefully. "I assume you have reason to think that might be unwise?"

Eddyn nodded. "First—and this is *not* a problem—if we stay with the river, we're guaranteed a modicum of shelter—from the camps, at night, and from the terrain in general—because the river usually flows between banks, which will keep the worst of the wind away."

Rrath nodded back, uncertainly.

"The problem's the weather. We've been incredibly lucky so far, but I'm not sure how much longer we can count on the weather to cooperate. If we got caught out on the plain with the wind and the cold—we're coming into the season of the long blows now—we could burrow in and maybe survive awhile. But it could easily blow for more days than we've got endurance or supplies. And the landscape's also more rugged."

Rrath cleared his throat. "You're right about the weather. But . . ." He paused and shook his head. "Never mind."

Eddyn regarded him sharply. *"What?"* But then realization awoke in his eyes, and Rrath knew he'd said too much. "You've trained as a weather-witch. You could find out what the weather's going to be for the next few days."

"Training to be a weather-witch and being one are two different things!" Rrath flared. "Do you think I'd have let us run afoul of that storm if I'd known it was coming? I know a little, but not enough."

Eddyn grinned in a way Rrath didn't like—a way that said he knew Rrath was holding back. "You knew enough to use the basic technique to locate Avall," he replied, all pretense of amiability vanished. "You were claiming to *be* one back in the boathouse," he went on. "Beyond that, *I* know that weather-witches can only work in private. I know you and one of the ghost priests disappeared every night after we'd made camp. If privacy's all you need, you can have it."

"One needs a lot more than privacy," Rrath retorted. "One needs a high place, a certain *kind* of high place. Beyond that, I can't say."

"Water from the appropriate Well?"

"So *you* said."

Eddyn's face went hard as stone. "If you can witch, I'd thank you to do it."

"I'll do what I can," Rrath conceded at last, with a sick feeling in his stomach.

"Think of it as minimizing our time together," Eddyn noted slyly. "The quicker we get to Tir-Eron, the quicker we're rid of each other."

"What about Avall?"

"What about him?"

"If he went into the river, and we *leave* the river—"

"I've considered that," Eddyn replied cryptically. "Never doubt that I've got a plan. The point is, the more options we have, the better our chance of success."

"I can't guarantee a lot."

"Try." Eddyn's tone brooked no argument. "How much time do you need?"

"It's only possible four times a day," Rrath informed him. "Dusk, dawn, noon, and midnight. And that assumes I can find an appropriate place, which is *not* a given."

"Try," Eddyn repeated. "If you're not back by two hands past noon, I'm going on without you—and I'll have your gear with me. If you take longer than that, you'd better like fish, and you'd better like cold."

Rrath didn't say what he was thinking: that he already liked both better than Eddyn syn Argen-yr.

Rrath hadn't lied in any meaningful way about weather-witching, but that didn't mean he'd told all the truth. Some things about that art were common knowledge; some were not. The time of day, the use of a high place in which to conduct the rite, the need for privacy—if not widely known, neither were those facts suppressed. Nor was the use of water from Weather's Well. But there were other, more subtle aspects to witching out the weather that were unknown beyond the craft.

Trouble was, even the most blatant of them applied only to witching at its most fundamental: determining major weather patterns before they manifested. As to *changing* the weather—few indeed could manage that, and even then in only the most limited manner—else why would Eron suffer the tyranny of Deep Winter that forced half the population to hole up in the gorges, and the other half to hide in the fastnesses of the winter holds?

Rrath had no illusions about changing anything. He had few about his facility at the simpler form, for that matter—but had to try. Eddyn, when sober, was good at spotting lies. What Eddyn didn't know was that Rrath might have to risk his life to realize even the most basic information.

And *that* depended on whether he could locate a certain something—and if he could utilize it properly if he did.

He was trying, however: trudging on the truest path he could muster due north of the fish camp, across what might, in warm weather, be a pasture or meadow, aiming toward a forested ridge that blocked most of the northern horizon.

East would've been better—or west. But the river lay both ways, and there were no high places on either bank that were out of Eddyn's sightlines.

So he tromped along, trying to ignore everything that wasn't part of the world itself—afoot, because to witch one had to be in touch with the earth as much as possible, and due north, because that increased the chance of finding what he sought.

The world was laced with lines of power born of the land itself—of the forces that moved in it, and those that moved it about as it tumbled along in space. That power ran everywhere, but certain types of geography focused it into stronger currents that webbed the whole landscape, as far as anyone knew. Certain things followed those currents without anyone knowing they were so doing—mostly because Priest-Clan alone knew they existed. They crossed each other, too, and Rrath had seen a map of all Eron with those crossings marked, and had noted how they corresponded almost exactly

with the locations of major winter holds, and the strongest, not coincidentally, with his own clan's fastnesses.

To witch the weather, one had to locate one of those currents. None of the
major ones lay near here, but there might be a minor one up on that ridge
ahead—because it appeared to run due east and west, and the rocks here-
about were of a particular kind and configuration.

Which supposed he'd be able to recognize one of those lines if he crossed
it. He might, and he might not. He'd practiced—all his clan had. And he'd
shown some aptitude. But that was when he'd been able to compare directly:
on the line and off it, and that sample line had been a strong one.

Still, he trudged onward, steadily uphill, hoping to reach his goal by
noon—and that noon would prove that goal to be worthwhile. For no clear
reason, he found himself imagining a scenario wherein he explained the
process to Eddyn.

*"Remember the theater at Acting-Hold? Remember how, when you stand at
the center-front of the stage and walk to the back, speaking all the while, you
reach a point where the sound comes back to you more loudly, though you don't
speak louder yourself? A sound you can feel in your chest and your bones? It's like
that, except that you're breathing a certain way, and walking at a certain pace
that exactly balances it, and if you can maintain proper concentration, and if
there's a line to be found, that's the way you can locate it—if you're sensitive to
such things."*

A hand before noon, he found it—beyond hope, or in spite of it. He'd
started the breathing halfway up the hill and the walk shortly thereafter, and
one step he'd trod on ordinary, snow-covered earth, and the next, something
came thrumming up through his bones into the fluids around his brain, and
he *knew*.

He'd followed it, then, and sure enough, it had led him to the highest
crest of the ridge. He still had time, too—enough to locate the largest section
of open ground between the skimpy trees, and to sweep that section bare of
snow in a circular patch a span in diameter where the current hummed most
strongly.

That accomplished, he found a fallen tree trunk and sat down on it, to divest himself of boots, leggings, hose—everything between his bare feet and
the natural world. Setting his jaw against cold that jabbed up into his flesh
from the frozen earth, he began to pace the circle in a slow clockwise spiral
from outside to inside, trying as he did, to get a sense of which way the principal current ran. Fortunately, he didn't have to complete the whole circuit
to tell. It was as he'd expected: near-right angles to the ridgeline, but on an
almost perfect alignment between the dome of the fish camp he could just
see behind him and a cleft in another ridgeline on the northern horizon.
He knelt there, marked that alignment with his dagger, then returned to
the log.

A fumbling at his waist produced a waterskin he'd managed to hide from Eddyn by virtue of its appearing to be empty, and he quickly unscrewed the carved ivory cap. Steeling himself, he tipped it to his lips, almost despairing before he felt that final welcome trickle. Just as well, probably, that this was all that remained. The stuff tasted more like leather than water, and had certainly lost potency since last he'd used it (the ghost priests had maintained their own supply), but he felt the effect already: a vague light-headedness, as though his brain were not quite connected to his body, yet conversely was more attached to his senses.

Then came the dangerous part—and the part most folks didn't know about. Moving quickly, he stripped off the rest of his clothes, noting as he did that his upper lip was already starting to ice over and his eyes to tear. The cold went beyond pain—and could kill him in less than a finger unless he found what he sought in a hurry.

Almost dancing across the frozen ground, he returned to the power nexus and lay down, arms outstretched along its major axis, heart centered over the crucial point. That accomplished, he closed his eyes, breathed a certain way, and tried to let himself go.

The cold bit at him, gnawing up from the earth, distracting him. Snow crystals pricked across his flesh, muddling his concentration. Anxiety made him sweat, and he could feel his naked shoulders, buttocks, and limbs being bound by new ice to the earth.

But that was also where the power lay, and he let it seep up into him through all that cold. Abruptly, the cold vanished—seemed to—and he felt himself at once suspended above the land and merged with it.

Now he had to merge with the sky. Another breath, and he sank deeper into trance—or else it took him deeper. And as he drank the air, he tried also to drink the sky, to feel the wind on his body not as coldness but as a play of pressures and moistures, and then to follow those powers, as the currents in the land flowed through him. It was not a matter of observing weather through time, but of seeing where it came from: of knowing how the winds swirled out there above the Oval Sea, or above Angen's Spine, and noting which were stronger and more like to come sweeping into the plains.

The rest he'd learned already: what a thunderstorm felt like a-borning. Or a long warm spell, or a blizzard. And as best he could tell, though two blizzards were building up their own power-swirls—one to the east, one to the west—neither would manifest for the next two days, which should be still and clear.

Which was what he'd set out to discover.

If only it hadn't cost him too much warmth. One thing about witching, one never knew how long one stayed out of one's body.

A breath felt like inhaling fire, and told him that bits of his lungs had frozen, but it also served to wrench him from that too-dangerous trance.

Another, and he sat up, feeling the earth tug at him, ripping shreds of frozen skin and hair from his body. He stood shakily, dashed to the tree, and slung his cloak around his shoulders, grateful for the way the sun had warmed the dark fabric. He dressed beneath it, as fast as numb fingers would allow. Patches of skin showed unhealthy reddening. He would itch tonight, but he doubted he'd suffered permanent damage. One thing was clear, however. He would *not* do this in the Wild again for anyone outside his clan, and only then under orders. And no matter what Eddyn threatened, he would spend an entire hand, once he returned to camp, sitting by the fire.

Eddyn didn't argue, however, merely watched in silence as Rrath strode into the common room and helped himself to a double portion of soup. Only when he'd finished eating did Rrath mutter a terse "It's possible." And go to sleep.

CHAPTER V:

GRINDING-HOLD

(WESTERN ERON—DEEP WINTER: DAY XL—EVENING)

～～～～～～～～～～

Rrath crouched beside Eddyn behind a snowcapped block of half-carved stone in a small granite quarry atop a low hill—and stared down at Grinding-Hold.

They'd left the Ri-Eron two shots back—as soon as the hold's lights showed—and veered off overland, the better to support Eddyn's sketchy plan. Eddyn had been here before, but the place was new to Rrath, and in spite of himself, he couldn't help being seduced by the vista before him.

The place *was* impressive. Like most winter holds, it was hewn into the land—in this case, the southern spur of a ridge that the river had bisected. Closer to the shore, additional buildings had been added, some of them aboveground, and a section of the flow had been turned aside beneath its icy crust to power a vast assortment of sheltered wheels and cogs. Year in and year out, they ground, reducing everything that needed such attention in Eron: metallic ores, sand for glass, and grains of every kind.

The only true bridge to span the Ri-Eron outside Eron Gorge arched on stone piers to the nearer side, giving, now that the river was frozen, the appearance of a road lifted above a snowfield. Torches showed along its railing, more for appearance than anything, for the span was empty.

The northern bank was their goal; the ridge was lower there, and the river shallower—too shallow for grinding. Yet that side was also inhabited.

Most holds housed their livestock in vast stables within their bowels; Grinding-Hold didn't. Atypically, a separate set of stables had been hollowed in the sweep of the northern ridge, presenting a dozen archways to an exercise ground between the stables proper and the river. It was there that Eddyn intended to secure mounts for the next stage of their journey.

It was his risk, more than Rrath's, but Rrath had already risked more than he was telling. A moment more they waited, then Eddyn muttered something unintelligible and rose. He tugged his tunic approximately straight, secured his skis and pole, then caught Rrath's eye. "One thing," he murmured. "If Avall's body has made it this far, there's a good chance these folks have found it. Let me do the talking. You look sick—from exposure, if nothing else. Anyone we meet will understand that. They may want to treat you, but I'll work around that. If we're lucky, there'll only be a couple of grooms doubling as guards."

"And if we're not?" Rrath challenged.

"Let's just say we'd better be."

Rrath smelled the food before he saw it. The odor—hot meat and spices—was wafting through a badly repaired chink beside the cold-door that filled the centermost of the outer archways, and the largest. There'd been no guard—Eron had no raiders, and banditry was all but unknown. Besides, it was Deep Winter, and even rogues and vagabonds had common sense. Eddyn's plan was to claim they were hunters who'd lost their way and sought a night's shelter without troubling the folk in the hold. Certainly their appearance could support that: dirty clothes, greasy hair, and fifteen days' worth of stubble.

Eddyn eased in front of Rrath, co-opting his position, but Rrath had seen enough. The cold-door opened on a winter-lock, with another door opposite— probably leading to an access corridor that paralleled the whole thirty-span length of the stables.

"Good a time as any," Eddyn murmured—and rapped the travelers' cadence on the thick oak.

After a long pause—and two more sets of raps—Rrath heard footsteps approaching. A small panel opened at head height in the main door. A pale face appeared, rounder than was typical of the Eronese, and, not surprisingly, young—winter holds tended to be staffed by those just beginning their years of service. Rrath waited for him to speak. And tried to look suitably ill.

"Travelers . . . ?" the youth blurted, utterly failing to mask his perplexity.

"Hunters," Eddyn gave back calmly. "Some beasts have winter coats that make even the cold worth the risk."

"I . . . see," the fellow mumbled, sounding as if he didn't.

"We lost our way, then saw the lights. We don't want to bother the folks in the hold—too much carrying on, and we stink. But we'd be grateful for a warm place to stay the night, and some of whatever's cooking. I'm afraid we don't have much to offer but dried fish. But if that will suffice—"

"Come in," the man sighed. "Wait while I shift the bar."

Rrath heard heavy boards being slid aside, and stood back as the door opened—sideways on rails, as it evolved. A brown surcoat barred with gold clothed their would-be host from neck to knees: the livery of horse sept of Beastcraft. It looked to be hastily donned, and Rrath guessed he was a groom, perhaps doing double duty as a guard.

They shook the snow from their clothing in the winter gate, before moving on to the vaulted access corridor, where a range of door-filled archways mirrored more like that by which they'd entered. Rrath smelled horses—their flesh, their droppings, and the dried fodder on which they'd subsist through the season. More importantly, he'd identified that other smell: fresh-fried sausage.

"I'm Den," Eddyn volunteered. "My friend is ill," he continued, ushering Rrath in before him as their host steered them toward a doorway opposite—probably a lip-service version of a guardroom. Eddyn had given his name first, Rrath noted: a sign of trust. That it wasn't his true name made no difference under the circumstances.

"It's been a mild few days," the groom replied. "I guess you knew that, or you wouldn't be out this far."

Eddyn didn't answer, content to let the two of them be shepherded into a stone-walled common room, with a fireplace at one end and a number of tables, benches, and low chairs set about at random, save for one pair close by the fire. Doors to either side likely led to sleeping quarters and the obligatory bath. The whole was surrounded by the invisible concentric ranges of stalls that fanned out from it to either side. It being too late to be cooking dinner, Rrath suspected the sausage was a late-night snack.

Another young man rose when they entered, scooting two more chairs closer to the fire, before motioning them to sit. His eyes spoke eloquently: curiosity, wariness, and mistrust, all masked by the rites of hospitality. He was a small youth, too, and wiry.

"I'm Gorrinn," said the fellow who had admitted them, his livery rendering announcement of clan redundant.

"Vil," his companion echoed, sitting back down to attend the sausages, which were starting to smoke.

"Ath," Rrath replied, through a cough he hoped would mask the lie. They were invoking hospitality here, and that involved certain protocols.

Eddyn shot him a glare their hosts missed, and joined them, scrounging in his backpack as he did. A moment later, he'd produced the brandy. "Donation for whatever meal you're cooking. We've fish, too, though better can surely be had in the hold."

"We thank you," Gorrinn replied formally. "We've all the sausage you can eat, though you might want to do your own cooking. Vil tends to burn things."

Eddyn nodded amiably. "I apologize for troubling you, but Ath and I have been out for days without seeing another living person. With him sick—"

"What troubles him?" Gorrinn broke in, sparing a glance at Rrath. Rrath tried not to scowl at being discussed in the third person.

"Fatigue, mostly, and he got a bit of a chill earlier today. Fell in the river, and it had a good go at him before I got him out and thawed."

Rrath coughed obligingly and tried to shiver.

"He's lucky, then," Vil snorted. "Most times it's so cold he'd have died before he dried. But it's been amazingly warm of late."

Eddyn nodded, and for a while the conversation turned, as it always did in Deep Winter, to the weather. It had, in fact, been unseasonably warm— which is to say, most days were only slightly below freezing.

"Thankless duty, isn't it?" Eddyn ventured eventually. "Exiled over here when there's so much more going on in the hold itself."

Vil scowled, shifted, and gnawed on a sausage. "Especially when it's punishment," he muttered.

"Which is as much as anyone needs to say," Gorrinn warned. "Our, uh, youthful high spirits got a little out of hand a few days ago, and they sent us over here to cool off."

"Wouldn't mind a look at the horses sometime," Eddyn said, overtly to change the subject. "Morning's soon enough, though."

"Too soon," Gorrinn yawned. "You lads are welcomed to stay up as late as you like—I'd recommend sleeping in here, as the fireplace in the spare room is smoky—but we need to go to bed."

Vil rose and scratched his side. "Gotta piss," he announced, padding off to the right.

"I'll see if I can find some blankets," Gorrinn added, also rising.

Eddyn grinned. "Fine. And I'll fix us all a hot toddy."

Gorrinn grinned back. "You do that. That's some fine brandy you've got there. We've got cider," he added. And with that, they both departed.

Eddyn acted instantly. As soon as the doors closed behind their hosts, he fished a phial out of the blue pouch and emptied a healthy quantity of the contents into the mugs the grooms had been using.

"Not so much!" Rrath hissed. "It's supposed to be burned. Concentrated like that—I don't know . . ."

Eddyn glared at him. "Now you tell me! Pass me that cider, if you don't mind."

Rrath glared back, but complied, watching as Eddyn added a good dose of brandy to all four mugs, and more cider, accenting the whole with a dusting of dried mint he hoped would disguise the flavor of the drug. He set the containers close by the fire to warm. It wouldn't take long. The cider had already been steaming.

Rrath hoped he knew what he was doing, but was too tired and brain-weary to argue. The morning's witching had taken more out of him than he wanted to admit.

In any event, their hosts returned soon enough, Gorrinn encumbered by a pile of fresh-smelling bedding Rrath was loath to foul with his filthy body. He wondered if it was too late to beg a bath.

Gorrinn dropped his burden in the nearest chair and accepted the mug Eddyn offered. He sniffed the vapors appreciatively, and smiled, an easy relaxed smile that troubled Rrath for its utter lack of guile.

Vil took the second drink with stiff grace, leaving the two untainted ones for Eddyn and Rrath.

"Health," Gorrinn laughed.

"I'll drink to that," Rrath chuckled back, earning a scowl from Eddyn.

"Long life," Eddyn countered.

"And a good night's sleep," Vil finished, quaffing at least half of his at one draught.

"Lots of bad dreams of late," Gorrinn confided offhand, smiling appreciatively.

They finished the libations quickly, and the two grooms trundled off toward one of the bedrooms—one less fire to keep going, Rrath supposed. They didn't look like bond-brothers or lovers. Barely even friends, if the truth were known.

Eddyn reached for the nearest blanket. "How long before that takes effect?"

Rrath glared at him. "I don't know—exactly. It's designed to be breathed in smoke, not swallowed. What you gave them was a *very* concentrated dose, so I'd say—no more than a finger. They'll be lucky to undress before bed."

"If we hear a thump, we'll know," Eddyn replied dryly.

Rrath didn't answer. He really did want to get *some* sleep before Eddyn had them out in the Wild again. Without waiting for any manifestation of Eddyn's subterfuge, he stretched out on a thick wool rug before the fire and pulled a blanket over him.

Eddyn stayed up, pacing.

He was still pacing when something woke Rrath. He sat up groggily, looked around, fighting the heavy languor that had claimed him.

Eddyn's face was unreadable. "They made it to bed," he said tersely. "I've checked the horses and found two that will do—hardy enough for what we plan, but not so good we'd rob the world of something wonderful if we rode them to death."

Rrath shuddered in spite of himself, but slowly began to untangle himself from the bedding. He yawned, stretched, and finished the last of his toddy—surprised to find it still warm.

Without saying a word, he followed Eddyn's lead through a series of doors into a long curving arc of stone-paved corridor lit with rushlights and lined with stalls from which the sounds and scents of probably two hundred horses issued.

Eddyn made short work of locating those he'd chosen, waiting at patient tether outside the tack holds. Nor was Rrath surprised to find them already saddled and bridled. He patted the nose of the rough-coated gray gelding Eddyn had chosen for him and was rewarded with a grateful whicker. Eddyn's was a big, rawboned mare with tired, trusting eyes—whose reins he took at once, leading her through a final gate and into the access corridor, pausing to wait for Rrath to likewise lead his through, before bolting the gate behind.

"I sure as Eight hope Gorrinn and Vil don't decide to wake up around now," Rrath muttered, as they slid one of the outer doors aside and eased into the night.

"They won't," Eddyn assured him, with an odd, strained edge in his voice that made Rrath pause in the act of climbing into his saddle.

"How can you be so sure?"

Eddyn's eyes mirrored the night sky: near-black, and clouded by a sudden gust of chill wind. "Because I looked in on them before waking you," he said softly. "One was asleep on the floor, as though he'd dropped down where he stood."

"And the other . . . ?" Rrath dared, as a cold fist squeezed his heart.

"It was the skinny one. He also dropped down in place—but unfortunately he seems to have hit his head as he fell. I'm pretty sure he's dead."

"Dead," Rrath echoed numbly. "Someone who helped us—almost befriended us—is *dead*?"

"Of too much drink, it will appear," Eddyn said quickly, as he, too, mounted up.

"Yes," Rrath replied. "We'd better *hope* that's how it appears, because if anyone finds that drug you used— Well, I wish you'd told me you were going to use it, because no one knows about that stuff but . . . those of whom I cannot speak."

Eddyn shrugged. "And how many times have I wished you'd told *me* things?"

"What we need to wish now," Rrath told him, as he kicked his horse to the fastest pace he dared in the knee-deep snow, "is that Gorrinn remembers very little about certain visitors."

Eddyn nodded grimly. "Too bad those doors bolted from inside—but they'll find the missing horses soon enough. If we're lucky, we'll be shots away by then."

Rrath stared stonily at Eddyn's back. "Someday," he said, "Luck is going to claim an accounting of you. And you'd better be placating Him with every breath, because I don't think even *your* connections will shield you from what's no more than a razor's edge from murder."

CHAPTER VI:

HIDING OUT

(Eron: Gem-Hold-Winter—Deep Winter: Day XLIII—late afternoon)

~~~~~~~~~~~~~~~~

It's already getting hard to hide you," Strynn sighed, as she deposited a tray of food atop the small table to the right of the slight, handsome youth who was at once her husband's best friend and bond-brother, and in some odd sense her rival. The meal had appeared an instant earlier: brought to the suite's common room by one of her younger clansmen, doubling as a hall page. She'd brought it here, to Avall's workroom, because no one except Avall, Rann, or she was legally allowed to enter such a place. But she wondered. Spies had spies of late.

Rann shot her a lopsided grin—an expression he usually reserved for Avall, which she found flattering. He raised the dome-shaped dish covers one by one, revealing fried blind-fish nuggets, fresh orange slices, hot bread, and a piquant sauce that was supposed to soothe pregnancy pains. His gaze promptly shifted from sauce, to lid, to Strynn's bulging belly. He tried to fit the lid against it, and grinned again.

"It passed that size some time ago," she growled, shooting the door bolt, then helping herself to a seat beside him. "But I'm serious, Rann. This is no life for any of us. We can maintain the facade for a while, but eventually I'll have the child, and then I won't have the excuse of ordering extravagant meals under the guise of eating for two."

Rann patted his flat stomach. "I'll eat less. If half an eighth in the Wild didn't kill me, a whole one on short rations won't, either."

Neither mentioned the way he had looked when he'd returned from the Wild the previous evening: like a skeleton sewn into a bag of skin. He'd been eating practically nonstop ever since.

Strynn took a deep breath. "I'm serious, Rann. It's starting to wear on me—and on Kylin."

Rann nodded and helped himself to a swallow of wine. "You think I don't appreciate this? I *know* the risk you're taking hiding me. Not that they'd be able to get anything out of me I didn't want to tell them—as if it would do any good now, if I told every sliver of the truth. But we have to remember that what we're doing is buying Avall time. I know we've discussed this before, but the fact that Eddyn and Rrath set upon us proves without doubt that there're others in this hold who know something. Those folks with Rrath—the ones who did the actual fighting—their clan tattoos were all obliterated except one. It was Priest-Clan, Strynn. But they had to have authority from somewhere, and the only place Rrath could've contacted them was here. Therefore, they have agents here, and if they have agents, you're at risk. I'm the black stone in the white. If they move against you, they won't have taken me into account. I don't have to remind you that I owe you absolute allegiance as my bond-brother's wife."

Strynn smiled in spite of herself. Jealous she might be, at times, but that bond was a beautiful thing: true devotion that transcended gender. Nor had she been denied access to it. Not after they'd found the gem.

"Still, it has to be wearing on you," she replied, "to stay cooped up like this. I know you'd like to be doing something for Avall—we all would. And we can't."

"We know he's alive. That's something."

"It's hope. But is hope enough?"

"Want to try again?"

Another deep breath. "I want to try every instant of every hand of every day. I know you don't believe it when I say I love him as much as you do, but I do. We don't have enough secrets from each other to matter now—none of us do. But Rann, I swear to you, if I could spend the rest of my life just lying somewhere warm with him beside me, I could be content. I don't understand it, but it's true."

"I feel the same," Rann replied. "But what *have* you heard about any of this? I hear nothing you don't tell me."

She regarded him wryly. "Only if you promise to eat while I talk, and not interrupt. We have *got* to get some meat on you, or Avall will kill me if—*when*—we survive all this."

"Not likely," Rann retorted. "He'd never get your like again, and he knows it. But for the sake of argument, go on."

Strynn poured herself a full mug of wine and settled back, letting her body lapse into the slump her pregnancy demanded. She was already barefoot, and only refrained from asking Rann for a foot massage from fear they might both find that distracting. "Very well," she began. "I know that Crim has already put far too much together, and The Eight alone know what the rest have puzzled out—especially Nyss, if what you said about Priest-Clan is true."

"And what are you giving out as the official comment?"

"Same thing that I told our Clan- and Craft-Chiefs: that Avall first and foremost serves his country and King, and that anything I say would put both at risk."

"You've not lied then? Not directly?"

She shook her head. "I know better. If this resolves as it ought, we'll have royal warrant for whatever we've done. No one here can command me directly, and I've said I'll tell anything they like—in the presence of Eellon, Tryffon, Preedor, and the King."

"But if they knew I was here, you'd have to tell the truth about me—as much as you know. So maybe I ought to think about leaving again. Ideally, we both ought to. Or all three, given that our departure would leave Kylin totally on his own."

Strynn rolled her eyes. "What a notion! A pregnant woman, a blind man, and a fatally idealistic scarecrow who'd blow away in a high wind."

"I'm still heavier than Kylin," Rann shot back. "In any case, we at least ought to consider the possibility before we completely dismiss the idea. Remember, we thought it was preposterous when Avall and I first proposed going out into the Deep. But then we found that at least two types of people do it all the time. Hunters, whom we sort of knew about, and whatever those screwy Priests were."

"Which raises the question. What about Div?"

"What about her?"

"Would she shelter us?"

"Of course! She'd adore you—and put you to work sharpening every blade in the place."

"And you're sure no one else knows about her?"

"Not here, I don't think; woodswomen like her tend to keep to themselves and trade only with the Tanners. And even as savvy as she is about the Wild, she'd never had reason to suspect the Priests exist, else she'd have been prepared for them.

"They know about *her* now, though," he went on. "Which is a reason we *shouldn't* go there. If they're watching her— Well, it'd be the three of us plus maybe some birkits, against the whole nebulous might of whatever group those fellows represent."

Strynn started to reply, but paused. A knock had sounded on the door to the outer chamber—her nominal sitting room. She waited until it repeated: three raps, then three again, then two. Fine: It was safe. She rose, hastening through the door even as Rann moved to lock it behind her. Strynn heard the bolt shoot home as she stepped from sitting room to vestibule.

A third cadence had begun before she was able to shoot all three bolts and heave the heavy panel open. It was Kylin syn Omyrr, of Music, with his harp in tow. He was a bit shorter than either Rann or Avall, which put him on the low end of average, and was elegantly—almost daintily—built. Typical for him, he wore house-hose and short-tunic of velvet, the textures compensating, he claimed, for his lack of sight. He also wore a sylk blindfold across his eyes, and carried a slender, silver-chased cane Strynn had made him from an aborted sword.

"Is this a bad time?" he ventured, wrinkling his nose—to catch the scent of her perfume: one of several ways he identified her.

"Not at all," she murmured, whisking him inside and resecuring the door. "In fact, Rann and I seemed to have blundered from discussion to actual plotting. We could use another head."

"Music helps the brain think more harmoniously," Kylin chuckled, his voice smooth as the fabric that covered him. He walked soundlessly in low velvet boots to the door to the workroom. Unerringly, Strynn noted. He paused there expectantly while she turned the key.

Rann shot the bolts from inside as soon as she began, and ushered them both in, helping Kylin to his own former seat, before locking the door again and securing another chair for himself. The light was failing and the room held a comfortable gloom that encouraged conversation. Kylin sniffed the food appreciatively and helped himself to a fish in sauce. "You eat better than I do," he murmured.

"Try getting pregnant and see how you're fed," Strynn shot back, with what she discovered was honest good humor. She didn't like having Kylin out and about in the hold—too many things could happen to him there. But he was the Hold-Warden's favorite musician, and also had other obligations, including those to his craft, in which he was both student and teacher. His quarters were here, however; Strynn had secured that as a clan boon after Eddyn's savage attack on the harper, the bruises from which were still fading.

In any case, her circle was now as complete as it could be without Avall and his twin: her bond-sister, Merryn. The wine was calming her, too, while at the same time sharpening her wits by filtering out extraneous worries. Which is how it worked with creative people.

"We were talking about leaving," Rann told Kylin, just loud enough to be heard above the harper's subtle melody.

"Who is *we*?" Kylin murmured. "And what, exactly, do you mean by 'leaving'?"

Strynn tried to glare at Rann, but couldn't without feeling a hypocrite.

"The three of us, in theory. We're not really safe here, and it's only going to get worse, especially for Strynn as her time approaches. Me . . . I'm ready to go back out if I have to, but Strynn won't let me. Plus I'm bound by oath to Avall to look after her. Oh, I could find somewhere in this warren to hide, and ghost about surreptitiously, but that would be a risk, if for no other reason because if I *was* caught, people would want to know why I thought I had to hide. Nor would I have a good answer. But perhaps I should—just to hear what's being said. I think . . . I can use Strynn's gem to help with some of that. With your permission, of course," he added, to Strynn.

"I'll have to think about it," she said.

"Surely you're not serious," Kylin yipped. "With your time almost upon you."

"Women have given birth in the Wild before," Strynn answered tartly. "I'm strong for a woman and we're not talking about going all the way to Tir-Eron."

"We weren't really talking about it at all," Rann grumbled. "This is getting a little too serious."

"Div?" Kylin guessed. "You were thinking of the three of us sheltering at Div's hold?"

"I was thinking of that *in extremis*—if we learned there was actual threat against us."

"It makes sense, though," Kylin told them seriously. "You *are* running a risk by staying here. You'd run far less risk there, and be closer to Tir-Eron when the thaws come. And don't think I don't know that you're going mad trying to decide what you feel about her—and wanting to get back."

"I could release you from your vow to protect me," Strynn offered.

Rann shook his head. "That's all I really have of Avall right now—beyond the fact that he's not precisely dead."

"Are we going to try that again tonight?" Kylin wondered.

Strynn shrugged. "I see no reason we can't go ahead and do it now—maybe at sunset, since that's supposed to be a powerful time of day."

"We've got half a hand, then."

Kylin looked at Rann. "Rann, forgive my rudeness, but what exactly *do* you feel about Div, now that you've built some distance?"

Rann closed his eyes and took a deep breath, then a long quaff of wine. "I shouldn't answer, because once I give one, I'll feel bound to it, and my feelings could alter."

Strynn kicked him gently. "How do you feel *now*? This does have a bearing on a lot of things—if nothing else, on whether we can consider her an ally. She may wind up in the clan, after all, or under clan protection. We've a right to know what we're taking to our bosom."

Rann took another deep breath. "I'm not sure I *love* her, exactly. She's too different from any woman—any person, actually—I've ever met. She clearly likes me, but I don't know if that's for myself or for what I represent—a chance to attach herself to a high clan. I *think* it's for the former, but I'm just not sure. She can't have children, though, so that might be a problem, since I still have to sire my three. But she'd probably be willing to share, since she has already."

"But only with Avall," Strynn cautioned. "Women are used to sharing their men with their bond-brothers, and vice versa. Would she share you with a woman?"

"She might. I won't really know the answer to any of these questions until I've spent more time with her. Still, I *do* think about her a lot. I miss her. I keep thinking of things here I'd enjoy showing her, but I'm not sure if that's love or simply the fact that it *is* fun to show off those things to those who don't have our . . . advantages."

"Enough to chew on, in any case," Strynn sighed, glancing at the time-candle, which had exhausted another finger. "If we're going to try to contact Avall, I'd suggest we be at it."

Rann put down his mug with a dull click, and rose. A tinkling run with impossibly nimble fingers concluded the piece Kylin had been playing.

The ritual had—almost—become familiar, yet Rann found himself apprehensive. Probably because every time he'd undertaken it before his return to Gem-Hold, he'd been partnered with Avall, using Avall's gem. Since then, he'd done it once—with Strynn and—effectively—Kylin, simply because adding people—people one was close to, at any rate—added to the strength of the sending.

Trouble was, Strynn's gem was smaller than the one Avall had found, and had a different feel—like the difference in taste between goats' milk and cows'.

Not that he hadn't come to value these moments of closeness, even as he'd likewise come to dread their aftereffects. At the moment, they were waiting for Kylin to finish bathing. It helped him relax, he said. Working with the gem made him nervous because his earlier encounters with it had been so traumatic—first when Strynn had been moved by sympathy to merge minds with him, so that he could see through her eyes, and later, when Eddyn had wrested that secret from him, with utter disregard for his mental or physical well-being.

He was running late, though, and Rann was getting fidgety. Strynn was as well, though she masked it by gliding about arranging candles and pouring drinks. She was, Rann thought, a vision of loveliness in her loose white robe, with her long black hair unbound down her back. Avall was a lucky man indeed.

He wondered if he was up to it. Linking was at once exhilarating and draining, and he'd had one mug of wine too many, so that he was poised on the edge of drowsiness.

They'd know soon enough, he supposed, because Kylin padded in from the bathroom, still damp across the torso, and with his hair plastered sleekly to his head. Like Rann, he wore only house-hose, because they'd learned that bare skin aided the connection.

Rann rose reflexively and steered the harper toward the bed, placing a pillow behind his neck and shoulders before scrambling in beside him—in what would become the middle. Strynn took one final look at the candles, nodded approval, and claimed the other side. Rann felt, rather than saw, her push up her right sleeve—the one on his side. A brief sound of fumbling he didn't bother following with his eyes, and she passed him the gem. He took it gingerly, studying the warm sparks of life within its ruby depths before setting it on his chest above his heart. Meanwhile, Strynn had taken the small paring knife they'd come to use exclusively for this rite and had made a tiny incision in her right palm. He heard her gasp as the blood began to ooze. "Done," she murmured, passing the blade to Rann.

He nudged Kylin with his free hand. "Do you want help, or can you—?"

"I can," Kylin whispered back. Rann eased the knife carefully into the harper's fingers. "Done," he echoed a moment later, returning the knife to Rann.

His turn now, and he dreaded it. Pain was never pleasant, though he'd grown used to this particular kind. A deep breath, and he closed his eyes and slid the edge across his palm.

It hurt less than expected, though it brought more blood—Strynn had obviously been at it with her whetstone since last they'd used it. He gasped as it bit, then passed it back to Strynn, who returned it to its sheath.

That accomplished, he found the gem and clasped his bleeding hand atop it. It began to draw immediately, but at the same time it sent an odd tingle of heat and energy into him, as if he were slowly being thawed after weeks of cold. He felt his senses altering as well: slowing down, so that he could watch each exaggerated flicker of the candle flame across the room.

"Ready," he murmured.

His partners moved, each laying a hand atop his on his chest. He felt their blood mingle with his, as they shifted again to bring their bare shoulders into contact.

And *he* was flowing, too: into the jewel, and through it into Strynn and an apprehensive Kylin. And with that flow, they likewise flowed into him. He balanced those tides by some method he couldn't have described if he'd wanted to, while at the same time admitting certain parts of them that awakened—or empowered—certain parts of him.

It was one of the things they now knew with reasonable certainty. Every person, regardless of sex, had a male aspect and a female, and each of those aspects responded more strongly to certain stimuli. This kind of link awakened and strengthened those things and made the whole mind—the whole *self*—stronger in turn. It worked best, Rann suspected, if one merged with a person of each sex—a second woman would probably have been optimal. Lacking one, this seemed the best configuration, and Rann was the guide because he had the most experience of the three. Both parts of his mind were also open, whereas if Strynn had claimed control, there would have been two male minds striving to fill space ideally suited to one.

Rann felt himself at once contracting and expanding, and tried to center his thoughts—and those shadow-thoughts that joined his from Strynn and Kylin—on a single goal.

He and Strynn had touched Avall's *self* briefly, last night: not awake, but not dead. All they'd felt was heart-stopping cold.

It was time to try again.

A deep breath, and Rann let himself sink further, until he barely seemed a discrete entity. At the same time, he let himself rise above himself and move outward—beyond the room, beyond the hold, into the high-arching dark. Strynn was with him, and Kylin—less fearful now. But they supported him, rather than directed, and so it was he who began the quest—down the local tributary of the Ri-Eron, and thence to that river itself.

That was where they'd seen Avall fall. That was where the fleeting touch they'd had of him yesterday had seemed to lead.

But Rann felt nothing.

He tried harder, felt his strength start to go thin, wishing he had access to Avall's stronger stone, or that he had some way to seek one of his own in the mines without being seen. Strynn no longer could, because of her condition; nor could Kylin.

He'd just started to withdraw when his awareness brushed something.

Something familiar.

Not thoughts so much as feelings such as the body experiences when it is alive but little more.

Cold.

Cold beyond cold, yet cold warmed with life.

"He still lives," Strynn breathed beside him.

"He does," Kylin agreed.

Rann took a deep breath. "Shall we try for Tir-Eron? Or Merryn?"

"Both," Strynn replied. "But quickly. I'm very tired."

Rann didn't reply. Drawing on the last strength he had, and knowing that even that was insufficient, he once more launched himself into the not-place that was the Overworld, moving toward what passed there for Tir-Eron. He could see it, but couldn't reach it. He shouted for Eellon anyway, at the same time building a picture of the old Clan-Chief in his mind.

It was like shouting from a mountaintop. The air rang with the effort, but the distance swallowed it.

He tried for Merryn, then, but even in the Overworld he could only glimpse, very far away, War-Hold's surrounding mountains.

"Tomorrow," he sighed—and gently shifted the hands off the gem, before folding it into Strynn's palm.

Kylin, he discovered, slept. Strynn didn't; he could hear her softly weeping. As carefully as he could, he rose from between them and climbed out of bed.

He shivered—once—twice. A third time. Somehow he made it to the bath, where he turned on the water as hot as it would go and spent the next half hand soaking. Trying to drive away the cold that had entered him from Avall. Wondering if either of them would ever be warm again.

Strynn was asleep when Rann returned from the bath. He'd likewise dozed off—in the tub—only to awaken when the water grew cold, which was too much a reminder of Avall.

Now he stood gazing down at her and Kylin. They'd moved closer in his absence, neatly filling his spot. Not that he felt right sharing a bed with Avall's wife in any case—not without Avall there. Their hands touched, he noted, and they looked at peace. He wondered if they were lovers. Stranger things had happened. Certainly they adored each other, and both were in desperate need of whatever comfort they could manage, here in the Dark Season. Avall might even approve. Probably would, he amended. It would take some of the pressure off him.

But he was sleepy, too, and so he steered his step toward the door to the common room. He'd already laid a hand on the latch, when something caught his attention from the corner of his eye. He paused, blinking, then realized that it was the gem lying on the rug beside the bed. By the way Strynn's hand was draped over the side, it had fallen from her grasp while she slept.

He picked it up, started to set it on the night table, then thought better of it. It was a comfort of sorts, and he needed comfort now. Tomorrow was soon enough to return it, and tomorrow would be too soon anyway.

As quietly as he could, he made his way through two sets of doors to the pallet they'd set up for him in Avall's workroom. The helm sat there, undraped, accusing him with empty eyes. Moonlight gleamed off the dented steel, the shattered bronze, the scoured gilding. Even damaged as it was, it was the most beautiful made thing Rann had ever seen.

Dropping the towel he'd worn from the bath, he stretched out naked on the pallet, letting the moonlight clothe him. A deep breath, and he laid the gem on his chest, with either hand beside it, so that two fingers from each barely touched it. He had no reason for so choosing, it simply seemed right. As if to reassure him, the gem rewarded him with a pulse of heat.

He felt guilty about this, though. It was Strynn's gem, after all. He had no right to co-opt it, even for such harmless use as he made of it now. It really *would* be nice, he thought, if he had one of his own, one he could study; that was tuned to his unique thoughts and needs and desires. Maybe he *would* dare the mines, if he could find some time when they were attended by no one who knew him.

Except that the gems came from Argen's vein, not Eemon's, and about such things the Wardens were strict. No way he could search Argen's vein unnoticed.

Still, it would be nice.

Very nice indeed.

Pondering that, Rann slept.

He awoke in darkness, shivering uncontrollably. Yet he couldn't move— not so much as a finger to drag cover over him. His teeth were chattering.

Yet there was heat, too: a burning centered on his chest above his pounding heart, as though someone had lit a fire there that had drawn all other heat from him.

But he had to move, *had* to. Gritting his teeth, he tried.

Couldn't, even as the fire grew worse.

He fled from it, but it followed. He wanted nothing but to be warm. To be utterly enclosed with warmth and never be cold again. To be part of the earth.

The heat increased, yet so did the cold, so that he became a being of absolutes. And he suddenly couldn't breathe, though it didn't seem to matter, because there was something warm ahead of him, something that drew him on. It had no color but he gave it one anyway. Red. Red was warm, or warm was red. He reached out for it, touched it, felt it grow warmer yet, even as that wilder heat that had never left him flared hotter yet.

And then both those heats collided around his heart, and the heat consumed him. Maybe he cried out; certainly he knew no more.

Voices woke him: concerned cries from the half-open door. He blinked through his shivers, and made out the shapes of Kylin and Strynn standing there, each robed against the cold that pervaded the room—a cold that seemed to emanate from Rann's own body.

"What—?" Kylin began.

Strynn cut him off. "By The Eight!" she cried, dashing forward to kneel by Rann's side. Heat pulsed from her, yet he knew that she was cold, too, if not as cold as he. Goose bumps patterned her flesh. She reached for his face, then shifted her hand to his chest. Air swished, like a glacial wind, and the flame that had burned there departed. Something hard rattled on the floor.

Rann didn't care. Heat—*life*—was washing back into him. Slowly, oh so slowly, yet it was blessed balm. He could breathe again. His teeth no longer chattered, his limbs no longer shook. Strynn slumped down beside him, awkward in her pregnancy, and folded her arms around him.

And Kylin . . .

Kylin had tipped his head to one side, as though listening, and was now pacing slowly across the darkened room. Rann expected him to join him and Strynn, but instead, he knelt a span away and began running his hands across the floor. "One," Rann heard him murmur, as though to himself. Then: "Two. No—three! Wait . . . *five*! There are five of them, Strynn!"

"Five what?" Strynn called. "Kylin, we need to tend to Rann!"

Kylin didn't reply, simply walked to Rann's pallet and sank down there. He held his hand out for Rann and Strynn to see.

Red gleamed there, visible even in the moonlight.

The same red as Strynn's gem. And Avall's.

But there were five of them: two exactly the same size, one slightly larger than the rest, two smaller.

Rann swallowed hard and reached toward the smallest stone. "I'm not sure, Strynn," he breathed. "But I think this one is . . . mine."

"Tomorrow," Strynn whispered. "Tomorrow. For now, we need to get warm again. All of us."

Half a hand later, wrapped in their thickest robes, full of hot cider, and sitting by a fire punched up so hot it was like a forge, they slept. Even Rann.

But the gem—*his* gem—was still clutched in his palm when he awakened.

By the light, he guessed it was shortly before midnight. Kylin was still with him, but Strynn was gone.

"She wanted to be alone," the harper murmured sadly. "I don't know why."

CHAPTER VII:

UNEXPECTED GUEST

(ERON: TIR-ERON—DEEP WINTER, DAY XLIII—SUNSET)

. . . eyes . . .

. . . bright or dark. Red or blue. Single, or paired.

Eyes: the first things Avall truly recognized when he returned to himself after being dead.

There was an eye of fire fixed upon him from very nearby indeed: bright and indistinct, a nimbus of gold around dimmer crimson. Two more eyes regarded him at middle distance, these dark blue and hooded by level black brows in a young male face, tensed with concern. The last eye was also of fire, but brighter and ruddier than the nearer. It gleamed amid a wash of topaz splendor: a perfect round ruby atop a crown of snow-veiled mountaintops.

"Sun," he whispered. "Sss—" His tongue gagged him. Air mixed with liquid brought up by his lungs to his throat. He choked, gagged again, felt his lungs take fire. Something ripped free, and he choked once more—endlessly. Flexing muscles that hadn't moved in days—that would surely fracture like river ice if he used them—he wrenched his torso over the side of whatever soft, warm thing he lay upon and vomited a thin stream of water onto the floor.

Hands found him—related to the blue eyes, he assumed—and some sense of self returned, as he found himself utterly helpless, gagging and retching into an earthenware bowl strategically inserted between his mouth and the rug.

Heat washed the top of his head—the nearer fire—the *lamp*, he identified—come too near. Hair sizzled, the stench acrid yet strangely comforting. He shivered. And shivered again, though his body was warm—on the outside. Inside—he doubted he'd ever be warm again. His blood was clogged with ice crystals, every one of which hurt as it thawed.

"Don't fight it," a voice cautioned—loud beyond enduring, when he'd heard nothing but his own languid pulse for countless ages. "I got what I could out of you, but you'll have to bring up the rest on your own."

Avall did, choking, retching, spitting: weak as a newborn, and desperately grateful for that warm, solid presence beside him, arms wrapped around his shoulders (bare, he noted), one hand stroking his hair away from his face even as that hair soaked his benefactor's tunic.

Eventually, the heaving stopped. He signaled its cessation with a spontaneous relaxation and a whispered "No . . . more."

But he didn't fight as the dark-eyed youth helped him lie back into what he'd determined to be a narrow but comfortable bed in what bleary vision proclaimed was an equally narrow but comfortable room with a fireplace somewhere beyond his head, a sturdy wooden door a span beyond his feet, and a thick-paned window opposite. Which made that direction west, for that was clearly a setting sun.

"Sun," he said again. Numbly. Unwilling—or unable—to think because the only thing *to* think was impossible.

"There *is* one," the youth agreed. He seemed barely older than Avall's own twenty years, dark-haired and slender, and clad in what reflex as much as memory told him was Stonecraft black and silver beneath a tabard of Warcraft crimson.

Avall nodded weakly.

The youth's eyes narrowed with a combination of fear and concern that Avall wasn't certain he'd ever seen before. He had a narrow face, too; more quirky than handsome. His mouth twitched, as words fought to escape and were recalled, but Avall was too tired to aid his struggles.

After all, hadn't he just been dead?

"Are you warm enough?" the youth ventured. "I can stoke up the fire or get you more cover . . ."

Avall finally realized, by the sensations along his body and the items of fur-lined clothing steaming in an untidy heap before the fire, that he was naked. Which meant that this fellow had probably undressed him. And while that wouldn't normally have bothered him, it did now, because it implied that this . . . *stranger* had seen the gem.

"I'm fine," Avall croaked.

"Hungry?"

"I don't know."

Eyes narrowed further. "I have brandied cider warming by the hearth. You need to get something sweet inside you. And warm. Then we have to talk."

Avall nodded weakly. He would deal with *now,* he decided. He would deal with how he came to *now* later; otherwise, he'd find himself staring hard at madness. "My wife's Warcraft," he whispered. "Her bond-sister and my twin are at War-Hold." Neither of which facts he'd been aware of until they'd simply appeared there, on the tip of his tongue. But now that he'd said them, a horde of information came stampeding back. *Wife . . . Sister . . .*

No! He loved them, but dared not think on them now. He closed his eyes, felt sleep drag at him, comfortable twin to that terrible unconsciousness that had claimed him since . . .

Since when?

He remembered being dead, and before that he remembered being cold. And before that he remembered . . .

He knew, yet did not know, for that way lay fear. And behind it, responsibility and things he had to do that he dared not think of now, but that had to do with—

His fingers struggled to his chest, fumbling for what ought to lie there in a nest of wire against his flesh. He found it, and felt warmth and comfort and something he could only call recognition pour into him from that strange smooth stone.

Steps distracted him, and he eased his hand away, as the youth scooted a stool beside him. Scents came with him this time: woodsmoke, soldier's soap, and hot spiced cider. All at once his mouth was watering. Warmth joined the scent as the youth brought a stoneware cup to Avall's lips. He sipped, almost choked again, then drank deeply as the fumes wound their way to his brain, which then told his throat it was allowed to swallow. Avall drained half of it before the youth removed it.

"Good for you," he said. Then shifted his gaze to Avall's chest. "That thing burned me," he continued. "One more thing we have to talk about— *Avall,*" he concluded after a pause.

"You know me?"

"I know *of* you. I've seen you around Tir-Eron."

Avall sighed, feeling at once remarkably more focused, and more alert and wary. "And you are—?"

"Myx. Stonecraft sworn to War, and thus, apparently, double-bound to you. Your mother is Stone, is she not?"

"Clay," Avall corrected numbly. He had no energy to spend puzzling out genealogies—not with a generation mostly absent from them, courtesy of the plague. "How did I get here?" he asked instead.

Myx shook his head. "Better I should ask you that."

"The last thing I remember," Avall dared, "is falling."

Myx countered with a lopsided grin. "The first thing *I* knew was that I came in here a finger ago to find you lying by my fire, soaking wet, with no way you could've entered this place unseen, never mind this room, since that door was certainly locked."

"So no one knows I'm here?" It was safer than confronting what Avall was still barely able to comprehend.

"No one but me—so far. But I'll have to report you at some point. I'd rather have my facts straight when I do."

"Where am I?"

"You truly don't know?"

"I'm too weak to play games, Myx."

Myx nodded warily. "On that I agree. And on the fact that you've been in very cold water a very long time. Unfortunately, the nearest source of that much cold water is the Ri-Eron, which is a shot away—across empty land. And if you'd come that way, the lookouts would surely have seen—"

"I'm in a tower," Avall announced abruptly. "It fits. Your garb, these quarters, the quality of light: sunlight on expanses of snow. The question is, which tower?"

"Drink some more."

Avall wanted to refuse, but the idea was suddenly insanely appealing. He finished the cider—under his own power—and extended the mug for more. Myx scurried off to oblige. Avall scooted higher in bed, tugged the fur coverlet close around him. Birkit fur, he noted, with a shiver of revulsion. He knew things about birkits no one else did—more things he dared not think on now.

"Eron Tower," Myx conceded.

"The one at the top of the gorge?"

"There *is* only one Eron Tower."

Joy welled up in Avall so forcefully he would've started from his bed had Myx not restrained him.

"You haven't told me how you got here," Myx reminded him, with a forcefulness that was almost, but not quite, a threat. "I'll have to explain your presence, and craft-kin or no, I *can't* explain it."

"I don't know myself."

"You were wet. You weren't frostbitten, however, or frozen—beyond your hair."

Silence.

"The only thing that makes sense . . ."

"What?"

"Is that you simply appeared out of thin air."

Avall rolled his eyes in mock dismay, even as his heart gave a twitch. He truly did not know himself—but even if that notion was preposterous, it also had an insidious sort of logic.

So people didn't spontaneously . . . place-jump. They didn't talk mind to mind, either. Or travel to the Overworld.

Except that *he* did—with the assistance of a certain magical gem.

A gem that had, apparently, mustered a desire from somewhere to save him.

And delivered him into friendly hands a stone's throw from his goal.

"I have to leave," he cried.

"You'll do nothing of the kind! Not until I have answers. Besides, it's almost dark and starting to snow again."

Avall couldn't resist a contemptuous snort. "I have no fear of the weather—not any longer."

"What's that supposed to mean?"

"If I told you, you wouldn't believe me."

"I know you've been outside, if that's what you're getting at. I saw your clothes; I saw the frostburn on your face and hands. I saw scars on your neck. You've got secrets—but not as many as you'd like."

"I'd prefer to have none," Avall flared. "But I don't have anything like as many answers as you think I've got, either. For instance, I truly have no idea how I came here."

"But you have suspicions—you have to."

Avall nodded slowly.

"It would seem," Myx ventured, "that we need each other."

"Meaning?"

Myx shrugged. "You need care, for one thing. Anyone who sees you here will ask the same questions I have. And some of them will be people who won't take kin-claim, sketchy as it is, as rationale for silence. Eight, man, I could keep you here and starve you and make you tell your tale that way!"

Avall almost laughed aloud. "No you couldn't! You have to have friends here; you'd have to keep them away, and anything you did to that end would look suspicious. On the other hand, you need me to remain discreet, so as not to cast aspersions on whoever was on guard tonight, who's almost bound to be a friend of yours."

Myx nodded slyly. "My bond-brother, actually. He's the reason I didn't raise the alarm first and ask questions later."

"Are you going to tell him?"

"Of course! I haven't yet because by the time I got through tending you, you'd come around."

"You could've called someone when I showed up! That's what I'd have done."

"Would you? You walk in your room and find a near stranger in a puddle of water on your floor, unconscious and maybe dying? The dead answer no questions. And no one's up here but me; they're all on duty or at supper."

"Which means they'll be looking for you."

Myx shook his head. "I'm known as a bit of a hermit. And I've not felt well of late."

Avall took a deep breath and closed his eyes. He was tired. So tired. And confused—easily as confused as Myx. But he was also close to the goal he had set however many days ago it had been. He hated to delay now. If he could only travel a few more shots. Or send a message.

But there was no one here he'd trust with one, and in any event he could navigate the distance himself in little longer than it would take to find a messenger, send him off, make the necessary connections and decisions, and return with someone Avall *could* trust.

Except, he realized suddenly, he had no idea how much time had passed between then and now. They—he, Rann, and Div—had been attacked. There was only one reason for that attack. Therefore someone from Gem-Hold had the same reason for reaching Tir-Eron that he did.

"What day is it?" he asked abruptly.

Myx grinned at him. "Why should I tell you? Why shouldn't I trade information for information?"

"Because information can get you killed," Avall replied flatly. "Because what you already know can put you in debt to a very powerful craft and clan, and earn you some very powerful enemies as well. I've nothing against you, but I make a better friend than foe—and nobody needs enemies."

Myx gnawed his lip. "Can we make a deal?"

"Maybe."

A deep breath. "I won't say anything to anyone except my bond-brother, and I'll swear him to bond-oath. You stay here tonight. And tomorrow night—or sooner, if we can—I'll help you get away from here."

"I sense conditions impending."

"You're no fool. Neither am I. There's a mystery here, and if I'm going to be involved, I want to be on the right side—or at least the winning side. At the very least I want you to promise me—when you can—to tell me the truth about everything."

Avall regarded him steadily. "If the King or The Eight do not bind me with vows that supersede it, I will do that thing. In a year and a day, I will do it."

"Good," Myx grinned. "Now . . . I'll go seek my brother."

Avall wanted to rise to stop him, but when he made to do so, his muscles failed—not so much from weakness as from pain. It was as though every fiber were laced with ice. It would be a long time, he suspected, before he was free of pain again.

And he wasn't certain he had a long time. He had to get word to Eellon,

Chief of his clan, about a certain revelation. And it truly was something he was better equipped to deliver in person. Never mind that Eellon was among the few with sufficient influence to silence whatever random speculation might emerge from what was even now transpiring.

But in spite of himself, he almost slipped into sleep again—or unconsciousness—though he did hear the click of a key in the lock when Myx departed.

As soon as he was alone, he took a deep breath—it was like breathing fire—cleared his throat again, and pushed the coverlet away. Another breath, and he got his feet over the side. Two more, and he could sit up. Darkness swam behind his eyes, and for a long moment he thought his body had erupted in flame. He closed his eyes, tried to regain some control over his breathing, then recalled what his masters at War-Hold had taught him long ago, information which Merryn had drilled into him endlessly in later days: that pain was not truly real, and could, at need, be ignored.

The deepest breath yet, while he tried to think on something else entirely, and he managed to half lunge, half fall across the space between the bed and the window, so that his fingers found the hard, cold stone of the sill.

He faced west.

The sun was all but gone now, but he could see the mountains that masked it: a saw-toothed bite from the horizon. He'd been among those mountains not that long ago: a simple goldsmith, newly married, happily engaged in crafting a war helm for the King, while working in the mines one-quarter of the time.

Where he'd found the gem that now thumped heavily against his chest. Opal but not opal; ruby, yet not that, either. Red, but with a sparking heart like crystal fire.

He reached for it, but that upset his balance, and he had to slap both hands back on the sill. It was darkening out there as he watched: the last of the sunlight being sucked down by the endless shots of snow that lay between him and the forests. Forests that themselves covered half the distance between here and where he'd so recently been. Shots he'd traversed by a means no one should've been able to effect.

Unless they had access to what he had little choice but to call magic.

The magic of this gem.

The weight of that knowledge caught him unaware and made him gasp. For a moment he wished he'd died in truth, so that he would no longer have to bear this terrible burden of responsibility. He closed his eyes—to conjure darkness or escape it, he had no idea. *No,* he told himself, firmly. He had two things yet to accomplish, *then* he could rest. A day, at most. Half that if he pushed himself to the limit. In fact, he realized, he could probably do one of those things right here.

If he was strong enough—and had appropriate gear.

A quick look-round showed nothing obviously useful, and he knew he hadn't the strength for a search. It wouldn't take much. A cut in his hand: merely enough to draw blood—maybe not even that, were it not for the distance involved.

He saw nothing. But then sense caught up with desire, and he recalled that his gear was still in the room. He slid down the wall, then crawled on all fours across the thick sheepskin throw rug to where his snow breeches lay clumped before the fire. Myx, reasonably enough, had undressed him in haste, and spared no time for niceties, so that Avall's belt was still attached to his breeches, and his knife to the belt. He found it, worked it free, and lay there panting, listening for Myx's return, mustering strength for that final trek to his bed.

This close to the fire, its heat beat at him in waves, pain and pleasure so mingled he couldn't distinguish them. He suppressed an urge to crawl right into the fire itself, and complete the thawing of his body, mind, and soul that way.

Or maybe the gem could do that.

Back to bed then? Or should he simply remain here, since whatever he did would be obvious. Here seemed as good a place as any, and was better use of time in the bargain. And with that, he found the knife and dragged the edge clumsily along his palm just enough to bring forth blood, then clasped his hand upon the gem.

Warmth lapped at him, stronger but less fierce than the fire, and it was as though he were being filled with . . . *himself,* it almost seemed: some vital component of his being that had dispersed and now returned. He felt stronger at once, and more energized. His breathing slowed and steadied, and his heart lapsed into a less frantic pace. Calm came with it. He closed his eyes tighter, and . . . wished.

Wished to see Strynn, to tell her he was all right. Wished to see Rann and tell him the same. And Merryn. He was inside himself and then he wasn't, and that frightened him beyond reason. But then logic made him recall something he should have thought of earlier. And in that final moment before panic made him return to himself, he pictured another face in his mind. Eellon, who was very close by indeed. And who was kin. And with whom he was linked by affection as well as blood.

Almost he had it. Eellon's face swam before his inner eye. But Eellon was engaged in dinner, and wasn't paying attention to what disparate thoughts might come prying at his mind. And so he missed Avall's frantic plea.

And then panic caught him again, and sent him roaring back into himself. He had only sense enough to free his hand from the gem before darkness found him in truth.

(TIR-ERON—ARGEN-HALL)

"... nor is it to be assumed that a finite number of integers exist, yet an infinite number can be part of a greater infinity. For instance, when a man walks to his door, he faces an infinite number of futures. Go right, or left, or straight ahead, at any of a thousand angles, each of these also offers an infinite number of possible choices, yet each choice diminishes the number of ways his life may fall—yet there are still an infinite number. Frinol syn Meekon has this to say about ..."

Lykkon syn Argen-a jerked his head up with a start, gazing blearily at the book propped on the desk before him. Wine cooled to his right in a cup Avall had made him for his last birthday—his nineteenth. A plate of meat morsels sat to the left, mingled with small loaves and various dipping sauces. It was all he had time for now, amid this mass of scholarship.

Perhaps, he reflected, he wasn't cut out to be a Loremaster after all. Not if lore involved much in the way of mathematics. He liked *concrete* things—or history, which was *about* concrete things. But this! Abstract numerical theory that connected to not much of anything. That existed only to confound the minds of nineteen-year-olds, as best he could tell.

But he had to finish this treatise tonight. He had an exam on it tomorrow a hand after sunrise—which sunrise he suspected he'd be awake to witness.

Sighing, he rose and snared the wine, quaffing it absently even as he realized that was foolish. It would make him sleepy when he needed to stay awake. Oh well; it was getting dark anyway. Time to raise some light—and put on a pot of cauf. Pausing to stretch his lithe body, and to wipe an inky forelock out of his eyes, he sauntered to the fireplace, lit a splinter from the stash there, and used it to light two candles on the mantel, and two more to either side of his desk. That accomplished, he returned to the hearth, found the small cauf-grill set there, lit it, then filled a pot with water and set it on to boil. Rising again, he started to return to the book, but concluded that a bit of exercise might better set his blood flowing. With that in mind, he doffed the long house-robe that staved off the random chills that found their way inside, leaving him clad in maroon house-hose and short-tunic. A series of bouncing steps brought him to the thick glass door that looked out on his balcony. A glitter of snow showed on the pavement beyond, and more mounded on the rail, while icicles as big as his arm depended from the rafters beyond. The door itself was frosted with rime, and his breath turned it white where he paused to look out on Tir-Eron—what he could see of it, beyond the crenulated roofs of Argen-Hall. Steam rose from the Ri-Eron, for the air above it was warmer than the water, and very dimly he could discern, on the opposite bank, the impertinent spire of Lore's tower, which was the tallest structure in Eron Gorge, because some nameless Lore Chief years ago had got both a King and a Priest to agree that thought ought to come above all other things.

He wondered if that included infinite numbers.

Shrugging, he turned away and busied himself with a series of knee bends and stretches, wincing as a bruise he'd collected at sword practice twinged along his right hip.

At least he was awake again—he thought.

A pause to check the water—not quite ready—and he settled back into the chair before his desk. He only had a page to go. He'd read that, make cauf, then start over.

He managed two lines, only to find his lids easing closed.

Nor did he fight; the cauf-pot would sing when it was ready, and that would awaken him. Instead, he let himself drift, enjoying the comfort of the chair and the warm light of the room.

His eyes closed in truth. Almost, he slept. But it was an odd sort of sleep, as though sleep—or unconsciousness—had gained sentience and was reaching out to embrace him. It scared him—but it was curious, too, and so he let himself be drawn to it.

And while he floated there, in a place that was not precisely bound to his body, he heard someone call. Not to him, but to Eellon. It sounded like Avall, he realized with a start. Avall, who was his hero and his friend, and would've been his choice of bond-brother had he not been kin, just slightly too much older, and already taken by Rann.

It was a dream, of course, but a very odd dream.

Or was it? He tried to follow that call—and found himself swept out of himself, and looking down at the Ri-Eron, and then at the snow-covered plain above it, and then at the tower that stood guard at the river-road approach to the gorge. Avall was there, he knew at once. Which was impossible.

"No!" Avall—screamed. Then: *"Help me!"*

And he was gone.

Lykkon's eyes popped open, all traces of fatigue replaced with a desperate urgency he wasn't at all certain was his own. He stood abruptly, upsetting the book, which tumbled to the floor. He barely heard that thump, because he was already halfway to the door.

Before he truly realized how preposterous this all was, he was stumbling into Eellon's private dining room. A few folk looked up—maybe a dozen: the old man's healer, and assorted family and clan or craft functionaries, dropping by as part of some complex rotation. Lykkon ignored them. Pulling himself up to his full height, and wishing he had a man's bearing, he marched up to the Chief of his clan, who was more than four times his age, and looked him straight in the eye. "If you never do me another favor in your life, Clan-Chief," he burst out, "give me fair hearing now."

(Tir-Eron—Eron Tower)

Avall had been awake for a while, but hadn't let on that he was. It didn't take much effort—he was tired as a relay runner, weak as a newborn child. A large portion of him still required convincing that he *was* alive. And he hurt where his body continued to awaken: tiny explosions coursing through him as though his blood itself were aflame. But there was comforting warmth, too, from the room itself and the coverlet over him. And softness: a true mattress beneath him, for which he'd longed since starting out on this ridiculous quest all those days ago. Myx and his bond-brother—Riff—must have returned him to bed as he slumbered.

But there was warmth and softness of another kind, too: of simple companionship when he'd known the loneliness of not being. They were concerned for him, he knew, and he knew also that he ought to pretend to awaken so as to allay that concern. But if he slept—or pretended to—they wouldn't plague him with questions he couldn't answer.

So he let them wonder, converse softly among themselves, drink a fair bit of beer, and refuse visitors at the door under the guise of Myx's very real fever that ought to have *him* in bed instead of wrapped in fur robes by the fire.

Besides, it gave him time to continue the call. That was all it was now: a simple linkage to someone who registered in his brain only as "familiar person/blood-kin/friend." There was too much activity there—too much sheer mental energy for him to determine more. But he'd made his call, and reinforced it, and every now and then—when he had the strength to face that brief burst of non-being—sent it forth again.

Still, he was not prepared when voices and booted feet sounded on the stone stairs outside, instants before a sharp knock pounded on the sturdy oak door.

Riff was on his feet at once, and he heard Myx swear, then call out a terse "Who The Eight is it?"

"Let me in, boy!" a gruff voice thundered, for all that it was female. And even Avall recognized those tones. It was Lady Veen of War, who was also master of this tower, as well as a renowned singer—of male-intended roles. Another voice joined it, calmer, but more familiar and blessedly comforting. "I have reason to think you have a guest therein, and Lady Veen has reason to think I'm mad; I'd as soon settle the matter."

"Eellon!" Avall yipped in spite of himself, as he dropped his masquerade. Myx glared at him, while Riff—a compact blond lad who looked too young to be a guard—shot eye daggers at him as he reached for the bolt.

"Avall!" Another voice burst out, younger and clearer, and by that time the bolt had been thrown and three people crowded into the room.

They could not have been more different. Veen—in full Tower Warden garb, including a raised hood—was short and stocky. Eellon was past ninety and thin as a post; his body all angles, as was his face—save for the sensual curves of lips and eyes. He moved carefully, efficiently, but not at all like most old men. Few knew that beneath all those robes, an intricate strapwork of metal and leather helped him remain upright. At the moment, he was wearing a winter robe and cloak of Argen maroon, with hood raised, again to show that he acted in official capacity.

With him was his page—squire—whatever Lykkon was. A handsome, lightly built, black-haired lad who looked enough like Avall to pass for him when required. He was also cloaked, but not robed, and wore a fur hat as big as his head, with flaps pulled down across his ears. His fair skin was seriously windburned. He was also grinning like a fool. Veen looked angry, puzzled, and put-upon, and Eellon simply looked vastly bemused.

"I told you he was here!" Lykkon crowed, sounding like a boy half his age as he bounced over to sit on Avall's bed, thereby sparing Avall the problem of rising.

Eellon raised a brow. "So it would seem," he replied, eyeing Avall dubiously before reaching around behind Veen to close the door and shoot the bolt. "At least I didn't come up here in vain," he added with a warning look at the eager-faced Lykkon, whom Avall was trying, unsuccessfully, to hug.

Veen settled herself into the chair Myx hastily cleared for her and folded her arms expectantly. "This," she said loudly, "is very strange." Her gaze fixed first on Avall, then on Myx. "I take it there is some explanation?"

Myx cleared his throat, not looking at the Warden, his gaze shifting uncomfortably between Avall and his bond-brother. He was sweating, too, but whether from the heat of the room, anxiety, or his own light fever it was impossible to tell.

Eellon's eyes had never stopped moving, though they'd spent a fair bit of time on Avall's steaming clothing (now spread out), on Avall himself, and on Myx's clan tabard. Avall felt a little hurt that his two-father and mentor hadn't acknowledged him more properly. Then again, Veen was right: This was a very strange situation indeed, and Eellon was playing it close—a fact confirmed when Avall caught a clandestine wink in his direction.

"I could breathe if you'd let go of me, Lyk," Avall managed finally, trying to force Lykkon away with indifferent success, born in part by his desire to keep the gem hidden, which meant keeping the fur as high as he could.

"Glad you're back," Lykkon managed with reasonable formality, and rose, to be replaced by Eellon, who merely uncovered his right shoulder far enough to reveal Avall's clan tattoo. "You look like you," he said. "You can tell me if you *are* you when we get back to Argen-Hall."

Veen bristled at once. "Not tonight, you're not! The snow—"

"We'll do fine," Eellon assured her. "And so will you."

"Me?"

Eellon nodded, then indicated his raised hood. "I'm sorry, Lady, but I have to claim Chief-right now, and ask that everyone here accompany me and my escort back to the gorge. I claim this on my authority as Clan-Chief, and am willing to stand by this decision, should any here wish to bring it before the King and the Council of Chiefs. But it is clear that strange matters are afoot, matters that would seem to involve the clan which has been entrusted to me. Until I know what these matters are, I would prefer to control the flow of information."

"Oaths sworn here mean as much as those sworn in Argen-Hall," Veen protested.

"Yes," Eellon agreed, "they do. But if we exchange them before our departure, you would wonder. If you wait until we're in Argen-Hall, you may have answers to salve your oath. And I will have answers as well, since there are four stories here, at minimum."

Sparing no pause for protest, he rose and turned to Myx. "You look about his size. Do you have any clothes he could wear?"

Myx nodded nervously. "Aye."

"Good. You, your brother, and Lykkon get Avall dressed and ready to travel. I'm sorry to do this to you, lad, but I promise we'll make it worth your while—and have a healer assess that fever. You know our clan is in your debt . . ."

Myx nodded uncertainly, and Eellon nodded back as he offered his hand to Veen. She shook her head, denying the ritual, as women of Warcraft traditionally did, and rose on her own.

"It would seem, Lady, that we have a few things to discuss as well," Eellon murmured, as he started toward the door.

Avall couldn't contain himself. "Lord—Chief—Eellon—Two-father. I probably shouldn't say this now, but . . . this really is important."

Eellon regarded him levelly. "I know."

CHAPTER VIII:

HOMECOMING

(Eron: Tir-Eron—Deep Winter: Day XLIII—late evening)

A vall didn't remember much of the journey from Eron Tower to Argen-Hall.

Or perhaps he chose not to recall. That was easier than making decisions, easier than trying to be circumspect about what he said around three near strangers as the close-sledge swept along the snow-covered trace. Rather, he pondered the landscape—wrapped to the chin in fur blankets above Myx's best fur-lined travel clothing—staring through the thick, rime-patterned glass at a featureless white plain marked only by the tracks the sledge had made in transit to the tower, and by the route poles that showed red at twenty-span intervals to mark the way and show the depth of the snow (almost a span, in places). He didn't want to study faces—either those of Eellon and Lykkon, who sat beside him, or Veen, Myx, and Riff, who slumped opposite, looking by turns fiercely angry, put-upon, utterly confused, and scared. Lykkon, irrepressible as ever, had made stabs at conversation, but Avall had rebuffed him with terse replies. "I'm fine—as much as I can be. Strynn was fine the last time I saw her. I'm not sure about Rann. We were on our way here and were attacked."

And that was all. Even at that, he saw Eellon fix his gaze on him sharply, as though to say, *Hold your tongue, boy! Your very presence already says too much!* He was therefore left to lie in a semistupor and wonder what information he should impart first, and to whom, and how Eellon would handle the presence of these others. With that, he was struck anew at how alert the old man was. As Clan-Chief, he was the eldest mentally competent member of the clan, of either sex, much as Craft-Chief was the most accomplished artisan of any age past twenty.

Eellon also had a mind like a spring lock, tuned to a fine balance by years as Craft-Chief. He'd survived the plague that had taken most of his children and almost all his male descendants, down to Avall's generation. He'd helped make a King, and kept that King on the throne for two years, in the face of opposition from a sept of his own clan. What Argen would do when he died, Avall had no idea. Descend into chaos, probably, which condition could precipitate Avall into a craft-chieftainship, which would be no reward at all. He was a maker, not an administrator, and chiefs rarely got to make anything but peace.

And the disturbing thing was that a great deal of how all that resolved could well depend on what he himself revealed in the next few hands. He didn't like having the fate of most of his kinsmen on his shoulders.

Still, Eellon had been nothing but good to him, and hadn't goaded him as Tyrill had Eddyn—not that he hadn't been expected to excel past reason. But Avall's loyalty was unshakable in where it lay. To land, to King, to clan, to sept, to craft, then to his sister, his bond-brother, and his wife, in that order—which he didn't always feel good about, but couldn't change.

All in all, he concluded blearily, it was too much to think about. And so he chose to lapse into a drifty languor that only altered when the sledge slowed to begin the slow, tortuous trek down the Winding Stair to the floor of Eron Gorge.

A glance out the window showed the endless white snowfield turned to empty space full of drifting flakes as the plateau broke off at the edge of the gorge. Avall couldn't see the floor, for the driving flurries and the steam that rose from the Ri-Eron and the hot springs around it to render the gorge habitable. Already the air felt warmer, or perhaps that was an illusion, since there was still snow under the runners, and banks of the stuff to either side, in defiance of daily removal crews.

And then they reached the first switchback, and the view shifted to raw rocks glazed with ice, and he dozed again. He didn't wake until he felt the sledge jolt, and heard the grating of metal runners against stone instead of ice. "Wake up, boy," Eellon intoned softly, giving Avall a gentle shake. "We have to change transport here. It won't be long now."

Avall nodded groggily and let himself be helped out the door, down into slush two fingers deep, then up into a wheeled carriage painted in Argen maroon. The activity helped him regain sufficient alertness to know that they were no more than two shots from home.

A moment later, they'd passed the Citadel: the seat of government for the entire Kingdom, where High King Gynn lived. Not long after that they were navigating the mostly deserted promenade called the River Walk, with the Ri-Eron steaming to the right, and the halls, holds, and gardens of the major clans and crafts passing on the left.

And then they were flanking Argen's compound, and he could see the low, crenulated walls and higher, trapezoidal towers that marked the heart of his reality: the place he'd grown up, the place where the bulk of Clan Argen and its three septs——a, -el, and -yr—lived, intrigued, and made wonderful things out of metal. Before he knew it, they were passing through the massive gates, startling a gate-warden at his post, then veering left, toward the stables, into whose warmth and shelter they disembarked, only to assay a set of narrow stairs and a dozen corridors and come, at last, to the main apartment level. Avall remembered it clearly—but from an odd angle, as Lykkon and Riff had stuffed him on a litter and carried him, with Eellon himself striding ahead to clear the corridors, most particularly of anyone from Argen-yr, but also of Argen-el, the King's own clan.

Eventually Avall found himself in a small, comfortable room cut into intimate groupings by the intersecting vaults of the low ceiling. One wall was a parabola of windows, and showed the main audience hall below, while another was mostly fireplace. Lykkon scurried off to secure food at Eellon's request, and the rest busied themselves stripping down to indoor clothing. All the while Veen gnawed her lip, and Riff and Myx took comfort in staying close to each other, as bond-brothers were meant to do. In due course, Lykkon came trotting back with an enormous tureen on a cart, as well as bowls, bread, and spoons. He also had a companion, his thirteen-year-old half brother, Bingg, whose presence he explained by stating he'd found the lad in the kitchen and couldn't shake him.

Eellon filled a bowl of soup, which he gave to Avall, then opened a bottle of almond liquor and served everyone, followed by hot mulled cider. "Don't you have studying to do?" he asked Lykkon mildly.

Lykkon nodded. "But this is more important, don't you think? Besides, do you really think I'd be able to study? Besides, do you want to have to explain all this to me again? Besides, it's to do with lore, and that's my craft of choice. Besides . . ."

"Besides, I'll have to explain why you were missing to your chief," Eellon grumbled. "But that'd be easier than keeping you happy, I suppose, so you might as well stay—with your ears open, your mouth closed, and your tongue bound by Clan Oath, where that applies, and Council Oath, where it doesn't."

Veen whistled under her breath. "You don't take chances, do you, Lord Eellon? I've heard that pair invoked once in my life."

"I'm trusting you with a lot," Eellon acknowledged. "Like I said, I'd rather have you know and be bound than be speculating indiscriminately."

Veen looked pointedly at a time-candle, which indicated it was two hands shy of midnight. "I think," she growled, "it's time we actually *did* some knowing. Something tells me I've just been made to take sides in a clan feud without recourse to full information."

"Not by choice," Eellon gave back. "In any case, you can always claim neutrality."

"Let's hear Avall's tale," Lykkon broke in.

Eellon regarded Avall keenly. "You up for it?"

Avall studied him as carefully, from where he was alternately sipping thick, savory soup and rich-scented cider. He felt unaccountably refreshed, and had an idea why. "You put something in this, didn't you?" he accused. "To perk me up."

"Nothing that will do you lasting harm," Eellon retorted, settling himself onto a low sofa. "This has to be important, and time is of the essence."

"If it was that important," Veen inserted, from where she sat flanked by the two guardsmen, "you could've started in the sledge. Oaths would've been as binding there."

Eellon rounded on her. "Look at the boy, Veen! He's worn beyond worn, and not just from . . . whatever happened that brought him to your tower so precipitously. The Avall I know isn't supposed to have hollows under his cheekbones like that. Or haunted eyes."

Veen's mouth popped open, but she didn't reply. Avall almost laughed aloud. He'd forgotten the effect Eellon had on people who weren't used to him.

Avall found eyes looking at him, and cleared his throat, wiping his mouth as an afterthought. "I actually do feel better, but if Eellon's potion was what I suspect it was, I'll sleep for a day after this, so I'd best get started. I'll also warn you that the best way to prove some of my story is by demonstration, and that some of the things I have to demonstrate may be hard to believe."

Eellon nodded gravely.

"Very well," Avall began, "I'll give our . . . guests the background later. It's pretty complex intraclan politics," he added, to Veen. "Suffice to say the situation really began when I happened to be working in the clan vein at Gem-Hold-Winter one day—and found something a bit out of the ordinary."

Veen started to speak again, but Eellon silenced her with a warning hand. "Do you need privacy for this?"

Avall took a deep breath. "Lyk, Myx, and Riff already know part of what I'm talking about because they helped me dress. So do some folks from -yr, and—I fear—from Priest, so it's unlikely to be a secret long. I suspect *you'll* be off to Ferr before the night's over, if I know you."

"I defer to you," Eellon said carefully, but with a clear note of caution in his voice.

"Well," Avall sighed, fishing into the neck of his tunic, "as I said, I found something . . . interesting. Specifically, I found . . . this."

And with that he slipped the chain that held the gem over his head. A twist of nimble fingers freed the stone so that it glittered on his palm.

Eellon leaned forward to inspect it. He did not, however, touch it. Lykkon was practically breathing down Avall's neck, he was craning so far forward, as was Bingg. But Myx was having no part of it, and Veen and Riff seemed to be taking their cues from their fellow guard.

"Not a ruby," Avall said. "Not a garnet. Not a red variant of any gem we know."

"Inner fires like an opal, though," Lykkon noted.

"Touch it—gently," Avall told him, easing it in his direction. He heard Myx inhale sharply, and recalled that the thing had burned him. But Lykkon didn't know that, and Myx was none the worse for wear, as far as Avall could tell.

Ever curious, Lykkon eased closer, holding his breath as he cautiously extended a finger toward the softly gleaming gem. A pause, and he touched it, drew it back, then touched it again.

Avall studied his face, raised an eyebrow in query.

"It . . . likes me. Or something. I—" He paused. "That doesn't make sense, though, 'cause *things* can't feel."

"I'm not sure if it is *just* a thing," Avall replied, closing his fingers around the gem and cradling it in his lap. "Nor am I sure that it so much likes you as knows that you like me. As best I can tell, the only folks besides me that can touch it with impunity are folks I care about."

Eellon regarded him impassively. "This is interesting," he murmured. "But I don't see that it justifies a trip overland in Deep Winter."

Avall shook his head. "No, but something else might—several somethings, actually. Lyk told you how he found out I was in the tower, didn't he? Obviously he did, or you wouldn't be here."

"He told me he was convinced that you were there and that if I ever did a favor for him, it would be to go there. That's all. I thought it was The Eight speaking through him. That happens sometimes."

"And we may now know how or why," Avall replied. "Or we may know that The Eight really aren't The Eight at all, but simply someone with a gem like this putting notions in the royal head. Just because they don't show up in records anywhere, doesn't mean this is the only one."

"It . . . lets you speak *mind to mind*?" Eellon gasped abruptly.

Avall spared a glance at Veen. "You shouldn't have said that. But yes. I'm not sure exactly how, when, why, or what the limits are, but that can happen.

The other person has to be relaxed—optimally asleep—or very empathetic with the sender. I found out about it accidentally. I was in bed, wishing I had Merryn to talk to—and then suddenly I was somewhere else—someplace that really isn't—and then I *was* talking to her. I caught her asleep, and it was odd, and we've never managed contact again, really. But it *was* her."

"Merryn!" Lykkon blurted. "But she's at War-Hold, you were at Gem. That's hundreds of shots."

"Yes," Eellon mused. "It is. But if you've found a way for people to communicate that far instantaneously . . ."

"It would upset many balances of power," Veen put in. "Suddenly I'm glad I'm here. I'm not sure I want to know what I just found out, but if it means what it could . . . I think I just found myself on the side of power."

"Maybe," Avall replied. "But there's more. It lets you mind-speak to at least some animals. Specifically, to birkits, which are—in some way—intelligent. We denned with a pack on our way here. It's the only thing that saved us."

Eellon shook his head. "This is a lot in a hurry, lad. I wish I was writing it down."

"I am," Bingg piped up from the corner. "Making a list. Like Lyk told me."

Eellon snorted loudly, probably sensing another defection to Lore. "So we've got mind-to-mind communication between people and between people and animals . . ."

"Between *some* people," Avall corrected. "I think you have to either be kin or share some bond for what happened to me and Lyk to work. But there's another way, too. Two-father, I think you're the best one to rule on this—but it's not without cost."

"You've already cost me a night's sleep," Eellon growled.

"Do you have a knife?"

Eellon nodded, and brought out a small, sharp one.

"Cut yourself just enough to bring blood," Avall instructed. "I'd suggest the hand, then pass the knife to me."

The scowl deepened, but Eellon made a neat gash in the heel of his left hand. Blood welled forth in a series of beads. "You didn't need that much," Avall murmured, as he took the knife and made short work of opening the gash he'd made before. That accomplished, he retrieved the gem, laid it in his palm atop the blood, felt the gentle drawing that entailed, then extended his hand to Eellon. "Put your hand on the stone. And close your eyes."

Eellon did. Avall felt him start and stiffen. And then he felt himself flowing into the gem and out into Eellon, while Eellon likewise flowed into him. But Avall consciously held himself back, unwilling to plunder Eellon's secrets, though they were all laid bare for his inspection. Yet Eellon was in *his* mind, too. Avall steered him this way and that, providing a rambling sample of what could happen when minds were joined.

And then he slowly eased Eellon's hand away and broke the link. His *self* retracted, and he saw Eellon sitting across from him, eyes wide, mouth wider, as his chief took breath after breath, half-dazed.

"Not something to share with just anyone," he whispered. "Thank you . . . I think."

"I've shared it with Rann, Strynn, and a woman we met on the trek named Div—though that last was an accident."

Eellon drained his cup of liquor, poured another, and drained half of it. He eyed Lykkon speculatively. "Lyk," he said. "Go get the King." He tugged a ring from his right index finger. His Clan-Chief's signet. "Tell him I need him to administer a Sovereign Oath, and that it would be better done here."

Avall felt his heart skip a beat, as Lykkon's face went white. No one had administered a Sovereign Oath in his lifetime. Which meant that Eellon thought his discovery was even more important than Avall imagined.

"Does this toy do any other tricks?" Eellon wondered wearily, when Lykkon had departed.

Avall shrugged, feeling fatigue sneaking up on him again. "It heals wounds. I think it can draw strength from other people. I think maybe, it can make people . . . jump from place to place instantaneously."

Myx leapt to his feet, startling them all. "That's impossible! Except that it's the only thing that explains—"

"Yes," Avall broke in. "It is. But I wasn't conscious, so I don't know. The last I knew I'd fallen into the Ri-Eron and was drowning. Then everything went dark, and I woke up on your hearth."

"Why there, I wonder?" Eellon mused. "Forgetting how preposterous that is, I mean."

"Because it was the closest source of comfort?" Veen suggested. "From what your boy's said, that thing seems to take care of itself. And to take care of itself, it has to take care of whoever has control of it."

"That was my thinking, too," Avall agreed. "Obviously it has many powers—there's another one, for that matter, but since Lyk's gone for the King, perhaps that ought to wait until he returns."

Eellon sank back in his chair, his face lined with thought. "Aye, lad, maybe it should. But tell me again: Does *anyone* else know of this beyond this room, besides those you've mentioned?"

Avall counted on his fingers. "Rann was there when I discovered its power. Strynn helped me test it. And . . ." He broke off. "I forgot that another effect is that it slows down your senses and muscles relative to time, so that you can, for instance, hold your hand steadier than any normal person could. Which I used to good effect on the helm I'm making."

"Other people," Veen prompted.

Avall cleared his throat. "A harper named Kylin. And . . . Well, evidently Eddyn somehow got into my workshop and saw it. From what I've pieced together later, he was so amazed at the enhanced quality of my work that he became suspicious. He also told a Priest named Rrath. Young fellow, still in his service."

"Each of whom probably drew the same conclusion you did."

"Which was?" Veen broke in.

"That this was too important to wait when someone else might not, so that whoever first got word of it to their clan-kin would, at minimum, increase the prestige of his sept."

Avall nodded. "We all know that Eddyn's Tyrill's creature, and that she's determined to bring down the King."

"As if she didn't already have more power than anyone reasonably needs," Eellon grumbled.

"We *were* attacked," Avall noted. "And the nature of the attack wasn't such that it seemed like random banditry."

"Eddyn," Eellon spat. "It'd be just like him. If he was desperate or felt cornered . . ."

"But not alone," Avall stressed. "If it was him, he had allies."

"Priest-Clan," Eellon breathed. "Oh Eight!"

Avall nodded again. "That might be another problem. I've got proof that some animals can think. Therefore, by our definition, they have souls. But The Eight say animals don't have souls. And . . . no, I won't say more until the King arrives."

"Please don't," Eellon sighed. "I need to puzzle over this for a while. The rest of you . . . I'd advise some very strong drink."

Avall closed his eyes, as weariness came upon him again, and with it an odd new fire that he thought, perhaps, might be the magic stone keeping him alive.

"Wake up, boy!"

Avall started from the drowsy reverie into which he had fallen while he, his kinsmen, and three near strangers awaited the arrival of the King. It took a moment to realize that it wasn't him being addressed, but his cousin Bingg, who'd evidently nodded off amid his copyist duties, to judge by the smudge of ink pooling across the parchment on which he'd been taking notes.

"Wake up!"

Bingg jerked, yawned, then appeared to doze again. Eellon shook him— then looked at him intently and laid a hand on his brow. "He's cold as ice!"

Veen joined him beside the boy. "He's breathing, though," she observed.

"But this *is* . . . odd." Her gaze shifted to Avall. For his part, now that he was awake again, Avall felt alert. He took a deep breath, and then he, too, felt Bingg's brow. "I think," he ventured, "this is another function of the gem. As I said, it seems to protect me somewhat. And I noticed when Rann and I were on our way here that it would sometimes steal energy from him to fortify me. It nearly killed him, actually. Myself—now—I don't know what condition I'm really in, but I suspect that it's drawing on Bingg, either because he's sitting closest, or because he's healthiest among my kin. In any case, he should be fine soon enough. You might want to wrap a cloak around him, though, and get some of that soup in him." He paused, studying his cousin curiously. "How *do* you feel, Bingg?"

Bingg blinked sleepily, then yawned. "Cold, tired, and like . . . I'd had too much to drink and was kind of floating outside myself. And I've got a headache all of a sudden."

"So do I," Eellon acknowledged.

Avall gave Bingg a rough hug. "I'm sorry, cousin, but it's not a thing I can control. In a way it's a compliment that it picked you. And you *will* be fine, I promise."

Eellon eyed Avall keenly. "Yes, but are *you* going to be fine?"

A shrug. "I hope so. As far as I can tell, all I need is lots of food and lots of sleep, which I intend to get as soon as tonight's over, Eight willing."

"Speaking of which," Myx announced from the door, where he'd stationed himself—mostly, it seemed, so he'd have something to do besides sit and wonder—"someone's coming."

Eellon was there faster than Avall could have imagined, given his age, edging past the guard to throw the door bolt and peer into the hall. Avall saw the tension leave his shoulders, and by then he'd identified the tread of two pairs of feet.

A moment later, Eellon stepped back, managing a sketchy bow in the process, which prompted Avall, Bingg, and Veen to rise—followed, a confused moment later, by Riff, who only just found his feet as the King of Eron strode in, trailed by Lykkon, looking very pleased with himself.

The King of Eron did *not* look pleased. Avall noticed that beneath the dark travel cloak he was already doffing he wore a short version of the Cloak of Colors and carried the Crown of Oak, which meant he was there in official capacity. Eellon had put up the hood of his robe, signifying that he likewise acted officially.

"Sit," Gynn said offhandedly, motioning them all to their places. His gaze flitted about the room, coming to rest on Avall. A brow shot up. "For some reason, I thought you were elsewhere, cousin," he continued with somewhat forced courtesy.

Avall couldn't help but grin. "I was."

"And the reason you're here is the reason I'm here?"

Avall nodded, only then realizing that the King had arrived with no more entourage than Lykkon. Which he suspected meant that, irked or not, the King realized that Eellon wouldn't have summoned him without good reason.

For his part, Eellon took a deep breath. "Well, Your Majesty," he began, "how do you feel about impossible things?"

Gynn helped himself to some of Eellon's liquor. "I assume that these impossible things may not be so impossible, else I wouldn't be here."

"Some of them remain to be tested," Eellon admitted. Then, carefully: "I think, however, it would be best if they were revealed only under Sovereign Oath, and that you further swear everyone here to the same retroactively— commencing at"—he paused, looked at Avall—"sunset, I would say."

"A hand before," Myx corrected. "If you want to be safe, from my point of view."

A royal brow quirked upward again. "Very well. I would have you all kneel before me." With that, he reached for what had heretofore been hidden beneath the Cloak of Colors: a very old and very keen sword. The Sword of Air, in fact, having come, so legend said, with The Ancestors out of the air. Avall had never seen it, though even now his wife labored to complete its descendant.

And then he was kneeling himself, just behind Eellon, who'd taken the lead, with Lykkon supporting him, and Bingg aiding Avall, accented by a wary grin.

"Touch the sword," the King commanded.

Avall reached out with the rest, stretching past Eellon to rest his fingers lightly on the shimmering metal. He felt an unexpected thrill course through him at that, which he doubted was born of excitement alone. Indeed, it was not unlike that which the gem produced in him under certain circumstances.

Gynn cleared his throat. "I, Gynn syn Argen-el, for this time High King of Eron, and first of that name, do hereby command Sovereign Oath upon you gathered here, that nothing that is seen, witnessed, or referenced here, having occurred since one hand before sunset this day until dawn tomorrow will be discussed beyond those gathered here without my consent, on penalty of death for treason. Excepting those whom I, in my guise as voice of The Eightfold God, do deem it necessary to inform."

Avall cleared his throat. "Majesty," he ventured.

"What?" Gynn snapped.

Avall swallowed hard. "There are four who already know much of what has been discussed tonight and of what remains to be revealed. I would have freedom to include them in this as well, as those to whom it may be necessary to speak freely."

"Who are these four?"

"My wife, Strynn san Ferr; my bond-brother, Rann syn Eemon-arr; Kylin syn Omyrr; and a woman named Div of Common Clan, who saved my life and Rann's."

The King scowled, but nodded. "I will have their oaths of them when I see them. For now, your oath for them will suffice." He cleared his throat. "Each of you will now swear as I have commanded, one at a time so that all may hear and witness, and so that none may say the others nay."

And so they began, starting with Eellon, who came first in precedence, then continuing through Veen, Myx, Riff, Avall, Lykkon, and Bingg, the last of whom could barely keep his voice from cracking. Avall found himself wondering how it would feel to witness such events from the threshold of adulthood.

"I accept these oaths," Gynn acknowledged when they had finished— whereupon the sword twitched. A wash of pain coursed across Avall's fingertips, matched by a pulse of warmth from the gem. He found himself rocked backward, gazing at fingers that bled, though he'd have sworn they'd never touched an edge. A quick check showed the others likewise ensanguined.

So, he decided, there was magic in the world beyond that wrought by the gem and The Eight.

"Now," Gynn said, settling himself on the sofa Eellon had cleared for him. "What are these impossible things that have brought me from my bed?"

Avall told him.

To Gynn's credit, he listened without judgment or comment save to request clarifications, and even took Eellon's word that it was possible to join minds when Avall would have allowed his King to share his own.

In spite of the excitement of the evening, Myx was nodding when Avall finished, which reminded them that the young guardsman had a slight fever and had been promised a healer. "At dawn," Eellon vowed, though he helped Veen lay the yawning youth on the remaining sofa and covered him with a double portion of furs. Riff helped where he could, then took over Myx's post as door warden.

"Well," the King said when they'd finished. "These are all very interesting things, and you did right to call me here, never mind the time and the season. But you spoke, I believe, of one more thing."

Avall took a deep breath. "Indulge me a moment, Majesty," he replied. "You sometimes speak with the voice of The Eight in One, who, it is said, dwells in the Overworld. Tell me what you know of that place."

Gynn took a deep breath in turn, looking distinctly unroyal, though perhaps that was a function of his having started out in a sept of this same clan before being Raised to the Throne by the Council of Chiefs. He was barely more than twice Avall's age, anyway, so Eellon had probably seen him as a pink, naked babe. *Surely* had, Avall corrected, Eellon had been stationed at one of the remotest holds when Gynn was born there, which was how he'd survived the plague.

"The Overworld," Gynn began, rousing Avall from his reverie. "It is the place The Eightfold God dwells when He does not dwell here. It is a place where time and space are as He chooses to make them, so that those things may cease to exist at need."

"Is it a physical place?" Avall inquired. "I know you're not a Priest, nor privy to all their mysteries, but you sometimes function as one. Sometimes the God speaks through you."

Gynn shifted uneasily. "Some of these things are *hard* to speak of because there's no vocabulary for them. It's like trying to describe a color. Red isn't blue, but how to explain the difference? The Overworld isn't this world, but how to explain the difference?"

"You've seen it, then?"

"I've seen a place—visited a place—where I can see all this world at once, as from a great height. But I've never been able to move where I would there. Rather, it's as though I were dust blown before the winds."

"Are there people?"

"Shadows, maybe. Perhaps those parts of people here that exist there. I think it is as if . . . as if The Eight live there and are reflected here, and we live here and are reflected there."

"So The Eight may only be people from that other place?"

"Blasphemy!" Veen cried.

Eellon regarded her mildly. "Not blasphemy if it is only an idea. And tell me that you have not questioned the existence of The Eight every day of your life."

"*I* certainly have," Lykkon dared. "What Avall has said of the gem makes it possible to suppose that someone has another gem of like kind, through which he or she manipulates events by—forgive me, Majesty—manipulating the King. *If* we have found such a stone, and Priest-Clan knows we have, that would go far in explaining their desire to prevent Avall's appearance here."

Gynn stared at him incredulously, then at Eellon. "Are all my kinsmen this accomplished?"

Eellon shrugged and ruffled Lykkon's black hair. "You merely meet the more accomplished. In any event," he continued to Avall, "what was it you had to say about the Overworld?"

Avall took a drink, pausing to let the warmth flow through him, wondering how long he'd sleep when this was over. Finally, the pressure of gazes upon him grew too great. "At one point on our journey here, Rann, Div, and I sheltered in a birkit den. It was a bifurcated cave, and the beasts had one fork and we the other. Eventually the three of us found ourselves joined through the linkage of the stone—joined with ourselves and with the beasts as well. We didn't *intend* that to happen," he emphasized. "But it did. In any event, we found ourselves going . . . somewhere else. Not in our physical bodies, I don't think, we were more like . . . shadows of ourselves. It was the place I go when I speak mind to mind—and yet it wasn't. It was both more material and more abstract. I'll tell you one thing, though, it was frightening as the Not-World—so much so that I wanted to leave. I think I was the . . . leader then, that whatever Div and Rann experienced was only a reflection of what I did, perhaps because it was my gem that was taking us there. Anyway, we fled back to our bodies, but before we left, I grabbed a hand-ful of . . . something—I don't know why, maybe I was just trying to hang on to anything solid so as to stay sane, or maybe I wanted proof. But when we came back—whatever it was—exploded."

Lykkon's eyes went very round, and Bingg's, if possible, even rounder. "You weren't hurt?"

"Knocked out," Avall replied. "Who knows what would've happened had we not been linked to the gem and so, presumably, under its protection?"

"We wouldn't be having this conversation, for one thing," Veen supplied tartly. "But what you're saying *without* saying is that what you've found is—or can be—a weapon. It can allow speech across impossible distances, which would certainly aid any army, especially if a means could be found to use it reliably. And now this other thing."

"And we know nothing about what it can really do—when, how much, how often, with whom," Eellon observed.

"And from what Avall said," Gynn finished, "both Argen-yr and Priest would like to have some say in its use as well."

"Gem, too—probably," Eellon sighed. "They're bound to find out about this eventually; *they'd* have a claim it would take a score of Law Priests to disentangle."

"Never mind that for all we know they've known about this kind of thing for years, and that it could as easily be them manipulating The Eight—assuming that's what's happening—as Priest. Or they could be in league with Priest."

"The mind reels," Gynn groaned. "I don't *think* The Eight are merely a function of some plot such as you've suggested, but it's definitely some-thing we need to investigate. But one thing this does imply is that ordinary people may have access to what could be the Overworld, which by extension means they might have direct access to The Eight, which Priest has tradi-tionally claimed as their right alone. So Priest is doubly threatened: Animals have souls—some of them—and the rank and file can access the Overworld directly."

"Assuming," Avall broke in wearily, "that more gems can be found, or even exist."

"The boy's right," Eellon agreed. "Our problem is to find out if more exist, and if so, how to control and use them. And if not, how to make best use of the one we have."

Gynn nodded. "I may have to bring Ferr into this, since he's almost into it anyway. I won't invoke my sept-chief, because the clan politics of this are complex enough, and a three-way struggle for power in a major clan is more than any of us need."

"There's also the small matter," Avall noted bitterly, "of the fact that if Gem *has* been withholding information, which we've now stumbled upon, my wife, bond-brother, and an important Warcraft heir might all be in danger."

Eellon nodded. "But you can contact them, right?"

Avall shrugged. "I've been too weak to try since I . . . came to myself."

"How *did* you do that?" Gynn wondered.

Another shrug. "I don't know. I wasn't conscious at the time. I think . . . maybe it was something the gem did of its own accord."

"So maybe the *gem* is an Avatar of The Eight," Veen ventured.

Gynn studied her seriously. "Lady Veen," he said thoughtfully, "you seem to have an interesting take on things. And since you know more than you ought already, it is perhaps wise that I take you into my personal service, and these two lads as well, since one of them needs a healer anyway. Therefore, I would have you return with me to the Citadel. I'll send someone to replace all three of you at the tower, and to retrieve your gear, if that pleases you."

"And if it doesn't?" Veen countered bravely.

"You'll do it anyway. We're talking about the fate of the Kingdom."

"Aye, Lord," Veen replied meekly. "As you will."

"Strange bedfellows," Eellon muttered.

The King yawned. "And it's time I sought mine, lest I be missed. I took a . . . secret way here. One"—he gazed fiercely at Lykkon—"you no longer remember."

Lykkon grinned, but nodded.

"I don't suppose you have a secret way out of here?" the King continued. "I'd as soon no one know I've been here, and there'll be more of us leaving than arrived."

Eellon shook his head. "Not from here." His breath was still fading into the suddenly silent air, when a sharp rap sounded on the door. Riff jerked as if he'd been struck, which meant he'd dozed off. He reached for the bolt, then hesitated, looking at Eellon.

"Who is it?" the Chief of Argen called.

"Tyrill!" a harsh female voice cracked back. "Am I going to have to stand out here all night while you try to hide from me?"

Eellon stiffened, face purpling into a rage only Tyrill could impart in him, but Gynn swiftly edged past him to shoot the bolt and wrench open the door.

Confronted with her sovereign, which was clearly more than she expected, the Craft-Chief of Smith staggered back a pair of steps, and would have fallen had she not had the support of two female squires. Half again her size, though slender for all that, the King whisked the old woman away from them. "Go . . . now!" he thundered. "Return in a hand. And remember: This hasn't happened!" And with that, he snatched Tyrill into the room. "Riff," he added, "stand guard outside. It'll raise questions, but the main questioner is right here, so maybe Luck will tend to the rest."

Riff nodded mutely and slipped into the corridor as Lykkon courteously helped Tyrill to a seat—tactfully far from Eellon, who had regained a semblance of calm, but only a semblance. "How much did you hear?" the King demanded.

"I heard nothing," Tyrill snapped back. "If I'd been spying, I'd not have knocked. As any fool would know."

"And you often attend Eellon's apartments late at night?"

"I do when I see sledges leaving at odd times and returning at odder, with gate-wardens ignored; then hear of the sudden use of back passages and food being conscripted by someone who's supposed to be somewhere else. And—"

She blinked, having just that moment noticed Avall—or perhaps having realized who he was, and the implications thereof.

"Sovereign Oath," Gynn said simply. "I would have Sovereign Oath of you, as I have had it of these others."

"To what am I swearing secrecy?" Tyrill growled back. "I don't like secrets."

"Unless you contrive them," Eellon burst out.

"It's important," the King told her, "else I wouldn't be here. I have no intention of involving anyone further, nor of informing you of what has lately transpired until I have time to do some thinking. In the meantime, you will mention this meeting to no one—and yes, I know I'm a fool to deny you information. Then again, I *am* your King. You can speculate all you want, but you will say nothing. Now—I would have your oath."

"Suppose I refuse?"

"Refusal to swear Sovereign Oath is treason."

"So are other things I can name."

"Name them if you will, but not until I give you cause. I'm warning you, Tyrill, if I have to have you drugged and dragged out like a ceremonial puppet, I will. Some things are beyond your need to know. Now—*swear!*"

And with that the King withdrew his sword again, recited the oath, and heard it back from a white-faced Tyrill. Not until the ritual blood sheened her fingers did the King speak again. "I know that keeping you ignorant is more dangerous than having you armed with knowledge, but some things are worth that risk. When I feel free to inform you further, I will—probably soon. Now go. Riff will escort you to your quarters. And return here at once with those maids—squires, whatever they are—who henceforth will be in my service."

Tyrill looked as though she were about to explode, but finally realized she might possibly have met her match in a room full of strong youths and powerful men. "I *will* know," she hissed, as she rose to leave. "It would be better if you told me than if I hear otherwise."

"We would all have been better had you remained asleep," Gynn retorted. "Now go. Be assured I will follow hard upon your heels."

Tyrill spared one final, all-encompassing glare, and departed.

"One final thing," the King called to her back. "There is not now, and never has been here, tonight, anyone who looks like, sounds like, or whom you have cause to think might be, Avall syn Argen-a."

"I would," Tyrill gritted back, "there never had been."

CHAPTER IX:

MAKING CONTACT

(ERON: TIR-ERON: ARGEN-HALL— DEEP WINTER: DAY XLIII—NEAR MIDNIGHT)

A vall stared blankly at the door through which his King had just departed, along with Myx, Riff, and Veen, all three of whom he suspected he'd see again—in the guise of Royal Guards.

And felt all the false energy that had sustained him since he'd returned to Tir-Eron start to ebb away. His eyelids seemed made of lead; his limbs had a distant quality, as though they were not quite part of him. A moment only it would take to fall asleep.

He'd welcome it, too, because if he stayed awake he would think, and there were too many things to think about already. Nothing was *ended,* he realized; he'd just set something larger than he could imagine in motion. Something he prayed would not become his task to bear.

But he was almost alone now, with good food and two people nearby who liked him and, more to the point, cared about him. Three, if you counted Bingg.

Eellon was settling himself wearily into the chair next to Avall's, and Lykkon was puttering about with the remains of their hasty repast. Not, incidentally, without helping himself to the odd tidbit.

Avall was more tired than sleepy.

So tired . . .

"Hold on a moment longer, boy," Eellon urged softly, "and we'll let you sleep as long as you want. I won't let even the King disturb you."

Avall shook his head stubbornly, wondering where the energy for even that had come from. "Whatever you put in the cider, I need more. I have to stay alert for at least another half hand."

Eellon regarded him sharply, and Lykkon actually gasped.

"On one condition," the old man conceded finally. "That you take the smallest dose you can get by with—and that you do it in Lykkon's quarters."

"Mine," Avall protested weakly.

"No," Eellon replied flatly. "First, there's no fire there, since we didn't know you were coming and left in haste. Second, your return should *not* become common knowledge until we've had time to confer a bit more about some things—*we* being, at minimum, you, me, the King, and Ferr."

"Besides," Lykkon continued, "Bingg's been lonely since I started spending most of my time at Lore. And since I have to get back there soon anyway—probably tomorrow—"

"*Definitely* tomorrow," Eellon corrected. "I'll write you a letter, but don't expect it to do more than spare you a thrashing. Still, I'd as soon someone stayed with Avall tonight. I can't—I'm tired to the bone. And Bingg's still too young, even if he wasn't half-asleep."

Finding any protest likely to fall on deaf ears, Avall merely shrugged and let Lykkon help him to his feet. Eellon, for all his age, took the lead, and stood guard at every intersection as they made their way to Lykkon's suite. Since the youth often served as Eellon's squire, it was only one level away. Mercifully, they saw no one save a distant cousin out to raid the kitchens, and she was easily evaded.

Eellon held the door while Lykkon steered Avall into the vestibule, then right, into the bedroom itself. The place was a near twin to Avall's apartment except that there were two beds, each smaller than the single one in Avall's quarters. One was made up, the other looked hastily abandoned.

Avall let himself be led to the fresher one, and Lykkon got him undressed down to his shirt and house-hose. While a somewhat revived Bingg poked up the fire, Eellon emptied something from a phial into the last of the cider, which he'd brought with him, sending Bingg back to the meeting room to retrieve the soup.

Avall had almost fallen asleep again when Eellon sat down on the bed beside him and held out the doctored mug. "I'd appreciate it if you'd tell me what this is for," the old chief grumbled.

Avall's reply was to drain the drink to the dregs, then extend the mug for more as he wiped his mouth on his sleeve. "I have to contact Strynn—or try. She must be mad with worry. I have to let her know I'm alive, and I have to tell her about Rann."

"What about him?"

"That he may be dead."

And with that Avall fell silent. He'd been avoiding that topic since he'd returned to himself, but now he'd voiced it, and that had made the notion real. Rann had been with him during the attack. Rann had yelled at him to look out. Rann had been injured even then.

Which meant there was a good chance he *was* dead.

Maybe when he finished with Strynn he'd have strength enough to try and contact Rann, anyway. He'd *certainly* try, he amended. No one needed to know. There was no way anyone *could* know, unless he told them.

"Mind if we watch?" Eellon inquired from the candlelit gloom, as he retrieved Avall's second mug of cider—which Eellon didn't remember drinking.

"Nothing much to see," Avall replied—then paused, staring at Lykkon. "Lyk, if you're up for it, I could use you for this. If you're willing to endure a little pain, and something that could scare you to death but won't actually hurt you."

"You don't even have to ask," Lykkon gave back instantly. "Where would you rather I cut?"

"If you've got a scab, that'd be fine. All that seems to be necessary is that the gem have access to your blood. After the first time . . . not even that is always required."

"Are you sure you're up for this?" Eellon cautioned.

"No, but I'll rest better if I make the attempt. Just this one thing, and I'm going to forget the world exists for a while."

Lykkon, meanwhile, had been busy stripping down to the house-hose and shirt that were typical garb for a young man in his own quarters. He untied a sleeve and pushed it up, searching for a likely wound, but found none. Shrugging, he snared a dagger from a rack by the bed, set his mouth, and made a short incision in the heel of his palm. Avall was impressed with the determined ease with which he accomplished that—in one sure slice, with no false starts. Thus prepared, he settled himself onto the bed beside Avall. Avall couldn't avoid a twinge of sorrow at that, for the boy looked—and acted—remarkably like Rann. A lump rose in his throat.

No! He couldn't think about that now, not with another, more pressing obligation at the fore.

Closing his eyes, he removed the gem from its holder and clutched it in his palm. The cut was still open from his earlier bonding with Eellon, and he felt the gem start to draw at once. "Lyk," he whispered. "Give me your hand—put it atop the gem so that the blood touches, and then . . . just try not to be afraid. I don't know what you'll see or feel, but try to give me control. If you want to help, wish as hard as you can to see Strynn."

"Won't she be asleep?"

"I hope so—which is why I wanted to do this now. It only seems to work when the other party is asleep—or when they're actually with you. Or if they know to expect it."

"Lots of 'ifs' there, cousin," Lykkon chuckled.

Avall's eyes slitted open to see Eellon still watching from his chair, and the newly returned Bingg sitting attentively at the foot of the bed, like a pet, resilient, if nothing else.

"If anything goes wrong," Avall began, "break off contact. I don't know what kind of damage that would do, if any, but it's probably the safest thing." Without waiting for reply, he sank back on his pillow and, with Lykkon beside him, murmured, very softly, "Now."

He felt the warmth of Lykkon's hand clasp his own, with the gem between, and then . . .

He *was* Lykkon—briefly—but didn't dare linger there. This was still much a catch-as-may process, but he was beginning to know his way around his own brain in a way he'd never imagined possible. As such, he was able to resist the temptation to prowl through Lykkon's mind, save to note that it was amazingly ordered, passionate, and loyal. Instead, he neatly installed part of Lykkon's self in that part of his own being that drove his own strength of will. That accomplished, he tried to picture Strynn as she should be at this hour: asleep, of course—pale-skinned, her face beautiful beyond beauty, with dark lashes and dark brows precisely complementing the angles of cheekbones and chin. She'd be visibly and heavily pregnant, too, and probably sleeping on her back in a light night shift, with a warmer robe around her in one of those jewel tones she preferred.

There'd be candlelight in the room, and he wouldn't be surprised if Kylin was present, as de facto guard, if not actually Strynn's lover—which made him jealous, though he had no right to be.

But with that thought, his desire for her began to quicken, and then he was out of himself and looking down on all the cold sweep of Eron—and then on Gem-Hold; and then on his and Strynn's suite; and then on Strynn herself.

She was exactly as he'd imagined, save that she lay on one side, an arm curved protectively around her belly.

Strynn, he called: *Strynn!*

She didn't stir—though her brow furrowed, and Avall felt a brush of consciousness as the patterns of her mind began to alter.

Strynn!

Again.

Strynn!

She awoke at that, blinked wide eyes the color of sapphires, then sank back to her pillow, brow furrowed with thought. *Avall!*

And with so much passion Avall gasped aloud—for she had seized his thought with her own, fiercely, protectively. As though she would never let him go.

Strynn!

You're alive? I knew you were—yet I didn't! I knew . . .

He plucked the thought from her mind before she could think it. *You knew I was injured?*

I thought you were dead! Rann said you'd fallen during an attack!

Rann! He's alive, then? He's unhurt?

He made it back here, with the help of a woman named Div. Oh, but Avall, where are you? What's happened?

I . . . died and then I came back, and I . . . somehow I floated down almost to Tir-Eron. I only came back to myself tonight. I still don't understand most of it.

The important thing is that you're alive!

And that the King knows what I intended, as does Eellon.

How are you?

Tired beyond belief—I'm going to sleep until I wake up—Lykkon's helping now, and I don't know what kind of effect this will have on him, weak as I am.

Best be safe.

But tell me about you. How are you? How's the child?

I've been wild with worry, but I'm doing as well as can be. The child's fine, but far too frisky. Rann will be happier than you can imagine that you've survived.

So, you know about the attack?

Oh yes. There's been a bit of an investigation, too, and I've had to answer hard questions, as has Kylin. Eddyn's gone, as is Rrath.

Which confirms what I suspected—that they were behind the attack.

There's more. And with that Strynn told him about the ghost priests.

But the weather—Maybe, if we're lucky they're—

Strynn shook her head, which Avall felt as much as saw. *I don't think so. It's been mild, for the Deep. They could've survived if they were careful.*

And might be almost here, if they moved quickly.

But if they do show up, there's something you should know: something that may give you an advantage if this gets as political as it could. She paused, but he caught the thought as she "voiced" it. *It's your masterwork, Avall: the helm. Eddyn had a fit before he left and—damaged it. Badly. Maybe you can fix it; I'm not sure. We think that's one reason he left.*

Avall reeled—felt the contact waver and stretch, as a sickness he'd never experienced before made his gut twitch. His masterwork: the helm he'd been commissioned to make as part of the royal regalia. The finest piece of smithwork he'd ever attempted by far—ruined. He could make another, maybe, but the passion would be gone—

Yet along with that despair came a surge of anger at Eddyn, a fierceness he'd not felt even when Eddyn had raped Strynn. Because Eddyn had now, in effect, raped him.

And then the enormity truly did register. Destruction of art was a crime. A *capital* crime, in fact, depending on how great the slight. Eddyn was already on prickly ground over the Strynn affair, and had only narrowly escaped exile then. This was too much for the Law to ignore. It wanted only proof, which Strynn could provide. So Eddyn would be returning to . . .

Prison, Avall supposed. At least an investigation he doubted even Tyrill would be able to spare him. Yet he was coming anyway—apparently.

Avall had to respect him for that.

Unless his rival was dead, which would solve a great many problems.

Maybe as soon as he was strong enough, he'd seek Eddyn with the gem and try to make sure.

We'll try, too, Strynn inserted unexpectedly. *Rann, Kylin, and I—but we're none of us as strong as you, or else our gems are weaker.*

Gems? What—?

We've found more gems, Avall. We—

Avall felt something stir at that—a sense of discomfort coming from Lykkon.

I have to go! he broke in. *I'll try to contact you again soon—or you can. We've succeeded, in part, but now I have to rest.*

Yes, Strynn agreed, *you do. But oh, Avall, I'm so glad you're with us again!*

Me, too, Avall agreed. *Tell Rann I love him—but no more than you!*

Never doubt that I shall!

Farewell.

Until the next time. I'll rest tonight as I haven't since you left.

And I.

Love.

Love.

Avall broke the contact—or had it broken for him, by Eellon slapping him smartly on the cheek.

Avall blinked into the light, disoriented, as one room replaced another. Eellon looked tired but concerned. Lykkon also looked tired—and was shivering besides. Bingg's eyes were big as saucers, but he also had sense enough to pour three mugs of cider—one of which he thrust into Avall's hand, one into Lykkon's, and one into Eellon's. He drank the dregs himself straight from the pot, and put on more to heat, along with the soup.

"Well, lad?" Eellon urged through a shiver of his own. "Did you succeed? Those of us who don't know how this works need to be told these things."

Avall sank back wearily, wondering if the whole night was going to consist of "one more things." Still, the cider helped. He took a long draught, and noted that Lykkon was still shivering. "Cover him," he said, likewise shivering. "It's the same thing that happened to Bingg earlier. Something to do with the gem . . . eats your body heat, or something. Talking distances does that, for one—and can also give you a headache."

"I know," Lykkon muttered, rubbing his temples as Bingg snugged a fur coverlet around him and stayed there, one arm around his brother. The boy was shivering, too, but trying not to show it.

"I'm sorry," Avall told him, feeling his head start to pound in earnest, though the sensation seemed oddly distanced.

"You contacted her," Eellon persisted. "I hate to push, lad, and we all need to rest, but there's too much at stake here to delay, and we both know what time does to memory."

Avall nodded. "The major things I learned are that Rann made it back to Gem-Hold and told Strynn everything. And that Eddyn and Rrath did indeed leave, apparently because they also know about the gem, and that—"

"Eddyn," Eellon broke in. "It always comes back to him, doesn't it? Somehow he winds up in the middle of all the confusion. But Rrath—he's Priest, you said? Quiet little fellow, smooth-faced? Was your roommate for a cycle somewhere or other?"

Avall nodded. "*Too* quiet, evidently. One of those who misses nothing but reveals nothing, either, though I think he really did admire me for a while— probably because he's attracted to power, especially if what Strynn just told me about certain allies of his is true."

Eellon regarded him sharply. "Allies?"

"Rann says he somehow hooked up with some secret cabal within Priest-Clan, and they're the ones who attacked us."

Eellon slapped his chair arm so hard the cider pot rattled by the fire. "Why am I not surprised? I *knew* there was more to that group than rumors, and I've tried to tell Gynn as much. But what I don't understand is the risk they're taking now—effectively revealing themselves."

Lykkon leaned forward attentively. Eellon noticed the movement and rolled his eyes. "I'm a fool," he muttered. "Here I sit discussing state secrets in front of a pair of boys."

"Very loyal boys," Avall countered. "And you can always have another Sovereign Oath put on them if you think the other doesn't apply."

Eellon glared at his two kinsmen. "You will not speak of this," he said flatly. "You only think *Tyrill* is awful in her wrath."

"But if I may ask—" Lykkon began.

"What?" Eellon snapped.

Lykkon cleared his throat. "If they're revealing themselves now, whoever they are, it implies that they have no choice—that something's forced their hand."

Eellon nodded. "Which therefore implies that they see a bigger threat in this than we've suspected. That there may be factors at work about which we know nothing."

Avall nodded in turn. "There's more, too, something that once again gives us a hold over Eddyn: He destroyed the helm I was making for the King."

Lykkon set down his mug with a thunk; Bingg's mouth dropped open. "That's—a capital offense," they gasped as one.

Avall almost laughed. "I could almost feel sorry for him—if it weren't my work he damaged. Not that I can't fix it," he added stiffly.

"No doubt," Eellon agreed. "And I intend to alert the King to that very fact—and to the fact that Eddyn may be on his way here. In fact, I intend to ask His Majesty to arrest him on sight—that's my prerogative as Clan-Chief."

"What about Tyrill?"

"She has a right to know—but that's not to say she needs to know immediately. Never mind that I'm sure she'll want to know where we came up with such a preposterous notion."

Avall studied his mug. "You'll have to tell her sometime, Two-father. This rivalry of yours—this may be the thing that finishes it. I think we're fast approaching a time when the two of you will have to work together. In case you haven't noticed, we may have just made a major enemy out of Priest-Clan."

"Time to see who's most powerful," Lykkon agreed. "Priest or the Smith-War-Lore coalition."

Eellon leaned back and closed his eyes. "I think, lads, that I'd just declare myself incompetent if it weren't for the fact that there's no successor I'd halfway trust. But dammit, I'm too old for this!"

"And I'm too young," Avall yawned, feeling his strength starting to fade again.

Eellon snorted, but Lykkon seemed to have shaken off some of his malaise. He prodded his brother. "Lord Argen," he intoned formally. "Perhaps Bingg could take word to His Majesty. There doesn't seem to be anyone else equipped to do that right now, and if Avall's tally of events is even halfway accurate, Eddyn could be here literally any moment. Waiting a hand could make a difference."

Eellon nodded wearily. "Can you remember all that, boy? Can you give a clear accounting?"

"I'm Argen-a," Bingg replied stiffly. "Of course I can."

Avall couldn't suppress a smirk as he exchanged glances with Lykkon and Eellon. Eellon was already slipping off his Clan-Chief's signet ring. "Use this as security," he said. "They won't let you in to see the King without it. Don't let anything stop you, either. If the guards give you grief, remind them of the connection between Argen and Ferr."

Bingg was already half out the door, pausing only to snare a cloak from Lykkon's stash. "I'll report when I return."

"See that you do." Eellon shifted his gaze to Lykkon. "Lad, I hate to do this to you, but Avall can't be moved and I don't have the energy to get back to my quarters, so I'm going to have to claim the spare bed. Either you two snuggle up there, or you find a place by the fire. I'm sorry, but right now . . ."

A yawn ambushed him. Then another.

Lykkon yawned as well. Then Avall.

By unspoken consent, each moved to the place Eellon had assigned. And when Bingg returned a hand later, it was to find all three of them snoring.

"Mission accomplished," he told Eellon, once he got the Clan-Chief awake. And then he curled up by the fire and slept as well.

CHAPTER X:

SUN AND SUBTERFUGE

(THE FLAT—DEEP WINTER:DAY XLIV—MORNING)

～～～～～～～

Merryn had forgotten what clear air was.

Then again, she'd forgotten many things.

Like time. But it was hard to tell time when the gloom that surrounded her was always the same: thick tent walls lit with candles in the corners, just enough to see by—until they'd put a mask across her eyes, so that even that stimulus was denied her. Day . . . night . . . had long since ceased to matter. They fed her erratically and let her drink, but that was all.

But since the first day, the air had never been free of imphor smoke. They'd surely burned a tree by now, but whoever was supervising this must know his or her business, because there was a fine line between building a resistance to the stuff, and succumbing to it. Or between either of those and madness from overdose.

She must have *breathed* a tree by now, too. Still, she was glad that she could think at all, even if those thoughts were shrouded deep in that part of her brain that had little to do with her imprisoned body.

Her body . . .

Her thoughts . . .

Her memories . . .

Her self . . .

She dragged herself up from the last to the first, trying to breathe as little as possible as she once again tested her restraints. A slight tug at each limb in turn, focusing on the degree of resistance, hoping that she'd be rewarded with some change that might be the first slow step toward escape.

She had to be careful, though. She was guarded. Not in the imphor-filled room, granted, save once a finger when someone poked a head in to check on her. But she had no doubt the tent was ringed on all four sides by others, full of soldiers.

The questions—there'd been none for a while, which puzzled her. And she seemed finally to have become numb to their suggestions—the ever-more-graphic and disturbing hallucinations they fed her.

It wouldn't do, she supposed, for them to return the King of Eron's cousin less than intact in mind or body. Which might be all that was saving her.

Except, she realized, there was a new presence in the tent. She hadn't heard the sound of canvas moving, either, and people who moved silently worried her. Or maybe this figure wasn't moving at all.

In any event, it scarcely mattered. Whoever it was wouldn't stay long. The imphor fumes would prevent him.

She wished she could *see,* dammit. One thing she did note, however, was a scent that had entered with him: smell of the desert that reached her nostrils even through the fumes. Not the odor she'd grown accustomed to.

She focused her hearing—tried to. Whoever it was sat down, close by her shoulders. Something tickled her nostrils. She twisted her head aside, tried not to sneeze, but a hand grasped her jaw firmly, and she hadn't strength—or will—to fight, as some kind of hollow reed or stem or pipe was set against each naris in turn. She tried to hold her breath as the most pungent imphor reek she'd ever experienced roiled in—but in the end, she failed.

Reality spun away. Merryn floated. Drifted. Experienced every sensation available to her at once. She discovered that she had nerves in her nostrils that could actually *see* the spirals of the imphor smoke as she inhaled. Why, they could even count the individual grains as they passed, and revel in their shapes and subtle colors.

And that was only the smoke. There was the rug beneath her skin, whose vivid hues she could actually feel fading. And there was a whole spectrum in the shades of reddish gray that was all she could see through the mask. Her saliva tasted like wine, and she could taste everything she'd eaten since coming here as shadow tastes upon her tongue.

Wind sighed like the finest music, while the rustle of the tent flap was like timpani and thunder. And then a voice. Soft and soothing, but with an air of absolute command. Each word took an age to enunciate, and each sound and syllable was an epic poem to be savored for itself alone.

"Your name is . . . ?"

She gloried in the elegance of the question. Found the terminal pause exquisite. Appreciated the variations in stress and tone as though they were secrets of ages revealed.

"Merryn," she said eventually. The movement of her tongue, jaw, and lips was like perfect combat and perfect sex combined: everything moving with absolute precision toward the goal. And the sensation in her throat as her voice box vibrated—Words could not describe it.

"Merryn," that voice echoed, soothing as waves on a shore.

"Merryn," she repeated, just to feel that sensation once more. "Merryn san Argen-a."

"Argen-a," that voice murmured. "They rule . . . ?"

Again that subtly made a question. Like dessert on the feast that was the sentence. She couldn't help but answer, so much joy was there in speaking.

"The working of precious metals."

"Ah!" (Like a sighing of wind in spring foliage.)

"Ah,"—because she'd grown so fond of the sound of speech.

(*Do not answer! another part demanded. They have won you—they will ask what you dare not answer. But you* will *answer, and that will destroy you.*)

But that inner voice was like a rusty hinge in a hallway of well-oiled doors. She ignored it, eager for other sounds, other questions.

"But the King is Argen-el, which rules . . . ?"

"Tools and machines."

(*No secret in that, she advised her conscience. Everyone in Ixti had access to that information.*)

"So you are kin to the King?"

"Aye."

"And why did you leave Eron?"

"I was pursuing Krax."

"Kraxxi?"

"Perhaps. I sometimes thought that's who he might be," she continued dreamily.

"For what purpose?"

"Because I love him."

"You do?" The voice sounded startled. Merryn savored that variation.

"Aye."

"Was that the only reason?"

"Because I hate him."

"Is that all? Surely there is more."

"He left without reason. I had to know what that reason was."

"Did you find out?"

"Only in my imaginings."

"Ah, and what *did* you imagine?"

"That he came south to tell his father about the gem."

"What gem?"

"The gem my brother found. The gem that lets one speak mind to mind across great distance."

Breath hissed, like rain across stone-paved streets in a storm.

"Tell me of this gem," that voice purred, no longer quite so pleasant. "Reach into your memory and tell me everything you recall. From the beginning."

Merryn didn't want to. But then that reed was at her nostrils again, and she was breathing in more imphor, and so she did.

It was a long time before she realized she was no longer speaking. A long time in which to ponder silence.

Then that voice again. Like balm on her ears. Soft and soothing as rest.

"And you say you and the Warden of War-Hold left in secret?"

"Aye."

"How was this effected?"

"Through a passage that exits in a cliff a shot or so from the hold."

"And who knows of this passage?"

"I don't know. Those of us who were with the Warden. Three of whom were from this land."

"Ah!"

Silence, for a while, and then that silence changed, as Merryn's visitor rose to leave. She heard the swish of robes and smelled again the scent of deserts.

He paused at the entrance, however, and spoke one last time. "You have done well, little Merryn. And in reward for that, I will let you live. And of course soon enough you will remember everything you have told me. And that will be the best torture of all."

And he was gone.

Merryn almost wept at that departure. At the absence of cherished sensation. But gradually she became aware of another voice demanding her attention. One that dwelt deep inside her, and that voice that would neither be denied or silenced was yelling louder and louder, "You are a traitor and a weakling and a fool!"

Sleep claimed her, then, but not freedom. Even her dreams consisted of everyone she knew surrounding her in a circle chanting, "Traitor! Weakling! Fool!"

The man thrust the last flap of tent canvas aside and stood blinking in the morning glare. He inhaled deeply. Once. Twice. A third time—to dilute the fumes. He'd have to be careful for a while. The trouble with imphor was that it was impartial as to whom it affected. Fortunately, those exposed the least amount of time usually had the upper hand. Or those who had conditioning.

He straightened his long tan desert robe, and shoved his mouth-mask higher to obscure his face, then felt reflexively for the serviceable sword that hung at his hip, and for his geen-claw dagger. A soldier, most would've seen: one of many on an errand from Lord Lynnz to one of his prisoners.

He chuckled at that, and rubbed the stump of a missing thumb joint.

Even Lynnz didn't know everything.

And chuckled again, at what he'd just learned where others, apparently, had not.

Chuckled *now,* perhaps. But soon enough would come some very serious thinking indeed.

In the meantime, he had another tent to visit.

There was no part of Kraxxi that didn't hurt.

Some parts were sunburned, from where they'd left him naked in the sunlight for hands at a time, in spite of the too-chill wind that had made him shiver as he burned. And some of those parts were already blistered or peeling.

They'd exposed both sides of him, too, so that the sand on which he lay abraded tortured skin whenever he moved.

And that wasn't counting the scorpions.

They danced about him constantly: attracted by the flakes of skin scaling off the worst of his burns, which they apparently considered a delicacy. Never mind that here and there his wounds leaked pus or even blood, which attracted the creatures in droves.

As for stings, in spite of his efforts, he'd garnered a few. One to the side of his neck. One between his fingers where an attempt at flipping one of the creatures away had failed. Two in his groin he was glad he couldn't see.

And true to his situation, his captors had ignored those wounds until they were almost infected, at which point someone had slapped a minimum of salve atop them—a salve almost certainly chosen for its ability to burn.

The only concession to comfort he'd been granted was a mask across his eyes during the worst part of the day, a single slice of dry bread every morning, and a cup of water every three hands.

And a minimum of sleep he could barely tell from unconsciousness.

But he'd told them nothing, of which fact he was very proud.

And in those moments when there was someone about to question him, he still managed to repeat only that one phrase: "I will speak only to my father."

And here came another: opening the flap and striding forward (probably in thigh-high scorpion-proof boots) to stand glowering down at him. Kraxxi chose to relish the shade and ignore the rest. By the scent, this seemed to be a common soldier, not Lord Lynnz. Someone come to bring him a drink, perhaps. He dared lick his lips. Dared, because more than once, he'd felt his tongue brush a questing scorpion.

But no drink seemed to be forthcoming, though his visitor hadn't moved.

"I will speak only to my father," he began weakly.

"Well then," replied Barrax, king of Ixti, "perhaps your father will listen."

Kraxxi inhaled sharply, straining against his bonds to remove his blindfold. It had sounded like Barrax, but Lord Lynnz was clever. This could be a trick. Or his mind could be contriving tricks of its own.

"Remove my mask and give me water, and maybe I'll believe you."

"You're in an odd position to make demands, but perhaps . . . I will."

Air swished around Kraxxi, and he felt a brush of warm darkness as hands fumbled at the ties to his mask, finally yanking it away. He blinked up at his father.

Though not as he'd ever seen him. Not in royal regalia, but in the guise of an ordinary soldier. Which made him wonder all kinds of things, including how many people knew their king walked among them so disguised. Whether even Lynnz knew, though surely Barrax would've had to show the royal signet to access a royal prisoner.

"Drink . . ." Kraxxi choked.

"When you've finished. I have none with me now."

Though he'd had days uncounted in which to ponder this meeting, Kraxxi was suddenly at a loss as to what to do. Barrax saved him the trouble.

"Why are you here?" he barked.

"To save lives," Kraxxi replied, feeling a modicum of strength returning.

"Whose lives? Your own? Surely you know you're under sentence of death for slaying your brother."

Kraxxi didn't reply, but his gaze quested down his father's body to his hands, where, indeed, showed the missing thumb joint that signified loss of a child past puberty.

"I know it doesn't matter to you," Kraxxi said at last, "but it was an accident."

"I have only your word for that, and your flight gives the lie even to that. If you'd returned—"

"—You'd have had my head without a trial," Kraxxi gave back, wondering where he'd gained the nerve to address his father so.

Barrax glared at him. "Perhaps."

Silence.

"So," Barrax said eventually. "What is this thing of which you will speak only to me?"

"Something I learned in Eron, that, I hope, will save many lives in both that land and this."

"And how will these lives be saved?"

"By convincing you that this war you want is even less wise now than heretofore."

"And how do you propose to do this?"

"I—" Kraxxi began, and fell silent. Now that the moment was upon him, what should he say? He'd rehearsed this conversation a thousand times, but now that he confronted it, he was terrified. Once he revealed his secret, his options decreased by orders of magnitude. "I have learned of a means by which certain folks in Eron can speak mind to mind across great distances."

"And if I believed this, what difference would it make?"

"It means their commanders would know in moments what might take yours days to discover. It would give them a clear advantage."

"And how is this . . . advantage effected?"

"By a gem."

"A gem? Surely you realize—if I believed you—that even if such a thing were possible, it would take more than one person speaking thusly to make a significant difference."

Kraxxi regarded him calmly. "It would depend, I would think, on who those people are."

"But there is only one of these gems?"

"Only one of which I am aware."

"And your purpose in telling me this was . . . to dissuade me from my war?"

"It . . . was."

"You had no thought for yourself? No desire to trade this knowledge you have so freely given for your life?"

"I had considered that," Kraxxi admitted.

"I see your time in the sun and the scorpions' maw has rendered you rather more . . . tractable than I recall."

Kraxxi closed his eyes. Despair filled him. He should've set out his desires first, *then* made his revelation. But he'd been tired and stupid and . . .

He wished he were dead. That was always his solution to situations like this: wishing he were dead. Then he wouldn't continue to play things so totally and completely wrong.

"I could kill you now," Barrax told him. "I could collect my own reward. But I think perhaps you and I might have other things to discuss by and by. So I tell you this. Die you will, but not until you can die in Ixtianos. I want everyone there to see what befalls a fratricide."

"And that will be . . . ?" Kraxxi dared.

Barrax shrugged. "As soon as I have conquered Eron. I have just been given two important keys."

And with that he strode from the tent.

Kraxxi closed his eyes against the glare, and pretended the sunlight was the only cause for his tears.

Barrax didn't bother announcing himself before he strode into Lord Lynnz's tent. The new one that had replaced, in all expensive particulars, the old one that Merryn had burned. Which alone told him a number of things about his captive, one of which was that she needed to be watched. Another was that she was a prize to be treasured: not something to be used casually and thrown away—and certainly not if she was kin to the King of Eron. A more worthwhile person, perhaps, than his son—though something had changed in Kraxxi, too.

Not that it mattered.

Lynnz rose abruptly from where he'd been perusing what looked like plans for a revitalized series of way stations along the Flat Road, complete with a nice wooden model. Barrax wondered idly which of his cowed courtiers was financing this one. *Not* Lynnz, he was certain. Lynnz looked angry, though. Then again, he'd never been one for interruptions.

"Who are you?" Lynnz snarled, reaching for his dagger. "Guards—!"

"Respect their king," Barrax said quietly, lowering his mouth-mask, and whisking off his helm. "I can show you the signet and missing digit if you need proof."

"Majesty," Lynnz managed with reasonable aplomb, as he searched for a chair for his sovereign. Doing a good job of not appearing shocked. "I thought you were in Ixtianos."

"That's what I want people to believe."

"But why—?"

Barrax claimed Lynnz's chair, which happened to be on a dais, along with Lynnz's clean plate and cup. He filled a glass of wine. Lynnz paused with his hand on the back of another, lower seat. "I ask the questions here," Barrax continued, offhand. "I am *your* commander, in case that has slipped your mind."

"No, Majesty."

"Sit. I need your full attention, and I won't have it while you're standing."

Lynnz obeyed.

"You didn't recognize me, did you?"

Lynnz shook his head. "No, Majesty."

"Neither did Kraxxi and . . . *Merryn,* whom I just finished interrogating."

"Ah, so that's her name. Did this interrogation achieve anything useful?"

"Enough. I'm surprised you had so little success."

"They told you—"

Barrax drained the mug and refilled it. "All in good time."

"Trust is necessary among commanders, Majesty. And kinsmen."

Barrax eyed him narrowly. "This is a fine force you have here. Finer than I had in mind when I asked you to assemble it. Fine accommodations. I was not aware of the wealth of the Army of the North."

"It fared better than the south during the plague," Lynnz retorted. "As my reports show."

"I have no doubt," Barrax noted dryly. "In the meantime, I have in mind to see if this force and another to which I have access are in fact soldiers as well as poseurs."

Lynnz leaned forward at once: interest gleaming in his eyes. "What did you have in mind, Majesty?"

"Why, to test Eron's defenses."

"Now?"

"You sound surprised."

Lynnz covered with a sip of wine. "No, Majesty—if you think it wise. But I would remind you that it *is* winter up there."

"And I would remind you of two other things. First, they are so used to hiding out in their holds during the cold time they never think someone might dare attack them then. And second, that warmth returns first in the south—and their first and strongest line of defense lies in the south."

"War-Hold."

"Exactly. If we were to attack it early—in the middle of the winter, say, when they least expect it—we could take it before word could reach the north. Then, as spring marches north, so do we."

"A brave plan, Majesty, but . . . forgive me, foolish. Forgetting the winter, War-Hold has never been taken."

"Nor has it been assailed in ten generations. And we know that Eron is under strength."

"So are we."

"But not so much. And our full army against one hold . . ."

"One *impregnable* hold."

"Not so."

Lynnz's eyes narrowed again. "Kraxxi told you . . . something?"

"He did. Foolish, naive, innocent boy that he is. I may even let him live—long enough to see what he has done."

"And what has he done?"

"Given me a reason to attack."

"And this reason is?"

Barrax smiled wickedly. "Well now, that is something you need to ponder for a while. Suffice to say that I learned some very interesting things from my interview with Merryn. A remarkable woman, that."

"Things that would benefit me to know?"

"Things that would benefit the army I command to know, of which yours is part." A pause, then: "Oh, stop fretting, Lynnz. I'm not out to kill you or relieve you of your command. I'd never hear the end of it from my sister if I did."

Lynnz shrugged. "You are my king. I can say nothing else."

Barrax laughed—loudly and without restraint. "Perhaps not. For now, however, we need to spend some time discussing how far we can move how many men how fast."

"You're determined to do this thing?"

"I'm determined to investigate it thoroughly. The rest—I may have to modify the timetable for all sorts of ridiculous reasons, but I will tell you this, Lynnz. I may be a dreamer, but I'm no fool."

CHAPTER XI:

COLD COMFORT

(NEAR TIR-ERON–DEEP WINTER: DAY XLV–PAST SUNSET)

~~~~~~~~~~~~

I 've forgotten what green looks like," Eddyn told Rrath, as the stumpy gelding he'd named Stamina labored up yet another snow-drenched hill. They were angling sideways, to keep the wind out of their faces and ease the slope a bit. As if it mattered.

Except that everything one did on the plains mattered, if it preserved one whit more warmth, strength, or determination. There'd been no snow for a day—for a change—and thank The Eight for the tents they'd had of the ghost priests, and for the horses the folk at Grinding-Hold kept. *Horse,* rather, because one of them was dead and buried in drifting snow, forcing the other unfortunate beast to bear double on those occasions Rrath and Eddyn both tired of walking. They tried to vary that task—taking turns on the horse and leading it when the going was especially rough, though both knew it cost them precious time to labor along in snow up to their waists, when both had skis. They moved slowly, but they moved. Every hand brought them closer to Tir-Eron. And decision.

"Remind me next time we start overland," Rrath growled, from where he sat behind Eddyn on Stamina's broad back, "and I'll be sure to wear a suit of motley, so you won't get bored."

Eddyn ignored him, having grown tired of arguing everything either of them did or said. Instead, he pondered the landscape: rolling hills covered with snow, dulled by a thunderous sky. A distant line of forest in gray-brown and midnight-blue, but not the dense foliage of the Wild. A ruined hold they'd decided wasn't worth investigating. And, for the first time, a gauzy whiteness against those glowering clouds that he prayed was steam rising from Eron Gorge. By straining his vision, he thought he could make out the square finger of Eron Tower: the guard post that marked the western road. They'd come in from the northwest, splitting the distance between the two principal means of ingress into the most habitable—and inhabited—gorge in Eron. Better that way, Rrath said, than to risk being sighted.

Eddyn wasn't certain he cared anymore. None of this was remotely real, nor had been for a while. It was all noble notions worn down to naught by the need for survival.

Rrath released his hold on Eddyn's waist and pointed past him, a little to the left. "Is that the tower?"

Eddyn squinted. "Should be."

"Then we should turn farther south, and wait in the shadow of that hill there until dusk."

Eddyn shivered. "I suppose you have a reason for depriving us of comfort for two more hands?"

"More than that, probably," Rrath returned offhandedly. "Distances out here are deceiving, as I'm sure you know, and dusk is when we're least likely to be noticed. The light's uncertain then, and two of the moons rise together tonight just past sunset, so there'll be all kinds of weird shadows out here, which I hope will confuse any sentries who actually happen to be doing their jobs. Too, the bulk of the tower staff will be eating then. And finally . . . I have to go that way to reach a certain route into Priest-Hold I'd prefer you didn't know about."

Eddyn reined Stamina to a halt, then twisted around to the right and caught Rrath in the ribs with his elbow—hard. The Priest "oofed" and did exactly as Eddyn had intended: fell off. He landed full on his back, spread-eagled in the snow, looking startled. Eddyn calmly paced Stamina around so he could stare down at his companion, who was trying to get his breath. "Eddyn!" Rrath gasped, eventually. "There was no need—"

"There's *plenty* of need," Eddyn shot back. "If you think I'm going to ac-company you to your clan hold, so that whoever is *really* in charge there can put me back in thrall, you're crazy! I've had enough of that to last my whole life. I had one goal when I started out on this insane journey, and for a while it was your goal, too, because I had no choice. But I *am* Clan Argen, and a smith. I have to consider our interests first."

Rrath glared at him as he tried to rise. Eddyn kicked him down again with a well-placed foot. "Stay there. When I leave, go where you will, but I'm through with you. Maybe you can protect me—or think you can. But I'd rather rely on Argen—and the King."

Rrath's glare intensified, though he didn't try to rise a second time. "They'll find out, you know, that you've destroyed a masterwork. We can protect you from that—"

A snort. "And how do you propose to do that?"

"If they can't find you, they can't try you. If they can't try you, they can't convict you."

"I'm hoping that what I have to tell them will overrule that."

It was Rrath's turn to snort. "Like you thought Strynn would name you father of her child instead of bringing charges of rape? Like you thought bringing word of the gem to Argen-yr before Argen-a got wind of it would make up for murder along the way, never mind destroying a masterwork?"

"It might, if that thing's as powerful as it seems. It certainly made the ghost priests go solid in a hurry to get hold of it—or the threat it represents," he added, to see how Rrath would react.

He didn't. But all Eddyn's pent-up anger for the last few days suddenly welled up in him. "You're scared to death, aren't you? Scared that once I get a finger alone with the King I'll tell him things that will bring your clan down completely."

"Or start civil war," Rrath countered. "Do you want to risk that? This isn't Argen-a and -yr, Eddyn. These are the two most powerful clans going at each other, and while we've a pretty good idea what resources the King commands, he has no idea of ours, nor do you."

Eddyn paced Stamina a step closer, so that the horse loomed over the Priest. "Somehow I doubt you do, either."

And with that he jerked back on the reins, even as he set heels smartly in Stamina's sides. Startled, the gelding vented an irate whinny and rose up on its hind legs. A better-than-average horseman, Eddyn not only retained his seat, but managed to direct where those heavy front hooves landed.

He heard Rrath scream, and the snap of bones, and then a muffled curse. "Stupid horse!" he shouted, from sheer desire to counter his own wickedness.

Whereupon rationality reasserted itself. Whether or not Eddyn liked it, Rrath was human, had been a friend, and didn't deserve to die like this in the cold.

With that in mind, and hating himself all the while, Eddyn jumped down from Stamina's saddle and waded to where Rrath lay, unmoving in the snow. His eyes were closed and a nasty gash in his forehead leaked blood, along with a troubling depression in his rib cage. He still breathed, though—barely.

So, what would someone do who'd had this happen by accident? Not move the body, but cover it and get help—in a hurry.

Without further debate, he tugged Rrath's cloak more closely around him, paying special attention to extremities that might get frostbite if the temperature fell very far. A pause, and he raised the Priest's mouth-mask, feeling the warmth of breath against his fingers, but hearing, also, a rattle in those ragged exhalations. Finally, he removed his cloak and tucked it around Rrath as snugly as it would go, so that no skin was exposed directly to the air. The cold bit at him without that protective layer, but he could endure at least another hand. A pause to line up landmarks—the tower and a notch in the horizon—and he was in the saddle again. Without looking back, he once more urged Stamina forward.

The Priest could live—or not. But in spite of circumstances, there was no way he could prove the horse's action had been anything but an accident. In the meantime, Eddyn would do the right thing and have help sent for his companion—from his own clan, if possible. In any event, he was rid of Rrath for a while. And right now, that was all that mattered.

The depth of the snow and a biting head wind slowed Eddyn, so that it took more than a hand to make his way to Eron Tower. But despite the mounting cold, that interval also gave him time to compose what he thought would be an adequate story. The place was close now: looming up out of the twilight; a great central finger with smaller cubes bracing it. The main gatehouse loomed ahead, and he'd had the guidance of the way markers for the last half hand. Yellow light glowed through thick glass in the higher rooms: proof of warmth and comfort he'd all but forgotten.

Closer, and he felt Stamina's gait shift as its hooves came onto the hidden pavement.

The sun was behind him, and the snow had gone luminous red and dusky purple where light contrasted with shadows. The tower blazed orange-red like an ember. Light flickered off movement on the nearer battlements, sunset finding polished spears and banner poles and helms.

The wind picked up, stealing warmth and breath as one. He urged Stamina to a quicker pace and tried to put an appropriate urgency in his voice when he yelled for help.

No one noticed at first, but soon enough the half-seen figures on the battlement began to move more quickly, and torches appeared from inside to augment those already flickering uncertainly at either corner. People clotted, then dispersed, and he urged Stamina faster yet—though the beast protested, and struggled through the heavy drifts. The gate, which had been closed for the night, was slowly opening, disgorging figures who rushed out to meet him.

"My friend—he's hurt," he yelled, as soon as the first green-cloaked guardsman came into range. He gestured frantically back the way he'd come.

Voices clattered back at him, masked to obscurity by the wind.

"He's hurt; I couldn't move him!" he shouted again, varying the litany as he'd rehearsed, over and over.

"Who are you?" A voice finally clarified from the howl of a sudden gust. "What're you—"

"My friend's hurt," Eddyn interrupted, gesturing again, even more frantically than before as he reined his mount to a halt. "He's—"

"What happened?" the first guardsman—a lad no older than himself—demanded.

"We were riding double, and got excited when we saw the tower, and he moved wrong, or something, and the horse reared. I must've yanked the reins when I twisted around and . . . the horse brought its hooves down on him. I—"

"When was this?" a second guard broke in, already scanning the darkening plain.

"A hand ago, maybe. I didn't dare move him. His ribs—"

"Was he conscious?"

"Not so I could tell. A hoof took him on the forehead. He was bleeding some. I covered him as well as I could and—"

He didn't finish, because Stamina chose that moment to expire. Eddyn barely had time to leap off his collapsing mount—which forced two new arrivals to leap out of the way. One moved toward the beast, the others—three now—regarded Eddyn.

Who, now that he was on a level with them, was suddenly aware of his height, and the fact that his mouth-mask had slipped down when he'd landed.

And that he was face-to-face with a lad named Merlicon, against whom he'd more than once played orney. Confusion flickered through the shorter youth's eyes—probably due to the fact that Eddyn wasn't where he ought to be and had a fair start on a beard. But the guardsman's companion was quicker.

"It's—" that one hissed.

"I *know*!" Merlicon rasped back, reaching for his sword. Eddyn started to reach for his as well, then realized that would give the lie to his ruse.

"My friend—" he tried again. "Rrath, from Priest-Clan."

"Eddyn," the third man said, tonelessly. "Eddyn syn Argen-yr."

Eddyn neither acknowledged nor denied the salutation, but he backed away a step, as though from reflex, wishing Stamina had proven worthier of its name.

The sword came free. Another joined it.

"Dead," said the man who'd been tending the horse. "Ridden to death."

"For a reason," Eddyn replied desperately. "My companion—"

"We'll tend to him," Merlicon, who seemed to be in command, said, glancing over his shoulder. Eddyn followed his gaze and saw five more guards issuing from the tower—which should be half the active complement.

"Where *is* this man?" someone barked.

Eddyn pointed toward the notch. "Between those hills: the double one and the single."

The man nodded and trotted back toward the tower—likely in search of aid, medical supplies, and a litter.

Again, Eddyn made to go with him, but suddenly found himself facing three drawn swords with matching grim expressions above them.

"Eddyn syn Argen-yr," Merlicon repeated. "You've changed, but no one your age has your height. Please acknowledge," he added, with ritual formality. "Eron Tower demands you identify yourself upon approach."

Eddyn didn't reply, and tried hard to keep his hands away from his sword. To attack would bring a counter—and his death, which, now he thought of it, might not be an unpleasant option.

"Acknowledge!" the man barked again.

"Why? When you've already recognized me. My friend—"

"We'll *see* to your friend," the horse tender snapped, as two more men arrived, and likewise drew their swords. "Meanwhile, we have orders to arrest you."

"Me?" Eddyn gasped, taken utterly off guard. "This makes no sense. I've just come out of the Wild, with an injured Priest!"

"We know," Merlicon retorted. "We were also told by the King himself to expect you. That's as much as you need to know, and as much as we were told, besides. Now, do you fight or come peacefully?"

Eddyn spared one glance over his shoulder to the night darkening across the snow and wondered if perhaps Rrath didn't have the better situation.

And then, for once, he did the right thing. He dropped his sword and raised his hands before him. "I don't know what I've done," he began carefully, "but if the King knows, I suppose he'll inform me in time. Neither of us is above the Law."

Silence greeted him, and by the time Eddyn had been escorted to the gatehouse, a dozen armed guards accompanied him.

It was warm, he noted gratefully, and there was even a small fire crackling behind a security grate in the cell to which they led him, two levels below the surface of the plain. It was austere but clean, and they let him eat as soon as they'd stripped him, searched him thoroughly, and given him a robe and a pair of thick house-hose.

But no one spoke to him—at all.

Not during the rest of that evening, nor during the night he spent there, nor the next day when, just past the morning meal, they moved him—under guard, in a windowless litter—to another cell. He had no idea where it was save by the impressions he gained in transit: across land, down the Stair, and north at the bottom, then down more stairs. He *suspected,* however, that he was in the dungeon beneath the Court of Rites—which was to say, beneath the forecourt of the Citadel.

But no one told him, and he'd never been down there to know. They fed him again, and locked the thick wooden door, leaving him in a room two spans to a side, lit only by light brought in by polished steel mirrors he couldn't reach.

At least it was the light of day. Eddyn wondered when he'd ever see the real thing again.

It was not quite noon, based on the quality of light, when Eddyn heard a commotion without: the stomp of booted feet, the rustle of mail, and, mostly masked by them, the softer tread of house-boots. No voices.

The sounds halted outside his cell. Keys jingled, locks clicked, and the door slid sideways, to reveal four guards in royal livery surrounding the slim, fit, black-haired figure of Gynn syn Argen-el, High King of all Eron.

The King wore the Crown of Oak and a tabard in the colors of his Cloak of State. He also carried a sword—unsheathed, as were those of his escort.

Eddyn rose automatically, for all he and Gynn were of the same clan. The crown meant he was there in official capacity. The movement raised Eddyn's head above the King's, which he doubted was advisable, given the circumstances, and so he fell forward to his knees, bowing slightly. "Majesty," he murmured, letting silence play into his hands. Impulsive he might be; he knew when he was outmanned.

The King leaned against the wall, dismissing all but one young blond guardsman with a wave of his hand. A deep breath, and the King spoke.

"Eddyn, Eddyn, Eddyn," he began, almost a sigh. "What am I going to do with you?"

Eddyn didn't reply.

"It wasn't a rhetorical question, Eddyn. You make things very difficult for me. You commit such acts that I am forced to come to you in your cell, lest word reach the wrong ears that you have returned."

"With what am I charged, Majesty?" Eddyn replied boldly.

"With destruction of a masterwork."

Eddyn felt his blood go cold, but was determined to brazen it out. "Which masterwork would that be, Majesty?"

"A helm I commissioned be made for the royal regalia by your cousin, my kinsman, Avall syn Argen-a."

"Avall and this helm should both be in Gem-Hold," Eddyn replied. "How is it that I am accused of their destruction?"

The King snorted. "You're testing me to see what I know of certain matters, which isn't wise. You have been accused."

"I have the right to face my accusers."

A brief pause, then: "Strynn san Ferr and Rann syn Eemon."

"They *told* you this?"

"In a manner of speaking."

"A manner . . ."

"A manner," the King repeated for emphasis.

"So you've no proof?"

"Not . . . conventional proof."

"Which implies that you're aware of a certain larger issue of which this, if true, is but an aspect."

Another sigh. "Eddyn, you were never a good liar. And I tell you frankly, you don't act like a man who's been caught off guard."

"I don't act like most men, anyway."

"True," the King conceded, "both for good or ill. But the fact is, I know why you're here."

Eddyn didn't reply, though his brain was working as fast as it ever had. The King knew about the gem, which implied that Avall had somehow made it here, impossible though that seemed. But the report of the desecration had to have come from Gem-Hold, from both Strynn *and* Rann. Which proved that Rann had returned to the hold. And Strynn and he had managed to get word to the King—word that had convinced him. Word he did not want widely known, even in Argen, else the King would not be here.

"How do you know it was me who committed the desecration?" Eddyn asked, finally. "What were the particulars?"

"I could find out the former under the influence of imphor, as I'm sure you know. I'd prefer not to have to do that. I have a story. If yours matches . . ."

Eddyn shook his head. "I'm sorry, Your Majesty, but I don't think it would be wise for me to say more. Not until I've faced my accusers."

"Which won't be until Sunbirth," the King spat. "Very well. In the meantime, I hope you enjoy your own company."

Eddyn raised his head. "Two questions, Majesty, if I may."

The King turned at the door. "Yes?"

"Rrath of Priest-Clan, and . . . Tyrill."

"What of them?"

"That is what I would ask."

A long pause. "I haven't told Tyrill you've returned, nor will I until I have more information to hand. Nor will I permit her to speak to you without myself and Lord Law present."

"And Rrath?"

The King sighed. "Sometimes, Eddyn, I truly do think you are two people. The Priest lives, and you did right not to move him, but the circumstances . . . are suspicious. Tell me," the King went on, conversationally. "Was he conscious when you left him?"

"He was breathing, but not conscious. I was afraid to move him for fear of broken ribs. We were riding double and he fell off the horse. It reared and came down on him. Simple as that."

"And possible, if not believable."

"Ask him yourself. He'd have heard me swear."

"I'm sure."

"And his condition?"

"That," the King replied coldly, "is for me to know and you to find out when I choose."

And with that he departed. Eddyn remained where he was, kneeling, not even looking up when he heard the door slam shut.

Eellon met the King in the small waiting room at the top of the dungeon stairs. He'd been drinking strong cauf and worrying about how much longer they could put off Tyrill, who had to know something mysterious was up. The King did not look happy as he flung himself into the seat next to Eellon's. "Something tells me," he said, "that I would save us all a great deal of trouble by arranging an accident for our young kinsmen in there. A winter fever, perhaps. Or an incurable flux . . ."

"Except that you'd have Tyrill on you like sun on ice, and I'm afraid even you couldn't survive that one."

"Sometimes," the King repeated, "I wish I were king of Ixti. I understand he has no such compunctions."

"Of the two, I'll take you," Eellon chuckled.

"How's Avall today?"

"Tired. Kind of sad and listless—which has me a *little* concerned. It's like he wants to be doing something, but doesn't know what that is. Beyond that . . . at some point you and I have to decide who else needs to know about this—besides those who know already."

The King stared at the sword still in his hands. "Ferr, because it's potentially a matter of defense, and one of their own is involved."

"By which logic you should also include Eemon, because of Rann—and Common Clan, for Div."

"Let's not—yet."

"Fine with me," Eellon agreed. "Of those already involved, then, there's also Priest—and whatever that group is that attacked our boys. Do you have any idea who that could be?"

"No group that exists officially, though one hears rumors. But one hears rumors about every clan. I know you've heard the one that I'm really my identical twin sister, and they only drag out my male persona when I have to stand naked."

"Which is just stupid—and also an aside. War. Priest—I guess. Who else? Oh, of course: Gem. This was found on their turf, even if in our vein and on our time."

"It also raises the question whether *they* might not have some secret group that already knows of and uses such things."

"It does, but it doesn't seem likely, based on the personalities involved: Crim's as honest as they come."

"Unless she doesn't know."

Eellon sighed expressively, then rose and started pacing. "I guess that leaves Lore, since they rule communications."

Gynn rolled his eyes. "That's a quarter of the Council right there, if you count Stone and Common. Something tells me I may have to call a conclave."

"With half the chiefs at other gorges?"

"I have to appear honest in this, Eellon. Eight, man, I *am* honest—as much as I can be. But there's so much I don't know."

"Such as how much Merryn knows, or has figured out, and who *she* might've told?"

"Has Avall—?"

"Not yet. He hopes to try again tomorrow, when he's stronger. Probably with Lykkon and Bingg to bolster him."

"Well," said the King, sheathing his sword and starting for the door, "I guess that gives me some excuse to wait."

"I wouldn't wait too long, Majesty," Eellon cautioned. "Things like this have a way of creating their own momentum."

"Yes," Gynn agreed sadly. "They do."

INTERLUDE I:

DECISION

(Gem-Hold-Winter—Deep Winter: Day XLVI—noon)

Strynn shot the bolt behind her, and paused only long enough to determine that both Rann and Kylin were present in her common room before she took a deep breath and spoke. "We're going."

Kylin's fingers stilled upon the harp strings, and Rann looked up, briefly puzzled—which feeling was replaced with a kind of awe at the image Strynn presented: arms folded above her bulging belly, effectively blocking the door, as though by that gesture she likewise blocked any thought of opposition.

"Going where?" Kylin replied mildly: the second figure in a verbal dance whose results they already knew.

Strynn strode forward to join them, seating herself neatly between the two men. Rann could almost feel the heat of her determination—or perhaps it was his gem picking up feelings sent forth by hers. In any event, her pronouncement didn't surprise him, though hearing it gave him a chill, because it made days of suppositions real.

"Into the Wild," Strynn sighed, taking a sip of Rann's cooling wine. "To Div's hold, if she'll have us. I've looked out the route, and—"

"We'd be insane to do that," Kylin protested. "You've reached the point where your child *could* be born early and still live. Rann only thinks he's recovered, and I— Well, that's obvious."

"Which is why we have to leave now," Strynn retorted. "The longer I wait, the more I risk both myself and my child. Rann and I have gems which ought, in theory, to look after us. And you. Between us, I think we can manage. We'd have to go slowly, but we'd need to leave at night anyway, when we'd have little advantage over you."

Rann gnawed his lip. "You may be right, much as I hate to say it. Think, Kylin," he went on, as though trying to convince himself as much as the harper. "We can spend every moment between now and the Thaws worrying about being asked questions, or dodging questions, depending; and sneaking food enough for three into a room where only two officially live; and starting every time there's a knock on the door, with me having to dive for cover whenever there's a visitor who can't be put off. Unfortunately, sooner or later Strynn will have to leave here with the spring trek, and that pretty much means I'll have to reveal myself and go along. And *that* means another two eighths of questions we *won't* be able to dodge."

"And I don't want to leave you here," Strynn finished.

"And instead of this," Kylin gave back, "you offer—what?"

Strynn reached to her side-scrip, fumbled inside it a moment, then produced a square of yellowed vellum. Unfolded on the low table before them, it proved to be a map of the area within five days' trek of Gem-Hold. Strynn grinned fiendishly. "I've been thinking," she began. "There's a hold less than a day's trek away, in good weather—which we're supposed to have for the next four days. But look here"—she pointed to the lower right corner. "This is the last map of this area made before the plague, showing all the way stations and private holds, and this hold here almost has to be Div's, based on what you told us. You said it took you five days to get from there to here, staying in birkit dens, right?"

Rann nodded.

Strynn nodded back. "But look. There's a way station less than a day away from here. And between it and Div's hold—on a road nobody uses anymore—there's another private hold indicated. According to this, it's made of stone, and there's a spring, so it should still be functional, but it's not on newer maps, so it's almost certainly not used."

Kylin's face brightened beneath his sylk eye-mask. "So you're saying . . ."

"What I'm saying," Strynn took up again, "is that we could hole up there, halfway to Div's hold, raid whatever supplies might survive, then push on to Div's when it looks best."

Rann shook his head uncertainly. "Dangerous, because it depends on too many variables. But that's not to say it's unworkable."

Strynn's brow furrowed. "I'm willing to consider alternatives."

Rann tapped the map with a finger. "How about this? Once we reach this halfway hold, you and Kylin stay there, and I'll go on to Div's, and bring her back. We're much more likely to survive if she's around, and I can make better time in the Wild alone than with you two."

Kylin looked troubled. "But we'd have to wait five days. We'd be missed from the hold by then. That's plenty of time for a search to find us."

"But they won't know where to look, and logic would have them scour the main road first, and we won't *be* on the main road after the first night. We can probably hide any signs of staying at the station."

Strynn puffed her cheeks. "I don't like it, but I like the idea of spending another day here under all this scrutiny even less. At this point, I just want to be doing something, not waiting for things to happen." She paused, looked at Kylin. "What about you, Kyl? You'd suffer most out there, and you've least investment in it. You've no obligation to us, save by your choice. I'm asking you out of love for you: I think you'd ultimately be better off with us than with anyone here—besides which, you'd be asked even more questions once word of our departure became known. But it would be unethical to force you. I feel bad about even this much intimidation."

"And once we're at Div's, what then?" Kylin replied.

"We wait out the winter, if we're wise. If the weather looks promising, we try to make our way to Tir-Eron in fits and starts. There's that birkit cave Rann spoke of—"

"And then days and days of the Wild before Grinding-Hold."

"In any case," Rann noted, "we'd be moving toward something we desire, instead of worrying about things we don't."

Strynn smiled like spring sunrise. "Good," she laughed. "Next thing, I guess, is to start a packing list."

"I'll wear the helm," Kylin chuckled back. "I won't be able to see anyway, so I might as well."

"That," Strynn replied, "actually makes more sense than you think."

"If *any* of this makes sense," Rann muttered. But he was already searching for paper.

CHAPTER XII:

SUDDEN FLIGHT

(Eron: Tir-Eron–Deep Winter: Day XLVI–night)

~~~~~~~~~~~~~~~~~

Three days of being pampered in bed was long enough, Avall decided—not that he objected in principle. He was still camping with Lykkon, to minimize knowledge of his presence in Argen-Hall, and certainly had no complaint about the quarters—which were always warm, and less drafty than his own. Nor with the company—Lykkon was his closest male friend after Rann, if kinsmen could also be friends. Nor the food, nor the clothes they'd spirited to him from his suite, nor . . . a lot of things.

But the fact was, he'd grown accustomed to taking an active part in his life, to making decisions without the knowledge, never mind approval, of anyone besides Rann and Strynn. And to having important things to consume his time—like working in the mines or on the High King's helm; like studying the gem; and like cementing his friendships with Rann, Strynn, and maybe Kylin. Two of these were no longer active options, and he was still debating whether to try to re-create the helm Eddyn had presumably ruined, or attempt to repair the remnants when Strynn returned it in the spring. The High King said either was fine, but he'd also said it in a distracted way that made Avall think he had more important things on his mind.

Which he probably did, now that Eddyn had returned. Avall didn't know what to think about that, frankly. It was bad form to wish anyone dead, never mind a kinsman, but it would certainly have simplified several people's lives if Weather had chosen to claim his cousin as a sacrifice, perhaps in exchange for the power of the gem.

As for that, he'd decided not to try distance contact again for at least another day, for a number of reasons—paramount among them that he wasn't yet strong enough to do it himself, and Eellon didn't want knowledge of the thing to spread wider than it already had. Which left Lykkon and Bingg as the main sources of energy to tap—which both would've eagerly provided had Eellon not warned them against it.

Lykkon had protested, but Eellon had been firm—except that he'd written the Chief of Lore to inform him that he would need Lykkon's services on royal business the next half eighth. Which was irregular, and would raise some brows, but not unheard of. What that business would entail was unclear—besides keeping Avall fed and entertained, and taking exhaustive notes while Avall tried various experiments with the gem. Lykkon was also surreptitiously scouring the Lore halls in Argen-Hall, Smith-Hold, Lore-Hold, and Gem-Hold for information on aberrant gems of any kind. So far he'd turned up nothing. Not even a reference to another strange red gem with properties of attraction Rann had heard about at Gem-Hold-Winter. Which had apparently gone south to Ixti, in any case.

Lykkon was nothing if not conscientious. The piles of parchment on his cousin's desk proved that, one labeled "history," one "temporal anomalies/concentration," one "communication: human," one "communication: beasts," one "physical aberrations/healing," one "power manifestations," one "priming-activation," and one "place-jumping." Set out that way, it looked like a lot—and was. The problem was that almost every bit of it was also a mystery. And since Eellon and Gynn were keeping quiet about it for the nonce, even those experts outside the clan who might know something weren't available for consultation.

At the moment, Lykkon was trying to determine precisely how Eddyn had become involved, and what that involvement entailed. As a function of that, they'd decided that Avall would answer all pertinent questions with the gem in his hand. Not primed—he barely needed that these days, as best he could tell—but so that any response it might have independent of him could be more easily noted. It *did* like and dislike certain people; that was a fact. But that seemed to be tied to how that person related to Avall.

Lykkon dipped his pen into the inkwell. "So the first you began to suspect was when you overheard Eddyn and Rrath in the fruit garden at Gem, correct?"

Avall nodded. "Eddyn was as drunk as I've ever seen him, and gushing all kinds of nonsense. But I learned two things: that he'd seen the helm—and seen the gem. And somehow, I don't quite know how, he'd made a connection."

Lykkon scowled. "Between—?"

"Between the fact that I was able to work much better and faster, and the fact that the improvement only began after I found the gem. It was a leap, and a fairly major one."

"How did he see the helm?"

"I assume he either picked a supposedly unpickable lock or somehow got hold of a key. It doesn't really matter."

Lykkon nodded sagely. "In any event, it was illegal. But I can just imagine what he was thinking. He already felt guilty over the Strynn affair. He'd had his self-worth crushed over and over by Tyrill. He had a commission from the High King, but that put him, once again, into a competitive position with you, yet it was also something he might actually best you at. And then you showed signs of bettering him—again. If you"—he paused, looked at Avall sadly—"don't take me wrong on this, cousin, you know which side I'm on, but facts have no side—If you hadn't been born, Eddyn would've had quite a different life. From his point of view, you're the source of all his problems. I think he wants to be . . . good. But things go against his expectations, and he just has to react."

Avall closed his eyes. It was all true—objectively. And if he'd had a less sympathetic mentor than Eellon, it could well be Eddyn sitting here discussing what a flawed casting Avall was. Still, it hurt to hear Lykkon rationalizing Eddyn's behavior, even in an objective context.

Lykkon hadn't *been* there, not for all of it. Maybe for the first ripples from the rape, since Avall had been out of the gorge then. But afterward . . . Lyk hadn't had to endure Eddyn's presence on the trek to Gem-Hold, or that strange little power game with Rrath, which seemed to have reflected back on him. Or the attack.

All at once *that* hit him. Eddyn had been at the station, Strynn had said. He'd probably led their attackers there. Quite possibly he'd pointed out who was who. Eddyn had conspired to *kill* him, and not only that, his bond-brother and Div, whom he held in ever-higher regard. Eddyn had wanted to take his *life*! Not in theory, but as an active, real event—like his rape of Strynn. And he'd hurt Kylin, and he'd hurt Rann—and even—now—Rrath.

Eddyn did *not* deserve to live. And if Avall had him here now, he wouldn't.

Without realizing it, he'd clamped his hand tight around the gem—letting the vision build: his hands around Eddyn's neck. Letting the anger he'd fought down for days flare hot as forge-fire, untempered.

"Avall—!" he heard Lykkon shout. "Avall—Wha—"

The word was cut off, because Avall was *not* for a moment, then came back into being feeling significantly colder. He also felt something warm and textured beneath his fingers, with something more solid under that.

And opened his eyes to find himself face-to-face with an equally startled Eddyn.

One moment Eddyn was calmly sitting in the single chair they allowed him in his cell, sipping soup from the single wooden bowl on the single table. The next he felt a curious disturbance in the air of the candlelit chamber, saw something appear between himself and the bed, like a sheet of advancing rain—and then felt something solid clamp down on his shoulders.

"Avall!" he shrieked—flinging the hands aside as he recoiled. The movement overbalanced him, and the chair toppled, sprawling him into the space between bed, fireplace, and table. His shin caught a corner, sending a burst of agony up his leg. Soup splashed across him.

"Eddyn?" a voice gasped in turn, and by then Eddyn had righted himself sufficiently to see that, in spite of what logic told him, it really was Avall standing at his feet, gaping stupidly in surprise.

Which was impossible. "What—?" he heard himself begin, but broke off. Something had fallen from Avall's right hand. Something red that flashed in the firelight. Something he recognized. Reflex sent him diving for it, as Luck—or Fate—set it bouncing his way across the floor. He snatched for it. Avall lunged after him—clumsily—clearly as shocked as Eddyn had been. "No!" he shrieked.

But Eddyn was closer and reached it first. He felt its smooth warmth pulse in his hands like a small animal resisting capture. He felt it disliking him, too, but held on grimly. Whatever else it might be, it was a bargaining tool, if he only knew how to work the negotiation.

"That's mine!" Avall yelped, as he finally got sufficient bearings to assess the situation. He'd frozen in place, as though torn between attacking Eddyn and his usual, civilized demeanor. Clearly this was no intentional visit. And the presence of the gem in his hand implied that the troublesome stone was, yet again, a factor.

"Mine, now," Eddyn spat, grasping the gem more securely as he rose to a wary crouch.

Avall's eyes were blazing. "Mine by any Law you name, Eddyn. The King knows—"

"This is how you got here!" Eddyn blurted. "Out of the river."

"Give it to me, Eddyn! You're already in so deep you'll never get out. Strynn. Kylin. The helm. The attack on me and Rann and Div."

"Then one more won't matter!" Eddyn raged—and snatched the wooden ale mug from the table. The room was small, and Avall was even more off-balance than Eddyn. Nor was there anywhere to dodge. Reflexively, he stepped back—and stumbled into Eddyn's bed. By which time Eddyn was on him. Avall raised his hands in defense, but Eddyn was stronger—and had anger on his side. A swipe with the mug raked Avall's knuckles, laying them open. Blood flashed in the uneven light. A backhand impacted a wrist. Avall tried to rise, but Eddyn had leapt full atop him, battering Avall's hands aside, before grabbing his right hand and holding it as Avall continued to struggle. A blow caught his rival's head—another.

A third, and Avall grunted, cursed, then finally screamed for help—by which time Eddyn was pummeling his skull with the mug, almost unopposed. Blood showed in Avall's black hair.

But someone was coming. He could hear footsteps and shouts, and the words "Keys" and "Eddyn" and "What's happening?"

And then Avall suddenly stopped moving, and Eddyn found himself staring down at the limp body of his rival.

He thought of ending it there—if he'd had a proper implement—but once again he stopped short of actual murder.

But they were still coming for him. And they'd find what he'd done, and take the gem away, and—

The gem. It had brought Avall here. Was there therefore any reason that power couldn't be accessed equally well by him? The gem didn't like him, but did that matter?

Only . . . how did it work? How *had* it brought Avall here?

He didn't know. But one thing he did know was that that door would open any moment and his choices would be gone. He wanted out. Away from this cell and the dreadful anticipation it wove constantly through his brain. Away from even the sight of his cursed rival. He wanted—he realized—to start over.

The gem pulsed in his hand, hating him. If it had been a mouse, it would've bit him, but he grasped it more tightly. Avall's it might be, but Eddyn had it now. It was his. He was the master—and he wanted out.

Reality jolted. The room grew dim, then clarified. Something rattled the lock. More shouts echoed, and the floor outside rang with approaching feet.

Eddyn couldn't face it. Not anymore. He closed his eyes, and . . . *wished*.

And for a long moment nothing existed save a burning pain in his hand, as though he held a hot coal. It protested, but he beat it back: overruling its desire with his own. He opened his eyes—saw *nothing*—which scared him ten times worse than he'd ever been scared before. Once again he wanted out—gone—over.

Nothing . . .

And then cold, and more cold. And something solid against his feet that unbalanced him.

Eddyn tumbled backward, opened his eyes, and saw darkness above and gray/blue/white rising around him. And had just time to think "outside" and "snowbank" before consciousness forsook him.

CHAPTER XIII:

FAR FROM HOME

(SOUTHERN ERON—DEEP WINTER: DAY XLVI—NIGHT)

~~~~~~~

Death wasn't at all what Eddyn had expected it would be, when he re-gained marginal awareness to find himself confronting it. Perhaps that was because he'd always hoped death would finally free him from car-ing whether he was warm or cold.

In fact, he was the latter, in no uncertain terms. But it was a *strange* cold: more than simply one that pulsed up from the compacted snow beneath him, oozed out from the fluffier walls that blocked all view to every side, and bore down at him from the chill sky overhead.

No, *this* cold was almost pleasant. *Almost.* And wasn't freezing to death *supposed* to be pleasant?

But in that case, the cold came from without: forcing the body ever more deeply into itself. This cold also came from within—as though something had sucked all warmth from him, slowing his heart, numbing his brain . . .

Save where something hot as a living coal pulsed in his right hand.

He jerked upright and flung it away reflexively, saw a small, hard dark-ness go spinning across the snow.

He felt marginally better. Until he realized that he'd just flung away Avall's magic gem—which had brought him here in the first place. He leapt to his feet abruptly, staggering forward to paw through the drift where he thought the stone had landed.

It was a moonless night, he noted. Priest-Clan said that nights when no moons shone were portentous, because at those times alone were The Eight completely uninvolved in the affairs of men. Anything effected then was therefore likely to have a more than average chance of success—if it depended solely on human endeavor.

Like staying alive.

He had no idea where he was, or even how long he'd lain there. He did, however, recall one of his guards remarking that they were coming up on the moonless night. Which meant he hadn't been unconscious very long.

A supposition reinforced by the fact that his fingers still retained some feeling.

If he recovered the gem, he had something with which to bargain, and—perhaps—a means of effecting his own survival.

If he could only find the wretched thing. Snow flew in flurries that would've done a burrowing rabbit proud, but he couldn't find the cursed stone. Or perhaps his fingers were grown so numb, he'd touched it all unknowing and let it pass. Certainly it was difficult finding something cold and slick amid that which was cold and slick already. But it was also red. He squinted into the gloom, feeling the wind gnaw at the nape of his neck. Wondering if he could command it to take him somewhere warm, now that he had some notion of how to control the thing.

There it was!

No—he'd merely dug down to raw earth and found an ordinary stone. But *next* to it—he felt its heat as a contrast to the cold. Snared it—and almost dropped it again, at the wave of anger it hurled at him. Ignoring that as much as possible, he closed his eyes and wished—what?

Warmer? That was a good idea. He wished to be warm, which required little conscious wishing at all.

But instead, he grew colder yet. At first he thought it was the wind, but then he realized that he could literally feel the warmth flowing from his body into the gem. Which meant—

Maybe that it had to draw its power from somewhere, and what it drew from was him. He opened his eyes.

More dislike, like what he'd seen in Strynn's eyes made palpable. He had no choice. He dropped the stone.

But he couldn't just leave it out here in the cold and the Wild. Yet he couldn't bear to touch it, either . . .

A quick search produced the belt-pouch no one had bothered to confiscate when he'd been captured. Maybe it would suffice. He opened it, wrapped his fingers in the hem of his robe, and picked up the gem that way. Thus insulated, he made the transfer. He could still feel it, but the sensation was manageable. Like traveling with a foe. Like the trek from Tir-Eron to Gem-Hold with Avall.

His hands were getting cold again. He rubbed them together, then thrust them into his armpits for warmth. And finally took true stock of his situation.

He had a minimum of clothes—undertunic of tightly woven wool to accompany his house-hose, indoor boots, and long, loose robe—and no survival gear. And it was cold enough for snow to be drifting down in the tiny random crystals that even a clear sky could produce.

He *wasn't* in Tir-Eron, that was for certain—or in Eron Gorge. Or in any gorge, for that matter. The stars told him he faced east, halfway down a gentle hill, the top of which was crowned with thick-grown evergreens. More hills rolled into white obscurity to north and south, while straight ahead the hills leveled into a plain.

A plain he recognized!

He sat down abruptly, as reality spun. Not only had he left Tir-Eron, but he'd somehow managed to jump cross-country all the way past South Gorge, which was five days' travel from Eron Gorge—in good weather.

Which he wouldn't have believed had he not experienced it.

More to the point, he was on Clan turf! Specifically, he was in the east meadow that was attached to one of Argen-yr's summer holds. The hold itself should lie among the trees at the top of the hill.

Maybe two shots away. Which meant he might survive if he hurried. The place would be empty, granted, but it would have both shelter and food.

Without further pause, he started up the hill.

"I still think we should've stayed where we were," Elvix growled at the nighted world in general, and her siblings in particular, as she led her weary horse up yet another snowbound ridge. "Dammit," she added, as the crest gave no encouraging view. The same view they'd had for what seemed like days, in fact: forest to the left, rolling hills straight ahead, ocean to the right, the last visible and invisible by turns.

Tozri, who went last, leading the other horse (a third had died two days back), vented a weary sigh and rattled the map he'd kept constantly to hand since sunset had set them—optimistically—on the road. "Where we were was a hovel I wouldn't keep geen shit in. The map says there should be a hold somewhere ahead—if we don't miss it in this confounded dark."

"It also said it belongs to one of the septs of Clan Argen, which, if you recall, is the clan Merryn belonged to. Do we want to risk the questions they might ask?"

"No hiding our accents," the third member of that party replied: Olrix, their sister. "They'll have questions regardless."

"And hopefully this time we'll have appropriate replies," Elvix snorted. "Which has nothing to do with whether or not we should've moved on or stayed."

"It was a choice of no roof versus quite a lot of roof and real stabling. And if you're worried about the place being inhabited, you needn't be. It's a summer hold, according to the map. Nobody stays in those during the winter."

"Houses just sitting around," Olrix sighed. "Such fools these northern folk can be."

"They're our folk, now," Tozri reminded her.

Elvix froze in place and peered around at him. And at her sister. She needn't have bothered, if it was to remind herself of how they looked. They were siblings of one birth, and as identical as three people of two sexes could be, with hard, wiry builds and black hair growing out from the clip favored by Ixtian soldiers, which they'd once been. They also had dark eyes and sharp, angular faces. Tozri had a beard because it kept his chin warm, but that was the only reason.

"I'm tired of arguing," Elvix growled. "It's my day to be leader, and yet I let you convince me to move when I didn't want to. This place had better be worth it, because I don't plan on traveling again for a while."

"Not even in search of our loving northern kin?"

"They can wait. I have no reason to assume they'll grant us any warmer welcome than we found in War-Hold."

"It *was* a warm welcome, though."

"Are you wishing we'd stayed?" Tozri inquired, moving up beside her, the movement setting them trudging onward again. Talking shortened the distances, so they talked a lot. But not about certain topics. Like Ixti and the reason they'd fled it. Like War-Hold and the life they'd led there. And certainly not about Prince Kraxxi, whose life they'd sworn to guard—and which responsibility circumstance had forced them to abdicate—because snow had driven them to shelter before they could begin pursuit after first Lorvinn, then Merryn, had tricked them, half an eighth ago.

Which had left two alternatives. Return to War-Hold, where they'd effectively been prisoners, or wander the Wild in search of their kin—their mother was a healer out of Eron—or in search of death. For, as their friend Kraxxi was fond of saying, suicide didn't have to be a rapid process—and going north into the heart of Eron in what was also the heart of Deep Winter was certainly a flirtation with the latter.

Except that it had been, by all accounts, a mild winter. Which did not, however, negate the possibility of blizzards, several of which they'd already endured.

"Another three shots, I think," Elvix announced. Then: "That's odd . . ."

"What?"

She rubbed her hand through her glove, where a ring with a strange red stone always rode upon her finger. "Oh, nothing. It was just that it felt like the ring . . . yanked at me just then."

Olrix cast a sideways glance at her, and took the horse's reins without comment. "What kind of yank?"

"Like it yanks when one of the others is nearby and hasn't *been* nearby for a while."

"Two of the other three are south," Olrix reminded her. "Very far south indeed—and likely getting farther."

Elvix shrugged. "I was merely reporting, except— Look."

Olrix did, and saw as her siblings saw, that Elvix's hand had drifted away from her body and was tending toward the top of the ridge ahead of them and to the left. "I didn't do that," Elvix informed them. "Not consciously. It was just . . . like your hands and feet floating up when you go swimming."

"You think . . . ?" Olrix dared.

"I don't know what to think, but I'm for following it. If there's no hold, there's at least a better chance of shelter beneath the trees."

"Lead on," Tozri sighed, and eased back to the tail of the file.

Half a hand later, they'd crested the next hill and were in sight of the hold: a squatty tower of dark stone whose battlements rose to the tops of the nearer trees. What part of the walls they could see sloped slightly inward so that each facet was less a rectangle than a very subtle trapezoid. Typical Eronese architecture.

But what was interesting was that, in spite of Olrix's predictions, a light showed within. Not much, granted—candles or a small lantern—but enough to pierce the night with implicit invitation to warmth and light, if not food and drink.

"Odd," Tozri mused. "Even if someone is there, that's not much light. Even if you allow for the shutters being closed. It's more like—"

Elvix shushed him by freezing in place. She was in the lead, and had the best view of the structure. "It's . . . burned."

Tozri indicated the flicker of light. "Burned? Or burning?"

Elvix surveyed the surrounding trees, noting how many of the branches were bare, and many more showed shriveled needles that daylight would prove to be brown. "Burned, I'd say. Maybe lightning. While no one was around."

"So who's made fire, then?" Tozri demanded.

Elvix shivered. "I don't know, but I'm willing to ask a lot of questions and beg on my knees if necessary to get out of this cold for a while."

"There's a good chance it's someone in the same straits as we," Olrix opined. "And there are three of us, and we're soldiers, when we remember to be."

"We should *also* remember," Tozri put in, "that Merryn was likewise a soldier and could probably beat anyone we know."

"Except Kraxxi at thin-sword."

"And she was mastering that."

"So," Olrix sighed, as Elvix paused, watching. "We stick with our standard lie?"

"I'd prefer to think of it as modified truth," Elvix answered. "But yes."

Tozri shivered in turn, noting the loom of partly roofed outbuildings to the left. "I'd say we enter that way, and hope."

"Luck," Elvix muttered. "Or Fate. The God of the Eronese."

"Luck," Olrix echoed, and followed her sister toward the darkened pile.

The stable yard was fenced and gated, but they left the gate open, and the horses tied in such a way they could quickly be released, as they made their way into the back of the hold.

The fire hadn't touched much there—flame would have a hard time catching hold, with all that stone. They passed through a kitchen that seemed intact save for a skim of soot, and into a hallway from which a stone staircase swept upward into what had been the common hall. Space roared around them as they trudged up the limestone steps: four walls rising to a roof spanned more with stars than ceiling, but reasonably intact for all that. An enormous fireplace rose to the right, but the light came from a door ajar beyond it. Motioning her siblings to silence, Elvix led them that way, trying to ignore the way her ring was also pulling her in that direction. One step . . . two . . . and she paused by the crack whence the light issued—which on this side was courtesy of a door that had loosened from one of its upper hinges. Closer, and she set an eye to the opening.

And saw nothing at first, save that the fire came from a fireplace that backed the larger one in the common hall. But then she noted that what she'd taken for a pile of rugs near the fire was in fact a man—curled up almost atop the hearth. And, as far as she could tell, alive.

Eddyn awoke to find a total stranger standing between him and the fire he'd coaxed into marginal being moments before fatigue—or shock—or some other unpleasant energy-sapping condition had claimed him utterly. Another stranger crouched beside him, feeling his forehead, in search, perhaps, of a fever he didn't have.

"Not dead," he managed, batting the hand away as he tried to sit up and failed. His head swam; he closed his eyes in hopes of assuaging a serious case of dizziness. When he opened them again, he reeled in truth, for the one by the fire had become two.

"Not dead," he repeated numbly.

The one who'd been inspecting him rocked back on his heels, to peer at him intently over a swath of unkempt beard. There was something odd about his eyes, too, and the general set of his features. It took Eddyn a moment to puzzle out that the eyes were brown—or very dark, in any event—and that the face rather resembled an Ixtian merchant he'd seen on trial back in the autumn, on Sundering Day.

"Who are you?" he blurted. "What're you doing in . . . my house?"

The nearer—the man—shot him a glare, but backed away to stand by his . . . sisters, Eddyn supposed. Twins, by the look of them—or triplets, which was odd, since Ixtians rarely even had twins. And they wore Eronese clothing—of a sort. Cold weather gear, too.

One of the women hunkered down beside him, concern hiding among more aggressive emotions in her face. "We're seeking shelter," she said, in accented Eronese. "Same as you. If this is your place—well, forgive us if we say so, but you don't act like the owner."

"My clan," Eddyn replied, wishing at once he hadn't. In spite of the fact that these folk were a good third smaller than him, they were three to his one, and he was worn out. And something about their bearing said "soldiers." Soldiers of fortune, he guessed. There was a story here, which he'd as soon they began telling, seeing how he was nominal lord of this manor, and—

"Are you sick?" the nearer woman demanded.

"No, but I've—you could say I've had an accident."

"What kind?"

Eddyn thought fast. "I was captured by thieves and held for ransom," he reeled off recklessly. "I only *just* escaped."

"Where are these thieves?" the man snapped, motioning to his sister to check the doors and windows.

"Attacked by . . . birkits," Eddyn improvised. "I was asleep, and—"

"You're lying," the nearer woman said flatly. "But that's no surprise, given that you seem to be squatting here. There'll be plenty of time to get your true story."

Eddyn glared at her. "If you think you're staying here—"

Metal gleamed. A dagger. "You plan to fight three of us? Big men like you are usually clumsy. And slow."

Eddyn resisted the urge to add, "And easy to underestimate," but held his peace instead. The woman was pretty in an exotic way. And, in spite of her gruff tones, not entirely unsympathetic. He needed no enemies now.

"I'm . . . Dyn," he volunteered, finally daring to sit up.

"Elv," the nearer woman supplied, motioning to herself. "Toz." The man. "Ole." Her sister.

"You're also from Ixti," Eddyn ventured. "I hope for all our sakes you're not spies."

"Refugees," Elv corrected.

"From what?"

"After we eat," Ole broke in. "Toz, go check the horses. I'll see if any food survived the fire."

"Fire," Eddyn echoed. "I didn't expect it."

Toz raised a brow, as he strode toward the door. "So you were waylaid by thieves, who just happened to be killed by birkits within staggering distance of your home hold?"

"Not my home," Eddyn corrected. "My clan owns it. It owns a lot. I owe you no more explanation when I've had none from you."

"After dinner," Elv reiterated. "I hope your new lies are better than your old ones," she added with a wicked smirk Eddyn couldn't help but find . . . enticing.

Tozri saw to the horses—bedding them down in proper stalls for the first time since leaving War-Hold. He fed them, too, with proper oats and hay, of which there was plenty. Meanwhile, Olrix did indeed find the makings of a meal: flour and a nice cache of salted ham and smoked fish. Wonder of wonders, there was also butter—and a completely untouched cellar full of wine, beer, and ale of a quality she knew, from her time at War-Hold, meant that this hold belonged to no poor clan. The map had attributed it to Argen, which was Merryn's clan. This fellow had claimed it was his. She wondered if they knew each other.

"Should we ask?" she queried her sister when the two found themselves alone together.

Elvix shook her head. "He's got a mystery to him you could cut and serve for breakfast, but I don't think we need to push him. Frankly, this doesn't look a bad place to wait out the winter. We've still got a lot to learn about Eron, and if we're sharp, we can get this fellow to tell us everything we want to know without him even knowing it."

"You clever wench," Olrix snorted.

"He's also easy to look at," Elvix grinned. "And I've never seen a man so tall this close."

Another, louder, snort. "Don't do it, sister. Kraxxi got an eye for Merryn and look where he wound up."

Elvix rounded on her. "You think I don't know? If it weren't for him, we'd be safely back at War-Hold getting fed regularly, and sleeping warm at night."

"We could also have gone south—if not for clever Merryn."

"Not Merryn," Tozri corrected from the outside door, by which he'd just entered. "That gods-damned snowstorm that came up before we could catch up with her. No way we could've chased her down after that."

"Greatest good for the greatest number," Olrix spat. "Yes, I know."

"There was still the hold."

"And questions every moment. Being watched every moment. We came to Eron to be free. That's what we're doing."

Olrix slammed a mug down so hard the handle broke off in her hand. "I'm hearing nothing I haven't heard before, and I'm sick of it. I say we go start dinner and then we'll talk. One of us will. The rest had better do some very good listening."

"I'll watch our . . . host," Elvix chuckled. "That shouldn't be hard to do at all."

Olrix's only reply was to roll her eyes.

A hand later, Eddyn had gone from lying semiconscious by the fire to slumping groggily in the remains of a low padded chair. He'd also gone from being cold to being nicely warm, courtesy of Toz's attentions to the fire, and he'd swapped the hopeless gnawing in his stomach for one born of eager anticipation, based on the odors issuing from the stew Ole was making.

Elv was simply watching him, in the guise of polishing her sword. Eddyn stared at it sharply. Swords were both a Smithcraft monopoly and a major Eronese export. He wondered who had made that blade. He thought of asking, but they were still playing the wary game—with good reason. He had secrets. Clearly these people did, too. But now, in spite of their superior numbers, he had control on his side.

Soon enough Ole was dipping out bowlfuls of a savory fish stew, heavily laced with butter. And soon enough after that, Eddyn was finishing his third bowl, feeling as content as he had since—

He couldn't recall when, actually. Certainly he'd not felt as in control of his life since his precipitous departure from Gem-Hold.

Toz yawned and refilled his mug. "Looks like we're all companions of the storm now," he mused, motioning toward the shuttered window, beyond which snow was beginning to fall, in flakes large enough to impress even Eddyn.

"Good time for your story, then," Eddyn prompted, as he sopped his bowl with a hunk of way bread.

"Our mother was Eronese," Ole began, as Elv shifted closer, both to

Eddyn and to the fire. "You can see that in our faces when you look, and in the fact that—"

"You're triplets," Eddyn supplied. "Ixtians don't have twins, never mind triples."

Ole glared at him. "Our story, if you would hear it. We don't have to tell you anything. We could kill you and destroy the remains and no one would be wiser."

Eddyn glared back, but refrained from further comment. "Go on," he said coldly.

"Briefly, then. Our mother was Eronese, and died when we were small, but before she did, she told us stories about our land. She—"

"Sorry," Eddyn inserted. "What clan?"

"She was a healer," Toz supplied. "I don't know who rules them."

"No one, much," Eddyn gave back. "They were decimated more than any except Weavers by the plague. Most who practice that art today are not of that blood, if you understand how such things work here."

Elv scowled. "I understood our mother's sept was extinct. That's why she fled to Ixti. To escape the memories."

Eddyn wasn't sure whether to believe her, but it made a certain sort of sense. Such things had certainly happened before.

"In any event," Ole went on, "we were due leave from the army and decided to see the north, so we hired on as guards for the last caravan out. Unfortunately, it was late leaving for reasons that would upset our digestion were we to relate them—and the upshot was that we hit the first snow earlier than expected."

"It *was* early this year, was it not?" Toz inquired a little too innocently.

Eddyn nodded mutely. "It was in the north. Can't speak for the south."

"In any event, a blizzard caught us in the Flat, and we weren't prepared for it. Many died. Finally a number of us guards decided we'd try to redeem the situation. Most stayed with the caravan, but we three chose to go north seeking help. We found nothing—"

"You should've found War-Hold," Eddyn noted.

"We weren't equipped to dare the mountains," Toz retorted. "In any event, we turned back—and found everyone dead."

"Why didn't you go back to Ixti?"

"Because we had failed at our duty, and didn't want to face the disgrace," Ole told him smartly. "We had few kin there, in any case."

"And wanderlust," Toz chimed in.

"So then you *did* stop at War-Hold?"

"Eventually. Their hospitality was reasonable, but . . . they suspected us of spying, which we didn't like. We stayed as long as we could tolerate, and then . . . moved on."

"I'm surprised they let you go."

Ole grinned wickedly. "They . . . didn't. We went out with a hunting party one day and simply didn't come back. They didn't seek us."

"I'm sure," Eddyn replied skeptically.

Ole shook her head. "Believe what you will. We kept moving north, looking for the road, but the weather was bad. Finally we decided we'd missed it."

"So you went to Half Gorge?"

"Again, no. We started that way, but one horse died, and then Ole twisted her ankle and couldn't travel, so we had to find what shelter we could. We saw a ruined tower and stayed there awhile."

"And by the time we were able to travel again, we'd decided to push on for South Gorge, since our mother claimed to have come from there."

"The rest you see."

"Storms," Toz inserted. "Snow. Getting lost. Hunger. Hunting that put us farther off the trail."

Eddyn nodded once, but by the time Elv had refilled his mug, this time with tart, mulled cider, he'd forgotten to ask his next question.

"And how about you?" Elv inquired. "You know the framework of our tale; the rest you can fill in as may be. How came you here? I thought your kind hid out during this sort of weather."

Eddyn stared at his goblet, wondering if the truth or a lie was better. He settled on possibility.

"You mean when I was robbed?"

"Whatever."

"I was . . . unclanned," he said at last. Which was almost true.

Toz's eyes narrowed. "Unclanned. That means . . ."

"That I'm denied any of the rights afforded those of my clan—the right to their comfort, their company, use of their facilities—including this one, except that no one knows I'm using it."

"And this happened . . . when?"

"Recently. I'd really rather not discuss it with strangers."

Ole puffed her cheeks. "As I remember, there are very few things that get you unclanned, one of which is destruction of a masterwork."

Eddyn felt his breath catch, but hoped no one noticed. "That's one. Crime against the clan, basically."

"Was that your crime?"

"I *don't* want to talk about it!" he flared. "Even if I did, there's no way you could prove the truth of what I say, and you'd only believe what you want to, anyway. I will tell you this, however. I don't consider myself an evil person."

"Well," Elv sighed from the floor, where she was already curling up for the night, "I guess we'll have time to find out, won't we?"

"How long until spring?" Ole yawned.

"Long enough, and too long," Toz concluded. "Long enough to winnow truth from any number of lies." And with that, he, too, stretched himself upon the floor.

Tired as he was, Eddyn couldn't sleep. He watched the triplets until the fire burned low and wondered if he should leave the hold that very night—there were certainly supplies available—or if he had found himself a new set of friends. He didn't know which notion was more frightening.

INTERLUDE II:

SUNRISE IN THE WOODS

(NORTHWESTERN ERON—DEEP WINTER: DAY XLIX—SHORTLY BEFORE DAWN)

~~~~~~~~~~

Kylin felt the tether tense toward the right, and shifted his weight accordingly, following that as much as Rann's tersely breathless directions, or the sound of his companion's skis, as Rann skimmed across the snow ahead of him. Air whipped his face, but not wind, for it was still, here among the evergreens. A blessing, that; it had been growing steadily colder since they'd set out at dusk. Too, the near silence allowed him to take better stock of their party—Rann in the lead, proceeding alternately by dead reckoning and a map they'd found at the first way station, that showed a now-disused road between it and the private hold that was their goal; and Strynn behind, continuing, as far as Kylin could tell, solely from strength of will. There was moonlight now, Rann said—two of the three had risen full at midnight—but that scarcely mattered to Kylin, save to increase Rann's confidence as he led their little party through the forest southeast of Gem-Hold-Winter.

It had been clumsy going at first—fearfully so. They'd set out at midnight three days back, but their departure from the hold had been ridiculously easy compared to the logistics of navigating those first crucial shots beyond—those in which they were still visible. Being blind, Kylin had been able to tell nothing about the terrain, save to take Rann's word that it was largely featureless as far as the top of the ridge that surrounded the vale in which the hold was lodged. But Strynn and Rann alike were handicapped by the darkness and the fact that they couldn't burn torches until out of sight of the hold. Kylin had actually had the advantage there, and once they'd managed those first two shots—which had taken almost two hands—the going had been better. Eventually they'd established a rhythm, with him tethered to Rann by a three-span rope around his waist, through which he'd eventually learned to sense the directions he needed to take by the play of pressures alone. In some ways, in fact, it had been better than walking, for skiing let one slide one's feet along, and that rendered progress less vulnerable to unexpected shifts in elevation.

Too, they'd acquired an additional advantage they'd neither expected nor could effectively define. It was a kind of . . . sense of where the others were, or what the others were thinking or doing. Rann said it was almost certainly a function of the way they'd been linked through the gems, the effect amplified by the fact that they were, so far as they could tell, alone out here, with only each other's thoughts to draw upon. Indeed, at times it seemed they were almost one being, which was also fortunate, because necessity had honed their reality down to three foci: the pure act of steering themselves along, the necessity of maintaining direction, and shrugging off the fatigue that had become a real presence halfway through the first night.

For all his wasted wiriness, Rann was strong, and had spent the previous half eighth in the Wild, skiing constantly. But Kylin got far less exercise in the hold, excused as he was from all but volunteer pedaling on the mining machines, which activity he'd abdicated of late. And Strynn— Though strong for a woman, much of that strength lay in her upper body, for she was a weaponsmith, accustomed to standing in one place and hammering; her legs weren't conditioned to steady action, and certainly not with the added, clumsy weight her pregnancy conferred. The upshot was that Kylin and Strynn had been forced to rest more than expected, and suffered shooting pains in their calves and thighs that required massages when they halted for meals or sleep. There'd been a small hot spring at the station where they'd sheltered the first night. But since then . . .

Well, it was getting worse, and they still had, by Rann's reckoning, half a day to go.

But dawn was approaching, for Kylin could sense a change in the atmosphere, a subtle warming, perhaps, or a shift in humidity as a tiny bit of snow evaporated. And there was a change in the light even he could detect, for they faced full into the sunrise, and the noonday glare that had burned away his sight as a foolish child had not taken all his vision, so that he could still tell extremes of dark and light. The snow went pink at times like this, Strynn said. But he had to work to recall what pink was.

In any case, Rann was slowing, and not only from the increased pitch of the slope they'd been navigating for the last half hand. Kylin likewise slowed, lest he impact his companion unaware. He heard Strynn swish up beside him as Rann came to a halt.

"Something wrong?" Strynn asked breathlessly. Kylin felt the warmth of her closeness, more real to him than the trees he only assumed loomed about.

Rann shook his head—Kylin could tell by the way his clothing rasped against itself. "I don't think so. But something feels . . . odd."

"Can you be more specific?" Strynn persisted, leaning against Kylin for casual support.

"Not really. Just a feeling that there's one more element out here than there ought to be. It could just be the presence of birkits. It has something of that feel. But my ability to sense them had all but vanished by the time I reached Gem-Hold."

"You didn't have a gem then," Kylin countered.

"That may be the difference," Rann conceded. "In any case, you two have been pushing harder than you ought since our last stop. So why don't you make breakfast? I'll check out that next ridge east. It should be full daylight by the time I reach it, and it's higher, so it'd be better for comparing the lay of the land with the map."

"I'm too tired to argue," Strynn sighed, fingers already working at the tether. The knot gave, and Kylin felt something less tangible diminish at that, as though that length of mingled hemp, sylk, and cotton had carried some sustaining energy between him and Rann. Not that he much cared at the moment, as he sank down against the tree trunk to which Strynn had deftly steered him.

"Back in half a hand," Rann called, and sped off down the slope.

Rann couldn't have explained the sensation any better than he had, and while it wasn't unpleasant, it was still cause for alarm. The Wild in Deep Winter *wasn't* empty of human activity, in spite of what one heard. There were people like Div, eking out an existence by trapping through even the coldest seasons. And there were the ghost priests, who were certainly prepared to dare extended trips outdoors at need. Never mind fools like him, Strynn, and Kylin. And Avall, but best not to think about Avall until they could be reunited. He still lived, and that was enough—for now.

In the meantime, he'd made it to the valley between the ridge where he'd left his companions, and the higher one that was his goal. Indeed, the terrain was smooth enough that he'd been able to build sufficient momentum to carry him partway up the facing slope. But now that he had slowed, he could hear something approaching from the opposite side of the ridge. He glided to a stop, listening, trying to winnow those other sounds from the hiss of his own breathing.

Footsteps, and breathing harsh as his own. Something big, somewhat clumsy, making no care for the noise it made, which ruled out all large predators. Close, too; whatever it was would crest the rise at any moment.

All Rann could think of were the ghost priests, and he had no idea what he'd do if he encountered a band of them out here, with Kylin and Strynn in tow. But this sounded like one entity, though that didn't negate it being a ghost-priest scout. Holding his breath and moving as quietly as he could, he crouched in the scanty shelter of a patch of snow laurel. Waiting. Grateful for the white cloaks he and his companions had affected.

Closer. Skis appeared, towering over a head so muffled in furs the features would've been invisible even had the face-mask not been raised. And then shoulders. It paused there, turning, searching the landscape, as though it too had heard someone. Once that gaze swept by his screen, but on the return, it locked on him. Hands dropped skis and snatched up a crossbow.

Rann's logic completed the picture. "Div!" he blurted. "It's me, Rann!"

Fortunately, he had sense enough to remain where he was, though impulse would've set him bursting through the brush—likely to receive a bolt from pure reflex.

"Rann?" the figure ventured, even as the crossbow came up.

Rann stood. "It's me—and two friends one ridge back. But what are you . . . ?"

The bow lowered. They met on the crest of the hill. Fingers fumbled at masks; breath ghosted into the air. Surprise and concern stole what joy would properly have marked their meeting. They hugged perfunctorily, almost shy with each other. "What—?" Rann dared.

"On my way to Gem to see you, of course," Div snorted. "It was know something or know nothing, and I chose the former."

Rann shook his head to clear it. "And we were going to your place. Things got too dangerous in the big hold. We'd heard of an abandoned private hold halfway between, and—"

Div pointed back the way she'd come. "Over that hill, no more than two shots."

Rann's laughter rang loud in the cold, still air, sounding almost giddy. She regarded him curiously. "What's funny?"

He grinned. "Nothing—except that you've just cut five days off our journey. Now come with me; you need to meet two of my favorite people."

CHAPTER XIV:

TROUBLE AFOOT

(ERON: TIR-ERON—DEEP WINTER: DAY LI—MIDAFTERNOON)

G ynn syn Argen-el had been High King of Eron for a little more than
two years, but had been a smith all his life. He'd spent most of his youth
in North Gorge, where lay the principal seat of his sept, Argen-el,
which ruled machines. He'd therefore been spared the bulk of the intrigues
that kept Argen-yr and Argen-a perpetually at each other's throats, and had
thus acquired a reasonable level of objectivity. So he thought. So Eellon had
also thought, when he'd conspired with the Sub–Clan-Chief of Argen-el
and the Chiefs of War, Lore, and Stone to put him on the throne when his
predecessor had revealed an invisible imperfection by proving unable to sire
even one child, despite three healthy, fertile consorts.

Gynn had no such trouble, and had given -el two boys and one girl, the
last of whom had cost her mother's life when labor had come an eighth too
soon and found pale, quiet Ortrarr becalmed, with the rest of her trek, at
Five Tree Station. The child had started out rump first, and there'd been no
choice but to cut her free. Which Ortrarr had survived. What she hadn't survived was the plague.

Neither had the elder son. The younger, now twenty-two, lived quietly in
Mid Gorge, where he was a subcraft-chief. The daughter was with her
mother's clan, learning how to heal. He'd had no choice. He'd cost them a
daughter; he was obliged to give one back.

Now he claimed no consort but Eron.

Yet sometimes he liked to recall that power and position—and royalty—had been thrust upon him, whereas he was first and always a man.

And with all those terrible revelations Avall had bestowed upon him to keep him awake at night, to the point he'd started making lists of projected allies and foes and votes and favors and opinions—well, sometimes it was nice simply to work with his hands, as he was doing now, in the forge beneath the Citadel.

Few outside his clan would have known him: stripped to the waist, with his legs cased in leather hose and his thick black hair bound back in a tail beneath a plain sylk scarf. He could've been any healthy man his age in Eron. Except there *were* almost no men his age, courtesy of the plague, which was another reason he'd gained the crown.

But that wasn't why he was here—pedaling happily away at a complex lathe that spun a rough-cast cylinder of a new alloy, while cutting edges trued it down to match a metal bore he'd already fashioned. No, he was here to indulge his first passion: making.

He'd been at it a good while, too, by turns pedaling and pouring oil over the involved surfaces lest they get too hot and warp. His legs were sore, his spare-muscled torso sweaty, but the pain was one of achievement, to be enjoyed, not endured.

Still, he'd have to stop soon. He had a meeting with Eellon about whether or not to tell Dallonn of Stone about Eddyn's disappearance, on which topic he'd changed his mind twice that day already. In any event, the cutting edge had worked its way to the end of the cylinder. It was time to replace it with a broader one, to remove the tooling grooves.

Sighing, Gynn climbed off the pedal platform. His legs were stiff—sign of a winter's inactivity—but the floor felt so cool beneath his hose that he didn't bother retrieving his shoes. Blissfully unshod, he padded to the tool cabinet and sorted through cutting heads until he found the one he needed. It looked more like a chisel than anything else, save that the edge was as keen as the sharpest knife and made of the hardest metal Argen-el had yet contrived—a secret his sept didn't share even with -yr and -a.

Perhaps he hadn't wiped all the oil from his fingers. Or perhaps his hand was a trifle numb from working the lever that moved the cutter. Whatever the cause, the head slipped from his grasp. He snatched at it vainly, swore in a most unroyal manner, then stared with dreadful fascination as the edge grazed the side of his right foot before he could dance away.

The leather parted neatly, and he thought he'd been spared injury—until his smallest toe informed him that it was, in fact, in pain. Indeed, once established, that pain was quite remarkable. Abruptly dizzy, he sat down on the floor, by turns grateful he worked alone and wishing one of his squires was present when he actually needed one. The pain vanished—returned—vanished again. Blood darkened leather and floor alike in troubling amounts. Holding his breath, he took his belt dagger and enlarged the hole in his hose far enough to inspect the wound.

It was hard to tell for the blood, but it didn't look as bad as he'd feared. He'd clipped the toe smartly, right at the joint—probably down to the bone. He might lose the nail, but it would grow back. For now, it was a minor inconvenience. He'd limp for a few days; that was all.

But he'd do no more smithing today. Another breath, and he levered himself up—and almost passed out, as pain waged war up his leg. He sat down again, and inspected the wound more thoroughly. Dared to probe the toe—and discovered to his horror that he felt nothing when he moved the tip. And then he saw what blood and a few doughty sinews had obscured. He hadn't clipped the toe at all; he'd all but severed the joint!

Which he was in no position to tend.

And then another thought struck him: one so dire his brain recoiled from it.

He was King of Eron, and the King of Eron must be physically perfect.

Which he would no longer be—if the toe could not be reattached.

But dared he have it tended? Word would get out, and that could spell disaster, with the matter of the gem still to ponder, most especially whether it should remain a secret or be made public knowledge. This was certainly no time for Eron to be changing Sovereigns. He would therefore wait. He'd limp awhile, but people did that. Broken bones were no deterrent to kingship, and he'd simply give out that he'd kicked a table while working barefoot.

Besides, the wound might heal.

And pigs could fly!

It took all the will Gynn possessed to bind his foot with his sweat-scarf, put on his shoe, and mop the blood from the floor. No point risking the questions such a mess might entail.

He snared his tunic and made for the door, dismissing the new guardsman, Myx, with a terse "I just kicked an Eight-damned table, and I want to be alone with my carelessness right now."

Myx fled, and Gynn eventually made it up a little-used staircase to his chambers. Fortunately, he'd been his own man longer than he'd been Sovereign, and was perfectly capable of scouring the bath after he'd cleaned the toe. He was also capable of sewing the edges of loose flesh back together, renewing the bandage, and throwing the old one in the fire.

It was harder to hide his naked feet from his squires, but he managed. It was not so easy to hide the limp.

Tyrill was well aware that even her peers on the Council of Chiefs referred to her as the Spider Chief. Nor was she concerned by that appellation—save, perhaps, as a compliment. She'd even gone so far—once—to wear a gown embroidered with spiders and their webs to a royal fete. It was therefore with a certain amount of glee that, after a number of webs of a less obvious sort had been cast, she began to reel them in.

They took the form of her squires—young women who, in many holds, would've been called maids, but which term she despised, because it seemed less in status to that applied to young men—like Lykkon—who performed equivalent duties.

Well, not precisely. A number of Tyrill's brood came from outside the clan, by way of rescues performed in the guise of good deeds, which coincidentally rendered these young women intensely loyal to her—or afraid, which had the same effect.

She was ready to receive the first one now, where she sat primly in her chambers, clad in clan maroon, with her Craft-Chief's silver tabard prominently displayed.

A knock sounded precisely at the appointed time.

"Enter," Tyrill called.

The girl who closed the carved oak door was named Lynee. She wore the beige of Common Clan, differenced with a sash of Argen maroon and a silver brooch of Tyrill's service. Lynee bowed solemnly, and took the ritual cup of meeting silently, before seating herself on a low chair beside Tyrill's high one. "It took me longer than I'd hoped," she said clearly, "for which I apologize. But there was need for . . . circumspection."

"There was," Tyrill agreed. "But what I need is results. Confirmation, rather."

"It is as you suspected," Lynee replied. "The Roll of Arrivals at Eron Tower has been altered since you sent me there on the forty-first. It appears the whole thing has been recopied."

"Which implies Lore's collusion—or else Eellon had Lykkon do it. I don't suppose you recognized the hand?"

Lynee shook her head. "I'm sorry, Chief, no."

"No matter. What form did these changes take?"

"The earlier roll listed a visit from Lord Eellon and Lykkon as his squire, a hand and a half after sunset. It recorded the departure of them a hand after that—in company with Tower Warden Veen and two guards named Myx and Riff—along with an unidentified person. The later version only includes the departure of Veen, Myx, and Riff."

Tyrill nodded sagely. "And that other matter?"

"I had to bribe a young guardsman to get this information, but it is also as you suspected. Two nights after Eellon's visit, a man was apprehended, having come out of the Wild with news of a wounded comrade. He was taken prisoner, and identified as Eddyn syn Argen-yr—before references to his arrival were altered. He—"

"Eddyn!" Tyrill broke in, lunging forward, as though someone had slapped her back. "But that's impossible! He'd have come straight to me upon leaving the tower. Unless—" She broke off. "Continue," she managed breathlessly.

"I was only *told* they were altered, Chief; I didn't see the earlier version. Later that same night, there was a flurry of comings and goings between the tower and Priest-Hold—messages sent first from the tower notifying them that one of their own had been found injured nearby, and then the arrival of several high functionaries from that clan, and another clandestine departure. Interestingly enough, the references to Priest-Clan comings and goings were *not* altered, only those to Eddyn."

Tyrill gnawed her lip. "Would that I could see these records myself, but that would draw too much attention."

"There is one final thing, Chief," Lynee said hesitantly. "No one would talk about it directly, but I got the clear impression that the King knew Eddyn was coming and had ordered that he be arrested immediately upon his arrival."

"He has no authority to do that without informing me!" Tyrill all but raged. "I don't suppose you heard the reason given?"

"I think it had something to do with destruction of a masterwork."

"Avall," Tyrill growled. "*Now* this makes sense—of a sort. Except that Avall being here at all makes no sense." She paused, having realized she was not alone. "You heard nothing I said since coming here," she said flatly. "You may go, with my thanks. Do not be surprised, however, if I don't find reason to send you away for a time, as soon as such can be arranged."

"As you will, Chief," Lynee murmured, and departed.

"Send in Nisheen," Tyrill called to her back.

Nisheen was most things Lynee wasn't. Though born to Argen-yr, her mother was Healer-Hold, and her gifts lay in that direction. Which would probably prompt a defection when the time came for her to state her official calling when she turned twenty, a year hence. She was also slim as a reed and intense, almost angry, though Tyrill had never found the source of that ire.

The obligatory greetings and drinks disposed of, Tyrill got right to business. "How fare things in Healer-Hold?"

"There are many things to tell you, Chief. So many I hardly know where to begin, and some of them things I was *not* dispatched to learn, but which may prove to be of more interest." At a sign from Tyrill she went on. "Briefly, then, as to the information I was sent to retrieve, I was able to learn no more about Eellon's condition than you knew heretofore. His body grows frail; that is no secret to anyone in this hold or hall. He hasn't been sleeping well of late, however, to judge by the increased requests his healer has made for certain ingredients useful in sleeping draughts. And he's apparently having trouble with headaches, which seem to coincide with periods of irregular heartbeat. He has refused drugs for either, because he says they dull the mind."

"And how do you know this last?"

"His healer requested the drugs . . . in case."

A brow shot up. Tyrill leaned forward in casual interest. "In case of what?"

Nisheen shook her head. "No one would say, though my sense is that they expect something to fail in him . . . eventually."

"If only he precedes me in that happening," Tyrill muttered. Then: "You spoke of other things?"

"Aye, Chief, it would seem that not only is Eellon in need of drugs, so is His Majesty, except that he is seeking painkillers—very strong ones."

Tyrill leaned back and gnawed her lip again. "I wonder if this is real information, or something planted by His Majesty for whatever reason."

"I think it is real, Chief. The request for drugs has not come from the Royal Healer, but from the King's own daughter, who is apprenticed at Healing. I don't know who the intercessor is between King and daughter, if there is one, but she seemed very concerned, though she wouldn't say why."

"I have some ideas," Tyrill mused. "More than that is not for me to say— to you."

"As you will. But there is yet one more thing I thought you should know. His Majesty has been sending his own healer to Priest-Hold to check on someone who apparently came out of the Wild several days back. He is unconscious, but His Majesty is keen to know if he raves in his stupor, and has given orders that word be sent as soon as the lad revives."

"Do you have a name for this boy?"

"Rrath syn Garnill. I know him vaguely."

Tyrill nodded slowly. "And you're sure you know nothing of the King's pain? Are you not bonded to one of his squires?"

Nisheen blushed, but then her face darkened with emotion of another kind. "I thought we agreed we were to keep that out of it. I *love* Barri; I don't want him to think I'm using him, and certainly not to someone else's ends."

Tyrill's anger surged in return, but she fought it down. "We did agree," she acknowledged. "But anything he volunteered without your asking, and to which he has not sworn you to silence, would violate very little."

Nisheen's brow furrowed in thought. "He told me out of concern, and I *will* tell you, but remember what I risk here, Chief."

"I remember," Tryill replied coldly.

"It wasn't much, really. He only said that he'd noticed that the King was not using his squires as much as heretofore, and that he had himself noticed that the King seemed to limp when he thought no one was around."

She paused. "Chief," she dared, "do you think there is a connection between the limp and the King going through his daughter to acquire painkillers?"

Tyrill stilled her face to calm. "If I were to answer that, which I will not—officially—I would say that there might very well be."

Tyrill did not confront Eellon the next morning, however. Nor the King. Rather, she acted on a notion that had been fermenting in her since hearing from her squires, but from which good sense had, so far, dissuaded her. That, and fear of what Eellon and the King might do, should she nose around their secrets too openly. Still, she had Nisheen in tow, and the girl had obligingly passed word of their intended destination to Argen-yr's sept-chief, so Tyrill doubted she'd find herself disappearing without at least a search, as Eddyn (so discreet inquiries indicated) apparently had.

Therefore, it was with dawnlight still spreading across the sky that Tyrill and Nisheen made their way from one of Argen-Hall's lesser gates to the promenade beside the river. Tyrill wore full clan regalia minus the too-distinctive tabard, but also a mouth-mask beneath it, the better to obscure her features. She wanted her presence noted for safety's sake, but not her identity. Nisheen simply wore gown, cloak, and hood in clan colors.

Their breaths showed white in the chill air, but boots, gloves, and layers of thick fabric made it tolerable, as they walked with casual briskness toward the southwest end of the gorge. Crossing the river on its last span before the waterfall, they soon found themselves facing the calculated wildness of Priest-Clan's precincts.

Unique in all Eron, Priestcraft had no ruling house, and was therefore clan and craft alike, drawing its members from all aspects of society, at, so they said, the Will of The Eight. And though its members were as educated as the other High Clans, and their tastes as urbane, they chose to present an outward face of ascetic austerity. For that reason, they'd hollowed their hold into the cliffs, leaving as much of the natural facade as possible. The interiors were as luxurious as any High Clan hold.

"Are you sure you want to do this?" Nisheen murmured as they paused before the rough-stone trilithons that marked the compound's formal entrance.

"No," Tyrill grunted. "But it's the only way I can find out what I want to know, without a lot of follow-ups and guessing."

"Nisheen san Argen-yr," Nisheen informed the gate-warden in the bored tones of ritual formality, "on business for that clan. And the King," she added—which in a way it was, though not in a manner to win royal approval.

The warden studied her warily, then nodded toward Tyrill. "And your companion?"

"This is royal business," Nisheen repeated. "Do we need to tell you more?"

The warden studied Tyrill carefully. Happily he squinted, which Tyrill hoped Nisheen would play to their advantage. "She looks familiar," the warden mumbled.

"Her identity is her concern," Nisheen huffed. "And the King's."

" 'Royal business' is not sufficient," the warden stated flatly.

Tyrill took a deep breath and broke in. "We've come to see Rrath syn Garnill, of Weather."

"For what purpose?"

Tyrill suppressed a scathing retort. This was more than ritual formality. Which likely indicated a hold on some sort of alert.

"To report his condition to the King."

"One normally sends the Royal Healer for such things."

"One normally sends the *ill* to Healer-Hold," Nisheen retorted. "Now do we go, or do you rouse royal ire?"

"You may go until someone else says you nay," the warden conceded at last. "I . . . knew Rrath somewhat myself. Promising lad. If you learn anything . . ."

Tyrill was glad Nisheen didn't reply. It had taken all she had to defer even this much authority, and wouldn't have done even that, were it not for her desire to attract as little attention as possible without resorting to actual subterfuge.

It was as though the cliffs had eyes, she thought, with a shudder, as they continued on, angling toward the left-hand face, not far from the hold's famous hot-pools. She could smell their sulfur already.

Fortunately for Tyrill's joints, they didn't have to continue up the tortuous path to the local sick-hall, for a sweet-faced young man in Weather's tabard fell into step beside them—from the direction of the pools, in which he'd been indulging, to judge by his damp hair. "I was wondering when someone from your clan would show up," he blurted, before Tyrill could dispose of him. "Forgive me, Ladies," he went on awkwardly, "concern has made me rude enough to grasp at any tidbit. I am Esshill syn Vrine. Rrath was my bond-brother."

"What makes you think we're looking for Rrath?" Tyrill snapped, unable to restrain her temper any longer. "I thought he was still in service. Gem-Hold-Winter, if I recall."

Esshill's features hardened. "The same reason the Craft-Chief from Smith knows where a neophyte from here was posted last Fateing. The same reason folks went storming out of here eight days ago, bound for Eron Tower—and came back with Rrath hurt and maybe dying. That's got all kinds of people coming and going here, from the Citadel and Healer-Hold, none with explanations. That's got everyone here looking over their shoulder for no reason anyone can explain."

"Which still doesn't explain what *you* think should be our reasons," Tyrill noted archly. "Or why you're volunteering so much to total strangers." She stopped in place and turned to face him squarely. "What, exactly, *do* you know, anyway?"

Esshill regarded her levelly. "You're from a powerful clan with some connection to this matter. I'm saying what's necessary to assure a maximum number of allies if things fall out as I fear. And, more to the point, I'm saying what I must in order to look out for my friend." A deep breath. "I know that Rrath and someone rumored to be Tall Eddyn were found near Eron Tower hard on the heels of Midwinter. Rrath had had an accident and was brought back here to recover. Meanwhile, Eddyn disappeared so fast it'd make your head swim. And then, so says rumor, disappeared again before anyone from here could question him. Not that I believe all that," he added. "No one from here seems to have actually seen Eddyn." He broke off, looking at his feet. Then: "Do you mean that he's not in Argen-Hall? But we assumed—"

"Not since he left," Tyrill sighed. "The King wants a report on Rrath," she went on irritably. "It would be good if you could provide one."

Another, deeper breath; Eshill was almost crying. Tyrill actually felt sorry for the lad, having been suddenly put in an awkward station. "He's unconscious but as healthy as he can be, considering that. Now and then he seems on the verge of awakening, but never does."

Tyrill nodded sagely. "Would they let us in to see him?"

Esshill shook his head. "No one save myself, his healers, the chiefs of this clan, and the King himself can see him."

"On whose orders?"

"Actually," the Priest confessed, "no one seems to know. But he's got guards. That's enough for most."

"Guards don't always help," Tyrill sighed. "Thank you for your assistance. I suppose we'd best be going."

She'd already taken a few steps down the path, when Esshill hailed her once again. "I hope," he murmured carefully, "that royal curiosity can be forged into royal protection."

"The Eight protect us *all,*" Tyrill replied, and strode away, wondering if she'd actually learned anything useful. And wondering, more to the point, why she was suddenly afraid.

CHAPTER XV:

SHARP EYES

(Tir-Eron—Deep Winter: Day LVIII—late afternoon)

~~~~~~~~~~

I still think you should move to your suite here and be done with it," Lykkon informed Eellon wearily, as he followed his sometime-mentor down one of the Citadel's least-used corridors. "It would save us all a lot of trouble—and you a lot of pain."

Eellon halted in a swish of robes. His Clan-Chief cloak swirled around him like a maroon tornado as he turned. "My health is my concern," he snapped. "Don't forget that."

"You're better company when you don't hurt," Lykkon retorted bravely. "Don't *you* forget that. As much as you've got on your mind right now, I think—"

He broke off, having seen the darkness that clouded Eellon's face. His Chief wasn't looking at him, however, but some distance behind, the furrows in his brow deepening by the breath. Lykkon twisted round to investigate.

It was the King, going the opposite way down the corridor at whose terminus they stood. He'd entered it, from a corridor farther on, and hadn't seen them. But Lykkon noticed something odd the same moment Eellon whispered it. "He's limping."

"Maybe he stubbed a toe."

"Perhaps, but right now we can't afford to take chances." And with that,

Eellon started down the hall in pursuit of his sovereign. Lykkon had to hurry to keep up, and heard the Chief's leg and back braces squeaking alarmingly as he strode along at a pace for which they'd not been designed. It had to hurt, nor did Lykkon like the way Eellon's breath sounded: all cramped and hollow. His face was disturbingly red.

But the King *was* limping, Lykkon confirmed as he grew closer. Or maybe not, for the King suddenly altered his stride to a much more confident gait.

"He's heard us," Eellon hissed under his breath. "That's all the proof we need—dammit."

Lykkon didn't ask "proof of what?" He already knew. The King wouldn't try to hide a temporary injury.

"Majesty," Eellon called, as with one smooth motion he swept his hood up, signifying that he now acted in Clan-Chief capacity. The King slowed to a casual—and perfectly paced—saunter, then paused by the door to an unused suite and waited, arms folded across his chest. He looked grim and angry, for any number of reasons Lykkon could imagine.

"Majesty," Eellon panted again, when they arrived. "I would speak with you a moment."

Gynn's eyes flicked from Eellon's hood to Lykkon. "Very well. But he stays here."

Lykkon tried not to glare as his King ushered his Chief inside.

"May I sit?" Eellon asked bluntly, noting in passing that the room seemed long disused, and recalling vaguely that the previous Sovereign's brother had lodged there. His sigils were still present, blazoned on dusty swags of drapery. Without waiting for reply, Eellon brushed off a chair and sank down in it. He'd exerted himself too much, he supposed; was breathless, sore, and his head felt funny. Still, there was nothing to gain by postponing the inevitable.

Gynn claimed a chair opposite, his face dark as thunder. "Clan-Chief?"

"Majesty," Eellon began, "there's no way to say it but to say it. You were limping just now. Nothing odd in that, of itself—people hurt themselves and people heal. But you, I noticed, changed your gait when you became aware someone was watching. I don't like what that makes me think."

Gynn's face was immobile. "And what *does* it make you think?"

"That you've sustained some injury that renders you unable to remain on the throne." The words rang like pebbles dropped on ice.

The King did not reply.

Eellon took a deep breath. "I put it to you bluntly, Majesty; on your oath as King."

No reply.

"Majesty, I warn you, tension among allies is never good. Certainly not at this time."

"Then why do you provoke tension?" Gynn flared. "Is my word not enough for you?"

"I have *had* no word from you. I have had silence and evasions."

"A King's silence is his own. His evasions for the good of the Realm."

Eellon sprang to his feet, face darkening with a rage he could no longer control. "The good of the Realm?" he gritted. "I wonder if you even know what *is* good for the Realm. If you do not, *I* do: a King who is trusted, a King who does not put himself above the Law." He paused for breath, relaxed a trifle, if only to still his own racing heart. "If I have noticed it, Gynn, then others of the Council will, and put you to the same question. Your choice is not *if* you reveal your . . . infirmity, but to whom and when. You have to know that to me and now are the best alternatives you're likely to have. But I *will* have honesty from you."

"And if I say no?"

A shrug. "I'll simply ask you to take off your boots and hose. The Eight know I've seen your bare feet often enough. You've no reason to deny me unless you *have* reason to deny me. Barring that . . . Well, you have to sleep sometime."

"And if I refuse?"

"I'll have War here, and Lore, and Stone. And if you still resist, I'll call in Tyrill."

Gynn chuckled grimly. "You must truly be desperate, then."

"I'm concerned for you, you whelp," Eellon snapped. "I'm concerned for the Kingdom, and for observing the ancient rites. If you're injured beyond healing, you have some grace. But Tyrill *will* find out, make no mistake. We need to plan against that eventuality, so the sooner those who made you King know the truth, the sooner we can take appropriate action."

The King glared at him.

"We will know the truth at Sundeath, in any case. You have that long. Would you rather stand alone or with allies?"

Gynn sighed wearily and slumped back in his chair. "You won't take no for an answer, will you? And I won't have an easy minute if I worry about you watching my every move. So . . ." He was already reaching toward his boot when he paused. "I seem to be doing this twice a day of late, but I would have Sovereign Oath of you on what I am about to reveal."

"You don't have the sword," Eellon replied mildly, sitting again.

"Then I'll have to trust your word as a man. But I beg you to think before you act."

"I will keep my own counsel, Majesty. But I would also remind you that my own counsel has rarely been at odds with the good of the Realm or the King."

"That's as much as I can expect, I suppose," Gynn sighed, and eased off his boot. "Forgive me if I don't remove my hose."

Eellon merely grunted. He'd seen what he needed to see: a flaccid emptiness where the King's smallest right toe should have been.

"It's healing," Gynn confided. "But not fast enough. I can fake an honest stride, but it costs me."

Eellon nodded grimly. "But it's an imperfection we won't be able to argue away. Which means we have a bit more than half a year in which to lay plans for your succession."

"I'd thought I might step down at Sunbirth."

"Not wise," Eellon countered. "Too many things are at odds right now. We need all the stability we can muster. At best, we can stall. At worst, your condition might render major policy issues subject to question. In any case, we've got time in which to agree on a reasonable successor—though I'm damned if I can think of one."

"I can think of plenty," Gynn snorted. "Plenty that could do the job. But I can't think of any that won't result in civil war. The next generation from Smith, War, and Stone are still young to assume the crown. Anyone else . . . I wouldn't enjoy seeing a Weaver or a Woodwright on the throne any more than you would."

Eellon spared a glance toward the window, noting the westering sun. "Majesty, I thank you for your candor. You have given me much to ponder, and little of it pleasant, but I hadn't planned to spend this time as I have. I must therefore be on my way. But I fear we must speak of this again, and soon. Have I your permission to tell Avall?"

"If you think it will do any good. But wait a moment," Gynn continued. "You were blunt with me, to the Kingdom's good. It is now my obligation to be blunt with you: Are you well? I know about the pain in your joints and back, that you overcome with braces and such. But you have seemed . . . tired of late. And your face often goes red or pale. Are you aware of this?"

Eellon took a deep breath. "My body is old and is quickly wearing out. My mind is as supple as it ever was, so it seems to me—though I confess to odd blanks in my memory now and then, but we all know that worry can provoke such things even in young men. Still, I do feel light-headed more than I ought. I feel my heart racing sometimes at night. I have more headaches than heretofore."

The King gnawed his lip thoughtfully. Then: "Whatever happens, Clan-Chief, I hope one of us is there to give the Kingdom guidance."

"I will be there until The Eight render me unable," Eellon assured him, rising.

The King took a deep breath. "One more thing, Clan-Chief."

Eellon paused in place, hands on the arms of his chair. "Yes?"

"Avall. I have seen him little of late. How does he fare after the . . . taking?"

"He says he fares well, but I don't believe him. That journey took much out of him, make no mistake. Without the gem, he probably could not have survived it, even with the aid he had. But now that it has . . . vanished. Well, you have seen him, Majesty. He is like a man spurned in love, like a man worn beyond endurance, and like a man who has lost his crafting hand all at once."

Again Gynn chuckled. "I know something of that last," he said. "I was complete, and it *made* me what I was, and now it is gone, and I will never *be* what I was."

"Nor, I fear, will Avall, until he retrieves the gem."

"Yet he makes no effort to that end?"

"He says he is not yet ready. He says he is waiting for Rann and Merryn to return."

"Which won't be until Sunbirth."

Eellon nodded ominously. "And they haven't contacted him, which has him concerned. He says they should be able."

Gynn started pacing, oblivious to his limp, though Eellon saw him grimace more than once. "Meanwhile precious time goes by and he does nothing, while rogue magic runs wild in the world, and I dare not send anyone to seek it, lest they, too, be tempted, as Eddyn was."

"You're assuming much of Avall's ethics, Majesty."

"At least he intended to give the gem to me. I cannot imagine Eddyn doing the like."

Eellon cleared his throat. "It might help if Avall were allowed to visit Rrath. They were friends—once. At least that way he might get answers where he had none. Betrayal by a friend, even a lapsed one, is hard to stomach. Avall needs answers now."

Gynn shook his head. "I can't let him go. It would raise too many questions. I already suspect Tyrill of muddying the waters there."

Eellon shook his head in turn. "It was a suggestion. Meanwhile, Avall is like a man who has lost both shadow and soul. He has the form, but not the substance. But he will have to heal himself; we cannot do it for him."

"Would that I could heal myself so easily," Gynn sighed, limping to the window. Rain streaked it now; sometime bane of snow. Eellon wished all their troubles were as transitory and as easily dispersed.

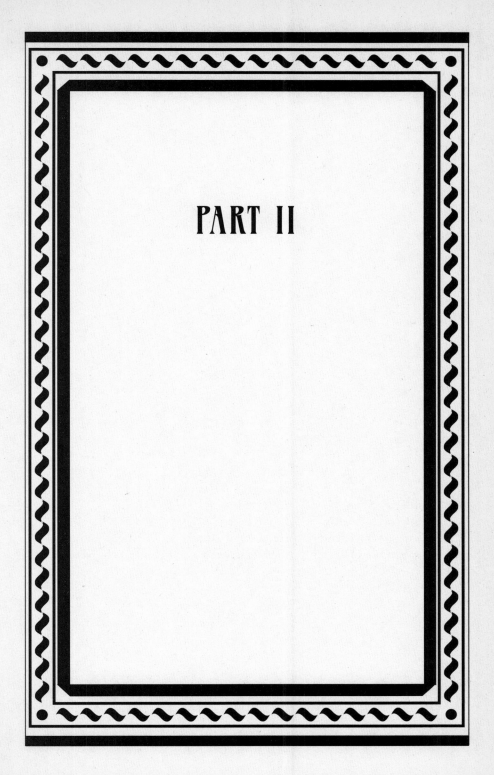

PART II

CHAPTER XVI:

INTERRUPTION

(ERON: WAR-HOLD-WINTER—
NEAR SPRING: DAY XX—EARLY EVENING)

~~~~~~~~~~

H old-Warden?"

The voice came hard on the heels of a tentative knock on the half-open door. Lorvinn heard the double raps echo down the empty hall outside her new quarters. Her new cell, rather. The voice was softer: male, and pitched for her ears alone.

"Hold-Warden?" More insistent. Maybe a little desperate. Or simply nervous.

"Not my title—now," Lorvinn called back, easing herself to a more poised seat in the hard-backed chair that was all she permitted herself, as the plain table was the only flat surface, and the narrow, sparsely sheeted bed the only other furniture beyond a minimum of toiletries and one book at a time. No thick emerald carpeting on the floor, no rich wood paneling, such as had adorned her former suite. No fine fabric robes. Only naked stone floor and walls, a single window, a candle, simple shoes—and a shirt of pig hide worn bristle side against her skin beneath old wool. "But come in anyway . . . Krynneth."

The door opened farther to admit a slim young man with piercing blue eyes that set even War-Hold women swooning. He wore a formal cloak-and-hood of War-Hold crimson, and dress mail—which meant this was no casual visit. Lorvinn composed herself for an audience. She had twice his years and more, but was lean and fit for all that. Her face was lined with age, however—and, lately, with worry.

Krynneth shut the door behind him. The latch clicked softly, well-made and tended. He looked troubled, Lorvinn thought, with a mental sigh. She hoped he hadn't come for the reason she suspected. Then again, she also hoped for an end to old age and yearly snow.

A deep breath from Krynneth, then: "Lady Warden, I am here of my own will as a man of this hold who has known you and worked with you and served under you and respected you since I was a boy. You honored me by including me in the Night Guard when you began to rebuild it. But now I am here to tell you that . . . this has gone on long enough."

Lorvinn kept her face neutral. "To which 'this' do you refer?"

Krynneth fumbled at his wide leather belt, from which depended his personal sword. More symbolism there. "Surely I don't have to tell you."

"Humor me."

Krynneth rolled his eyes in exasperation. "Oh, Lady, why are you doing this? It's to fortify the punishment you've laid on yourself, isn't it? Making me catalog your one failure in four years of Wardenship." He gestured around the austere room. "As if this weren't punishment enough. And don't think I don't know about the bristle shirt."

"Humor me," Lorvinn repeated.

Krynneth's eyes flashed. "Eight damn it, Lady, you *do* want me to say it, don't you? Very well. You think you betrayed the hold—first by letting Kraxxi escape, then by choosing to follow him yourself for fear word of that would come to light. And finally by including me, Merryn, and the triplets from Ixti in the pursuit."

"Which resulted in Merryn's escape—defection—who knows?—to Ixti. And our disgrace."

"We couldn't have helped it," Krynneth gave back. "Merryn's a rare woman and one most folks underestimate, including both of us. Hopefully Kraxxi underestimated her as well. If she found him, fine; if not . . . she'll either continue to search, or die. If the latter, she'll die doing what she thought was right."

"Which is what I'm doing," Lorvinn snapped. "I betrayed the hold and my position in it and my kinsmen and my craft and my clan. Maybe even my King, if Kraxxi was the spy I think he was. I do *not* deserve to command for that."

Krynneth flopped back against the wall, arms folded across his chest. "Whatever punishment you think you deserve, Hold-Warden, you aren't the only one to suffer because of it. By abdicating, you thought to forestall your disgrace, yet who would've done differently in your place? Who would've expected treachery from Merryn, for one thing? And which of those who have replaced you could have done better?"

stairs beyond the central arch. Men—and women, he supposed—in tabards of Warcraft crimson. The first real resistance they'd met. Barrax's men surged forward in turn, blocking the way, holding the defenders at bay on the stairs, raising square shields a quarter span wide and half a span high as they knelt so that spearmen could thrust their long deadly shafts between. A few archers dared shots as well—the high ceiling permitted that. Zrill could see little of their effect, though he moved toward that battle with the rest. Men shouted in Eronese—not in panic, but surprise. From what he could see from his vantage a dozen strides away, the Ixtian warriors were slowly forcing their way up the stairs. Which was part of the strategy: a strong force to fan out, ever renewed from behind, and with specific goals—to meet a force taken unaware, that must assemble from all parts of the citadel without any central command initially, and having only guesses as to where the invaders might be. All resulting in an uncoordinated defense.

A noise at his back made Zrill swing around—to find a wild-eyed stable-boy who'd evidently hidden through the preliminary sweep. To Zrill's dismay, he was armed with a pitchfork, and had in fact stabbed the soldier behind him in the thigh. The man went down in a tangle of armor, weaponry, and blood. Zrill was suddenly exposed. He stepped into the void, stabbing at the fork with his sword, knocking the weapon aside with reasonable ease, for it was too big and clumsy for someone who couldn't be much older than eleven. The boy's eyes widened in pain—likely from the impact—and Zrill pushed past his guard. He started to swing at the unprotected neck, which would be merciful, then thought of shifting to the heart-stab, which would be cleaner. In the end, he wrestled the boy down and cracked him smartly between the eyes with the sword hilt. Let someone else finish him if they would; he hadn't joined the army to kill boys. Someone gave him a hand up as he rose. He met the eyes behind the helm: his best mate, Trimm. What he could see of Trimm's face was grim. He nodded approval, and dragged Zrill away. Somehow they'd wound up near the tail of their group.

But the battle plan was clearer. The central half of the invading force, which was still being swelled by soldiers coming through the secret route from outside, were pushing their way up the stairs. He had no idea what the right flank was doing, save that it involved the doors on that side. But his own commander was mounting a massive assault on the heavy oak panels on the left, using one of the few siege weapons the Ixtians had perfected that the arrogant Eronese had not.

Giant's Fingers, it was called. It consisted of a narrow iron point that could be driven between the halves of a double door, or between a door and jamb, far enough to admit additional thicker points to either side. These were connected by a scissors action, and, when forced in opposite directions, could pull most doors far enough apart to spring whatever locks or hinges they might have. Or splinter wood outright.

Zrill heard the lock explode on this set, and the agonized rip of thick oak being torn asunder. A moment later, someone was brave enough to reach through with another, similar, tool and snap the bar.

Not until the doors swung back did they meet any resistance, and Zrill wasn't in range of that combat. What he could see, as he rushed forward with the rest, were shirtless young men sheened with sweat, wet rags wrapped around their heads. Most were fairly dirty, though their eyes were white and wild. Heat rode forward with them, with billows of steam and a stronger sulfur smell. The bulk were simply armed: a few swords or daggers, though many carried long iron bars. Perhaps they'd found the forge, Zrill thought, as he shifted his grip on his blade, seeking an opportunity to strike, but finding progress impeded by stone walls to the left. He stepped on something soft, startled to find it one of his comrades he'd not seen fall, in what was becoming a one-sided battle ahead.

"It's the heat plant," someone hissed. "It's how these folks survive the cold."

Zrill merely shrugged and struggled onward, as the skirmish ebbed and flowed. And then the man before him was falling, and he was in the front ranks. He leapt over the body, stuck his sword without thinking into the heart of an older man armed with a blade shorter than Zrill's, and then casually batted aside the wrist of the woman who took his place, a bloody dagger in either hand. She gave him the best fight he'd had—or the most dangerous, depending on how one looked at it—and fought like someone well versed in such things. In the end, Zrill had to cripple her, taking off one hand outright, and laying open her other arm from elbow to wrist. He left her in her blood, trusting to the heavy boots of those behind to finish what he'd started.

And then space roared around him, and he released a breath he didn't know he'd been holding, relieved at finding himself unconfined. He leapt to the left to accommodate those behind, and found himself staring up at rank upon rank of massive stone and metal blocks each four spans square, their tops crowned by countless pipes and ducts, many thrice as thick as his body. A complexity of valves and gears at waist level fronted them, serving some function Zrill couldn't fathom.

That they were important, however, was evident by the fierceness of the fighting around them. Someone jostled Zrill, and he started, then joined the rest—forgot everything except reflex, and succumbed to the ritual of advance, stab, parry; advance, parry, stab, and leap that quickly ruled his world. A final thrust into a naked torso, and then the slow rise of breathy silence as the battle ended. Zrill wiped sweat from his eyes with a finger through the eyeslots of his helm—and realized that the chamber was taken.

"Check for other entrances and secure them," the commander yelled. "Disable the controls on these, and follow me—we must rejoin our fellows."

"Disable?" someone challenged.

"Let them freeze," came the commander's reply.

Zrill, who by virtue of being one of the farthest from the entrance was among the last to leave, wondered if he was the only one to hear someone call in clumsy, Eronese-accented Ixtian, "No, you fools! You have no idea what you've done."

And then Zrill reached the entrance, and let the corridor enclose him with wet stone walls, but clearer air and cooler. And then they reached the stables again, and joined the upward battle.

Pain flowed down Krynneth's arm like a fresh-forged blade slicing ice. Except that he'd never planned to be on the receiving end of Eronese steel hilted by Ixtian smiths and wielded by an Ixtian soldier. He endured the pain stoically. To succumb would mean his life, and survival must come first. If only he'd thought to bring a shield to his meeting with Lorvinn—but that had been a ceremonial encounter. At least he had his sword and knew how to use it. Unfortunately, so did his opponent: a man about his size, face hidden save for dark eyes that caught the glare of the torches as Krynneth led what passed on this level as a charge toward the gate tower. Forget the central keep. It had fallen first, to forces welling up from the stables below, and down from the Warden's quarters in the topmost level. Whether Dormill, who'd succeeded Lorvinn, had survived, he didn't know—nor care. For good or ill, Lorvinn was his leader.

If only he could find her.

Steel flashed in from his right, the follow-through of the blow that had opened his left arm. He parried the blow, then twisted his blade beneath it, as he stepped back and ducked. And then stabbed: an economical blow, if one were strong-wristed. Not what the foe would expect.

His point found resistance, but he ducked again, and lunged, felt the foe's sword slide off his shoulders as he drove his point through mail and leather into flesh, then danced back to withdraw it. The man screamed and staggered. His chin strap broke and Krynneth got a glimpse of a face as young as his own, but gray with pain and despair. The sword slipped from failing fingers. The man raised his chin, even as he clamped hands across the gushing wound below his sternum. Krynneth read the gesture, and gave him the mercy cut: ear to ear.

But only because the battle had moved on.

He raced to catch up: along the corridors within the outer walls, where he'd hoped resistance would be less. If they could reach the gatehouse and hold it, they could isolate Barrax's troops *and* ensure their own escape.

Oblivious to his aching arm and the blood trail he was leaving, Krynneth careened around a corner, seeking a battle he could hear but not yet see. How bad his wound was, he had no idea. He might die of blood loss; might not. In either case, his duty was to the hold.

The corridor he stumbled into was short and lit only from the larger passages to either side. It took a moment to realize that he'd also stumbled onto Lorvinn herself, with a band of half-clad soldiers at her back, forcing a smaller force of Ixtians in Krynneth's direction. His comrades saw him—maybe. Silently as he could, he crept forward, holding to the shadows, trying to still his breath. Closer. There were six of them. With any luck . . .

One fell. The soldiers poured over him. Krynneth moved. A quick leap—slash—roll across the hallway took an Ixtian across the back of his knees. The one next to him got a continuation of the same blow across his left arm and back, and Krynneth managed to slam his fist into the side of the last man's head before he reached the wall. Fortunately that man was right-handed, and had any response blocked by the wall, which gave Lorvinn herself time to finish him.

With three men suddenly moaning on the stone floor, the remaining two Ixtians bolted. One fell to a bold Eronese spearman who jumped one of the fallen to stab the man in the back. The other made it to the end of the corridor and fled. Krynneth started after, but Lorvinn restrained him. Her face was awash with sweat beneath her crooked helm, and her sword was red to the hilt, with the same red staining the wool robe beneath her hauberk. "No," she rasped. "I have another task for you. And not one for a coward, though it may seem otherwise."

"Aye, Lady," Krynneth gasped, as half Lorvinn's small force moved past at a sign from her. Someone grabbed his arm and tied a rag around it near his shoulder.

Lorvinn spared a glance down the hall. "Someone needs to get word of this to the King. Others may have thought the same, but I order you to flee this place. There's a stair to the Guard-Hall near here that only the Wardens know about. Take it to there. Rally anyone you find, if any there still be—there's a chance they don't know of this. From there—remember the exit I showed you."

"But—!"

"Go!" Lorvinn shouted, giving him a push. "Third door, second chamber, press the black door in the tapestry twice. Now go!"

Krynneth started to protest, but Lorvinn was already striding away from him, following the Guard. Krynneth watched for a dozen breaths—long enough to catch his own—then followed the Warden's instructions. A moment later, with guilt a burden on his shoulders, only slightly salved by responsibility, he was following turn after turn of stairs down and down and down.

Lorvinn was fighting for two things. Her life—or her honor, which was effectively the same thing—and to protect the secrets of the hold. She was seeing fewer hold folk all the time, and fewer yet alive, while every turn seemed to bring her and her ragged band of loyalists into combat with an ever-increasing host of grim, dark-faced men in Ixtian livery. Worse, she hadn't managed to find either the acting Hold-Warden, or any of the sept commanders. Granted, most would've been in bed—or preparing for it. But surely this attack hadn't been so well planned it could've taken out all of them, especially as they varied their sleep schedule to a set rotation.

Not that it mattered as she strode along little-used corridors in one wing of the Middle Hold, intent on preserving one other thing. The hold itself might be lost now, but she could ensure that no more secrets fell into Barrax's hands than she could help. And so, she bent her steps toward the Lore hall.

Happily, the hall wasn't located in the part of the hold where the attack had been concentrated. If she was lucky—

She wasn't. She darted up an atypically wide and straight staircase two steps at a time—only to meet a force coming down: three men, in finer robes and better-weaponed than any she'd met before. She charged them, relying on loyalty to close ranks with her. Her sword clanged against that of the man who moved to meet her. A thrust from behind her took his life, and she hurtled on—almost to the landing. She returned the favor of a thrust an instant later, while someone grabbed the spear the third Ixtian had poked forward and yanked—catapulting him down the stairs, even as blows rained down on him. He reached the floor in pieces.

By then Lorvinn had moved on. The doors to the Lore hall stood closed across a corridor at the top of the stairs, but she heard other steps pounding toward her from the side: heavily armed men at a run. She fumbled at the catch—the place was never locked—and felt it give. More troops veered into view. She braced, then relaxed. They were her own people, under the command of Vorminn, Hold-Warden himself. Not many, but better armed than her band.

"You had the same idea I did," she shouted.

Vorminn wasn't looking at her. He was gazing back the way he'd come—while Lorvinn's troops kept watch on the larger chamber below. "Fire it if you can!" Vorminn shouted. "They're coming—everywhere!"

Lorvinn hesitated but an instant, then opened the doors and slipped inside. Her men would have to forgive her desertion. It was Eron's forgiveness she sought now, and no other. Scarcely looking at the racks of books and manuscripts towering around her on every side, she grabbed the nearest, strewing precious documents on the floor. A candle guttered nearby. She flung it atop the heap, not bothering to watch as she continued around the enormous room, adding fuel to the fire growing by the door. Once she ripped a tapestry down and added it, then found a cache of lamp oil and hurled it atop a series of particularly important codices. Most were duplicated at War-Hold-Main, but not all—not the latest research and theory. It would perish now, but maybe some of it could be reconstructed.

On and on she moved—halfway around the hall—while fire roared behind her, merging with the crackle of charring pages. Smoke filled the air. She coughed. Her eyes watered. She thought of fleeing, but she'd left loyal men and women outside, facing their doom; she could do no less. A quick survey showed a third of the room in flames. If she didn't hurry, it would be her pyre.

Raising her cloak across her face, she staggered through litter, sparks, and wayward burning pages toward the door. The heat beat her back at first— fire by the door had been a mistake, but she'd been working on reflex, not logic. Or maybe that had *been* logic: Deny access, and damn the consequences. A second try put her at the exit. Fire licked the hem of her robe. She beat at it absently as she set her shoulder against the studded oak. It moved— slowly, as though something lay against it. What, she dared not think.

But then she was through, though she could barely see for the tears in her eyes, or hear for her own coughing. Shapes swam into view from either side—but not until she heard them speak did she recognize them.

Not by their voices, but their language. The buzzy, hard-voweled accents of Ixti.

She grabbed for the door, intent on self-immolation.

Too late. A blow to her wrist numbed her hand. A press of bodies bore her to the floor, and then away. Her heels thumped against every tread as they dragged her down the stairs. "Send water," she heard someone yell— thank The Eight she had a good grasp of the Ixtian tongue. "Save what you can. If nothing else survives, we need the Lore hall!"

And then she was being dragged along smooth marble. Not without a struggle, of course, but a mailed fist to the head made her see stars and flirt with a darkness deeper than night.

Abruptly, she was jerked to her feet, and spun around, only to be thrown to the floor again. Unable to break her fall, her face hit the pavement— hard. Something shattered in her nose, and her throat filled with blood. Its sick/sweet odor fought with the smoke in her nostrils. Her head swam.

Someone knocked her helm aside and yanked her up by the hair. She saw boots: fine elegant boots of tooled leather, ornamented with gold leaf and jeweled filigree. She saw the hem of a gold-embroidered robe of black velvet, and then dared look higher—high as the belt, which was tooled to match the boots, but which also bore a fantastically worked geen-claw dagger. A hand clutched it, gloved in mail and black suede, but what caught her eye was the ring. Carved gold it was. Lorvinn looked closer, blinking through tears of pain her mind could not suppress.

It blurred. Cleared. Blurred again. And then she saw: the arms of Ixti.

"Your Majesty," she heard someone say, "we believe this woman to be the Hold-Warden."

Lorvinn grabbed frantically at the dagger—to what purpose she had no idea. Feet came down atop her, bearing her to the floor. A rib cracked. A boot stomped her hand and pain argued there with numbness seeping down from her wrist.

"My name is Lorvinn san Ferr-een," she gasped. "Kill me now, whoever you are, for I deserve to die."

"No," came a voice as cold as a wind off the northern ice. "I will not kill you, though die you will. But only when certain others can witness that dying."

And then something hit her head, and she saw no more.

Krynneth had to halt halfway down the stairs to sit down. He had no choice, really; the steady movement, the exertion of the descent, and the demands the steep treads made on his legs and balance required it. As did the queasiness rising in his stomach, that might be a response to pain, the tight spiral, or even the preposterousness of the situation. In any event he sank down on a step, barely able to see despite the feeble light of an ancient glow-globe some turns below. The silence overwhelmed him, and he thought briefly that he ought simply to lie there and sleep. Then, when he thought it was safe, he could sneak out again and slay the Ixtians in their beds. Probably that would happen anyway. War-Hold was a warren of secret rooms, halls, and stairs.

Which of course assumed Ixti's success, which wasn't guaranteed, though it seemed likely. Attacked at night, with no warning, from two directions, the battle wouldn't go in the hold's favor. Not in a place designed to be attacked from without, not within. And he knew who was to blame, too. If not Kraxxi's fault, it was his lover's. Merryn's.

Only six people he was aware of knew that secret exit, three of whom had gone north into Eron. He and Lorvinn were two more, which left Merryn. Merryn, whom Krynneth had admired almost as much as he'd admired Lorvinn herself.

Dizziness swam near. Krynneth bent over, removed his helm, and let his head fall between his knees. Darkness encroached, then retreated, leaving him marginally more alert. He donned the helm again but didn't buckle it, and rose—carefully, bracing himself against the wall.

And continued down.

He found the door before he expected it, and pressed a hidden stud. Stone slid sideways, revealing a large, dimly lit chamber hewn from solid stone: the assembly hall of the Night Guard, where someone was supposed always to be on duty.

Someone was—or had been.

Thirty of them actually: caught unaware and murdered by a force that had found the outer door but not the inner, which confirmed what Krynneth had suspected. That door, which he'd never seen opened, had given onto the secret corridor by which his foes had entered. He'd seen it from the outside the night of Kraxxi's escape and their aborted pursuit. Seen it and wondered. Clearly the invaders had as well—to the Guard's regret.

But there were other ways in and out, one of which Lorvinn had only revealed to him four days ago.

Stepping over the body of a woman named Vynyn, he knelt to press a series of floor tiles in sequence, and was relieved to see another section of wall slide sideways. He was in it before it fully opened, fumbling for the closure stud. Found it—and moved on—through pitch-dark, which forced him to shuffle along lest he stumble, while he raked the wall to his left with his less functional arm.

On and on he traveled, through the dark, sometimes tending uphill, sometimes down, aware only of the increasing cold and his own growing weakness, and, more and more, of a pounding in the silence that was the sound of his heart pumping an ever-decreasing supply of blood.

Kraxxi sat in a padded chair to which he was bound by golden clamps and golden chains two spans away from Merryn, who was likewise accoutered, and watched firelight flicker and flare over War-Hold. Men guarded them ten deep to every side. The land between the hold's crag and that on which they sat opposite the hold's southern side was plowed to ruts by hooves and the odd war machine, where a thousand of Barrax's elite troops had made their way by stealth through what once had been a secret gate and was no longer.

Cold wind bit at him; he shuddered even in the ceremonial fur and armor they'd provided to mark him part of this expedition. Stars rode overhead, but no moons, which was one reason the attack had been mounted when it had. Kraxxi wondered what time it was, and when this would all be over.

But more than that, he wondered about Merryn. He tried to catch her eye, but they'd bound her head in a padded vise so that she could only look toward the hold she had betrayed. Her mouth was gagged, but her eyes were open, held that way by clamps. A woman stood nearby, dripping water into them. It was Barrax's idea, not Lynnz's. Proof that a king could be crueler than any torturer.

At least they hadn't torched the place—not that it would burn anyway. Though full of fine wood, carpet, and tapestries, the bulk of the hold was thick stone. Even a major fire would be confined, though not its poisonous smoke, perhaps, or other noxious fumes. In any event, it had been four hands since the attack had begun, and resolution, if any, should be imminent.

As if in reply, a flare rose from the central tower, exploding overhead in a burst of green and white. Proof War-Hold was, to Barrax's satisfaction, taken.

Kraxxi wondered why his father had bothered to put himself at risk to lead the attack. It was foolish and rash.

But perhaps he was like Kraxxi. Perhaps he wanted a glimpse of the splendors their cold northern rival could produce during its forced confinement.

All Kraxxi knew was that he was sick—at heart, and almost physically ill as well. He had brought this to pass. People he knew and liked were dead or dying. People who'd trusted him, who'd sparred with him, who'd given him books to read, who'd treated him like a kinsman and friend.

All . . . dead.

He closed his eyes to shut it out, but was jerked back to attention by the pounding of hoofbeats on the slope below. Dark shapes showed, moving across the muddy grass, shapes that slowly resolved into riders. Long before they arrived, however, Kraxxi had identified them, by the glitter of gold on weapons, helms, and armor, as his father's personal guard. To his great surprise, however, they didn't veer to the right, toward Barrax's hastily raised tent, but galloped straight toward him, not stopping until they reached the ring of torchlight that turned trampled grass to molten gold.

The king himself leapt down, tossing his reins to a groom with practiced nonchalance, then gestured to his companions. Kraxxi squinted into the glare. They were helping someone from a horse, it appeared. A prisoner, he supposed. But why . . . ?

His father had doffed his helm and was marching toward him. His face was sheened with sweat and his hair was plastered to his skull like paint. Blotches of darkness on armor and clothing hinted at more stains than smoke. All at once, Barrax was before him. He reached to his waist and drew out his sword, thrusting it beneath Kraxxi's nose. Blood glistened on it, still wet for all it had been scabbarded. "The blood of Eron," Barrax sneered. "Given to me by you—or by your lady, who followed you!"

Kraxxi tried to close his eyes, to look away, but at a sign from Barrax, two of Kraxxi's guards seized him, forcing his eyes open.

Barrax grinned, and wiped the sword along Kraxxi's throat—not to cut, but to mark him there.

And then the king moved on to Merryn. Who ignored his taunts completely, as he repeated what he'd done to Kraxxi.

"Enough!" the king barked. "Bring the prisoner."

Kraxxi followed the sound of movement to his left, and saw the prisoner being hauled to Barrax's feet, a span to Kraxxi's right. It was a woman, and not young, in rough clothing splattered with blood and permeated with the stench of smoke. Still, she must be important. Kraxxi tried to make out the shadowed face beneath the grime. No one he knew. Or maybe— She'd sat back on her haunches now, and he had a clearer view.

Lorvinn! Warden of War-Hold. And Merryn's kin. He saw her stiffen, heard a muffled cry of alarm he suspected she regretted, given what it might have betrayed.

"Hold her," the king snapped, and moved toward Kraxxi. "Release him!" he continued, to Kraxxi's guards. "But keep him in chains. If he makes to escape, hamstring him."

At those words, movement seethed around him. Hands reached to unclamp his wrists and ankles from their fetters, leaving the manacles and joining-chains. But behind those who wielded the keys, he saw rank after rank of drawn swords and spears. And damn his father for it.

"Give him a sword," Barrax rasped. Then, when he saw a ghost of hesitation, he strode forward and thrust his own into Kraxxi's hands. Confined by the chains, and half-numbed by the clamps, Kraxxi nearly dropped it. Certainly there was no way to strike at his father. Which he doubted was the intent in any case. But what—?

"Bring him here," Barrax spat, motioning Kraxxi and his captors toward the kneeling Warden.

A flurry of confusion followed, and then Barrax himself eased beside Kraxxi and maneuvered him before the woman he once had known. Dimly he recalled how Lorvinn had looked down on him in judgment the day after he'd been brought captive to War-Hold. She'd tempered justice with mercy then. He owed her much. Or did he? If she'd had him slain outright fewer people would be suffering now. If only he could turn the sword on himself. But he knew he would be forestalled.

"Kill her," Barrax rasped.

Kraxxi blinked at him. He'd heard the words, and they made sense, yet they carried no real meaning.

"Kill her!" Barrax repeated coldly. "Or watch Merryn die a joint at a time as we march north."

Kraxxi closed his eyes, wishing this were all a dream—a nightmare, even. A delusion born of scorpion sting. Anything but what he would see when he opened his eyes again. But open them he did, when he heard the scrape of steel to his right.

He saw Lorvinn looking up at him. Her face was smudged and streaked with smoky sweat, yet her eyes were calm. No accusation showed there, only calm resignation.

"I can't," he choked.

Barrax slapped him hard. His cheek stung. Blood filled his mouth from a cut cheek. "Kill her, boy, or Merryn dies!"

Lorvinn said nothing.

Kraxxi took a deep breath—and dropped the sword.

Barrax grabbed it before it hit the ground, and forced it once more into Kraxxi's grasp. But this time he didn't let go. Rather, he stepped behind his son and with inexorable force secured his grip on the weapon—Kraxxi's hand on the hilt, but Barrax's hand on Kraxxi's—and with slow deliberation, pressed the blade into Lorvinn's breast. She recoiled reflexively— whereupon four men grabbed her and pinned her spread-eagled on the earth. Barrax wrestled Kraxxi forward until he stood above her, then, again, lowered the sword to her chest. Kraxxi tried to struggle, but to no avail. All he could do was try not to watch, try not to feel, try not to sense anything at all, as Eronese steel pierced Eronese mail and Eronese wool, and finally entered High Clan Eronese flesh.

At least he was able to exert a tiny twist of control at the last, so that it was quickly over.

Abruptly, the pressure was gone—as was the sword. He sagged back and would've fallen had hands not grabbed him and dragged him back to his chair.

Barrax hadn't moved. He was staring down at the first of what Kraxxi supposed would be many vanquished foes.

And he was still standing there ten breaths later, when a low rumble jarred the land, quaking up through their boots, and making tent poles and standards tremble. Kraxxi glanced up at once, fearing—or hoping—that the fire mountain on whose knees the hold was raised was voicing its protest. Or that, perhaps, he might be about to witness a physical manifestation of the so-far mythical Eight.

The rumbling increased alarmingly. An explosion lit the night. Fire was only part of it, however. Mostly it was pressurized steam released abruptly, as the untended heat plant beneath the hold did what Barrax himself had forbidden—and blew War-Hold-Winter, the guardian-gate to Eron's southern flank, to flinders.

Kraxxi watched numbly. They all did. Yet only when the sun rose did they grasp the true scope of the devastation. The central keep was gone, and with it a length of wall across which it had fallen. Fire sparked here and there. Maybe some survived—on either side; Kraxxi doubted Barrax cared. The power of War-Hold was broken. Spring was in the air, and the north of Eron waited.

Among those who rode out the following morning were a soldier named Zrill, who remembered someone saying in the bowels of the hold that they were fools, and a woman named Merryn, to whom breath itself was now a burden.

With them, and two thousand others, went a packtrain filled with Eronese war gear and Warcraft cloaks and armor.

Half a night ahead of them, a bleeding young man named Krynneth had also seen the explosion, but had not gone back to investigate. Rather, he set heel to the horse he'd found running wild outside the secret gate, and raced daylight and the armies of Ixti toward the High King of all Eron.

CHAPTER XVII:

MARKERS CALLED

(ERON: TIR-ERON: THE CITADEL— NEAR SPRING: DAY XXVII—EVENING)

A vall was making lackluster sketches for a new royal helm—and doing even that without conviction—when he heard footsteps approaching the suite in the Citadel to which he'd been spirited after the incident in Eddyn's cell. Officially, it was to protect him from Tyrill's inquiries, but of course she'd found out anyway—or found out enough. Eellon had told her about the gem sometime back, but not having seen it, she hadn't believed him until the Craft-Chief had reminded her that Avall's arrival there in the middle of Deep Winter constituted more than sufficient proof that *something* untoward had occurred. The matter of Eddyn was more difficult, because no one but a handful of guards and the King had seen him. But Avall *had* been beaten. And Rrath was back at Priest-Hold, which couldn't be denied, either. So Tyrill had been forced to accept that something *had* occurred, to which her Chief and her King were both witness. She'd also had sense enough to agree that the gem's purported qualities were more important than intraclan rivalry, and was as alarmed as the rest at Eddyn's sudden—and patently impossible—disappearance, though not necessarily for the same reason.

Not that it mattered now, when someone was approaching—under escort, Avall assumed, which usually wasn't good. At times like this, he needed Strynn and Rann, separately or together. Even Lykkon, to whom he'd grown much closer since his return, would do.

But this was almost certainly either the King himself, or—

"Chief," he heard someone mutter without, and surmised by the rapid steps that it wasn't Tyrill, who could barely walk since a certain escapade outdoors. Eellon, then, or Tryffon of Ferr.

He rose automatically, dismissing the sketches with a disgusted shrug that was typical of his attitude these days. The first knock sounded as he found his feet. He snugged the ties of his house-robe and made for the door. "Open, boy," came a voice from without. "It's me, Eellon."

Avall breathed a sigh of relief. He shot the bolt and heaved the portal open, to admit his mentor. Alone, save for the inevitable Lykkon, who somehow managed to continue his studies at Lore and play squire all at once. A pair of guards remained outside: Myx and his former commander, Veen— who likewise looked to have attached herself to Eellon permanently.

Eellon took a seat without asking. After giving Lykkon a perfunctory hug, Avall also sat. Lykkon opened a hot jar of cider, filled three mugs, then joined them, note-scroll in hand. He watched everything, Avall knew. Saw everything. Probably knew more than anyone in the hold except Eellon himself.

Eellon looked tired—which was typical of him these days. Still, his eyes roved across the sketches as a cook might sniff odors upon entering a strange kitchen. "Not your best work," he muttered.

Avall shrugged. "Hard to care about something you've already done."

"Do something else."

"It was the best work I've ever done. But I need the gem—"

"So you think. That only made it faster, so you said."

"It also gave me finer control. I—"

"That's for later," Eellon sighed, accepting a mug from Lykkon. "I'm here now as your Clan-Chief, though without my robe and hood."

Avall raised a brow.

"I need you to sit in Council tomorrow."

Avall shook his head. "I can't. I—"

Eellon slammed his mug down with a thump. "It isn't a choice, boy. I need you there to support your King and your clan. I need you there to support me! I need you there as proof—as a distraction, if you must know."

"From what?"

"Tyrill's making her move, fool that she is. She claims she's got proof of Gynn's injury and intends to demand he step down."

"Even with the gem loose in the world?"

"She's decided to blame Eddyn's disappearance on Gynn's commission."

"That's insane!"

"So is she, I sometimes think."

"That will upset—everything."

"I see you've grasped the implications."

"But he's not up for Proving until autumn. Even Tyrill knows that."

"He shouldn't be, but Tyrill's going to try to force the issue. If nothing else, she'll have groundwork laid for Sundeath."

"Meanwhile Eddyn—"

"Eddyn is the King's problem right now. Nor does he need this distraction. Which is why *we* need another one."

Avall shook his head. "I . . . don't know, sir. I'm— Dammit, Two-father, I'm just so—" He broke off and stared at his mug. "You have no idea how I feel, sir. Without the gem— Well, I had no idea how dependent on it I'd become. But it's like . . . like losing one of my senses. Like I'm only half-alive."

Eellon slapped him. Not hard, but it stung. Lykkon looked up with a start. "I'm tired of this self-pity, boy. You made an important discovery and did a brave and very foolish thing that was still, probably, the right thing. And you've suffered a loss because of it, but that doesn't mean you can play hermit for the rest of your life. Eight, lad, I see maybe a third as well as I did in my prime. I can't half hear, and everything tastes the same. You've seen the braces I use to maintain the illusion that I'm still vigorous, and you know how much *they* hurt. All you have to deal with is the lack of something you didn't *have* three eighths ago."

"It's like being blind, then seeing," Avall snapped back. "And then losing it again. Wouldn't you be bitter about that?"

"I'd be grateful it had happened at all," Eellon retorted coldly. And rose. "I will see you in Council tomorrow, sitting by my side, in full clan regalia. Even if I have to drag you there myself. I'm sorry it's come to this, but sometimes there's no time for nicety."

"And what shall I say if I'm questioned?"

"The truth," Eellon sighed. "The time for lies is over."

And with that, he swept from the room. Lykkon lingered long enough to give Avall's shoulders a comradely squeeze, then he, too, fled, leaving Avall to stare at indifferent drawings and wonder if he had once again attracted the eye—or ire—of Fate.

(THE HALL OF CLANS—NEAR SPRING: DAY XIV—MORNING)

"Slide your hood back a bit," Eellon growled, as he and Avall prepared to enter the Hall of Clans for the latest convocation of the Council of Chiefs, which met every sixteen days throughout the year. "We need you to be recognized. People pondering rumors won't pay as much attention to other things, if we're lucky."

Avall tried not to glare at him. Eellon was right, in his way: Avall had played hermit too long. Meanwhile the world was as full of mysteries as ever, and none would wait on him.

Eellon had timed his arrival carefully—with royal connivance, Avall suspected—so that most of the other Clan- and Craft-Chiefs were already seated when he made his way into the hall. It would be Avall's first time on the floor; the last time he'd been here was as a first-time observer at the High King's Proving, the previous Sundeath. He'd occupied one of the galleries then. But Chiefs were allowed aides, and a certain number of adults rotated in and out of the floor seats regardless.

The main difference Avall observed, as he followed Eellon down the carpeted marble of the particular spoke assigned to their clan and let the vast surge of stonework rise over him, was that the Stone on the dais was caged by a simple wooden throne.

The King himself wasn't present, nor would be until every Chief had deposited a ball in the counting chute beside his or her seat. Only when a quorum was tallied would he grace them with his presence.

In the meantime, Avall tried to match Eellon's dignity as he paced in measured steps toward Argen's wedge. A hush followed him, vanguard of a murmur of surprise that indicated Eellon still had his flare for spectacle. Avall hoped it also meant that some of those present didn't know he'd returned to Tir-Eron impossibly early. Unfortunately, too many people were accidentally privy to the odd events surrounding him, and even the King had no illusions as to the force of rumor. Or its accuracy.

Tyrill was already seated in her accustomed place on the craft side of the clan's section, nor did she stand when Eellon steered his way past half a dozen other mostly unoccupied seats to claim his own beside her. Avall took the one to Eellon's right—officially, as clan scribe—and followed his two-father's example in pulling his hood as far forward as it would go. "Regrettable," Eellon muttered. "It's supposed to symbolize the darkness of the ignorance that exists without debate—until the King comes in."

Barely had he uttered those words than the King arrived, clad in his cloak of state, and with the Iron Crown of Contention upon his hair, token, Avall supposed, of his mood. Two priests followed: Law and World, who would act as heralds and organizers. The King sat without fanfare. The Council followed his lead. After the usual welcomes, ritual blessings, and avowals of loyalty, truth, and service, he got down to business. Normally, those with matters to be brought before the Throne entered their requests with the heralds and were summoned forward in the King's good time. Today, however, Gynn simply cleared his throat and announced, "Lady Tyrill, I understand you have a matter you would like addressed?"

Avall saw Eellon grin, and imagined his Chief had seen what Avall had: that the King had phrased the challenge in such a way that she'd have to choose which of her agendas she'd present first. Whatever her choice, none would concern the gem directly, because that was Eellon's prerogative. Besides which, she knew next to nothing about it, and Tyrill always preferred to fight from a position of strength.

Rising stiffly, she made her way down to the Chair of Demands, which sat on the floor below the dais. She settled into it with a clumsiness that made Avall feel sorry for her. "Majesty," she began.

Gynn inclined his head with formal grace. "Chief."

"I will be brief, Majesty," she rasped, the room's perfect acoustics amplifying her voice. "You know as well as I that the Law states that the King must be perfect—in mind and body—in order to properly reverence The Eight."

"In order to serve as the most suitable receptacle for The Eight, when They choose to speak through him," Gynn corrected. "There is a difference. The King is always the King, but sometimes he is more than the King."

Tyrill sniffed. "And sometimes he is less than the King, which brings me to my business. Majesty . . . you have been limping since shortly past Midwinter. It is time you explained that. And," she continued, "if the cause be a matter which . . . compromises your perfection, you had best consider your responsibility under Law to step down from your throne."

Half the room gasped in surprise. Even Avall, who'd known what to expect, was shocked by the old woman's bluntness. Eellon was on his feet in a finely timed instant. "My Lady Chief," he cried, then waited for the King to acknowledge him. Gynn did, by pointing the dagger of state he'd chosen instead of his usual scepter—another sign he expected heavy wrangling.

"Lady Chief," Eellon repeated, when the room had fallen silent. "Did you observe the King limping when he entered?"

"One can endure—or mask—anything for a dozen paces."

"Or The Eight can," came a voice from Beast. An ally Avall hadn't expected.

Tyrill didn't reply—which was wise. To do so now would risk denigrating The Eight before the Council.

"Nor does it matter," rumbled Tryffon of Ferr. "The King has been Proven for this year. Autumn is soon enough to address these claims."

"But if I am right," Tyrill countered, "we will have more time *this* time to choose a proper successor."

"And if you are wrong," the King broke in casually, "you will have wasted a great deal of this Council's time, when there are more important matters to consider—including," he stressed, "yet more charges to be leveled at your two-son."

"Who is not present to hear them, which is his right."

"Whose absence is the *cause* of some of those charges," the King retorted.

Intrigued as he was by the pace of the events, Avall couldn't resist letting his gaze drift around the chamber.

Most councilmen looked utterly dumbfounded, as though this were the first time they'd heard of the Eddyn situation—either his attacks on Avall and Rrath, or his disappearance. Others—notably in War, Lore, Stone, and Priest—seemed carefully neutral. A few—mostly those clans to which Tyrill had applied for aid in opposing Gynn's raising in the first place—appeared angry at having their coup disrupted before it truly got under way. As eyes turned in Argen's direction, Avall scratched his head, which coincidentally let his hood slide back. A good third of the faces gazing at him registered shock or amazement.

Young Meenon of Glass was the first to respond aloud. "What's *he* doing here? He's supposed to be—"

"Serving his King," Gynn finished for him. "He was and he is, and he dared the Deep to do it."

A mutter of disbelief scampered around the room. "Alone?" someone else called.

"Not at first. He was accompanied by Rann syn Eemon."

"Who is . . . where?" Eemon's Chief inquired, though he'd known for almost two eighths.

"He had to return to Gem-Hold," Avall replied loudly, forgetting it was not his right to respond without royal recognition.

"We were speaking," Gynn broke in, "about Eddyn."

"He's part of this," Eellon retorted. A pause, to let that sink in, then: "Majesty, I think it's time we all heard Avall's story."

Tyrill stood abruptly, turning to address the assembly—and blatantly presenting her back to the King. "You are all fools," she snapped.

"Tyrill?" The King's voice was cold, but it stopped her in her tracks.

"Majesty?" she managed.

"You will have the answer you desire in due course, but until then . . . we both know there are more important matters to be laid bare, matters that will be even more difficult to prove than your accusation."

Not until Tyrill had found her seat again did any voice rise above a murmur.

"Avall syn Argen-a," the King said. "Come here. Your Sovereign would address you."

Avall felt a knot of concern rise in his stomach, but tried to mask it with a facade of calm. He rose and started toward the aisle—and had just edged past the last Argen-a subcraft-chief when the pain hit him.

He froze where he stood, one foot in the aisle. A strangled cry trickled from his lips.

Another pain, like the first. A griping in his lower gut as though someone had set a knife there and twisted. His first thought was poison; his second to wonder why he was suddenly so dizzy. And then a third pain hit him and forced him to his knees. Another followed. They were coming in waves, he realized blearily, as consciousness ebbed and flowed. But it was like no stomachache he'd ever had, nor was it centered solely in his gut; it was moving . . . lower.

"Help me!" he gasped. And sprawled across the floor.

"Eellon, if this is one of your ploys . . ." he heard Tyrill shout.

"No ploy," Avall choked—and darkness closed about him.

But not unconsciousness.

It was the darkness of another place—a *not*-place, to which part of him had journeyed under the aegis of the gem. But on those occasions, *he* had done the seeking; this time it . . . *something* . . . was seeking him.

And then a third darkness took him, and other senses wrested control of his own, and he was, quite simply, no longer himself.

But this darkness was another room, candlelit though it was day, and dark only by contrast to the brilliance of the Hall of Clans. And there were people looking down on him: two groups, one atop the other, one in hooded clan robes, cloaks, and tabards, and mostly unfamiliar; the other numbering but three: Kylin, Div, and—*not* Eellon, though he was there, too, looking concerned. But superimposed on the Clan-Chief's face was . . . Rann's!

He was two places at once, Avall realized dully, as he fought to regain some trace of reason, while pain after pain pulsed through him, setting him writhing on the floor, as someone pinned his limbs, and a healer set a stick of imphor in his teeth, as much to save his tongue as calm him.

And then thoughts fought their way through the pain and finally reached him: other thoughts—almost alien, it had been so long since he'd felt them.

"Strynn . . ."

Had he said that, or was it merely a thought? Did it matter? It was an acknowledgment of contact, and with that, the bond between them strengthened, and he was one with her across all that unseen distance. She was in agony, too—an agony he felt most keenly. But he now knew its origin. She was in labor, and not a moment too soon. And she had her gem, weaker than his lost one. She grasped it desperately, and cried out with the worst distress she'd ever felt—one that transcended intellect into raw instinct. Rann *was* with her, too, and Kylin, each holding one hand, and all those hands were bloody.

Avall relaxed into that contact, come at last after almost two eighths of silence, courtesy of Eddyn's theft. The Hall was gone, save as a distant clamor of voices. Avall was aware of being moved, but didn't care. He sensed a disruption in the thoughts about him, and cared even less. He was more Strynn than himself now, and she was in pain. Pain she was desperate to escape yet could not. It beat at Avall, making him want to scream. Perhaps he did. And at that, a barrier he didn't know he'd kept raised fell, and Strynn flowed into him. Not to contact him, or be one with him, but to find someplace where the pain was not.

He welcomed her with love and acceptance, not words. Certainly he made no move to ask the myriad questions that rose in him at that unexpected joining.

And so they balanced there. Her body in labor at . . . at Div's hold, he realized dimly; his intact and in transit to the Citadel. But their minds were another place, in perfect equilibrium. He took part of her pain, and she took part of his calm. And for a long time they barely existed.

CHAPTER XVIII:

NEWS

(Eron: Tir-Eron—Near Spring: Day XXVII—late morning)

~~~~~~~~~~~~~~~~

Avall barely knew enough to realize he'd been taken back to his suite in the Citadel when pain beyond any he'd felt before wracked him. Hands clamped down on him as he writhed, as others clamped down on Strynn.

A final pain, a final *push*.

And the agony flowed out of him, leaving only a hot, burning throb. He relaxed, then tensed again, for Strynn was moving away—flowing back to herself, not so much to leave him as to welcome another, whom he knew somehow instinctively was her . . . son.

But he wanted to see, too! And for a moment he let himself flow back into Strynn. Long enough to gaze with her upon a tiny, bloody, wriggling form that peered at him with calm, dark blue eyes, then squeezed those eyes closed and wailed. Avall made to gather him into his arms, but Strynn's desires were paramount now, and without meaning to, she thrust him away and withdrew her awareness from his. And without her desire, Avall could not maintain the link.

He gasped, blinked, opened his eyes, saw Lykkon staring down at him, and slowly sat up. And shivered, as a familiar cold assailed him.

"What—?"

"That's our question," Eellon said dryly.

Avall blinked again, and finally got some sense of his situation. He was indeed back in his quarters, and, by the light, it was close to noon. But whether the one immediately after the Council, or another, he had no idea. He'd lost that much time. And he was cold. So cold.

He reached for the coverlet, noted absently he still wore the clothing he'd worn to Council, minus his hood and clan tabard, and from that divined that no more than two or three hands had passed. Then all at once it hit him:

"I have a . . . son," he chuckled. Then, as realization dawned. "That is, Strynn has a son—"

"What?" someone inquired.

Only then did he observe how crowded his chamber was. Not only with Eellon, Lykkon, and the healers from the Citadel *and* Argen-Hall, but with Tyrill, Tryffon, and a dozen other Clan- and Craft-Chiefs as well, including everyone of note from Argen-a. Even his mother was there, which was unusual. So was the King, still in his robe and crown, therefore serving as an official witness. A very high honor indeed.

Silence, for an instant. Then, from Eellon: "Congratulations."

Tyrill snorted. "This is preposterous. I don't know what this was, but there's no way—"

"Yes there is," the King snapped. "I felt it, too—somewhat. A gnawing in my stomach that food wouldn't assuage. A dizziness."

"And I," Eellon confirmed. "And I'll bet Lykkon did, as well."

Lykkon nodded. "I didn't want to say anything, but . . . yes."

Eellon and Avall exchanged glances with the King. "So this means that—"

"Those of us who bonded with Avall before . . . connected again."

"With what?" Tyrill all but shouted. "This is—"

"Something we should be discussing before the full Council," Tryffon broke in tersely.

"One thing it is—or should be," the King observed, "is witnessed proof of a number of things Avall and I have already told you."

"Not to me," Tyrill challenged.

The King motioned to his healer. "Feel Avall's brow—and tell me what you find."

The healer did so. "He's cold, Majesty . . . very, very cold."

"Tyrill," the King continued, "I command you to do the same."

She blanched at that, but laid a rough hand on Avall's brow. He watched her expression carefully. Saw it change, though in a way he couldn't read.

"Well, Tyrill?"

"He does seem . . . cooler than he ought. But still . . ."

"Do you know any way to counterfeit such a thing?" the King asked his healer. "Anything that could be effected in the Hall?"

The healer shook his head.

Gynn nodded triumphantly.

"But—" Tyrill sputtered. "Strynn was due almost two eighths ago. This has to be preposterous coincidence."

"Children of War-Hold are often late," Tryffon informed her calmly. Strynn herself came sixteen days later than expected."

Tyrill spared him a haughty glare, but held her tongue.

Eellon nudged the King. "Majesty, if I may be so bold? I think it would be wisest to continue this discussion with the Council. We'll need to have everyone here witness what we've seen or experienced, including you. The Priests will probably want you to drink from at least one Well to determine what this portends. But I think Fate is dancing with us now, and if we don't partner him, we may all regret it."

The King gnawed his lip, then motioned to a guard who stood outside. Myx, as it turned out.

"Tell the Hall Steward to send word that Council reconvenes at sunset." He paused, looked at Avall. "You can rest until then—but I'll want you there. We'll do whatever it takes to keep you warm, but we have to have you. I—"

He paused, listening. Others cocked their heads as well. Myx dashed for the door. Avall sat bolt upright.

More steps. Boots at a dead run. At least two pairs. Myx glanced outside, then turned. "A guard, Majesty, and a messenger, and someone I don't know."

The King waited. The rest of those in attendance backed away.

"Message for the King," he heard someone shout from without. "Urgent."

An instant later, three men crowded through the door. The guard, the herald, and a third man Avall didn't recognize.

He was maybe five years Avall's senior, and would normally have been very good-looking indeed, with pale blue eyes that would get him noticed and remembered. Now, however, he looked terrible. His hair was matted, his cheeks stubbled. Scratches showed on a face as gaunt as Avall had ever seen on a living man, while his nose and ears both showed signs of frostbite. His clothing was in tatters, and mail gleamed through rents in a house-tabard that might once have been Warcraft crimson. His boots looked to have been of good quality, as did his sword. He wore no cloak, but had probably been relieved of it.

He also stank. Whatever word he carried must be urgent beyond belief.

"Majesty," he panted from the door, as a dozen hands moved to offer him drink. "My apologies for my unsightly looks and demeanor, but some things will not wait."

"Krynneth," someone murmured. "That's Krynneth. But he's supposed to be at . . ."

A swallow of cider and the man nodded. "Aye, Krynneth syn Mozz-een, most lately of War-Hold-Winter. Of which I have dire news indeed."

The King braced himself. "Not plague!"

Krynneth shook his head and dared another swallow. "No, Majesty. But maybe worse. Your Majesty, it grieves me to tell you that War-Hold was attacked in the night by the armies of Ixti—and has fallen."

"That's impossible!" Tryffon burst out. "The place can withstand any siege. It's impregnable. And the season—why, winter's barely over!"

Again, Krynneth shook his head, meeting no one's eyes. "There was no siege. It was . . . we think it was treachery from within."

"*We?*"

"Lorvinn. She ordered me here when I would've stayed to fight."

"Lorvinn," Tryffon took up. "What of her? Surely she—"

Krynneth wavered where he stood. Someone slid a chair toward him, which he claimed gratefully. "The short version of a long tale is that she showed some of us a secret way out, back in the winter. One of that company in all likelihood fled to Ixti with that knowledge. It's the only way."

"Traitor," someone muttered.

"Traitor," Eellon echoed.

Krynneth looked at him sadly. "Worse than you know," he sighed. "It was—we think it was Merryn."

"Merryn?" Avall cried. "No!"

Krynneth stared at him, as though seeing him for the first time. "You look—"

"She's my twin," Avall snapped. "There's no way in the world she'd—"

"Probably not by choice," Eellon agreed. "But there are more important things to learn now." He exchanged glances with the King, as though conceding the floor to him.

Gynn—almost—glared at him. "First things first then, Krynneth. When did this occur?"

"Seven nights ago," Krynneth replied. "I've been in the saddle ever since. I . . . I think they destroyed the hold, or it destroyed itself. But I know it was Barrax. It had been warm. He attacked us at night, when we weren't looking, from a direction we didn't expect."

Tryffon of War was about to gnaw his lips off. He glanced around the room furiously, then spotted Myx. "Go find everyone from War you can, from subchief rank on up, and have them meet me here. Anyone from Lorvinn's sept as well, if you can; they'll want to know. By your leave, Majesty," he added, almost as an afterthought.

The King snared a chair and sat down beside the weary warrior. "And now? Know you anything since then? Surely we would've had word?"

"There may be word in my wake," Krynneth retorted. "But I've done nothing but ride, through rain, snow—everything. I've killed three horses, two of which I stole."

"And maybe yourself," a healer grumbled, already fussing with potions by the window.

"It doesn't matter. Not with everyone I cared about . . . gone."

The King glanced at Tryffon. "Seven days. Men march more slowly than that, and the terrain's rough down there. Still, he'd have reached Half Gorge in five, faster than that, if he forced his men. Tell me, Krynneth, those you fought: Did they look fresh or weary?"

Krynneth shook his head. "Most wore helms, Sire. I saw eyes, but that was all. They fought well, though; and their armor was polished, their clothes clean."

"But Half Gorge—" Tyrill put in. "If they could reach there in five days, it—"

"May well have already fallen," Gynn finished, rising. "But we should've had word! By signals, if nothing else."

"He's following spring north," Krynneth offered. "With War-Hold fallen, they wouldn't have expected attack. They've always been small and weak."

The King looked at Tryffon again. "If you were Barrax, what would be your goals, and what would you do if you had just taken your enemy's main line of defense?"

"My goal would be Tir-Eron, because that's where political and administrative power is concentrated. What I would do? I'd march there as fast as I could, with enough forces at my back to subdue any resistance I met along the way. In the case of Half Gorge, I'd send a portion of my troops around it in secret, and rely on the rest to attack—from the south, as expected. If they won, I'd leave as many as necessary to occupy the place and order the rest onward—in effect two armies half a day apart, to confound my enemy's expectations."

"And if they couldn't quell Half Gorge?"

"They would, eventually. The northern force could simply double back, and take it by stealth. Half Gorge has many approaches, unlike this. Or South."

Gynn had started pacing. "And so . . . would they have reached South Gorge by now?"

Tryffon's face clouded. "Not yet—I'd say seven days, minimum, depending on how long they stayed in Half Gorge. Small as they are, they'd be bound to put up a fight, and they'd be a natural place to resupply."

"And it would take us how long to get any useful force there?"

Tryffon's eyes were cold as stone. "Seven days, at a guess."

The King slapped the wall with both hands. "Then we've no time at all."

He raised a brow at the lone Priest in attendance. "What can you tell me about the weather?"

The Priest regarded him calmly. "The snow melts, and the air warms. The Ri that feeds South Gorge always floods the plain above it in the spring, while half the country still freezes. That should keep Barrax at bay for days, unless he's fool enough to dare the mountains. But for you to muster an army . . ."

"And a third of your forces may already be taken or under attack," Tryffon noted. "We can send word to the northern gorges to meet us, but it would take an eighth to get them here, never mind to South Gorge."

"Which means that Eron Gorge will have to hold them," Eellon concluded. He looked at Tryffon. "*Can* we hold them? Until help arrives?"

Tryffon scowled thoughtfully. "In this place? If we're lucky, it won't come to that. If you mean our forces, there are several likely places between here and South Gorge—"

Avall had been listening quietly, still stunned from the triple shock of sharing Strynn's labor, gaining word of his sister's possible defection, and now a war none of them had expected. Which reminded him of yet another problem.

"Eddyn," he observed flatly, "has the gem."

Tyrill rounded on him. "What of it?"

"He's not here. Tyrill, believe me when I tell you that thing is very powerful indeed. It is *not* something you want in the hands of enemies."

"Enough!" the King snapped. "This is the wrong place for such discussions. We will meet in half a hand in the lesser council chamber: all Clan- and Craft-Chiefs, and the subchiefs of War, and anyone who knows anything about this gem. Avall, I know you're worn-out, but you come, too. We have to have your knowledge."

"Why?" Tyrill demanded.

"Because," Avall told her tersely, "there are at least two more of those gems—if they can be delivered in time."

"If," Gynn echoed grimly. And marched out, with no trace of a limp in sight.

CHAPTER XIX:

IDYL

(SOUTHERN ERON—NEAR SPRING: DAY XXVII—MIDAFTERNOON)

Elv studied the red-hot horseshoe she'd been shaping steadily for the last half hand—under Eddyn's practiced and far-too-critical eye. Sweat gleamed on her forehead, plastering her hair to her skull where it escaped the rag she'd tied around it. Stripped to a sleeveless undertunic in the crisp Near-Spring air, her arms showed muscles that had barely existed when they'd met. Eddyn grinned at her as she plunged the glowing iron into a bucket of snowmelt to one side of the small forge that had survived the fire.

"Will I ever make a smith, do you think?" she inquired, with a grin of her own.

Eddyn levered himself up with easy grace from where he'd been lolling against a second anvil, moving to stand close enough to feel the warmth of her body—a warmth that had nothing to do with the fire and a great deal to do with her being an attractive woman, with spring coming on. As he passed the door, he glimpsed Toz in the courtyard putting his horse through its paces. Ole was in the main hold, prowling through what was left of the Lore hall, which had come to be an obsession.

Nor was the shoeing a mere exercise in craft. It was a necessary adjunct to the plans they'd been making all winter: to continue north to Tir-Eron. All save Eddyn. He still hadn't revealed his true name, and still suspected he didn't have the right form of theirs. But sometimes it was better not to know about people, given that the ones who'd given him most grief in past years had been ones he'd known all his life.

All except Rrath, who was a special case entirely.

He wondered how the little Priest fared. He'd survived abandonment in the snow, so Gynn had said. But who'd found him first? Gynn's minions, which was to say Eellon's, or Priest-Clan's? More than once he regretted that he'd chosen not to tell the High King what he knew about the ghost priests. Had he availed himself of those sketchy opportunities, perhaps he'd be back in Tir-Eron, putting the final polish on the royal shield.

But would that life be better than this?

Elv tested her workmanship with a finger, then snared the prototype from beside the forge and compared the two. "Close enough," Eddyn chuckled, reaching casually around her.

She tensed, though they'd been playing Lovers' Tease for over an eighth now—far too long, by Eddyn's reckoning. But every time he got . . . eager, she warned him of the greater potency of Eronese men, and the greater fertility of Ixtian women. "I have no clan," she told him. "And as I understand it, you couldn't claim any child unless you wed me—and since you're unclanned, that would do you no good. Assuming," she added archly, "that you really *are* unclanned."

Eddyn flinched, which he knew at once was the wrong thing to have done. "I thought we'd settled that."

Elv rounded on him, abruptly all warrior. "Two eighths is long enough to live with lies."

"I haven't lied," he retorted. "I simply haven't told all the truth. There's a major difference—as I'm sure you *and* your siblings know."

"I know that I find it nearly impossible to believe that you would willfully destroy a masterwork—which is what you claim got you exiled. But that doesn't fit with what Ole's read about Eronese law in your own Lore hall. According to her, you have to be very High Clan indeed, to have been unclanned at all. Even so, it would require action of the King and Council of Chiefs, who only consider unclannings twice a year—at Sundeath and Sunbirth. You therefore couldn't have been freshly unclanned when we met—it was almost two eighths since the last appropriate Council met. And don't tell me it was a special session, either. You're not important enough to warrant that."

"I'm the best smith of my generation," Eddyn huffed.

"That's interesting, since word at War-Hold was that the best was a fellow from your same clan named, what was it? Avall?"

"Not my sept," Eddyn spat recklessly. "That makes an enormous difference."

A brow went up. "You knew him?"

"I've . . . met him."

"Was he as good as they say?"

"By most standards."

"And by yours?"

"He was a goldsmith. I was a weaponwright. Is a bowman better than a swordsman?"

"The books say you're required to be competent at all branches of your crafts."

Eddyn fished in the scrap pile for another bar of iron. "Your sister reads too much."

Silence. Eddyn saw Elv go tense and wary. "I don't trust this," she murmured.

"What?"

She gestured around the forge. "Everything. The fact that we've no one around but ourselves. And the woods. And the snow and the sky and the silence. This is the longest I've gone without seeing other people. It's not how people are meant to live."

"It's not how you'll live, when you get to Tir-Eron. Once you find your clan—"

"If they'll have us. From what you've said, we're more likely to find welcome at War-Hold or Lore."

"Maybe," Eddyn agreed. "But that's for your kin—your real kin—to arrange."

Elv put down her hammer and wiped her hands. "That's not all I distrust."

Eddyn didn't reply. Something about her expression indicated that it was for her to make the next comment. She took a deep breath, suddenly shy. "I . . ." She bit her lip. "I seem to have . . . I think maybe I've . . . fallen in love with you."

"There are worse things you could tell me," Eddyn replied carefully.

Elv scowled helplessly. "But I don't trust my feelings. I don't know if it's you, or the fact that you're different and exotic—I saw that happen back at War-Hold. Or if it's what you represent."

"And what would that be? Not security, I expect."

She shook her head. "Wildness, maybe. A lack of respect for rules—the same as Ole, Toz, and I have. We're all outsiders, in a sense."

Eddyn nodded, wondering in which of many directions this was leading.

She gnawed her lip. "But I . . . I've reached a point where I can't decide what I want to do about it, and can't make any decision until I have more information. And for that . . . we need to dispense with these secrets. I need to know more about you than the fact that you have no father, and have managed to destroy a masterwork. I know some of the whats, but I need to know the whys."

"You wouldn't like me."

"I'd prefer to have the choice."

"What do the others think about me?"

"You're trying to change the subject!"

"I'd still like to know."

Another deep breath. "Toz likes you well enough because he can learn things from you and because you help balance things—he's always had at least one male friend around, and he misses them. He doesn't like the secrets, either, but he understands the rationale."

"And Ole?"

"You're a means to an end. She's neither encouraged nor discouraged my . . . interest in you. But I will say this. No matter what happens between the two of us, you had better never hurt her—or my brother. I—"

She paused, glanced around, abruptly all nerves and alertness. Eddyn stood as quickly. They exchanged troubled looks as they dashed to the door. Toz had heard it, too—the sound of hoofbeats on the road below the hold.

Coming from the south.

"A trek?" Elv ventured.

Eddyn shook his head. "Unlikely. They move slowly, and we're off the main road from War-Hold."

Elv reached for the sword she always kept close at hand: a nice Eronese blade from a cache in the hold's armory, further refined and balanced by Eddyn's expert crafting. Her siblings had matching weapons. They'd be the envy of the Ixtian army—if they ever saw the Ixtian army again.

Toz met them in the middle of the practice yard, urging them toward the horse gate. Ole had noted it, too—to judge by the way she'd appeared on the balcony outside the Lore hall and was pointing south. They nodded, whereupon she disappeared, to return, sword in hand, at the top of the stairs leading from the court to the second level. By the time Elv, Eddyn, and Toz had gained the stone-and-oak gate, she was no more than a dozen strides behind.

"A party from War-Hold, best I can tell—" she shouted, though the thunder of hooves already made it hard to hear. "About a score, on horses. Red cloaks and helms."

Eddyn stiffened. "That's odd. It's too early for a casual mission. And a trek escort wouldn't bother with so much panoply through empty country."

"Maybe it's not empty,"

"Any war would take them south, not north."

"We'll know in a moment," Ole grumbled. "They're coming this way."

"Forage?" Elv dared.

Eddyn shook his head. "Shouldn't need to, though maybe—"

"The forge," Elv growled. "They'd have seen the smoke—and from what I hear, any sign of a hold in use is to be investigated."

"Do we fight?" Toz wondered.

"Should be no reason," Eddyn gave back. "But any lies you tell had better be better than the ones you told me."

Everyone exchanged troubled glances. Eddyn squared his shoulders and edged toward the closed gate. "Since this *is* my family hold, and there's no way word of my unclanning could've reached War-Hold, I'd best play host. I'll have to invite them to stay, but I'll try not to encourage them. As for you—remember this isn't your country and play everything carefully. Half-Eronese or not, these folks will see you as half-Ixtian."

The thunder of the approaching host drowned out further conversation. And riding with the hoofbeats now came the rattle of armor, the subtle jingle of mail. But no conversation.

The noise abated. Eddyn noted through the spy hole that the soldiers had assembled no more than three paces beyond the gate. Sunlight gleamed on helms, spears, and bright red cloaks drawn close against the chill. Mouth-masks covered most of the faces. Eyes glittered here and there behind intricate nasals, earpieces, and brow guards.

"Hail the hold!" the figure in the vanguard sang out formally.

Eddyn hesitated—but had no good reason not to respond as courtesy demanded. Straightening his tunic, he shot the bolt and raised the counterweighted bar from the gate. The triplets moved back to either side. A deep breath, and he stepped through.

Looking up at the horses and their mounted riders, he felt unaccountably short and vulnerable. "Welcome to Car Neezh: holding of Argen-yr."

"Which seems to have suffered of late," the leader observed. His voice was muffled—perhaps he had a cold.

"A lightning strike, which we came to attend. Winter caught us at work."

Gloved hands folded on the pommel of the saddle. "You are . . . ?"

"Eddyn syn Argen-yr." There, he'd said it: his true name, lest one of this host know him and call him on a lie. Already he was straining his gaze in search of Merryn. At least there was one less lie between him and Elv now. He'd face the repercussions later.

"May we enter?"

Eddyn had no choice but to agree, and had already stepped aside to admit them when Ole yelled from within. "No! Don't! They're from Ixti!"

Eddyn reached for his sword even as he made a frantic dash for the gate. But the leader was there before him, bringing heavy warhorse hooves to bear on the oak panel the triplets were rushing to close. He skidded to a halt, turning to bolt—not to flee or abandon his friends, but to buy them time. Another horse appeared from nowhere, blocking the way.

He slashed at it desperately, but it danced away, then advanced again. Another slash, and others moved in to either side, blocking movement.

Behind them, more were dismounting. There were shouts, too, in Ixtian, and mingled with them came the splintering of wood as the gate gave way. The horses pressed closer. He could kill the one before him, but to what avail? The wall was at his back. Mounted warriors faced him; others filled the gaps. And he had no armor. Nothing to turn aside weapons. No alternatives but death and surrender.

"Throw down your sword!" the leader snapped, lowering his own, and pointing it at Eddyn.

Eddyn hesitated, then started to accede. At the last moment, however, he flipped the sword around and presented it hilt first to the looming Ixtian. "This edge is too fine to sully upon the ground."

The man smiled as he snatched the weapon, then ran a finger along the gleaming steel. Brows went up as glove leather parted.

Eddyn smiled in turn. "One reason to keep me alive."

"Maybe the only one," the man laughed grimly. He barked a command in his own tongue, and two soldiers eased around to seize Eddyn's arms.

"If all men here offer as little resistance as you—" one began.

"Death should have a purpose," Eddyn gave back, as he let himself be hustled inside.

The triplets waited there, looking sullen, kneeling on the ground with two armed Ixtians apiece behind them.

The commander dismounted, tossing his reins to the young man who rode behind him. He stomped over to regard the three curiously. Brows went up again. "Stranger and stranger," he murmured to no one in particular, though the words were in Eronese. "I wonder . . ."

"That woman has a ring," the man's squire, or whatever he was, called, pointing.

The captain stepped forward. One of the guards snared Elv's hand and yanked it up for inspection. "I've seen these before," he laughed. He turned to walk away, then spun around again. "Elvix, is it? I remember you from the guard, though you may not remember me."

Eddyn felt as though he were about to explode, so many emotions roiled through him. Fear, frustration, danger of loss, betrayal—maybe, except that the triplets looked as taken aback as he. And mysteries were washing away like dust in rain. Elvix, was it? So the other two . . .

"Orlizz," Elvix challenged. "You seem a bit farther from home than I would have expected."

"Or perhaps home draws nearer," Orlizz countered archly.

Eddyn felt as though he'd been kicked in the gut. It was all falling into place—what he should've realized at once, had the notion not been too preposterous. These were Ixtian troops well into Eron. To get there they'd have had to pass War-Hold. But the man's cocky demeanor, his confidence and easy assurance indicated that—

No! It wasn't possible. War-Hold could not have fallen. He had kinsmen there. Folk he cared about. Even, in an odd way, Merryn.

It was as though Orlizz read his mind. "War-Hold is ours," he announced. Then, to the guards who held them: "We will stay here tonight and move on. Take the women one at a time. Strip them. Inspect every hem and seam for hidden weapons as well as obvious ones, then let them dress. Return in half a hand."

Eddyn watched impassively as two soldiers dragged Elvix toward the forge.

"Bring them," Orlizz rasped, indicating Eddyn and Toz. He strode toward what was in better times a smoking shed for meat, now roofless but with sturdy stone walls washed clean by snow and rain. Half his troop followed; the rest fanned out to secure the perimeter of the yard. The guards were neither ruthless nor kind, Eddyn noted, as he was hurried along.

And then he was inside. Orlizz himself blocked the doorway, while a dozen or so guardsmen ringed Eddyn and Toz.

"Strip," Orlizz told his prisoners. "I want no hidden weapons."

Eddyn glared at him, but reached for the laces of his tunic. And froze, with his fingers at his throat.

He was wearing the gem! It hated him, and made that hatred known at intervals, but he dared not let it out of his presence. Even when he and Toz bathed in the steam-house he was careful to bring it along in a pouch. Normally, however, he simply wore it on a thong around his neck. But if these men—

"Hurry up!" Orlizz warned. "Or we will be forced to help you."

Eddyn looked around frantically, noting that Toz was already down to his house-hose, and had sat to remove his boots. The spring light gleamed on his skin like morning on snow.

Eddyn had no choice but to stall for time. And with that in mind, he followed Toz's example and sat, tugging at his boots, making a show of removing the dagger tucked in there, hoping thereby to win his captors' trust, or at least make them drop their guard. In the meantime . . .

The gem truly *did* hate him. Yet once, in a panic, it had worked for him as well. Maybe . . .

One boot came free. The other.

He stood. And as he fumbled for his tunic ties again, he also felt frantically for the gem. Found it—and, even through the pouch, felt it protest his touch. He fought it—in his mind. Trying to summon sufficient desire for escape to invoke whatever had happened before.

To no avail.

"You're stalling," Orlizz spat. "Vorm, Snikk—help him."

Eddyn closed his eyes, slapped both hands on the stone—and wished as hard as he ever had.

Still nothing.

And then it didn't matter, because hands clamped down on him and his tunic was torn away. He lost his grip on the pouch, and could only stand helplessly as his undertunic followed—ripped away from either side, as they then ripped away his hose, to leave him standing naked beside Toz, who was also bare, but wearing that state with far more grace.

Already the men were inspecting what remained of his garments, but Orlizz had lunged forward. A gloved hand flashed out to finger the pouch. The gem evidently disliked *him,* too—for he flinched away in something between anger and awe. But then his eyes narrowed suspiciously. Abruptly he laughed out loud.

Faster than Eddyn could follow, Orlizz snatched the pouch free, and in one deft movement emptied its contents into his palm. The gem gleamed there like frozen fire.

"I know of this stone!" he cried. "And I know a king who will give a tenth of his realm to have it!"

He thrust the gem in a waist-pouch and turned abruptly, snapping orders in Ixtian to every side. Someone tossed Eddyn a ragged tunic as they hurried him toward the courtyard. Toz grabbed up his clothes as well, and for a moment they came close enough to speak. "What—?" Eddyn dared.

"South," Toz replied. "We go south, but that is all—"

"Silence!" Orlizz shouted, rounding on them. "Kinsman to your King you may be, Eddyn syn Argen-yr, but your life, until I say otherwise, is mine!"

CHAPTER XX:

INTERVIEWS

(Eron: near South Gorge—Near Spring: Day XXX—afternoon)

You know it's a risk, Majesty," Lord Lynnz told his brother-in-law through a languid exhalation of poppy smoke, a small cloud of which was slowly spiraling through the vent hole of the royal pavilion. From outside came the sound of tent pegs being driven and wagons unloaded, as the camp prepared to settle in. The scent of poppy twined with that of an unoccupied summer hold, burning.

Barrax chose to ignore the calculated arrogance of Lynnz's tone in favor of gauging the present thinking among his commanders and advisers concerning the invasion. He had no doubt that he was taking a risk that could cost him his crown, if not his life. He also had no illusions about the fact that he had been presented with a set of circumstances that would never occur again: an excuse to invade Eron, a means to inflict major damage to Eron's prime defense, and decent weather in which to effect it.

Of course the Gods were also known to tempt people with the easy path, so as to catch them in their snares. But that was also part of the pleasure.

"What would you do in my place?" Barrax replied, puffing on a water pipe of his own, though not filled with narcotic. "Don't fear to tell me what you think; that's why I have advisers. If one person tells you you're a fool, there're even odds who's right. If ten tell you that, you should consider the situation."

Another puff. Lynnz stretched his legs atop the thick carpet they'd looted from a Half Gorge craft hold before they'd burned it. "They're two separate issues, Majesty. At the moment, there's little reason to let Prince Kraxxi live. He's under death sentence for fratricide, which even he doesn't deny. Balancing that is what he told you of his own free will and the risk he took to impart that information, which frankly revealed more spine than I ever expected in the lad. But he doesn't like you, he doesn't support your causes, and he clearly cares for the Eronese woman. Which means that as long as he lives, he'll be a threat. The Eronese will see him as a potential ally, especially as his half-blood friends have some claim on the support of a powerful craft there. On the other hand, those factions among our own people who either dislike you personally or who disapprove of your policies, especially as regards this invasion, might see him as a rallying point around which to foment rebellion."

"So you think I should kill him?"

"The sooner the better."

"In spite of the fact that he knows more about some aspects of this country than anyone else to whom we have access?"

"He doesn't know anything you can't learn elsewhere at a price."

Another puff. "Suppose I simply want him to suffer? He cost me a son I loved."

"And a brother he loved a great deal more, by all accounts. That argument doesn't hold much force, I'm afraid. Not that that will aid you in the long run. People understand law and justice. They also understand cruelty and pettiness, but they never like them or approve of them."

"Then why do so many attend public executions?" Barrax countered. "Because they get a chance to see someone do what they wish they were free to do themselves."

"There's still the matter of Merryn."

"What would you do with her?"

Lynnz gnawed his lip. "She's a much harder call. She's the reason we took War-Hold, and there's no denying that. She's also a source of potential information, but the more imphor we give her, the more resistance she builds. Eventually we'll turn a vulnerability into a source of strength."

"More of that balance I was mentioning."

"Aye. But she's also one of your best hostages, since she's both kin to Eron's King and a shining light of her generation."

Barrax tried not to snap back at that. He had *not* planned on the destruction of War-Hold, which had taken with it a valuable source of potential hostages. Of those he'd acquired, most were Common Clan or clanless. Not one subchief from either the King's clan or War-Hold's ruling clan had survived. Which was the main reason he'd killed Lorvinn: to assuage his anger. But that execution, he conceded, had, perhaps, not been wise.

Lynnz was gazing at him curiously, his eyes slightly glazed, which suggested that fresh air might be prudent. "Have I told you what you wanted to hear, Majesty?"

"Maybe what I *needed* to hear," Barrax grumbled. "Especially if what you said is borne out by my other advisers—which remains to be determined."

Lynnz nodded, and rose. "By your leave, Majesty," he murmured, with a sketchy bow.

"The Gods watch you," Barrax replied absently. "Oh, and send in the embassy that arrived this morning. We've let them wonder if they're going to live or die long enough."

"It is done, Majesty," Lynnz said. And strode out.

Barrax took time to infuse the preponderance of poppy smoke in the tent with a small amount of imphor wood burned in a brazier by the door, in case those he was about to entertain should prove vulnerable to its myriad effects. Probably they weren't. *He* certainly wasn't. A word to a servant produced a selection of food and drink on small tables ranged between the low audience chairs around the room, so that by the time Barrax had resumed the crowned helm he'd doffed for the interview with his commander and positioned himself on his portable throne, he felt and looked suitably regal.

A moment later, the door flap was lifted by one of his younger guards, who simply said, "Your Majesty, the visitors from Eron."

Barrax nodded his assent, and the guard backed away, raising the door flap higher to admit three fit-looking men in white hoods and tabards—the former raised, per Eronese custom, to indicate that they functioned in a particular role.

Barrax studied them with interest, noting that their faces showed a fair bit of weathering, and that their hair, while black like that of most Eronese, was clipped shorter than he'd been informed was the norm. Nor did he miss the fine mail beneath the rich fabrics, nor the quality of their knee-high white-leather boots.

"Enter and be welcome to the presence of Ixti, which lies below you and above you and around you and before you," Barrax intoned. He did not rise—Ixtian monarchs didn't do such things—but he didn't bridle at the token bows they bestowed upon him, either.

"Majesty," the one in the middle acknowledged.

"Please be seated. Eat if you will, or drink. If you mistrust either, I will be glad to sample before you."

The leader sniffed the air appraisingly, raising a knowing brow, but saying nothing. "Caution is wise when one is not in one's own country," he observed in Ixtian, "but caution of this sort is futile."

Barrax grinned.

The man spared a thin smile. "There is Eronese law, and there is . . . ours."

"Perhaps you should state where the difference lies."

"You received our message?"

"I received *a* message that said there was a . . . I believe the term was 'invisible power' in Eron that wanted to have converse with me. I take it you represent that power?"

The man nodded.

"Do you have a name?"

"Names are less important here than titles, Majesty. Where I come from, I am called the Chief of the Ninth. It would please me if you styled me thus."

"The ninth what?"

"The Ninth Face of The Eightfold God."

"I sense an enigma."

"The other eight faces are those the folk of this land see, from unclanned up to the King. But who is to say that The Eight do not have *more* faces to reveal?"

"Ah, then your King does not know?"

"We are a shadow within shadows."

"To what end?"

"To our ends. Which are the same ends as yours, ultimately: the preservation of power."

Barrax leaned forward with genuine interest, enjoying this verbal sparring. Though certainly not part of the official Eronese government, these were the most high-ranking folk of that land he had actually treated with. At least until he could proceed with his attack on South Gorge.

"And if you lost this power, what would really change in your lives?"

"We would lose the freedom to determine our own destinies."

"If you are what I suspect—let me be blunt: a radical arm within the officially sanctioned Priest-Clan, known by few but suspected by many—you fear that you might have to do like all the other clans, which is to say actually produce something besides words, Wells, and rituals for a living."

The Chief's face was solemn. "Oh, but The Eight do exist, as does The Ninth. I have proof of that."

"So," Barrax sighed, suddenly impatient. "What is it that has brought you to me?"

The Chief sampled a pastry. "We serve, first of all, ourselves and The Nine. What King we serve, or speaks with Their mouth, concerns us less. You seem a practical man, Barrax of Ixti. I'm sure you know that the people will embrace your rule far more willingly if their lives change as little as possible. Most of Common Clan and the clanless believe unquestioningly in The Eight. High Clan, in spite of the genuine piety of the King, increasingly do not. But the people need The Eight and we—Priest-Clan and the Ninth Face alike—need the people. The people believe that we alone can intercede with The Eight. Let us say that a discovery has lately been made that challenges that belief—and many others. We do not need our efficacy questioned. In this the clan's public front is one with our own."

"Does the clan of which you are a part know you exist?"

"Most do not—and by telling you this, we give you a certain amount of power over us. Having said that, we have found ourselves in grave danger of having our existence revealed more widely—more publicly—than we desire. This would inconvenience us. If another King, with goals more in line with our own, sat the throne of Eron, we would feel more . . . secure."

"So you betray your King?"

"The King is the voice of the God and the personification of the people. He would agree that both those things should come above himself."

Barrax snorted in disgust. "Then that is a remarkable King you have. What is it you propose?"

A deep, measured breath. "That in exchange for our support—or lack of resistance—in your efforts to subdue Eron you help us destroy those people and institutions that would stand between ourselves and our goals."

"Which are?"

"Bluntly stated: The people must continue to approach The Eight only through us."

"There is reason to suspect otherwise?"

"There . . . may be."

Barrax nodded cryptically and settled back in his chair, stroking his chin. "I believe I require confirmation of that."

The Chief showed no emotion. "What I tell you I offer as proof of our loyalty—our potential loyalty, one might say."

"Go on."

The Chief took a sip of wine. "Very well. Some two eighths ago, we received word from a young but reliable source that a certain accomplished . . . friend of his from Smithcraft had discovered a most intriguing gem. One with amazing and, to us, troubling, properties, including, apparently, that of enabling men to speak mind to mind. We also have reason to suspect that this same gem can confer the power to . . . project oneself out of oneself, as the King and some of our craft do when they drink from the Wells. More specifically, we think it allows them to enter the realm of The Eight. Should the unclanned, the clanless, and Common Clan learn that we can access The Eight directly . . . Well, you recall what I have said."

Barrax steepled his fingers. "And can you describe this gem?"

"We have not seen it, but it is reported to be a red stone the size of the big thumb joint, smooth-surfaced and full of sparkling inner facets, somewhat like an opal."

"I . . . see," Barrax replied casually. "And you believe this? Enough to risk what you do on such preposterous suppositions?"

The Chief shifted in his chair. "There have been other gems with powers come out of that place, though few. So yes, until we know otherwise, we do believe."

"That's why we need priests anyway, isn't it? So we'll have someone to tell us we need faith."

The Chief's face was unreadable, though he tensed at that last. "Majesty, we have presented the bones of our proposition. We will remain to discuss them further, or withdraw so that you may take what action you will, at your leisure. But we have said what we came to say."

Barrax smiled. "You have indeed said interesting things, many of which bear further consideration. I trust, however, that you will not take it amiss if I offer you our hospitality until certain other measures have been enacted?"

"We expect no less," the Chief acknowledged solemnly.

"You may go. It is likely that I will summon you again before much time passes."

"Your Majesty of Ixti is gracious."

"Better say . . . curious," Barrax retorted. And sat on his throne unmoving as the Ninth Face of The Eightfold God departed.

A guard followed hard on their heels, however. "Majesty," he ventured. "Is there anything you require?"

A pause for thought. Then: "Send me my son."

"At Your Majesty's will."

Barrax indulged himself in a full glass of thick Eronese wine and a slice of buttered bread as he paced the room. It was times like this he needed someone to confide in. Some beloved kinsman. A bond-brother, perhaps, such as the Eronese had. Such as his son all but had. He had his own opinions on these and other matters, but he needed someone he could *trust,* dammit. Someone whose agenda mirrored his own, and who valued the same things he did.

Briefly furious, he flung the goblet at the nearest tent pole, not caring that expensive glass shattered. He was pouring another as the guard entered, with two others. Kraxxi stood between them, dressed in a clean belted robe of Ixtian cut and Eronese cloth, shaved and bathed and with his hair combed, but looking gaunt for all that. He was also barefoot and barelegged beneath the padded shackles that bound his ankles and his wrists. His eyes, however, were calm.

Without asking, the guards thrust him into the seat vacated by the Chief of the Ninth. Barrax wondered idly if it was still warm, and if Kraxxi would notice, as he'd seemed to notice other things Barrax hadn't expected.

"Lord Lynnz and I have been discussing your fate," Barrax rumbled, giving neither name, relationship, nor title, as he had vowed not to do in Kraxxi's presence.

Kraxxi, as was typical, did not reply.

"You are allowed to speak."

"I have already told you what I had to say."

"About the gem?"

"I gave you Eron. You should either give me freedom or end my life."

Barrax glared at him. "The woman gave me far more of Eron than you did. But tell me, what form would this freedom take? Would you go north or south?"

"Perhaps I would do neither. Perhaps I would go where there is none of this endless contention and playing of games. Perhaps I would go east, take ship, and sail until I could sail no farther. Or go west over the mountains, to the unknown land beyond."

"Alone?"

"I've survived alone before."

"Or I could kill you."

"We both know that. Clearly you have a reason for keeping me alive."

"More than Lynnz knows. Would you like to hear them?"

"No, but I suppose you'll tell me anyway, since they're bound to be things that would hurt me to know."

"You know me well, you think."

"I have known you long. That's almost the same thing."

"Very well, you've been frank. So will I. You're bait."

Kraxxi's eyes rounded ever so slightly, but Barrax caught the gesture. "I see you've guessed for whom: your friends the triplets. They also have sentences of death upon them. I would enjoy watching you watch them die."

"You enjoy watching death, period. Maybe that's because you're already dead inside."

Barrax all but leapt to his feet. "You dare! You hope to goad me into killing you."

Kraxxi shrugged. "I have little to lose by making the attempt."

"Your life."

"Such as it is."

"The woman's life. Don't think I don't know you love her."

"Did love her, perhaps."

"I keep thinking how interesting it would be to have her conceive a child by you. A child I could hold for ransom. Or a child I could use to torture you. A child you could watch cut from her womb. A child you could both watch . . . die."

To Barrax's surprise, Kraxxi looked less shocked than sympathetic. "Don't look at me as though I'm mad, boy," he raged. "I am entirely too sane, I assure you."

"Merryn's clan will kill you," Kraxxi said simply. "They—"

He broke off, for a warrior had burst into the room, fresh from the road, to judge by his travel-stained clothes. Still, he had doffed his sword before entering, which few had grace to do. It took Barrax a moment to identify him: Lord Orlizz. He'd been on patrol to the northwest. "Majesty—I apologize, but you had wanted to be told at once . . ."

"What is it?"

"Better I should show you."

Barrax thought of sending the man away, but something in his earnest demeanor made him reconsider. "Very well. Approach."

Orlizz stepped neatly past Kraxxi, reaching to a heavy leather pouch at his side. But when Barrax held out his hand, the man shook his head. "Better you should see it on the table."

King though he was, Barrax cleared a place among the wines, revealing an expanse of white-brocaded velvet lavishly stained with purple and red. Orlizz set the pouch there, undid the drawstrings gingerly, and upended it to let a second pouch roll free. That, in turn, contained another, of black velvet. Barrax's hair prickled unaccountably as he watched the last pouch emptied.

And found himself staring at a smooth red stone, in whose depths flecks of colors gleamed. Indeed, as the Chief of the Ninth had said, like an opal.

"Can it be touched?" Barrax inquired, trying to keep his voice calm, since he had no idea whether he'd been presented with a weapon or a threat.

"With caution, I would suggest. It doesn't seem to like certain people."

A brow shot up. *"Like?"*

"It's the only way to describe it," Orlizz replied uncomfortably.

Barrax refrained from touching it. And would continue to do so, until he'd taken certain precautions. Amazing coincidence, this: to discuss it and have it appear all in one day.

"How did you come by this?" he demanded.

Orlizz shifted his weight, and wouldn't meet his king's eyes. "By accident, actually. We were on patrol to the north. We happened on a fire-damaged hold where we found an Eronese man of whom you may have heard, and, more importantly, a set of Ixti-born triplets."

"No!" Kraxxi blurted out, strangling further reply with a sob.

The king fumbled a pouch of gold from a chest beside the throne and handed it to the warrior, who took the gesture as the dismissal it was, bowed, and left.

"Well," said Barrax to his hated son. "Maybe if I sit here another hand the King of Eron himself will walk in and hand me his crown. If not . . . I seem to have acquired three more prisoners you can watch die."

CHAPTER XXI:

AUDIENCE

(ERON: NEAR SOUTH GORGE—NEAR SPRING: DAY XXX—AFTERNOON)

A push from behind sent Eddyn stumbling forward into a deeper darkness than that he'd already endured, courtesy of being made to ride blindhooded for three days—ever since he and the triplets had been captured. He tripped on something and skidded forward on hands and knees, barking both painfully. His shackles clanked against stone flooring marginally warmer than that he'd previously trod. He was indoors, then. Someone grabbed him from either side, hoisting him up. Hands fumbled at the hood, and he could see again—enough to make out a small stone room and three other figures hunched on the floor. Daylight flooded in from behind, making him squint, and then he was thrown to the floor again. The door—a massive square of plain oak—slammed behind him. Bars showed in a head-sized vision-hatch at eye height. The only other light came from a tiny brazier in an otherwise empty fireplace. Water dripped to the right. And someone was breathing.

"Welcome to Ixti in exile," came a voice he hadn't heard since his capture. He jerked his head up.

"We didn't betray you," Elvix murmured, easing down to join him. "I want that clear right now." She wore the plainest wool robe imaginable, as did her sister, who remained where she was. Tozri was there, too. It was he who had spoken first, but his face was serious now. And puffy. Eddyn wasn't the only one who'd suffered hard use, though he doubted his ribs, knees, and half-frozen hands and feet would profit from company. Or his jaw, in which two teeth wobbled, courtesy of a cuffing he'd taken when he'd protested his condition.

"Where are we?" he dared. Almost afraid to speak.

"It's your country, so I have no idea. From what I saw when they put us in here, it looks like it might've been a cloister of some kind."

"Possible," Eddyn acknowledged, easing around to stretch out on the floor. Elvix sat beside him, close, but not too close. Their relationship had shifted again. He didn't know in which direction.

"You know this place?"

Eddyn shrugged—which hurt. "We rode south to meet the army, then north again; that much I do know. We've covered enough distance to be halfway to South Gorge, and there's a ruined cloister on the way there that Priest-Clan abandoned during the plague. It would make a perfect prison, with a little work, and I suspect Barrax has more prisoners than places to house them."

"You're right there," Tozri agreed. "I doubt they'd have quartered us together otherwise."

"Why bring us at all?" Olrix challenged. "We're under sentence of death in Ixti."

"Maybe because Barrax has something in mind besides simple execution," Elvix offered. "It would be just like him."

"Maybe he thinks we know something about Eddyn's gem," Tozri chimed in pointedly.

Eddyn glared at him. "There's nothing *to* know about it, it's just a—"

"This is no time for lies," Tozri spat, rising and starting to pace. "I don't know if it's the stone you had, but I know that woman I met at War-Hold has a special connection to some rare gem out of Eron, and I know you're kin to her."

"And how do you know?"

"Kraxxi told me."

Eddyn reeled at the revelation. "Kraxxi? You mean Barrax's son?"

Tozri nodded. "Once. Now in exile."

"But what—? Eight, man, if I'd known this back—"

"You'd have what? We all needed friends that night. We as much as—" he broke off, eyes narrowing—"That gem was supposed to belong to Merryn's brother. What were you doing with it? Or are there two? Is *that* the reason you were unclanned? Because you stole it?"

Elvix rounded on him. "Think, brother. It couldn't be. He wouldn't have had it with him if he'd been unclanned for stealing it."

Olrix whistled her dismay. "It's a powerful thing—*if* what Kraxxi told

Toz about it is true: that it allows people speak mind to mind across distances."

Eddyn didn't reply.

"Can it do that, Eddyn?"

"I don't know. All I know is that it can alter perceptions and let people share minds. It's proof the soul can exist independent of the body. Priest-Clan doesn't like that. Otherwise . . ."

"It's why we're alive," Olrix concluded tersely. "Barrax thinks we know how to work it."

Elvix regarded Eddyn levelly. "*Do* you know how to work it?"

Eddyn shrugged, remembering how it had place-jumped him, and then how it had failed him when he'd attempted that again. "I know very little. But one thing I do know: It doesn't like me. I doubt anything I'd be able to do with it—*if* I can do anything at all—would come to any good end."

Fright woke him.

Eddyn stared blearily at the guard who'd that moment opened the door to the cell. Light lanced in, but it was the long light of afternoon. Black shadows stretched across the pavement. Stone and flesh alike held a fiery glow.

"Which one of you is Eddyn?" the soldier demanded, squinting into the gloom. He peered first at Tozri, then at Eddyn. Eddyn jerked awake, fumbling for any semblance of a weapon, even as part of him sought to recapture the dream he'd been having. It took a moment to realize his situation. "I am," he said before sense suggested that might not have been wise. Then again, he was Eronese. Among his coprisoners, that much would've been obvious.

"You are to come with me."

Eddyn started to balk, but then noticed that two more guards stood ready outside, with others undoubtedly close to hand. He rose carefully, meeting the man's eyes with proud challenge—the Ixtian was half a head shorter than he, he observed with smug satisfaction.

For a wonder, they didn't blindhood him as four of them escorted Eddyn out of what was indeed the cloister he'd supposed, and into a sea of tents that seemed still to be spreading along a vale he recalled as being three days' trek south of the Gorge. They steered unerringly for the largest, an extravaganza of exotic sylks veiling more serviceable canvas with a riot of gaudy color. The flag of Ixti flew above, bracketed by golden streamers, to indicate that the king was in residence.

The lead guard disappeared briefly, but quickly returned, whereupon he and his fellows ushered Eddyn into a tunnel-like antechamber. "Kneel," one hissed, forcing his shoulders down. "You must greet his Majesty of Ixti on

your knees." Eddyn glared at him and knocked the hand away with sufficient force that all four men reached for their daggers. By which time he was
striding forward—into the king's audience tent. He stopped just inside,
hands folded before him, standing as tall as he could. Whatever advantage
the king of Ixti had over him, Eddyn was taller—and intended to play that
advantage.

The king, however, was enthroned on a dais two steps above the floor,
which put their eyes on a level. Nor did the king react as Eddyn risked the
first of what he'd decided might be many affronts. Whatever else he was, he
was High Clan Eronese—in his own land—and would yield to no invader.

Barrax merely raised a brow and dismissed the soldiers who'd been Eddyn's escort with a careless wave of his hand. A hand from which something
bright depended: a cage of silver wire hung from a silver chain.

The gem!

"This should look familiar, Eron-man," the king announced, letting his
gaze shift from the gem to Eddyn, and back to the gem again.

Eddyn didn't react.

"There are many ways to reach the truth," the king drawled. "Truth
from the start would be best for all involved."

"Trinkets on chains are common in Eron," Eddyn dared. "Or did you
loot that from one of the border tombs?"

Barrax tensed ever so slightly, but his hand never stopped slowly spinning
the gem. There was smoke in the air, too: braziers burning green imphor
wood, to lower his inhibitions, he was certain. He'd have to be careful what
he said, and even then might not be able to hide what he knew—which
wasn't a great deal.

"It doesn't like me," Barrax continued. "I wonder, does it also dislike
you?"

"I have no standard by which to gauge such things," Eddyn replied somewhat more circumspectly.

"Oh, but I thought magic gems were found in every stream and cave in
Eron."

"You thought wrong."

"Do you *want* to die, Eron-man?"

"There are worse things."

"I'm considering several right now. It would be best if you cooperated."

"How?"

"Show me how this thing works."

"Gems don't work, they simply . . . are."

"Geen shit!"

Eddyn started at the coarse phrase. The level of commerce seemed in the
process of changing.

Barrax leaned back in his makeshift throne and stroked his geen-claw dagger meaningfully. "Two more people have spoken to me of this gem," he said. "One had only hearsay, but the other . . . there is reason to suspect she had firsthand experience with some of its powers. Since you actually had the thing in your possession, I thought perhaps you might know . . . more."

Well, Eddyn thought, *that certainly made a few things clearer.* Unfortunately, he really did not know how to work the gem—except possibly in one way—and even that had taken him by surprise, as it clearly had Avall. But maybe . . .

He tried not to grin as a plan took form. "I might be able to do something," he conceded. "But whatever you think, I am not the master of the gem. Nor, it would seem, are you."

"Then how came you by it?"

"By rankest accident. I . . . fought with the owner and wrested it from him. Not so much to possess it as to thwart him."

"Should I believe you?"

"I know what these fumes are. Do you believe them?"

Barrax glared at him, but rang a tiny bell. A pair of guards appeared instantly. "Bring this man closer," the king commanded. Though surprised, Eddyn didn't resist as the guards snared his arms and ushered him none too gently to a small chair across the table from the king. "Hold him," Barrax said. "And if he does *anything,* kill him."

"I may not be *able* to do anything," Eddyn protested, taking the seat, still thinking furiously. "I truly know almost nothing about this thing save that it is . . . important."

"Enough to precipitate a war, it would seem."

Eddyn ignored that. Once again, he'd found himself balanced on the fine edge between heroism and treason. If he could succeed at what he hoped, he might—*might*—be able to redeem himself. If not . . . well, traitor would make a nice cap on rapist, vandal, thief, and murderer. And if things went as they could, he at least might be able to trade a slow death for a fast one. "I will need to touch it," he said.

The king—who did *not* touch it, Eddyn noted—laid the gem and its accoutrements on the white-velvet tablecloth.

Eddyn stared at it briefly, then closed his eyes, silently uttering one of his rare sincere prayers to The Eight for whatever aid they might feel inclined to bestow. A deep breath, and he slid his hands across the fabric to bracket the stone. Slowly, tentatively, he moved his index fingers inward to where the actual surface of the gem showed within its cage of silver—partly in fear of what he might find himself, but also hoping to invoke an atmosphere of dread that might catch the king off guard.

Another breath and he touched it—right, then left. He did feel something, too: a pulse of anger and dislike, but along with them a vague sense of . . . familiarity, like a known enemy met in a room full of even more hostile strangers.

But what did he do now? He only knew how to do one thing. And what did Barrax know? Probably that one could use it to communicate over distance—which was its most important military advantage. But Eddyn didn't know how to do that, though he'd tried over and over to contact Rrath and Tyrill—unsuccessfully. Nor had the gem proved helpful; in the end, it had given him no more than a headache.

The one thing he did know was that he was going to try again right now.

A third breath, and he tried to focus on two things alone: the power he could feel in the gem, which blazed there like a hot coal enclosed in cold iron—present, and warming, but not available to light any fires. And his desire for all this to end, to free himself of this dangerous southern king who threatened everything he held dear. And so, he simply *wished* at the stone, trying to turn off his intellect so that the raw force of emotion ruled—as it had done, to his detriment, far too often.

For a moment nothing happened. But then . . . it warmed. Or something; the sensation was impossible to describe. Abruptly, he felt something tug at him. Not at his physical body, but at his *self,* his consciousness. He tried to control it by raw desire. It resisted; he tried harder. But he had managed to activate it, which meant he might be able to act on his desire.

Out, he thought desperately. *Away. Gone from here. Escaped.* And with that, he tried to imagine being gone. Freedom around him. Familiarity. Security.

But the image that came to him was of Merryn: asleep—possibly drugged. Without intending to, he moved toward her—a familiar face in an alien country, a person whom he knew to be strong and free. A potentially valuable ally.

Avall? she queried, unbelieving.

Eddyn.

He recoiled from the wash of anger. Yet with it, hiding in it, was a sort of resigned hope.

I'm here and prisoner, he dared. *Barrax has the gem, and—*

Avall should have it!

Not at present. It was an . . . accident.

If you've hurt him . . .

In no way he can't survive. But there's no time for this. Barrax is watching me. I was trying to escape.

How?

In trying to explain it to her, he found himself thinking images at her that were not limited by words. She grasped some of it—maybe more than he wanted, for that history was bound up with his assault on Avall.

"Eron-man!"

The words came from without, grabbing at him. Seeking to wrest him away from the first hope he'd had in days.

I have to go. I'll try to work with this thing again. Maybe we can get out of here.

Maybe.

"Eron-man!" that voice thundered.

Eddyn opened his eyes, noted a roaring headache, and closed them again as he found Barrax glaring at him. He shivered uncontrollably.

The king's glare became a stare. "I don't know what you did, but that thing glowed slightly, and I felt . . . colder. It's not what I wanted, but maybe it's enough to let you live."

The king reached for the gem, but paused, and grasped the chain instead. Ever so carefully, he lowered it into a pouch, which he placed in another and stored at his waist.

Then he looked at Eddyn.

Eddyn wasn't looking back, however.

He seemed to have gone to sleep or fainted. Barrax wondered if it was normal for people to shiver in their sleep like that.

CHAPTER XXII:

PRELUDE TO WAR

(ERON; NORTH OF SOUTH GORGE— NEAR SPRING: DAY XXXVII—MIDAFTERNOON)

~~~~~~~~~~~~

In spite of what his scouts had told him, High King Gynn was approaching the pass called Eron's Belt with trepidation. Lodged between the ragged peaks of Angen's Spine on one hand, and the cold Oval Sea on the other, his kingdom consisted mostly of an unbroken line of forested hills following the roots of the mountains, above an open plain of varying width, which in turn slid down to the coast, all split by the six principal gorges, running northwest to southeast. Just ahead, however, mountains, woods, plain, and shore pinched together, giving the country a kind of waist, which was both its vulnerability and its potential salvation, now that War-Hold had fallen. North of that narrowing lay four gorges, in order from the south: Eron, Mid, Dead, and North. Below were South Gorge and Half. The Belt was maybe a quarter way up the land's length.

It was also the last place short of Eron Gorge itself where Gynn could expect to meet Barrax and hold him—and the best place from which to ride to the defense of South Gorge, if it wasn't too late already. Even that assumed a certain predictability on Barrax's part: namely that he and his south-born army would take the safe route along the coast, leaving the Eronese, with their greater tolerance for cold and snow, to claim the heights. From what Gynn had heard, Barrax, though rash and headstrong, was no fool.

Unfortunately, he had one advantage Gynn lacked. Barrax was ruler absolute. He could demand every live body in Ixti walk naked across raw ice, and expect to be obeyed. Even in war, Gynn was subject to reelection and the Rule of Law.

Not that the war-call hadn't gone out in haste and in force; conscripting levies from every hold within reach—even sleds to North Gorge, which would be icebound for another eighth. Warcraft, in particular, had responded better than expected, though he suspected he'd pay the price of that support in favors if he survived this mess.

At least he wasn't sitting home playing bureaucrat.

Without really thinking about it, he reined in his steed—an icy white stallion named Snowmelt—and motioned the troops to a halt behind. His elite guard rode vanguard there, a neat line of gold-washed helms and bright swords and spears, all in the crimson cloaks of War-Hold-Prime. Both Tryffon and Preedor accompanied that host, though one was properly too old; unfortunately, there'd been no time to argue.

In any case, the sun was high in a cloudless sky, and the road gleamed with a mix of water and melting ice between the well-laid paving stones. More snow showed among the pines to either side, but the plains looked largely free of the stuff. It had been with no small relief that Gynn had watched the snowpack shrink from waist high, to ankle deep, to splotches of clear ground as he'd led the army south. And now there was a high meadow just ahead, nestled in a bowl between the approaching gap and a higher, final declivity, from which one could look down upon the Ri-Ormill that fed South Gorge, roughly two shots away, down an intimidatingly steep slope. The head of the Gorge itself was farther to the east: two more shots, at least.

The army would bivouac there. The site allowed maximum flexibility. And, depending on the quality of Barrax's advisers—and prisoners—his foe likely didn't know it existed.

Impulsively, Gynn slid off his horse and strode forward through the slush, tossing his reins to a squire in Beast-Hold livery beneath War. At that moment, a rider appeared atop the rise ahead. Gynn reached for his sword reflexively, but the man stretched his arms straight out from his body in token of identification, then started down the track.

Tired from the saddle, Gynn marched out to meet him, motioning his advisers to follow. Orders to dismount flowed up and down the line. Already men from the baggage train were rushing up with camp seats and food. Gynn claimed the flattest place he could find, pouring two mugs of hot cider while he waited. He sipped his gratefully.

The scout dismounted when he came within the requisite three spans, then knelt at two. "I need news more than ceremony," Gynn told him calmly. "Come, sit. Or stand if you will. We need to know what lies beyond."

Probably *not* attack, Gynn reckoned, for the scout—he recognized him now: a lad named Whyllor, and, like most of his kind, a Geographer out of Lore by way of War—was fairly composed and in nowise out of breath, though he'd recently knelt in mud, to judge by his tunic, cloak, and hose.

Whyllor pushed back his hood and took the mug from the King's own hands.

Gynn waited while he drank, noting a disturbance in the ranks to the left and a flash of green and gold that meant someone in messenger garb was pushing through the assembled multitude. Good: He'd have two reports at once.

"How lies the land beyond?" Gynn asked when the man had emptied his mug. "And how lies my enemy upon it?"

Whyllor wiped his mouth self-consciously. "It is as we suspected from his seizure of Half Gorge: He has split his force in two. One part even now infests the tree line beyond the Ri, most likely to come upon the tower and the gorge from the west as soon as the floods recede. The other waits a day's ride to the south."

"And the size of this force?"

"The nearer is smaller than yours. The farther—we were unable to get close enough to tell, though, of course, we're still trying."

"And the Gorge itself: Does it know?"

"It does. As has always been the plan in case of such attack, the people who inhabit the Gorge's upper reaches will move toward the Tir-Vonees at the coast, then turn north where the cliffs lower, and join you. The cost will be in buildings and position."

"But Barrax has not yet reached the river?"

"His scouts surely have, but the floods were early this year and therefore extensive enough to fill Ormill Vale right up to the roots of the mountains. Barrax will expect a plain and find a lake. Nor do I think they know we're as close as we are—yet. We've been very thorough. We know the land, they don't. And they'd have to skirt through the mountains."

Tryffon cleared his throat. "Unfortunately, the floods hold us off as well as our foe, and during the floods, even the bridges across the Ri-Ormill are drowned. Still—if I may offer advice, Majesty—we *could* slight the causeways to them. We may not be able to disable them all, but if we concentrate on those at the top of the Gorge, the bulk of our folk could still escape to the north, and we could force our enemy either to cross the river at flood, or go into the mountains, where we will have advantage."

Gynn nodded. "So I was thinking. Yet it seems too simple. Barrax looks to have relied mostly on surprise and the fact that he has the weather on his side. But his supply lines are much longer than ours, even if he relies on pillaged stores—of which, I fear, there are many. He will also find his flanks harried. Only a twentieth part of our people dwell in Half Gorge at the best of times, but I doubt many of them will take to Barrax's rule. Every adult down there has spent time at War-Hold; they know how to fight. Even if no trained leaders survive, leaders will still arise. If we can hold them here until our own numbers are up to strength, we can win this thing. They are a hard wire of arrogance stretched across our land, with new filaments added now and then. We are a forge growing ever hotter. We will melt them if they come too close."

"Unless our fire goes out."

"And," Tryffon sighed, "don't forget about Eddyn—and the gem."

"Wherever Eddyn is, he surely has sense enough to avoid the armies of Ixti."

"Unless he seeks to throw in his lot with them. He would have a powerful bargaining tool in the gem's communication abilities alone. And we've given him little cause to remain loyal to us."

Gynn nodded. "A rape. An assault. A defiling. A possible poisoning. Two more assaults. The theft of a national treasure. It is as though the man is trying to cut his own throat."

"Maybe," Tryffon acknowledged. "But surely we have other concerns than Eddyn syn Argen-yr."

Another nod. "One of which is to set up camp, and ring that camp with the best spies and scouts we have. Barrax *will* be sending feelers north. We must see that none succeed—though even failure to return will tell him something."

Tryffon motioned to a young man in his entourage and muttered a few words to him, whereupon he left at a run. "You should have a roof over your head in less than a hand. There's a ruined hold on one horn of the gap, which overlooks the vale, but it would take some work—"

"The tent will more than suffice," Gynn replied frankly. "But have someone assess the hold, just in case—it *would* be a more comfortable place in which to plan."

"My thinking exactly, Majesty."

A noise in the ranks proved to be the herald Gynn had noted earlier, jostling his way into the royal presence. His horse was lathered and his face flushed. Gynn hoped the lad was not the bearer of bad news.

"Vallyn syn Morvall," the youth panted, "with word from Tir-Eron."

"Word for good or ill?" Gynn demanded formally.

"Mostly good. Mostly from the Council of Chiefs."

"Give me the gist now," Gynn said. "You can give your full report at tonight's council." And he would, too: every word anyone said, with descriptions of body language at need. Unfortunately, he'd only be able to do it once.

"There was only one significant item of Council business," Vallyn began, "which is to inform you that the Priests of Fate and the Chiefs of Lore have agreed that this spring's Fateing can be altered as you asked."

"*Exactly* as asked?" Tryffon inserted.

Another nod. "Everyone entering the Fateing for the first time must list War-Hold as his or her first choice. The rest are encouraged to do the same, and those with only one choice remaining, and that not War, will be given four free choices—if we survive this thing. Those with two choices remaining will be given three for free, and so on. The result will be chaos for a while. But if we fail . . . it won't matter."

Gynn grinned his satisfaction. "Exactly as I'd hoped. These new levies should begin arriving soon, then?"

The herald looked uneasy. "That was one thing to which the Council would *not* agree—Priest-Clan, more precisely. The Fateing will fall as the Law demands."

The grin became a scowl. "Which is still within the eighth, though I'd hoped to have them sooner. And another eight days for the first to arrive . . ." Gynn turned to Tryffon. "That is how long we have to hold them."

"It can be done."

"Are you certain?"

Tryffon gestured at the sky. "Nothing, my King, is certain."

Gynn rose to go, but the herald once more cleared his throat. "Majesty, there is one final item it was thought you might need to hear, though it will not make you happy."

"And that is?"

"Lord Eellon syn Argen-a, Clan-Chief of Argen, is ill. His head and heart have troubled him since Avall's return, though it is said he tried to hide it. Since then—"

"He's pushed himself relentlessly," Gynn spat. "And tried to hide *that*. Dammit, why couldn't he have taken better care of himself? I knew he couldn't travel down here with the army, but I was relying on him to keep the Council in line—to keep Priest-Clan in line, in any event. If he dies—"

"The next eldest member of that clan is old Fallora, who was in North Gorge, last we heard," Preedor muttered.

"Which would mean the ranking subchief in Tir-Eron would have to take over—who is, I'm afraid, from Argen-yr."

"If Tyrill doesn't try to seize control herself. It would be just like her."

Gynn shuddered, and not from the wind. "She's still loyal—to the land. But if we survive this and Eellon doesn't . . . I don't want to think."

"The trek from Gem-Winter has arrived," the herald murmured, almost as an afterthought. "Tyrill says to tell you she has the shield."

"Good for her," Gynn growled. "I hope it doesn't adorn my tomb."

CHAPTER XXIII:

ARRIVALS

(Eron: Tir-Eron—Near Spring: Day XL—late afternoon)

Remember the eyes . . .
Eyes reveal all . . .
Avall was trying desperately to keep those admonitions in mind as another pair of dark blue eyes met his from behind the eyeslots of a plain war helm. Breath hissed loud within his own steel equivalent; sweat ran in torrents down his spine. His arms were numb from throwing blows and deflecting them. His palms throbbed from impacts against his blade. Endlessly.

He saw an opening, and twisted slightly, drawing his opponent out, then feinted beneath his foe's arm, only to launch a true blow at the helm. Metal clanged satisfyingly loud. An edge scraped down the back of *his* helm as well, sliding off padding worn above mail.

His foe crumpled with a grunt and a jingle of armor.

Avall bent to offer a hand up. "I knew I could take you if I made you wait long enough," he told Lykkon, as the younger man thrust his practice sword into its scabbard before reaching for his chin strap. "Merryn said you were good for exactly a hand, and then impatience intercedes. She was right, too."

Lykkon had his helm off by then. His hair—cut short in anticipation of combat—was plastered to his forehead in a fringe of points. "I was distracted," he panted, with a disarming grin.

Avall glared at him as he removed his own helmet. "That grin won't save you," he warned. "And distraction can cost you—"

"If you're going to lecture, at least do it over wine," Lykkon chuckled, as he strode past Avall to the darkest part of the arcade that surrounded the Citadel's war court.

Avall had no choice but to follow, helm in one hand, the other wiping his brow with the tail of his surcoat. Lykkon was already filling goblets when Avall reached the small table. He snared a stool and absently watched a dozen other sets of young men and women honing their combat skills.

Lykkon nodded toward them. "You really think it'll come to this? Folks that young, I mean?"

"Folks as young as *you,* you mean?" Avall snorted, scowling at his drink, as though it contained something foul. "No one's going to make you fight but you, Lyk. Not on the front, anyway. But if Barrax and his friends come pounding on your gate, I doubt anyone will ask your age before he runs you through."

Lykkon wiped his face on a sleeve and sprawled backward, absently fumbling with laces and ties. "I'm not afraid to fight, 'Vall. But you've said yourself, some things simply aren't real until they make themselves real. Like battle—or sex. No amount of simulation can prepare you for the genuine article."

"Speaking of . . ." Avall smirked. "Have you . . . ?"

Lykkon turned redder than his surcoat. "What do you *think*?"

"I think you're like I was at your age: not with a woman since your Manning, and only then with an unclanned courtesan, which really is *not* the same at all."

Lykkon studied his wine in turn. "Unfortunately, I'm not into casual liaisons. But more unfortunately, there's no woman I love, and I don't have a bond-brother. Plus, I'm not important enough politically for what happened to you to be repeated."

"That's not what Lore says," Avall muttered. "Besides, I wasn't trying to—to— Dammit, Lyk, with things like they are, maybe you should. Maybe we should all abandon caution for once, and live . . . *intensely*. Fateing or no, you could be dead in an eighth. Aren't there things you want to do before you die? Things there's no reason *not* to do except that they carry the weight of implicit disapproval—not legal prohibition, mind you—merely traditional assumption of avoidance."

Lykkon buried his face in his hands. "It isn't supposed to be like this, 'Vall. We have this neat, predictable life worked out for us, with everything established by Law and enforced by our elders. It's safe and secure and a little boring, but it also gives us freedom and life experience we might not get otherwise. More to the point—for now—it renders us much more informed and accomplished than the average Ixtian can ever hope to be. Still, we're supposed to be able to look ahead ten years or thirty or eighty, and have a clear idea of where we'll be doing what with whom. And now none of that's a given. There're folks in Half Gorge right now who'll spend the rest of their lives rebuilding what they've lost, and trying to superimpose their needs atop a system that isn't designed to support them. It's—"

Avall couldn't help but laugh. "You think too much, cousin."

Lykkon regarded him steadily. "I think about those things to avoid thinking about others—like Eellon."

Avall's face clouded. "Have you seen him today?"

"Of course."

"And?"

"He's sicker than he admits, but claims he's pacing himself. He says you can endure anything if you know how long you'll have to endure it. He says this spring and summer will tell the tale. He says if Gynn doesn't hold the gap, the only thing that can win this war for us is the weather."

Another snort. "Well, it's sure as bloody cold not helping now! Not with the top two gorges still frozen in. I guess that's the price we pay for a mild winter."

"Which at least saved you. I wouldn't have wanted to lose you, 'Vall."

"Nor I you." Avall studied the courtyard. "There's time for another bout—"

Lykkon shook his head, but then his eyes went very round, and his chin all but clanked against his chest, he was so slack-jawed.

"Lyk, what—?"

Lykkon closed his mouth enough to speak. "Avall," he whispered carefully. "Look . . . behind . . . you . . ."

A chill trotted down Avall's spine—precisely as he felt something brush his mind. He recoiled instinctively, already reaching for his sword as he rose.

But then an impossibly joyful freshness washed across his consciousness like rain across parched earth.

"Strynn!" he blurted, as a tall figure emerged from the shadows behind him and stepped into the light. Hair like liquid night framed a face of porcelain-white before tumbling across shoulders clad in Argen maroon. He was dumbfounded anew at her beauty, wondering how he could have forgotten it in the eighths since he had seen her. Wondering if perhaps she had grown more beautiful because of all that had transpired, that had fortified already incredible fairness with strength.

"Avall."

She smiled with absolute joy, absolute conviction. And that joy reached out to engulf him as he had not been engulfed since leaving Gem-Hold. It was like emotion solidified, and he wrapped himself in it, even as his more physical aspect wrapped himself in her arms and she in his. He was vaguely aware of a sudden silence from the court, and of Lykkon starting to laugh, long and loud and recklessly.

Other laughter joined in: his own and Strynn's. No one spoke—yet communication continued unabated. Finally Avall eased away. "I'm not going to kiss you until I can do it without interruption," he murmured, as he drew her back into the shadows. "But—there should've been word of your approach. I didn't think you'd be with the trek, but I've been asking everyone I could find who was on it, anyway; never mind going out of my mind since . . . Well, I'll tell you about *that* later—" He broke off, wishing he hadn't said even that much, for it was like extinguishing a candle he'd only just ignited.

"Don't apologize," Strynn shot back far more seriously than expected. "I know what you're going to tell me. The rest—it was Eellon's decision. As soon as word came of our approach, he sent my cousin Veen to outline the situation, and—"

Avall stiffened. "Why would he do *that*?"

"Because, sweet man that he is, he didn't want to sully our reunion with politics—which we're doing anyway. We'd already heard so many terrible things, he . . . we just wanted something good to happen to you, something you wouldn't fret about until it happened. He wanted to surprise you!"

"But you know . . ."

"About the war and the attack on War-Hold. And—" She broke off, eyes bright with tears. "Oh, Avall, poor Merryn—"

Avall reached out to take her hand. "I don't think she was there—for reasons I'll explain later. You'll have to trust me on this—and Merryn."

Strynn nodded bravely, glancing around lest she be overheard. "I also know about Eddyn."

"And the gem . . ."

Another nod. "Eellon met us at Argen-Hall and briefed us there. It— He says it's affected you."

Avall shrugged. "Maybe. I can't tell."

"I can."

Avall started to reply, then froze in place. "I . . . have a son—"

And then he froze in truth. He did *not* have a son. Strynn had a son. The boy was no blood of his, nor bone. He was Eddyn's forever. Anything Avall made of him—he and Strynn—would be a patina on someone else's casting.

Yet in spite of what she must have read in his face, Strynn grinned and squeezed his hand, while Lykkon dutifully filled every goblet in sight. People were approaching, Avall noticed, lured to Strynn like moths to flame. "A very handsome son who takes a vast interest in everything he sees."

Avall let go her hand. "I have to . . ."

"He's at Argen-Hall, as he should be," Strynn went on quickly. "You'd have to fight your mother for him. Besides, he's asleep, and I dare even *you* to wake him, given how much trouble he was—as Rann, Div, and Kylin can attest."

Avall caught at a pillar, as realization rocked him. "Rann, Div, *and* Kylin . . ."

Another grin. "They're waiting in your suite. We ran into Bingg, and he suggested it, clever lad. Rann said to tell you he loved you dearly, but that he thought you'd love him more if he had a bath first. Kylin's having one as well—and not with Rann, lest you worry."

"And Div?" Avall repeated, both relieved and terrified, given what had passed between them, if only once.

"We wouldn't be here without her, that's for certain. Pacing the spring trek out of Gem, while keeping us safe from them. Being as good a friend to me as I've found since Merryn."

"And she and Rann?"

A shrug. "I don't know. Sometimes they are; sometimes they're not. This whole thing has blindsided him."

"What do *you* think?"

"That she knows what she is and isn't, and that Rann knows as well—but that they don't always agree on how those things fit together, or which is more important."

Once again Lykkon burst out laughing.

They stared at him. "Lyk . . . ?"

Tears stained his cheeks. "Do you have any idea how silly all this sounds? You two haven't been together for even a finger, and you're already dissecting your friends' relationships."

"They're safe," Strynn informed him stiffly. "In any event, I've been dying to find out what Avall thinks about our little overland initiative."

"Well, I'm not sure I *approve*," Avall replied darkly, "given the risks I suspect you ran. But it's bound to be more pleasant than discussing the infernal war, if only because we know it resolved successfully."

Strynn's face clouded, but she did not reply.

"The baby—" Avall began again. "I should—"

Strynn's eyes were sad—and very, very tired. "I—I have to speak frankly," she whispered, "even if it hurts us both; I've no energy for games any longer. I didn't bring him here to meet you because I didn't know how you'd react. He's not your child, and you can't hide how you feel about that. Argen-Hall was on the way, and your clan will have his fosterage in any case. I wanted—I wanted to let *you* choose the time."

Avall shook his head to clear it. "This is a lot in a small space, Strynn. You, Rann—you're *real* to me. The child's never been real. I'm sorry if I don't seem happier; and I appreciate your understanding more than you can say. There, I've given you truth for truth."

Strynn nodded through a failed attempt at a smile.

"I'll send for him when he wakes up," Avall continued. "If no one's made it clear to you, I'm living in the Citadel now."

"Another reason I didn't bring him," Strynn confessed. "I didn't know what I might be interrupting."

"Nothing that couldn't wait," Avall sighed—in relief, as much as anything.

"Well," Lykkon announced decisively, "I say we should reconvene in Avall's suite at once."

Avall raised a brow. "We?"

Lykkon raised one in turn. "*Someone* has to be a neutral observer."

Fortunately, it wasn't far from the war court to Avall's quarters. He and Strynn spent that journey holding hands and trying to make light conversation, but a pall of seriousness haunted even that inconsequential patter. There were still unresolved issues between them, after all—more than either of them realized, it appeared. Too, now that Strynn was here, he had no more reason for inaction. If she'd brought the helm.

It was as though she'd read his mind. "I did bring it. There was no reason not to, and I thought . . . maybe you could reconstruct it from what remained—if you had the heart for it."

He sagged against her. "I don't know if I've got the heart for anything, Strynn."

"Well, don't tell Rann that," she cautioned with an edge of anger in her voice that hurt to hear, so soon after their reunion. "Don't forget what he risked for you. And don't forget that you owe all four of us an explanation of how you managed what you did."

"Everything in due time."

"Let's just hope due time still exists. I've heard about the Fateing."

"There'll be time," Avall repeated. "I promise." And then they turned down one final corridor, and Avall saw the door to his suite ahead. Guarded, as was always the case these days. He chuckled grimly. "Gynn considers me a national treasure," he told Strynn. "More precisely, he considers what I know about the gem to be a national treasure. Even though I no longer have it," he finished bitterly.

Lykkon, who'd been following a discreet distance behind—though not so far he couldn't eavesdrop—swerved neatly around them and darted ahead, likely to proclaim their arrival. To no surprise, the guard was Krynneth. Gynn had steadfastly refused to let the young War-Holder join him at the front until he recovered from his mad ride, but had attached him to Avall in compensation. Krynneth bowed slightly and opened the door for his cousin, Strynn, to enter. Avall followed, through the vestibule into his common room.

No sooner had he crossed the threshold, however, than strong arms enfolded him, and he was lifted off the floor and spun around. Lips brushed his cheeks. Avall caught glimpses of several more people in the room than anticipated. But by then he'd recognized that grasp, the feel and scent of that body . . .

"Rann, you fool—"

"I will *not* put you down," Rann laughed, continuing to hold Avall aloft until Avall tickled his ribs. Rann released him so suddenly, he fell to the floor with a thump. Which gave him time to note who else shared the chamber. Strynn, of course, and Lykkon. But Bingg and Eellon were there as well—looking bemused—as were Div and Kylin, the latter still with wet hair, but already having unearthed his harp.

Avall's glance danced between the woodswoman and his bond-brother. Rann looked glad to see him as only Rann could. He also seemed happy and content—and far healthier than the last time Avall had seen him, when days in the Wild had led to the gem's sapping Rann's vitality.

"You're alive," Rann said simply, as he helped Avall to his feet. "Only now do I believe it—I think."

Avall's gaze slid back to Div. Though well dressed—in women's clothing, for the first time since he'd known her—she looked ill at ease. Which she probably was. She was Common Clan, after all, those around her very High Clan indeed; she'd naturally be reserved. Never mind what the two of them had shared, along with Rann, one night in a birkits' cave. As for the other thing that haunted him: the fact that this might be the person with whom he'd forever have to share his closest friend—that was for him and Rann to puzzle through when they had time. If they ever *did* have time, which to judge by Eellon's impatient glower, they might not.

Bingg was playing squire for the nonce, standing solicitously beside Eellon, as Lykkon had done not so long ago. Drinks had been set out, Avall noted—as he likewise noted that he still wore sparring leathers. "I'll change," he apologized, then noticed Lykkon's similar attire. "You, too, Lyk. This could be a long one."

Lykkon sniffed an armpit, grimaced, and followed Avall into the bath. The air was still damp, and it took Avall a moment to recall that Rann had just availed himself of that luxury. Rann—who joined him quick as thought, and helped him and Lykkon divest themselves of their padding and mail, not stopping until they'd splashed themselves free of sweat, toweled down, and donned clean house-hose and short-tunics.

Much refreshed, Avall rejoined his companions, by which time someone had produced a light snack. A covered dish occupied the center of the table, which roused Avall's curiosity. He sat down wearily, took a sip of wine, and reached for the lid, then hesitated. "Strynn, if you'd like to do the honors?"

She smiled at him. "Actually, that's a delicacy we brought specially for you from Gem-Hold. At great peril," she added, mysteriously.

Avall regarded her askance, then shrugged and lifted the lid.

And almost dropped it at what he saw revealed.

"*Four* of them!" he gasped. "They . . . are the same, aren't they?"

"So we hope," Strynn replied, as Avall stared with a mix of hope, horror, and relief at four stones identical to the one he'd lost. And Strynn had a fifth, which meant— He reached forward reflexively, but Rann snared his wrist before he could touch any of the gleaming red objects.

"None is . . . activated, as far as we know," he said. "But we don't think anyone *ought* to activate them until we know who's best to master them. Besides, you've already got one, and we don't know if a person *can* master two."

"But Strynn and you—"

"Used yours after you'd . . . bonded to it."

"Until we each got our own," Strynn added, offhand.

Avall masked his confusion with a deep draught of wine. "Waiting's probably wise," he conceded.

"I'd think so," Eellon agreed, pausing to cough.

Avall tried not to think about Eellon's presence here, when he was so ill. He hoped his Chief knew what he was doing. "Where'd you find these?" he asked, to distract himself.

Another cough from Eellon. "That *would* be good to know. If they're from the clan vein, that's one thing. But if they were found elsewhere—well, Gem would have a claim over the stones themselves *and* whatever use they're put to. And I don't feel like contending with them right now."

Rann exchanged glances with Strynn. "They're ours," he assured them. "Though exactly how we acquired them is a longer story than we have time for at the moment. In any case there's nothing to stop others finding more. What happens then . . ."

". . . we'll worry about when it occurs," Eellon concluded. "For now . . . there are things we must discuss."

Once again Rann's gaze found Strynn's, but then he looked at Avall. "Strynn and I had an idea," he began. "It's really an outgrowth of a notion of yours, but now that we've learned about the war—I have an even better idea, though it's also more . . . urgent."

Strynn nodded. "It's also something we don't feel equipped to decide ourselves, and one of those scary points where clan and craft converge. In the absence of the King, and much as I hate to suggest it, I think we'd better summon Tyrill. I'm not sure she can help in this case, but we're wiser not to exclude her."

Eellon shifted uneasily—and coughed again. "Send for her, if you think best." He motioned to Bingg, who left at a run. "Accept no excuses," Eellon called after him. "Tell her it's about power."

"Tell her to bring Averryn," Strynn chimed in. "Maybe that'll cut the edge off her temper."

"Averryn?" Avall wondered.

Strynn managed a lopsided grin. "We had to call him *something* until you and I can confirm a name for him—since you're still his father, under the Law . . ."

"Averryn," Avall repeated thoughtfully. "I think that will do very well indeed."

Averryn, in fact, arrived ahead of Tyrill—with Avall's mother, who'd evidently laid permanent claim to him. And would be in charge of him for the next eight years, in any case—until his parents finished their first term of Service. He was duly admired, poked, and prodded, weathering all with admirable restraint. Avall felt a number of things at first, but it was hard to feel anything but joy when confronted with Strynn's delight in the tiny, bright-eyed bundle. His own perceptions were mostly objective: more black hair than expected, and impossibly smooth baby skin. Still, he would try to love him, as he loved Strynn. And he *did* love her, too—though sometimes it took absence to prove it.

And then Tyrill arrived, and affairs took a darker turn entirely.

"It's about power," Rann echoed Eellon, as the Craft-Chief settled herself among what Avall realized was as impressive an assemblage of clan authority as he'd seen in a while. Especially as most of the subchiefs from clan and craft alike were away in the south with the King.

"What kind of power?" the old woman snapped primly.

Rann glared warning. "I take it you know about Avall's gem?"

She nodded suspiciously. "I know some things. Not enough. I always said that thing was too precious to trust to one half-grown boy."

"It apparently makes its own decisions about trust," Avall shot back. "I don't know that it would've worked for you even if I'd wanted it to."

"It worked for Strynn and Rann, so you said."

Avall studied both warily. "I think that's because it reacts to people who try to use it based on how those people relate to me. If someone I like tries to use it, it cooperates, if not—"

"What about Eddyn?"

Avall shrugged. "We've gone over this before, Craft-Chief. All I can think of is that it also runs on emotion and desire, and maybe some other factors we haven't discovered—like fear for one's life. It acts to protect itself, I think. When I thought I was drowning out in the Ri-Eron, it protected me, and when it couldn't—when the only thing my *self* wanted in the whole world was to get away from the cold—it took me to the nearest aid. Eddyn wanted away from . . . whatever he feared would happen to him for yet another crime, and—"

"It doesn't matter now," Eellon inserted. "Rann said he had an idea."

Rann indicated the gems. "We know they can manifest some kind of physical power, though not much about how that power is activated or directed. But we were thinking—especially now that it appears Barrax may have access to the original—that we might be able to counter him if our King had power of his own that really was *his* power. Gynn's already used to working with power to some degree, when he becomes vessel of The Eight. We thought that if we could tune these gems to him, he might be able to use that power Avall and I invoked."

Tyrill's eyes narrowed. "Assuming this power exists, how do you propose to go about it?"

Strynn took up the tale. "As we've said—and proven, I think, to reasonable satisfaction—the gems work to preserve themselves, which they seem to do by serving those who protect them. They also seem to function as foci of desire. So we thought that if we could bond three of these into the new royal regalia, in such a way that they could access Gynn's blood, and he could access their powers in turn—"

Avall's face brightened with excitement. "So you think that if you put a gem in, say, a sword, which one uses for offense, it would . . . read Gynn's desire for offense and act accordingly?"

"Something like that," Strynn agreed. "And yes, I know it's a stretch, but it's all we have to go on."

Rann studied Eellon and Tyrill carefully. "Do you think the King would agree to such a thing?"

Eellon took a deep breath. "I think he'd be a fool not to try. That said, he's very busy. Will he have time to master a whole new set of skills?"

"We can teach him," Avall and Lykkon volunteered at once. "*Someone* will have to," Avall went on, "else he could be at risk. You're suggesting that he try to master several gems at once, and we've no proof that can be done, or that they won't work at odds with each other."

Tyrill set down her goblet with a noisy thump. "Power," she huffed. "I've no proof this power of which you spoke exists."

Avall glared at her, then shifted his gaze toward Rann and Div. "It only happened once," he admitted. "We were very, very focused—centered on each other to the exclusion of all else. We were just wanting . . . *more* and it gave us more the only way it could."

Eellon interrupted. "You said, however, that you think you reached the Realm of The Eight? The King might be able to verify that, since he has contact with Them."

"As does Priest-Clan," Tyrill growled.

"Whom we dare not trust, and certainly dare not bring into this now."

Avall nodded vigorously. "So, to jump ahead, it sounds like you're saying he could use the gems as . . . as portable Wells."

Rann shrugged. "But the Wells control him, so we think. He has to be able to control this . . ."

"But if he desired to go to the Overworld—" Avall began.

"And could go there when he would . . ."

Lykkon, who'd been observing the proceedings with sharp interest, cleared his throat. "I've been thinking about that: what Avall said happened. Correct me if I'm wrong, cousin, but you said that you went to another place, and when you started to leave, you wanted proof you'd been there, so you picked up a stone. But when you returned, the stone vanished. Turned to energy, as it were."

Avall nodded uncertainly. "That's how it felt. Rann and Div were with me; they can verify."

"So," Lykkon went on, lacing his fingers before him, "suppose we're dealing with a simple inversion here. Two worlds that meet but don't touch, if that makes any sense. Each with matter and energy, so we assume, because we can't imagine anything else. So maybe matter in one world becomes energy in the other, and vice versa."

Avall's eyes went huge. "That's a major leap, cousin."

"It would be worth it to prove. Besides which, if Rann's right—if we could find a way for Gynn to gather stones in the Overworld and throw them at the enemy here as . . . fire—"

"It almost killed us," Avall protested.

Div shook her head. "No, it merely knocked us out—and we weren't prepared for it. Remember, Avall, the gems look after whoever owns them. They aid healing. In fact, Rann and I enjoyed some of those benefits even after you fell. As though it left some residual power even in us."

"Healing!" Lykkon mused. "You think . . . That is . . . Is it possible it might help Eellon?"

The Chief of Argen looked startled. "From what I've seen, it only draws strength—and I have none to spare."

Strynn gnawed her lip. "But it made my pregnancy less difficult, I'm certain. And I *know* it speeded my recovery after Averryn's birth. Enough that we could leave Div's hold three days later."

"And Rann and I both healed more quickly after we were wounded," Div chimed in, less reticent by the moment.

"Well, I certainly wouldn't complain if I felt better," Eellon acknowledged, "but I don't want anyone using what may be finite power to improve my condition. Besides, you said these gems aren't activated, and you've already spoken of using three in the royal regalia. Strynn, I know, also has one, as, evidently, does Rann. What were you planning to do with the fourth?"

Rann looked him straight in the eye. "Give it to Avall, of course."

"Assuming I want another!"

"Don't you?"

Avall shrugged. "At this point . . . I don't know."

Rann raised a brow. "Someone also has to try bonding with two. Someone besides the King."

"Someone more expendable than the King, you mean!"

Rann's eyes went hard. "I've got a gem of my own, Avall. I'm willing to make the effort if you're not. I thought you'd *want* the chance. I know what the gems can give you; I can't imagine that taken away." A pause. "Think about it, in any case—brother."

"What about Div and Kylin?"

"We've refused," Kylin said quietly.

Eellon cleared his throat. "There's still the matter of the regalia. If I recall, only one piece might possibly have been finished: the sword Strynn was going to make. Can someone give me a report?"

Strynn nodded. "I still have a bit of engraving to do—and honing, of course—but not so much I couldn't finish fairly soon, depending on what we do with the gems. The pregnancy threw off my schedule, and since Averryn was born . . ."

"I assume you brought the helm?" Tyrill inquired archly.

Strynn regarded her levelly. "I did. Avall can either fix it or duplicate it. If it comes to that, we could always use something that already exists, except we've come to think that the gem might sense its own . . . magic at work in whatever we make, and . . . resonate with it better."

"In any event, I'd like a go at finishing the helm," Avall conceded.

"Which leaves the shield."

"Which Eddyn was working on."

"Did you bring it with you?" Lykkon asked innocently.

Strynn shook her head. "We didn't have access. But I heard -yr's subchief say he was going to bring it with the trek. From that, I assume it's safe at Argen-Hall. But it needs someone to complete it, someone who's a master. Without Eddyn—"

"It *is* safe at Argen-Hall," Tyrill announced unexpectedly. "As you surmised, it arrived with the trek some days ago. I . . . I suppose I should have told you, Clan-Chief," she added, with uncharacteristic humility. "But it was Eddyn's last work—and his finest."

"Then you can finish it," Eellon retorted. "I'm too sick, Avall and Strynn are already busy, and Merryn isn't to hand. I don't trust anyone else. But a Craft-Chief as accomplished as you should have no trouble collaborating with her protégé."

Avall started at that, listening carefully for any trace of sarcasm. He heard none. It was true, anyway: Rivals Eellon and Tyrill might be, but the Clan-Chief had never had trouble bestowing either work or favor where it was due. If anyone could complete the shield properly, it was Tyrill. If nothing else, she ought to know by now how Eddyn thought.

"Are you up for it?" Eellon inquired.

"I . . . am," she replied faintly, still looking more than a little shocked.

"Well, then," Eellon grinned, "I suggest those objects be retrieved and work begun as soon as possible—in the royal forges, because the King wants us under his guard." A pause, while he eyed the assembly. "I expect quarters can be found for Rann and Div nearby. You, too, Tyrill. Lyk, you'd best stay on as scribe. Someone needs to watch these people."

"Speaking of which," Avall inserted. "As interesting and important as all this is, I'd like to spend some time alone with my wife."

Strynn raised a brow and sniffed pointedly. "Not until you've had a *proper* bath, and I've had a nap—which sounds like somewhere around dinner. Rann, you and Div come by later. Kylin, I'd love some music if you feel like a bit more playing."

Avall looked briefly startled, then caught first Strynn's eye, then Rann's—and finished his wine at one draught. "Well," he announced smugly. "I think my life may finally be moving again."

Eellon started to reply, but all he could do was cough.

Avall shook his sodden forelock out of his eyes, but continued teasing Rann's chest, where he lay a step below him in Gynn's—and the Citadel's—second-best steam chamber. He'd already given Rann release, and now they simply sprawled there, amid a wonder of mosaics and colored tiles neither of them noted.

Rann sighed gratefully and reached up to stroke Avall's arm. "I wish you'd let me—"

Avall stopped the hand's advance. "I wish there were two of me, brother. Truly I do. But I'm married to Strynn, I owe her the best I have, soul *and* body. Certainly I owe her that much tonight, when we've been apart so long. You, on the other hand, have had Div for days uncounted, to relieve—"

It was Rann's turn to interrupt. "You're making an assumption there."

Avall propped up on his elbow and regarded Rann curiously. "How so?"

"You're assuming Strynn's been celibate."

"Hasn't she?" A pause. "Granted there was tension between us. Granted, more to the point, that she knows you come before her in my affections. Granted she knows me well enough to know I wouldn't protest overmuch if she and someone—"

"Kylin."

"Do you know this?"

"Not with my eyes or ears, but with my heart. I know she needed comfort. I know I couldn't give it to her. I know Kylin would've been willing. I know they've been a way down that road if not to the destination."

Avall flopped onto his back and folded his arms across his sweaty chest. And sighed. "Why does that bother me, Rann? It's no more than fair turnabout, for you and me and Div and me—especially now that she doesn't have Merryn. And I like Kylin a lot—enough that *I'd* share with him, I think—if you and Strynn consented. But—dammit, Rann, I'm not supposed to love Strynn this much. It was supposed to have been a marriage of convenience. I don't need to fall in love with her. I'm not good enough for her, because she truly *is* good, and she deserves someone who'll treat her that way."

"Who better than you?"

"You've already answered that question: Kylin."

Rann sat up abruptly, which let him look down at Avall. "Forgetting sex, which is only a small part of any relationship. Forgetting that—do you think she'd ever find a better match? She and I can talk about a lot of things, so can she and Div. But it's making where your hearts are joined more surely than any meeting of the flesh. If you lost that—either of you. Well, I'd be very sorry."

"Maybe."

"No, think, Avall," Rann went on urgently. "Even with this wonderful bond between you and me, there's a place where you and I can't go, because I'm not so much a maker as Strynn is. That's what you need to treasure."

"And I do treasure it. But she's given me so much—indulged me so much on this madness about the gem, and all. This once I have to put her first. Oh, she'd understand if you and I shared tonight, but tonight of all nights *I* have to give her the best I have."

Rann chuckled softly. "You're right, dammit. As much as I'd prefer otherwise, you're right. From an absolute sense, she has first claim on you."

"I'm *not* dreading it, Rann. And please believe me when I tell you that adding something to my life doesn't diminish what's already there. This is in-addition-to, not instead-of."

Rann sighed dramatically. "That much more I can give Div, I guess."

"I doubt she'd complain, no matter how much—"

"Watch it!" Rann warned. But his face was merry.

Avall shifted again. "I have a suggestion, if you're feeling adventurous."

A brow lifted. "Oh?"

"Lykkon. He needs closeness, Rann. He needs what he could get from a bond-brother now—if he had one. I can't give it to him; we're too close kin. But you and he—"

Rann chuckled wickedly. "Devious, aren't you?"

Avall shook his head, sending droplets flying. "That just occurred to me, but I think he'd welcome it, especially if you told him it was my idea."

Another chuckle. "Well, he's certainly not hard to look at. I like him a lot. And there are definitely worse ways to stay warm."

Avall laughed in turn—loudly. "Oh, and I just had a really great idea. When you're finished with him, you could pass him on to Div. The three of you—"

"I can think of worse things," Rann repeated. "If nothing else, I suppose I could ask her."

"Which only leaves Kylin."

"Not for long," Rann laughed in turn. "To judge by the way Krynneth was looking at him!"

Avall rose and started toward the door. "Strynn should be awake by now," he said. "And I'm hungry, and not just for food."

"Well," Rann observed, as they headed for the cold-pool, "it should be an . . . interesting night for all of us."

"And all because of the war," Avall replied darkly.

"The war," Rann echoed. "But you know, at this very moment, I'm not even sorry."

CHAPTER XXIV:

SMITHING

(Eron: Tir-Eron—Near Spring: Day XLI—morning)

~~~~~~~~~~~~

For all that High King Gynn had been raised and trained as a smith, the forges beneath the Citadel were rarely used. Indeed, excluding Gynn's private forge, they hadn't been touched, save for routine cleaning, in more than a generation. Even Avall, who'd been all but incarcerated in the Citadel since his return, hadn't been there, and had no good expectations for what he might find. Such structures were typically designed and built by architects, not by those whose crafts were actually involved. As such, they tended to be triumphs of form over function.

He'd said as much, too, as he and Strynn made their way there at far too early an hour—after a night's lovemaking had kept them up far too late. Still, the helm, the sword, and the shield should be there even now—transported in the night by trusted Smithcraft minions under royal guard. It would be strange, Avall thought, to work so openly on what he still considered a masterwork. And while there'd still be opportunities for privacy, he and Strynn would probably be sharing a forge for the first time since their wedding, and for the first time ever as adults.

"I wonder where Tyrill is," Strynn murmured, as they strode along corridors in the depths of the Citadel—the same level that housed the dungeons, had they known. The walls were straight, and smoothly hewn from solid rock, but completely unadorned. The same for the floor, though the texture was rougher there, to improve footing. Even the ceiling was plain, arching in a simple barrel vault a span above their heads. Other corridors intersected at precise right angles. The main difference between analogous spaces in other holds was the fact that the light came from more and newer glow-globes than Avall had ever seen.

He tightened his grip on his tool kit as he strode along—sure token of an anxiety he was trying to mask. "I don't know," he yawned. "She could as well be wildly early as wildly late, depending on what suits her."

"She's *old,* Avall,"

"Not as old as Eellon, and he gets around decently."

"Not without those braces he thinks no one knows about. But you're right, it'd be just like her to lie in wait for us with a list of criticisms of our work ready to go."

Tyrill was in fact lying in wait, but with a hot cup of cauf clutched in her gnarled old hands instead of the much-feared list. Indeed, she was sitting calmly in a leather-cushioned chair to one side of the master bellows, having drawn two more seats to join hers around a small refreshment table. Still, Avall almost missed her amid the splendor of the forges. Forging was dirty work, that was a fact. It depended on fire, which produced smoke, ash, and noise. These were utterly clean. Fresh coats of gleaming whitewash covered every stone surface save the floor, and there was plenty of light, both from glow-globes and a bank of glass-brick windows giving on a light well that must be in the very back of the Citadel. As for the forges themselves, none had yet been fired, but Avall already knew they were a minor matter to ignite.

For the rest . . . tools gleamed everywhere, all in neat rows; along with machines for shaping metal in ways goldsmiths didn't usually have to assay. And of course one whole wall was lined with books on smithing. Probably every book on the subject ever written, duplicating the libraries at Smith-Hold and Lore-Hold alike. And with a fourth set secreted at a remote location, just in case.

In case of *war,* Avall realized with a shudder, as he finally ceased gawking and allowed himself to be seated beside Tyrill. She poured him cauf without comment and motioned toward a plate of scones and honey. Only then did he note that she was dressed for a hard day's smithing—in thick but supple leather over wool. Her hair was pulled back severely and pinned beneath a cap. She even wore a smith's apron, which Avall hadn't seen her sport since his tenure in her tutelage two years back.

"Chief," he said eventually, because it was polite. Strynn echoed him somewhat more forcefully.

"Smiths," she replied formally, including both. "Whatever your accomplishments, and I know them to be considerable, you are bound to recall with every breath that I alone rule this craft. I will expect no argument as far as matters of design or technique are concerned. In the matter of these gems . . . I will learn from you, but even there, I expect to be heeded." She nodded toward three shrouded shapes arrayed along a table between them and the nearest wall. "Now then," she sighed, "let's see what's had my curiosity dancing since I got here—almost a hand before you did, I might add."

"We came when we said we would," Avall grumbled.

"But with making, one should always want to arrive as soon as one can," Tyrill snapped back. "You're supposed to be in *love* with making, aren't you, boy?"

Avall tried to ignore her, as he moved toward the first shrouded shape. "This would seem to be the sword," he said. "Strynn, would you do the honors?"

Before Tyrill could protest, Strynn carefully raised the pall of white velvet, then unfolded the wrapping she'd placed around what lay underneath.

Light literally flashed around the room.

Avall whistled in amazement at the revelation of that blade, and even Tyrill's eyes widened, though she tried to hide that fact. A casual observer would've considered it complete. But a close inspection, as Strynn grasped the hilt and flourished it aloft, then laid it across her forearm, showed file marks still visible atop the myriad folded layers, and that the incised inscription still needed some minor engraving. As did the hilt, which was a separate bronze casting. Strynn didn't *like* casting, and that dislike showed here. Not that it still wasn't fine work. It simply wasn't finished. She'd left room for a gem in the hilt, however: positioned just so that a wielder's hand would close over it. A tiny hole ran inside to the tang.

"In case we still need blood, that's a means of making a direct connection between blood, gem, and blade," Strynn explained. "Like Rann said, it's a guess, but it's easier to insert such things now."

Avall nodded, and Tyrill stroked her chin thoughtfully. "Nice work," she conceded, motioning Strynn to put it away. Avall realized he hadn't complimented it, either. "Better than you've ever done," he acknowledged, and moved down the table to where Tyrill was uncovering the shield.

Since Avall hadn't officially seen Eddyn's aborted masterwork, he made a show of active surprise when he finally got a good look at it. In form, it was an ordinary heater shape, subtly curved to embrace the body. A good size for a man of Gynn's height and build, but the proportions had long since been spelled out in treatise after treatise, so there was no art there. And since Gynn had wanted a functional shield, that had also been taken into consideration, which meant that surfaces most likely to be impacted were made of hardened bronze over iron, in panels that could be removed for replacement. But between those panels, worked in thin sheets of a light alloy whose making Argen-yr would not reveal even to the other septs, a fantasy of interlacing shapes had been wrought. Shapes that started out with complex, if formal, geometrical precision at the heart, then became more amorphous toward their edges, like patterns of frost. Exactly like the frost-flowers Avall had utilized on the helm.

Still, it was excellent work, and most of what remained involved duplicating extant bits in mirror image. And affixing the gem, of course, which would require some modifications, discussion of which Avall didn't want to contemplate.

Nor did he look forward to confronting what lay beneath the rounded lump at the end of the table, and therefore waited patiently for Tyrill to stop grumbling over the shield. A final grunt from her, and he took a deep breath and raised the cover from what should have been *his* masterwork.

It was no longer. Eddyn had pounded it into the stone floor of Avall's workroom back in Gem-Hold—not once, but many times. Joints had cracked open. Panels were dented. A few had popped free. Almost nothing remained unscathed. "Some of the understructure is intact," Strynn advised. "Still, I think you'll have to take everything off and straighten about a third of it."

"Replace," Avall countered. "I'd as soon replace outright as try to fix what shouldn't have been broken."

"The rest—"

He shrugged. "If the cartoons survive, I might be able to duplicate some of it." He paused, looked at Strynn. "You're almost done with yours. If you could help with the casting . . ."

"Lykkon can help with the casting," Tyrill broke in sharply. "He's all tied up in Lore, but he's as good with lost wax as we've got to hand right now."

Avall stared at her. Was she actually being helpful? If so, why? What was her real agenda? Or was *this* her real agenda? With the country under attack, had she finally sublimated her massive arrogance?

"Well, then," Avall replied, "if no one objects, I'll take the table to the left, there. I see no reason not to get started."

A pause, and he reached for the shield, remembering how much such things weighed, and that Tyrill was old. She started to protest, then grimaced, and let him carry it to the table to the right, which left Strynn the center.

"Mostly I'll be working on parts, not the whole," Tyrill informed them. "For the rest . . . I'll not be afraid to ask for help."

Avall—almost—grinned.

Strynn did grin, and carried the sword with quick dispatch to a place by the light well. She left it there and went rummaging for appropriate tools.

Avall spent the rest of the morning dismantling the helm to the last twisted rivet.

· · ·

It was good to work again, Strynn conceded, as she set down the latest of the myriad very-high-quality files with which she'd been relentlessly honing the sword's edge. It wouldn't be long before she switched to stone, polish, and more stone. But not yet—not until she had everything else to her satisfaction. Trouble was, the light wasn't good for working on the inscription. One really needed daylight for that, which both Tyrill and Avall knew. For now, however, it was enough to be home again—in more ways than one. Home in the literal sense, for she'd been born in Eron Gorge; home in the sense of working at what she most loved; and home in the sense that most of the people she cared about—save Merryn—were once more close at hand.

As for Merryn . . . well, she'd address that matter anon. She and Rann had tried to contact her with their gems, of course—as they'd tried to contact Avall repeatedly. But the new stones were either too weak, different in kind, or else they'd consistently done something wrong. Perhaps Avall could do better, once he had a gem again—if she could convince him to bond with another, which he'd said last night he was more than a little afraid to do.

But if Avall wouldn't, there was always Rann or Div—or Eellon or Lykkon. Maybe even Tyrill. The Eight knew she had strength of will aplenty.

A clatter to her left made her look up, to see the Craft-Chief of Smith hefting the shield back onto its stand. Strynn blinked, letting her vision shift from close work to far, wondering if she might not soon need a pair of those lenses the folks at Glass were always trumpeting.

Tyrill caught her watching, scowled, and wiped her hands on her thighs, as she slumped back into the special stool that let her stand upright for long periods of time.

Avall noticed, too, and put down the rivet punch he'd been wielding with ruthless determination. Lykkon, who'd appeared midway through the morning, slammed his book of notes with authority.

"Time to come up for air," Tyrill sighed and, without further ado, marched toward the door—only to be all but bowled over by Bingg frisking in, with a breathless, sweaty Rann not far behind, looking like he'd been in pursuit. Bingg's movements spoke of unbridled excitement, but his face was troubled, as was Rann's. Bingg, Strynn realized with a start, wore the tabard and hood of a royal herald. He flipped it up as he skidded to a stop.

"Anytime," Rann muttered. "It's not like I haven't been trying to catch up with you for three levels."

Bingg cleared his throat. "First, be it known that by royal appointment this day arrived, I, Bingg syn Argen-a, am appointed royal herald assigned to Lord Eellon syn Argen-a, Clan-Chief of Argen, Steward of the Citadel, and acting head of the Council of Chiefs in royal absentia."

"Second, in that capacity, be it known that the results of the Fateing for this eighth have been posted, as is custom, in the vestibule of Argen-Hall, and all of that clan are advised to seek them there."

And with that, he flipped his hood back and relaxed into his usual boyish demeanor.

Lykkon obligingly clapped him on the shoulder, then eased aside for Avall to give him a hearty hug. "Nicely done, young one!" Lykkon crowed.

Which was all well and good, Strynn thought, scowling at Rann uncertainly. "Something wrong?" she inquired, for all it spoiled the mood.

Lykkon scowled in turn, and even Tyrill looked puzzled. Avall looked stricken indeed. "Oh, Eight, I'd forgotten," he whispered, aghast.

Rann nodded grimly, and joined his friend. Together they sat down next to Strynn.

"What . . . ?" Tyrill snapped, reaching for the inevitable glass of wine from the refreshment table. Bingg obligingly filled it for her.

Rann stared at the floor. "You don't recall, Craft-Chief? I'm an eighth older than Avall. I was in the Fateing before the one that sent him to Gem-Hold, and was also assigned to that hold. My service in that place therefore expired an eighth ago. I'd normally have had the eighth just past free, and now be entered in the present Fateing, had I not chosen to extend my stay at Gem, which should put me in the *next* Fateing. But I wasn't exactly around to *tell* anyone of that decision. Therefore my name and choices were entered as a matter of course. I'd already chosen War-Hold as my next service, anyway. But regardless, I must make certain." He grasped Avall's hand seriously. "I fear, brother, that the next skill I learn will be that of soldier."

It was Bingg's turn to look sheepish. "It is."

All eyes turned to him. Bingg shifted his weight uneasily. "I . . . cheated," he confessed. "I delivered the list to Eemon-Hall, and stayed to wait. I couldn't *help* it! Rann, you're called to the front."

Rann shrugged listlessly. "No more than I expected. Nor is it something I dread. But the timing—"

"The price of carelessness," Tyrill huffed.

Avall glared at her, and reached over to hug his bond-brother. "Whatever happens, I'll be there with you. I can do what I do anywhere there's heat, light, and tools. Besides, something tells me the King would like to have all of us to hand."

Strynn felt as though she'd been slapped, but managed—she hoped—not to react. She even understood the reason. But so soon after their return. So very soon. She'd hoped to have a little time without chaos, a little time to work in peace. To spend with her child before he became the child of her husband's clan.

Still, this *was* war, and so she squared her shoulders and stood. "I likewise can do what I do anywhere," she announced. "So, Craft-Chief, what about you?"

Tyrill was putting away her tools. "I was born in South Gorge," she gritted. "If I was ten years younger, I'd be on my way already. As it is . . . what do you suppose?"

"I think," Avall replied, also rising, "that it's time to test what we've always been taught. War is an art, they've said. I think it's time art went to war."

(Argen-Hall—late afternoon)

Strynn felt Avall's presence before she heard the soft pad of his boots on carpet, the swish of the loose robe he'd taken to wearing instead of a short-tunic, or the slightly anxious hiss of his breathing. Maybe it was the warmth of his body, felt more keenly now that she had a gem. Maybe it was the warmth of his mind itself—or its force. In any case, she wasn't surprised when his arms went around her from behind and he drew her against him, resting his chin on her shoulder as he likewise looked down at her child.

Averryn was sleeping, having been fretful most of the day, so Avall's mother said. Which was good. She wanted simply to look at him for a while. To wrap him in her mind and memory so that she could then let go. It made sense, she knew, letting a child's one-parents care for it, which freed its parents for endeavors more suitable for the young and active. Certainly the system had worked for years uncounted. It had even worked for her and Avall—and Merryn and Eddyn and everyone else she knew. That in spite of the plague that had eaten a generation.

But she wondered if every mother felt the pangs of impending separation she was feeling. Then again, most mothers didn't share ten days in the Wild with their newborns. *Most* mothers kept their offspring by them for the ritually prescribed eight days, and then saw them when the Fateings posted them near enough to allow such things.

But most mothers didn't have to play a major role in a war.

"This is bad for you, isn't it?" Avall whispered into her neck, even as Averryn gave a little twitch and snugged a chubby fist to his mouth.

She shrugged. "No worse than for any other woman, I suppose. Nor is it a thing I want to avoid—if I think about it rationally. But motherhood isn't rational, Avall. It's instinct. It comes from somewhere else. I wonder about this system, sometimes: this clan fosterage we all undergo. It gives us many parents, in a sense, and it allows bonds to form with those with whom we're most compatible, and it frees us to be ourselves earlier than might otherwise be the case. But I wonder if we don't miss something, too. I wonder if it doesn't set a part of us adrift, looking for what we should've had from birth."

"Maybe that's why we're makers," Avall murmured. "Maybe we look for a special bond with someone early in life, and not finding that, we bond with our crafting. That's what we're encouraged to do, anyway."

"And maybe it's cost our country its soul," Strynn gave back. "Maybe we're all form and no substance. Maybe we deserve to lose this war because—well, because we need a good shaking up."

"We had one a generation ago. It was called the plague."

"And maybe we should've taken it as a sign."

"Like Averryn's name?"

She tensed ever so slightly. "You noticed that, then?"

He nodded. "Avall and Merryn, merged into one. I guess I was a little surprised."

"That I tried to link it that closely to you? Maybe it was a mistake, and we can still change it, up until Sundeath. But I thought . . . maybe. Avall, I know it's going to be hard for you to love him, even though you won't see him that often. But I wanted to give him that tie. I want him tied to you, if possible. Certainly now that Eddyn's gone. I don't want his father's disgrace to shadow his whole life. If he grows up like you, I'll be proud."

"Distracted and indecisive and distant? I hope he does better than that."

"As long as he knows what he is and isn't, and gets a chance to be whatever he wants to be, I'll be happy."

Avall heaved a sign. Averryn whimpered at that, as though he knew he was being discussed. Which given all those gem-bondings while he was in the womb, might even be the case. "You're still determined to go to the front?" he whispered.

"Where you go, I go."

A deep breath. "What about Kylin? This is one thing he really can't be a part of."

She tensed again. "He wants to stay here and play for Eellon. He says it's the only thing he can do. Krynneth will look after him. You *know* Krynneth was in love with Merryn?"

"Like everyone else, apparently."

"Poor Kylin."

"He's happier than we are, in some ways. He's found his place where he can make a difference without losing who he is. That's all he wants."

Silence, for a while.

Avall peered down at Averryn. "Well," he sighed. "I guess we've got one *more* person we have to make proud of us, now."

"I guess," Strynn chuckled sadly, "we do."

CHAPTER XXV:

MACHINATIONS

(Eron: Tir-Eron—Sunbirth: Day 1—dawn)

~~~~~~~

On the first day of The Eight-day festival called Sunbirth that divided the dark half of the year from the light, the sun rose above a particular point on the eastern horizon exactly as it did every year at that time. But this year its beams lanced over a landscape still mostly clad with snow—and rapidly priming for war. Movement was afoot in clan and craft alike, and five times as many treks as usual plied the icy roads, over half of them heading south under various banners, each commanded by a subchief from War-Hold.

But that light also did something else.

At precisely a breath after dawn, a beam entered the easternmost window of the eight that made a lantern above the Hall of Clans. It struck a mirror there, which bounced that beam to another, then another and another, so that raw light laced the air between Sarnon's famous dome and the rough, empty weight of the Stone, which was the seat of the High King in council. At the start of the dark half of the year, at Sundeath, the light that filled the chamber was white. This was ruddier. Fit for a kingdom at war.

And as the sun rose, that light shifted, so that eventually it focused into a single narrow beam, centered on the Stone like a red dagger stabbing the land. And then it was gone.

So was the King, for the nonce. Gone from Eron Gorge, Tir-Eron, the Citadel, the Council of Chiefs, and the Stone . . .

Esshill, who'd turned twenty during the dark half of the year, and was therefore entitled to sit as Witness in Priest-Clan's official box during this, the first day of Sunbirth, was more than a little disappointed he would *not* get to see High King Gynn.

Unfortunately, some things carried even more force than ritual, and His Majesty had felt it his duty to take himself away to defend South Gorge, leaving his kinsman, Eellon, in charge of the Council of Chiefs—for all that Eellon was old, sick, and a powerful ally who would no longer be able to vote in the King's favor, save in the case of ties. It was a flaw in the government, Esshill had heard voiced more than once: that Eron had no established provision for a second-in-command after the Sovereign. No chancellor, no royal steward. Nothing.

Eellon had been appointed before the King's departure, with no one's approval but Gynn's own. Then again, Eellon was not a man to be trifled with, even by Esshill's clan.

Which didn't mean his presence on the dais wasn't an insult. Traditionally these ceremonies were orchestrated by Priest-Clan, most lately by Grivvon of Law. But the die Grivvon had rolled to open the ceremony had conferred that function on World, who was the weakest and least charismatic of the Priests of The Eight. Also the most intelligent, so everyone said, but his was knowledge without sense to back it up—or aggression.

Which fact Eellon had seized upon in his first official act as de facto regent. He had, in short, co-opted the floor on the assumption that it was easier to get forgiveness than permission.

"My Lord and Lady Chiefs," he began, "those of you old enough to understand language—which I believe is *most* of you present"—he garnered a few chuckles at this—"should know that there is here, as in all things, a fixed form that defines the order in which our business ought to be conducted. Like Sunbirth, certain events and concepts ought properly to be addressed in their own time and season."

He paused and coughed into a cloth. From his high vantage point, Esshill thought he saw blood. Certainly there were rumors: headaches that had the old man screaming. A heart that ran fast with no reason. And now this . . .

"Still," Eellon went on hoarsely, "many of those rites can be properly conducted only by the King in his capacity as Voice of The Eight, and those rites neither I nor anyone here dares usurp. Yet King Barrax of Ixti has dared to usurp a portion of this *kingdom*! Therefore, in riding to our mutual defense, the King performs his primary duty. In short, rites that exist only to function *as* rites should wait until they can be properly conducted.

"But that is only a small part of the function of this Council," he continued. "The greater part, in terms of time invested, lies in debating how affairs in this land shall be conducted to our mutual benefit and good. And that role does not require the King's presence so much as ours. I therefore ask if any here have business to lay before the Council that does not require attention to rite, writ, or royal seal. *Real* business, in other words."

An uneasy rumble of voices ensued, which Eellon overruled with a loud rap of his staff upon the bronze "silencing tile" between where he stood and the Stone. "If you have business, drop your insignia balls into the tally holes in your seats. Fate will determine the order in which you speak."

Esshill strained forward. It was hard to tell who intended business and who didn't, though he did see two members of his own clan remove red balls from pouches and deposit them into the specified holes. A system of gears, chutes, and shuttles beneath the hall would arrange the balls in random order—or the order demanded by Fate, depending on whom one asked.

The results were already appearing: rolling from beneath a marble sleeve into the palm of Fate's statue, which, along with representations of the other Faces, made a semicircle behind the dais. World retrieved the first and handed it solemnly to Eellon.

Eellon read it calmly. "Lord Law, it is you whom Fate would first have say his piece."

Law rose from the ranks of Priest-Clan, adjusting the mask he wore instead of a hood. He stood very straight. "Are you familiar with the Law of this land, Lord Eellon?"

Eellon regarded him narrowly. "I have read every word of it that is written down, have heard or read the Prophecies for longer than you have been alive, and have watched it played out here for seventy years in one guise or another."

Grivvon nodded gravely. "And what is the rite that opens Sundeath?"

The briefest of pauses, then, "The Proving of the King."

"To what end?"

"To assure that the King is perfect in body and mind, so that he may be a perfect vessel for The Eight when he drinks from the Wells and reveals Their will to us."

"And is the King perfect?"

A rush of silence filled the Hall. The Council had reached this point once before—almost. Before Avall had pulled . . . whatever it was with that attack.

And yet that silence lingered. More than one brow was creased in thought. More than one chief was caught, like Eellon, at the balance between the abstractions of Law and the hard, clear fact of the war.

"He limps!" someone said at last, from the segment of Beast.

"He commands!" someone retorted.

More silence, and then Eellon rapped his staff again.

"*Is* implies this present moment," he said. "And since His Majesty is not present, there is no way to determine such a thing. Nor would it serve any-one if he were summoned here for that purpose." A pause. Grivvon started to speak, but Eellon preempted him. "And now, my Lord Law, I would ask *you* a question about the Law: a question any child could answer."

"And that is?"

"When is the Proving of the King?"

"The first eighth of the first day of Sundeath."

"Which, I believe, is half a year from now."

"Still," Grivvon gritted, "I raise the question now for a reason."

"That being?"

Grivvon snorted derisively. "One has only to look around this room at the seats left empty because those who should fill them are mustering them-selves and their halls and holds for war. At the faces that would not normally sit here at all, but that those who rank them are absent, and someone must take their seats. There are sub-subchiefs here, Lord Eellon. And the wit-nesses in the galleries—some are mere children."

Eellon nodded gravely. "If you like, we can spend the rest of the day in-specting the credentials of those in attendance. I think even you might sug-gest better ways in which to spend that time."

Grivvon stiffened. "I would *suggest* we spend it debating whether or not there is some connection between what I strongly believe to be an imperfec-tion in the King and the fact that our land has suddenly become afflicted."

"Remember the last invasion," someone from Wood chimed in. "Ventarr had gone blind."

"—In High Summer, while Ixti suffered drought," a woman from Lore shot back. "Who would *not* invade a rich neighbor then?"

"And the Queen during the Year of Four Feints was judged perfect four times that same year—by a Council as stupid as this!" Elvrimm, the ranking chief from Warcraft, snapped.

"Barrax has wanted war since he took the throne," Ekalynn of Eemon rasped in turn. "There is no correlation."

"Aye," said Morkeen of Stone. "Whatever Barrax does now, he would have had to lay the foundations eighths ago. The King's limp has only mani-fested since the waning of Deep Winter."

"And not always then," someone from Water whom Esshill couldn't identify put in.

A second Priest rose from their ranks. Aged Nyllol, who was Rrath's sometime mentor. Light gleamed on his bald head as he stood there un-hooded and unmasked, save for a strip of white sylk across his eyes. "Never-theless, it is a thing we should consider."

"I think we should let *Fate* consider it," Lady Vyreen of Wood shot back. "If the King is given victory, *then* we should decide."

"I am amazed," Eellon broke in quietly, his voice clear in the room's perfect acoustics, "how we can sit here debating the King's right to the Throne when that King is the only reason you aren't this moment watching the hordes of Ixti pillaging your homes."

Grivvon cleared his throat. "Does anyone here recall whom our clan serves? Does anyone here recall what any clan or craft serves?"

"The people!" came a voice from the ranks of Healing—a very young and minor voice, to judge by the uncertain tones.

"Exactly. We do not exist to serve ourselves, we exist to serve the people. Frankly, I've been uncertain for a while whether Gynn does in fact serve the people."

Eellon folded his arms. "I would be glad to hear the origin of these doubts."

"It is rumored, Lord, that even as the High King rides to war, there are those in his very household—in this very citadel—who seek to espouse what we can only term heresy."

"Heresy?" Eellon looked aghast.

"Heresy."

"And what is the nature of this . . . heresy?"

Grivvon smiled, visible even behind his mask. "Why, that Gynn has begun to espouse the fact that the soul can exist independent of the body, and that he knows of certain . . . means by which that separation can be accomplished."

"In effect," Nyllol added. "That anyone can access The Eight."

"Instead of merely Priest-Clan—in the interest of the rest of us, of course." From Eemon, again.

"We do not," Grivvon growled, "know what will happen if everyone begins storming the Overworld with their prayers directly. Perhaps The Eight will withdraw themselves from us. Or perhaps they will retaliate. Perhaps they already have."

"Perhaps you will shit golden turds," came another young voice from Lore.

"Whoever that was is out of line," Eellon thundered. "Even if you may be right. But, Lord Law," he went on, "you're missing a rather important point. You seem to be neglecting the fact that were the rest of us free to petition The Eight on our own, your clan would quickly become . . . not superfluous, but perhaps less . . . powerful."

"Assuming this is true," Tyrill said abruptly. "There is another matter we must consider. As best I can tell, the means by which this . . . access is effected is limited indeed, and only free in theory. In practice, the King controls it; therefore, he controls who can access The Eight. Is this a power he either needs or deserves?"

Eellon glared at her. "The Wells exist, Tyrill. Nothing save guards, fear, and tradition keeps anyone from drinking from the Wells when they would. This has not happened, and access to the Wells is far easier than access to . . . what you reference."

"What *does* she reference?" Moole of Wax inquired innocently.

Eellon looked as though he could have eaten Tyrill alive, and even she looked frightened, as though she'd slipped and said too much. "It would appear that we keep secrets better than I'd thought, or else that Sovereign Oath carries more force than I expected," Eellon replied, pausing to cough again. "Very well, then: During the season just past, certain members of my clan and two others discovered a number of peculiar gems whose properties may be important in every way imaginable—especially if we recall the Prophecies last fall. These clansmen did not choose to make these discoveries, nor have they profited from them in any way, nor have my clan or theirs profited from them, nor do they plan to do so. But now is *not* the time to discuss this, not without the King himself to hand. I would beg your indulgence in this."

"Priest-Clan knows," Nyllol challenged. "It knows far more than you think it does."

"Good for you," Eellon shot back. "I trust you also know the meaning of judgment, especially as this information misapplied could lead to civil war."

"It already risks that," Wood replied, "if Smith withholds information that ought to be given to all of us by right."

"By the King's command," Eellon shot back, coughing again.

Elvrimm of War rallied to Eellon's defense. "If you want to speak of civil war when we face a very real war of quite another kind, I suggest you consider what might happen if Common Clan, clanless, and the unclanned learn that we of High Clan have withheld from them direct access to The Eight. They already outnumber us ten to one. And I assure you their blades are very real, and if not their blades, their stones. If I had to choose between fighting Priest-Clan and fighting Common Clan, there would be no choice—if I wanted to retain my position."

"Priest-Clan *could* even be sacrificed," someone else spoke up boldly. "They have no real existence, in the sense that no one is born to them. Not a man or woman is there among their ranks but could be absorbed back into the other clans."

"Fools!"

Grivvon's shout silenced them all. Slowly he turned in place, surveying every living thing in the room. "Did I just hear what I thought?" he hissed. "I spoke of heresy earlier, but this indeed is heresy I hear now. Smith, War, and the King deny us all information that is ours by right. They seek to set themselves up in place of the Priesthood; to *become* Priests, if you will. But they play a dangerous game, for they also control information that could bring us all down."

Ilfon of Lore rose for the first time. "Lore stands with the Crown and with Smith and War. Until we have defeated Ixti that is our only choice. This Council must present a united front against this larger threat. I, for one, would rather the lowest unclanned Eronese put me out of my house than the king of Ixti himself. I think most of you would agree. And," he added in a tone of dead seriousness, "we cannot let word of this potential schism leave this room. Not until we have driven Ixti from our ground."

"You expect miracles," Eellon drawled, "but you're right. We must—"

"*We* must do nothing!" Grivvon roared. "*We* are a thing made of smaller we's, and the *we* that is Priest-Clan will have no part of this until we have addressed the King to our own satisfaction. Until then . . . we will withdraw. If the people come to us for intercession with The Eight, we will deny them. We will tell them to ask the King and the Smiths, and the Lords of War and Lore. Perhaps they will be patient, perhaps they will not. But we will have no part of this war."

"Grivvon, stay where you are!" Eellon roared back, his face alarmingly red.

Grivvon ignored him. Already he was edging toward the aisle, with the host of Priest-Clan behind him. An elbow in Esshill's side prompted him, and he, too, rose, joining a swelling tide jostling toward the corridor that encircled the witness level.

Esshill made it to the hall before he found himself pushed back by a flood of men and women in Warcraft livery. "You are under arrest," one said. "For treason. Any man or woman of Priest-Clan will be detained here until proof of loyalty to the Crown can be ascertained."

Esshill found himself looking down on the floor. Chaos reigned there as well, but already a third of the cloaks swirling above the pavement were Warcraft crimson, under the leadership of Krynneth and Lady Veen. Of the remaining Councilors, a third were congregating around the dais, most notably the Chiefs of Smith, War, Stone, Lore, Glass, and—somewhat reluctantly—Gem. The most powerful ones. The rest looked uncertain, but most were being apprehended by doughty warriors in royal livery, quartered with War and led to the exits. Only Priest-Clan was surrounded, unable to depart. "Eron cannot risk what you risk," Eellon called. "Time is critical, and we have no time for political games such as you would play. We will see you cared for here, but here you will remain until Priest-Clan gains some sense. The rest of you . . . we seek no enemies, though we know we have just made some. But the sorting of that is for later. For now . . . Eron needs you. If you feel inclined to battle, I would suggest you take yourselves south."

"And you, Lord Eellon?" someone dared. "Do *you* plan to go south?"

Eellon didn't answer.

Esshill caught a final glimpse of him, however, as he slowly crumpled to the floor, only to be swept up by two sturdy Royal Guards and carried from the hall.

The last thing he saw was Lady Tyrill, hesitating for only a moment before she, too, joined her clan.

"I'm cold."

Vyyk had been dozing, and so it took him a moment to realize that someone had actually spoken, and more than a moment to realize that it was the patient who had uttered those words. Rrath syn Garnill.

From Half Gorge, he thought, though he tried not to think such things because, as a healer, he was supposed to maintain objectivity. Even here in Priest-Clan's sacred precincts.

And then it dawned on him in force. His eyes popped wide open, and he moved in a breath from the chair where he'd started out doing vigil and wound up napping, to the narrow cot in Priest-Clan's brightly lit infirmary. The patient—Rrath—looked no different than heretofore: a slim, wasted form covered to mid-chest, with his hair grown long, and his body stubbled all over because, with most of the healers gone to the front, there was no one to shave or wax him.

At that, he'd filled out since they'd brought him here, unconscious from a gash in his head that was reported to have been caused by a horse's hoof. Unconscious indeed, but not so much that he couldn't be force-fed nourishing soups and thin gruels.

Yet now his lips were moving, and his eyelids were fluttering.

And then, suddenly, popping open—to reveal irises of startling blue.

"I'm cold," Rrath repeated more strongly, clutching the covers. "I'm—"
He broke off, studying Vyyk intensely. "You're not Eddyn."

"I'm Vyyk," Vyyk volunteered. "I'm your healer."

"You're too young to be a proper healer."

"As are you to be a proper Priest, but I'm what they've left, what with the war—"

Rrath sat straight up in bed, eyes wild and desperate. "War?" he choked. "What war?"

Vyyk feared he'd excite himself overmuch and lapse into coma again. He reached for a pot of cauf. "Nothing that need concern you now."

"That's my decision," Rrath managed giddily, trying to rise again, to swing his feet out of bed. "Where's Nyllol? I need to see Nyllol!"

Vyyk scowled. "He's gone to Council."

"He's not *on* the Council."

"He is now. Most of the senior members from all the clans are away or occupied."

"But—"

"No," Vyyk insisted. "You need to rest. You need to eat everything I can get in you, and then, maybe—"

Rrath took his hand desperately. "What about Eddyn? Do you know Eddyn? Eddyn syn Argen-yr?"

"The smith? I heard he was in prison."

"But—"

Vyyk fumbled for the food tray behind him. "No more questions until you eat. Then we'll see."

"Only if you'll tell me about the war."

"Very well," Vyyk sighed. And did.

He'd muddled through the attack on War-Hold and had reached the part where the King had ridden off to defend South Gorge, when he heard alarms of excitement coming from outside, mixed with shouts of protest. "Hold for a moment," he told Rrath, and rushed to the window. Like the rest of Priest-Hold, the infirmary was hollowed into the rocks of the gorge itself, and its windows were set with careful regard to maintaining the illusion of natural cliffs. Thus, the one he found was high and narrow.

Still, it was enough to show a frantic knot of men in Priest-Clan livery making their way from the entrance toward the main assembly hall. He could hear shouting, too, in anger and confusion.

For an instant he thought war had come to Eron Gorge, but that was preposterous. There would've been advance warning. But then he saw that the Priests were followed by a phalanx of men in Warcraft colors, surrounding what was clearly a royal herald.

Desperate to hear, Vyyk acted impulsively and broke the window with a heavy ceramic mug, which let in cold air, but also the herald's words.

"Hear me! Hear my voice, which is the voice of the King of Eron speaking through the Council of Chiefs this day in session." And the same repeated twice, until those who'd rushed in slowed, and people began to approach. The herald cleared his throat, safe behind his barricade of soldiers.

"Hear me," he cried a third time. "This day has the Council of Chiefs in Tir-Eron, acting in lieu of High King Gynn, under the stewardship of Eellon syn Argen-a, declared all those of Priest-Clan in attendance at said Council to be potential traitors to Eron and to the King, for which reason they are to be incarcerated under royal guard until such time as inquiry can reach the King as to their proper disposition. Should any here seek to aid them, or free them from their confinement—which will be made as comfortable as possible—be it known that they shall likewise be styled traitor, and any resistance they dare be treated in like manner. The Council regrets this and asks that those of you who are true citizens of Eron go about your business, or show your loyalty by going south in support of your King."

And then the whole thing repeated.

Vyyk turned away. A chill ran up his spine, for all Priest-Clan was not his clan. But Rrath apparently had heard everything as well, for he stood shakily at the foot of his bed, naked save for a loin wrap.

"War . . ." Rrath whispered.

Vyyk nodded. "War. But you should—"

He didn't finish, for with no warning at all, Rrath slammed the food tray into the top of Vyyk's head, then followed that blow with another as he crumpled.

Rrath didn't stop to check for pulse or breathing; he was too busy relieving the healer of his clothes.

CHAPTER XXVI:

WORRIES

(Eron: Tir-Eron—Sunbirth: Day I—afternoon)

~~~~~~~~

Avall had never been so frightened in his life.

Not at the prospect of going to war, however. That was still remote and unreal, though he heard about it constantly—from everyone he met. And observed its ripples as well, from the increased pace of movement on the streets, to the cloaks of Warcraft crimson that were suddenly everywhere— with those of High Clan War who remained in Tir-Eron given deference formerly reserved for the crown.

Besides which, he had survived Deep Winter and the icy depths of the Ri-Eron, and had been more than once in what he supposed was the Overworld. Death itself therefore held little sway over him.

Yet he was still scared of death past reason.

Not his own.

Eellon's.

That Argen's Chief was ill was no secret, Avall knew, as he paced the corridors of the Citadel with a confidence he wouldn't have believed half a year gone by. That Eellon was over ninety and simply could not last much longer was likewise a foregone conclusion, if one regarded the situation with the cold eye of logic. That he had managed to defang Priest-Clan that morning, at the risk of civil war, only to collapse immediately after, was merely typical of the man.

But he *had* collapsed, and though his headaches and dizzy spells had been alarmingly frequent of late, he had not recovered so well from this latest occurrence, which was by far the worst. Never mind that both were increasingly complicated by a fever in the lungs that might've had its origin in Myx's long-gone illness.

Which—war or no war, helm or no helm—meant that Avall had delayed as long as he could in seeking what he dared not think might be his final audience with his lifelong mentor, protector, and . . . friend.

And yet he lingered at Eellon's door. There was still time to imagine things as they were. Once he passed that portal, *might-be* would become *is,* and his life would never be the same after. He wondered idly, as he pondered the elaborate strapwork hingeplates, if he was doomed to spend his whole life confronting change at the frantic pace that had typified the last few eighths.

Then even that decision was taken from him, as the door swung silently open to reveal a tired-eyed Veen in full guard livery, evidently returning to her post from some errand inside. At least it was no stranger. The King—or Eellon—was playing his hand very close indeed, making certain that those who knew the full extent of the unseen factors behind the recent events were kept more or less in one place.

Which might itself be dangerous, he conceded, as he absently acknowledged Veen's slight bow and, before he could think more about it, strode into Eellon's suite.

It was bigger than his own, but the layout was the same, which meant he had to turn right to enter the bedchamber. A low buzz of voices led him there—too many voices, and too many people, had they been any others than those who congregated there.

There was the obligatory Royal Healer, of course—Gynn's daughter, in fact—arranging an array of potions across the whole length of what should've been Eellon's reading table.

And there were a number of minor subchiefs from all three septs of Argen, looking fretful and concerned—as well they might be, given they could well have a new chief before the eighth was out.

Beyond them, there were Strynn, Rann, Div, Kylin, Lykkon, and the evermore-attentive Bingg.

And that was it. Eellon had survived his brothers, his sisters, his son, his one- and two-sons, and most of their spouses.

But not for very much longer.

The Lord of Argen-Hall was not in bed, however, but reclining in a loose house-robe of clan maroon on a long sofa, his torso propped up with embroidered pillows. Nor was he asleep—or even resting. Rather, he was plowing methodically through a pile of parchments, dictating occasional notes to

Lykkon. And completely ignoring everyone else—most of whom cringed every time he coughed, which was often.

He looked up, however, when Avall cleared his throat—which he hadn't meant to do. A smile beyond wonder filled his face, and Avall almost wept, to know he was so important to one such as Eellon. That he dared that smile so openly before witnesses also said more than he wanted to contemplate. Strynn, who'd given up on secrecy and was filing away on the sword by the window, looked up and gave him a smile of her own, while Rann, sitting cross-legged on the floor, raised his gaze from repairing a mail hauberk and shot him a troubled grin as well. Kylin played softly on his harp. Div simply smiled.

But none compared with Eellon's. Forgetting everything, Avall stepped forward, to kneel at the old man's side, taking his hand in a grip he feared might crush the brittle fingers. But words failed him utterly, and he could only stare.

"It will happen," Eellon whispered, raising a hand to brush Avall's hair from his eyes, moving it down to stroke his cheek. "I remember when there was no stubble there. No roughness. I wonder if that's why men grow beards: to shield the boys they were from the hard things of the world."

Avall felt his heart catch, exactly as he realized that even now, Eellon's cheeks were shaved as smooth as a child's—as smooth as little Averryn's, he suspected.

"It's good to see you, boy, nor am I the only one here who thinks so," Eellon murmured. "But I have work to do, and so do you, and Fate casts a dim eye on sentiment."

Avall held his hand a moment longer, then nodded. "You're a great man," he told his two-father. "Eron will remember you forever." And with that he stood.

He found Strynn by the windows, his eyes awash with tears. She took his hand as he approached, and he heard, rather than saw, her slide the sword aside. "Avall," she said softly. "We have to talk."

With that, she rose. Avall wiped his eyes with a sleeve, and saw Rann likewise rising, along with Div, who seemed to have found a place among the local Tanners, and was helping everyone in sight mend leather armor, horse tack, and scabbards. A moment later, they'd passed through the vestibule into Eellon's workroom.

Avall flopped down in a deep-cushioned chair. Rann slipped in beside him, with Div at his feet. Bingg took a place by the door; close enough to be paged, but not so close as to overhear.

A deep breath, and Strynn spoke.

"Avall, my love . . . I don't think we can wait any longer."

He blinked at her through burning eyes. "For what?"

"For you to confront your fears."

"Eellon—"

"I'm not talking about Eellon," she sighed, "for all that we all love him. No, I'm talking about you and the gem. I know—we all know—that you've been through more than any of us can imagine. But it's time to stop feeling sorry for yourself. You have to be aware that you know more about the gems than anyone else alive. You know that at bare minimum they can aid communication. You know that at least one king thinks that's sufficient excuse for war. And yes, I know we're working like crazy to find out if they can be used as weapons. But there're things we *do* know about them, things that would benefit the crown. Yet we dare not use three of them because they're committed to the King. There's a fourth, however. We—Rann and Div and I—want you to try bonding with it. At minimum, it might give you back some of . . . what you lost. At best, it might give us a chance to make the crucial difference to the war. Think of it, Avall! One of us rides out with scouts. He sees the lay of Barrax's army. Fast as thought, he sends word to another, with the King, while a third keeps watch somewhere else. Faster than horses, more coherent and subtle than mirrors."

Avall shook his head. "Maybe Rann—"

Rann grabbed his arm, and not gently. "Look at me, brother," he snapped. "I agree with Strynn. You've lost your fire, somehow, your energy, your . . . spark of magic. You act like a shell, but I know the man I love more than life is still in there. And I know why you're hesitating, too, and it doesn't have anything to do with fear of what might happen if you try to master two gems."

Anger flared in Avall. "So tell me what I want!" he challenged. "Tell me how I work, because I sure as Cold don't know anymore. All I know is that I was . . . without everything for too long. There's nothing that can fill me."

"Not even making?"

"*Re*making," Avall snorted. "Trying to repair a ruined thing."

"That's all Strynn and I are trying to do," Rann murmured, shifting the hard grip to a soft embrace across the shoulders, easing his bond-brother's head down onto his chest. "You're *not* ruined past repair, if only you'd see."

"I'm . . . afraid," Avall whispered.

"We know. But you have to name that fear, Avall. There's nobody here going to judge you. We've—all of us—been in your mind. We've shared your thoughts. Your loves, your hates. We know your body as well as anyone can. There's nothing in you to be ashamed of. Nothing in you we haven't felt as well."

"I've lost more," Avall managed, his voice perilously near a sob.

"What have you lost, brother?"

"I lost the gem," Avall said finally. "And with that I may have lost us all . . . everything. I may have ruined more lives than I can count."

"Maybe," Strynn conceded. "But I know one person who will never think that about you. Because of what you found, Kylin could see again—if only for a finger. If we could repeat that, for those who truly need it, it would mean . . . everything."

A long silence. "I was . . . saving it," Avall dared at last.

"Saving it? For what? For whom?"

A deep shuddering breath. "For Eellon. I thought if we could get him to bond with it—to master it, as you say—it might do more good."

Strynn nodded; a gesture more felt than seen. "Oh Eight, Avall, I . . . think I see."

Avall nodded back. "He's stronger-willed than I am, Strynn. Who knows what he could do with a gem? He's lived ninety years and made wonderful things, not the least of them Clans and Kings. He's raised up Smith above all other clans save maybe Lore and War. He survived the plague. He survived the death of almost everyone in the clan he loved. And he's suffered with his body of late, though no one knows. With will to endure all that, I thought he was the man to master that one spare stone."

"And," Div said softly, but clearly, "you thought if you could get him to use it, that it might heal him."

"It—one of them—healed me. It healed Rann and you and . . . Strynn."

"It did," Div acknowledged. "But you're young and strong. Did you ever stop to think that it might sense that Eellon is dying—forgive me for the force of that word—and reject him? It might not work for him at all."

Avall reached up to wipe his face. "Let me see the gems," he said dully. "All I can do is try."

"Get Lykkon," Rann hissed to Bingg. "You take his place with Lord Eellon. And tell Veen to let no one through that door."

"I love you," Strynn murmured into Avall's hair.

"So do I," Rann added.

Avall took both their hands and kissed them. "Tell me that again when this is over."

Avall acted without thinking; it was the only way he could endure what he was about. One thing at a time. He needed a table, and so he found a table—a small round one in a corner, existing only to support a statuette of Fate. He needed chairs—one, he thought, but there were four in the room that matched, and so he set them in a circle around the table. He had his own knife.

And friends. "Strynn, Rann, sit, please, to either side of my chair, and Div across from me. I'll do this alone, but you need to be there to manage—whatever you can. Lyk, ask Kylin to play for us—I'll need all the soothing I can get—then watch and record. If one of us tells you to do something, no matter how absurd, do it."

Lykkon nodded, wide-eyed, and left to fulfill his instructions. A moment later he returned, settling himself into Avall's former seat. Kylin found a chair in the corner. A tinkle of minor strings, and he began a slow, subtle melody. Strynn's favorite: "Winterqueen's Lament."

A deep breath, and Avall sat down, facing the window. Strynn sat to his right, Rann to his left. Div sat opposite, looking very uneasy—with reason. She'd suffered as much for this as anyone. More, perhaps. He'd seen the scar the arrow had left in her back in spite of the first gem's healing.

"Strynn, lay out the gems," Avall murmured. While she fumbled with the pouch that never left her side, he rubbed absently at a water stain on the lustrous wood. The grain fascinated him, as the patterns of ice crystals had fascinated him when he'd begun the helm, as the whorls of Strynn's fingertips had fascinated him, which he'd never told her about, either. It was something else to explore. When he had time to explore again.

And then all he saw were Strynn's hands, laying a strip of fabric atop the stain, and slowly upending the pouch over it. Stones clinked against each other: four smooth ovals of murky red, lit with inner fire. The smallest was the size of the end joint of his little finger, the largest the size of a human eye—bigger, by a bit, than the one he'd lost. Using the tip of his dagger, he arranged them in a line, then passed the dagger to Rann. Another breath, and he slowly touched each gem in turn, seeking any reaction.

There wasn't—at first. But he tried again, sweat now dampening his fingertips. The smallest one was dormant. The next two were much of a size, almost twins—like him and Merryn. He hesitated between the two, then moved on to the large stone. It—rejected him. Not with dislike, but with a strange, gentle firmness, like a mother denying the breast to a child that had grown too old.

Back to the twins. He closed his eyes. Touched one, then the other. Then the first again.

"That one glowed," Rann murmured. "I saw it, very faintly."

Avall opened his eyes. "Knife," he whispered.

Rann handed it to him.

Steeling himself to enact a rite he hadn't undertaken in far too long, and the repercussions of which he both anticipated and dreaded, he drew the blade along the tip of that same finger. Once, twice, before blood showed. Then, taking yet another deep breath, he rested his wrist on the table and touched the bleeding finger to the gem.

Fire ran up his arm—not a flame of pain, but of greeting. It was like he felt when he poured himself into Strynn and Rann, except that something in the gem was responding to something in him that was *not* him. And that conflagration was spreading, racing through him like fire through straw, or dye through water, leaving him forever changed. Forever brighter, forever deeper, forever . . . stronger.

He gasped, for his heart had been too startled to beat, and then had been unable to beat as that power wrapped around it. It reached his brain and with it his *self,* and his soul, and began to flood out there.

"Rann, Strynn—" he choked.

And that part of him that could still feel, felt their hands fold over his wrists. Part of him knew, too, that there'd been no time for them to cut themselves, to contribute their own blood. Yet there was still a joining.

Even better, he felt Strynn and Rann experiencing what he'd just experienced himself, but through their own stones. And once again there was that eerie spark of recognition, as though something in him but not part of him joined in celebration with a part of them that was not *of* them.

Somehow Div was there, too, and Avall felt . . . strength—or power—or energy—or magic—or whatever it was, start to flow in a circle between them, from him to Strynn to Div to Rann and back to him, each time stronger.

But each circuit forced him farther away from himself as well, and closer to what he called the Overworld. That place where strange things happened he was not yet ready to confront.

But the energy was there, as well, and he knew he had to use it.

He never knew whether it was *his* thought that focused it, or Strynn's or Rann's, or maybe even the gem's itself, but all at once they were out of themselves entirely, and looking down on all the vast length of Eron, with one goal alone in mind.

Merryn.

We have to include her in this, came Strynn's thought. *It is too wonderful to restrict to us.*

Whatever pleases you, Rann replied. *I'm only here to be.*

Merryn, was all Avall thought. Simply *Merryn. Merryn. Merryn.*

For a moment they spiraled through nothingness, and then Avall felt something familiar, that to his companions in nothingness must surely feel passing strange. He felt them all four lodge in another mind. But this time that mind was not asleep. This time their strength was such that they had reached her full awake.

Avall opened his eyes, but the eyes he gazed through were his twin's.

"Brother," she whispered into the gloom of what looked like some kind of ill-lit cell. "Where are you?"

Within you, sister, Strynn replied.

A confusion of startled joy clanged through Avall, so strong he almost withdrew. *We must be quick,* he said. *We have found more gems. We are . . . I suppose we are seeking the other.*

The one Eddyn stole? from Merryn.

How did you know that?

He . . . told me.

He is there?

Yes. But oh, Avall, War-Hold has fallen, and there is war everywhere and I am captive and—

Slowly, sister, Avall advised. *Tell us where you are and how you came there and what of the traitor Eddyn.*

He's no traitor, Merryn shot back. *They seek to use him in every way and he resists. He did not come here of his own free will.*

But he has the gem.

He could almost feel her shake her head. *Barrax has the gem. He wants us to show him how to use it, but we don't* know *how.*

But—

Remember how it was before, Avall, Merryn broke in, her silent impatience like shouting. *We did not* need *to use words to explain what had happened. And it was both clearer and faster.*

The vehemence of that admonition rattled Avall—*he* was supposed to be the expert on gem lore, after all—but then he thrust his vanity aside and "told" her as much of what had transpired since their last contact as he could manage—not as narrative so much as pure bursts of images and emotions. And then it was her turn. Avall felt memories slide into his brain and lodge there that he knew he'd be able to sort out later. For now it was enough that he'd found Merryn. Enough that she and Strynn were finally able to share some of the closeness he and Rann had shared.

More and more information she poured into him, and he into her, and they reveled in that contact after so long apart. Yet every moment took more effort, more strength that no longer felt quite so inexhaustible, now that the first flush of joy had faded.

More effort, and then more yet, and Avall had to work to sustain the link, and then he could *not* sustain it. He grabbed for it frantically, to no avail.

And then sudden cold enfolded him and the link was severed, and he blinked back to Eellon's workroom to see Lykkon standing beside him, clutching a pitcher of water he'd just splashed over the four of them. To his horror, some of it was freezing as it touched his skin.

Lykkon looked frightened beyond reason. "It was all I knew to do," he stammered through chattering teeth. "I felt cold, and then colder, and then cold enough to scare myself, and there was ice in the air around you. And . . ."

"Eellon!" Avall cried, rushing for the door. Bingg met him there also shivering, but his cheeks were more flushed. "He fainted just now. I was coming to tell you."

Avall seized him savagely. "But he lives? Tell me he lives!"

"He lives, but he's very, very cold. As were we all. But that means it . . . worked. Right?"

"It worked," Avall agreed dazedly. "Maybe it worked too well. But let's pray we haven't paid too high a price for that success."

"Aye," Rann acknowledged. "But at least we know Merryn is alive."

"I'm not sure I *want* to know where," Strynn added grimly.

"Doesn't matter," Avall replied. "No matter where she is, we'll have to get her out of there."

Rann regarded him strangely. "Well," he yawned, "I guess one thing at least is . . . better."

Merryn was lost.

Utterly and completely lost. Not from anything as prosaic as landscape, either; she was lost from her very *body*. Her senses told her nothing. Sight showed not blackness, but an utter absence of color. She heard nothing. Not wind, not the low drone of voices that had been her constant companion for days uncounted. Not the distant clank of weapons being cleaned or practiced with, or honed. There was nothing to smell because there was no air. Nothing to taste save the fear that welled up in some distant part of her.

Nothing to feel but cold.

Yet even that was distant.

She was nowhere: a thread stretched too tight in the night, then severed, left dangling in winds that didn't blow, beneath a sky that *wasn't*.

And only a moment before she'd been oh-so-firmly anchored by Avall, by Strynn, by Rann—by someone she didn't know, but for whom they all held deep regard. She clutched at it desperately. She hadn't finished what she had to say, dammit, and she wanted that comfort back.

But something sought to draw her away as well: a second, more substantial anchor, which reached to this not-place to torture her with cold.

Which, at least, was a feeling.

Avall? she cried one last time. *Strynn, my sister. Rann* . . .

Silence answered. Silence within a greater void.

But the cold was stronger and she acquiesced to it, let it reel her in like a fish on a line. Back and back and back, to where sensations slowly returned.

Where there was a redness behind closed eyelids.

Where men shouted encouragement in endless weapons drills.

Where the air smelled of smoke and sweat and horses and drying dung. And spring.

Where the taste of fear in her mouth was like wine in its intensity.

Where she was cold beyond reason.

So cold . . .

Too cold to live. A vibration in her bones, a clatter in her ears like thunder, was her own teeth chattering. A pain like twin daggers in her breast was her lungs fighting to breathe ice. Her heart beat wildly, as it tried to pump frozen blood.

She blinked once at a world where even the most minor stimulus was orders of magnitude too intense.

And then found a place inside herself to hide.

In every sense but one, she died.

Only her will remained alive. Fighting stubbornly to bring warm air to fight the cold in her lungs. Reveling in the warmth of the circle of sunlight into which she'd fallen.

For fallen she had, in a noisy clatter of wooden crockery.

Rhyxx min Mykkix stood at nominal attention halfway down the columned arcade that had once been some kind of cloister, but which now fronted twenty make-do prison cells. That was the exact number, too; the Gods knew he'd counted them often enough since being stationed here. As he'd checked the locks and hinges often enough as well—new hardware fixed to thick old wood, with everything on the *outside,* so as to keep prisoners confined. Ironic, that: The priestly former occupants had bolted the doors on the inside, to protect their contemplation.

He supposed he should consider this post an honor—these were very important prisoners, after all, including the king's son himself. Still, maintaining vigilance while doing nothing was more tiring than one thought. Why—

He froze. He'd heard something. A rattle and a thump, like someone falling, down in the corner cell, the one occupied by the Eronese woman. Probably nothing, besides which, someone else had duty down there. He scratched an itch under his armor, sighed, and tried to stand up straighter. And waited. There was no sign of Keexin moving to investigate. No sign of Keexin at all, in fact. Then again, Keexin had a notoriously strong appetite, which often resulted in fluxes the next day. He'd certainly indulged himself enough the previous evening; probably he'd gone to the garderobe. Still, he should've told someone before disappearing.

But suppose something *was* wrong? These prisoners were mostly High Clan and therefore well behaved, as well as being important enough—some of them—to be summoned to audience with the king himself. Any atypical noise should therefore be investigated.

Especially when it came from that cell in particular.

A deep breath, and he signaled Keexin's counterpart, Tymm, who was stationed down by Kraxxi's cell, at the opposite corner from the noise, motioning the younger man to join him.

Tymm shouted something unintelligible, then shrugged, and started up the arcade. Meanwhile, Rhyxx had gone on ahead, and was fumbling with the suspect cell's tiny spy hatch. It took longer than expected to open, and longer again for his eyes to adjust to the gloom inside. But then he saw Merryn, sprawled from her stool into the scanty patch of sunlight provided by the cell's far window.

Horror filled him. She was—

She couldn't be.

"Tymm," he hissed. "Keep watch, and if anything is amiss—"

Tymm peered past his companion, and scowled. "Your call, Rhyxx, but she's surely too smart to expect that old ruse to succeed."

Rhyxx glanced around in search of the missing Keexin, saw neither him nor his own counterpart on this side, and grimaced irritably. With Tymm looking on from outside, he unlocked the door and—with dagger drawn just in case—knelt beside the woman's body. Her skin looked odd—gray, like a dead person's, though he could've sworn steam rose from her flesh where sunlight struck it. A hand to her throat found . . . nothing.

He checked her wrist—and shrank back. She was as cold as any corpse he'd ever buried. Removing his helm, he laid an ear to her chest. Heard nothing. He checked her wrist, then her neck again. No change.

He paused, staring. She was too cold to have died recently, yet she was certainly dead. But then why the noise? Perhaps she'd had a seizure while eating and had only now slipped to the floor. Perhaps she'd even been poisoned. Lynnz was wise in the way of such things, and he and Barrax *had* been at odds over the disposal of the prisoners. Perhaps Lynnz had acted unilaterally.

In any event, he had a duty to perform. Prison space was at a premium—there were those half-blood triplets, for instance, who really should *not* be housed together. And the dead required no confinement.

"Tymm," he called. "She's dead. I don't know how or why, though I've some idea, but—"

"What?"

"Confirm my opinion first, then—I guess we'll have to tell the king."

"He'll have our heads!"

"He'll have Keexin's first. In any case, he's free to inspect the body. He'll find no wounds or trauma. It will be for him to have her checked for poison—not that anyone will be able to tell. If she was poisoned, it was by Lynnz. And if it was by him, he's too smart to use one that leaves traces."

Tymm shook his head. "I'm just a soldier," he muttered, as he carried out his own cursory inspection. "We'll need a stretcher," he continued, rising. "And we'll need to alert the warden. Let *him* do the dirty work. You can tell him," he added. "Since you rank me—*and* Keexin."

"And leave her here?"

"The king might notice things we wouldn't. Until I hear otherwise, I've no intention of touching her."

Rhyxx stared at her curiously. She was quite beautiful. And remarkable in other ways, it was said. It was certainly a waste. "I don't want to leave her like that."

"Suit yourself."

Without reply, Rhyxx swept off his cloak and swirled it across Merryn's body, where it lay like a swath of desert sand. The sunlight made the nubby fabric glitter like hot gold.

Merryn didn't so much awaken as melt back to life. It was a strange sensation, actually. Not like sleep, where you dreamed, and then felt that dream shatter, and all at once you were awake with everything working but your mind.

This was the opposite. Her mind worked just fine, there in her innermost recesses. It was everything else that had slowed.

Yet warmth soaked into her at every shallow breath. And enough heat fought its way through cooling blood to warm her heart, prompting it to pump more vigorously. Her skin prickled, which wakened reflexes. She jerked, and blood raced stronger. Her mind made sense of what her ears had lately told her.

She was dead.

Had been dead.

No . . . Barrax's men *thought* she was dead. They'd left her to rot like a slaughtered pig in the sun.

Maybe without a guard.

That awoke her in truth. She made to move, and pain shot through her like ice breaking. But still she strove. It required effort enough to shift a mountain to make a finger twitch—but she managed, and the hand attached to it. Felt the texture of the pavement beneath her. An eye cracked open, and she saw . . . nothing but the weave of fabric backlit by the sun.

Someone was breathing, however—close by. And something about the air and the quality of light told her that the door was open and but minimally guarded.

She knew she was acting from instinct, with no regard for sense. But she'd never have a chance like this again. Not in this lifetime.

A flurry of movement that was like an earthquake of pain, and she sat up. The cloak slid away, so that she could see part of a soldier's back, where he stood, half-in the doorway, half-out. Paying little regard to anything in particular.

She thought fast. She had a corner room, farthest from the gate. One guard had gone to seek the warden, who was quartered by that same entrance. There was typically one guard per side, and one per corner. But one of them had left before Avall's contact, and another had apparently followed just now, which lowered the odds. . . .

Slowly, oh so slowly, she rose to a wary crouch, suppressing a gasp as pain took her, and then again as the act of breathing was like inhaling knives of ice. But what now? She still felt groggy, like coming off a three-day drunk. Every thought was like swimming through ice floes. But she *did* think, and the act of that cleared her head.

Only an instant she hesitated. It was barely two strides to the door, and the guard had his back turned . . .

More from reflex than thought, she lunged forward, whipping the cloak outward, so that the lower corner snapped around the guard's head, briefly blinding him, and stifling his startled cry.

She had him by then: an arm around his neck, another around his head, and a twist, followed by a sickening crack, and a groan that segued into the soft, sad hiss of life escaping. Miraculously he didn't fall, merely slumped against the wall, looking almost comfortable. Pausing only to relieve him of the sword he'd been fumbling for, she left him there, amazed at her own luck.

Only an instant she hesitated—then ducked back into her cell. Her clothes were of Ixtian cut, fabric, and color—which was good. But she saw nothing of use save a lone wooden spoon and a pewter mug with a handle. She snared them, then stumbled over something.

A cup?

No! *A cap helm.* The one the guard had removed when he'd examined her.

And surely a gift from The Eight. Quick as thought, she snared it and crammed it on. Too big—no surprise—but she pushed it back, and returned to the light.

So how did one escape a guarded cloister? She scanned the arcade, found the two closest sides still unguarded—and dashed across the shaded pavement to brace herself against the back side of one of the stone pillars that supported a pair of arches.

Well, this *was* a cloister, and cloisters weren't meant to serve as prisons, save in the most general way. And if this was the one she thought it was, the dormitory had been built beside a river—a tributary of the Ri-Ormill that watered South Gorge, in fact. They'd stopped by the outer precincts on their way south to War-Hold in the autumn. Which meant . . .

She peered down the arcade.

She was right. There was a stair to the rooftop at the next corner, maybe sixty paces away. And the man who should've been guarding that corner was standing dead two spans across from her.

And it was in the shadowed side.

A deep breath, a pause to square her shoulders and stand as erect as possible but with the cloak pulled tight around her, and Merryn strode toward those stairs.

Halfway there, she heard voices rising at the gate and saw a tall man without a cloak or helm arguing heatedly with two more, while a pair of men in servant's livery lugged a stretcher out of the gatehouse.

She had to hurry—and dared not.

In any event, the altercation had drawn the notice of the guard from the next side. He stepped from it into the cloister square itself. Fairly close to her, too, as though he'd been on his way to investigate his fellow's absence.

She didn't alter her course, made no move to walk quietly. "What is it?" she called gruffly, in muffled Ixtian.

The man spared her but casual notice. "Some tripe."

Though still in the arcade, she angled toward him, as if she shared his interest. Then, when she was close behind him, she raised the pewter mug and slammed it smartly into his chin. His head snapped back, even as his body slumped forward. The weight of his helm brought his head forward again, exposing his neck. A second blow connected the juncture of skull and spine. Maybe a killing blow, maybe not.

She didn't wait to see.

A pair of strides brought her to the narrow, twisting stair. She paused there to catch her breath, then had to sit down in spite of herself, as reality threatened to spin away. Pain washed over her in waves.

"Merryn!" a voice rasped from the spy flap in the door to the corner cell.

She froze, head awhirl, caught between fatigue, fear, the need to escape, and—perhaps—love.

She was on her feet at once. "Kraxxi?" she gasped. "Kraxxi, is that you?"

"Yes, and don't waste time with me you don't have."

She could see his face between the bars. Tired, and scarred from scorpion stings, but with a certain nobility she hadn't seen there before.

"I can get you out. And there's a second sword—"

"He doesn't have keys, if that's what you were thinking," Kraxxi countered. "I just"—he paused, breathless, face like a serious boy—"I just wanted to tell you that I'm sorry I've messed things up for you so badly. I'm sorry I got you into this. I'm sorry I've brought war to your country."

"I'm sorry, too," Merryn murmured, casting her gaze about. "But I also know that very little of this is your doing. The groundwork must've been laid long ago. You were just the catalyst. Or I was."

"The gem was," Kraxxi corrected. "If you want to spare both of us blame."

Merryn was still watching both adjoining corners *and* the gate. She had so little time . . . "We've a lot to talk about," she said finally. "That should give us both something to look forward to. Some reason to . . . go on living."

"Enough for me," Kraxxi sighed. Then: "I have to say this, Merryn, because I don't know if I'll ever get to speak to you again, and I couldn't stand parting in anger . . . I love you. I truly do."

"Tell me that again when we're both free," Merryn replied solemnly. Impulsively, she reached out and clasped the fingers that protruded through the bars.

"Luck."

"Luck."

She turned away before he could see that she was—almost—crying. The stairs beckoned. She charged up them. Behind her, someone vented an uncertain shout. Footsteps followed at a run.

She pounded on: two steps at a time, though she barely had energy to move, and shivers wracked her. Yet somehow, an instant later, she was easing somewhat more circumspectly out of the turret that covered the upper landing, with pain crumbling away like clay from a new-cast dagger hilt.

She barely noticed the roof, save to note that it was flat and empty, as she barely noticed the sudden sweep of landscape around her. The cloister tumbled off to the left, with the camp surrounding it on three sides: a crazy-colored maze of tents, flags, and pavilions.

To the right lay empty land—

She made the edge in two breaths, peered over the limestone parapet.

She'd guessed correctly. The river flowed below. A dozen spans straight down, and flooding up onto the opposite bank: typical of the season.

But what was the bottom like? She could survive the drop—but only if there was some depth to absorb her fall.

Still, even a broken neck was better than execution. Better than being made to breathe imphor fumes until she'd betrayed everything she knew about her country. Better to risk in hopes of seeing Avall and Strynn again.

Perhaps she was still groggy, or perhaps the still-incredible pain fogged intellect in lieu of instinct. Whatever the motivation, she threw caution to the winds—and jumped.

The cloak belled out around her—an odd image she glimpsed as though in slow motion. As she saw the face of the cloister become sheer rocks, laced with moss, grass, and springtime flowers.

And then she hit water, and life was nearly knocked out of her a second time in one hand. The cloak dragged at her, and she sloughed it off regretfully, and then water was fighting to gain access to her lungs, and all she could do was let go of herself and use what energy remained to help her rise.

To her surprise, she surfaced close to the fast-moving central channel, and far enough downstream that the shore showed not cloister wall but tents.

Another breath that she prayed wouldn't be her last, and she dived once more, let the current carry her on, its pace accelerated by the fact that the river was swollen by the spring floods.

When she found air again, it was to see open land.

And freedom.

Kraxxi slumped back against the cool stone of his cell wall, closed his eyes, and took three long breaths.

Breaths of relief.

He opened his eyes again, staring at what he clutched in his right hand.

A simple wooden spoon that had accompanied his last meal. It had been a different, harder wood than typical. More importantly, it was a kind of wood he'd recognized as leaving a keen, hard point when you broke it. Which he'd promptly done, intending to thrust that tip up under his sternum and into his heart.

They'd been very thorough about such things, his guards had, fearing, probably, for their lives, and this had seemed to be the only option. *Not* hanging—he could make rope aplenty from his clothes, but the ceiling was utterly smooth, so there was no way to attach one there if he had one. Or anywhere else that wouldn't result in slow strangulation, in lieu of the quick snap-death he desired.

But now . . .

Merryn was free. He'd seen her, briefly, had proof of that. And for now that was enough excuse for him to, as she'd said, go on living.

Another deep breath, and he crossed to the narrow, barred window and flung both bits of spoon as far as he could. And stayed there until it was full dark, staring at the tiny bit he could see of a glimmering line of water.

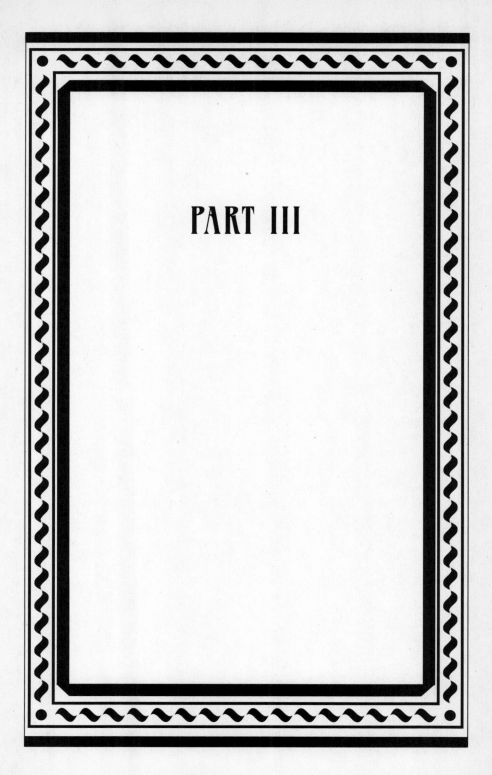

PART III

CHAPTER XXVII:

BIVOUAC

(ERON: NEAR SOUTH GORGE—SUNBIRTH: DAY VII—SUNSET)

War was far more than battles, Avall had discovered somewhere between sunrise six mornings ago, when he, Strynn, Rann, Div, and Lykkon had ridden out of Eron Gorge and sunset today, as they approached Gynn's bivouac at Eron's Belt. They'd attached themselves to a force comprised mostly of stonesmiths from Mid Gorge, which had finally made it through a late-season snowfall to swell Eron's ranks. Amid their black-and-silver livery, Avall's brighter colors stood out more than he liked.

Not that he would've changed them, symbolizing as they did all that he was. He wore a tabard of Argen maroon quartered with Smith gold, but he also wore it barred with Warcraft crimson to signify whose command he recognized, and he wore it above the best mail hauberk, gauntlets, and coif Smith-Hold could offer up from its vast stores. He carried a sword and shield he'd made himself, and matched daggers he'd had from Strynn. And wore a grim expression he'd adopted, all unknowing, from everyone around.

And so he looked like a warrior. How he felt was another matter. War was everywhere. When he looked at a clear blue sky, he wondered how fair weather might influence the time of battle. When it misted rain or spat snow, he wondered how that would affect supply trains that might have to travel muddy roads. Plains of grass suddenly became domains of fear, because one was visible in the open. But forests fostered other anxieties, for enemies could hide in the woods, and they had only the word of scouts as surety that battle still lay ahead, where Gynn and Barrax glared at each across the Ri-Ormill that fed South Gorge. Barrax held the south bank, and the river was still very much in flood. But that wouldn't last forever.

Gynn claimed the heights to the north, ready to swoop down at the first movement across the river. Meanwhile, South Gorge emptied itself, to east and north, adding to Gynn's forces by a very welcomed third, even as more forces poured up from the south to swell Barrax's ranks.

Their supply lines were long, but Ixti had already taken Half Gorge, and their granaries were full, never mind the livestock industry concentrated there.

Yes, war was everywhere—even in the air, because every breath seemed to smell like smoke, and every wind seemed to bring the sound of battle. The air was . . . tense with it, Avall supposed. It was as if every single object in Eron was involved. Why, the merest stone could be a weapon, the slimmest blade of grass the one that kept a crucial horse from starving.

And none of it seemed real. Not the landscape, which was fairly rugged between Eron Gorge and South, where the mountains swung closer to the coast. And not the company he kept, save his friends. Reality had narrowed to a steady pace on horseback with far too infrequent breaks. There was little chance of conversation, and little time to work on the helm, though it rode on the saddle behind him, in its proper shape again, and with some of the panels reaffixed, if not restored.

A glance ahead showed Strynn moving left to talk to an old friend from War-Hold, her tabard identical to his own. Rann rode to his right, in Eemon midnight-blue barred with Argen maroon, quartered with Stone black-and-silver. Div was with him, in a tabard of Common Clan beige barred, yet again, with Argen maroon, but with no craft quartering, though she was a hunter, and had been married to a Tanner. Finally, Lykkon brought up the rear, in Argen maroon quartered with Lore's bronze, though he hadn't officially linked to that craft.

Avall thought to hail the lad and ask his thoughts on all this, as he'd been watching everything with keen interest, and writing for hands at night in his journal. Keeping a record of the war, he confided. In case no one else bothered.

But just as Avall began to twist around, movement from the corner of his eye drew his attention back ahead. He rode in the middle of a company of some two hundred, which fanned out in a rough triangle across the slope behind. The way ahead narrowed as it grew steeper, with trees close on either side. A figure in royal livery had just appeared at the top and was addressing the company commander.

Avall reined his mount to a slow walk, urging him closer to Strynn, with

Lykkon in tow, and Rann and Div more to the right. He found himself straining his hearing for the sense of that meeting, but heard only the clop of hooves, the low murmur of speculation, the rush of the wind, and a random equine whicker.

Soon enough, however, word spread down the ranks: The royal camp lay four shots away, over the rise. They should be there in time for supper.

Avall studied the sky, noting the deepening color to the east, as twilight began to assert itself. Darker clouds bannered the sky, their ragged edges limned with crimson and fiery gold that contrasted impressively with the dark green trees and the black shadows among them.

And then the file was moving.

Avall and his four companions crested the rise together, and beheld the main army of Eron spread out below them. It was roughly three shots from the gap in which they paused to the higher one beyond, which looked down on South Gorge itself. The space between was a wide vale between two ridges running east and west, and framed with trees. A stream bisected it, threatening to overflow its banks, and it was along that that the camp had been erected—a sea of tents and pavilions in every conceivable color, but laid out in a neat order for all that, with the multicolored mass of the royal pavilion taking pride of place in the center. The whole was encircled by a palisade of pointed stakes as high as a man was tall, pierced by portable gate towers at intervals along the way, and with what almost looked like proper towers where the road entered.

The company was reduced to single file there, as the gate-wardens checked each person's name, clan, and craft in turn, adding them to a muster list that would be analyzed and turned over to the King once a day. It was tiresome work but necessary, for any number of reasons. Avall, as nominal leader of their group, had found himself in line ahead of the rest—just in front of Strynn—and was alternately gazing at the sky, as though daring the stars to appear, and waiting for his stomach to growl as they ambled along.

Just now the duty watch was changing: an older man in Tanner livery looking anxiously at someone in Warcraft crimson, who emerged from a clot similarly attired to stride purposefully toward him.

Avall recognized that confident saunter a half breath before Strynn did, but for all that, they cried out in unison.

"Merryn!"

Avall barely remembered to toss his reins to Div before his feet hit the ground. More pounding right behind was Strynn and Rann, all three of them ignoring the protests of their erstwhile companions as they were shouldered aside.

For her part, Merryn looked as startled as a person could, then scowled, then finally realized who had hailed her, and was suddenly behaving as irresponsibly as the rest. They might have been at a summer dance instead of a war, for all the discipline or decorum they displayed.

And then they reached her and there was an awkward moment as Avall and Strynn deferred to each other while Merryn dithered over whom to hug first. Finally they made it all three, with Strynn easing in ahead of Avall for the first solo. Rann and Lykkon held back, but only briefly. Div alone was not involved, content to watch with grave interest.

"What're you—?" Avall began. "I—we—thought you were captive. We were on our way to try to—"

Merryn cut him off with one of her smug combinations of shrug and grin. "That won't be necessary. Thanks to you," she added mysteriously.

"But—" Lykkon began.

"Forgive me, but I have a duty to perform right now. I promise to give you the whole story as soon as I get off. I expect you'll have tales to tell as well. In fact, I pray Gynn doesn't decide to attack tomorrow, because we'll need all night and then some."

"Merryn!" That was the voice of the outgoing gate-warden. Nor did he sound pleased.

"I'll see you when I can," she apologized. "Meanwhile, if I were you, I'd check in at the royal tent."

Avall was more than a little surprised to find Myx and Riff standing guard outside the royal pavilion. Both looked grim and competent in their royal livery, but their faces lit when Avall hailed them, though whether from surprise or joy was impossible to determine, so quickly did they resume the requisite dour demeanor. Still, it was difficult to regard any of this as real. Any of it as more than boys—and not a few women—playing soldier.

No one in Eron remembered Ixti's last incursion, and what few experienced warriors existed had gained their expertise fighting geens and birkits, or keeping the lesser clans in line when they now and then threatened to revolt. His only comfort was something their commander—a hard-faced woman from War, and one of Strynn's cousins—had offered: that no one in Ixti had been to war, either. Avall wondered suddenly why no one had tried diplomacy. Or had they—and failed? Perhaps Gynn and Barrax—who were of similar age, though Barrax was reported to look older—really were assuaging their royal boredom doing what they supposed kings were expected to do.

In any event, Avall told Myx to inform the King that they'd arrived and would like to attend him at his leisure. Lykkon sidled up to him while they waited. "Correct me if I'm wrong, cousin, but didn't you used to be *afraid* of the King? When did you and he become so . . . familiar?"

Avall blinked at him, then realized that he'd stated a fact. A season ago, he'd known that the King recognized him on sight and had been both flattered and alarmed by that attention—and that was all. Since then, he'd found himself too much in the royal eye, for he had no doubt that it had been Gynn's intervention that had got him posted to the remoteness of Gem-Hold-Winter. But he'd also had a royal commission, and while he knew that had come in part to placate Eellon and Tyrill, no sovereign ever bestowed such things lightly. "I . . . really don't know," he said at last. Honestly.

Lykkon merely rolled his eyes. "Well, figure it out when you can. It needs to be in the chronicle."

Avall started to reply, but Myx chose that moment to reappear. "His Majesty will see the lot of you at once, but he advises that he has little time just now."

Avall nodded, and let Myx hold the door flap for his party to enter. Only then did he recall that Strynn and Rann hadn't seen the King since their return, nor did they know him very well. As for Div—the poor woman was clearly in awe. He'd have to see that she spent some time with Merryn. His active, strong-willed sister would be a good companion for her. And then they were entering the inner chamber, and Avall found himself once more in the presence of his King.

Clad in a simple black surcoat over light mail, Gynn was sitting at a plain, sturdy table alternately poring over charts and trying to make his way through a meal that was rather too ornate for his present circumstances—if the number of small gold dishes and wine ewers strewn about was any indication. And the exotic spices, of which Avall could identify but three, by scent.

Nor was the King alone. Tryffon of War sat behind a smaller table, with a plate of victuals growing cold in their sauces to his right hand. A clay pitcher of ale sweated moisture at his left. Flanking Tryffon were two more men in War-Hold livery, neither of whom Avall recognized. There was also a weather-witch. One Avall hoped was trustworthy.

The King stared at the chart one final time, stuck a crimson pin into a certain location, then looked up. His eyes were tired, his hair greasier than Avall had ever seen it, but he still managed a smile as he preempted their bows with a sweep of his hand, indicating that they should take seats. Avall found a folded camp stool and claimed it for Strynn, then joined his companions in taking places on the floor.

"Greetings, cousins," the King intoned formally. "I trust your journey here was productive." He paused, as though waiting for reply.

Avall swallowed and nodded. "It was as fast a ride as that size trek could make, once we'd decided that the best thing for us to do was join you—not that Rann had any choice," he added, with a nervous grin. "But if by productive, you mean have we learned more than we knew or finished certain things, then the answer is no." He broke off, staring intently at the strangers. The King clearly read his meaning. "We need privacy," he informed them. "All but Tryffon, who knows as much of these matters as I did when last we spoke."

Avall availed himself of the ensuing confusion of bodies to procure drinks for himself and his companions, and found himself in a somewhat less crowded chamber as he finished. "I forget myself, Majesty," he began. "Since we know your time is precious, what would you know of us?"

The King munched a morsel of smoked meat. "First of all, how fares Lord Eellon? I've had reports, of course, but you know him better than anyone. Did I do right in leaving him in charge of the Council?"

"You did right," Avall acknowledged. "But, forgive me, Majesty, I fear you did the man himself no good. We all forget how old he is. I"—he paused, swallowed again—"I have never seen him so weak. You know he collapsed on the floor of the Hall?"

"I know. Two questions there, then—no, three. Who is really running the Council? What is the situation with Priest-Clan? And what use is Tyrill making of all this?"

Avall took a deep breath. "Three very large questions, Sire. First . . . Eellon is still managing to run affairs though, often as not, from his rooms. The sept-chiefs are proving to be much more cooperative than expected, or else they've rallied behind the situation for the nonce; it's hard to tell. Tyrill is . . . herself. I think she still despises you, but she seems also to have remembered that she's Eronese first of all. And I think she's glad to have something to actually make. Something that she can contribute—but that's suitably showy—to gain her recognition."

"And Priest-Clan?"

Avall shrugged. "Who knows? One thing I do suggest, however, if I may advise Your Majesty, is that as soon as this war is over, you examine that clan with the finest gaze you have. There are at least two layers of power there, and who knows how many more. My sense is that very few people in that clan know the entire pattern. As far as the prisoners are concerned, they're well fed—though a few have refused food—and well guarded. The bulk of the clan are keeping good behavior because, as it happens, the chiefs of Common Clan have noted that they don't seem to actually have much to do besides intercede with The Eight and perform ceremonies—which doesn't get them much sympathy when loved ones are marching off to battle."

The King smiled wanly. "That always happens. Religion tends to fade in importance when faced with real life. Until one stares down the dripping blade of death, when one finds religion again."

"Maybe we can prevent that, Sire," Avall murmured.

The King took a long swallow. "Maybe we can."

A pause, then: "You know Merryn is here."

The King nodded.

"Have you spoken to her?"

"At length and often, but less of her escape than of what she saw there and en route here. I do know, however, that you were able to contact her with a gem."

"One of them," Avall corrected. "Your Majesty also knew that Strynn and Rann arrived with more?"

"That's *all* I know, though I certainly wouldn't have minded being better informed."

Strynn cleared her throat. "Not counting the one Eddyn stole, we now have six, Majesty. I have one which is bonded to me, as does Rann. Avall bonded with another just before we left—which leaves three, which we thought to incorporate into the royal regalia if you would consent to having them bound to you."

Gynn's expression was an odd mixture of excitement and wariness. "I would certainly *like* one bound to me, for very many reasons. But three? Can someone be bound to three?"

Avall shrugged. "I'm bound to two, though not entirely by choice. But as to that, it brings us to the real reason we're here. We've"—he paused for a deep breath—"we've been trying to hone our communication skills— Strynn and Rann and I have. Lykkon and Div have helped. Rann's done some really spectacular theorizing, and—" He broke off again. "You haven't met Div, have you?"

The King shook his head. "I trusted your judgment in bringing her here."

"She saved our lives," Rann supplied simply. "She kept us alive in the Deep."

"I've heard some of that tale," Gynn informed them. "For now—what I need to know is whether you can communicate well enough to send the kind of word I need back and forth?"

"We can," Avall affirmed. "Before, when we only had one jewel, one party really needed to be asleep or distracted. With two, we can both be alert. And if we could take you into the bond as well—"

"It would be a risk," Strynn added carefully. "But I think it would be worth it."

"It would," the King agreed. "Provided mastering this skill doesn't distract from more pressing duties. But tell me, what of that other thing? The power—the *real* power—you said the thing displayed. Have you mastered that yet?"

"You mean the ability to reach into the Overworld and bring back power from there? We're working on it, but not to our satisfaction. We hope, however, now that we're in camp, to give it more attention."

The King scowled. "What're the problems?"

Avall shifted to a more comfortable position. "First of all, we haven't found a way for one person to go there alone. It requires the support of at least two others—Rann thinks one male and one female—but we haven't tested that yet, because we've been on the road since the morning after I activated my stone. There hasn't even been time to try to reconnect with Merryn, or we'd have known she was here. Second, we haven't found a way to go there quickly. And if the thing is to be used as a weapon, we must be able to determine when, where, and how it acts. Rann thinks willpower might be able to direct it, but again, he has little to back that up."

The King regarded him steadily. "Make that your first priority. Loath as I am to use such a wonder as a weapon, I see no choice if we're to stem Ixti's advance. The river will start to recede in a few days, so I'm told. We must be ready. Anything you need—most especially privacy in which to work—you may have. I'll have a tent set up next to mine, so that you may consult me at need, or apprise me of any developments."

"It could be dangerous," Avall advised.

"So can war in general, but do what you can. For now, I'd suggest you rest. Get food. Meet with your sister. Get her tale. I'll join you when I can."

"For what, Sire?" Rann blurted.

"To be bonded," Gynn retorted. "We don't dare wait any longer."

Avall sensed in his tone a dismissal and rose. "By your leave, then, Sire, we all have work to do."

"And mine not the greatest," Gynn replied. "Go, young kinsmen, and be at it."

A moment later Avall and his companions walked into the twilight.

Merryn met them there. "I begged off," she chuckled. "Actually, I explained the situation and found someone with more desire for authority than sense, and set him taking the gate toll. Now," she continued, "you look even more tired than I feel, so if you've no other duty—which I suspect you don't—you can join me in my tent and eat while I tell my tale, and then you can tell yours."

"Your tent," Strynn said pointedly. "How do you rate that?"

"I've become one of the royal intelligence officers, among other things, courtesy of my stay behind enemy lines. The King keeps me close by in case he needs to know something about affairs in Ixti. Not that I know as much as he'd like; still, it's more than he'd know otherwise."

Lykkon was fumbling in his pack for his journal as they made their way into the tent Merryn indicated, which was indeed located within a moment's summons of the royal pavilion. It was also conveniently close to the kitchens, to which Lykkon, as youngest, was summarily dispatched.

Merryn's tent wasn't large—one more person would've crowded it—but there was room for a camp bed, along with a small table and a stool. Bits of armor and harness lay about, as well as a set of saddlebags. Avall wondered what had become of her faithful horse, Ingot, which she'd ridden off to War-Hold after their first Fateing. Probably nothing either of them wanted to contemplate.

For her part, Merryn wasted no time in stripping down to her undertunic and house-hose, wiggling her toes gratefully as she stretched out on the bed. "I can't believe you're here," she sighed. "I truly can't. So much has happened since the Sundering. You rode north and I rode south, and somewhere in between the world changed. This spring is nothing like I'd expected."

"For none of us," Avall broke in, easing aside to make room for Lykkon, who'd returned in record time, with a large tray in hand. It was simple fare—hot bread, roast meat, and boiled grain. And both wine and ale— from the royal steward, he confided. He set the meal on the table and joined the others. The food could be eaten with fingers.

"I was just telling my sister that the Dark Half was not what any of us expected," Avall informed his cousin. "I expected to be returning about this time with the helm finished and a fresh new child in tow. I was looking forward to showing what I'd done to the King. But I never had any idea that what I'd actually be showing him would be something of such power no one can imagine—and of which we'd never even heard a year ago."

"I never thought I'd have dared the Deep," Rann chimed in, reaching over to clasp Div's hand. "And I sure as Eight never thought I'd meet anyone out there like Div."

"We also know that Priest-Clan has darker aspects than we'd ever suspected."

"But that's not why we came here," Lykkon broke in. "We're here to hear Merryn's story, first of all."

Merryn rolled her eyes, as she hastily swallowed a chunk of bread and meat. "The question is, where do I begin? With my arrival at War-Hold? With me happening to be on patrol when we picked up four weather-worn fugitives from Ixti? With having the bad luck to fall in love with one of them at the same time my brother was discovering that gems are sometimes more than gems? Dammit, I want to tell all this blow by blow and breath by breath, and I can't! There's no time. Trouble is, this is the first time we've all been separated by so much, both in time and distance and—worse— experience."

"What I want to know," Strynn said decisively, "is how you escaped from prison. Surely they had you guarded."

"Heavily," Merryn affirmed with a wicked smile. "Word got out that I was kin to the King of Eron, which is perfectly true, and that they'd be fools to kill so valuable a hostage. And then"—her face darkened and she wouldn't look at them outright—"they found out about the gem. I told them—" She pounded the bedding with a fist. "I *told* them!" she repeated. "They tortured me, and I thought I could stand up to it, but I failed. They found out that I knew about the gem, which maybe saved Kraxxi—"

"Kraxxi?"

"The king of Ixti's son. He was my . . . lover. And such a strange mix of naive and wise. So different from the men here. I don't know what it was about him, but even after he betrayed me, there was something. I guess there still is. Anyway, to make a very long and unpleasant story short, Kraxxi found out about the gem—and no, I didn't tell him, Avall; all I can think is that he heard me talking in my sleep. In any event he found out about it and fled south, I assume because he'd made the same assumptions about the military applications of the thing that you and the King have. I followed, at first purely to get a full accounting out of him because he'd lied to me. Bad luck caught me out, but I survived winter on the Flat—by virtue of being captured by outriders from Ixti intent on probing our southern border. Turns out they were part of a secretly assembled expeditionary force. I was tortured, but they brought me north with them—me and Kraxxi both."

"To—?" Lykkon prompted.

"To the Cloister of the Winds, half a hard day's ride below South Gorge. That's where Barrax had set up his command, since the valley was already flooding when he got there. In any event, to tell you what you asked, your last contact almost . . . killed me."

Strynn's face went white, and Avall actually gasped. *"Killed you?"*

Merryn nodded. "You're aware that using it consumes body heat?"

"I know it draws energy from those around you, and yourself if you're alone. We haven't had a chance to fully test and observe the effect—to Lykkon's chagrin, I might add."

"Well, it either froze me to death or the next thing to it, but I survived. The important part is that they took me for dead long enough for me to escape. Trouble was, the only escape was into the Ri-Vynn. I was already cold, and nearly drowned, but something about the fact that I had been nearly dead made me more willing to dare things. I gave myself to the river, pretty much. I floated past the camp, and fortunately, there was a hold on an island halfway between the Vynn and its juncture with the Ri-Ormill. Both were in flood, of course, and as cold as the Not-World. Anyway, the holders had gone—probably in fear of Barrax—but they'd left a boat, which I commandeered. It took me to the tower at South Gorge, where I got off. Being an island, too, this time of year, it was mostly deserted—everyone but the garrison had fled to Tir-Vonees down on the coast, or else joined the army. Still, it was no problem getting from there to here. Though I have to say, after this year we do have to propitiate Weather, because only the flooding of the

Ormill has bought us enough time to make ready at the only place we could really stem an invasion."

Silence.

"And that's all," she sighed. "I'm sorry, but it really wasn't much of an adventure. The mechanism of my escape— Now *that* was less an adventure than a miracle." She paused again. "Avall, what do you think is going on with those gems? Are they truly magic? Are they some aspect of The Eight, or are The Eight really only an aspect of them, or what?"

"You've never even seen one, have you?" Rann blurted. "We've become so complacent about them, we forget."

Strynn was already fumbling at her throat for the chain that held her gem, even as Avall did the same. Both stones appeared simultaneously. They glittered in the half-light. Merryn reached first for one, then the other. "Can I . . . Is it safe to touch them?"

Avall nodded. "As far as we know, though I'm happier doing it because you're my sister. Eddyn . . . got hold of mine and . . ."

"How?" Merryn asked sharply. "I know he got south with it, but I never knew how—"

"Basically, he just vanished. Place-jumped, evidently, to some place where the king of Ixti found him."

"Well, that explains a few things," Merryn said. "I hate to say it, but I wish I could've brought him with me."

"In any event," Avall went on, "the gems appear to 'like' whomever I like. What Eddyn did seems to indicate that someone who doesn't like me can likewise master them, but only in necessity. They also speed up your perceptions—which is one reason we think they might benefit the King."

"If he had some set into his regalia," Div supplied—the first time she'd spoken.

"If," the King echoed, slipping into the tent to join his kinsmen on the floor. "And don't worry about being overheard. I have keen ears, I knew what to listen for—and Myx won't let anyone within three spans of this place on my orders."

Avall took a deep breath and regarded his companions. "Does anyone know any reason *not* to do this now?"

"It takes energy," Rann cautioned. "Even if the rest of us aren't in the link, the King may draw on us, depending on what he intends to do. Having said that, I'm no more tired than anyone else present. And if *all* we're going to do is bond His Majesty to the gems, there should be no problem."

Avall nodded solemnly and raised a brow at Gynn. "You should tell your second what we're about. He needs to know he may have to take charge if anything goes wrong. And . . . I want him to know absolutely that there's no foul play afoot. I don't want to be accused of regicide."

Gynn smiled grimly. "I've already told him. I've also told him that any word that comes from anyone in this tent is to be taken as royal command."

Avall suppressed a chill at that: the realization that he was a breath away from being King in function if not in fact. That more rode on his shoulders—their shoulders, for he was not alone in this—than he could imagine. He wondered if this was how Gynn had felt when he'd first been proposed as Sovereign.

Strynn cleared her throat as she loosened the pouch from her belt. "Majesty, I feel compelled to ask: Have you tasted of the Wells? Have The Eight made Their will known in this?"

The King smiled. "I feared what they might tell me," he replied. "Ever since the autumn I've feared it, and everything they've said has been ambiguous. But if this goes as it may . . . I may soon be in Their realm. Perhaps They'll grant me an audience face-to-face."

Avall didn't know whether to believe Gynn or not. Nor whether the King spoke blasphemy. But he'd certainly been somewhere else—some place he preferred to call the Overworld. "Perhaps you'll find this altogether a more familiar experience than I," he said at last.

"There's also one crucial decision you have to make," Rann broke in. "One that we can't really advise you on."

"And that is?"

He shifted uncomfortably. "Whether to bind you to all three gems at once, or one at a time."

Gynn gnawed his lip and looked at Avall. "You're bound to two, but in sequence, correct?"

Avall nodded. "But others can use them even so. In fact, we thought of binding all three of these to one or the other of us, but we weren't sure whether that might cause some problem in the long run."

Gynn chuckled grimly. "This is learn as you go, isn't it? This is the kind of thing that'll be in the histories a thousand years from now: what we did, how it turned out. I'm not sure if I like making history, though."

"No," Merryn and Avall chorused as one, in that eerie way twins had. "Adventures are much better to read about than to live."

"But we can either work with what we know," Gynn retorted, "or we—I—can expand our knowledge in some small way. Fact," he continued, "we don't know if the gems you've found aren't all there'll ever be. Therefore, this may be the only chance in the history of the world to *try* to bind three stones at once. I'd be a fool to try it, but I might be a worse fool not to."

" 'Knowledge outlives Kings,' " Lykkon quoted.

"Thank you for reminding me," Gynn replied dryly. "At any rate, my life hinges on the next few days—or even hands. I might die sooner this way, but that death will certainly be more interesting."

At some unspoken sign, Strynn spread the gems on the table. They glittered in the firelight, as if in anticipation.

"You know some of this," Avall said. "You cut yourself, you . . . feed the gems blood. After that—you wait to see what happens."

Gynn shrugged resignedly. And accepted the knife Strynn passed him.

They think they know what I risk, Gynn told himself. *They have no idea. Not my life as it is now, but my life as it is for all time to come. Gynn syn Argen-el, who saved Eron or lost it.*

Or who made it greater than it ever was before. And all for a little pain, a little risk. A day from now I will be someone else.

They were waiting for him to take that risk, too. Eyes watched him. Young eyes that had still seen so much. Faces—minds—bodies—that had suffered more than he ever had at that age. *He'd* only had to survive the plague.

Sparing his comrades a wry smile, Gynn used the point of his knife to array the gems in a neat line, a hand's length apart. Then, steeling himself, he grasped the blade in his left hand, and with his right pulled it smartly down. Merryn had edged that blade, so it was sharp beyond believing. He saw the blood before he felt the pain, but by then he'd swapped the hilt to the other hand, and was repeating the ritual to bloody his right. He'd been conditioned since birth to seek patterns—symmetries. This was one of them. Another breath, and he returned the dagger to Strynn, who wiped it on the tablecloth, and slid it into its sheath. A pause, and he reached for the two outside gems, taking one in each hand.

And saw the God.

Or *was* the God.

Was *everything*. Avall had said that the first effect he'd had from the gem was a sense of being energized. Coupled with that had come an attenuated time sense, along with a much tighter focus of concentration.

This was like that, only more so. Time slowed down at once. At the same time, his senses expanded, and he realized that for this moment he had all the time in the world—time to examine everything in the room in the most minute detail. He could count the threads in the table cover by eye—by texture if he ran his fingers across them. By the sound his nails would make as they brushed that surface. Or all three at once. And he could feel the . . . powers of the universe, he supposed, as though his body had grown a second set of nerves that responded solely to the unseen.

His companions were no longer mere solid bodies seated close by, but complexities of systems, large and small, some of which he could touch with parts of himself that he hadn't known existed. He'd shared minds with Avall before—and in that, had shared his body. But that had required touch. This didn't. He saw Avall and the others, and then he saw Avall's mind. He saw fear and wonder, and a dreadful slowness he realized numbly was Avall's mind frozen in time relative to his own. But that mind was open, trusting, wondering. He couldn't resist, and slipped in there, ignoring those things he had no right to know, but moving unerringly toward anything that spoke of the gems. And there, for the first time, he saw Avall's whole memory of what it had been like to enter the Overworld. Not as a set of words or images, but as a pattern in his thoughts. Along with it, he saw how that pattern joined with Avall's mind itself, like a webwork of invisible scaffolding binding earth and sky. And more important, he saw how that connection was made.

And could therefore be remade, over and over. Endlessly.

But he also saw that no words existed to explain those things. Whatever communication occurred had to take place at a level that had not, heretofore, existed. Nor could Avall perceive the pattern—because he was within it, as one could not perceive the shape of the world while immersed within the sea.

Almost he lost himself, as he stared in awe. And then slowly, oh so slowly, came a rolling growl of something he only dimly recognized as words. They were like tides, so slowly did they ebb into his ears. Yet still he heard them. "Try . . . the . . . other . . . ," they proclaimed.

Gynn hesitated. *Other what?* And then knew. *The gem.* But he was so perfectly balanced, with a gem in either hand, and the power they contained flowing perfectly. And though he knew he could prime them, he feared to upset that oh-so-perfect balance.

But then his precise new reflexes thrust rational thought aside and took total command of his body, so that it was with exactly enough force and direction that he slammed his forehead down atop the third gem hard enough to break skin. Hard enough to feed that stone the blood it needed to awaken all those wonders.

Reality promptly swung into even sharper focus. Order imposed itself on chaos, as left and right merged and mingled, and his mind became one again. But it wasn't safe, he also realized. There was too much power at work here, unless that power had some focus. And what must that focus be? What did he want most strongly?

He wanted to save the land, and for that he must wield the power of the gems. But that power was too great without a structure. Yet he *had* a structure—had seen one—lodged in Avall's memory. He needed only to duplicate that.

Which he couldn't do, because he had no time in real time for such things. But which Avall could manage, if he could see the pattern.

But what *was* that pattern?

There were several, actually. Yet it seemed that the one that would do most good in the context in which their conscious minds were accustomed to working was one that would feed the power of the gem to his nervous system most effectively.

He couldn't explain the pattern—but he could show it. And so he dived into Avall's memory, and set that pattern there. Not in a place where words or images could find it, analyze it, and set it forth. But deeper: down where instinct lived. Where one simply did art, not described it.

And that was all he *could* do, he realized, as his body let it be known that far too much of him was not accustomed to such stress.

Slowly, oh so slowly, he raised his head, and with that, energy flowed out of him, then shifted to a new balance.

He opened his hands and saw the gems drift down like stately drops of crimson rain to the snowfield that was the tablecloth. They glittered as they fell, their inner facets winking at him, one after another, as though they were tiny gods each sharing a secret with him. Maybe they were. Maybe instead of The Eightfold God, he had met The Eight-million-fold. A languid rush of air was his companions breathing, and then the gems struck the fabric. The noise was like soft thunder.

Reality shattered, then realigned. If he tried, he could assess the world at a normal pace. And while part of him danced through his own brain, as though through a Lore hall and a gallery of wonders all at once, a denser, duller part was aware of his companions spinning around in place, to stare at Tryffon standing in the doorway, his face hard with concern.

Gynn heard the words that nested around the major ones and softened the blow, but the ones that registered most forcefully were contained in two sentences: "The river will be back in its banks tomorrow" and "Barrax's army is moving."

Gynn nodded a slow reply. But the person he spoke to was Avall. "You know what to do now, without knowing."

"I'm cold," Avall replied numbly. And then, quite suddenly, was asleep.

Gynn stared at the hand-high phial before him. It glimmered in the darkness, its iridescent glaze reflecting the light of the single candle that was the sole illumination in his tent. He was naked—not only because he'd just had the bath that was prescribed for Sovereigns on the eve of battle, but because he was about to petition the God. For the phial held water from Fate's Well.

Gynn paused with his hand extended. Did he truly want to do this? He was tempting Fate already—twice over.

The wound was one way. But he truly had thought it might heal, and by the time he was certain it wouldn't, affairs were moving swiftly toward war. And since that war would, indeed, have been long in planning before his injury, blame for it could not rest on his indiscretion. As for stepping down now . . . Ritual gave him some leeway, but it finally boiled down to choice. He could abandon his kingdom in its time of need, and thereby placate the letter of the Law. Or he could give his country everything he had to give, and hope that the Law—and The Eight—would forgive him. Especially if what he placed on Fate's altar was his own life.

He'd been fortunate so far. Rumor of his deficiency was still confined to the Council, or to High Clan, at best. And High Clan were increasingly dubious about the existence of The Eight anyway. The northern gorges were still blissfully isolated, unless the couriers he'd sent with the war report had gossiped, which he didn't think they'd do. As for the other two, one had already fallen and the other been busy evacuating itself when rumor, if any, had gone south.

At bottom, few knew, fewer would have told, and by the time rumor became widespread among the troops, the battle for South Gorge would be over.

Maybe *then* he'd drink from Fate's Well. As for the other—what he'd done just now with the gems—that was temptation of another kind. Maybe it was compensation: a risk to his self in exchange for the risk he was forcing on the land, in case The Eight were *not* pleased with his failure to abdicate.

He shrugged and ran a finger down the side of the phial. It all came down to choices, didn't it? And he'd made one choice, which might go against the Law, and now another in recompense. It was balance, he supposed. It always was. Then again The Eight had long since named him the King of Balance. And maybe that was enough.

Sparing one final wistful glance at the phial, he returned it to the portable altar in which it was housed.

If Fate wanted his attention, Fate would tell him. But for now, it seemed, Fate spoke mostly through Avall.

CHAPTER XXVIII:

THE HERMIT OF PRIESTS' GORGE

(ERON: TIR-ERON—SUNBIRTH: DAY VIII—EARLY MORNING)

~~~~~~~~~~

Rrath had fallen into a crack.

Two cracks, actually. There was the literal crack in a slab of stone into which he'd just stumbled, as he made his way through the rocky wilderness that comprised the extreme south end of the rugged spur gorge that housed Priest-Clan's main precincts. *That* crack had cost him no more than a scraped ankle, a bloody elbow, and a certain amount of dignity—that latter gone to waste, since no one had seen him anyway, nor would have, the way the rocks were piled around here, ornamented with clumps of hardy plants the same color as his robe, and the whole wreathed often as not with puffs of steam billowing from vents in the main gorge lower down.

The other crack was figurative. He'd regained consciousness at precisely the best moment to effect a disappearance. Exactly when no one was concerned with him.

Not with the elite of his clan imprisoned in the Hall of Clans, including his mentor, Nyllol, who'd introduced him to the Ninth Face. *Mentor indeed!* he snorted, as he picked himself up and assessed his skinny self for damage. Nyllol had used him ruthlessly, playing on his combination of ambition and naïveté to effect certain ends that were not Rrath's own. But Nyllol wasn't accessible now. And he doubted anyone else had energy to spare locating a young man who'd escaped from the infirmary. Not when he was eking out an existence where no one would think to look—or dare.

Nor did he want to be found.

Not by his clan, for his clan contained a secret inner clan, and he had no way of knowing who was which. If the Ninth Face got hold of him, he'd never have peace again. There was no end of the things they could do to control him, and Rrath had had enough of being controlled. And if they even suspected he was no longer loyal to them, he would die quickly and invisibly, with no chance whatever of survival.

But the King was gone, so there was no way to beg royal protection in exchange for information. As for the remaining powers in the gorge—well, it was mostly Argen and Ferr, and the people he'd hurt most grievously were of those lines. Eellon might listen, but that would be all. And Eddyn—

He didn't want to think about Eddyn—wherever he was. Eddyn who'd maybe been his friend and then tried to kill him, not once but many times. With cause, perhaps, for the first—but Rrath figured that only made them even.

Fear and ignorance were his friends, he concluded, as he started down the path, sparing a glance at the glowering sky. Ignorance, because few even among his own clan knew what was kept prisoned in the upper reaches of Priest-Clan's gorge. And fewer, he suspected, actually thought about those prisoners. Which was just as well, with Nyllol incarcerated, since Nyllol had maintained charge of them.

Maintained for the last half year, rather. Before that, they'd been in Rrath's care, under Nyllol's supervision.

Those prisoners.

Those things everyone else feared.

Not that he didn't fear them as well, but he had so much else to fear that they, in their predictability, were comforting by contrast. They were also the lone powerful things he, in some wise, controlled.

The beasts in the clan menagerie.

The geens.

The route he followed to their enclosure was a mirror of the one he'd taken half a year gone by when Nyllol had asked him about his observations of the geens, and whether they were intelligent, and then followed those queries with more probing ones about how he felt about knowledge and power.

That path had taken him up from the hold proper, through a sort of rock garden, to a saddle in the rocks, beyond which, in the most steep-sided, dead-end canyon in all of Eron Gorge, lay the geens' enclosure. But teeing off that saddle to the left was a tunnel that opened into another canyon, where the goats on which the geens were fed, were kept. Beyond *that* was wilderness. And caves, in one of which he'd chosen to dwell, with a few supplies filched from uninhabited suites under cover of night. As for food, he had vegetables and grain stolen from the stores intended for the goats, and goatflesh itself, when he dared cook it, which he did at night on the smallest fires he could manage. He hadn't spent a warm night in what seemed like forever. But spring was upon them now, and with it . . .

Change.

Somewhere.

Not here.

Now was all he cared about. Eating, drinking, sleeping. Perhaps he was a little mad. Certainly he lived mostly in *now*. For the rest—he no longer cared.

Except about the geens.

The trail that was not a trail had leveled off into the upper pasture of the goat corral, and he hesitated beside a spur of rock before continuing. No one was about, save the usual herd of worn-out old bills and nannies. The crippled, the blind, the sterile. Too old to eat, too useless to milk or shear for wool. Like him, he supposed. Alive, but with no part in the world any longer.

One ambled up to nibble the hem of his tunic when he paused too long. He batted it absently, noting as he always did its odd, square-pupiled eyes. Wondering if that affected how it saw the world. Perhaps *he* had odd-pupiled eyes now. Certainly the world he saw wasn't the one he'd seen a year gone by.

In any event, he didn't want to linger—not in the daylight. Someone was still feeding the goats—and the geens—after all. Probably some terrified half-boy like he'd been when he'd found his way to Priest-Hold: an orphan, because the whole generation ahead of him had died of the plague.

He didn't want that child—whoever it was—to see him. Then he'd have to kill it, and that would draw attention.

With that in mind, he skirted left, through the shadows that lined the canyon and so came to the near end of the tunnel. He didn't enter it, however, but eased farther left, where a half-hewn stair snaked up the slope beside it, ending a dozen spans above his head. He climbed it nimbly, agile for one who had been ill so long. Nor was he even slightly winded when he reached the top. He crouched there briefly, feeling more breezes beating at his body than were typical in the closer quarters at his back. They brought scents, too: smoke, and the sulfur stench of the steam from the hot springs that heated the gorge. And, ever so slightly, baking bread. Unfortunately, that made his mouth water and his stomach growl, and so he scurried left again, down the slope of the rock dome, to where he could look down on the geens' enclosure.

It was maybe two shots long and half of one wide, with a stream along one side and enough spotty growth to provide needed cover for the reptiles.

Also enough cover to support a modest population of small animals that supplemented the geens' diet of derelict goat.

On which one of the beasts was feeding now, a haunch grasped in one knotty forearm. It nibbled at it absently, exactly like a man gnawing a roast fowl's leg.

They were actually no larger than a good-sized man—about Eddyn's size, perhaps—and shared more than size with him, too, Rrath thought sourly. Essentially lizardlike, they nevertheless walked on their hind legs, which put their fanged heads a span above the ground. Their long tails were mostly for balance, and their eyes were in the front of their heads, like most predators. Their skin was smooth and mottled, rather than scaled, and made high-quality leather. And their claws were dark blackish green—and prized in Ixti for use as dagger hilts.

Why were they here?

Officially because Priest-Clan maintained a scholarly function as well as a spiritual one. Which, though it put them in competition with Lore, also helped validate their existence among the increasing ranks of unbelievers.

And perhaps for a second reason.

Canon taught that anything that had intelligence also had a soul. Dolphins had been given their own god, just in case, because their actions were ambiguous. But in recent years increasing attention had been devoted to certain other animals that seemed to display traits that while not distinctly human, yet did not seem to be entirely derived from instinct. Reason and the use of tools were two of these. And maybe language.

Or memory, or loyalty, to judge by how the birkits had acted when they'd attacked his Ninth Face companions back at the station. Avall, and maybe the rest, could speak to them mind to mind—of that he was almost certain. But geens seemed even more warily alert than birkits. And if he could somehow access *their* wicked little minds . . .

Well, he might not *need* Ninth Face allies any longer.

And so he watched and waited, sprawled upon his rock.

Eventually the second geen appeared. The male. It spared what looked almost like a contemptuous glance at the feasting female, as though to say, *Fool of a woman! Why dull your teeth on stale meat when we will soon have fresh?*

Disgusted, it ambled off toward the south side of the canyon, which brought it directly under Rrath. Apparently its goal was the shade there, for it curled up in a compact ball, all its elaborate armament of claws and fangs obscured, save the row of hand-sized spiky plates down its back.

Rrath edged closer.

A stone moved under his hand. He flinched back, but didn't fall. The stone did, however, landing directly atop the geen's head. It uncoiled at once, leaping to its feet faster than even Rrath—who'd observed them steadily for over a year—could imagine.

And not only upright, it leapt up the cliff—straight toward him.

The walls were sheer—fortunately—so the beast could find no purchase. But even so, the movement brought its head uncomfortably close to Rrath's own before it fell to earth again.

Terrified yet exhilarated, he eased back to his former perch.

The geen was looking up at him, teeth bared.

Impulsively, Rrath bared his in return, trying to look as fierce as flat face and minimal dentition allowed.

To his surprise, the geen cocked its head.

Their eyes met.

For a long time they stared at each other.

Rrath wasn't sure what the geen was thinking, but he no longer had any doubt whatever that something besides raw instinct lurked behind those intense yellow eyes. It was exactly like staring down a bully or a rival. An establishment of power hierarchy.

Rrath knew that. And he suspected the geen knew as well.

Knew that one-on-one and naked, the geen could rend his life away in instants.

Knew that with any number of longer-range weapons, Rrath had the best of it.

And that Rrath controlled the food.

And maybe that Rrath regarded them with something besides fear and loathing.

For almost a finger they remained that way. Barely blinking, not moving. Only when the female flung the shank bone at her mate did he turn away. And even as he pranced off to meet her, he looked more than once over his shoulder.

CHAPTER XXIX:

FROM ON HIGH

(Eron—Eron's Belt—Sunbirth: Day VIII—midday)

~~~~~~~~~~~~~~~~

It doesn't look like a battlefield, Avall told himself, as he shifted to a more comfortable position on his perch: a bare stone shelf three spans wide, high above Ormill Vale. Pines ringed the place, and spring flowers bloomed amid the laurel thickets that masked that part of the ridge. A lightning-blasted stump to his left made decent cover, now that he'd obscured his gaudy livery with a gauze-thin cloak and hood the same anonymous gray-brown as the rocks. The sky blazed overhead, impassive.

And below . . .

Below stretched a great bowl of a plain, eight shots across north and south, and half that east and west. The river divided it unevenly, a quarter to the north, the rest to the south. The north side—this side—was steeper, too, for the tree-clad heights behind which Gynn's army nested swooped down sometimes dangerously precipitous slopes to meet the tall plain-grass halfway. Those same heights curved west as well, into the higher wall of Angen's Spine, which ventured closer to the coast here than anywhere else in Eron. More stone than wood showed there. It was not a place for a battle, for all that a ruined hold claimed a prime vantage point on a particularly impressive crag.

South, beyond the river, the vale stretched flat for a fair distance before giving way to a series of forested hills. Barrax's forces lurked among them, invisible behind the nearer knolls. They'd seen their smokes, however—and vast smokes they were, too.

Southeast—left—lay the gorge itself, its western terminus veeing in to meet the river at the obligatory waterfall that characterized all five inhabited gorges. Unlike fallen Half Gorge, however, or Eron Gorge, South Gorge's principal city, Tir-Vonees, had not been built at the west end of the gorge, with fields spreading between it and the sea, but at the coast. This end was mostly lake as well, the few islands marked with mills and assorted villas—all deserted now—with the land between being the province of small Common Clan farmers, many of whom now swelled the ranks gathering beyond the rise. There'd been talk of moving the forces east, to defend Eron's third most populous city. But such a diversion would have been wildly out of the way. Besides which, Barrax hadn't marched *his* army there.

Or into the gorge.

There were two reasons for that. One was that, like the vale below, the gorge's west end flooded in the spring, which was also why Tir-Vonees was on the coast. The second was that Barrax was no fool, and while it was easy enough to enter the gorge from the south, the northern cliffs were ever so much steeper, and no commander worth his sword would lead his army into such an obvious trap, especially when the defenders could rain whatever they wanted upon them with impunity.

To control South Gorge, then, one had to control the plain around it and the water that flowed into it. The valley was the obvious place for the armies to meet.

Avall wondered about the wisdom of battle now, given that the river was still in flood, though receding every hand, and the flats to either side would surely be reduced to a slippery snarl of grass-laced mud. Not the best terrain in which to wage war, either on horseback, or afoot.

But battle, so the scouts said, there would be.

As soon as the bridges cleared.

Which could be any moment, Avall decided, as he squinted through the distance lenses Gynn had provided. The view was hazy and distorted, for the lenses were a new thing Glass had contrived, and not yet perfect in their operation. Still, he could see the river clearly: a mud-colored shimmer amid fields of grass only slightly less luminous. The bridges were still drowned, but the rails showed on all three intact ones, and the uppermost, which was also the narrowest, was probably covered no more than knee deep.

But they'd slighted the causeway that led up to it, as they'd slighted all those higher up, never mind that it was out of the way, and too narrow. Any army crossing there would have to go single file. And the waters were too deep to ford a-horse, even without opposing fire.

A movement in the underbrush behind him made Avall tense and reach for his sword before he heard a familiar hail and saw Merryn trotting up what passed for a path behind him. Like him, she wore a gauze stone-cloak, but the flimsy fabric did little to disguise the glint of steel and heraldic fabric beneath. Her eyes flashed fire.

"Merryn!" Avall began, with a grin that faded when he saw her grim expression.

"I didn't want to be here," she grumbled. "I'd planned to get in there and fight till I could fight no more, since a good hunk of this is my fault anyway." She flung herself down beside him. "But then the King got wind and said, 'Oh no, *you're* going to defend your brother, since he may not be in a position to fight if he's threatened. *You're* also going to advise him on what he sees, since you know more about tactics than he.' " She cuffed him so roughly he wasn't entirely sure it was play. "So here I am, your trusty adviser/guardian. I hope you appreciate it."

Avall regarded her seriously. "You shouldn't feel guilty—not about War-Hold. There's not a High Clan man or woman alive who hasn't been subjected to imphor. It was the wood talking, not you."

Merryn pounded the rock beside her. "Yes, but *I* was a member of the Night Guard—or was training to be. A little longer, and I'd have worked up an immunity. But I had to get impatient. I had to go running after a man. A stupid, conniving man!"

"Save your anger," Avall advised. "That's also something they teach at War-Hold, isn't it? At least you're here with us. At least you're getting to fight on the proper side."

"I wouldn't be fighting at all if I'd kept my mouth shut!" Merryn shot back.

Avall resisted the urge to reach over and hug her. Neither could spare the distraction. "I'm surprised you aren't with Strynn. She's playing spy over on the other side." He pointed west, to where their ridge met the mountains by the ruined hold.

"I asked to be, but the King said you were more important than she was, based on what you know. I didn't argue. But I made him send Div—who's *quite* something, by the way—with her."

Avall couldn't help but giggle. "Yeah, I figure she's *almost* your equal as a warrior."

Merryn huffed contemptuously, and settled into a more comfortable slump, but her face told Avall this was no time for talk.

Especially when that conversation might be the last either of them ever had.

"I'm going to try to contact Strynn, Rann, and the King," he said sometime later, with the vale as empty as ever, but his nerves somewhat more frazzled. "If I do anything weird—stop me."

Merryn nodded, moving in close enough to subdue him, should that become necessary. "If you start getting cold," he cautioned, "either move away, or bring me around. I don't know how much power this will take, but it may very well draw on you. I'd hate for you to be too tired to save my skin when the real battle comes."

Merryn snorted, but did as instructed. For his part, Avall reached into his tunic and fished out the gem. Per a suggestion from Rann, he'd made a new casing for it that included a spring-loaded spur that popped out when one touched it a certain way, thereby negating the need to constantly cut one's hand. That wasn't strictly necessary anyway, he suspected—he hadn't always needed it with the old gem—but this one was still largely untried, as though the two of them were getting used to one another. A pause for breath, and he closed his eyes, even as his hand closed around the gem. The pressure released the catch, and he felt a prick of pain as his hand was blooded. With it, too, came the now-familiar rush of warmth and familiarity and . . . liking.

And power enough for what was needed. Working with the gem at odd moments during the last few days had taught him considerable discipline, so that he was able to enter the proper frame of mind with relative ease. A breath. Two—and he'd blanked his mind sufficiently to conjure Strynn. Not as she looked, however, but how she felt when he was in her mind. The image clarified, and then he reached for her—

And was there.

It works.

A mental chuckle. *Div had just suggested I send to you! I'd just pricked my finger, and was starting—*

Maybe we were linked already.

Maybe so. Can you see anything?

Avall blinked, trying to distinguish among what he saw with his interior eye, the impressions he was receiving through Strynn's, and what he could see with his own true vision.

Use my eyes, she suggested. *Close yours and try to see what I see. And then I'll reciprocate.*

Avall did—and felt the intensity of the contact increase. At the same time he truly did see with Strynn's eyes—she was gazing at a very quizzical-looking Div. She blinked at him uncertainly, then spoke. Her words had an odd quality to them, like a muffled echo in a metal-lined room. "There's been a change," she said. "The King didn't think it would be wise for him to be distracted by whatever communication you two managed to get to him. More to the point, he wasn't certain he could receive what you told him without him actively bonding to a gem, which he didn't think was smart in the heat of battle. So he's . . . just sent word for Rann to join him. He'll have a guard, and he'll report whatever you tell him to the King."

Avall's fury—concern, or whatever—nearly severed the contact. *So he's going to endanger Rann? Does he think Rann can ignore the distractions of combat any better than he can?*

Probably not. But he's more used to it. I . . . think it'll be like picking up a single voice in a room full of speakers. Difficult, but not impossible.

Maybe, Avall conceded. *In any event, I don't want to waste any more energy on this than I have to. But take care of yourself—all of you. Remember that I love you.*

And I you.

A pause. Then, from Strynn, *Can I have a look at Merryn?*

A short one would be wisest, but you were going to test this back.

And with that, Avall opened his eyes. Reality roiled and shifted, and it took a moment before he felt solid again. His head also felt clogged, as though with a painless hangover. The pain would come later, he suspected. In spite of his confusion, he spoke to his twin. "She's here, Merryn. She can't speak to you directly, though you might feel the resonance. But if you've anything to tell her, now would be a good time."

"She knows what I'd have to tell her."

"I know, but she needs to hear it."

Merryn puffed her cheeks. Then: "Everything after today will be easier, but simply knowing we're both free again and fighting on the same side makes *everything* easier."

Avall felt twin waves of emotion wash through him, one from close by, one from afar. It was more than he could bear. And with that the contact severed. Nor did he trust himself to contact Rann. *That,* he suddenly knew, truly would be more than he could bear.

It began as a glint on the horizon just before noon. Just as the narrowest bridge finally stood free. Just as the water on the other two reached knee height. Just as sections of wall became visible along the riverbanks.

A glint that hadn't been there before. And then a glitter of light: sunlight on a burnished helm. Avall tensed at once, saw Merryn fall into reflexive guard beside him. He fumbled the lenses free and checked to make certain. He'd hate to call down an attack on some poor misguided tinker with a donkey. Eronese tinkers also wore burnished helms.

"Is it—?" Merryn hissed beside him. He watched a moment longer, then passed her the instrument.

"It is," she concluded grimly.

Avall's hand had already closed on the gem. *Rann!* he shouted into the ether. *I think it's begun.* He blinked then, and in that moment glimpsed Rann running toward the High King, who was just starting to climb atop his horse. The armies of Eron spread around him. Beyond him was the crest of the ridge to the right. A mirror signal could have marked the movement, but not been so precise. "Your Majesty," he heard Rann cry, "it's started."

The King fairly leapt into his saddle. An instant later he was galloping. Avall withdrew from Rann's mind. But he had no doubt whatever that his bond-brother was also mounted.

When he blinked back to his own place again, it was to see Merryn all but crawling down the rock in her eagerness to see more. "If there's anything the King should know, please tell me."

"Tell him," Merryn said at once, "that the foe has twice as far to ride as we, but that the ground is marshier on this side the last shot or so, which will slow him down. Tell him that the bulk of the force seems to be angling toward the bridge closest to the gorge, though the water is highest there. Tell him that I see banners of Ixti's minor houses but not that of their king."

Avall closed his eyes, and relayed all those things, and for that one moment, his world was the pain in his hand, the one in his heart, and the one in his head.

Nor did he know if the King even heard Merryn's last observation. Because by the time Avall had relayed it, the vanguard of the Eronese army had crested the ridge and started down the hill, with the King clothed in the Cloak of Colors, riding unhelmed in the center.

It was like ants swarming toward a line of fresh blood, Avall thought. Eron's first charge consisted of alternating sections of foot and horse, the idea being that the horse would arrive first, and slow the enemy until the foot—mostly archers at this point, and most of them Common Clan men, women, and youths of either sex from South Gorge—got within range to effectively use their bows.

Certainly there'd be no massive impact; the terrain would see to that. What Barrax was doing attacking so early, he didn't know, either. But perhaps the king of Ixti knew something they didn't.

"They don't value life as much as we do," Merryn offered, as though she'd overheard him, which, given the intensity of Avall's emotion, she might have. "And they've surely been promised booty. There's much for the average Ixtian to gain in Eron. There's precious little for us down there, unless you want to fire all the sand in the Flat into bricks and build a wall around them."

The first cavalry had almost reached the bridges by then, and Avall suddenly realized that every third one of those men had ridden double, and that most of the co-riders were armed with stone-hammers and carried pouches of quick-fire. Arrows flew from the fore of Ixti's ranks, for Barrax had sent almost entirely cavalry—on stolen Eronese horses—and most of them carried bows. Shafts arched high into the air, then down in a glittering rain of death. Raised shields caught most of them. But one horse died just as its rider reached the bridge. The body toppled into the river. The rider managed to leap free, but his steed caught the footman beside him and laid him low. Nor did he rise. First blood to Ixti, then, though the blow had come from friend, not foe.

Avall found his attention drawn away, as Gynn put his plan into play.

His strategy was simple. To take Eron, Barrax would have to cross the Ri-Ormill. That meant taking the bridges. This was not his country, and the longer he remained in it unsubdued, the more vulnerable his flanks—and supply train—would become. Without the bridges, Barrax would have to wait—or dare the gorge. And if he could be made to wait long enough, other forces already in transit could be sent around to attack him from the flank.

Why did Gynn not cross the bridges himself, and take the war to Barrax? Because that meant abandoning the high ground, for one thing. More importantly, it meant moving his force by small increments into a place where attack could come from any quarter, for the land was wider south of the river.

But if he could lure Barrax here, the foe would have almost no maneuvering room.

And if they could destroy the bridges before the foe reached them, it wouldn't matter. Any further movement north would be subject to attacks by a swelling horde of Eronese intent on protecting their land. Gynn's hope was in attrition. And buying time. And a superior knowledge of Eronese men, land, and weather.

And then suddenly the battle congealed, as isolated clumps of men and beasts came together. Ixti's army had always moved as one, unlike Eron's, which consisted of more specialized groupings. And for once Avall was grateful that everyone who completed a tour in Wood-Hold was required to finish at least ten double eights of arrows. They were using them now; the sky was thick with them. But if they were stemming the approaching Ixtian tide, he didn't see it.

The bridge crews were having a hard time as well, finding the marshy ground much harder to navigate than they'd expected. Nor had the bridges been made to slight easily. It didn't help when one pouch of the precious quick-fire powder exploded prematurely.

Yet all that observation occupied but a fraction of Avall's time. The rest—he forgot what he was put there for, and found himself straining his gaze in search of Rann—or Lykkon, or the King. The latter was easy to spot. Half a shot back from the front, and surrounded by a ring of armed War-Hold knights, which ring also encompassed his friends. He was seeing everything, missing nothing.

And then, without warning, Merryn began feeding him information. "Tell the King that a group has broken off the west flank and are moving toward Narrow Bridge. Tell him—"

Avall didn't truly hear the words. He simply closed his eyes, linked with the gem, and through it told Rann everything Merryn dictated.

And for moments on end was more his bond-brother than his self, to the point of feeling the horse shift and paw beneath him, as he sat unmoving while the battle flowed around him. Rann was heavily armored—in almost full plate, since he wouldn't be in a position to fight, except in defense. Yet he was still vulnerable to the ever-raining shafts. Fortunately, few reached him, and of those that did, all but one slid harmlessly off the metal. The other caught in his surcoat. He picked it up absently, studying the workmanship.

Shafts made from inferior wood, with points cast in batches, and rough-filed in haste to a modicum of sharpness. Painted gold to produce an illusion of splendor when they rode the air.

Avall blinked back to his own head.

Both armies were clumped along the banks now, both having trouble with mud and wet grass. Horses were sliding down, and men barely had better traction. It was still raining arrows, but both sides had their shieldmen in place, and few of those shafts got through. Neither side was shooting as often as heretofore.

But the bridges were still intact. And no one had dared step upon them.

Too late Avall saw why the enemy had not advanced.

Bows were raised, but bigger bows than earlier, bows capable of shooting farther than the standard measured shot that was the basic unit of Eronese distance. Bows strong enough to shoot *behind* the body of Gynn's force, who were clumped around the bridges. Which meant they were also strong enough to target the open ground between the bridges.

Where the ground was covered with long, dry grass.

Spring was the dry season in Eron. And while the river had been in flood, that water had been snowmelt from the highlands that surrounded them. The grass itself was ripe to take fire from arrow flame.

Which Barrax had just sent hurtling northward in masses so thick it looked as though the sky was blazing.

The grass ignited at once.

And Gynn found his army assailed from behind, even as access along the banks between his phalanxes suddenly became difficult.

Those closest to the flames turned to fight them. But men who turned to fight fire at their backs were men who must turn their backs on their foes. And while shieldmen went on plying their trade, the number of available archers Eron could bring to bear was suddenly diminished by a tithe.

Smoke roiled into the sky, briefly obscuring vision, until the high winds began to fan it away. Which also, unfortunately, fanned the flames toward Eron's back. Maybe *this* was why Barrax had waited.

Merryn was shouting observations faster than Avall could comprehend, but he thought it was getting through. What was also getting through, however, was the raw emotion welling up in him. His rage at seeing good men die, and the land assailed. His disappointment in seeing Gynn's ploy start to fail so easily. An irrational notion that this would be just the grist Tyrill needed to see him unthroned. But all the while he was talking.

It was chaos down there. And in the middle of that chaos, Barrax's most heavily armed knights pounded onto the bridges, as an ally with a thousand lives and no heart at all to show mercy fought half his battle for him.

"It doesn't look good," Merryn gritted. "Damn, but I wish I was down there with them."

"You may get to fight sooner than you thought," Avall retorted. "Did the King hold any in reserve?"

"A few. Most are Common Clan, though, and underarmed. Our best are on the field."

Where there was fighting. Where there was noise and stench and death. Avall heard it as loudly as though he were there, perhaps because his link with Rann was never entirely severed; perhaps because the emotions and images on the battlefield were strong enough to strengthen their connection and reach him without Rann's volition. But even there on the mountainside, over two shots away, he could see the flash of spears, and the steady push of Ixtian cavalry.

A bridge blew—finally. But it was Narrow Bridge. He reported that fact dutifully, as he reported the fact that the forces sent there were returning to the main battle. And all the while the fire crept closer. Men fought it, and some had sense enough to soak their clothing, or cake it in mud, and run through the flame. But the smoke was a terrible distraction to men already pressed for air inside their helms. That the smoke also troubled Ixti's army was small comfort.

And then an Ixtian force broke through—not at what Avall had started calling King's Bridge, but at the other. And the battle realigned as men who'd been unable to find foes found them in great abundance.

He couldn't stand it. Not sitting here doing nothing, observing calmly, while people he knew and loved or might someday know and care about risked their lives a dozen ways every breath.

"I'm going to try something," he announced. "Forgive me. But don't try to stop me."

And with that, he closed his eyes, and gripped the gem as hard as he ever had. But instead of trying to contact Rann or even the King, he thought only of his desire for power. He had the trick of it now: the knack for getting to the Overworld alone. Gynn had given him that much the previous evening, all unknowing. But he'd never *gone* there alone, nor did he dare rely on Merryn. Not consciously. The gem would take what it would in any case. Maybe a mistake, that, but only one, and only once.

And that way was clear, too: clearer than he recalled, as though someone had opened the path before him, so that he found the way unencumbered. But it still took every bit of will he possessed, like climbing a sheer slope. More than once he wavered, fighting the urge to return to his body, to reject that terrible aloneness he found here, where he had only been with his closest friends.

But he *was* there. A place that wasn't and yet was, that terrified him. And he took what he'd come for: a handful of sand from the not-beach on which he'd found himself. And then he fled.

For the barest instant he noted the solid world, and in that instant, while that part of him that visited that other place was still partially there, he tried to fling that remnant of Overworld matter upon his enemy.

An explosion of fire did indeed bloom among the ranks beyond the nearer bridge. But much closer and more intense, and ultimately impossible to endure, was the explosion that occurred in his head.

He saw the ground slamming up to meet him, and had just time to recall that the gem had saved him more than once. And then he was unconscious.

Merryn woke to equal portions of panic and pain. Her head ached as though, like the stump beside her, it had been splintered by lightning. The rest of her hurt as well, but that was mostly concussive force, or the minor bruises and abrasions she'd suffered from hitting rock too hard.

The panic was born in equal parts fear for her country and for Avall. She sat up groggily, but that was enough to determine that her brother sprawled beside her, his fingers still clamped around that infernal gem. And that on the plain below what had never been much of an advantage was in danger of becoming a rout, as the armies of Ixti flowed inexorably toward the bridges, and then out again to clamp Eron's warriors between themselves and the smoking plain. That was a risky ploy, too, but it seemed to be succeeding, though a fair number of Eronese were electing to brave the river for short swims or rides downstream. It wouldn't win the battle, but it might put them in position to fight again. If there *was* an again.

But that was there and she was here, with a brother who she prayed was only unconscious. She scrambled toward him, reeling before her vision cleared, wondering why she felt so cold. And then she saw his chest rise and the twitch of pulse at his throat.

"Avall!" she cried, shaking him as she sought to revive him. He didn't answer. She slapped him. Hard—but enough to warn his body it was in peril. To no avail. Gritting her teeth, she found her water bag and sloshed water in his face. He grunted and groaned and fought at it, but did not truly waken.

"Avall! You have to get up. I don't think this is going to last much longer. I think it's going to be a rout. We have to get back to the army."

"Duty," he mumbled. Which relieved her and irked her all over again.

"Not now. The King needs you alive and with him. There's no good you can do up here now."

He moved, twitched, tried to rise, then collapsed once more. Merryn dared another glance toward the plain, searching for the King's party and finding them still mostly intact, though she had no idea which of those ant specks was Rann. As for Strynn, over on the other point, she had no time for her now, though Avall's blast had surely affected her as well.

Avall moaned. She looked down at him, cursing him for making her choose, for denying her access to her all-but-sister when she might also be in danger. But Avall's eyelids were fluttering now, and his color was better, his breathing more certain. He tried to sit up again, but slowly, oh so slowly.

And dared look over his shoulder.

"It didn't work," he groaned. "I did what I could—all I could think to do, and it failed. There's no more."

"There is while there's hope and will," Merryn flared, frustration paving the way for an unfocused rage she'd fought all day. "But probably not here, and probably not now."

Again Avall tried to rise, and shook his head. He indicated the swirling chaos of horses and men and steel and blood and flame that oozed out from the river across the valley. "You're right. We have to return to camp. They won't wait for us. But I . . . I have to rest a little longer. You have no idea . . ."

"A finger," Merryn sighed at last. "If I can stand it. If nothing changes. After that . . . if I have to, I'll carry you."

Rann felt a chill surge through him, and then a tightening in his thoughts that made him think his head was going to explode, or his *self* simply snap like a too-taut bowstring. And then he saw a flash of light somewhere across the bridge, and felt the air pulse toward him like the aftershock of a lightning strike. He rocked in his saddle, but worse was what he felt in his mind—his soul—his head. Wherever the power of the gem took hold. That part of him had been strong all morning, alive from his ongoing link with Avall. Suddenly a vital part of it had vanished, as though he'd had one leg cut from beneath him. Avall wasn't dead—but something—

"What . . . ?" From a white-faced Lykkon, beside him.

"He used the gem," Rann gasped, reeling, as were most of those around him. "I've felt it used that way, you haven't. He used it—against our foe."

"Did he . . . ?" Lykkon dared.

"I can't tell. There's some chaos over there, but—"

The King, who'd stationed himself ahead of them in anticipation of a foe that hadn't reached him yet, twisted around in the saddle, his face taut with hope mingled with despair. "He did something, but . . . I don't think it was enough. It wasn't controlled. It had a feel of desperation about it. What—what does he say about it?"

Rann regarded him squarely. "Nothing, at the moment. He's . . . not dead, but whatever that was, it cost him."

"Us, too," the King spat bitterly. "I know he meant well, but that did them little harm, and us little good."

Rann nodded mutely.

"But maybe it's a distraction we can use," the King added, whirling his mount around, and setting heels to the horse's sides. "Eron!" he shouted, drawing his sword, as he and his ring of guard surged forward, as though they were one being.

Rann rode with them because he had no choice. Beside him, he saw Lykkon set his jaw and draw his sword as well. Rann syn Eemon-arr was no coward. Though born of Stone, his one-mother was from War-Hold, and had made sure that he learned swordwork as he'd learned to walk. He was as competent as most of his peers—though by War's standards, no more than adequate. Still, he gave no thought to shirking the fight, and indeed felt a rise of exhilaration as he found himself bearing down on a small group of Ixtian horse that had ventured too far from their fellows. A gap loomed in the ring of Royal Guard around him, and he forced his horse through—and found himself yelling at the top of his lungs at the startled man who swung around to meet him. His foe was left-handed, as was he, and their blades met and belled in the hot, smoky air. The impact surprised him, but only long enough for him to compensate and dare another blow, as the man like-wise shifted his seat. The slash angled past the man's guard and down the cheekpiece of his helm, grazing his mount's neck on the downstroke. Rann used the force of that impact to bring it back around toward his foe's face.

The horse bucked as blood fountained. The man flinched back—and started to slide sideways. Rann stabbed at his throat—and hit something solid, but whether bone or steel he wasn't certain. He saw the man's foot wave into the air, and by then was jerking his horse away from the injured steed—and toward the downed soldier. Trained warhorse hooves found the Ixtian as he tried to rise. But by then Rann was parrying other blades.

He stabbed one inattentive man where he sat, then sliced neatly through another's neck, and laid open the thigh of a third before a shout from

Lykkon informed him that he was separating himself from his group. He retreated. In that too-brief respite, he saw that Lykkon was also acquitting himself decently, with deft if workmanlike strokes against a man older and larger than he. Myx, who had little use for horses, had jumped off his and was having at whatever foes in similar straits he could find. Which, though brave, put him at too much disadvantage. "Get back on your horse," Rann yelled, as he passed, only to see Lykkon likewise unhorsed—though not by choice, his mount having grown a pair of arrows in its hip. The boy slipped in mud when he landed and fell, whereupon a pair of Ixtians, also afoot, bore down upon him. He tried to rise and slipped again, but by then Rann was there, wheeling his horse between Lykkon and the startled men, then spinning it around again to slash at them. Lykkon, who tended to think very fast indeed, needed no prompting to grab Rann's hand as he finally made it to his feet. And though neither he nor Rann was particularly strong, both were lithe and nimble, and with fear as goad, Rann got the younger man up behind him.

Riff galloped in on the left, and together they hurried toward the ring of guards that had been forced uphill to the right by another push from the bridge. He saw the King—fighting now, though the Ixtians seemed to be avoiding him. Gynn's sword flashed down all clean and silver then rose again, rank with dripping red. A line of droplets flicked across the King's face. He licked at them absently, then saw Rann watching and grinned. "Regroup," he yelled. "Make a wedge."

Rann found himself face-to-face with Gynn. "You're a fool," the King snapped. "A brave one, but I can't risk you. Get to the back. All of you."

For the briefest moment Rann thought to defy him, but then he saw the glint in his Sovereign's eyes, and remembered that he was the King of the land and people of Eron and that he was Gynn's to command, and so he complied.

And by the time they'd regrouped, and Lykkon had vaulted atop a riderless horse that happened by, and they'd got Myx on one to stay, they were once more spurring forward.

Merryn had managed to get Avall roughly a quarter of the way back to the camp. It wasn't the shortest route, but it was the only one she dared, because of the precipitous terrain. That it also permitted a constant view of the battlefield was not lost on her, either. Not that it helped to look that way. It was a disaster. Gynn should've made them come to him on the heights, where he'd have had the advantage.

But that would've ceded South Gorge to Ixti, and he wasn't prepared to do that. She wondered idly if the fact that Argen-el had more holdings here than either of the other septs had anything to do with it. Probably not; Gynn could be coldly logical at need. But still she wondered.

At least he was alive, and as best she could tell so were Rann and the rest. It was hard to see, because of the distance. And because the added exertion of lugging her brother along made her sweat, which, in spite of her padded coif, ran into her eyes.

She paused to wipe them, leaving Avall propped against a convenient oak. This was a particularly good vantage point and she risked a moment with the distance lenses. Right to left—and there was the King—and—

She sensed movement as much as saw it: something from the corner of her eye. There to the left, beyond the main field of battle. Over by the gorge, in fact.

She swung the lenses that way, fighting with the recalcitrant focusing gear. A project for Smith for sure, if they ever survived this. For Argen-el, in fact. Maybe for Gynn, if this cost him his throne.

She had it now—and wished she hadn't. Swearing vividly, she looked up, as though her naked eyes would deny what augmented senses swore was true.

Men were pouring out of South Gorge. More to the point, they were pouring out of it on the *north* side—Eron's side. Nor did she need more than an instant's pause to determine that these were not allies come to give aid. Not with those gold-washed helms and sylken banners.

But how—?

And then she managed a closer look at the style of dress and armor those in the forefront sported.

And knew.

Sailors' garb.

Which suggested two possible options. One was that Barrax had launched a fleet in midwinter, to sail around the Finger of Rhynn and meet with him today. Which was an all-but-impossible feat of coordination—especially since she had a hunch that Barrax hadn't made his decision to attack until it was too late to send a fleet anywhere.

But Eron had a fair-sized fleet in Half Gorge, both a fishing fleet and a few warships. And Half Gorge had fallen. It wouldn't have been difficult for any sailors among Barrax's troops to sail down to the sea, which was clear this far south this time of year, and then back up the coast to where the Ri-Ormill flowed out of South Gorge at Tir-Vonees. Maybe they'd have taken the city, but there'd probably have been word of such a thing, or at least a telltale smudge of smoke on the horizon. But they could've slipped by in the night—especially in Eronese ships. Or they could've landed up the coast from the Ri, and marched overland the whole length of the gorge. It would've been diffi-cult, but it could've been done in the amount of time they'd had.

In any event, they were here.

A second force, moving to flank Gynn's already outnumbered and dispirited army.

And thanks to the screen of smoke, she doubted anyone had seen them. Probably not even Strynn.

She had to get word to Gynn *now*.

But how?

"Avall," she snapped, for all that he was a span away, still leaning groggily against a tree. Eyes open, and breathing, but not functioning much beyond that. "Avall—if you've never done anything in your life you have to do this one thing. You have to warn them."

"Warn them . . . ?" he mumbled, looking up at her as though that effort took all the strength he possessed. She shivered, and not from the cold that still ravaged her.

She grabbed him savagely, heaved him up, slipped behind him, and took his face roughly in her hands, peering over his shoulder, her head close beside him. "Do you see that? That's Barrax's army. A whole second force we didn't know existed. And it's going to cut Gynn off in about a finger. Do you think you might be able to do one more thing, even if it kills you? Do you think you *might* be able to alert Rann?"

"Rann . . . ?" His eyes cleared, then glazed again. "Too tired. Too tired . . ."

He sagged earthward in a way that alarmed her, but she dragged him up again, ruthlessly. And as she did, her finger brushed the gem, which had become fouled in a fold of his surcoat. She flinched from it reflexively, before she realized it had . . . responded to that contact. It scared her, given what the thing could do—but she knew she had no choice.

Slumping to the ground with her brother still before her, she set her back against the tree, clamped the gem in her fist, felt a shock of pain as the barb stabbed into her flesh—and braced herself for whatever occurred.

She didn't know much about the gems at all. But one thing she did know was that they responded to will. And she had that to spare—especially now, when she wanted two things in the world: to alert the King, and then get down there and fight. Avall . . . could take care of himself. And if he couldn't, the gem would.

And then it didn't matter, because reality was shifting and she felt everything with heightened clarity. Avall weighed as much as ten men, yet was weightless, and the simple fact of that weight was a wonder and a glory. It was not unlike an imphor high, but with more control.

Almost she lost herself in wonder. Fortunately, her eyes had gone right on observing, though she seemed to see much better now. And so she shut her lids, took a deep breath, and simply *wanted*. Wanted Rann to hear her—or Gynn—or whoever might happen to heed her.

For the briefest instant she was nowhere—the same nowhere in which she'd almost died—and that terrified her. But she also knew it could be survived, and that on the other side, and not far away at all, lay Strynn. Strynn would help her. Strynn knew what to do, how to master all this impossible mental complexity—

Strynn . . .

Merryn . . . ?

Strynn?

Where's Avall?

Alive. That last foolish effort cost him. But . . . Strynn, I've no time for this. Tell Rann to warn the King that his east flank is under attack. Tell him they've come up the gorge in secret. Tell him—

Strynn's answering surge of panic all but broke their link, as she, along with her bond-sister, gazed to the west. She saw nothing, but she trusted Merryn—Merryn felt that trust so strongly it was almost as though she had lost herself.

Tell the King to sound retreat now!

You already have, came another contact altogether. It took her a moment to recognize, but she'd somehow reached the High King himself. He seemed confused by that communication—at the force of it, apparently. But he also showed no inclination to hesitate. Signaling his trumpeter, he bellowed that awful word.

"Retreat."

Merryn heard it with Strynn's ears, and then with her own as it reached her. And with her mission accomplished, she rode that sound back to her body.

And had another shock.

Avall had passed out in her arms.

A chill shook her, but she shrugged it off and stood. And this time, she managed to sling her brother across her shoulders. It was a long walk back to camp thus encumbered, and her legs were already protesting. But she could do anything if she knew how long she'd have to do it.

Besides, even if she gave her life, she doubted Eron would ever forgive her for what she'd done already.

What she'd told the foe.

What had cost them War-Hold.

And maybe the rest of Eron.

CHAPTER XXX:

OPPORTUNITIES

(ERON: THE CLOISTER OF THE WINDS— SUNBIRTH: DAY VIII—NEAR MIDNIGHT)

~~~~~~~~~~~~~~~~~~~~~~~~~

A completely unnatural quiet had settled upon the cloister. Not the true quiet of death—or the soft quiet of snow falling on more snow, with no wind. But certainly an unnatural silence for what had, until shortly before sunrise, been an armed camp. Maybe it still was, but Eddyn could see nothing through the tiny barred opening in his door save the empty cloister yard, and that but dimly, for it was approaching midnight.

All he knew was that something had changed. The casual energy that usually pulsed out there, even this late, in the form of impromptu weapons drills and other interchanges, had vanished. Maybe there were still guards about, he didn't know. Eight, maybe the whole army had departed the previous night and he'd been left here to die of slow starvation with the other prisoners, whose number he didn't know, save that somewhere in this complex of courtyards and buildings Elvix, Olrix, and Tozri still survived. And Merryn—he hoped. And, by report, the king's son himself, under some kind of sentence of treason he'd been unable, after all this time, to understand.

It was nice, though, in a way. The weather had turned warm and dry, after the cold damp of the winter, and he'd overheard enough from his various guards to know that Barrax had been waiting for something to happen before launching his attack.

Probably for the vale above South Gorge to be a vale again, instead of a springtime lake. He bet Barrax hadn't thought of that. In fact, the floods were not a regular occurrence, but depended on how much snow fell where, melted when, and how fast.

Why, this might even be the silence of defeat—for Ixti. Maybe Gynn's forces had massacred Barrax's so utterly there was no one left to tell the tale of prisoners.

Eddyn snorted disgust at his own fancy and slumped back against the single pillow they'd allowed him, at the head of his narrow cot. He poured himself a mug of water from the jug they'd brought last night, but it was tepid and flat-tasting. And if things went as they might, he'd probably be wise to ration it anyway.

Perhaps he dozed, relishing the late-night silence.

He awoke to the slap of footsteps echoing down the arcade, someone in a hurry, but not quite running. Someone still armored, to judge by the creak of leather and the rustling jingle of mail.

Someone angry, too—because Eddyn had himself been angry often enough to know how angry footsteps sounded.

He wondered who the recipient of all that rage would be.

But was still sufficiently groggy to be surprised when a key rattled in the lock and an armed man strode into his cell.

Eddyn blinked in startled confusion, but by then the man had grabbed him and flung him to the floor. A foot slammed down on his chest, driving the air from his lungs. A sword sliced the gloom to lodge at his throat. Torchlight in the arcade outside lit the man from the back, obscuring his features. But the gold on his armor and the insignia on his surcoat were unmistakable.

"You will tell me how he did it, and you will tell me now!" Barrax of Ixti roared. The sword dug into Eddyn's flesh just above his sternum. A flick of Barrax's wrist, and any number of unpleasant things could happen.

"How who did what?" Eddyn choked, as panic burned away lethargy. He thought briefly of fighting back, on the theory that, while he would surely die, he might at least harm Barrax in the process. But then Barrax barked something in Ixtian, and four more men strode into the room. One promptly grabbed Eddyn's feet, while two others neatly prisoned his arms, giving the king a chance to back away. But Barrax was still furious.

"You will tell me," Barrax raged, wrenching off his helm, "how someone in Eron managed to call down lightning on my army!"

Eddyn's heart leapt. Maybe Eron *had* won. But then what was Barrax doing here? And what was this business about lightning? He knew nothing about such things.

"It was one of those gems, wasn't it?" Barrax snapped. "It had to be. I knew there was more to them than communication. How many of those things does your King have, anyway? Does he have a mine full of them? Does he—?"

"He had lookouts posted," a calmer voice inserted. "They gave the word about the flanking—"

"Silence, or I'll have your tongue!" Barrax flared, rounding on the speaker. "I know something alerted them sooner than I'd hoped. But that isn't the issue here." He turned back to Eddyn, eyes glittering in the torch-light. *Mad eyes,* Eddyn thought. Not the eyes of a rational man. This man would do anything. From anger or from fear, he couldn't say.

"I don't know what you're talking about," Eddyn managed. "Give me imphor if you don't believe me. What you saw—I don't know what it was, or how it was done. None of my kinsmen can call down lightning." Which was probably a foolish thing to tell a frightened man. But Eddyn was fright-ened, too, and had no mind for lying.

"It wasn't exactly lightning," one of the others dared. "There were no clouds, and it . . . it was like a flare of fire in the air. It knocked men down beneath it. Some died of—"

"I *know* how they died!" Barrax shouted. "What I want to know is how I can do that in turn. Or how to defend against it. This man here—!"

"I know nothing!"

"You know something! You have to! You and your scholars and your artists. There's no way you could *not* know."

Eddyn had no reply.

"Bring imphor," Barrax spat. Then paused. "No, wait. Imphor brings pleasure, too. This man is better broken by pain."

Eddyn felt that awful twitch in his groin that spoke of fear unalloyed.

"Cut off something," Barrax rasped. "I don't care what. But something he can see. Something small, but painful. I don't want him bleeding to death, but I don't want him treated."

"A finger? A toe? A . . . testicle? His manhood. Or maybe just part of it?"

"From what I've heard, he deserves to lose it," Barrax laughed. "But no, make it . . . a finger. A joint of a finger. For my son. He's a craftsman; that will pain him more than anything else he can lose."

Another chill. And then somewhere Eddyn couldn't see, the man who held his left hand against the floor began to fumble at his fingers.

"I'll do it," the king snapped. Eddyn closed his eyes, but he heard the rasp of the king's geen-claw dagger clearing its sheath. And he felt the touch of the blade.

The pain washed all that away—that and a hatred that transcended hate.

Eddyn saw the finger, held dripping in Barrax's hands, but he didn't bother to notice whether the king had it with him when he departed. Proba-bly because he'd heard his last words to the guards upon leaving. "I don't care if you've had a man before or not. I want every one of you to rape him. Over and over. Until you're all dry of seed."

"I *don't* know what you want!" Eddyn screamed, to the no-longer-silent night. And then someone dragged a gag across his mouth, and tied his arms to the bedposts. And that single strip of fabric drank up an entirely different kind of screaming.

The agony in his finger was a distraction he found he needed.

If drugs wouldn't succeed in breaking the Eronese lad's infernal silence, and if pain didn't produce prompt results, either, perhaps humiliation might do the trick, Barrax concluded, as he strode away from the prison and toward his quarters. He had the victory—the plain above South Gorge, anyway, with the Gorge itself, and Tir-Vonees to collect at leisure. His forces were ranged just below the heights of Eron's Belt—those that had constituted his main strength, anyway. The rest . . . Gynn would not be sleeping well tonight, because Barrax had made sure that word got out that the ships that had sailed up the Ri-Ormill weren't the only ones he'd captured at Half Gorge, that another fleet even now sailed for the Ri-Eron. It wasn't true, but Gynn didn't need to know that. A man fighting imaginary foes was a man with an unquiet mind.

Meanwhile, he had other things to do.

Like master that infernal gem. He'd had enough of caution. Enough of trying to learn how to use it the scholar's way. He was a warrior—as he was beginning to discover—and by the Gods, he would master it as a warrior should—by force!

Not only that, he'd do it tonight, while his army celebrated their victory across a hundred shots of Eron. Sure, they'd miss him for a while, or his commanders would, but the double ration of ale he'd granted the former would take care of them, and the latter were accustomed to his caprices. He was king after all. It was their duty to wait for him. When he appeared, he would be the gem's master.

He'd reached his headquarters by then—a tent, though he could've stayed in the much more spacious, substantial, and potentially luxurious quarters that had belonged to the cloister warden before this place had been abandoned. Two guards stood sentry outside, trying not to look as though they'd be happier reveling with their brothers a hundred shots to the north. He wasn't the only one here, however; Lynnz's adjoining tent likewise blazed with light. Perhaps his brother-in-law felt the same anxiety he did—that today was not a victory but bait for a trap. This invasion had all been too easy.

Even the fall of War-Hold.

And curse the woman, Merryn, for her escape. He'd have Eddyn raped for that, too—just in case.

By the time he'd reached the middle chamber, he'd doffed his helm and gauntlets. The surcoat followed, with the mail hauberk. But then he could wait no longer. Reaching for the pouch inside his tunic where the gem always resided, he drew it out, and rolled the stone onto a table.

"I *will* master you," he growled. And snatched it up.

He almost dropped it again, so fierce was the dislike that pulsed from it, like a small animal caught, and fighting for escape. But this small animal had teeth—maybe even poison. He closed his eyes, trying to fight it in his mind—he could feel his will pushing at something, which scared him beyond reason. Minds weren't meant to do such things. Man had mind, a body, a soul—and that was it. But the mind controlled the body; it was not a thing apart, to do battle on its own.

Yet he was doing that.

Which gave him hope, for how did one master something? By force of body, or of will. And so he wished at the gem. Wished very hard, wished that it would answer him, that it would do what he desired. And while he did that wishing, another part of his mind was haunted by what he'd seen today: a blossom of fire taking form in the sky and smashing down like an invisible hand, flattening men where they stood for a dozen paces around. Killing those in the center. Pounding their bones to pulp.

That was what he wanted—for his enemies.

He squeezed harder.

Wished harder.

A blister he'd barely noticed broke in the palm of his hand. He felt the pain almost like pleasure. A wash of fluid followed.

The gem awoke in truth at that.

Which told him something.

He wanted—

No, the *gem* wanted: A pulse of raw hatred flowed into his hand from that shard of what should be inert stone. Up his arm, into his shoulder, into his throat. And there that force split, and one half went to his brain, while the other half went to his heart.

And clamped down.

It fought as the gem had fought, but this time the small trapped animal was the organ that drove his blood. It fought like a cornered geen, like a birkit queen defending her cubs.

It lost.

His mind outlived his heart by a dozen breaths. And then, like stars winking out, it, too, started dying. The last thing he knew as a conscious entity was what sounded like a million souls—or a million grains of sand—every one laughing.

. . .

Lord Lynnz, Warlord of Ixti and chief of torturers, was getting very impatient. The king should've summoned him by now, to assess the day's victory, to toast it afterward, and then to join the soldiers in the celebration they would be expecting.

Not that such things were Barrax's style; he was a known recluse. Still, he'd made no mention of wanting to be alone tonight, though it didn't surprise Lynnz, as angry as Barrax had been when he'd left the battlefield. Left Lynnz in charge of it, in fact, responsible for securing lines and seeing that the fronts were manned and guarded. After the day's events, there was no certainty the cursed Eronese wouldn't call the sun back to the sky to smite them in the dark.

Which was probably why Barrax had ridden half the night to return here, and was now in his tent, sulking.

Which, Lynnz reckoned, he'd indulged long enough.

A pause to finish the wine he'd been drinking while studying the revised charts they'd acquired that day from an abandoned villa in the near end of the gorge, and he started out of his tent. This would be an informal meeting and shouldn't take long—not as long as the one he'd have afterward, at any rate, during which he'd have to brief his subcommanders, review charts and supply lists, and generally do those things it really took to win a war. The things one did when one didn't have the dubious added distraction of being king. Probably the men—whoever was left in camp—would be wanting to see flash, glitter, and royal panoply, and so he paused in the outer room to don his cloak, helm, and sword. Thus attired, he stalked into the night.

"Is the king within?" he asked the closest soldier, as he reached the outer entrance.

The man nodded solemnly. "He is."

"For how long?"

"He's been there—" the man paused uneasily "—for some time. He went to see the prisoner Eddyn, and returned very angry."

"No surprise," Lynnz muttered. Nor was it. The man was a thorn in Barrax's side. Someone who lived because he knew too much to be killed. But perhaps it was time Barrax reconsidered.

Which probably meant the king *was* sulking. Lynnz started past the guard. The man hesitated, then thrust his spear ahead of the commander to block his way. Lynnz smiled warning, and pushed the shaft gently aside. "The king has these moods; you should know that. But I think he'll see me."

The man exchanged glances with his companion, who looked younger. "It's you who'll suffer if you interrupt," he dared.

Lynnz thought of killing him right there. Instead, he marched straight down the short entry passage, through the common room, and into Barrax's private quarters, where the light was strongest.

"Your Majesty," he began, even as he dipped his head in the obligatory courtesy bow upon entering. He'd glimpsed the king but briefly, a dark shape behind his table. Lynnz's eyes scanned the rich carpet.

Your Majesty," he began again, eyes not moving. "I apologize for this intrusion."

Silence.

He looked up, angry. Tired of indulging monarchs who ought to know what was expected of a king who would also be a soldier.

The king looked back at him, unmoving. Staring.

Gape-mouthed.

Not moving.

Not breathing.

Dead.

"Dead," Lynnz whispered, not believing.

And then he was acting. A quick inspection told the tale. It was that infernal gem. He should've known. Should've read the signs of the king's growing obsession with what Lynnz mostly considered a conjurer's trinket, its reported powers a dream conjured by Kraxxi and Merryn during a night of lust.

Yet he was still wary enough not to touch the thing directly. Drawing on his thick war gloves, he removed the stone from Barrax's clenched fist and replaced it in its pouch, which he then, on impulse, stored inside his tunic.

And then it struck him like a blow. *The king was dead!* On the night of his first victory, the king was dead. The armies were half a world from home, and the king was dead. Which meant . . .

Well, meant that Kraxxi was king—legally. Sentence of death or no, he was still Barrax's heir. But that was an impossible situation, and frankly not one he was equipped to reckon with at the moment. Not on the eve of a crucial battle. *That* was the important thing. Never again would they have so good a chance to subdue Eron. And he would certainly not be the man who threw that chance away.

But what, then, was his best option? The king had no brothers, so his heirs were his sister's sons. And though Lynnz was married to one of those sisters, he had no sons himself, nor would. The others . . . they were boys. Younger than Kraxxi. Back in Ixtianos being schooled. One of them toddling about in baby robes.

So who was the strongest man in Ixti now?

Himself.

And if he wanted to secure that power, he'd have to act quickly. He'd have to act tonight.

It took but an instant to formulate the plan, for like many brilliant men, Lynnz acted best when he acted out of instinct. And so, with that in mind, he returned to the outer room, where Barrax had left his cloak and helm. It required but a breath to swap his cloak for Barrax's cloak of state, and his own helm for Barrax's scarcely more ornate one. Fortunately they were of a size, and not unlike in age, visage, or carriage. And so the soldiers saw what they wanted to see when he passed. "Lynnz is checking some charts for me," he murmured, slurring his words as though he'd been drinking, which Barrax was wont to do when angry. "He should be finished anon. Meanwhile, I require your escort to my meeting with my commanders."

Accustomed to royal caprice, the guards nodded mutely, and marched off smartly in Lynnz's vanguard.

Fortunately, the war council met in one of the cloister halls, neither Lynnz nor Barrax having a tent large enough to accommodate them comfortably. Fortunately, too, Lynnz's tent was right next door. "I need a chart from here," he told the men, who waited dutifully while he ducked inside. And though he did indeed retrieve a chart from those piled in his sleeping quarters, what he brought with it was far more important. A certain bottle of wine he'd been saving for an appropriate occasion, just in case it was needed.

A moment later, they were off through the night once more.

The war council was awaiting him when he entered, leaving the guards outside. And since there was a short corridor between their station and the chamber, Lynnz had ample opportunity to store his royal finery. So it was that it was once more as himself that he entered the room—a long, low, comfortable chamber where whitewash was fading off sturdy stone beneath groined vaulting. He moved with ease to his accustomed place midway along the table. The other commanders—eight of them—rose as he found his seat, but he nodded at them to sit again. Most did not look happy. Nor did he blame them. Riding half the night to indulge a royal whim was enough to sour anyone's disposition.

"I apologize for my tardiness," he yawned carefully. "Especially at so late an hour, after such a tiring day. Unfortunately, I had . . . business with the king. And we have business tonight as well—some of it unexpected. But before we get down to the serious talk that must come before we can engage in the celebration I know we all desire, let me propose a toast, with the king's own wine he has sent here. He will attend later, he hopes. For now . . . he is indisposed."

And truly the wine did bear the royal seal. And so Lynnz filled his own cup and passed the bottle down, watching with absent but keen interest as each goblet, mug, or other vessel was filled in turn. There was nothing left but dregs when the bottle returned, which was perfect.

"Gentlemen!" Lynnz intoned, rising. "I give you . . . victory."

"Victory," they echoed in various cadences. And once again he watched as they drank. All of them. Good soldiers. Good at taking orders. At doing what they were told.

"Now then," he continued pleasantly, settling himself into his seat. "I have several things to tell you, and none of them will please you."

Lord Eezz, who sat nearest, stared at his cup, and then at Lynnz. "Ah, Lord Lynnz, has it come to this, that you think for us now?"

"I think *of* you," Lynnz corrected. "More important, I think of Ixti, which stands on the threshold of a greatness and prosperity we had not heretofore anticipated."

"And this news?"

"The king is dead—of his own recklessness."

It took a moment for the words to sink in, and then the room exploded into noise.

Lynnz silenced them with a shout. "I found him not a finger ago. He tried something he should not have, and . . . failed."

"Then . . . Kraxxi is king."

"Kraxxi is a traitor. Do you want him in charge, here on the eve of battle?"

"So who, then? The heirs—"

"Are in Ixtianos. Mere boys."

Eyes narrowed suspiciously. "You are kin to the king, by marriage."

"Have I ever led you wrong?" Lynnz inquired neutrally.

"Never," a younger man conceded.

"So is it this?" asked old Lord Arl. "Are you saying you are taking the throne?"

"I say that I take charge of this campaign. The throne is as safe as it was a day ago. The throne is in Ixtianos. We are here. We stare victory in the face."

"But you are not the heir."

"I am still your commander."

"Until you have Kraxxi killed . . ." someone dared.

Lynnz glared at him. "There is something else I need to tell you, something you will like even less than what I have just conveyed."

"And that is?"

"Most of you have served with me a long time. Most I know since childhood, as teachers, friends, or students. But a man in my position must trust no one entirely. Therefore, I feel it my duty to . . . ensure your loyalty. For that reason, I regret to inform you that you have all been poisoned.

"You won't die," he continued, shouting over the ensuing din. "It was I who administered the drug; it is I who control the antidote. Indeed, this poison is an odd sort. It doesn't kill you, only . . . its absence. Serve me as you have been, and you will have your ration of life. Kill me, and the secret dies with me."

A stunned silence filled the room.

"Nothing has changed," Lynnz said at last. "Not really. What Barrax promised you upon completion of this invasion, I promise you as well. Ixti will be ruled as well by me, as . . . regent, as by Barrax—and with more attention to men such as you. We cannot bring him back, but the war must continue."

Another pause. Then: "And I tell you true, this makes no difference in your lives. None at all. But it might make a difference with the soldiers. Therefore, I require your absolute trust. Word must not get out that the king is dead. Ill, yes: and indisposed, but not dead. The men who came with me here will leave with me—cloaked and helmed as the king. I leave it to you to see that they do not find their beds alive.

"I hope I have made myself clear."

Silence again, then, from the far end of the table: "The king is dead, but we have the king's work to do. Gentlemen, I suggest we be at it."

"Good," said Lynnz brightly, unrolling the chart he'd brought. "Now, does anyone have an accurate count of our losses?"

Kraxxi was dreaming of blue skies and hot sun on dusty streets. Of yellow and orange and red, and a white so bright those colors reflected there. He was dreaming of the ocean and smooth golden sands, of the susurration of waves, and the sough of wind drifting out of green-clad mountains.

And then all that shattered with the sound of a squeaking door. He was on guard in an instant—not that it availed him much, given that his cell was as empty as his hope right now. He'd roused from his slumbers some vague time back, to the sound of someone cheering Barrax's victory out in the cloister square. But there'd been no bonfire—probably because the bulk of the army was gone: up to South Gorge in pursuit of battle. Which pretty well dissolved his hope of rescue.

And now—

He tensed, preparing to fight if need be, for if Barrax had won, there was less reason than ever to keep him alive.

Another squeak, and the door opened fully. Kraxxi's heart sank, to see it occupied by four hooded soldiers, who more than blocked the entrance. And there was no way he could fight his way past them into the darkness beyond.

And then he had no more time for speculation, for they surged forward in a rush of cloaks and mail, and before he could so much as cry out, he'd been gagged and a hood had been drawn over his head as far down as his upper arms, which were bound, none too gently, behind his back. They left his legs free long enough to walk him to some sort of wagon, before loading him inside and tying his ankles.

Silence for a moment, broken only by the sound of his own breathing, amplified by the hood.

Almost he dozed again. It was safest, when the only things to think were things it frightened one to think, when one was an exiled prince kept alive on sufferance. But then he heard the sound of more boots approaching, and a muffled exchange of conversation. By straining his hearing, Kraxxi could make out part of what was being said. Maybe the crucial part, to judge by the phrase ". . . follow half a day's ride back? This makes no sense."

And the chuckled reply: "Lynnz's orders rarely do."

"Better we should kill him outright and be done."

"I think they want him alive to witness the final battle."

"If you can call that in there alive."

"I call it torture, if you ask me. But you didn't hear me say that. In any case, we leave at dawn. Be ready."

Ready for what? Kraxxi wondered.

Eventually the wagon began moving—unaccompanied, it appeared. But that was no true answer.

CHAPTER XXXI:

DARKENING DAYS

(Eron: Tir-Eron—High Spring: Day V—early afternoon)

Bingg was drowsing on a long padded bench tucked in an arched alcove beside Eellon's door when a very tired and dirty Avall found him. Not that Bingg looked much better, as far as the tired part went. Lads his age ought not to have dark smudges under their eyes, nor rumpled hair, nor clothes that looked like they'd been slept in for five days running. Still, his smile was as bright as Lykkon's best when a cough from Avall roused him.

Avall was *not* expecting a hug, however—nor for tears to replace joy in Bingg's eyes. "You're back!" he managed through a flustered fumbling with clothes and hair.

"Just this moment," Avall replied, "and as tired as you are, I suspect. But much as I'm truly glad to see you, I have urgent news for Lord Eellon." He nodded toward the door for emphasis.

Bingg looked troubled, though he tried to stand straighter, like a proper page. "I'll tell him you're here." Yet still he lingered. "Avall . . . I'm sorry. But I have to ask: what about Lyk . . . ?"

"He's at the front but safe, as is Rann, who's keeping an eye on him."

"Well, that's a relief," Bingg sighed. "What about the rest of you?"

"I'm here, with Strynn, Merryn, and Div, all of whom are intact and on various quests to execute royal orders. As for my report . . . you're free to listen, for all I care."

Bingg stared as if dumbfounded. "Merryn . . . ?"

A nod. "Surprised us, too. Now—"

Bingg eyed the door as though he were afraid to open it. "I'll tell the Chief at once."

Avall suppressed an urge to simply bypass Lykkon's younger brother and barge in, as was more or less his custom. But Eellon had far more in the way of responsibilities now than heretofore, and far less strength with which to conduct them. Avall was worried about the old man, too—more than worried, in fact. Still, protocol was protocol, and he was at present merely a messenger. And so he waited while Bingg ducked through the door.

He didn't stand, however; he was too tired for that. Six days' travel in four did that even to a healthy man, and Avall was not at all certain he was healthy. Not after what had happened when he'd tried to call down the fires of the Overworld on Ixti. But he didn't want to think about that now. He'd have to relate the whole tale to Eellon, anyway. In the meantime—well, the mere thought of it made him shiver.

He was rubbing his hands briskly up and down his arms when Bingg returned. His handsome young face looked troubled. "He'll see you . . . ," he began. "But he's very tired. I just wanted to warn you. Maybe you'll give him what he needs, but I'm not certain. He's"—he shifted his weight nervously—"not been the same since you left. Nor really since the night you linked with Merryn."

Avall grimaced at that, though it wasn't Bingg's fault. Facts were facts, and guilt wasn't something he needed to entertain right now. Merryn had her guilt; this was his.

A pause to straighten the soldier's surcoat he now wore most of the time, and he pushed through the door. Bingg followed. And would probably stay until someone ran him out.

In any event, he took comfort from the fact that Bingg directed him not into the bedchamber, but to the workroom. Still, Avall found himself holding his breath as he entered. His first impression was of light, for Eellon sat in front of a window wall of glass bricks. A fire burned to the right, however; the Citadel was cool this early in the year. Wine mulled there as it always did. Avall wondered if that was one of Bingg's duties, or if some other Argen-Hall youth had been conscripted to wait on his Chief. Without thinking about it, he stole a pastry from a tray by the door.

"Still the sweet-thief," Eellon's voice rumbled, from where he sat in a heavy house-robe behind a table covered with parchments, books, and scrolls. His face was shadowed by the light behind him. His voice held a raspy quality Avall didn't like.

Before he knew it, he was dashing forward, slipping around the table to enfold his ancient two-father in a cautious hug. Tears started in his eyes. "Two-father—"

"For about the next half finger, and then you have to be the royal messenger you claim to be, and I have to be Steward of Eron."

"How are you?"

"Surviving."

Avall wiped his eyes and finally got a good look at his lifelong mentor. Though barely a dozen days had passed since he'd last seen the old man, that interval had laid years on the Chief of Argen-Hall. Never a big man, Eellon had nevertheless lost weight. His craggy features looked ravaged and worn, the hollows deeper, especially those around his eyes. His skin looked paper-thin, too, and held none of the flush of health. Even his mane of white hair seemed to have thinned, though Avall suspected that was a function of its not being washed and combed very often. A trace of stubble also lined his jaw, which was something he'd never seen.

"I'm sick," Eellon said, matter-of-factly. "But I'm glad to see you, Two-son. Not that you look the picture of health yourself."

"I'm not sure if it's health as much as fatigue," Avall sighed, rising to claim a chair to Eellon's right. Bingg handed him a mug of hot cider he hadn't requested. He tasted it gratefully. There was stronger liquor in it. The fumes danced through his head, warming him. Another of those and a hot bath, and he might feel almost human.

"You said you had a message," Eellon prompted. "I surmise by the fact that it's you delivering it, not one of His Majesty's more typical couriers, that it contains information that might not be suitable for every ear."

Avall nodded. "You've heard about the battle? The light relays should've passed on word of that."

Eellon nodded in turn, toying with a pen. His fingers were stained with ink, Avall noted, all the way up to the second joint. "I know the gist of it: that both sides had to wait until the floods subsided, that the King intended to destroy the bridges but was thwarted. That it wouldn't have mattered because half of Ixti's force came up the Ormill. That his forces were hamstrung by fire behind him—which was a damned fine idea if I do say so."

"Since then—?"

"You'd better tell me."

Avall took another sip of cider. "I . . . don't remember a lot. I was—I tried to call down the fires of the Overworld. We were losing, and I couldn't stand watching it, and it was all I could think to do. Gynn—the King—had decided to use Strynn and me as observers, to relay information to him through Rann. Merryn was guarding me and—"

"Merryn?"

"That was Bingg's reaction," Avall laughed. "The short version is that she escaped. The long version . . . ought to wait."

"You be the judge," Eellon managed through a cough.

"Well, the important thing is that she was feeding me reports to pass on. We weren't in the battle itself, though right now I wish I had been. But anyway, once I did what I did, I don't remember a lot. I know Merryn saw that it was a rout—I *think* I heard the retreat trumpet sound myself— and started back to camp, half-carrying me. She got another view, though— that's when she noticed Ixti's reinforcements. It was she who saved what could be saved. She snatched the gem from me and used it to contact Rann, who was down on the field. She kept the King from being cut off."

"But he lost the vale, and with it the gorge."

Avall nodded. "He fell back to Eron's Belt that night, awaiting battle that never came. I don't remember a lot of that, I'm afraid. Apparently using the gem like I did isn't good for one person to attempt alone. As best we can tell, it draws . . . energy from anything alive around it—anything warm-blooded, anyway. That's why we get cold. And the fewer people, the stronger the effect. In an army . . . we're not sure, just as we're not sure what the range is. But in a battle, maybe it would draw on so many people the effect would be negligible on any given person."

"You may have to prove it, though," Eellon observed, glancing around. Probably for Bingg, who, like his brother, Lykkon, was always making notes about such things. Avall hadn't the heart to tell him those things were already recorded. "So, what's the situation now?"

"You know better than I, if the light relays are working."

"I know that as of a hand before you arrived Gynn was still holding the Belt—relinquishing it a span at a time, rather say. He's had reinforcements, too, for what that's worth. And there's something else that should give you heart. What you did—whatever you did, and the relays are understandably vague on the point—it could only have helped."

"That's what Merryn tried to tell me all the way here."

"She's right," Eellon affirmed, before Avall could elaborate. "It's a double-bladed sword. In our favor, it heartened our forces because they know that, somewhere, there's a power we can draw on at need. They don't know where it came from, and given that your connection to it isn't widely known, it could be interpreted to mean that The Eight themselves have interceded on our side. That's especially useful, given the number of Common Clan we've had to conscript, and the situation with Priest. Fortunately, rumor of Gynn's . . . deficiency hasn't reached much beyond this gorge, and even here most of the lower clans prefer not to believe it. In any case, the presence of this mysterious power of ours ought to dispirit the

enemy; they have to face a weapon they've never seen and don't understand, and whose limits are completely unknown. That *could* be a big
advantage."

"No more than knowing that somewhere, somehow, you have the power
to destroy the enemy completely—but can't access that power."

"You will. I have faith. You will."

Avall shrugged.

Eellon helped himself to a deep draught of wine. Avall caught a whiff of
it and wondered if it didn't also contain some restorative drug. Eellon
cleared his throat. "And now I have a more personal question. Besides the
obvious need for recuperation, what are you doing here? Surely the King
has couriers less likely to be useful at the front."

Avall shook his head. "Two things. First, the King *has* bonded with the
gems—with all three of them, in fact, though we've brought them back here
to incorporate into the regalia—it's just too chaotic at the front to get any
work done there, never mind the need for secrecy. In any case, we can contact him if need be through Rann. And there's a reason we might have to,
which is the second reason I'm here."

Eellon looked troubled. "I suspect I know why, too—but tell me."

Avall cleared his throat. "You'll have heard what happened at South
Gorge: that Barrax used captured ships from Half Gorge to sail up the river
on the side away from Tir-Vonees, and managed to sneak a whole second
army in on Gynn's flank. Well, Gynn's afraid he's going to try that again.
He's afraid Barrax has either sent more ships here, to Tir-Eron, or else that
he'll use the same fleet he sneaked by Vonees to attack here. Strynn's supposed to alert him if that occurs. We're faster than the light relays, and a lot
more informative. In fact, she's leaving for the coast tomorrow. She finished
the sword on the way back here—as much as she *can,*" he added cryptically.
"But the effort wore her out. She has to rest tonight—and she wants to see
the baby."

Eellon sighed dramatically. "This is *not* a good time to be a mother."

"No," Avall agreed sadly. "But it's not a good time to be much of anything."

"Not even a Mastersmith?"

Avall shrugged. "I don't know. As I said, the sword's completed, except
that I have to add—" He broke off, having found himself about to explain
things he wasn't certain could be explained to someone who wasn't bonded
to a gem already. "Gynn . . . got into my head when we bonded, and figured
out what happens when we reach into the Overworld. He thinks he's set that
pattern in my mind so that I can see it, then make the . . . connections that'll
let that process . . . just happen. Only I don't know it consciously. It's something going on . . . in the deep levels of my brain. The way he explains it is
that I'll just know, the same way I know how to draw something, or design

something. That it's locked in there and when I reach the right place in my work, it'll happen."

Eellon snorted. "He's placing an enormous amount of faith on magic."

"Which, however, never seems to exhaust itself, once tapped. I on the other hand—"

Eellon patted his hand. "Get some sleep."

As though cued by that admonition, Avall yawned.

"Use my bed," Eellon told him. "I have other work to do while I still can. I'll see that you're not disturbed."

Another yawn. He blinked sleepily at Bingg. "You can admit Strynn, Kylin, or Merryn. But that's all." Then back to Eellon: "And I'll trust *you,* oh Steward, not to let me sleep if anything comes up I need to know about."

Eellon chuckled grimly. "Ah, my boy, you should know better than to trust anyone in this clan by now."

A third yawn ambushed Avall, and a twin from Eellon seemed to be a sign of dismissal. "Eellon," he dared, as he rose.

"What?"

"It's good to see you again."

"It's good to see anything I care about these days," Eellon replied ominously. And reached for another sheet of paper.

(ARGEN-HALL—MIDAFTERNOON)

"He may be the only person in Tir-Eron who's smiling," Avall told Strynn, as he peered down at her son, who lay in the same ancestral baby nest that had cradled Eellon, his son, and one-sons. Not Avall and Merryn, because they were twins and it was deemed bad luck to separate such pairs before a year had run its course.

Against the quilted cotton pad of clan maroon, Averryn looked very pale, especially in his white child-robe. But his dark eyes danced, and his smile curved in a way that reminded Avall far more of Strynn than Eddyn. He wondered what they would tell him when the subject of his conception arose. That tale was already translating from gossip into legend, simply from the weight of things that had become attached to it.

About which Avall didn't want to think.

"He has much to smile about," replied his nurse, who also happened to be Evvion san Criff: Avall and Merryn's mother. Around whom Avall was never comfortable.

Not that she was, either. They'd been born not long before the plague, but their father had been in service to the Fateing at the time, and had seen little of them—or her, either; contrary to custom, they'd not been posted together.

Already resentful of the restrictions of motherhood as opposed to father-hood, Evvion had never felt children for husband to be a fair trade, in terms of time spent together. And when Valleen had succumbed to the plague two years later, with her barely having seen him since the twins' birth, it had drained all the love out of her. She'd essentially withdrawn from life: craft, clan, and family all.

Until little Averryn had—against all logic, for the child was no blood-kin—given her something to hold her interest again.

Avall resisted the urge to challenge his mother's assertion, seeing that it looked like even odds that Averryn might grow up speaking Ixtian, assum-ing that, as a High Clan child, he was allowed to grow up at all. Still, for now . . .

It was as if Evvion read his mind. "He has nothing to worry about," his mother murmured. "He doesn't know fear. He doesn't know want or dis-comfort or deprivation. The blood of great men and women runs through him. If those who oversaw his arrival in the world survive the next half sea-son, he'll have a very amazing world in which to grow up, and amazing folk to teach him."

"His generation will grow up knowing of the power of the gems," Strynn acknowledged from Avall's side, reaching down to tickle the child beneath the chin.

Averryn's smile widened. Dimples appeared that would break women's hearts in far too few years. Avall wondered how the boy would manage that. For he had no doubt whatever that Averryn would inherit his mother's fa-mous looks, as well as his father's height.

Evvion regarded him keenly. "It would be best if you grew to love him, and best if you made another—a brother or sister—for him to love. Child-hood can be a very lonely time."

Avall almost protested that he did love him, as much as he could love something so remote from himself, and almost followed that up with a re-minder that unique among men of his time—and maybe all men forever—he'd shared the pains that had brought a child into the world. Finally he smiled at Strynn. "Lady," he said simply, "you never cease to amaze me with your ability to make wonderful things."

Strynn smiled back, but that smile proved transitory, as the stark serious-ness that had become her mask of late once again shadowed her features. "Speaking of wonderful things, shouldn't you be about one?"

"You should join me."

She shook her head. "I can't. As far as I'm concerned, the sword's fin-ished. This other thing you have to do, with the gem and the bloodwire, and all—I know you have to do it, but I can't watch you."

"This isn't like you, Strynn."

She gestured at the child. "Neither is this, but the sword's finished; Averryn isn't. And—" She paused. "This isn't artistic vanity, Avall—not that I'd enjoy watching even you modify something I'd crafted. But it's—" Another pause. "I don't like the idea of you going somewhere I can't."

"I'm willing to show you," Avall replied. "If I can," he added. "I've never done this, either. I might get down to the forges and find that what Gynn claims he's left in my head won't work. I don't even want to think about that! But as I said, I'm willing to show you, but you'd either have to watch me do it, or I could try to show you mind to mind, through the gems."

Strynn frowned. "Be practical, Avall. I'm leaving tomorrow—I have to, by royal command. We have no idea how long these changes will take. Suppose I wasn't finished when I ran out of time? And if I had to . . . to read whatever I had to do from your mind, that would still be one degree more distance from the source than if you do it, with a corresponding increase in chances something could go wrong. And—"

He cut her off with a raised hand. "You've thought about this a lot, haven't you?"

She nodded. "And I'll be honest with you, Avall. I'm at war with myself over this. Part of me wants it so bad I can taste it, but part of me knows that the best thing for the kingdom is for me not to have it. The sword's finished; therefore it should be the first to get its gem. You have time and the skill to do that. I—at present—do not. You may be pushing it as is: to do this and complete the helm."

"It *shouldn't* take more than a night. Maybe not even that."

Again Strynn shook her head. "It's still ultimately my choice. And for this night, I choose Averryn."

Avall took her hand again. "You're trusting me with a lot."

"No, my love," she whispered back. "I'm trusting you with everything."

(THE CITADEL—LATE AFTERNOON)

Avall wondered if there'd always been so many steps between his suite and the Citadel's forges, as he took himself there after a second nap that was far too short to have accomplished anything. Strynn had shared it with him— and Merryn and Kylin: the first time all four of them had partaken of that degree of intimacy. It was a completeness, he'd realized, for Strynn, who had the company of a bond-mate and a spouse. He and Merryn and Kylin should be so lucky. If only Rann had been there, too, instead of at the front, where the Fateing had placed him. At least Div was there as well, so he'd have someone to look out for him, now that she'd located some of what passed in her life as kin.

But, as Strynn had said, they had important work to finish, though even now it was hard to believe that the fate of the kingdom rested on what they had little choice but to consider magic—and that they were themselves the wielders of that power. It was funny, Avall thought, as he bent his way down yet another level of the tower, how, when one read stories of wizards and magicians, they already had their magic in hand; their spells, their books of potions. He'd never stopped to consider how those potions, spells, and cantrips were contrived. Would that record Lykkon was compiling even now someday be the founding arcana for the magi of some distant time?

If so—why, then, magic was a mix of rank carelessness, ongoing frustration, and blind luck.

Or, as the Priests would say, Fate.

And then he reached the final turning, and strode into the corridor outside the royal forge.

He heard the hammering long before he opened the door. And almost as quickly knew who wielded that most ancient of smithcraft tools, simply by the force and rhythm of the blows. Blows he'd heard since childhood. Blows he'd never stopped hearing—unlike Eellon, who'd been forced to choose Clan over Craft, and rarely got to forge iron anymore.

Tyrill's blows.

Holding his breath—one never knew what to expect when one encountered the Spider Chief—he pushed through the door.

If she'd moved since the last time he'd seen her here, he had no proof. She sat braced into a high stool patiently applying a hammer to a strip of glowing metal fresh from the forge to her left. Avall frowned. She was supposed to be working on the shield, and the only parts of the shield left undone, when last he'd seen it, were some of the intricate filigree panels, most of which were purely for decoration. The understructure had been completed long ago. Hadn't it?

He cleared his throat to announce himself as he approached. Tyrill spared him a half glance, then refused to pay him further heed. He cleared his throat again, as he came within the ritual distance for speech. "Craft-Chief," he began, "I thought—"

"I thought better," Tyrill broke in before he could complete his comment. "Eddyn's design for this thing was magnificent, and followed the King's specifications to the letter. But the King designed it before he confronted the possibility of taking it to war—and for that, it's too heavy."

Avall regarded her warily. "And how do you know the King plans to use it thus?"

"The Clan-Chief told me. He told me everything, in fact. And no, I don't know what that means, nor do I care to speculate—though I've some ideas. More to the point, he told me about your plans for the gems. As functional items, then, the sword is fine—as I'd have expected of Strynn—and the helm will surely be acceptable. But the shield—I don't have to tell you that gold, bronze, and steel are heavy. If the King would wield this thing, it behooves us to make it as light as possible. Therefore, I've started remaking the frame from a lighter alloy, the existence of which I've been . . . saving for some optimum moment which now, alas, seems to have arrived."

And without further commentary, she assailed the strapwork once more.

Avall didn't need to squint to see the effort it took her simply to raise her hammer, and the way she set her mouth to a hard grim line to bring it down where she wanted. She managed that, too: Her control was excellent. But at what cost? She was younger than Eellon, but not by much. She couldn't continue like this indefinitely. Nor, given the elementary nature of the work she was presently about, should she have to. It was work any apprentice could do. Rann could do it, probably, and he wasn't even a smith. Unless there was something tricky to this particular alloy, in which case, Avall owed it to himself to master it.

"Craft-Chief," he heard himself say. "I can't help but see the effort this is costing you. If you will show me—"

"On my deathbed perhaps, but not before. The making of this metal, and its working, is a secret I will otherwise show but to one person, and that is Eddyn."

"Who's Barrax's prisoner, if he's still alive," Avall replied flatly. "I don't think you can count on him."

"In the meantime, I'll do it myself," Tyrill snapped, raising the hammer again.

But this time she couldn't disguise the way her wrist and forearm shook. Beads of sweat appeared on her forehead that had nothing to do with proximity to the forge. She set it down again. And almost dropped it.

Avall took the wooden handle gently from her fingers and set it aside. "We both know that working when tired rarely makes anything but messes. I've heard you say that since—"

"You were about eight years old," Tyrill snapped. "But you're right. This time."

"Go take a nap, Craft-Chief. There are rooms for that purpose near here."

She scowled at a time-candle. "I'm due to discuss weapon tallies with -el anyway. I suppose I could consider that a rest."

"Do it," Avall insisted. "But I hope you're aware of how risky it is for anyone to withhold knowledge right now. We could all be dead tomorrow."

"You've a helm to complete, as I recall," Tyrill retorted airily, as she started out of the room. Once she'd have made that a grand gesture, an arrogant sweep of movement, which she managed to achieve even when assisted by pages. But now, she moved as haltingly as he'd ever seen. "Do you need help?" he called.

"I'll manage," she replied. And did, though once again the effort cost her. Fortunately, a page appeared not long after, navigating the corridor as part of a routine sweep.

Avall watched the girl assist the old woman away and, as soon as the door had closed behind her, crossed to a certain table and picked up the sword Strynn had, for half a year, been making.

It was finished—though he doubted Strynn was remotely satisfied with the edges. Beyond that, it only required one thing for completion. Insertion of a gem.

That and certain other things he knew yet did not know. Reaching into his tunic, he retrieved his gem and separated it from its clasp and chain. This might be necessary and might not, but he was inclined to err on the side of caution. Better new techniques be tried with the gem's explicit involvement. A deep breath and he closed his eyes, and squeezed just hard enough for the barb to prick his hand. He held it there, even as the euphoria swept over him. Time slowed. Storing his gem once more, he located the one the King had held in his right hand—since that was the hand that would wield this weapon. It took a moment to insert it—not in the juncture of hilt, blade, and quillons, as Strynn's original design had specified, but in one of the bulges that spiraled the hilt like rope.

That accomplished, he swung it experimentally, since even that negligible mass could affect balance. He could feel no difference, though Strynn would have final say. Impulsively, he flourished it more vigorously, reveling in how exquisite it felt in his hand, even knowing it had been designed for the King's stronger wrists. It was a pity to put it down, especially as he could almost see the air parting as it passed, even as the gem showed him the sensual stretch/release of every single muscle he brought into play.

But there were still things to do. Things that had never been done. *Magical* things, perhaps.

The first was to alter the setting Strynn had cast into the grip to accommodate one of those clasps he'd devised that could automatically stab a palm to bring forth the blood the gem evidently craved. After that, things got more complicated, as even thinking about what he was about to assay eased him into uncharted parts of his brain.

Mostly it included the attachment of the thin hollow wires he'd taken to calling bloodwire to the gem's housing, then running them to points he could sense as much as see upon the hilt. Places where pressures, inputs, and sensations would register just so.

His hands did the work for him, tucking the hair-fine silver wire into channels he made where there were already indentations, then filling them with molten gold, and shaping the surface so that those channels didn't show, never mind the wires.

Save at their termini, where he set smaller versions of the trigger barbs. If this worked correctly, whoever wielded the sword—would feed the jewel blood at a certain rate, and receive that power at a certain pace in turn. Maybe.

All he knew was that, early in the process, he'd found himself reaching for certain materials, notably the fabulously expensive bloodwire, and using it a certain way. Reasonably enough, he'd started to analyze his actions, but that only brought on a headache of the fiercest kind. In the end, he was reduced to doing what Merryn had taught him: finding a place where the headache wasn't, and directing his attention there. And if he worked while he did that, and let his gem involve itself as it would . . .

Things started happening that he knew were simply . . . right.

Twice he had to prime his gem with blood, not daring to mingle blood for that purpose with blood required by the sword.

And all the while time, to all intents, stood still.

Suddenly there was nothing left to do. Nothing left to show for half a dozen hands' work save a pile of metal filings and a few lengths of hollow wire.

And a sword like no other sword had ever been, that lay gleaming on white velvet before him.

As a weapon it probably had one of the keenest edges in history. As more . . . it had yet to be verified.

But was he qualified to do that? Strynn had made it to suit the subtleties of the King's hand, but it had been the pattern of the Overworld journey the King had observed in *his* mind that had determined its design. And since it was made for the King, he had no way of knowing how it would react to him. To him wielding it in anger, in any case.

No, much as he wanted to try it out right here, he really needed witnesses—if for no other reason than fear that the thing might turn on him. And the best witness he could think of, of those on hand and not otherwise employed, was Merryn.

It took Avall longer than he liked to find his sister, and at that, he almost missed her. She was sitting guard at Eellon's door: relieving Bingg, who'd evidently have stayed there until he collapsed entirely—or starved to death. "He's too young to be useful in the war," Merryn confided through a yawn. "But that doesn't mean he doesn't want a part. And since Veen and Krynneth are taking turns as Guard-Chiefs, no one seems to be attending to the details of who goes where these days."

"I noticed," Avall replied wryly. "People seem to be using this as an excuse to do what they want, without regard for process."

"Nice, isn't it?" Merryn grinned. "Proof we can function without a ritual to mark every breath."

In spite of Avall's haste, she made him sit with her, discussing ordinary things until Bingg returned, clean and fed, and with a pot of cauf as big as he was, just in case.

Then they were back in the forges. Avall noted how eerie the place felt late at night when no one was about. Eerie but not truly empty, for it was as if the vast chamber were haunted by the spirits of everyone who'd wielded a weapon made there, or died by one. He wondered if they were there in protest. What he and his friends were crafting might end war for all time. There'd be no more spirits to join these, then. So perhaps they feared loneliness. Or maybe they thought that with no one else to watch over, they'd finally be free to seek the Overworld. Or perhaps there were no presences at all save the minds of other folk in the keep, linked with Avall through the gem.

Merryn whistled when she saw the completed blade, though she was wise enough not to touch it. "Here, or . . . ?"

Avall wrapped the sword in its velvet shroud. "I was thinking the Royal War Court. It should be empty this time of night."

Merryn regarded him dubiously, but followed him up the stairs.

A moment later, they strode through a high-arched door, across the enclosing arcade, and entered the courtyard proper.

Typical of such places, it was somewhat austere—until one noted the construction, proportions, and details, whereupon the place became a wonder of subtle design. Stars gleamed down from on high, and only one moon was up, yet the walls and pavement themselves were sufficiently pale to provide enough light to see by, while at the same time imparting a cast of blue to stone and shade alike that made the place seem otherworldly.

The court wasn't entirely empty, however, nor entirely neat. An assortment of wooden pells had been erected, some bearing replica soldiers, both afoot and on horseback. A group of three stood nearby, backed by a barrier of piled stone whose purpose Avall couldn't fathom.

Scarcely daring to breathe, Avall unshrouded the sword. An exchange of looks with Merryn, a brief "Luck," murmured by both parties, and he took the hilt in his hand.

The gem nestled comfortably into his palm, like an old friend. But it wasn't yet activated. A deep breath, and he squeezed the gilded bronze a certain way. And felt the merest prickle of pain as the catch in the gem-shroud released. With it came the wash of blood, and another rush, at once more familiar and more strange, as the gem's power coursed into his blood. And did *not* find the King it expected, and . . . hesitated, before determining that Avall was both one in blood to its proper master, and had a bond of affection with him.

But something else was happening, too. Power was flowing into him from . . . another place. No, not so much flowing, as . . . waiting. He moved the sword, and felt more things move than the blade and his body. It was as if that motion drew not only on his own blood, nerve, muscle, and bone, but also reached somewhere else, that was *like* his mind but not his mind, and tapped something there as well. And as he knew that when his brain demanded, his body would react a certain way, so he knew that when another part of it demanded, the sword would respond in kind.

And more than the sword.

He swung it once, and air parted in the expected swish.

That was all.

But then he swung it again—and swung with that *other* part as well.

Lightning flashed, crackling across the pell men he'd made his target. The air smelled of storms, and Avall felt an outflow of energy that left him weak and staggering. Nevertheless, he swung again—to the same effect— only then realizing that working with the gems altered one's time sense, and that Merryn might not have seen much at all.

But the pell men . . . Smoking stumps showed where they'd stood. And the stones behind them were smashed and tumbled.

A deep breath, and he stepped forward. Struck an intact pell directly.

And felt no resistance whatever as the sword clove neatly through, though even then the air crackled and stank.

A final swing—at nothing. But this time he was observing himself.

Once more power exploded from the tip of the sword. Power he could feel pouring into parts of him that were like nerves and blood vessels but not those things, and then flowing onward into the sword, where it was refined and focused, and then flashed out again.

But that required a balance. And that balance he could not quite find. It was as though his mind were standing on a log that was rolling back and forth. He could control it, but it took effort. It needed other logs to brace it. Two other logs, in fact.

Or two other gems.

Gynn was the King of Balance. And when the helm and the shield were complete, balance should be achieved.

And then, abruptly, he sat down, for all strength had left his legs.

He retained the sword, however, while Merryn moved toward him— slowly at first, then more rapidly. He shivered, and when she sat down beside him and took him into her arms, he could tell she was shivering as well.

But the look on her face was unmitigated joy.

"It works," he gasped. "But it needs the other gems to complete it. It's very much Gynn's sword." And then—he couldn't help it—he was laughing. Giddy with relief that what had been so abstract as to be unfathomable had suddenly become real. *He'd done it! Had made a . . . magic sword. A sword of Power. A sword to end all swords.*

A magnificent creation, built off Strynn's masterwork.

Merryn studied him seriously. "I was going to ask to try that thing myself, but that might be a mistake, since I've never properly bonded with one of those things. But . . ." She paused, then grinned abruptly. "It *does* work, Avall. And you—and Strynn—may have made the most wonderful thing ever."

Avall was beyond exhaustion, yet found energy to wink at her. "I don't know about that," he teased. "There's still the shield and the helm."

Merryn rose abruptly, hauling him up with her. "What?" he gasped again.

"We shouldn't stay here. People will have heard all that noise, and this is still supposed to be a secret. Besides, we have to tell Eellon."

"Eellon . . ." Avall murmured, through a shiver. "Right."

In spite of weariness, they started for the Steward's quarters at a run.

And met Bingg where a staircase terminated in an arcaded corridor. Happy as they were—consumed with the flush of joy—it took them a moment to notice that the boy was in tears. "Bingg—What?" Avall breathed. And then Bingg had flung himself into Avall's arms, and all they could hear was sobbing.

"Bingg—" From Merryn.

"Eellon," Avall breathed. "It has to be." Slowly, carefully, he slid to his knees, gently easing Bingg away, so that he could hold the boy by the shoulders and still look him in the face. "Bingg, what's happened?"

"He's . . . not dead, I don't think. But he was working, and we all felt a rush of cold, and—"

Avall's heart flip-flopped, as tears of his own found him. A rush of cold. That could only mean . . .

"I should've known better," he choked. "I keep forgetting how much that thing . . . draws."

"And more from those to whom it's connected," Merryn added, face as grim as Avall had ever seen. "I . . . think it must take the easy route to minds before the hard."

"Maybe," Avall managed. "But Bingg . . . does anyone else know?"

"I left him with the healer, and went to look for you. You were all I could think of. But Lyk . . ."

"Is somewhere else. We'll find him. But for now, let me be your brother. And come with me while I see to my . . . father."

Bingg nodded, wiping his face on the tail of his tabard.

. . .

"It's a coma," the healer said flatly, as they trooped into Eellon's quarters. It was very late, and no one was about save those who had to be, or thought they did. Avall tried to look at nothing as he stood there, feeling Merryn and Bingg easing in behind him. He did *not* look at the bed. Nor at the healer, for what he might see there and wasn't certain he could face, if events had gone as he suspected.

"Will he recover?" Merryn asked, sounding as shaken as he, for all her cheeks were dry.

The healer shrugged. "Maybe. But he's old and tired. He's been pushing himself beyond reason."

"Maybe he just needs sleep," Avall murmured, wishing he believed what he'd said.

The healer regarded him levelly, concern softening what were hard features for a woman. "He won't wake up. Nothing wakes him. He lives; he breathes. That's all."

Avall sank down in the nearest chair, locating it by feel. He wondered if the chill in the room was real, or merely a tangible echo of what he felt in his soul.

Merryn touched his hand, lightly but firmly. "What happens now?"

Avall shrugged, aware that Bingg was rising. "I'll . . . go get Veen and Krynneth," the boy whispered.

Avall nodded absently, not daring to look at his two-father save obliquely, from across the room. Enough to see that he lay on his back with his hands atop the coverlet to either side. But even there, they could hear the rasp of his breathing.

"Bingg?" Merryn called, as Bingg reached the door.

"What?"

"Much as I hate to say it, you'd better also bring Tyrill."

"Tyrill . . . ?"

Avall nodded in turn. "Power has to transfer, just in case. She's not the next oldest in the clan, but she's the next oldest we can get hold of right now, with Half Gorge and South Gorge fallen. She'll have to act the role. And maybe . . . be Steward, until we can find someone else, probably from Ferr."

"Preedor returned five days ago," Merryn noted.

"Then we'll need to contact him, too," Avall replied. "He's the only one I'd trust who's not too close to this thing. We'll send Veen or Krynneth. I don't want to leave here."

Merryn shook her head, and took his hand, squeezing it hard. "He's strong. He'll make it. And we have good news to temper the bad, whatever happens."

Avall squeezed back, and then another thought struck him, so strong he gasped.

"What?"

"Tyrill," Avall whispered. "Suppose whatever . . . I did also hit Tyrill. She's old, and physically weaker than Eellon."

"We'll know soon enough," Merryn said matter-of-factly. "But she's never linked with a gem, has she? So that should protect her some."

Avall shivered. And then shivered again, as an even worse thought struck him. He rose abruptly, starting for the door.

"Avall—"

"Averryn!" he retorted. "I've linked with him before, through Strynn, when she was pregnant. I—" He crumpled into his sister's arms. "Oh, Eight, Merry, I may have . . . killed my son."

Merryn slapped him. Not hard, but enough to draw his attention. "You'd have heard by now," she told him. "Whatever happened, happened at once. Strynn would've been racing Mother to the forge . . ."

Avall bit his lip, trying to believe what he didn't dare, because to believe was to hope, and he wasn't sure he could stand to see hope shattered.

"I'll go get them," Merryn said quietly. "I'll have them bring Averryn here. You could use both of them and . . . so could I." For the first time Avall noticed that his sister's eyes were misty. He tended to forget that she was as close kin to Eellon as he; that they had as much history, shared as much of what passed in their clan as love.

"Go," Avall replied. "I'll stay here. I . . . need to look at him."

"If you're sure."

He tried to smile at her. "I am. But one thing, Merry. One thing. Tomorrow when Strynn leaves, I want her to take Averryn with her. I can't risk him otherwise. I just can't."

Merryn looked as though she was about to say something and thought better of it—probably to remind him that Averryn was no blood of his. Mercifully she held her tongue. And departed.

"I'll go, too," said the healer. And Avall was left alone with his two-father.

He waited until their footsteps receded, until the only sounds in the room were his breathing, and Eellon's. And then he rose slowly and crossed to Eellon's bedside. Even so, he didn't look full upon him, perhaps fearing that the old man's eyes would pop open to fix Avall with an accusing stare he far too well deserved.

But they didn't. And then Avall was beside him, and taking his hand.

He started to speak, but that was stupid, so he simply sat there, unmoving, feeling the steady pulse of Eellon's life.

Without really meaning to, he reached out to him with his mind. Not through the gem itself, but by ways the gem provided. Unfortunately, there was nothing where he looked, no bright thoughts darting just below the surface. Whether they were gone or simply obscured, he had no way of telling. But it filled him with dread beyond reason.

This was his fault. Through nothing more than rank carelessness he'd worked the doom of the second most important man in the kingdom. Anything that fell out from here would be his fault because any decision made henceforth would lack the considered stamp of Eellon's massive, passionate intellect. He'd cost the world something precious, and if he'd also given it something of worth in the gem, well, he wasn't sure that was a fair trade.

But maybe it was another balance.

Why couldn't someone else have found the gem, dammit? The gems, he amended. Someone from Lore, for instance, who would've known how to exercise appropriate patience. Whose controlling clan was not so fractured by power politics. A clan that had no Avall and no Eddyn.

And then, in the solitude of Eellon's room, with his hand still clasping the old man's, he wept in truth.

Fortunately, he heard Tyrill approaching. And more fortunately, the old lady had never been able to manage much of a pace, so that he had time to wash his face and reclaim his original seat before the Spider Chief was ushered in—with what looked like half of Smithcraft, but was in fact merely those members of the clan lodged in the Citadel. And those with claims on Argen folk, like Strynn, Averryn, Evvion, Veen, and Krynneth.

A moment only it took the Acting Clan-Chief of Argen to assess the situation, before motioning to the healer to resume whatever efforts she could. That accomplished, she fixed everyone else with an all-inclusive stare, and uttered one terse word: "Workroom." Whereupon they all adjourned there.

A large table stood to one side, rarely used, but Tyrill had it moved to the center of the chamber, and chairs found to range around it. "The other sept-chiefs should be here soon," she said, "but some things need to be said beforehand that won't be appropriate later. Bingg told me the gist of what happened, which I understand without approving. But does anyone else have any questions?"

To Avall's surprise, it was Krynneth who responded. "Chief," he said clearly, "we know the sword is finished, and, so I've heard, works. I know that Avall's spending every free moment working on the helm. But what of the shield? Now that you're Clan-Chief, will you have time to complete it, among your other duties?"

Tyrill looked as though she'd like to pluck out his eyes and use them for earbobs, but though she stiffened, she controlled herself.

"This is no time for anyone to feed their vanity," she said at last. "Decisions made now cannot be remade, but may be regretted for ages. Most of you here know who I like, who I don't, and why. That doesn't change the fact that many of you are kin and all of you have the good of the realm in heart and mind alike. But unless someone else comes forward—yes, I'll have too much to do to finish the shield as I'd like."

"What about the Stewardship?" Merryn and Strynn chorused as one. "I'd think someone from Ferr," Merryn continued, alone.

"Tryffon's at the front," Tyrill replied. "And while Preedor *is* back here in Tir-Eron, he has his hands full organizing the flow of men and supplies *to* the front. Eellon was running everything else, including seeing to the acquisition and manufacture of supplies and armament. I can do that, and function as Acting Clan-Chief, but it will take all the time I have."

"So Strynn, then?" Merryn dared. "For the shield, I mean. She's the next best functioning smith here, besides Avall, who's already committed."

"Someone also needs to take the sword to the King," Krynneth noted.

"Not yet," Avall countered. "The thing works, granted, but it's . . . out of balance, which could make it dangerous. The shield and helm have to be finished as well. I don't know how I know that, but I do. Trust me."

"So the sharp edge," Tyrill said, "is that you can finish the helm or the shield, but not both."

"Not in the time we have," Avall agreed. "And Strynn—"

"Is under royal command to go downriver at first light, in order to observe."

"And take Averryn away from my destructive influences," Avall added bitterly.

Tyrill gnawed her lip, scowling furiously. "I don't like this," she growled. "I don't like it at all. There are too many things that need doing, and not enough people to do them."

Avall puffed his cheeks. "I know what you mean. Much as I hate to say it, it's times like this I wish we still had Eddyn."

"Don't mention that name," Tyrill gritted. "I've had enough of him. I tried and tried, but . . . No, don't get me started, or I'll wind up like Eellon."

"So the shield . . . ?" Krynneth dared in turn.

Tyrill closed her eyes. "I don't know," she whispered. "I'll let you know tomorrow."

"Tomorrow?" Veen snapped. "Do we have that much time?"

"We've no choice," Tyrill replied. "I hear footsteps, which can only be our delinquent folk approaching. Which means other decisions. I'll let you know at breakfast. In the meantime," she finished, "you, young man,"—she pointed to Avall—"have, at the very least, a helmet to complete. I'd suggest you be about it."

Avall started to reply, then thought better of it. He considered leaving with Strynn and Evvion, when Averryn started fretting, until a warning glare from Tyrill changed his mind. But all through the ensuing meeting, during which Tyrill was confirmed as Acting Clan-Chief of Argen, he was sketching determinedly, trying to figure out where best to route the wires that would tie the King's blood, bone, and brain to a mass of inert metal.

CHAPTER XXXII:

RAIDERS IN THE NIGHT

(ERON: TIR-ERON—HIGH SPRING: DAY V—NEAR MIDNIGHT)

~~~~~~~~~~

Merryn had no idea what time it was—only that she'd been very sound asleep indeed—when she was abruptly awakened. Someone was in her room, the door to which she clearly remembered locking. As would any rational person, given the situation. She rose in one smooth rush, squinting into the scanty moonlight. Her hand found a dagger, but she didn't bother with clothes. Modesty was no use to the dead.

By the time her feet hit the floor, she'd determined that the invader was standing unmoving in the doorway.

"Merryn," it—*she*—hissed, "it's me, Strynn!"

Merryn's tension drained out of her so fast she nearly collapsed. Eight, but she was edgy! Still, if anyone was going to catch her with her guard down, better it was Strynn. She sat down on the bed pad with a thump, reaching absently for a night robe she'd left on a nearby chest.

Strynn had said nothing—probably waiting until she was certain no attack was forthcoming—then strode forward, moving with surprising confidence in the dark.

Merryn fumbled to light a candle, sensing that it was not yet time for speech, though whatever had called Strynn here in dead of night was bound to be important. Light flared. Strynn found a chair and a bottle of wine—and drank deeply before extending it to Merryn.

Merryn took it gravely. "Couldn't sleep?" she ventured, cocking a brow.

Strynn shook her head. "I need to sleep, but it's one of those times when you know you won't until you just go ahead and do what has to be done."

Merryn regarded her keenly. "That bad?"

Strynn nodded.

"So bad you couldn't even tell Avall?"

Another nod.

"One of those things that you don't dare mention because you know he'll forbid it, but you know you have to do it anyway?"

Strynn chuckled. "You've become a mind reader now?"

Merryn shrugged. "Maybe. I think working with the gems even a little improves one's abilities that way. But surely, sister, you know by now how very well I know you."

Strynn took another swig and wiped her mouth on her sleeve, rough as a man. "We have to do something dangerous," she said at last. "And we have to do it tonight."

"Tonight? Why? What—"

"Because there'll be no one to stop us. Avall's in the forges exorcising his frustration after that damned meeting. Tyrill's being Tyrill. Eellon's—better not to speak of him. No one else matters but Averryn. Tomorrow I'm supposed to leave for the coast. I may be able to delay a little—but with time as important as it is—"

"What *is* this thing?" Merryn demanded, her voice more forceful than was her wont.

Strynn swallowed hard, looking at the bottle instead of at her bond-mate, her face as grim and determined as Merryn had ever seen it. "We have to rescue Eddyn."

"Eddyn?" Merryn cried, mouth gaping into an O. "Eddyn's in the south, Strynn. Last I knew, he was imprisoned in the same place I was."

"And before that?"

"I don't know. Avall says he was here. He says he place-jumped out of prison."

"With the gem."

"With *Avall's* gem."

"I have one, too. It's weaker, but—"

Merryn snared the wine and filled herself a goblet. "You're saying you and I should . . . place-jump down past South Gorge and rescue Eddyn, so that—"

"He can finish the shield."

Merryn shook her head. "But surely it doesn't have to be *that* shield, if all you have to do is fit a gem—"

"No, I think it does, and so does Avall. Sure, on one level all that has to happen is that the gem be wired to the shield and the wielder alike in such a way that the proper connections are made. But there's more to it than that. Avall can't explain it—he says there aren't words for what happens, any more than one can describe an emotion or a color. But he says it's something to do with . . . art. The same parts of our mind that make art without thinking about it are the ones that carry the power of the gems—at least the aspect he's talking about. And somehow that power gets put into the object while it's being made, and . . ."

"So you're saying," Merryn broke in, "that though any shield would suffice, one made by a master like Avall or you or Eddyn would be much stronger."

"Maybe not so much stronger as more balanced," Strynn corrected. "Avall thinks the trio of helm, sword, and shield, if activated at the same time, will make whoever wields them very powerful indeed. But if one of those elements doesn't match—"

"But Tyrill's already remade most of the framework."

"To Eddyn's exact design, however. Plus she's a master in her own right. And she taught him everything he knows. If anyone thinks like him, it's her."

"And how is Eddyn going to learn all this?" Merryn demanded. "If even Avall doesn't know it until he does it?"

Strynn shrugged again. "Mind to mind, as best I can tell. If Gynn was able to see it and show it to Avall, then maybe Avall can show it to Eddyn. If not . . . he can still do the artistic work, and let Avall do the final connecting."

"Ha!" Merryn snorted. "That's assuming he'd do anything at all. He's no cause to love anyone up here now."

"He loves Eron," Strynn said simply. "I've never doubted that."

Merryn frowned. "But this is all speculation."

"I know. But it's also the only thing I can think *to* do, given that I have to leave tomorrow. Otherwise, *I'd* try to finish the damned thing, and get Avall to show *me* how to make the wretched connections. But if we could place-jump—"

"That's a large 'if.' We've never done anything like that before. I've barely worked with the gems at all."

"But assuming—"

Merryn reached over and took Strynn's hand. "Sister, what are you thinking? He *raped* you. He bared your body and stuck his thing in you and took from you what he had no right to take—and with that he took away most of the choices you had left in your life."

"Do you think I don't know that?" Strynn shot back, eyes bright with tears. "Do you think I don't think of that every moment of every day? Every time I see Averryn? Every time Avall and I make love? He's always there, like a shadow on the sun. But it wasn't entirely him, Merryn. It was also the imphor he'd been chewing and the game he'd just lost, and all that pressure Tyrill's laid on him since he was born. I can see how one wrong thing might break him."

"That sounds like you're excusing him."

"Never! But maybe I understand him better. Besides, this isn't about me, or him. It's about the survival of the kingdom."

Merryn took a deep breath. "So why don't *I* do it, then? You can lend me your gem, and—"

Strynn chuckled grimly. "I figured you'd say that. But we don't know if it can even take two people that far, never mind bring three back. What we do know is that the two times place-jumping worked were through will and desire. It has to be the *only* thing one wants for that instant, Merryn, and that's why I have to go. I'm the only person with enough of a bond to Eddyn. Even then, it may not succeed, but I think I can focus the desire— or the anger, or the hate; whatever it takes—strongly enough to get me there."

"But not alone."

"I can fight," Strynn replied, "but I'm no fighter. You've been where he is; you know the lay of the land."

"Does it have to be tonight?"

"I don't have any nights left. Besides, this late, he's unlikely to be heavily guarded."

Merryn felt an urge to laugh. "And of course you're also a master lockpick."

"Well, I certainly intend to take my tools."

"So the plan is to jump down there, pick his lock, and jump back?"

"That's it."

"You're forgetting one thing."

"What?"

"The energy factor. We'd be drawing enormous amounts of power. It could kill Eellon."

"No, actually I considered that," Strynn chuckled. "If we do it in the stables, we'd have the horses to draw on first—and they're bigger, warmer, and stronger."

Merryn gnawed her lip. "And in the cloister we'll have the army . . ."

"Some of it. The bulk has moved on. But there'd be guards, prisoners. Leftover baggage train—"

"Maybe."

Strynn finished the wine and set the bottle down. "Merryn, it's the only chance we've got. Even if we die—"

"We won't," Merryn countered fiercely, rising and starting to pace. "I have to think about this, Strynn. Not long, but I have to puzzle this out alone. Meet me in the stables in half a hand, and I'll give you my answer."

Strynn rose as well. "That's as much as I can ask for. And at that, I know I'm asking a lot, Merry."

Merryn gave her a brief hug, but didn't watch as Strynn passed through the door, her mind already spinning with implications.

There are people who don't live as well as these horses, Strynn thought, as she paced around the stables. Certainly the stonework could have graced any palace, and the hardware and accoutrements were as well-made as those in the King's own chambers. Tucked as it was into an angle between the royal herb garden and one of the war courts, it even smelled nice. And very clean.

Not a bad place to wait, if one felt like waiting.

Strynn didn't, which was why she was pacing the perimeter of the arcade that surrounded the exercise court, and glancing all too frequently at the sky.

It was past midnight, though not by much. Avall would be returning to their chambers soon. He'd miss her. He might even come looking for her.

She had no intention whatever of letting him know what she was about until she'd accomplished it, either. And she was as ready as she'd ever be, clad in supple black-leather hose and short-tunic under light mail and a plain black hooded tabard, with black gloves and black boots to complete the ensemble. Decent protection, while still being good for stealth and allowing freedom of movement.

For armament, she had a short sword, daggers in each boot, a third at her waist, and a small buckler for defense. And her lockpick's tools.

But where was Merryn?

Once again, she started pacing. Counting the horses this time, wondering if the gem could indeed draw on their life force to power what she and Merryn would shortly be undertaking.

Or she alone, if Merryn didn't show.

She fingered her gem nervously, where it hung exposed in its filigree clasp from a chain around her throat. It thrummed at her, like a cat purring. Which startled her.

Maybe it approved. Or maybe—

Footsteps. Purposeful, and with Merryn's distinctive cadence.

Strynn hastened her own steps to match them—and met Merryn coming through the door.

And couldn't help laughing. Her bond-sister had dressed almost exactly as she had, save that there was more quilted fabric and less leather.

Then she noticed the weapon at Merryn's side. "Eight save us!" she whispered, even as Merryn grinned. "You've brought *that* sword."

The grin widened, joined by a smug nod. "I've seen it work—and Avall conveniently measured it for me, to pattern for a scabbard. I was going to surprise you," she added sheepishly, not quite catching Strynn's eyes.

For the second time that day, Strynn fought down a surge of possessive jealousy. It was *her* work, after all, save for Avall's augmentations—and she'd begrudged those, though hadn't told him. "Are you sure it's safe to use?" she hissed back. "If we lose it—or ourselves . . ."

"We won't," Merryn informed her. "Besides, I'm not trusting it any more than you're trusting your stone."

Strynn regarded her levelly. "You're sure you want to do this?"

"I am now. But we haven't got much time, so I suggest we be at it." She eyed the nearest stall dubiously. "What do we do?"

Strynn dared a wry smile. "We go to where the concentration of horse-flesh is thickest."

"Lead the way."

Strynn did—to a section along the opposite wall where retired warhorses were kept in smaller stalls than those beasts still in active service. Which meant they were closer together. And more expendable.

There was also a pair of benches in a corridor between two of them, and it was at these that Strynn stopped. Without pause, she sat down on the nearer, motioning Merryn down beside her. "I'm not sure how this works," Strynn admitted, as she freed her gem from its clasp. "Avall didn't prime it with blood, but that was Avall. I don't know about Eddyn, but I think *we* should, because that seems to be how the things generate the most power."

"And there's the small fact that I haven't worked with your gem."

Strynn nodded absently while she found the dagger at her waist. Merryn took the hint and removed one glove, thrusting it into her belt. Strynn did the same.

"Ready?"

"As I'll ever be."

"I've removed the stone from its setting," Strynn murmured. "There's only one barb, and there're two of us, and—well, mostly it just seemed better to do it the old-fashioned way, if only for the enhanced closeness."

"I understand," Merryn whispered back. "Now—let's to it."

An instant only it took Strynn to make the requisite cut, purposely following the line of the scar from her and Merryn's bonding rite. Merryn did the same and returned the blade solemnly.

"Desire and emotion," Strynn stressed. "To the exclusion of all else: That's all we can figure does it."

"So I have to *desire* to be with Eddyn? I don't know if I can do that."

"Then this may not work. But what if you desired something *near* Eddyn? To be with Kraxxi, perhaps."

Merryn snorted. "I don't know if I'd kiss him or kill him. I change my mind twice a hand."

"Well, want one or the other," Strynn replied tersely. "Now."

Without waiting for further response, she closed her eyes, found Merryn's bleeding hand by feel, and folded it, with her own, around the gem.

Reality shifted. Time slowed, reflected in the attenuated beating of Merryn's pulse. Dust drifted in the moonlight, describing a slow dance whose individual members Strynn could observe both together and discretely. She sensed a barrier pressing against her self, and realized it was Merryn, trying to join her. She dropped her guard at once—and felt a surge of power as Merryn rushed into her mind. They met joyfully, and then she was merging with Merryn, and their souls and selves and maybe some of their blood were not only separate entities, but halves of one much more powerful being.

Nor did either of them command the other to remember their preposterous mission. Indeed, their sharing gave it more force. Merryn had doubts about being able to desire Eddyn's company, but Strynn showed her memories of the rape, and that knowledge roared through Merryn like flame. With it went an almost irrational desire to be revenged on Eddyn once and for all. *If I had him here . . .* , she found herself thinking. *If I were where he is, I could put an end to him. . . . It's my right, not the king of Ixti's.*

Strynn found that anger and fed on it, joining it with her own. But she also found something else: Strynn's feelings for Prince Kraxxi, who should still be incarcerated in the same place as Eddyn. And as Strynn, she wanted to meet him, whereas as Merryn, she wanted to love him and hate him, and demand answers of him she knew he would never be able to give.

Reality shifted. Pain filled them—and cold. For an instant they looked down on Tir-Eron. But then their senses wrenched again, and they were back in their own bodies.

—Hearing footsteps fast approaching, even as agitation filtered through the surrounding steeds.

Someone—

Who?

Someone we dare not let see us!

We have to—

Even as Strynn thought that—or Merryn, or both of them together—reality jerked again. And this time it stayed jerked.

For a timeless moment they were nowhere, in a place of cold beyond cold, heat beyond heat, pain beyond pain, and pleasure beyond pleasure. They wanted to stay and to escape at once.

And for a moment became lost indeed, when Merryn recalled the panic she'd felt when she'd lost herself seeking Avall.

But Strynn found her there and soothed her, in a flash of thought that lasted an eternity. Neither reminded the other of their true quest. There was no need for that; they were one in their desires.

And then reality shifted again, and they felt cold beyond knowing.

And smelled smoke instead of horseflesh and hay.

And were looking at a bonfire.

Or rather, *Strynn* was: a bonfire viewed through iron bars set in a massive oak door. A bonfire around which men in strange armor danced drunkenly, pausing now and then to fling what looked like bits of shattered furniture atop the hungry flames.

Flames that limned Merryn's face in red and gold.

They had arrived inside a cell. Stone walls. Dirty stone floor. Another opening behind them that let in the softer glow of moonlight.

"We made it—" Strynn breathed.

But then an appalling stench found her, overruling the eerie beauty of the fire, and she saw Merryn's face. Her bond-sister's eyes were growing wider by the moment.

Strynn felt the hand that still clutched the gem bear down so hard she feared the stone would shatter between them, never mind her finger bones. "Merryn—"

"Strynn," Merryn whispered, barely moving. "Turn around very slowly, and whatever you do, don't look down until you're sure you're ready."

Thoroughly confused, Strynn nevertheless obeyed, slowly easing her hand free of Merryn's, while Merryn's other hand quested for the sword hilt. And then the stench found her in truth. Dirt. Human sweat. Sour fabric. Excrement.

Blood.

All mixed with the cleaner scent of the smoke from outside, where someone was now burning cedar.

A deep breath, and she let her gaze slide down.

It was merciful that they were in darkness, yet even so, she gasped. Even the gloom showed too much.

A man—tall and dark-haired. And naked: facedown and spread-eagled across a filthy cot, his skin pale, save where shackles of black iron showed at wrists and ankles, binding him to the bed.

But a deeper darkness glistened between his legs that she couldn't bear to look upon, and yet could not resist.

Blood.

The same blood that leaked from gashes across his back and buttocks.

Strynn's senses reeled, forcing her to grasp Merryn for support, as that image merged with one she had almost—*almost*—banished from her memory.

"He's been—" she blurted.

"Don't say it," Merryn warned. "Strynn, you shouldn't see this."

"Is it—?"

"It's Eddyn. I can see his clan tattoo."

"Is he—?" As Strynn's gorge started to rise.

"He's alive, but I don't know for how long."

"Why would they do this?"

Merryn finally moved, pushing past Strynn to kneel beside the figure. She felt for a pulse. Turned his head to confirm identification in the tenuous light. "Humiliation—obviously. They were probably trying to find out what he knew about the gem. Of course the irony is, the only thing Eddyn knows how to do with it is escape—if he had it."

"But torture . . . I thought you said Barrax was more humane."

"A matter of opinion," Merryn gave back, rising again and eyeing the door. "I think he's running scared."

"But he's winning."

"Maybe. But every shot he advances puts him deeper into enemy territory and farther from home. And he knows we have a weapon he doesn't have. That would scare me to death."

Strynn was doing everything she could to avoid looking at Eddyn. "So what now?"

Merryn shook her head. "More than you expected, sister? Well, there's nothing we can do for Eddyn here that can't be better done in Tir-Eron, if we can get him there. And something certainly has to be done. We dare not waste any more time."

"If it doesn't kill him," Strynn gave back. "The cold . . ."

"We have to risk it. In any case, we've two things to do before we can leave. You have to pick the locks on his shackles—"

"And you?"

Merryn grinned cryptically, her face demonic in the wavering fire-light. "If they've done this to Eddyn, whom they in some sense need, I don't want to think about what they might have done to Kraxxi, who's basically superfluous."

Strynn nodded grimly, then peered at the door. "But that's locked from the outside—which we should've considered in the first place, given where *we* are."

Another snort. "We're lucky to have come this close. Imagine if we'd shown up in the fire."

"Might've converted some Ixtians," Strynn laughed nervously.

"Or replaced The Eightfold God with the twofold goddess."

Eddyn groaned.

Strynn took a deep breath, and steeled herself. She was finally getting over the shock of the situation—though the irony wasn't lost on her. Maybe Balance was a more important aspect of Fate than she'd assumed.

"Go," Strynn said decisively. "If you need help with the door . . ."

Merryn grinned again and reached for the hilt of the sword protruding from the scabbard. "You might want to turn away, just in case."

Strynn watched long enough to see Merryn's hand tighten, and note the way she flinched at the tiny prick of pain from the hidden catch. And then Merryn was leveling the sword at the door. She closed her eyes, took a breath that Strynn felt with her, so close were they still bound.

A tap, a wrenching of something that felt like wind, air, and stone all at once—and the door ripped asunder.

Merryn staggered back as the flame from the sword's tip died. Strynn caught her, though she, too, had felt the force of that blow. Eddyn groaned again.

She fumbled for her picks, while Merryn stood blinking dazedly at the blade, then set her mouth, squared her shoulders, wrenched the smoking oak aside, and strode through.

Strynn watched her go: a tall shape in black silhouetted by fire and framed by the deeper black of the arcade. And then she was gone.

A chill wind invaded the cell in her wake. Strynn shivered, and not only from the cold.

Night enfolded Merryn, and with it air that, while thick with smoke, was still sweeter than the stench of Eddyn's cell. Part of her was furious about that—that a king should use anyone so, much less a High Clan prisoner who was kin to a rival King.

But fury had to contend with other emotions now, as she paused warily in the shadows beside the door, trying desperately to regain control, to let what she'd learned in her aborted Night Guard training take precedence.

She failed.

She'd show them the power of Eron. The power of Merryn san Argen-a. The power of Strynn's sword. Why, that one casual blow had been like wine and combat and sex all at once. Like a drug—but one she made inside herself. A drug she'd barely tasted and was desperate to try again.

All at once she was running. Clinging to the shadows, but reckless for all that, as she made for the corner in which Kraxxi had been housed.

Ten spans . . .

Eight . . .

Five . . .

Her footsteps sounded loud as thunder as her boots slapped against the paving stones, yet she could also hear the voices of the men by the fire as though she were there with them—and each voice separately, at that.

She even felt the separate stones beneath her boots, the pulse and pull of the wind. The textures of the fabrics against her body. It reminded her of the imphor high she'd endured for days uncounted.

But this was courtesy of the gem—of the hot pain that pulsed and throbbed and—almost—protested against her palm. Of power waiting there, latent, but eager to burst free.

And very nearly out of control.

Two . . .

One . . .

She was there. She slammed into the door and pressed her face close against the bars, trying to see within.

Darkness.

"Kraxxi!" she hissed. Or thought she did, for her voice seemed loud as thunder.

"Kraxxi!"

Silence.

She pounded the oak with her fist.

Nothing.

Perhaps a tap with the blade . . .

But then she noticed the catch. Unlocked.

She flicked it irritably, pushed at the door.

It opened easily.

And though dark inside, there was yet sufficient illumination for her to see that Kraxxi was gone.

Apparently permanently, since the bed was completely bare.

"Damn!" she spat into the darkness. And the fury rose up in her again— or frustration—or a return to the ambivalent anger she'd felt for her former lover since he'd abandoned her. Without really thinking about it, she swung the sword at the door—not with the full force of her limbs or the strength of her will, but still not casually.

The door exploded. Lightning flashed across the room, turning it stark white. The mattress pad blazed up in a froth of flame, as other flames took root on the wooden ceiling.

She danced away, shielding her face from the flames she'd called. From the lightning that had come from her fingertips.

From the anger that threatened to overwhelm her as power she'd never known danced through her body.

She wondered how Avall had resisted this. How he'd been able to swing the thing time after time and still be willing to put it down.

And though instinct warned her that something wasn't right, that she was in danger of abandoning rationality in favor of this odd new giddy high, she ignored it, overwhelmed as she was by all the emotions that had tormented her since the war began.

. . . *since her affair with Kraxxi had begun.*

Since Strynn had been raped, in fact.

That jarred her.

Strynn . . .

She'd left Strynn alone with Eddyn. And guards were now approaching . . .

She ran.

But though she pounded along as fast as she ever had in her life, she still had time to study everything with the same considered languor as before. And among those things were doors: which ones were locked, and which not. And every door that was locked, she smote with the sword, not bothering to see if anyone emerged.

Behind her, she was aware of flame roaring up to the skies—and finally, of the men in the courtyard noticing her handiwork and starting to react. A few were running toward her, at least as many away.

It didn't matter. The latter were cowards, the former—she could use a good fight, to burn off some of this energy.

And to bring bodies closer to fuel what must be done, a more rational part of her appended.

A casual sweep of steel smashed another lock, and the follow-through took down a pillar of the arcade.

Stones rolled into the courtyard.

And then she was back at Eddyn's cell.

She skidded to a halt, breath coming fast, heart pounding, as every sound within a shot echoed in her ears.

And every smell and image.

Strynn loomed large as a giant, where she prodded expertly at one final lock—the one that prisoned Eddyn's left arm. He was conscious, too—enough to open his eyes and moan.

Strynn's eyes were huge, her mouth tense with frustration.

"Hurry!" Merryn rasped—though it took a day to sound.

Strynn tried to. The picks flashed and clicked, and then the clasp broke free. "Done!" she cried, trying to get a shoulder under Eddyn, while the other hand sought frantically for the gem.

The first soldier was in the arcade now—a young man, half-armed, and seriously drunk, to judge by what Merryn could smell on his breath. She leapt toward him, sword bright against the sky, as the blade stole flame from the bonfire.

A slash, a flare of lightning—and he collapsed. His fellows slowed. Two turned to run.

Merryn started after them—

Arms reined her back, hands moving expertly to pin her in a wrestling hold she'd learned when she was nine. Fingers pried at the sword. "Merryn! Enough! We have to get out of here."

She tried to retain the weapon—but it would not be held. Strynn wrenched it away. She whirled as she felt that precious power start to ebb. Saw Strynn's blazing eyes . . .

Strynn slapped her—hard. Pain bloomed through her like dye in water.

"Now! While they're waiting."

Merryn started to protest, but Strynn tugged at her with all the strength she possessed, and Merryn felt herself dragged inside, where a naked Eddyn lolled in a clumsy slump on the side of the bed.

"Help me!" Strynn gasped.

Merryn blinked, but then instinct took control, and she sat down at Eddyn's side, while Strynn took the other. Red flashed in Strynn's hand: the gem and the blood that woke it. Another red ghosted around: the fire.

"There!" A man yelled, impossibly close.

Merryn reached for the sword, but it wasn't there. And where anger and arrogance had been, fear rushed in, as she realized she was weaponless in a burning building with half a drunken army bearing down upon her.

And then Strynn was grabbing her hand, with Eddyn an awkward, stinking mass between them, and pain bright in her palm.

An armed man appeared in the doorway, grinning. Before he could take another step, however, Strynn's will reached out and tore into Merryn's mind, finding the one thing there it needed.

Out!

Away!

Back to Tir-Eron—though that was a secondary consideration.

Reality wrenched and whirled. And all the wonder of the Overworld was back: the cold, the heat, the pleasure, and the pain. Maybe Eddyn was there, but if so, he was no more linked to them than their clothes might have been.

Behind them, dimly, Merryn sensed a rush of cold air, as their panic sucked all the heat from the men who pursued them, leaving them cold as ice before the fire. One died—she was sufficiently linked to know that.

She recoiled reflexively, and Strynn, who was the only rational mind among them, seized that and used it to bear them home.

Darkness . . .

. . . then light again, but the softer light of a moon.

They were back in the War Court—a few strides from where they'd begun.

And Eddyn was with them. Cold as death, but breathing.

Merryn looked at Strynn, who was meeting her gaze with as grim an expression as Merryn had ever seen her bond-mate wear. "This stays with me," she gritted, shoving the sword into her belt. "You can get a healer, or I can."

"I'll go," Merryn replied meekly.

"Get two."

Merryn started off at a near run, then froze abruptly, and turned. "I hope Gynn knows what he's in for. I hope to Eight Avall knows some way to truly master that thing."

And then she was gone: a pounding of boots in the night.

Strynn watched her go—then took a deep breath, eased Eddyn down to the stones as carefully as she could, and threw her cloak over him. That accomplished, she found an unused water trough and threw up—copiously.

When the healers finally arrived, she was sitting calmly by Eddyn's side, staring at the increasingly thick flakes of a late-season snow.

She had taken three baths before Avall returned to their suite, just before sunrise.

"Eddyn's back," she mumbled.

"I heard," Avall replied stonily. "Merryn told me. It was a brave thing to do, but also very stupid."

"Fate and Balance," Strynn said for no reason. She let her lids slide closed and did not open them until noon the next day, when her escort downriver pounded on the door.

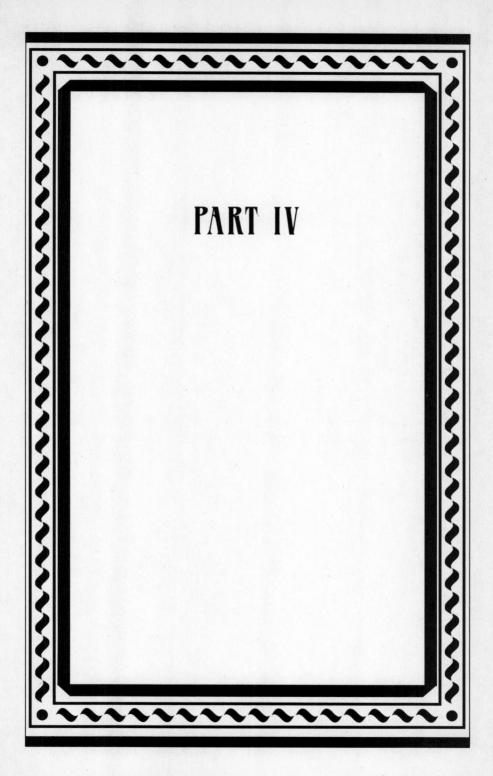

PART IV

CHAPTER XXXIII:

WAITING

(ERON: SOUTH OF ERON GORGE—HIGH SPRING: DAY XII—NIGHT)

~~~~~~~~~~~~~~~~~

Lord Commander . . . ?"

The voice was tentative, as though the title stuck in the speaker's throat. Or as though he were deathly afraid, which he well might be, speaking as he was from the door to Lynnz's suite in this sprawling ruin that passed for a headquarters. Lynnz resisted an urge to give the man cause for that fear. His hand eased to the geen-claw dagger at his belt, just in case. It had sounded like Lord Morrill, one of his half brothers-in-law. Which could be good or not.

Lynnz sighed and glared up from behind the desk at which he'd been studying supply manifests. It was Morrill, indeed—one of the few people given permission to meet with him directly.

The king was indisposed, so rumor said. Too busy to meet with more than a handful in person. Once they took Tir-Eron, which was to say Eron itself, *then* the king would show himself. So the story ran.

Morrill took a step into the room, inclining his head in what was a bow to equals, not that of subject to king. Yet.

"What is it, Morrill?" Lynnz snapped, reaching for a pot of hot cider laced with spirits. The fire popped obligingly, as though to stress his demand.

Morrill—who, like Lynnz, was wed to one of Barrax's sisters—always looked grim, but at the moment he seemed less so than usual. "Lord," he began, folding his arms across his chest, "the weather-witch says that not only has the snow ended, but that it will be warm as true spring by tomorrow morning."

"He says this, does he?" Lynnz growled. "Then why didn't he predict this cursed-be snow to start with?"

"*That* one is dead," Morrill observed wryly. "This one seems more competent."

"Or more eager to please. Or more eager to lie to the enemy and tell him what he wants to hear."

"This one," Morrill purred, "was sent by your allies."

Lynnz could barely suppress his rage. "Allies, indeed! We haven't heard a word from them since they came slinking into Barrax's camp with all that talk of secret alliances and such. It's just my luck I found out—drinking with the king does have its advantages."

"Lord, I believe the rest of the clan are still under arrest."

"Not all of them. They can't be." Lynnz leaned back in his chair, studying the map before him, letting his gaze drift now and then to the darkened window. As if to taunt him, a few snowflakes drifted down, close enough to the mullioned panes to see.

"That may be the best place for them, though, if you think about it. If things go as they might, we could be fighting in Tir-Eron this time tomorrow. If we were to free them . . ."

Lynnz glared at him. "Would you trust men who go against their King?"

A brow quirked upward.

Another glare. "I meant open defiance, not necessity of the moment."

"As you say, lord." Morrill bowed again, mockingly.

"Thank you for your report," Lynnz said coldly. "I will see you in the morning."

"Your lordship intends to attack?"

"As soon as it is light. We dare not give Gynn any more advantage."

"Get some rest, lord. It appears you need it."

Lynnz nodded dismissal, and, when Morrill had departed, rose and strode through a door to his left, and thence through another set of doors. These let onto the second-highest parapet of what had once been, someone had told him, a royal summer hold. Before the plague had rendered such luxuries superfluous.

Cold hit him as his boots crunched on snow the sweepers had missed. He shivered and drew his cloak around him as he made his way to the nearest embrasure and gazed out into the Eronese night.

If I could crave one boon of the Gods, Lynnz thought with a shiver, *it would be to never see snow again.*

Certainly he was seeing enough of it now: It was High Spring—the beginning of the light half of Eron's year, just past the equinox—and men back in Ixti would be working bare-chested and barefoot, already complaining of the heat.

But here—he was staring not at the lush green foliage that had greeted his victory at South Gorge, but at a late-season snowfall that had begun five days earlier and forced them to take shelter in these heights, instead of pressing on to Tir-Eron.

Not that such a respite was necessarily bad. He'd pushed his army hard—especially since the rout at South Gorge—and Gynn's soldiers had been forced to retreat north, as Ixti's army drove them ever closer to their capital and the heart of their realm. They'd fought like madmen, too, but there was an odd lack of cohesion in Eron's ranks as well, or perhaps a confusion, as though no one were precisely in control.

Still, Gynn had had war thrust upon him; Lynnz and Barrax had had seasons in which to prepare.

But if not for stolen Eronese supplies, he'd be in dire trouble now.

It was full dark, but the moon was bright, shining on ramparts where snow still shelled most horizontal surfaces, for all the blizzard had stopped earlier that day.

Trouble was, that moon also shone on thigh-deep snow in the valley before him. And it shone on what he'd been told had been another royal castle and was now Priest-Clan's summer hold, clinging to the heights opposite, which heights were the last barrier between his army and Tir-Eron.

That fastness—roughly four shots away—seemed to glare at him, too, poised as it was on an equal height to this, with but twenty shots of clear land between its back and the gorge itself.

Which was goal enough for one war. Once he'd taken Tir-Eron, he'd stop for a while, consolidate what he'd gained, beef up the sea war. And pick off the Eronese fastnesses as the season permitted.

That was his main advantage. Cold it might be, and the weather miserable, and he and the army nearly two thousand shots from home. But there was no end to them; indeed, sources said, new recruits were being fed into one end of the vast supply line faster than he exhausted them.

Whereas close to a third of Eron's population was still snowbound. He chuckled at that. Folks from the northern holds might well return to Tir-Eron to find it in the hands of the enemy. He wondered if they'd surrender peacefully, or if he had an extended war on his hands.

He'd be meeting Gynn soon, in any case—probably tomorrow, if he knew his adversary. And although torture was his specialty, Lynnz knew that the best way to subdue something past doubt was to cut off its head.

After all, *he* still had Prince Kraxxi. There *was* no royal heir in Tir-Eron.

And, if things went as he hoped, soon no Council of Chiefs to elect one.

Unless, of course, they could make that decision without their heads attached to their bodies.

. . .

Rrath peered around yet another snow-crusted boulder, and saw yet another sweep of snow-covered plain. It was a cold night, though not so dire as the last several had been, when he'd grown so chill huddled in his cave he'd thought he might freeze to death—since he, like everyone, had been caught unaware by the late-season blizzard.

As best he could tell—from a great deal of spying, lurking, and general overhearing—its sole virtue had been to buy the King time. Gynn's first battle had dispirited him—all agreed on that. He'd rallied as best he could, but his early loss had forced a slow retreat into open country, where Ixti's larger army could stretch his to the limit. He'd resisted valiantly, but in vain—until he'd reached Priest-Hold-Summer, which was the only remaining place to make any useful stand. Most of the land south of Tir-Eron consisted of long rolling ridges running almost due east and west, covered with grass and used for forage during the summer—though those closer to the city still retained their forests, and that closest south was almost, but not quite, a true mountain. Not that dissimilar to the situation at South Gorge, actually; Barrax would have to win through a guarded pass or go around. And the latter led through a marshy lowland that didn't rise to open plains until close to the sea.

But that wasn't Rrath's concern.

No, once he'd amassed enough information, mostly from haunting pubs that catered to the unclanned (which Rrath, in effect, had become), he'd had one thought in mind.

Geens.

Not the ones back at Priest-Hold in Tir-Eron, either, but another, larger population that had long been housed in secret near the very hold in which His Majesty might well be making his final stand. A *breeding* population.

Why he was concerned with the scaly beasts, he had no idea. Indeed, they might not even be there now, given the chaos that had marked the last eighth. He'd only seen them once, and that with Nyllol.

They could be *dead,* for all he knew. And even with the court effectively on top of them, there was still a good chance no one outside his clan knew they were present.

But he *had* to know how they fared. People—he no longer trusted them. They were at once too simple and too complex. Eager to manipulate, but blind to manipulation: both sides of which art Rrath had experienced too intimately.

Geens, however . . . you knew where you stood with them. They . . . Well, they never *loved* you, but at least you knew how any one-on-one encounter with them would resolve.

So Rrath, who had nothing else to do and no loyalties to anyone any longer, was acting on impulse alone.

Steeling himself, he stepped from behind the rock and marched off across the plain. It was night, but the place was alive with campfires, for most of Eron's army was bivouacked between the south rim of the gorge and Priest-Clan's Hold. The bulk, of course, was farther on: clumped about the foot of the small mountain atop which the hold was situated, and climbing in ever thicker numbers up that slope, so that the whole ridge looked like a dark forge with embers showing through the black. The bulk was straight ahead, where the hold guarded the pass. But smaller concentrations showed to east and west, where forces had been massed to protect the flanks. To the right, where the nearest bridge across the Ri-Eron lay, Rrath could see a steady line of flickering lights where, even this late, forces continued to filter in from north and west and east.

Closer in . . .

The nearest camp wasn't far away, a square of tents around a small fire, with the banner of one of the fishing holds flying above it. Whalers from the mouth of Mid Gorge, he imagined. The army was vast and shifting and not well organized, for all the Eronese prided themselves on such things. And this close to the gorge, there were few sentries, nor much need for any. Once Rrath got inside the camp proper, he'd have no trouble. His countrymen all looked alike, and most of this force were male and within ten years of his age. He could wander from camp to camp with impunity. And once he reached the ridge that bore the hold . . . *Then* he had another option entirely. One few in his clan knew about, and none outside, so far as he was aware.

So two hands passed, and midnight raced two of the moons up the sky, as Rrath syn Garnill made his way through his country's camp. Someone hailed him once, and he stiffened, until he realized it was a case of mistaken identity. Once, too, he shared a cup with a drunken young man, since that was the only way to dispose of the fellow. Finally, he accepted a kiss from a clanless woman someone had smuggled into a camp of Brewers. He kissed back—then, on impulse, had her quickly. And didn't regret that indiscretion. Tomorrow they might all be dead.

Eventually, he found himself at the camp's western edge, where a series of boulders thrust up from the earth. It was an abrupt shift of terrain and there were few campsites about, so he had little trouble making his way past the last one—though he did have to mumble something about needing to piss to the bland-faced young woman on sentry duty—to disappear among the tumbled, snow-shrouded stones. The laurel and rhododendron that would normally have sprouted between those boulders had been harvested for firewood, but the trees above and around them had not. Rrath therefore had a fairly easy time making his way with no source of light save the moons.

The ridge rose to his left, ever more abruptly, and he angled toward it until he came to a place where a sheer wall of stone rose up from the woods. He followed it west, running his hand along the rock to brace himself, for the forests were darker than the plain, and he could no longer see nearly as well as heretofore.

So it was that his hands informed him of what he'd found before his eyes did.

A cleft in the rock, through which a slender Eronese man could squeeze.

It was no secret—not really. This close to a major city, there was no way young Eronese folks would not have found it—not with centuries of afternoon rambles to provide time and opportunity.

But what he sought . . . Almost no one knew about *that*.

A deep breath, and he slipped inside the fissure, still working by feel as he followed the tight squeeze first left, then right. Soon enough it opened into a small cavern, which he sensed by a change in the air, for the place was utterly black. A quick fumble at his waist produced a candle and quick-fire to ignite it, and in the flare of golden light, he made out another fissure.

So it looked, but Rrath knew otherwise.

Taking a deep breath, in anticipation of he-knew-not-what, Rrath knelt before it, and inserted four fingers. It took a bit of probing before he found the matching depressions, and a bit more to get his fingers properly seated upon them. And then he pressed in a certain order.

And withdrew his hand.

The same fingers inserted in a crevice in the opposite wall rewarded him with a click, whereupon, with a slow grating rumble, a series of cracks on the wall he'd first assayed grew darker, eventually forming the outline of an irregularly shaped opening.

Stale air rushed out, but not as stale as one might have expected. And in the candle's wavering glare, Rrath saw steps he'd seen but once before. Steps going up.

When another set of depressions had closed the portal behind him, he followed the stair for what seemed longer than he remembered, until he reached a landing where archways opened to left and right. His goal lay to the right; he could tell by the odor that issued from there. He'd even started that way when something gave him pause.

Voices. Distant, but voices for all that, coming from the other archway. And along with them, the sound of hammering.

And since Rrath had no desire to be discovered on his nocturnal ramble, he decided it was best to investigate—especially when he thought he heard someone call out to . . . Eddyn.

CHAPTER XXXIV:

FINISHING TOUCHES

(ERON: PRIEST-HOLD-SUMMER—HIGH SPRING: DAY XII—NEAR MIDNIGHT)

~~~~~~~~~~

Avall's mouth was set in a thin, grim line. Sweat poured off him, though he worked bare-torsoed, with a sylk sweatband binding back his hair. It *should've* been easy, this fixing of gold-leafed plates to the steel backing frame of the helm, which he'd only completed the evening before. Four had been salvaged from the version Eddyn had smashed. The rest were new. Probably more complex than need be, too—for the purpose for which they were contrived. Or maybe not. The gems, it seemed, loved complexity, whether that complexity be the bodies of the humans they . . . co-opted—Avall was never certain if he controlled his gem, or the gem controlled him—or the complexity of the things they made. Somewhere in his brain were theories of how the two interacted; he could feel them in there when he worked. But whatever else they were, they were lazy about manifesting. For what he did now, he had to rely on the fact that he could simply stare at the pattern awhile and know where the bloodwire should be laid.

Trouble was, the only place to work in private these days was in the forge beneath Priest-Hold-Summer. It was a royal caprice, but Gynn was the King, and when he said he wanted Avall—and Eddyn and Merryn and a Strynn he'd recalled from the coast when he finally got a count of the numbers arrayed against him—absolutely as close to hand as possible . . . Well, when the King said that, you obeyed.

And if that meant doing what still had to be secret work in the heat of the forges, while less accomplished weaponwrights beat out more prosaic objects in the open smithy outside the room Avall had claimed. Well, there were still worse places to be.

If only it weren't so hot. Not because of the heat itself (and who could complain of heat when yet another blizzard had just finished assailing Eron?), but because the heat made him sweat. And when sweat got in his eyes, it made it hard to do close work—in spite of there being more glow-globes blazing here than in any place he'd ever been.

Except in the adjoining chamber, where Eddyn likewise labored, similarly driven and similarly constrained.

More driven, actually. He'd never seen a man work so hard.

But Avall had no time to ponder Eddyn. He was almost finished, he'd suddenly discovered, after emerging from a haze of work to stare at the pattern, where the bloodwires snaked around the helm like veins in a human body, joining certain parts of the helm to certain triggers, all leading to a cast-gold boss between the eyeslots, where the nasal met the thick steel band that arched across the skull. There was irony there, too, for that was where he'd first considered placing it, back when it was only a curiosity he'd found in Gem-Hold's mines. He'd rejected that location then, fearing it might look like an enormous carbuncle that had risen between the King's eyes. A small adjustment in the overall design had altered that, so that it now resembled a third eye, all-seeing, all-knowing, and unblinking.

Only one thing to go now, but not quite yet. He rose, stretched, and blinked into light that approximated day but wasn't. A deep breath, then another, to calm himself. Reality shifted, whether because of the gem under whose influence he worked, or for some other, more obscure reason. Certainly he was still obsessed with his senses. Sight, at first, which had occupied him since shortly past the noon meal. But now, his attention shifted abruptly to sound: the continuous clankings of his clan-mates at work in the forges, repairing old armor and weapons and crafting new in equal numbers. If he listened carefully, he could hear the cadence of their breathing as well: gentler echoes of the roar of the bellows that heated the forges. And once his hearing was *that* finely tuned, he could distinguish one smith's technique from another. Why, he could almost hear the patter of sweat drops falling, the hiss of evaporation when they hit hot metal.

But not much talk. His clan worked silently, intent on their work. Too aware of the importance of their art to distract themselves with unnecessary commentary.

There *was* music, however: harp music from a small girl named Toree, who was a prodigy from Music. She was good, and her melodies had the desired soothing effect. But she was certainly no better than Kylin.

Kylin . . .

He'd been caught up in this as well, though the flow of time seemed to have swept by him. As a blind man, he wasn't subject to the Fateing. Kylin went where he would.

But not the rest of them. Not yet.

Not when he still had work to do. He was resisting that, he realized, holding off finishing the helm because . . .

Why?

Because it was the best thing he'd ever done and he might never equal it and could spend his whole life trying?

Because he couldn't imagine what project could occupy his time after he'd set that final stone?

Because the King depended on it to save the kingdom, and that was an impossible burden for any man to bear?

Actually, he conceded, it was all those things and more.

Yawning, he stepped left, to where an archway in the corner led to a cubicle half a span square. Not bothering to remove the house-hose that were his only garment, he slipped in there, turned a handle, and let cold water pound him for a dozen breaths.

The cold awakened him—and also drew him back to more typical perception of time. He almost raised his hand to the gem that still hung around his neck, a lump of spiky gold encasing its crimson heart. But no, this last thing he would do himself. As Avall syn Argen-a.

He flipped the handle. The cold spray ended. He snared a towel from the supply by the arch and dried himself, though the heat brought sweat as fast as he vanquished it.

A pause, while he listened. No more pounding next door, but a softer, scraping sound. He followed it through another archway and into a workroom identical to his.

By custom he stood in the entrance and watched silently, waiting to be acknowledged. Art was not to be disrupted save by the artist's time and inclination. Even this intrusion stretched courtesy.

But Eddyn must've heard something, or noted a shadow or a shift of light. He looked up, showing no expression at all.

Avall met his gaze, and in his eyes saw anew what the last four eighths had done to the man.

Eddyn had aged ten years, it seemed. His features were craggier, etched with lines. His cheeks were gaunt, where captivity had ground away their fat in the absence of other food. His eyes were sunken caverns, scored with black in what Avall saw for the first time was almost a single brow. Probably he'd kept it trimmed in the past. But that *was* the past. There was no time for vanity now.

Certainly he was smithing with a purpose, apparently at almost the same stage Avall had reached. And like Tyrill, Avall noted, he was standing in a brace.

Because of what had been done to him.

Barrax's men had taken their order too seriously. Even now, his nether regions leaked blood. Never mind the finger joint they'd amputated. Which should've affected Eddyn's skill but didn't, save that it meant he worked in pain.

Avall swallowed hard, to see his adversary laid so low. But not without his pride, or his skill—and that was what Eddyn really was. Not the other things, which were born of circumstances he'd barely avoided himself.

The gems heal, he reminded himself. *Maybe one will heal Eddyn, when we get time. When Eddyn has time. If there ever is time for anything useful again.*

Eddyn gave something a final stroke with a buffing tool and laid down the implement. Only the back side of the shield was visible. Simple, yet perfectly proportioned.

The other side . . .

"All finished with the bloodwire," Eddyn said, his voice void of emotion. "I take it you are, too?"

Avall nodded, not surprised at Eddyn's perception. And certainly not after what had occurred during the linkage he'd had to make in order to fix the bloodwire's pattern in Eddyn's mind.

He recalled that event, even as he walked forward.

Eddyn had been sitting up the first time Avall had seen him after his return. After he'd calmed his fury at Strynn and Merryn's preposterous act sufficiently to confront the result of that endeavor. "I've spent the last ten days reclining," Eddyn had informed him before he could ask. "I can heal as well this way as any."

Avall had bit his lip and scowled. "Strynn told me."

A grim chuckle. "Balance."

"I need to talk to you, Eddyn . . ."

And then the explanation of why they'd risked so much to free him, coupled with what, exactly, needed doing with the shield.

Eddyn's only reply had been a nod. But he'd held out his hand where blood showed on his wrists, and half of his right little finger wasn't. "If this will do for the bonding . . ."

Avall had steeled himself and done what was necessary: joined minds with Eddyn. But only a little, only enough to show him what could not be shown or explained by any other means: the direct path to the Overworld.

The next day Eddyn had been in the forges. And when he'd left, they'd found a puddle of blood where he'd stood.

Now Eddyn was looking at him with the strangest expression Avall had ever seen. They could never be comrades or friends. Would certainly go back to being rivals if they survived the war. But something had changed between them. A link existed where none had been before, and both were stronger for it.

"I'm finished," Avall said. "All save one thing."

Eddyn nodded. "The last thing."

Avall fumbled in the pouch he always kept with him now: the pouch that contained the last two royal gems.

He touched them carefully when he tumbled them into his palm, noting automatically which was which. Wordlessly he crossed to where Eddyn sat, and laid the gem for the shield beside his rival's hand. He didn't look at the shield—completed now. One did not look at another's masterwork without permission.

"A hand from now we'll be finished," Avall whispered. "We should go together to inform the King."

Avall barely heard Eddyn's reply, perhaps because his rival had turned away. "I'm sorry, Avall. I can't. I have other plans."

"Congratulations," Avall replied in that same whisper. Then: "Good luck, Eddyn. It's time."

"Luck," Eddyn replied clearly, and sat up straight. It was as though in that one movement half the age that had lain upon him dissolved. He smiled briefly.

Avall smiled back, then spun on his heel and departed.

The helm was looking at him when he returned. Gold and steel in equal parts showed upon it; simple steel strapwork between panels of gilded bronze cast in patterns that evoked frost crystals and fingerprints, yet still incorporated traditional motifs. And gems.

Once he'd thought to use stones of every color, but he'd settled on red, to match the master gem.

The one he still held in his hand.

He studied the helm a moment longer, then set his mouth and reached around behind it, like a man supporting the head of a lover. And then he set the gem in the cavity provided for it, and secured the clips that bound it there.

It was finished.

The best thing he'd ever done.

The best work of smithcraft *anyone* had ever done, he reckoned—not with pride but practicality.

He suppressed an urge to don it, and march the halls of Priest-Hold thus arrayed. He'd been willing to test the sword. But this was for the head: the place where thought drove the jewel, and the jewel empowered thought. To wear something this powerful that wasn't designed for him was simply far too risky.

A final, thoughtful stare, and he whisked a velvet shroud across it, picked it up, and stepped into the outer forge.

Heat struck him, but he ignored it as he marched to the stairs that led to what was now being used as the royal armory, where the helm would join the sword already waiting, in a small room two floors and two corridors away from the High King's quarters.

Eddyn knew when Avall finished the helm, but how he knew, he had no idea. Nor did he care, when he was likewise on the threshold of completion. Maybe the gem warmed in his hand ever so slightly when its fellow clicked home in its nest of bloodwire. Maybe.

In any event, no more than ten breaths passed between the time Avall completed his commission and the time Eddyn snapped the gem he'd just been provided into the place prepared. Perhaps it glowed. Perhaps it didn't.

Maybe the air pulsed with power. Or perhaps that was simply relief pulsing through his veins. Whatever happened, it was finished.

Eddyn's first impulse was to show it to Tyrill. Maybe *this* would convince her that he could do equal work to Avall's, and do it quickly as well. She'd worked on the thing herself; she had a right to see it done.

But it was late, and Tyrill was old—and in Tir-Eron besides. There'd be time for accolades later.

Still, it would be nice to show it to someone.

Unbidden, Elvix's face sprang to mind. So like her sister's and so different, all because of the conflicting expressions the two habitually wore. It hadn't lasted long, that thing they'd had—if they'd even had a thing.

Where was she? he wondered abruptly, heartsick when he recalled how Merryn's rescue had neglected to locate them.

All because he'd been too woozy to tell her that all three triplets were probably prisoners in the same cloister that had housed him and Kraxxi.

She'd opened doors, she said. Maybe they'd escaped then.

And maybe, one day, he'd see Elvix again. And show her what he was good for.

In the meantime, the shield had to go to the King.

There'd be battle tomorrow, rumor said; the King would want it there. Ideally, he'd try it out first, but there might not be time for that. He'd have to take the field with the regalia untested, but possessed of might no human had ever seen.

If everything worked.

If.

Speculation would avail him nothing. And so he eased the shield into the velvet-clad case he'd commissioned when he was still back at Gem. And with it tucked under his arm, he followed Avall's footsteps, at the best pace he could manage, to the armory.

Avall was turning the corner at the opposite end of the corridor when Eddyn reached the last landing and entered that same hallway. Avall was empty-handed. Eddyn was therefore the first to see the entire ensemble.

Helm, sword, and shield. All under velvet shrouds of red, white, and black respectively. The best works of their age.

Weapons and armor fit for a King.

Finished.

And waiting.

But *he* had no time to wait, if he would fulfill the task he'd laid upon himself the night he'd returned to find Eron at war. And so he took himself to the tiny suite that had been set aside for him here in the place where everything he knew might end.

The rest was ritual: something he'd planned for days, yet utterly instinctive.

Having locked the door, Eddyn syn Argen-yr bathed, letting heat soak the pain from his body, though the water was soon tinged with blood.

A hot bath first, then a cold one, and then he rose and dried himself. And shaved, and combed his hair, wishing he'd had time for a haircut and body wax, so as to look his best.

Still, he had clothes that fit. Not the ornate garb of his station, however, but some he'd bought from a tall soldier he'd happened across on one of his infrequent strolls through the camp.

The garb fit him well—rusty black hose and tight-shirt, worn under a leather tunic and mail hauberk, with a mail coif for his head, and a plain beige Common Clan surcoat that went over all. Vambraces joined it, and greaves, and a cap helm, and simple leather gauntlets.

Nor was the sword he girded to his side ornate. Still, it had an edge Strynn had honed for him in happier times, and would cut nearly anything. Better no one saw such a weapon until it was necessary. Scowling, he thrust it into a worn leather scabbard, adjusted the folds of his surcoat, and tightened his belt a notch, so that the mail would hang better. And with his hood pulled far over his face, to shroud it in the late-night shadows, he left his rooms. But he did not go as Eddyn syn Argen-yr, cousin to the King, weaponsmith of legend, thwarted lover, convicted criminal, liar, betrayer, fool. Not as any of those things did he leave the back gate of Priest-Hold-Summer. Rather, he went as a plain man at arms he'd chosen to call Eed. And as Eed, it was no problem to find a corps of Common Clan archer-footmen who'd welcomed a swordsman from "the north" into their midst.

Dawn awaited.

CHAPTER XXXV:

RUDE AWAKENING

(Eron: Priest-Hold-Summer—High Spring: Day XIII—before dawn)

~~~~~~~~~~

Div wondered how she'd wound up among the mighty. A year ago, she'd had her hold, her hunting—a kingdom big as all the Wild, if she'd thought of it as such, if a kingdom was a place one did as one would with impunity. And now she had no place at all in any real sense. Nothing that hadn't been bestowed on her by courtesy or convenience.

But there'd been no one in her life, either. No handsome young Rann lying beside her in an enormous bed in the co-opted citadel of one of the most important clans. She had friends for the first time, too: friends who truly *were* friends. Why, the King himself knew her to sight, where a year ago her own Clan-Chief would've been hard put to recognize her. But there was also Avall, who'd made her part of the tale of the changing of the world, and Strynn, who'd become like a sister, for all Div had once shared Strynn's man. And Merryn, who was even more like her—enough so that she wished one might have two bond-mates.

Even Avall was not so lucky. Avall had Rann, though not so much as heretofore, because he now had to share him. And Strynn was becoming more and more her own woman, as was Merryn, so there was also a distancing there. Maybe he and Lykkon were closer, but Lykkon had his own path to take in Lore, if he survived the war.

If any of them did.

It was strange, she reckoned, to lie here amid all this luxury—all the fine fabrics, thick rugs, and good food no one seemed ever to buy or prepare; the warmth and hot baths, and the books to read and weapons to practice with and skills to hone to perfection—strange to lie among it and know it might all end in less than a day. That they walked on the razor edge of something that could change history forever.

And she was doing nothing to prepare for it.

Well, she amended, she was resting—trying to, for come tomorrow, if there was battle, she'd be out there with the Royal Guard, in the place the High King had found for her when he'd asked if there was a boon she craved for helping his kinsmen survive the Deep.

Trouble was, she couldn't sleep. Not that anyone could, she reckoned, facing what they did. But she could stand inaction no longer. Moving with a silence and stealth Merryn would have applauded, she left Rann's side—though she spared one lingering glance at him, where he lay sprawled on his back in the moonlight, naked—utterly exposed, peaceful, and abandoned. Utterly trusting.

As open to her as anyone had ever been.

And beautiful beyond reason, with his flesh like marble, and the accents of black like night incarnate. One could make a shawl of his eyelashes.

How could anyone kill such a thing?

But they could. Barely more than a quarter ago, she'd seen a man smash a cudgel into the back of Rann's head. He'd survived—the gem had helped. But how little more force might have smashed his skull and leaked all his genius onto the ground?

And all his love.

She shivered where she stood, wanting this moment to last forever. Even the fear that hid four shots behind the window at her back was something she would treasure, for it seasoned all other emotion to a fever pitch.

And then she could look no longer. It was two hands before dawn, and the Royal Guard were meeting the King in a hand. She would be ready. She would make her clan proud. More than that, she would make Merryn proud. And Rann.

Silent on bare feet, she strode to the window that looked south across the valley where the battle would almost certainly be fought.

Another hold stood there. A fortress, really. Lights showed there, too. Sentries, or maybe King Barrax himself, contriving their defeat.

She wondered if another Div also stared out one of those windows.

And then she could wait no longer, for the stars closest to the eastern horizon were fading.

.   .   .

"Your Majesty," Lykkon said solemnly, "it's time."

Gynn syn Argen-el, High King of all Eron, looked up from where he'd spent the latter part of the night: sitting in a comfortable chair in his comfortable quarters, staring out the window at the empty plain to the south. He was remembering the prophecies he'd made last year: that this would be known as the Winter of Blood. Well, winter had passed, and blood had certainly been shed.

Not only the literal blood of men, but also the figurative blood of the land. When *had* Barrax taken War-Hold, anyway? He couldn't recall—or hadn't bothered to at the time. That was for Loremasters—such as young Lykkon here was like to become—to number and record.

He studied the boy for a moment. Not boy, really, he amended, save only in the passion with which he embraced life and in his tendency to expect forgiveness for indiscretions committed with good intent. Certainly there was much to admire there. A handsome face and lithe body, like all his kin. Intelligence and politeness. Loyalty.

What kind of world would be his? Where would he be at the end of his time?

What he, Gynn, did in the next half day would determine that. He and those half-mad young genius cousins—assuming they hadn't let him down. The new regalia was all but finished, Avall had said when he'd stopped by the royal suite just past midnight. The sword was done—and had been tested. He'd just completed the helm, and Eddyn, he was certain, would have the shield done in another hand. Would His Majesty care to see them?

His Majesty had chosen not to. The sword, helm, and shield were part of tomorrow, when things would forever change because of them. For then he'd wanted to live a little longer in the Eron he knew.

So he'd eaten a little, and drunk a little, and held late court in his rooms for anyone who still needed advice. He'd had a late report on Eellon—still in a coma—and another from Tyrill—still keeping things running in Tir-Eron—and from Veen and Krynneth, whom he'd stationed at the Hall of Clans to keep tabs on the captive priests (they were considering a hunger strike, but cooperative otherwise—which Gynn considered very strange). And then he'd dozed.

And now it was tomorrow, and all those things were over.

"It is time," he echoed. And rose.

Lykkon, who seemed to shift roles as capriciously as a prism shifted light, had brought his brother Bingg to assist with the vesting. Which suited Gynn fine. Born a smith, he resisted ceremony, though he could play that game with the best.

Now was such a time.

He dressed in Smithcraft gold and Warcraft crimson—the first because of what he was, the other because of what he'd been forced to become. Hose, shirt, and undertunic of the former, then mail the color of moonlight, followed by a surcoat of the last. His gloves were crimson, too, and his boots— all dyed the same shade, and reinforced with steel. Over all, he threw a short version of his Cloak of Colors, a riot of color depicting every sigil and device in his realm—one for each of the twenty-four clans and the crafts they ruled.

On caprice, he hung a scabbarded geen-claw dagger from his belt: a gift from Barrax himself upon his ascension to the Throne.

And then he had no more call to hesitate. "Well," he grinned at his squires. "Let's go see what our kinsmen have wrought."

Somewhere between his suite and the armory, Gynn acquired an entourage. It was still a while until dawn, but he'd already decided that first light would see him in battle. This was his country, after all, his terrain. He'd let Barrax force him back for any number of reasons that made nominal sense at the time. But he had the advantage now. His soldiers were used to snow. And he had—or soon would have—the weapon to end all weapons.

Barrax had no idea it even existed—unless by some chance he'd heard of its part in that escapade of Strynn and Merryn's. Indeed, few of his own forces knew about it, and fewer beyond the lords of Smith and War. A few from Stone. A few from Gem, Priest, and Lore. That was it—in theory. Not even all his guard knew, though that number had swelled to include Myx and his bond-brother, Riff, and Rann's friend, Div.

In any case, there was a fair number trooping down the hall. And not only his Guard, for a smattering of the younger Craft-Chiefs had joined him as well, along with everyone from War-Hold who had a title and could raise a weapon, save Preedor himself. The hallways rang with their tread: an increasing tide of force that alone could subdue many foes. Swords flashed and helms gleamed; cornets and signs of rank were everywhere, as was the complex heraldry of clan and craft.

This was it, everyone seemed to think, without it having actually been voiced.

But there was a different feeling in the air. Not only because the weather had turned, but because something had been finished. Avall had said strong feelings could be sent out and received by those sensitive to such things. And the relief Avall had felt might well have infected them all, the same way chill did when they worked with the greater powers, as Lykkon had begun to call them.

So it was with a high eagerness he continued to the armory.

And had just turned the last marble corner into the last marble hall when he heard someone approaching at a run. Avall, as it turned out.

His cousin wore full armor and heraldry, like the rest of them. But in spite of everything he'd endured, Gynn had never seen him look so grim. It was as though something had sucked out his soul, leaving him a hollow man. Gynn's first impulse was to wonder whether something had happened to Strynn or Rann. But something about Avall's face and demeanor told him this was worse than that.

"Majesty," Avall panted, skidding to a stop the requisite span before him. His face was ashen. "Majesty—there's no way to say it but to say it. The regalia—the new regalia—is gone."

Gynn heard those words, yet did not hear them—but something went out of him: a long sigh that was like hope dying away on the wind. A low buzz filled the ranks behind him, and some—including Lykkon—swore. Div swore, too, but Gynn barely noticed. Ignoring the stricken Avall, he was rushing past him down the corridor, intent on the armory door, wondering why he'd neglected to post a guard over something so precious, and when he'd ever stop trusting people too much.

"Who . . . ?" someone dared. "What?"

He ignored the latter. As to the former, he had a few too many ideas. "Eddyn—maybe," he gritted to Avall, who'd managed to catch up.

"I don't think so, Majesty—I—"

Gynn rounded on him. "Who then? Who is mad enough to do this thing? And even if he's taken them, to what end has he done so? To weaken me on the edge of battle? Or on some fool heroic quest to redeem himself?"

"He could barely walk, Majesty," Lykkon dared.

"From midnight until now a man could crawl a long way," Gynn retorted. By which time they'd reached the armory.

It was true. The table that had been set aside for the new regalia was bare, though the three velvet shrouds lay there, neatly folded.

And then it hit Gynn all over. It really *was* true. His hope was gone. He would have to meet Barrax purely as a man, with no more advantage than he'd had all those other years when he'd discussed the theory and doctrine of war. He was still stronger—probably—brought up a smith, with arms, shoulders, and endurance to match. And close friends in War-Hold who'd taught him everything.

Yet still he stood there aghast, while a wondering silence spread from him to infect the guard and the others gathering outside.

"Majesty," Ganeen, subchief of Armor, called, from where he'd been performing a quick inspection. "There's other armor gone as well. Enough to make a set, but only a piece here and there, as though the thief wanted his theft unnoticed."

"As any thief would," Gynn replied dryly, surprised at his own grim humor.

"A small man," Ganeen continued. "That's all I can say. We can search."

"Do so," Gynn commanded. "In the meantime . . . I have come here to put on my armor, and armor I shall put on."

"Do you still intend to attack at dawn?" Tryffon of War inquired.

Gynn fixed him with a steely stare. "I intend to attack when I said. Even without this new magic on my side I am surely the better man, and my army the better as well—and my men and women, and my advisers, and my chiefs."

And with that, he strode to an armor stand to the right, where someone had arrayed the former royal war regalia. Helm and shield and sword: All looked fabulous. Yet still Gynn hesitated, his hand not quite touching the sword. It was five hundred years old, and only once in that time had any King carried it into battle. Which was maybe why he'd not fared so well, earlier. He'd chosen to use his own weapons and armor before. Perhaps The Eight frowned on that. Perhaps they thought it was pride.

In fact, it was practicality. The official war regalia was old and precious, granted. But it was also far too heavy and clumsy, for it had been made for one of Eron's largest kings, and no one since then had dared resize it, lest they ruin its wonderful workmanship.

Nevertheless, he reached for the sword. Then paused again, searching those gathered around until he found Myx. "Go, boy," he said. "Back to Tir-Eron. Bring me the Sword of Air."

Silence followed, of men too stunned to speak.

"The Sword of Air, Majesty?" Tryffon dared at last. "It wasn't made for battle. Its function is to compel truth—"

Gynn glared at him. "It nevertheless has power attached to it. I've felt it when I've used it. It's not the same power as the gems, but it's closer than anything I've got. And I'll take any advantage I can get right now."

"It's better balanced than that old thing, anyway," Tryffon conceded, indicating the royal regalia. "Now—"

He broke off, for a rumble of voices was filling the ranks behind him. Someone was running. And panting. Someone even more panicked than Avall.

"Majesty," the nameless man shouted.

Gynn turned, to see a young man in Warcraft livery, flush-faced and out of breath. "Majesty," he gasped, "Barrax is moving. The whole ridge around his hold is walled with shields, swords, and helmets."

"Eight protect us!" Gynn cried, while Lykkon and Riff grabbed frantically for the royal regalia. "Give the order to advance as we'd planned. I want soldiers moving when I do." He caught Tryffon's gaze, but said nothing. And then he thrust his arm through that ancient shield, and waited while Lykkon set the crowned helm of his predecessors on his raven hair. And found himself peering out of eyeslots as he said the final words. "I've often wondered why Priest-Clan thought they needed all those walls around this place. It's time we got an answer."

"Eron!" Tryffon shouted, banging on his shield.

"Eron!" Div echoed joyfully.

"And High King Gynn!" from Lykkon.

And then everyone in the entire room was running.

Less than a finger later, every wall of the three that faced Ixti's armies was crowned with War-Hold crimson.

CHAPTER XXXVI:

ALLIES UNAWARE

(Eron: Priest-Hold-Summer—High Spring: Day XIII—dawn)

~~~~~~~~~~

Why had he done it?

Rrath had no idea.

All he knew was that it was done. There'd been the urge to watch, of course—innocently at first, but with a delicious thrill of the forbidden, for he did it unobserved from the secret passages Nyllol had shown him. And it *had* been forbidden, too: not the spying on the forges, so much; but the spying on Avall and Eight-cursed Eddyn, both of whom he'd seen casually enter the common hall, then depart for the locked workrooms nearby. Locked to bodies, anyway, but not to eyes that could see through concealed spy holes.

And so he'd found himself witnessing the creation of masterworks, which was a crime—*theft of inspiration,* it was called. As though he'd ever aspire to anything like those two young men could do! And curse Eddyn for that, too—to have caused so much pain to so many and still be the master he was. There ought to be a correlation between virtue and accomplishment.

Shouldn't there?

Rrath paused in the secret corridor to rest, for that which he carried was heavy. How long had he had it, anyway? There was a gap in his memory that could easily embrace several hands.

And why did he have it now?

Once, when he'd been under the healers' care, back in Priest-Hold, he'd awakened sufficiently to hear without being otherwise aware, and what he'd heard had lodged in his brain. *"If he survives—if he revives—there's a good chance he'll be mad. No one takes a blow like his and emerges unscathed."* Perhaps part of him had taken that to heart. These were mad times, anyway, so maybe that meant they were times made for madmen. And so he'd begun to play the role in earnest, there in his hermits' cave above the geens.

And then one day it had come to him, clearly, like a bell. Geens were the one thing in the whole world he knew more about than anyone else; they were therefore his means to power and prestige, and therefore the things he loved most. And with that realization had come another. Everything that was wrong in his life was due to those cursed gems. And—

That was why he had this bag of secrets! Because of what they contained. What he'd do with them, he had no idea. Destroy them, perhaps? Or was that even possible?

What were Avall and Eddyn doing with them, anyway?

He'd seen them inserted in a certain shield and helm, but only after complex preparations. Which made no sense, unless, with battle imminent, they might be more than mere ornaments—perhaps even weapons. Why, they might even save the land! But in so doing, they would aggrandize one very undeserving man in particular at the expense of Priest-Clan and all they held dear.

By doing what he'd done, he was therefore serving his clan. More than that, he was making up in threes what he'd failed to deliver earlier.

Not only the gems—but the means by which they could be mastered.

Besides, if The Eight hadn't wanted it this way, they wouldn't have visited Eron with weather that allowed the regalia's completion. Or put him where he could spy on Avall and Eddyn at exactly the right moment. Or let him know where the secret door to the armory was, through which he had lately passed.

On his way where?

The Ninth Face ought to have a sanctum here, but he didn't know where it was, since he'd not been a member when Nyllol had shown him the route to the secret geen pens. Which was why he'd come here in the first place, he recalled, as he paused again to shift the bag he'd made of his cloak, in which sword, helm, and shield clinked and rattled together.

Maybe he should find out how they worked. Everyone else with whom he'd become entangled seemed to have experienced their glamour firsthand. Why not he, who had lost so much because of them?

It was rash and foolish, but Rrath was tired of being circumspect and wise. And so he trudged on to the first place he encountered where there was any light in that secret hall. Not a room so much as a widening of the corridor where another intersected. A tiny light slit in what must be an outside wall provided minimal illumination.

It was enough. He deposited the bag that held his burden and began to don the armor.

Which is when it occurred to him that he might *well* be going mad. Curiosity had driven him to follow Eddyn to the armory. But something else—a whole different part of himself, apparently—had wanted to get out there and fight the enemy. And since he had no armor himself, but was conveniently near a source of a very great deal . . .

He shook his head. It was as though he had two selves, one of whom was still the sly, fawning, scholarly old Rrath, the other this rash newcomer. Often as not, the two were at war. But the old Rrath was tired; the new Rrath, who thrived on impulse, passion, and energy, was in the ascendant. And while part of him knew that his actions were those of a desperate man—a man with nothing else to lose—he had no way to resist them.

And so, standing alone in the half-light of a hidden corridor, that in some odd way mirrored the way the controlling parts of him were hiding in his own mind, he began to don the stolen armor.

Mail hauberk. Greaves. Vambraces. But no gauntlets or coif because he wanted to feel the metal and leather that made the regalia special.

A breath, and he picked up the helm—and slowly, almost reverently, set it on his head. A moment of darkness followed, while he found his vision blocked, but then it took its seat, as invisible adjustment joints molded it to the shape of his skull. A click—and pain jabbed into his forehead . . .

And then he felt . . . *everything* . . .

A sheet of white, a sheet of blue, and an irregular, waxing line of gold and black between them: That was what Lykkon saw. Snow beneath blue sky, with Ixti's army moving steadily—if slowly—through the juncture of the two.

But he saw that only for an instant, as he marched with the rest of the Guard beneath the topmost portcullis, then down a hundred steps to the next wall down the slope—and through that the same distance to the next, where the King and the Guard and most of the archers would be stationed. A final wall girdled the bottom of the hill, its line of seamless stones sweeping away to east and west, with low towers rising above at intervals. Each wall was higher than the next one down: The lowest was four spans; the next, five; the highest, six. A long way to fall, or to climb. Lykkon tried not to look down as he found his place at the embrasure. His job, for the moment, was to watch, wait, and let Ixti pour out its lifeblood on the slopes below. He'd only enter the battle when the battle came to him. Or on the King's command.

And so he stood there, nineteen and a half years old. Handsome, smart, quick. Clad in Argen maroon augmented by the embroidered crown in gold that marked the Royal Guard. His right hand held a sword Merryn and Avall had made for him a year back, one completing the blade, the other the hilt. His left rested on a shield he'd made himself, for he, too, was a smith.

A questing hand found a niche beside his knees, which contained a bow and arrows. Smart thinking that: weapons made ready in the dark of night, that didn't have to be carried. That the enemy might not see being stored.

And still Ixti's army advanced.

Lykkon waited. Anxious. Feeling his stomach knot and twitch. He wished he hadn't had so much cauf that morning, in spite of the hour. Cauf made him fidgety, and he was already too high-strung for his own good.

The wind shifted, coming more fully from the east. It stirred the light snow into glittering flurries that bit into Lykkon's face like tiny arrows, though the air itself was warm. Most of the snow had been swept from the battlements on which he stood, but more was melting, running into rivulets that gathered in channels around his boots, making islands of the paving stones.

His gaze went everywhere, never resting long in any place. Ixti hadn't made it far—the drifts were deeper on their side, and they were having trouble. Gynn had been wise to make them come to him. Snow was not the enemy's element, and wading through it tired the troops. Why *had* they attacked so early?

Because the sun would turn this field to slush? Or for another reason? Second-guessing soldiers was not a game for which Lykkon had any aptitude.

Yet still he looked about. Seeking familiar faces—familiar heraldry, at any rate—among all those forces thronging the walls. Steel flashed down there, for the ramparts had grown a whole sharp crop of spears and swords and bows.

But where were the folks he knew?

Avall—he had no idea. He'd lost him after the fiasco in the armory. Last he'd heard, he was to have been stationed to the left flank, to inform the King of what transpired, with Rann as his second, since he'd lent his gem to the King. Strynn, newly arrived from the river, did the same thing to the right, with Merryn, whom he doubted liked that duty any more than before.

As for the troops . . . Gynn had spread them evenly, though he was saving the cavalry, posting them at the back gate lest Barrax try a flanking maneuver across the eastern plain. Like the battle at South Gorge, Gynn had the mountains on his side to the west. Barrax might try to come through them. But if he did, he was a fool.

A rumble of cries reached him. Lykkon snapped back to attention, leaning into his embrasure, squinting into glare as sunlight flooded the snowfield. Metallic fire leapt from gold-washed helms among the foe as they continued to advance. They had come maybe an eighth of the way now, marching close together, shields raised against Eron's deadly archers. The line of darkness between land and sky had widened.

Or the line of death.

Briefly—it might be the last chance he got—he closed his eyes, counted breaths, letting each one slide deeper into his lungs, holding it there, and exhaling slowly. Merryn had said to try not to think at all. Thought gave you doubts, and doubts would get you killed. Marginally calmer, he opened his eyes and shifted his grip on the sword.

The armies of Ixti had crossed a third of the valley.

No longer in a regular line, however; no longer like syrup pouring down a mountain of flavored ice.

Points were forming: one to the west, one straight ahead, and one to the east, where the ridge faded into the plain. The wall continued around there, as it circled most of the ridge, but it didn't continue far. Whoever had built it had stopped construction on the northeast side, perhaps feeling that no enemy would get that far. Not that it was entirely without defense. A wooden palisade two spans high ran all the way back to Eron Gorge, and parts of the Gorge were fortified anyway—for many private holds rimmed the southern edge of its escarpment, not a few of which had at one time or other been walled, if not actually crenellated. But if the battle got there— Well, Lykkon didn't want to think about that. Because by then there would be no battle, merely a house-to-house brawl.

Another eighth traversed.

Waiting . . .

Watching the black tide advance . . .

Waiting . . .

Hoping for gaps to appear in the flood still coming over the opposite ridge. Wondering how Barrax could put a square fourshot of men on the field.

Waiting . . .

Breathing . . .

Feeling his hands start to sweat . . .

As Barrax's army began to move faster . . .

. . . pain jabbed into Rrath's forehead, and fire followed hard in its wake: a rush of energy that galloped down his nerves like ice oxen on a rampage, that roared through him like spring melt that had burst a dam, that enflamed him like a river of liquid fire rolling down from the burning peaks of Angen's Spine.

For a moment, he saw nothing. Not black, not white. Not the colors that lived behind shut lids; no sense of light at all, the way he could not see his ears or the back of his head. And then he saw *everything:* not only the gray of the wall beyond the helm, and the black shadows that lurked around it, but the grays *within* the grays, and the colors of the grains that made those grays, and the colors that made those colors. His head roared with the noise of that place of silence, where the only sound had been his own breathing, the rasp of fabric against fabric, and the scrape of metal against metal.

But now his blood thundered, and he could hear his skin stretch as he moved. He watched in fascination the slow motion of his hands—bare hands, on whose backs he could count the hairs, on whose nails he could see landscapes among the ridges, and on whose fingertips he could lose himself beyond recall if he dared ponder the mazes there—

. . . his hands. The right moved toward the sword, which glittered like frozen sunlight even in the gloom, with the jewel halfway down the hilt like fire crystallizing and melting and forming anew.

. . . and the left, to the shield, where the gem was set not in the boss upon the face, but in the grip.

And then both those gems touched the sensitive flesh of his palms, and he squeezed back and bore down.

Pain flicked into him, like scorpion stings. Right hand first, then left. Normal pain, but perceived abnormally, as though a spike the size of a tree was being driven into a palm the size of a battlefield. He could feel it slide in: an instant that lasted forever, roots of a tree joining earth and sky.

And then the power erupted again—rushing into him from both hands, rushing along his nerves and through his blood and his muscles and across his skin, so that every hair on his body prickled. And then somewhere behind his eyes, those three waves of—*magic*—collided.

His brain caught fire, and he watched with his inward eye, watched with dreadful fascination as armies small as dreams took form in his head and started marching. They assailed thoughts and built desires. They dragged out memories and examined them, and set them aside or discarded them. They found scruples and ignored them, wishes and made them strong. But they were not *him.* Not Rrath syn Garnill.

Not in any real sense. They were searching, he realized, for something they would never find, some indefinable spark of recognition called Gynn, whom they had come to help. Maybe, if they couldn't find him, for another called Avall, or one called Merryn. Or Rann. Or Strynn.

But not for him.

Not for poor Rrath.

They hated him.

They despised him.

They devoured his *self* from within.

Except for a very few things.

The things that were strongest in him.

The things that were most ingrained.

Rrath opened eyes he didn't know had been shut. Saw light that might not exist suffuse the chamber.

And remembered why he'd come here.

All at once he was running.

His *body* was, as the magic drove him on . . .

His self . . . ?

What remained of him found, deep in his brain, a cave.

And hid there, quaking.

You're a weather-witch, something down there whispered.

"I'm scared," Avall told Rann. "What if it happens again?"

Rann simply looked at him, dark eyes like a moonless sky above fresh-fallen snow. As calm, and as clear. The eyes of his friend above all friends. His bond-brother. The person to whom, without guilt or fear or agenda, he'd given what might prove to be too much of his love. He could die here, or Rann could. That bond could be forever severed. It had almost been already.

"It won't," Rann said at last. "You know what to expect, and you won't let it happen."

Avall let his gaze sweep past his friend, to the right and down. Off the tower on which they stood, along the three undulating walls, to where the Royal Guard clustered around the King himself before the gates of this citadel. Three snakes. Three rivers of stone. Three chains. The images were endless.

But endless, too, were the armies of Ixti as they continued to march across the snow—like a hand slowly opening now, thumb going west toward the mountains—toward Merryn and Strynn.

Little finger hooking ever so slightly toward him.

Avall closed his eyes, brushed the gem for reassurance, and stepped out of himself and found Strynn.

The King was there, too—alerted by the touch of thoughts he'd touched before. Together, Avall and Strynn showed Gynn what they saw.

Wait, he replied. *Wait until I—*

He broke off. If thought was a pool of still water, and their selves three fish therein—this was as though someone had dropped a stone among them, so that ripples skimmed across the surface in intangible, ethereal rings.

Power, one of them thought—it didn't matter which. *But from where?*

But other eyes—human eyes—saw as well. And Lord Tryffon of War said, very quietly, "My Lord King, they are now a long-shot from here."

• • •

Lykkon heard the sharp drumbeat of command. Held his breath, and waited. But only for an instant. A rustling rose up behind him, then a thrum in the air like the most subtle and distant thunder. A rushing hiss, and the sky went dark with arrows shot from the rearmost ranks toward Ixti's advancing army.

They were barely in range, but arrows flew and arrows fell.

Shields rose to meet them, but not all those shields were placed correctly. A few men in Ixti's first rank fell. Blood ran across the snow. And in that brief gap, other arrows scoured the sky, from the second wall—Lykkon's wall. They struck farther back in Ixti's host, some of them into men left unprotected by those who had fallen before them.

And a third flight, farther back in turn. Shields bristled with crimson fletching.

But no arrows were launched in return. Bows required two hands. Ixti, it seemed, was relying on force. On what Lykkon feared most: combat hand to hand.

It was one thing to draw and fire on a shape far off that only looked somewhat like a man. It was something else when that man's breath was in your nostrils and his sweat and blood mingled with yours.

And then more arrows flew. Lykkon considered for only a moment, and then he, too, reached for his bow.

And paused, for there was movement far to his right.

Every step was agony for Eddyn, but standing still was worse. Pain from where Barrax's men had used him pulsed through his bowels every time he moved, for they'd not only stuck their man-parts there, but other things as well. Things that had hurt him past enduring, and yet he'd survived. But there'd been no time for healing, and little time for thought. Time enough, however, to know his life was ruined, that there was only one way he could ever clear his name, which was to make the shield to end all shields, and then die, with that as his legacy.

So here he was, moving at an ever-increasing trot to the west, where the commander of the group of Common Clan lads he'd joined had pointed him. He grunted, but no one heard. Felt blood start to ooze down his leg again. Maybe it would show, and maybe it wouldn't, but he wore a long surcoat, and that would hide a lot.

Yes, it hurt past enduring, and he was scared past ability to tell. Yet there was joy in it as well. He was free: free of expectations, because none of his comrades knew him. Oh, a few had remarked on his height last night, when he'd joined them by their fire. But they'd offered him food and beer, and the comfort of their tent. And he'd accepted everything without concern for what anyone else would say.

Here there was no Tyrill. No Avall. No Merryn or Strynn.

Here, he was a fighter—a warrior without excuse. And that was enough. Tomorrow . . .

Maybe he'd be Eddyn again.

Or maybe he'd stay Eed.

Maybe he'd be dead.

And then he forgot all that and was simply a soldier: jogging along the muddy, snow-pocked ground between the lowest wall and the middle. Jogging west.

—Where a wing of Ixti's army was advancing toward the farthest tower.

The tower, he realized with a start, where the High King had stationed Strynn.

Strynn's eyes hurt already. It was early morning—scarcely past sunrise— and the point she'd been assigned was the farthest one to the west. Which meant she had to look east to reconnoiter—straight into the sun. Double sun, really, for its rays lanced across the snowfield and reflected back. Yet she couldn't raise a gauze mask, because she had to be alert for every detail. For any aberration on Barrax's western flank that might be of use to Gynn.

So she squinted and scowled, and watched Ixti's army advance.

It *was* advancing, too. And more to the point—as Merryn had predicted and Gynn had feared—what had heretofore been a uniform front was starting to diffuse, with one part starting to stretch toward this very corner, where the fortifications ended in a rock escarpment that could, however, be scaled by the determined. And which it was nearly impossible to defend until those attackers leapt down in one's midst.

But there weren't many of them yet, and they moved in a risky formation: slogging through the snow one before two before three, and so on. The closer they got, the more disordered they became.

And they *were* close, too, she realized with alarm, when Merryn prodded her, and told her that perhaps the King should be alerted *now*. Closing her eyes, she reached for her gem, found the welcoming pain and the more welcome power, and then reached for the King in turn.

He was otherwise occupied, and she had to force her way to his attention. And then suddenly, she felt that link solidify. *Show me!* he demanded. And then he was looking through her eyes, and, without either of them willing it, sharing her brain. But he/they couldn't see as much as he desired—not quite. It hadn't been wise to station the western lookout on the lower rampart instead of the upper. The plain undulated there, so that whole groups of men could be hidden until they were alarmingly close.

Perhaps if he were higher . . .

And so Strynn—who was much more Gynn, at the moment, for it was he who controlled her mind and body—reached out to steady herself against Merryn's shoulder and stepped up into an embrasure.

Which made her a perfect target.

It was impulse, not sense, Strynn knew—*both* of them knew—immediately, which was an aspect of using the gems that one tended to forget: that they sometimes acted on stronger hidden desires in lieu of weaker, more overt ones.

It was too late, in any case. An arrow whizzed by her, even as she moved to step down, even as Merryn screamed a warning at the top of her lungs. And at that moment, she lost her balance on a patch of uncleared ice and fell.

Outward.

Reflex asserted and smoothed the fall into a clumsy jump. But that jump was still over three spans, straight down into knee-deep snow. She tried to stretch out before impact, and at the same time tried to roll. And so hit hard, but felt no incapacitating pain.

The wind rushed out of her, however, and the impact dazed her. She'd wound up on her side, a span from the tower's base—but all herself again.

Panic hit her. She was alive, but the enemy was bearing down on her, and the tower that had seemed so low when she'd leapt now seemed impossibly high. And the nearest Ixtian was no more than a quarter shot off.

Her head spun, cleared, spun again. She stood and fell once more, as a knee didn't work as intended. Forgetting the gem, she reached for the sword at her side, that Merryn had made her wear, at the same time wishing she wore women's garb, because Ixtians might pause before killing a woman who was not overtly a soldier.

Bows twanged and arrows flew in both directions. Merryn was bellowing from atop the tower. Others bellowed back, in what sounded like far-too-eager Ixtian.

And then she saw the shadow floating down beside her.

"Cover me!" Eddyn shouted to a very startled Merryn, as he rushed past her and jumped.

He'd seen it all coming together, even as he and the rest of his group had begun to run. He'd heard himself muttering, *Oh, Eight, no!* And heard his companions remark about stupid women and unwise Kings, and his nominal commander yelling at him to come back.

But he'd had none of it. This was it. This was his unique chance to do one good thing to redeem all his past crimes.

He had the barest glimpse of Merryn's eyes peering out of a half helm as he passed, and the barest sense of air rushing past his face as he vaulted out and over. Something ripped inside him as he twisted and stretched, and then the ground came up and kissed him, barely cushioned by the snow.

If Merryn covered him, fine. If not . . . he wouldn't blame her—though failure to do so would cost her her best friend.

He landed in a bent-kneed crouch, rolled forward and came up, sword in hand, a span in front of Strynn. There was blood in the snow where he'd hit, but *his* concern was for the group of three Ixtian soldiers who'd broken away from the advancing forces and were running as fast as he'd ever seen men run in snow away from the mass of the charge—and straight toward him.

Arrows flew at them, but none hit, and even as Eddyn rushed toward Strynn, he saw something that astonished him. The three had spun around in place, drawn short Ixtian crossbows, and were shooting at their own troops, then ducking, running, and burying themselves in the snow to avoid being hit themselves.

By their own men.

That didn't stop those above, however, and someone took a shot at the centermost, fitting him with an arrow between the shoulders.

None of which made sense. These were foes, but they were acting like allies, and he could finally make sense of what they were yelling: "Friends, friends, friends!" Punctuated by what was clearly a woman screaming, "Oh Gods, sister, they've shot you!"

Eddyn paused with his hand on his sword, even as, from the corner of his eye, he saw someone toss down one of the rope ladders every tower had for just this eventuality. But then his attention swung back to the two remaining Ixtian soldiers. "We surrender!" one cried, and there was something familiar about the voice. Something familiar about everything, but he couldn't tell, because pain was rolling up from his groin in waves, and he had on a helm that masked sounds, as did theirs.

But the deserters' comrades had finally tumbled to attack from within and were raising bows of their own, though most were staying in ranks, or straying only a few strides in their direction, which indicated better discipline than Eddyn had expected. Better than his own, in fact.

Could he trust them? He shifted his grip on his sword and raised it before him as he crouched behind his shield, easing sideways to put himself between the foe and Strynn, whom he hoped had presence of mind to climb up the ladder. He'd be a target, but less one than otherwise, and maybe Merryn could get down there with a shield—

"Friends, Gods damn it!" One of them—the nearer—shouted again. Maybe. But the roar of the Ixtian's former comrades, and the roar of the Eronese gathered on the walls drowned all but the most rudimentary inflection.

An arrow twanged. Air parted as a black shaft ripped by. Fletchings sprouted in the shoulder of the figure on the right. The closer one. The . . . male, Eddyn discovered, and suddenly felt a vast sickness well up in him.

A sickness confirmed by the name the unwounded deserter wailed.

"Tozzzriiiiii!" A long, agonized cry in the wind.

Eddyn froze where he stood. Dropped his sword to his side. Lowered his shield to peer over it uncertainly.

And felt pain beyond any he'd ever imagined, as a hammerblow slammed into his chest. An arrow came with it: buried to the fletchings below his right collarbone. Grazing a lung, he was certain, as he felt something bubble into his throat. He gasped, and winced at an explosion of pain. But somehow was moving again. Ducking behind his shield, while part of him determined what had happened, which was that a bolt intended for one of the deserters—for Tozri or Elvix or Olrix—had found him instead.

Tozri or Elvix or Olrix . . .

Elvix or Olrix . . .

One of them was dead. The last woman he'd loved. The only woman in years to have even halfway loved him. Dead in the snow. Or not.

With Strynn standing behind . . .

They had no idea who he was or who Strynn was, and probably not Merryn, armed and helmed like that. Fighting the pain that tore through him, he wrenched off his helm one-handed, fumbling to retain his sword.

Then came chaos indeed.

Shouts rained down from above. He could hear wild cries as his former comrades leapt or climbed down to join him on the ground, while a rain of arrows kept the Ixtian troops at bay. It was a waste of arrows, but he knew what he had to do. "The ladder!" he yelled. "It's your only chance." Then, to the Eronese soldier who'd come up behind him, "They're half ours. They're friends. Get them up—and get Strynn up. Forget about me, you fool! Any one of them is worth a dozen of me!"

"Eed!"

"I'm dead; I just don't know it," Eddyn snapped, and raised his sword again. The motion jogged the arrow, and something else ripped inside. Blackness waved a flag before him. He staggered. Saw Merryn herself jump off the end of the ladder and reach for Strynn. Saw the remaining two triplets rushing back to retrieve their fallen sibling.

More darkness.

He fell. Rose to his knees in snow that came to his waist, and which was now splattered with red for spans around. His legs were awash with gore. He welcomed that, because some of the pain flowed with it.

He was getting light-headed.

Blackness again, and an arrow narrowly missed him, and two men were trying to get him up, with no idea how much pain they inflicted.

"Leave me!" he spat, fighting them off.

And then he was on his feet once more. "Elvix?" he shouted—not daring to hope.

One of the deserters turned. "Aye?"

That was it, then. There was one last thing he could do.

A quick glance showed Merryn with Strynn on the ladder, and men on the ramparts hauling it upward, even as the women climbed. Arrows rained down, but most fell short, and his group had found sense enough to send a half dozen shieldmen down.

As for the Ixtians—they seemed to be digging in. But not for long. This minor skirmish had drawn Eronese from farther along the walls. Already the bulk of the force was moving toward that perceived attack.

"Eddyn!" Merryn shrieked. "Come on. There's nothing else you can do!"

"Oh yes there is!" Eddyn called back. And ran—toward the tower. He caught the ladder just before it swung out of reach, and with force of will he didn't know he possessed, half walked up the walls, half climbed it over-hand, so that his body shielded Strynn's.

An arrow caught him in the thigh—which would've struck hers other-wise. Another caught him directly in the spine. His legs went numb, but half the pain went with them. Somehow he hung on grimly until they'd reached the top. He waited until he saw Merryn scrambling over the rampart to safety, and hands reaching out to receive him—and Strynn.

And let go. Fell backward, arms outstretched, as though he intended to fly. The last thing he saw was the flag of Eron above the tower, waving in a clear, and very blue, sky.

The last thing he heard was the crack of his neck as he struck ground. And Elvix's anguished cry.

"How long is he going to wait?" Div muttered to the young Guardsman be-side her. His name was Krynneth, and he was almost as handsome as Rann. Almost.

She shifted her weight anxiously, gaze sweeping left and right—as it had been for some time now.

There'd been a flurry of movement over to the west that she'd not been able to see well, by virtue of the men around her being taller, and a flagstaff being in the way. The King had gone strange then—almost had fallen, but then had shaken himself, and said, "Enough." And gone back to watching.

"Not much longer," Tryffon answered behind her, having overheard. "He'd be a fool if he doesn't move soon."

As if in answer, the King leapt atop a step, putting him half a body length higher than anyone else. "Mount up," he said quietly, "in case they get through the gate—or try to go around."

"*Yes!*" Tryffon murmured, already moving toward the stair that laced up the back of the tower. Div was moving, too, though she had vast misgivings about fighting from horseback. Now if Gynn had someone he wanted skinned . . . But then she was pounding down the steps with the rest, and entering the corral where their horses waited. She found her mount, and leapt up, then rode through a gate in the middle wall and down to the lowest bailey. To wait again.

But not long. She heard a roar beyond the wall and, by rising on tiptoe in the stirrups, could see that the spreading black tide of Ixtian soldiers had reached the walls.

And then all she could hear was shouting.

For maybe two breaths before enemy arrows blackened the sky, and all she could do was raise her shield, duck beneath it, and pray.

Somewhere below, maybe twenty spans away, something struck the gate. She heard it boom hollowly, and heard also the crack of timber.

And shuddered.

Rrath ran—or his body did, while his self hid down there in the cave it had carved in the heart of what he might once have called his mind.

. . . ran down corridors of darkness that might not be anywhere, because they were hidden in the larger body of the hold.

. . . ran, because he was aware, at some level, that he was moving, that feet were slapping the floor, and that he was lurching from side to side from the uneven mass of the armor he wore, and the weaponry he wielded. Every time he impacted, he heard the scrape of irreplaceable craftsmanship and precious metal.

His body was on fire. Every tiny portion of it was being burned alive by the power that had flooded into him, that wanted out, and that apparently thought he had to be dead to do it. He was mad, but part of him still knew what it wanted.

Part of him kept on pushing . . .

. . . making him run . . .

. . . to the last things in the world he cared about.

He could smell them. Or maybe, mad as he was, with his mind no longer firmly anchored to his body, he could reach out and touch their minds in turn. Feel his way into the terrible hungry, angry, ravening pits where they lived. The geens.

His mind was there ahead of him, drawing him on.

They welcomed him, because he was somehow in all of them at once—all . . . forty, if he could still reckon numbers.

It lasted but an instant. Long enough for Avall to clap his hands on his head, stagger back a step, and utter a panicked "Oh Eight, no, not Strynn!"

Long enough for him to clamp his hand hard around the gem that hung prisoned on his chest. For his face to twist in something between fear, rage, and desire—

And then he was gone.

The air exploded where he'd been, making small thunder as it struck itself and resounded. A chill coursed through Rann that made him stagger in turn, and reach out to brace against a stone merlon with one hand and the man beside him on the tower with the other. That man's eyes were big as fists: big as the buckler he carried. He twisted sideways to dodge a stray arrow that had found its way there, as though being nearly impaled were of no consequence whatever, compared to what he'd just observed.

Eight, it shook Rann, too, and he knew it was possible.

"What . . . ?" the man asked shakily. And shivered indeed, as did everyone else around him.

"Reason to trust our King more than you fear the king of Ixti," Rann retorted, through a shiver of his own, yet even as he spoke he was straining on his toes, trying to see what transpired a shot away, at the west tower. He could see nothing clearly, for Avall had taken the distance lenses, never mind the intensifying hail of arrows pouring down on them.

More intensely every moment, it appeared, for he found himself having to crouch behind the rampart, with his shield raised over his back like a turtle, while arrows hissed and slid across leather and wood and steel. One landed beside his foot; he jerked it back reflexively. And then the air rattled again, like a flock of birds taking wing, as the archers in the citadel itself, and in the top ring of walls, once more came into play.

Relieved of the need to guard Avall, he was left simply to be a soldier. Which was better in many ways, since if you were defending yourself or looking for targets, you had no time in which to be afraid—or worry.

With that in mind, he peered through the arrow slot in the nearest embrasure—and felt a chill that had nothing to do with Avall's departure. The ground had gone black with Ixtians, and something complex was occurring down at the main gate that involved ladders, and men scaling those ladders only to be cut down on the walls or knocked off again.

But something was happening closer to hand as well.

He squinted. The force that had been pointed toward them had halted, and the front several ranks had raised their shields to hide frenzied activity on the ground. Rann saw a flurry of movement, but nothing clearly until the air suddenly resounded with furious barking and the shouts of soldiers, not all of them happy—whereupon the quarter shot of pristine white between wall and invading army was disrupted by a double dozen dark, low-slung shapes that raced across the melting snow so quickly they barely sank in.

War hounds.

Heavy as a small man, and oft-rumored but seldom seen.

Hounds that had, apparently, been caged and muzzled until now.

But for what possible reason?

Why assail stone walls with beasts?

Forgetting himself, Rann shifted enough to gaze through the embrasure proper. And saw more clearly. The dogs wore spiky armor on heads, necks, and shoulders. But there was something on their backs as well. Something that leaked darkness on the snow in their wake.

On and on they came—to what end, Rann had no idea, as he had little more notion how they could tell friend from foe under these conditions.

But then they reached the wall, just to the right of his tower, and were leaping and yelping and barking like black demons, as they sought vainly to scale the stone. An archer took one. Another fell in its tracks. A particularly well-placed shot killed two with one shaft. Bodies piled along the wall, dark in the snow.

The wind shifted. Rann smelled something. Something familiar yet strange—in this context.

Just as arrows flew from the Ixtian force.

Flaming arrows.

Impacting the mostly dead dogs and those odd, leaking casks upon their backs.

"Duck!" Rann yelled desperately, yanking at the man beside him, as he threw himself flat on the stones.

"What—?"

"Quick-fire! They must have raided every store they could find in South Gorge. They—"

The world turned to impossible light and deafening noise. The tower shook. He heard a boom, followed by another and a yelp cut off with a heart-rending whine, and then men shouting in both Eronese and Ixtian.

And then a lower rumble, and, very distinctly, someone shouting, in which the only intelligible words were "the wall."

A sound like an avalanche . . .

. . . panicked shouting, and the clang of weapons falling . . .

. . . and a joyful cheer from Ixti's army that chilled him to the bone.

A cheer that grew louder by the instant, to rival the stony thunder of collapsing walls as that army rushed wildly forward—toward a breach Rann didn't need to see, which had been blown in the adjoining wall.

He was there . . .

Who was?

Oh, *he* was: Rrath. Rrath syn . . . Garnill. Yes, that was it. That was him. Rrath. And Priest-Clan. Weather. Weather-witching. And he wished he could witch away the pain in him right now, which stabbed through his skull, and between his eyes, and ran up to meet that pain from either hand, connecting each other in a triangle of something beyond pain. Something that wanted to be somewhere else.

But where was it *now*?

Oh . . .

The geens.

He'd found the geen pens, which turned out to be where *there* was. He'd found them and . . .

Yes, indeed, there certainly were geens down there.

He blinked back to partial sanity, as he stared down from the landing he'd just blundered onto—down at the cavern-enclosure that roared out and away before him. Light showed at the opposite end, maybe a quarter shot away—the place was that huge—and he could see bits of trees.

Which made no sense—until he recalled that the tunnel he'd taken ran *beneath* the hold, clear through to a narrow valley beyond. One with walls too steep to climb, except in one place which . . . Nyllol (if that was the name that went with the face in his memory) had shown him.

The geens were looking at him, too: all eager eyes, hungry teeth, and grasping finger-claws. And he could feel their thoughts even more eagerly, and knew they were feeling his as well—and relishing his pain even as they withdrew from it. There were only two inside; the rest were gathered over by the light, as though daring each other to venture into the snow.

More geens.

That would be good.

The landing became a ledge that ran toward that opening. He followed it, holding his breath as the stone dipped lower—almost low enough for a geen to leap up and grab hold. Which gave him an uncanny thrill.

Come on, he thought at them, brandishing the sword. *I am armed the same as you. I have things that can cut even you in twain.*

And then he lost himself again as he thought about all this fabulous armor and how wonderful it was to wear it, wondering where it had come from and for whom it had been made.

Abruptly, he was at the entrance.

A cleft in the wall moved him from dark to light, still above the geens' level. Ahead and to the left was the stockade tower through which the beasts had initially been admitted. The only point of egress from the valley. And the only safe way down to see his friends.

He took it, lost himself again, and only returned to what he might once have considered awareness when he was on the ground, facing the massive portcullis beyond which *they* lay.

They knew he was there, too. He could feel them buzzing and gibbering in his head. Looking at things that made him what he was—who he was. And learning.

From nowhere—for surely such a thing could not be *his* thought—came an incessant driving desire.

free us free us free us free us free us free us . . .

Like drums in his head, which made the pain there even worse.

Without thinking about it, he found the quickest solution. Forgetting the complex apparatus that drove the portcullis, with all the safeguards that went with it, he raised the sword, which he seemed unable to release, and slammed it against the oak.

Light promptly reached out and grabbed him, carried him backward, and hurled him to the earth.

Which didn't hurt, because he was unconscious by the time he hit.

When he returned to himself, which was a little *more* himself than heretofore, it was to observe a sea of leathery legs flashing by his face.

. . . us free us free us free us free us free us free us free . . . came the litany, but louder by far was the rasp of deadly claws.

Rrath had sense enough to roll beneath a stone trough set against a wall.

Beyond hope, none found him there.

But then the last one paused, lowered its head, and sniffed right up into his sweating, steel-framed face.

And moved on—after a casual swipe of foreclaw found the collar of his hauberk and ripped down, as if in irritation.

Laying Rrath's chest open to the bone.

The pain was epic, and he truly expected to die. Instead, he flailed feebly with the sword. More lightning answered. A growl and a half scream, half yelp, and the thing danced away.

Leaving Rrath alone with his pain.

It was the worst thing he'd ever felt, as he lay there in his own blood, while power that could not be released nevertheless fought for release within him.

Even as another, very subtly, began an equally incessant call.

Darkness found him, but not the darkness he'd flirted with before; this was a deeper kind, like standing on the edge of an abyss, in which, if one threw oneself, there would be no pain, no pleasure, no worries. Nothing at all but falling.

But he didn't want to do that. Part of him still wanted to be Rrath. And that part had reawakened. Somehow, too, that part sorted the fractured chaos of Rrath's memories into something that made marginal sense. Eron was at war. Ixti had invaded. The only way life would ever be as it was before all these terrible things had happened was if Eron won.

If . . .

There was nothing he could do, however, but lie here and hurt and bleed.

You are a weather-witch, that voice reminded him again.

And the ground upon which he lay whispered back agreement.

Rrath agreed as well. By the power he could feel in the earth itself, this was the perfect place for a witching.

The pain in his head likewise knew it. But it also knew that an even more powerful place from which to drink of the land lay nearby.

Power welled up in him.

CHAPTER XXXVII:

FROM BEYOND

(ERON: SOUTH OF ERON GORGE—
HIGH SPRING: DAY XIII—EARLY MORNING)

~~~~~~~~~~~~~~~~

Gynn's horse slipped as the ground grew steeper, revealing a stretch of ice that had not yet melted, though water was everywhere.

Even his kingdom was melting, he thought grimly, as he let the aptly named Snowmelt find his balance. Even these walls, which had been built "just in case" the last time Ixti invaded. Even his plan of defense, which had depended too much on three untried youths, an uncertain King, and an unproven weapon.

Well, he still had steel. The Sword of Air, in fact, for Myx had that moment returned with that blade. Would it be enough, however? Would its own odd magic prove to be boon or bane?

At least there was something to do besides stand around and give orders that were better given by others—like Tryffon. Trouble was, the people needed someone to follow, and while Tryffon of War was by far their best tactician, Gynn—or the title that rode with him—was far more charismatic to the rank and file.

He also needed activity at the best of times, and certainly needed it now.

And since Snowmelt had his pace again, and the ground was flattening, he was able to lead the Guard toward the breach that had suddenly appeared in the walls, likely wasting five years' production of quick-fire.

Sacred quick-fire, the Priests said.

They'd give him grief for it, too—if he survived. If anyone ever let them out of the Hall of Clans.

Barrax would have fun there—if he got that far. Or Priest-Clan would have fun with him.

And then the terrain flattened before him, and all at once he was closer. Reality narrowed to the pounding of hooves, the rustling jingle of mail and armor, and the flash of crimson tabards on the two young Guardsmen to either side.

The wind shifted, and he caught the first shift of smoke, and saw the first dead Eronese soldier lying flat on his black with a stone as big as he was across him, while another, pinned down by an arm, thrashed and groaned and shouted at his side.

And then more stones—and fire—and yelling and cries. A surge of soldiers came tearing through a rent in the walls three spans wide, and for the first time, in truth, Gynn syn Argen-el faced the armies of Ixti.

He had his horse, armored and padded better than he, and that horse had been well trained in War-Hold, by Tryffon himself, whose mother was out of Beast, and so knew more about such things than anyone alive. Thus, the horse did most of the work—kicking, rearing, and kicking again; hooves slamming into heads and shoulders, hips and haunches knocking men about. Tearing at faces and necks with the fantastic metal spikes on his chamfron. Blood splattered the air like rain, from swords that were flashing down to meet swords flashing up in turn. He saw faces—a few—hard, tanned men from Ixti who might never have seen their own king as close as they saw death from a foreign sovereign.

He had to be careful, though; he dared not get too close. He was the King, and without him this could all collapse—for beyond Tryffon and four of his subchiefs, there was no clear chain of command. Another thing for the next Council—if it ever reconvened.

"Majesty!" A young voice, full of warning. Gynn whipped his head around, barely in time to dodge a spear someone thrust at him—the first of those they'd encountered. He batted the shaft aside with a metal-clad forearm, and saw it glance across the horse's chamfron, then lodge between two of its articulated plates. The horse jerked, then charged ahead—wrenching the shaft from the wielder's hands, leaving him defenseless. Gynn left him for someone else to cut down, and spurred to the heart of the battle. That gave him a brief glance uphill toward the citadel, where his troops were converging on the breach like water through a ruptured dam.

Soon enough, those few Ixtians who made it through the wall would find themselves facing three Eronese to every one of them. It would be slow going, but there was no way they could win.

But there was also a hole in the wall, and no way to patch it now.

Still, he had two more walls behind him, *and* the citadel.

But then he heard something that chilled him. Distant, but not as far off as he liked.

More barking.

He paused, alert for the explosion.

And heard a whistling-hiss instead.

A crossbow bolt had found him.

It was good he'd opened his mouth to yell an order, because the point sailed between his teeth without touching them, and exited through his left cheek, just behind the guard. The pain was preposterous, but what bothered Gynn more was the fact that he was gagging and couldn't speak.

Having no choice, he hauled his mount back, letting the battle surge ahead of him. Clamping his teeth over the shaft, and against the pain, he sheathed his sword and reached up with his free hand to grab the arrowhead. There was no point in breaking it in two, with the flesh of his cheek so thin. A yank got it partway through, but he almost passed out. His stomach twisted and threatened to revolt.

Another jerk, and the fletching tickled his tongue.

He did vomit then—an ignominious thing for a King—but a final yank freed the bolt. Blood coursed down his face, but he had no time to worry about that. "Eron!" he yelled hoarsely, to let them know he lived.

"Eron!" the Guard roared back, and then more soldiers, as everyone in earshot took up the cry.

But another cry eclipsed all others, as a second explosion sent a section of wall farther on crashing down, isolating the tower that stood between. Gynn watched helplessly as blocks of stone as big as his head rose into the heavens, then rained down once more.

He ducked, tried to raise his shield, but choked on blood running down his throat and botched the movement. A block caught his shoulder and it went numb.

So it was that he was unable to shield himself from another that grazed the back of his skull. He saw the ground rush up to meet him, but Gynn never impacted.

Rather, he kept falling and falling and falling . . .

The Sword of Air had tasted blood but twice.

Avall was still reeling from being one place and then another, fast as thought. And still shivering from the effort. He blinked, staggered, found room for himself as men and women moved away from where he'd suddenly appeared in their midst. "Strynn," he blurted, almost a demand: the first word off his lips being the last thing he'd thought before the gem had given him a wish he didn't know he *had* wished, and brought him here.

He saw it all, too, in dreadful slow motion. Acts that took but instants to occur: Merryn pawing her way over the rampart, looking like death and resurrection together, eyes going wide as she recognized him, but dismissing him with a raised brow as she twisted around to help Strynn over the edge while crossbow bolts peppered the battlements and everyone along the edge who could raised a shield to cover those in the center.

He also saw Eddyn's face—though Eddyn didn't see him—as his rival let go and began his backward fall.

Peace was what he saw there.

And what he wished on his rival, when he dared look where he sprawled bleeding in the snow.

Strynn was too shocked to notice him, besides which, he wore war gear, which didn't render him instantly recognizable.

While Merryn tended her, he turned to help two others—deserters, he assumed—over the wall. The last man's foot brought the last bit of rope ladder with it, and the tower was suddenly too full.

Especially when they heard the explosion to the east.

Where Avall had been. *Rann,* he thought in panic—but did not touch the gem. Instead, he wrenched off his helm, knelt by Strynn, and saw her grin at him, looking as savage as he'd ever seen her. Until her face clouded abruptly.

"Eddyn . . . ?"

"Dead," Avall answered dully, wondering why he felt loss instead of relief. In spite of Eddyn's flaws, there was one less genius in the world. One less man capable of making wonders.

Merryn laid a hand on his shoulder. "Piece of wall went down over there. You might want to . . . on foot."

"King's moving," someone else cried.

Yet still Avall hesitated, eyeing the captive Ixtians who were being summarily stripped of weapons and interrogated, while someone tried to tend the arrow that transfixed the man's shoulder. He looked pale beneath his tan. But not familiar.

"Tozri!" Merryn cried. "Oh, Eight. And . . . Elvix?"

"You killed Olrix," Elvix said bitterly. "And . . . Eddyn?"

All at once she hurled herself at Merryn, who simply reached out and grabbed her forearms, while a larger man from War-Hold moved to restrain her. "Not now," Merryn spat. "I didn't recognize you and I'm sorry, and I'll make it up to you however I can. But not now. If you're deserters, grab a sword. If not, we'll have to take you prisoner. You have two breaths to give us whichever proof you can."

"Where's Kraxxi?" Tozri coughed instead.

"Not here," Merryn growled, with an uncertain look that gave Avall pause indeed.

"Nor with us, either," Elvix gritted, still acting like two souls possessed her—one with sense, the other bent on vengeance. "There was the night the lightning came down and destroyed our prison. The night it leapt from door to door."

"That was me," Merryn chuckled, not bothering to explain. "He was already gone then."

Tozri eyed the battlefield. "He could be anywhere. Barrax would have brought him along so he could gloat."

"Maybe," Elvix snorted. "Or he could be rotting beside a road somewhere. Gods, but I wish we still had our rings."

Avall started to reply, but a second explosion split the air. Even there, a shot away, stone rained down. Avall felt something wrench at his mind, and sat down abruptly. It was as though something had been there and was no longer.

"The King," Strynn managed, scooting back to lean against the rampart. "He's . . ."

"Not dead, yet not alive," Avall managed. "I'd better get back there. I—"

His comment was cut short by the most terrible sound he could imagine.

A long, honking, screeching cry—the cry that haunted the sleep of many an Eronese boy or girl for eighths after they first heard it. Avall shivered as it was repeated, then doubled, and redoubled, to comprise a cacophony of dread.

Geens!

His hair prickled. Chills that had nothing to do with place-jumping danced across his body.

Scrabbling sounds joined those cries, as they became nearer and clearer—almost on top of them. And with those cries, now, came fleeting bits of sensations, instincts, and emotions, slashing across his mind like whips.

. . . us free us free us free us free . . .

Geen thought.

Not unlike birkit thought, actually, but rawer and less disciplined.

But clearly with intent behind it . . . and, buried deeper, desire.

More shrieks—

Then the impossible.

Avall could do nothing but stand and gape as dark shapes appeared atop the ridge above the escarpment where the wall ended—paused there briefly, cut out against the sky . . .

And leapt down.

Ten spans.

Into snow.

Legs like steel springs took that impact, while feet with dagger claws spread more force upon the ground.

And suddenly the Ixtian army found itself at war not with a kingdom's worth of scholar-artisans, but with the rawest forces of ravening nature itself.

Arrows flew, and crossbow bolts, but few struck anything. Those that did caught leathery flesh and lodged—which only provoked wilder anger.

A pair of claws flicked out. Blood spurted as a man's head snapped back with no throat to support it. Another geen leapt straight up and kicked out with both hind feet, sending soldiers sprawling—from force or desire to escape. A second leaping kick followed, and this time its talons trailed something shiny and bluish that Avall recognized as human entrails tangled with the gleam of mail.

But where had these things come from?

For that matter, was there any reason to assume they wouldn't turn on the Eronese?

And even if they did not, would this number, large as it was, be sufficient?

The beasts were taking wounds now, and one was down. The air stank of blood and fear, viscera and voided bowels. But the Ixtians were falling back in disorder. Few dared to fire their crossbows lest they hit their own comrades. Never mind that the geens moved too fast to make good targets. Nor was there room for the kind of maneuvering needed to fell the beasts.

Avall watched with Merryn to one side and Strynn to the other. He'd forgotten the rest of the battle. Forgotten the King and Rann and the war and the stolen gems.

And then he forgot in truth as, from nowhere, lightning hit the air. A burst of stark white followed—a white so pure it was almost without color; yet so strong it well-nigh burned out his eyes. Directly atop it came thunder.

It was like the cry of all those below, but redoubled and powered by the strongest gale, the most impossible winter hurricane. It shook the earth, and it shook the sky, and it shook that very tower.

A noise too huge for human ears to encompass.

The geens on the ground screamed challenge. Avall felt a mix of recognition and raw terror flash through his consciousness. And though still half-blind, he had sense enough to realize that the lightning had come not from the cloudless sky, but from somewhere closer and to the right. The west. From whence the geens had come.

He looked up, then down, then up again, not believing.

A man stood atop the escarpment, legs braced wide, arms outstretched, cut out against the heavens.

A man bearing stolen weapons, and wearing stolen armor. And even as Avall watched, that man raised his sword, then brought it down again.

And with it brought the lightning.

"Eight!" Strynn breathed beside him.

Avall fumbled for her hand, but dared not stop watching as the figure once more raised the sword. But this time he did not lower it, this time he flung himself flat on his back atop the cliff face and pointed the sword at the sky.

The wind changed directions, as if confused. Clouds rode in with it to ring the sky in darkness. And then came lightning indeed.

Something reached out and slammed into Avall's mind like a gust of dire wind—save that it struck his thoughts, not his body. He reeled, fought for consciousness as impossible powers flicked out at him. *Gem power,* he realized, as he fought to retain control of his thoughts in the face of emotions assailing him from everywhere.

Nonhuman ones. Blood and kill and revenge.

And with them, one that *was* human—or had been. One who drank the power of the gems, and—as best he could tell—likewise drank the power of earth and sky themselves.

"Avall . . ." Merryn began.

He opened his eyes, not knowing when he'd closed them—and wished he hadn't, for that skewed time sense was haunting him, though he no longer held his gem. And with that, he *felt* the earth beneath him, though it was not his flesh that touched it. And he felt the sky respond, as something that lay between continued to call down lightning into Ixti's army. Over and over. Endlessly, carving the world into quick-flashed images of black and white.

Which was impossible.

Avall swallowed hard, fumbling for his gem—for anything with which to regain some sense of focus.

It burned him, yet at the same time it sent a pulse of recognition flashing through him with so much force he fell. And stayed where he was: crouched in the angle between the parapet's western and southern walls.

He closed his eyes to shut out one set of impressions, for he was seeing with more eyes than his own. Something had got hold of him, like being too near a fire and being swept up in it, or a piece of metal too near a bell, chiming in sympathy. Desperate, he tried to find himself, reached out and took Strynn's hand, and forced a bond with her through the gems they both were wearing.

She resisted at first, evidently under as much assault as he, then dared to welcome him. Clarity returned, but not that feeling of being more than one person more than one place, with geens' thoughts gibbering around his mind, the same way their cries gibbered in his ears.

Nor did it help that the earth likewise spoke there. And the heavens. And maybe, it seemed, the one who commanded them.

Even without looking, he saw the man on the cliff.

The lightning warrior.

Saw him raise the sword again, and call down more lightning, and send it marching through Ixti's ranks, burning men where they stood, or slamming them to the earth with flaming weapons.

More lightning, and stronger, and the air was hot with the stuff, as bolts stabbed down like arrows. And then it was more like a dance, for a series of bolts hit raised spears and arched between them, leaping from spear to sword to helmet in an ever-widening reel of heavenly fire.

Never mind the geens that, half-mad with fear and rage, and ecstatic with bloodlust and unholy glee, still cut their own swath through Ixti's levies.

There was no rain, save one of blood—from fangs and claws and talons.

And one of fire from the heavens.

Yet all the while arrows flew—and spears—and crossbow bolts. But one could not shoot a storm. Nor could anyone target the nameless figure sprawled atop the ridge, because no one on the ground could *see* him. Yet still the lightning danced, in a widening sweep centered on the escarpment, but never once hitting inside Gynn's citadel.

Ixti was turning, too. They had no choice. No one could stand against the wind and the earth and the sky. A few threw down their weapons and ran for Eron's walls, crying out "surrender," demanding that ladders be lowered. A few responded. A few climbed. One was knocked away in transit by a bolt that scoured the battlements.

The black mass was moving, though—in utter rout.

And the soldiers farther down had noticed it, too, as the lightning storm moved onward, bearing down on the gate.

Merryn grabbed Avall to haul him up. He rose groggily. Reality spun, as he sought to see through two sets of eyes, even as he tried vainly to wrench his mind away from whatever had captured it.

Not a geen. Or more than a geen. Or something human that had briefly controlled the geens, until it had answered the stronger call of the land.

No! There was too much chaos, too much jumble, too much that made no sense in his head.

Elvix, at least, was running—jogging as fast as she could along the wall-walk, following the geen's track through Barrax's shattering army, while the Eronese archers finally got sense enough to pepper men who'd forgotten they were there with arrows like a hailstorm of black-shafted pain. The dead lay everywhere. And the dying. And those who wished they were dead and would not be that day, though they'd live sixty more years with missing limbs.

But where was the King? Surely he would've seen what transpired and issued some command. Surely now was the time for a sally: Rally the horse and the rest of the army and put Barrax's invasion to flight.

But then Avall remembered the explosions. His heart flip-flopped. He—and Strynn, who was still at least half him—reached out to the King.

And couldn't find him.

Not as an active mind.

They found something that could've *been* him. They found a memory of surprise, and a memory of fear, and a memory of pain. But they dared not go there. Even with what they faced, what they'd already seen, it was too terrifying.

Yet they were powerless to resist starting toward the gate, what with a third of Barrax's army running in rank terror, a third unable to do anything at all, and a third involved with the battle at the rent in the wall. Even there confusion reigned, as soldiers tried to win through from fear as much as desire for conquest.

It was more than Avall could stand. Too many things too fast, and worse for him than for others, who had only to watch in awe and fear, and remember how to use their weapons and die like honest warriors.

Not be seeing everything as though one *was* all things, with the simplest sounds become like pipes and thunder, and the scent of burning a thing to be pondered for years. With half of one's self wrenched away by someone who was certainly insane.

Avall fought it, tried to build a shell around himself, careful to bring Strynn with him, and Merryn, such as she could help. Or maybe that was Strynn building the shell. Or even Rann.

He didn't exist. He was stretched too thin, like the rainless storm out there.

But that was diminishing. Or at least he sensed it less clearly, as though a wind were dying down. It was losing its hold on him, too, and as it did, reality clarified.

Avall looked back at the man on the ridge.

He had risen now, but his sword no longer stabbed the heavens. Indeed, his stance looked shaky, as he let sword and shield slump to his side and gazed out across the valley. Dead men sprawled below him, in snow trampled to mush, amid which green grass showed in equal parts with black-clad bodies and crimson blood.

It was Strynn who named him, as the warrior who might have saved Eron toppled forward, touching nothing until his body slammed into the snow at the foot of the cliff—revealing the battered, bleeding, half-naked form of a man, clad in remnants of clothing, weaponry, and armor.

Rrath—with the sword and the shield and the helm.

"The King . . ." Avall said from reflex, though he dared continue neither word nor thought.

Strynn scowled. "If he's not dead, he might as well be."

Merryn glanced toward what passed for a battle at the ruptured wall. "It has to be you," she said, far too matter-of-factly. "The tide's turned in our favor. We dare not lose the advantage."

"You're the warrior," Avall countered, glancing another way. Rrath wasn't moving.

"You're the master of the gems," Strynn gave back. "You know more about them than I do. More than anyone. And they like you better."

A pit of impossible fear yawned in Avall's stomach. What she said made sense—if only it weren't *he* that had to do it. "You saw what they did to Rrath."

"I saw what they did to someone who was unprepared, who had no idea what he was doing, and who was probably half-mad anyway. Who, last I heard, was unconscious somewhere in Priest-Hold."

"Obviously not," Strynn snorted. "But you're right." She regarded Avall steadily. "It has to be you. And it has to be now."

Avall returned that gaze, and knew that everything they'd worked for and suffered for, fought for and worried for during the last few eighths all distilled down to this moment. And to him. "Let's do it," he said at last. And wondered if he'd thereby named his doom.

Strynn nodded solemnly and reached out to hug him, then turned her gaze to Merryn. "If you'll help him get the armor, I'll try to get hold of Rann. Eight, but I wish he hadn't given Gynn his gem."

Merryn nodded back, as solemn. "He'll want to know, if he doesn't know already."

Strynn gave Avall one final, brief hug and dashed away.

Avall followed her with his eyes for maybe a dozen steps, then looked back at his sister. No one else was around to give orders or forbid them. No one could. Not the King, wherever he was. Not Tryffon, who was preoccupied. Not Eellon, if he still lived, or Tyrill, if she still ran the Council.

Merryn cuffed his shoulder, as she'd done since they were children. She was grinning like a child, too.

"There's another gem somewhere out there," Avall whispered. "We have no idea if Barrax knows how to work it."

"Not from me and not from Eddyn," Merryn informed him, then lifted a brow, inclining her head toward the parapet. The requisite rope ladders were piled there. The grin widened. "Should take maybe a quarter finger."

Avall shrugged, and stepped to the rampart, then reached down, grasped one of the ladders and heaved. Merryn was right beside him, pausing only long enough to tell the nearest guardsman to be ready to hoist if either of them got into trouble.

It was strange, Avall reckoned, as he eased himself into the embrasure then over the side, how calm he felt. And how calm everyone was, here amidst what was surely the greatest battle Eron had ever seen.

And then he was descending, hand over hand, foot below foot.

He jumped the last span because Merryn did, and then the two of them were sprinting across the field, with the remnants of Ixti's army starting to regroup only now that the lightning storm had dissipated. A quick glance showed the geens still at work, but tiring, and a few arrows starting to fly again. And then they reached Rrath.

There was no time for nicety, no time to assess his condition save that Merryn said he still lived, though ripped from throat to belly, with disturbing things protruding. Never mind what the fall had surely broken.

All Avall needed was the helm, which was intact. He loosed the strap roughly, not caring if he hurt Rrath, while Merryn busied herself prying sword and shield from tight-curled fingers.

This was it: what Gynn would've done had he ever had the chance, and which *Avall* was the only other possible person to do. A pause, while he stood, and then Merryn stood as well: magic sword and magic shield clutched in either hand.

"Luck, sister," he said, with a grin. And crammed the helm over his head. He fumbled briefly with the strap, then held out his hands. Merryn nodded solemnly, and passed him first the shield, then the sword. Both settled into his grip as though made for him.

"Luck," Merryn whispered, and hugged him. Then: "For Eron."

And with that, Avall squeezed sword and shield a certain way, then reached up and pressed the front of the helm into his forehead.

Something clicked.

He held his breath while power beyond all power flowed through muscles and blood, bone and skin and brain to welcome him.

He wasn't Gynn, however, and the power expected Gynn. But he was *kin* to Gynn, and was lord of the master-stone, and so he was found acceptable. And then the true glory of everything that had transpired sneaked up and fell on him.

Avall roared that glory and that power. Then raised his sword and cleft the sky asunder.

CHAPTER XXXVIII:

DUEL

(Eron: Priest-Clan-Summer— High Spring: Day XIII—early morning)

~~~~~~~~~~

It took a moment to get the balance right—appropriate, since the regalia had been made for the King of Balance. But while Avall was not Gynn, neither was he Rrath, and the three gems seemed willing to tolerate him. Even so, it was a near-impossible task: absorbing so much power without succumbing to it utterly. Avall sank to his knees as energies crackled through him. He fought it—had to, to retain his self—but eventually he recalled how it was supposed to be. The gem in the helm tapped into the brain. It was the coordinator, the thing that sorted the demands made by the rest of him.

The sword was the outlet. When he reached into the Overworld with his mind, that was where the power he found there and released here had to go.

As for the shield: it took whatever force was applied to it and channeled it back to the Overworld in turn, so that balance between the two was maintained. All of which he knew more or less instinctively.

In truth, there was no language for what occurred—yet. If Lykkon wanted to chronicle it, he'd have to pluck the sensations from Avall's mind. Which would be a daunting task.

Avall had a more daunting task before him.

His first slash—across the sky at nothing—had been reflex. A test flourish, nothing more. Yet it had called down lightning.

If he was careful he could call down something much more dire.

And so he started forward, first at a jog, then at a run. Some of Ixti's braver troops were starting to regroup, and the sight of this preposterous Eronese lad hard on their heels must surely be amusing. Few had seen Rrath's wielding of this incredible, impossible weapon; and fewer still had seen Avall's reprise. Most probably thought it merely another explosion, or one last sally of that unexpected storm. But they were turning now, a few were drawing bows. He scowled. *Enough of this,* he thought—and reached into the Overworld. Finding what passed for substance there, he gathered it up with the phantom sword that existed there as well, then brought both through the barrier between. A prayer to Fate for guidance, and he swept the sword before him, at the same time releasing what it held. It was something between flame and lightning—not the natural lightning Rrath had called—and it flashed from the sword's tip in a smooth, bright swath of thunderous power. It struck the men nearest and cut them, burned them, and blasted them with lightning all at once. Those in the forefront died. Shields availed little. He strode forward again, and the tide of enemy moved back. He was ten spans from the tower walls now, and fifty spans from the gate. The nearest live men were ten spans or more from him.

Behind him, he heard Merryn yelling—and cheering the Eronese on.

Avall didn't dare look back, for a volley of arrows arched his way. He raised the shield reflexively, and let instinct and the gems do the rest. He wished those arrows gone, their force reduced to naught, and so it happened. Any that neared the shield simply *weren't*. Or else an onlooker might see them lose their force and fall, an ineffectual rain of sticks. Avall could follow them farther, to where the force they commanded was siphoned to the Overworld to replace what had been stolen from there.

He was, he realized, invulnerable, as long as the shield drank the force of incoming blows or missiles.

That gave him confidence—though he was scared to death, for the gems seemed to glory in what he was about. Which revolted him. He'd never been one for violence, though he could swing a sword as well as the next man. But killing men or women— How many would he have to slay before Ixti surrendered?

Perhaps he should seek Barrax himself. Barrax who had the master gem, and might be fool enough to wield it.

What would happen then? Would it be gem against gem, with people reduced to vessels of power? Or would that first and strongest gem overwhelm the combined might of the rest?

For now it didn't matter, because the nearest part of the Ixtian force had turned again, this time under the command of one of their more impressive officers, and were charging.

Once again he raised the sword, and sowed death and Overworld fire through the foe. Few emerged unscathed, for the force penetrated as deep into the ranks as there was straight-line access.

Men screamed and howled, and those in front who survived threw down their weapons. Some were cut down by those coming up behind, but often enough those, too, turned to flee.

The commander had lost his horse, and the leather on his thighs was smoking, but still he advanced: brave, if nothing else.

Avall moved to meet him. Six spans . . . five . . . three. Avall could see his eyes as he approached.

Avall hesitated, then moved in. Two spans . . .

They closed.

The man swung his sword.

Avall met it—he thought—for there was a flash of light and the tiniest resistance, and then his blade sheared through.

The Ixtian threw down the stump, and launched himself straight at Avall, drawing his geen-claw dagger.

Avall parried with his shield, not wanting to kill a man whose eyes he'd seen.

The man struck the shield. Fire exploded, and the man went hurtling back, minus several finger depths of armor, skin, and flesh.

Avall dared not look at him, though he wondered how he had mouth and throat enough to manage so much screaming.

Thought as much long enough to call down more Overworld fire and end the man's agony, at any rate.

There was little resistance as Avall waded farther into the foe. He had forces at his back now: Eronese warriors who took captives or harried those who lingered. He could hear horses galloping up, too: probably Royal Guard. They would, he realized grimly, have to choose a new High King.

Yet still he strode. Wondering what it would take to ensure Ixti's surrender.

Wondering what Barrax was doing and where he was doing it.

Wondering . . .

On and on he walked, through snow and mud—and grass that was wet with melting snow and blood.

And, increasingly, through bodies. Some were burned and smelled of smoke, hot leather, and cooking meat. Others were the grisly legacy of the geens

But where was Barrax?

Where was Ixti's thrice-cursed king?

Almost he found himself wishing, in that troublesome way that tended to take one to the object of desire, that the gems would take him to Barrax.

But it was Merryn who elbowed him in the ribs and pointed west, where a party in gleaming gold and black were advancing out of the chaos that had been Ixti's army.

By their panoply, most particular the twin set of armored banner-bearers, Avall knew he faced the one he sought.

Unlike Gynn, however, who'd worn a half helm with intricate nasal and ear pieces, Barrax min Fortan wore a full helmet, through which his eyes alone were revealed. Which Avall thought strange, given that most of Ixti's soldiers wore helms similar to his or Gynn's. Yet this certainly was Barrax: the heraldry proclaimed it—and the weaponry, and the arrogant bearing.

He also rode horseback while Avall stood there on foot, weapon to the ready, wondering if this was an ambush. Wondering if he would have to kill a man in cold blood and reap the whirlwind that came after. Wondering . . .

Merryn stepped up beside him, fixed him with a stare that could've melted metal, her eyes glittering with a wild light even in the recesses of her helm, as though two coals banked there, eager to awaken new flame. "Brother," she rasped, "I claim this man as mine."

"Merryn . . ."

"I claim this man as *mine,*" Merryn repeated, louder, taking a step closer, which put her ahead of Avall. No longer addressing him, either. Her voice was calm, and she stood straight and so firmly planted on the earth it looked as though she'd grown there. The wind whipped her surcoat about her. Argen maroon, Avall noted for the first time. Not Ferr crimson.

Silence, save for the wind snapping Ixti's banners.

"I claim this man's *life* as mine," Merryn amended. "I've no use for his body."

Avall heard a low, nervous chuckle behind him—once, then amplified into tens and hundreds, as he realized that a good chunk of Eron's army stood behind them, having forced their way through the slighted walls. Even Tryffon. Hopefully even Strynn and Rann and Lykkon and Div.

Silence . . . still . . .

Which maybe wasn't good. And Merryn had never been one for patience.

Avall moved the sword ever so slightly: a brush of contact with that other place, withdrawn instantly. Thunder rumbled. Lightning sparked from the sword's tip to the ground.

Murmurs filled Ixti's ranks.

"Who are you to claim this?" Barrax called back, in accented Eronese, voice rendered muffled and tinny by his helm.

"One who has known your hospitality," Merryn retorted. "One who would give as good as she received. Better, even, for whatever pain I cost you will be over very soon indeed."

"While you spend the rest of your life recalling how you betrayed your people?" Barrax shot back, with a wicked chuckle. "How you traded love for indiscretion, and so sealed your country's doom."

"I see no doom," Merryn snorted. "Now come, Barrax of Ixti. Fight me, or run away. My brother could slay you where you stand, if it pleased him. It pleases me to have him forgo that thing."

"Where is your king?" Barrax spat. "I see only soldiers—and boys. And one too-forward woman."

"*There* is our King," someone yelled from the Eronese ranks. Someone with a very strong-voice. Tryffon, probably.

Avall turned to see who was meant, then understood. He reeled as the import of that phrase washed over him. And the trouble was, he couldn't deny it. Not and save what must be saved. This was a game of feint and parry, as much with words, daring, and pride as with blades. And Merryn, so far, was winning.

"By the King's leave," Merryn continued. "I will fight this man. If I defeat him . . . well, somewhere in Eron the Heir to Fortan still lives."

"Does he?" Barrax taunted.

Merryn raised her sword and pointed it straight at him. "If you have harmed him . . ."

"Enough," Barrax roared. "I will fight you."

"Here and now!" Merryn shot back.

"Here and now."

"Afoot. With whatever weapons you name, so they *be* weapons."

"As you say, foolish woman," Barrax replied, already tugging at the clasp of his cloak.

Merryn could see the other commanders making their way through the ranks to gather round. Some stayed on horseback; most did not. She did not see Lord Lynnz, however, which was troubling.

Silence, then, throughout that multitude. War or peace rode on what happened next.

"Weapons," Merryn prompted. "Unless you claim cloaks at four paces, which is as much as you've evinced so far."

Barrax eyed her up and down, then reached—slowly—to his belt, until his hand rested on his geen-claw dagger. "Duels in Ixti are usually fought with these, but I doubt you are familiar with this weapon."

Merryn shrugged. "A dagger is a dagger."

Barrax surveyed those gathered around. "Will no one lend this woman suitable arms?"

There was rumbling and fumbling among the ranks, for the geen-claw dagger was a sign of highborn Ixtian's manhood, and never lent to anyone. Someone coughed. A young man pushed his way through the ranks, already removing his dagger sheath. A final deep breath, and he passed the assembly to Merryn.

She smiled at him, for no clear reason. "Your name, most courtly man of Ixti?"

"Vrill."

"Well, Vrill, you have my thanks if no one else's." She took the dagger one-handed, undid the peace-catch, and returned the scabbard to the soldier, who melted into the ranks of his countrymen.

Merryn tested the blade against a finger. And nodded. "It will do." She looked up at Barrax. "To the death, I assume?"

Barrax nodded in turn, motioning the rest of the army—both armies—to back away. Standing very straight, he strode forward until he was no more than two spans before her. A stride more, and they were within range. He still hadn't drawn his dagger, however; she could see it glittering beneath his hand.

Then, finally, he reached down to grasp the hilt.

Merryn paused, breathless.

Squinting in uncertainty within her helm.

And then tried very hard not to let her mouth pop open.

Barrax inclined his head. "When you are ready."

Merryn flung her dagger to the ground.

A gasp filled the ranks, but her voice rose clear above it. First in Eronese, then in Ixtian. "You are not Barrax."

The eyes in the opposing helm flashed. With danger, despair, or warning, she was unable to ascertain. "Barrax was missing part of his thumb. You have yours." She said it loudly, this time in Ixtian first.

The man froze, then relaxed ever so slightly. Which still betrayed too much.

"Take off your gloves," Merryn said coldly. "And your helm. Or taste my brother's blade."

Barrax hesitated the merest moment—until Avall shifted his hand again, and thunder once more crackled.

A rumble of confusion flowed through Ixti's ranks. Avall found himself following the gaze of everyone present. Barrax wore gauntlets. But, so Merryn had informed him, he'd sacrificed a thumb joint to mark the death of his son Azzli, who was also Kraxxi's brother. Gauntlets could hide the lack overtly, but not the effect it would have on a grip. Merryn had noticed that; Avall had not. Seeing what he expected to see, he supposed. But what of the other soldiers? And what of Barrax?

Avall moved the sword again, and this time . . . whoever it was responded. With a vicious yank, he tore off his left gauntlet and flung it to the ground beside Merryn's dagger. The right followed.

"He has all his fingers," someone hissed, in Ixtian.

"The helm," Merryn prompted, voice like ice. "And then you will tell me who you are, and where Barrax is, for it is on him I will work my vengeance."

The Ixtian impostor didn't move.

"We'll know, whether you be live or dead," someone called from Eron's ranks. "It is for you to choose."

Still the man hesitated, then slowly reached up, undid his chin strap, and with the warriors of two armies looking on, raised his helm.

Avall didn't know the man to sight, any more than he knew Barrax. But he heard a name spread through the assembled ranks. "Lynnz." "That's Lord Lynnz." "Barrax's war commander."

Weapons rustled, and not only among the Eronese.

"Where's Barrax?" Merryn demanded.

Lynnz's lips curled into an arrogant sneer that told Avall he'd rolled one die too many and was ready to accept whatever occurred, but would perish *knowing* he was the better man. His jaw tightened as prelude to speech—and then his eyes went wide.

Shouts followed, but what Avall heard was the swish of a crossbow bolt passing far too close to his right ear—to embed itself in Lynnz's throat. Blood gushed from his mouth instead of explanation, and he toppled backward. Avall twisted around, to see one of the Ixtian defectors he'd met at Strynn's tower—he thought her name was Elvix—lowering a crossbow she'd snatched from one of the less-attentive Ixtians. Her face was grim as death.

Avall raised a brow into the ensuing silence.

"He tortured my lover and my brother and my sister and our best friend," she said simply. Then squatted in place, and, her eyes never leaving Avall's, laid the bow on the ground before him.

He started to reply, but a growl of voices drew his attention back to Lynnz.

"The king," Merryn was shouting. "Where is your Eight-damned king?"

"Dust in the ground and smoke in the wind," came a voice in accented Eronese from one of the mounted men Avall had assumed was some kind of auxiliary commander.

"And we with him—soon," the man beside him added.

They looked at each other briefly, then exchanged nods, whereupon the former spoke. "There is no king in Ixti now, and no war commander, and very soon no royal house, nor others empowered to wage war. It is therefore best that"—he paused, as though the words stuck in his throat, which they might well have—"I, Lord Morrill, who seem to be the ranking person here, surrender, and ask that we be allowed to return to our homes in peace."

Silence followed. No one seemed willing to receive those words. Finally Tryffon, Craft-Chief of War, strode forward to stand beside Avall. "We have only slightly more King now than you," he said. "But in the name of old Eron and new, Avall and I will accept your swords."

"We hope you will accept our deaths as well," Morrill replied, as he drew his weapon with a careful flourish and held it before him two-handed, before breaking it across the pommel of his saddle.

Avall cleared his throat, sick of all this killing. And while it might not be the wisest response at the moment, and him with no more authority than the moment conveyed, still he spoke. "And why your death? We have no desire to kill anyone who will leave this land in peace."

Morrill was on the ground now, and striding forward, to drop the halves of his sword beside Lynnz's body. "Because without the secret this one knew, every commander you see here is doomed to die of slow withdrawal from poison."

"Maybe we can heal you," Avall offered

"You're welcome to try," Morrill replied. "But as I understand it, you have about a day. By your leave, we will search Lynnz's quarters. But we do not expect to find the antidote. Lynnz was far too subtle."

Morrill turned then, and addressed what remained of the Ixtian army. "I have surrendered in the name of the only man of House Fortan who still lives: in the name of Prince Kraxxi. I would suggest you do as I have done, and likewise surrender your weapons."

Avall blanched at the enormity of the request. But then the remaining commanders slowly dismounted and strode forward one at a time and unsheathed their swords and left them in a pile around Lynnz. Some spat upon his corpse. One dropped his blade so that it impaled Lynnz's outstretched hand.

"Kraxxi!" Merryn dared, to anyone. "He—"

"Is prisoner within yon citadel," Lord Morrill answered. "I imagine he will be offered the crown by noon."

"But—"

Avall bent close to his sister. "Not now, Merry. We've won the roll of the dice. Or Fate has won it for us—or Luck. But Eron must come first. If Kraxxi lives, there'll be time in which to conclude your business with him."

"Maybe," Merryn muttered, and slowly turned away, not stopping until she'd rejoined Strynn, who was one of a circle of mostly familiar faces who'd made their way to the forefront and now stood around the place where a proclaimed King stared down at one forever uncrowned.

Avall named them without looking. Merryn. Strynn. Rann. Div. Lykkon. Tryffon. Myx. Riff. Krynneth. Veen. Tozri, maybe; and bereaved Elvix. But his eyes, still, were fixed on Ixti's army.

And then, by ones and twos, those troops dispersed. A hand later, there was nothing left of that massive invasion force but a field of swords, spears, and daggers stabbed into the earth and abandoned.

In grass and snow and blood.

There, at the balance point between winter and summer.

CHAPTER XXXIX:

OF CROWNS

(ERON: PRIEST-HOLD-SUMMER—
HIGH SPRING: DAY XIII—LATE AFTERNOON)

~~~~~~~~~~

I t was good to be warm again, Avall thought. And indoors, in the company of good friends. And clean—of blood and sweat, if not of fear of responsibility.

Good to be—almost—his most basic self.

He was sprawling in the blue-tiled splendor of the steam room off the bath in what had been the Royal Suite in Priest-Hold-Summer. The suite to which they'd brought him much against his will and over his protests, after the morning's events. He'd claimed two hands for himself. Two hands in which he intended to rest, maybe to eat, certainly to clean up. But otherwise to do nothing. No one was running Ixti at the moment. Tyrill was nominally running Eron. And that was sufficient.

Meanwhile, he hunched forward, elbows on his knees, studying the forms and faces of those who'd joined him. Rann and Lykkon. Strynn had gone to bathe with Div and Merryn. The rest, for this time and place, didn't matter.

For now the only priority was letting the heat soak the morning's distress from his limbs, most of which he didn't recall acquiring. Some came from exertion or *over*exertion. Some from impacts he didn't remember. Some from—

It didn't matter, especially when Rann eased in behind him and began massaging his shoulders, good bond-brother that he was. It was hot and damp and close. Much like a womb, in fact. Like the place they'd sheltered in the birkits' den all those eighths ago. Once again, Avall realized, he was about to be reborn into another phase of life.

But that was for later. Now it was enough to enjoy what Rann's fingers were doing, finding hidden nodes of pain and tension beneath his shoulder blades.

"You should be watching this," Rann murmured to Lykkon, who lolled placidly on the floor, save when now and then he plucked at a long gash in his arm he couldn't decide if he ought to have stitched up or not. He had a bruise on his forehead, too, and a black eye. "If you're going to be Avall's squire, you'll need to know what he likes."

"I'm not going to be King," Avall muttered back. "I said there'd be no discussion of that in here. Besides which, I've got a headache. Those damned gems—"

"Merryn found your old one all trussed up like a present inside Lynnz's armor," Lykkon supplied. "No one from Ixti would touch it. Said it was bad luck."

"For some," Avall snorted. "Eddyn and Rrath, at any rate."

Lykkon looked up. "Eddyn is dead, correct?"

"Very," Avall assured him. "I expect he'll warrant a hero's funeral, too, in spite of everything."

"Was that Avall talking, or the almost-King?"

Avall shrugged. "I don't know. Don't care, actually. This is what I want. Comfort and friends."

"Lean back," Rann murmured into his hair. Avall did, scooting down on the stone slab until he could lay his head in Rann's lap. Now and then he looked up at him. Blue eyes beneath dark hair looked back. Rann turned his attention to Avall's temples. "A lot of the pain is from the gems, and I can't help you there. But that from muscles and from squinting . . ."

"It's enough," Avall sighed. And, for a while, it was.

At some point Avall reciprocated Rann's ministrations, before turning their efforts as a team to Lykkon, who hadn't so much as whimpered for attention. Eventually, however, they could delay no longer. Having sweated away their fatigue, they entered an adjoining room for showers, then sauntered into the dressing room, pink, smooth, and clean-skinned as adolescent boys.

Only to find themselves face-to-face with Chiefs Preedor of Ferr and Tryffon of War, who were presently the most powerful men in the kingdom. Sitting side by side on a bench by the outer door, both men were dressed in full clan regalia, with their hoods up, signifying official purpose. Avall froze in place, with Rann and Lykkon flanking him a short way back. Since none of them had been expecting visitors, all three were bare. In spite of himself,

Avall blushed. Especially as he felt the old men's eyes inspecting him. "Turn around," Tryffon barked. "Slowly."

It took Avall a moment to realize what they'd said, and why, even as his body acquiesced. The King of Eron must be physically perfect. Even if Gynn survived—which could still occur, for the Healers had not given up hope on either him or Rrath—he would not have been allowed to retain the Throne, because of his disfigured foot—of which there now was proof. Avall found himself wishing he'd suffered some similar disfigurement. So far as he knew, he hadn't.

"Looks just like Gynn," Preedor said roughly. "He'll do."

"Good," Tryffon replied, rising. "I'll go tell Tyrill."

"I'll let you," Preedor chuckled. "I know another way out of here."

Only then did Avall recall that Preedor had sworn when Eddyn had first raped Strynn never to be in the same room with Smith's Craft-Chief, save by the King's direct command. He raised an eyebrow. Preedor caught the gesture and winked. Avall chuckled. Rann did as well, but Lykkon simply looked confused, abruptly a boy once more. Avall clapped him on the shoulder. And laughed louder.

The next problem was twofold. One was simply dressing. Did he put on the colors of Argen and Smith, which he normally would have done? Or did he don what looked to be royal regalia someone as uncertain as he had also left out, just in case. "I'm not King yet," he told his companions at last, and chose the former.

The other problem awaited him without, and the trouble was that he knew it awaited him, but not what form that problem would take—save that there'd certainly be one. That problem's name was Tyrill.

The Acting Clan-Chief of Argen was sitting primly in a chair in the suite's common room, placed precisely to be seen upon entering. She, too, wore clan regalia, her hood so far overshadowing her face as to render it unreadable. Still, she'd come of her own volition—crossing twenty shots of snowy, muddy land plowed into worse shape by Eron's army. Avall tried to remember the last time she'd left the Gorge.

He suppressed an urge to kneel before her, so like a queen had she presented herself. Instead, he gave her the prescribed nod of clansman to chief, and found a chair opposite her, by feel. Rann and Lykkon stood behind him, de facto men-at-arms. Myx and Riff, he assumed, guarded his outer door.

"You might do," Tyrill conceded. Her words, if not her voice, an eerie echo of what Tryffon and Preedor had just espoused.

"I don't want it," Avall replied flatly. "It was the thing to do on the field—Eight, I'd have probably done the same thing those soldiers did, if I'd seen what they saw."

"A hero King."

"A King who had no idea what he was doing, who let something bigger than he was control him."

Tyrill cocked her head. "*Was* it bigger than you, do you think? Was it The Eight interceding in our behalf?" She sounded serious, not confrontational.

Avall shrugged. "I've never met The Eight. Not the way the King does. Not when he drinks from the Wells."

"You may."

"I don't want it," Avall repeated. "You know what I'm good at, Tyrill. I'm good at making things—better than I thought, apparently. But I'm no good at all playing diplomat, and I really do *not* like power. There are maybe half a dozen people who really like me, and I in turn love them beyond reason. I don't want everyone else to fear me. I don't want to be Eellon, or, forgive me, you."

Tyrill chuckled. "A wise choice, that. I haven't been happy, either, you know."

"Not even now that you're Clan-Chief?"

"Acting. Acting Chief, I suppose, and acting in general. There are still those who have a claim before me by virtue of their age and presumed competence. Besides which, now that I've got the job, I find I'm too tired to enjoy it. I'm having to learn new things, to start with—administrative things that require a lot of intraclan diplomacy, which I don't give a cold forge about, nor have the stomach for. I *know* how to run Smith-Hold, Avall. I know how to teach my craft, keep my subchiefs in line, and how to tell good smithwork from bad. I don't care where the food in the Clan-Hold comes from, or who cooks it." A pause, then, "I'm like you, Avall; all I *really* care about is making—even if it's only teachers."

"What about Eellon?"

Her face darkened. "I've effectively outlived him. Our rivalry ends at that. I've won. That's sufficient—and, I find, rather empty."

Avall stared at her.

"Surely you understand rivalry, boy," she snapped. More her old self than heretofore. "It ate up my life with jealousy and disliking, but it assured my legacy for future generations. I'm twice the smith I'd have been without Eellon to goad me. I suspect you'll find it's the same for you, now that we've lost Eddyn. However fine a smith you are in your own right, you're a better one because you've had to keep an eye on him. You've raised each other's standards."

Avall cleared his throat, uncomfortable with so much revelation from one who normally kept her own council, yet wondering which of the questions he wanted to ask should come first. "Surely somewhere," he said at last, "there's a better choice than me for Sovereign. Maybe someone in Ferr."

"Maybe," Tyrill echoed. "But for now it's you. Everyone who saw the battle thinks you're more god than man. Half of Ixti's army wants to desert and settle here."

"There are worse things," Avall gave back, surprised to find himself stating an opinion so matter-of-factly. "Maybe we should proclaim as much. We need people. If anyone from Ixti will settle here, we'll grant them citizenship in . . . five years, if they show good faith."

Tyrill grimaced.

Avall sighed. "All right, I know it was a bad idea, but it just came into my head."

"It was *not* a bad idea," Tyrill countered. "It made very good sense. Which is why you might actually make a viable King. My objection to Gynn was always that there was an equally good choice in Argen-yr, which Eellon blocked when he should've been neutral, for no reason beyond his own pride. But you're as good as either of those two lads already—and you've had to make harder decisions. You made the hardest today: to risk everything for your country."

"So did Gynn."

"But he didn't risk as much as you did, because he's not as accomplished. And much of his life, for all he isn't that old, is behind him."

"I don't want to be King," Avall repeated.

"If not you, who?"

"Someone from Ferr, like I said. They're our strongest allies. With what they can do, and what we know . . ."

Tyrill shook her head. "It's you until Sundeath, in any case. Maybe then we can make a rational decision. The folks in North Gorge still know nothing of this."

Avall cleared his throat again. "And what about you—and the clan?"

"By which you mean 'what about Eellon?' To answer that . . . I doubt he'll recover, because I don't think he really wants to. He might live a while longer, but he can't be Clan-Chief. He has to be mentally competent for that, and he isn't. He's had a brain seizure since you saw him."

Avall groaned—and returned to what was for the moment the less stressful option. "So . . . I'll act as King for half a year—maybe. And you act as Clan-Chief that long, and then . . . ?"

"You become Craft-Chief," Tyrill said flatly. "It's an elected position, and no one would protest if I stepped down in your favor. That's as far from the public eye as you're going to be able to manage."

Another sigh. Avall shifted in his chair. "This has been . . . interesting, Chief—and not what I expected."

"I've pride enough to fill a river," Tyrill replied tartly. "But I'm no fool. And I'm eminently practical. You'll need an adviser. Someone to show you things that wouldn't have occurred to Eellon."

Avall took a deep breath. "Speaking of which, what of the Priests?"

"The captives?"

Avall nodded.

"Frankly, I'm not sure *who* has the upper hand there. But I think we have thin justification on which to hold them. We called treason, but half of that was treason to a King who is King no longer. The rest . . . their credibility with everyone will have suffered, both from their actions and the questions recent events have raised about the nature of the Overworld and The Eight. They'll have plenty to do without fighting the Council and the Crown."

"There's still their secret face."

"That mask is growing thin as well. But it may still be our greatest threat. That's what you need to keep your sharpest eye on—when you're King."

"When," Avall echoed. And rose. "Thank you," he said from the door. "Shall I see you out?"

"I brought my own guard," Tyrill replied, as she, too rose. "Your Majesty."

Avall watched her leave by the visitor's portal. But didn't smile, even when Rann passed him a cup of walnut liquor.

(ERON: IXTIAN COURT-IN-EXILE—MIDAFTERNOON)

"I've come to see King Kraxxi."

Said in Ixtian, but the voice was Eronese and sounded impatient and strained alike, there in the corridor outside what for now passed for Ixti's embassy in Eron. Or their court-in-exile.

Merryn shifted her weight on the bare flagstones of what had never been a luxurious hold and waited, staring at the worn oak planks of the door between the two tired-looking guards in barely cleaned Ixtian dress armor that stood to either side.

"Half the world wants to see him," the left-hand guard replied.

"As with my King," Merryn gave back, adjusting the dress surcoat she'd donned over formal armor. "But I think he'll see me. Tell him it's . . . Merryn."

The guard scowled, but ducked inside. Merryn tried not to stare at the disarray around her. Half of Ixti's army had gone to chaos. A third had gone entirely: melted into the land. The remainder were trying to maintain some semblance of decorum and honor. Kraxxi had been found, released, and, as predicted, offered the crown. That was all she knew. But he would have a million things demanding his attention, just like Avall. She would take her time, have her say, then leave him to his own affairs.

The door opened.

"He'll see you," the guard said in Eronese. "But he has little time. He apologizes in advance."

"I accept," Merryn grunted, and strode forward.

Kraxxi rose when she entered the second room of the suite. A quartet of guards—or whatever—stood behind him. He dismissed them with a wave. Merryn's breath caught. He looked terrible, worse than Eddyn had, perhaps. What had they done to him, anyway? Eighths of sporadic torture had left no visible scars on his body, but what she saw spoke loudly of torture of the mind. A hungry stomach and a hungry heart were two different pains entirely. And fear of death hurt worse than death by sword.

Kraxxi grinned wryly. For a moment Merryn thought he was going to rush forward to embrace her. For a moment she started to rush toward him. In fact, she dared a step, then caught herself and blushed.

"I don't know," he said abruptly, in reply to no question she had asked. "I have no idea."

Merryn looked around helplessly, then finally found a chair and sat down, forgetting with whom she kept company. "About what?"

"About us. That's why you're here, isn't it?"

"*Is* there an us?" Merryn countered, raising a brow.

"Think of me as Krax," Kraxxi offered, as though he hadn't heard. "If it will help. I never wanted to be king, and certainly not to take the throne in a foreign land."

"You've no choice, I suppose," Merryn replied. "No more has my brother."

"I'd like to meet him. He and I surely have much in common, a least right now. I'd like to end all this hostility and suspicion between our lands. There's no reason for it. We both have things we could give the other."

Merryn nodded slowly. "And you and I? Do we have anything to give each other?"

Kraxxi shrugged. "I never lied to you about my feelings. I only lied about the rest because I had to. You'd have done the same."

"Maybe. But this isn't my suite in War-Hold."

"No more than this was my war."

"It wouldn't have been *anyone's* war if Barrax had been willing to talk!" Merryn flared. "It was his Eight-damned pride."

"A problem for all of us," Kraxxi conceded. "But that's not what we were talking about."

"No."

"What do you want?"

A deep breath. "In an ideal world? I want you and me together. In this world . . . that can't happen. You have a country to rule. You have no choice. But I can't be your queen and remain who I am, and I won't be your concubine."

"Why not my queen?"

She looked him square in the eye. "You know the answer to that, and it has nothing to do with duty or responsibility."

"You can't be tied," Kraxxi replied slowly. "All these Eronese rites chafe at you like the manacles we all wore. My court—probably any court—would be the same."

A nod. "I could be High Queen in Eron, if I wanted. *If,*" she stressed. A pause, then, "But I'm a warrior at heart, Kraxxi, not a courtier—or courtesan. I can get away with that here, with only the odd raised eyebrow. I couldn't in your land. I'd have to spend half my time explaining myself, and that would drive me crazy. Never mind that I've only just become free of my family and education—legally. I'm still bound to the Fateing, but even that provides tremendously more variety and experience than I'd ever get in Ixti. That's what I'd lose if I were your queen. Choices—when I've only just gained any."

Kraxxi wouldn't meet her eye. "You're welcome in my court anytime, for as long as you like," he said at last. "That's as much as I can give you."

"And as much as I'm wise to accept," Merryn acknowledged. "But it's sad, Kraxxi. All those things we did together. Many of them were things we did for the last time and didn't know it. It would've made them—"

"Not better," he finished for her.

A shrug. Merryn didn't want to follow where that might lead. "One thing I still have to tell you," she said instead, "and then I'll leave you to those awful things I know you'll have to do. But honor compels me, and desire fuels that compulsion."

A brow lifted. "And . . . ?"

"I owe you a life," Merryn confessed. "I killed your friend Olrix without meaning to. I didn't know who she was, and all I saw were Ixtians threatening my bond-sister and a valuable countryman."

Kraxxi chuckled grimly. "And I—as my country incarnate—don't owe you lives in return? What about the dead at War-Hold?"

"You'll have to pay for that," Merryn acknowledged. "I don't know what Eron will want in reparations, but I know that repair of War-Hold will be one of them. We'll probably want hostages until that work is complete."

Kraxxi scowled, but for all that, looked somewhat relieved. "I've no idea where we'll get the money, but that's fair. It's no more than I expected. But we were talking about Olrix."

Merryn nodded. "I could take her place in service for a time. If Elvix and Tozri will have me. I—we rather liked each other, before all this."

"But you won't be my queen?"

"That was choice; this is honor."

"It might take a while to convince them," Kraxxi mused. "But you may have a while."

"Oh?"

"They're staying here. They came here for personal reasons. I'm making them remain—and not from pure altruism. For the time being, they're going to be my ambassadors."

Merryn chuckled in spite of herself.

"What's funny?"

She grinned at him. "All us twenty-year-olds making these decisions about countries. It's ritual and the momentum of tradition that's letting us do it, and that's all; the fact that we're *called* kings and princes and ambassadors. But there're stronger people around who could do more with those titles—if they wake up and realize they can."

"Lynnz realized."

"And died for it."

"But that's not why you were laughing."

Merryn shook her head. "Half a day ago you were hungry and dirty in a cell. The triplets were hiding in the woods, spying on Ixti's army and looking for a way to join it until they could make a break. Avall was smithing like a crazy man, and—"

"Do you know how they found me?" Kraxxi interrupted. "In what state, I mean?"

Merryn shook her head again.

"I was bound behind a window in the topmost tower of this place, so that I had to look out on the battle. On what I'd been promised would be the death of everyone I knew—especially you. They were going to make me watch all that. They were going to capture you, and kill you before my eyes—or make me do it. And that would've been it. They'd have killed me then. But Lynnz waited too long—this time."

A cautious knock sounded on the door. Another, and then one of the guards stuck his head in. "Majesty—I—"

Merryn glanced at the time-candle in the corner. "I've got some of what I came for, which will have to do, I guess—until we can both do more thinking." Without asking leave, she rose.

"I'll see you again," Kraxxi told her.

A third time she shook her head. "Those eyes may see me, when you meet with my brother as I understand is already being planned. But I've seen the last of the Krax I knew. Good luck to you, *Prince* Kraxxi."

And with that, Merryn withdrew.

She held off the tears until she was back on her horse and riding toward Eron's camp. That way, she could blame them on the weather.

(ERON: PRIEST-HOLD-SUMMER—LATE AFTERNOON)

Avall closed the door behind him, and locked it, trying not to grin too much at the look on Morl syn Meneke's face, whom he'd left gaping on the other side. There'd be time later to discuss the state of Eronese brewing. He turned and joined the others waiting where he'd summoned them: on the high eastern terrace atop Priest-Hold-Summer. The wind was brisk there, but the sun was warm that afternoon. Had it been so few hands since the war had ended? *That* didn't seem possible.

He'd chosen this place deliberately. Gynn had been the King of Balance, and this was a place of balance. He could look south, and see the battlefield. The snow there was melting quickly, and being trampled to mush more rapidly yet, as the more responsible survivors of Ixti's army retrieved the bodies of their dead. Weapons on bodies would remain on them. Weapons left on the ground or abandoned were wergild. But no one was keeping records. Pyres were burning, too—beyond the Ixtian embassy. Discreetly out of Eron's sight—not that it mattered. Both sides burned their dead in season. And both sides had dead to burn.

Balance . . .

Avall could also look north from there, where his own army remained neatly in place—just in case. Tryffon had suggested it, and he'd approved because it made sense. There could still be trouble. Ixti's army had lost its former head, and no one much knew—or trusted—the new one. Kraxxi had more friends in Eron than his own land. Eron had best be prepared to support his claim.

But there was movement in Eron's camp as well: a steady stream of horses, wagons, and people on foot along an avenue that had been cleared between the gates of this citadel and the Gorge. Already that way was lined with folk who had nothing to do with the battle but a great deal to do with welcoming a new King to Tir-Eron.

Avall hoped they couldn't see him up here. For now, he needed to spend time with his friends.

His advisers, he amended. Those he most loved and trusted.

They sat there looking attentive, smiling some of them, or grinning outright, or looking surprisingly sober. Strynn. Merryn. Div. Rann. Lykkon. Bingg, in whatever capacity he served, which at present seemed to be tending a small double brazier, on one side of which cauf was simmering, on the other side Avall's favorite hot wine. There were curls of fried fish, too, and oranges fresh from Gem-Hold-Winter.

"So," he said briskly, as he seated himself between Strynn and Rann, and reached for a goblet already filled for him. "What do we do first?"

"What do you want to do?" Rann, who looked most sober, retorted. "I know better than to think you want this. You've already said as much."

Avall shrugged, and quaffed a long draught. "I just want you to know—because there's some chance you might actually listen to me—that there's no reason in the world I should be King."

"You saved the country," Div countered.

Avall shook his head. "You saved me once. Should you then be Queen? Rann gave me half the good ideas I had—including the business of incorporating the gems into the regalia. If anyone deserves the Throne he does, just for that. And I could say the same about any of you. Merry, you'd be a magnificent Queen because no one would ever be able to predict you. Strynn, you'd be wonderful as well—and will be, for a while at least—because you never do anything wrong and never will." He paused for another drink. "Even you, Lyk. You've half a year before you're an adult, but you know more actual information than anyone I've ever met. If experience of government as it works behind the scenes is what's needed, you'd be perfect."

"He's got Royal Steward written all over him," Strynn laughed. "Anyone want to give odds how soon he becomes Craft-Chief of Lore?"

Merryn cleared her throat. "This is interesting, folks, but we all know what's going on here: small talk to hide from big."

Avall shifted in his seat. "But there's so much big talk there's no way to choose."

Rann raised a brow. "Maybe we shouldn't do anything at all, and let the big things find their own place. Their own . . . balance."

Bingg rubbed his chin, where the merest trace of boy stubble showed. "I wonder what you'll be," he mused. "The King of . . . what?"

"The gems, probably," Strynn replied restlessly. "Though that's rather obvious."

Avall told them what he and Tyrill had more or less decided. "You have to admit it makes sense," he said. "Me as Craft-Chief. Something I'd actually be good at," he added sourly. "If I *have* to have a title foisted on me."

"In half a year," Merryn stressed. "A lot can happen between now and then. You might even discover you like being King."

Strynn poked him in the ribs. "And since I'll be consort unless you make me Queen in my own right, who's to say I won't decide *I* want to stay on and rule, with you as my consort? Stranger things have happened."

Avall rolled his eyes.

A movement from Merryn—or maybe a touch of her mind—drew his attention. Her face was grim and serious, as it had been for most of the day. "Do you think there'll be peace?" she wondered.

Avall didn't answer at once. It was a good question, and the right time for the asking, and not at all what he wanted to face just then. Still, she deserved a reply.

"If Kraxxi manages to retain his throne, there could be. We're different, Ixti and Eron. But we've also a lot in common and there are certainly things we can give each other. The Flat makes it unlikely we'll ever chafe at each other's borders, but there'll be people there, and probably some powerful ones, who'll feel they've given up their autonomy and are living on our sufferance."

"Which," Strynn added, "assumes *we* don't face civil war, which could still occur. Smith and Argen have lost power for all they've gained some, too. But Gem and Priest are still going to be furious, and who knows about the others?"

Avall gnawed his lip. "Whatever happens won't be boring."

"What about the gems?" Rann asked pointedly. "They're our bliss right now, but they could well become our bane."

Merryn looked at him askance. "How so?"

He cleared his throat, obviously preparing to deliver a speech he'd spent some time rehearsing. "Because they're too powerful. They'll make everyone afraid of us—and by us, I mean the few of us here, plus maybe a dozen others. But one thing to remember: we don't control the source of the gems, and we've no guarantee there won't be more, nor who'll achieve control of them. War with gems is fine—against a common foe. But what if it comes to war of gems against each other?"

"What indeed?" Div agreed. "The very notion chills me."

"Speaking of which," Strynn observed, "I wouldn't mind going inside."

"Neither would I," Merryn agreed, rising. "Besides, if I recall correctly, we've still got a coronation to plan."

Avall rose as well. And looked south again. And then north. And then east, where the sea could barely be seen as a glimmer of silver slicing the horizon. "West," he said, turning to face that way, though a mass of building loomed between. "Maybe we've ignored the land beyond the Spine too long."

"Maybe," Merryn acknowledged, as she linked her arm with his. "That's one thing more for you to think about—when you're King."

"When I'm King," Avall echoed, with a wistful grin. "When I'm King."

The next morning, precisely at sunrise, an untitled Priest chosen by random lot placed the Crown of Oak on his head, and he was.

Avall syn Argen-a, High King of all Eron.

ABOUT THE AUTHOR

TOM DEITZ grew up in Young Harris, Georgia, a tiny college town in the north Georgia mountains that—by heritage or landscape—have inspired the setting for the majority of his novels. He holds BA and MA degrees in English from the University of Georgia, where he also worked as a library assistant in the Hargrett Rare Books and Manuscript Library until quitting in 1988 to become a fulltime writer. His interest in medieval literature, castles, and Celtic art led him to co-found the Athens, GA chapter of the Society for Creative Anachronism, of which he is still sort of a member. A "fair-to-middlin" artist, Tom is also a frustrated architect and an automobile enthusiast (he has two non-running '62 Lincolns, every *Road & Track* since 1959 but two, and over 900 unbuilt model cars). He also hunts every now and then, dabbles in theater at the local junior college, and plays *toli* (a Southeastern Indian game related to lacrosse) when his pain threshold is especially high.

After twenty-five years in Athens, he has recently moved back to his home town, the wisdom of which move remains to be seen. He has published sixteen novels to date, and is currently at work on *Summerblood,* the third book in the Chronicles of Eron.